THE SILVER CALL

Trek to Kraggen-Cor

The Dawn-Gate and the Dusk-Door are the entries to the evil-ridden caverns of Kraggen-Cor. And through one or the other, King Durek's army must go to reclaim the ancient Dwarf realm from an insatiable evil. One entry is sealed by a monster's wrath. The other leads to an uncrossable chasm that stretches to the very heart of the world. These are but the first of the barriers that Warrows, Dwarves, and Men must attempt to overcome on their desperate mission to conquer the vile Spawn of Kraggen-Cor. . . .

The Brega Path

The Brega Path is the only sure route through Kraggen-Cor. Yet within this maze more than darkness lurks beyond the flicker of a Warrow's torch. In the roots of the realm, deep as very Hèl itself, Spawn-home and Gargon-lair stand before the Path. Trapped in a netherworld of fissured stone and unnatural dark, a small band of Warrow, Dwarf, and Man must fight their way through chambers measureless and caves of peril with the very hope and fate of Mithgar in their hands. . . .

The Saga of Mithgar
by Dennis L. McKiernan

The Dragonstone
Voyage of the Fox Rider
Into the Fire
Into the Forge
Dragondoom
Tales of Mithgar
The Iron Tower
The Silver Call
Eye of the Hunter
Silver Wolf, Black Falcon

Other Novels
by Dennis L. McKiernan

Caverns of Socrates
Once Upon a Winter's Night

THE
SILVER CALL

DENNIS L. MCKIERNAN
for the First Time Complete
in One Volume
and
with a New Foreword
by the Author

(previously published as two separate titles
in the *Silver Call* duology)

A ROC BOOK

ROC
Published by New American Library, a division of
Penguin Putnam Inc., 375 Hudson Street,
New York, New York 10014, U.S.A.
Penguin Books Ltd, 80 Strand,
London WC2R ORL, England
Penguin Books Australia Ltd, Ringwood,
Victoria, Australia
Penguin Books Canada Ltd, 10 Alcorn Avenue,
Toronto, Ontario, Canada M4V 3B2
Penguin Books (N.Z.) Ltd, 182–190 Wairau Road,
Auckland 10, New Zealand

Penguin Books Ltd, Registered Offices:
Harmondsworth, Middlesex, England

Published by Roc, an imprint of New American Library,
a division of Penguin Putnam Inc. Previously published in two volumes as *Trek to
Kraggen-cor* and *The Brega Path*.

First Roc Printing (*The Silver Call*), December 2001
10 9 8 7 6 5 4 3 2 1

Cover art by Jerry Vanderstelt
Designed by Ray Lundgren

Printed in the United States of America

PUBLISHER'S NOTE
This is a work of fiction. Names, characters, places, and incidents either are the
product of the author's imagination or are used fictitiously, and any resemblance to
actual persons, living or dead, business establishments, events, or locales is entirely
coincidental.

CONTENTS

Book Two: The Brega Path

FOREWORD ANEW

The Silver Call is the very first fantasy I ever wrote, and although it was my first, it was published *after* the second fantasy I wrote—*The Iron Tower*—but make no mistake: this truly is the first one written[1], and there is a special spot in my heart for *The Silver Call* for two primary reasons: 1) it kept me sane, for I was flat on my back in a cast that went from my armpits to my toes, and it gave me something to do while recuperating; and 2) it is the first story I wrote wherein Warrows appear.

Why was I in that cast? What happened? I was run over by a car; it shattered my left femur, broke it into at least fifty pieces. One way to heal a bone break is to use a cast to immobilize the joint above the break and the joint below it. For a femur, that means immobilizing the hip and the knee, and at the time the only way to do that was to go from armpits to toes with the cast. How did I get run over? While riding my dirt bike, a car came around a blind corner on my side of the road. QED.

Okay, enough of that. What about the Warrows? How did I come about them?

Well, I knew that a Mithgarian adventure should include Elves and Dwarves and High Kings and brave warriors and Wizards and Rûcks and Trolls and Gargons and other beings fair and foul in a tale set in perilous times, for they are the *stuff*

---

[1] Like many writers, I have learned a lot since penning this tale, and as a result I think I have become a better writer.

of high fantasy, and have been such going back to the days when stories were spoken and not written.

For example, many an Irish and Norse and Celtic and other such tales tell of tall and fair Elves (e.g., the Sidhe), and doughty Dwarves (Germanic and Norse tales in particular), and monstrous Trolls and Goblins (Scandinavian folklore is replete with such), and High Kings and brave warriors and such.

Yes, but what about wee folk? What about Warrows?

Well, many of these oral tales featured "wee folk" too; for example, long before the "white man" came to the "new world," my Cherokee ancestors told stories of wee folk, just as did my Irish ancestors in their own realm . . . and just as did many a tale teller in countries spread throughout six of the seven continents.

But Elves and Dwarves and all the others—including the wee folk of legends and folk tales and fairy tales—are usually people of "power," whereas I needed a folk of "heart" to be my surrogate, to be someone like "me," someone with doubts and weaknesses and lack of lore, someone with whom the reader could identify, yet also be someone who could, when pressed, do whatever was needed in the defense of all he or she holds dear. Thus were born the Warrows of *The Silver Call,* beings like us who generally seem somewhat insignificant in the grand scheme of things, but who, when driven by circumstance and peril and need, will rise to the occasion, for, after all, desperate times do produce unexpected heroes. And you and I both know that we ourselves on occasion can become heroes, and so we are indeed like the Warrows . . . with our weaknesses and naïveté and doubts and strengths . . . but most especially our "heart."

In many ways, we are also like hobbits and kender and other such wee folk, but unlike them, Warrows can become quite deadly, quite lethal when pressed. Oh, don't take me wrong: as I said in the introduction to the omnibus edition of *The Iron Tower,* I love the wee folk of longstanding legend and of other authors' tales, especially the hobbits of J.R.R. Tolkien's magnificent saga, *The Lord of the Rings;* and let me acknowledge here and now that a couple of things within both *The Silver Call* and *The Iron Tower* are written in homage, in tribute, to Tolkien . . . in particular, the titles of the opening chapters, as well as parts of the journey through the Dwarven-holt of Kraggen-cor, of Drimmendeeve, of the Black Hole. Wonderful tale tellers like Tolkien come along not once in a generation, but rather once in a lifetime, and then only if we are lucky. Fortunate are we that he set his story down in writing; fortunate are we also that his work lives on after he himself is gone. Like other authors, I can but pray that my own efforts will live on after me, though when I began I never expected such.

Little did I know some twenty-odd years ago as I lay in a cast from my armpits to my toes that this very first tale of mine—*The Silver Call*—and the follow-on Mithgarian adventures would transform my life forever, would lead to a career change and to an age-spanning series. However, when I penned *The Silver Call*[2], it was a place for me to escape being totally helpless, completely bedridden, when I was living, in effect, in a cement block. And escape I did, traveling across a wonderful place—even though quite perilous at times—and I am so glad to have journeyed therein.

Glad, too, am I that so many of you—new readers and old alike—have chosen to travel across Mithgar at my side, though not in a "cement" block[3].

A simple "thank-you" doesn't seem nearly enough to express my gratitude for your company, yet it will have to do, for I can think of nothing else to say that would better convey my heartfelt appreciation.

Let me also say that, just as I did with *The Iron Tower*, I wrote *The Silver Call* as a single story. It was my editor at the time (Pat LoBrutto) who decided *The Silver Call* should be a duology. And so it was done that way: two books to tell the tale. But you know, like *The Iron Tower*, I always felt that this story, too, should have been published as written—as a single book and not two. Well, here we are, whole at last, the omnibus edition of *The Silver Call*. And with this tale now in print as it was written, as it was meant to be read, let us all get comfort-

---

[2]Rather, when I penciled it, for in that cement block, all I could use to write the tale was pencils and tablets.

[3]By the way, I do *not* recommend getting run over by a car as a way to start a writing career.

able in our favorite rooms, in our favorite chairs or lounges or beds, in whatever and wherever are our favorite places to read, and open the pages to the (oh-so-familiar, for some of us) opening words and experience all over again the tale for the very first time.

—Dennis L. McKiernan
Tucson, Arizona, 2000

A WORD ABOUT WARROWS

Central to this tale are the Wee Ones, the Warrows. A brief description of this legendary Folk is given in the appendices at the end of Book Two: *The Brega Path* (p. 419).

JOURNAL NOTES

Note 1: The source of this tale is a tattered copy of *The Fairhill Journal*, an incredibly fortunate find dating from the time before The Separation.

Note 2: The Great War of the Ban ended the Second Era (2E) of Mithgar. The Third Era (3E) began on the following Year's Start Day. The Third Era, too, eventually came to an end, and so started the Fourth Era (4E), and then the Fifth (5E). The tale recorded here began in October of 5E231. Although this adventure occurs some four millennia after the Ban War, and more than two centuries after the Winter War, the roots of the quest told herein lie directly in the events of those earlier times.

Note 3: There are many instances in this tale where, in the press of the moment, the Dwarves, Elves, Men, and Warrows speak in their own native tongues; yet, to avoid the awkwardness of burdensome translations, where necessary I have rendered their words in Pellarion, the Common Tongue of Mithgar. Some words, however, do not lend themselves to translation, and these I've left unchanged; yet other words may look to be in error, but are indeed correct—e.g., DelfLord is but a single word though a capital L nestles among its letters. Also note that waggon, traveller, and several other similar words are written in the Pendwyrian form of Pellarion and are not misspelled.

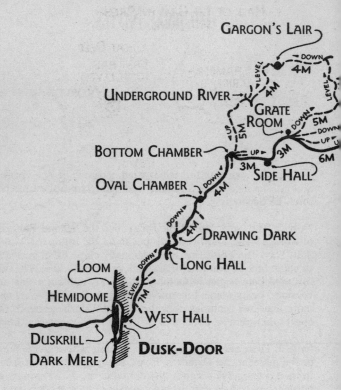

GARGON'S LAIR

DOWN
4M

LEVEL

4M

LEVEL

UNDERGROUND RIVER

GRATE
ROOM

DOWN
5M

DOWN

UP
5M

DOWN
UP

BOTTOM CHAMBER

UP
3M

6M

3M

SIDE HALL

OVAL CHAMBER

DOWN
4M

DOWN
4M

DRAWING DARK

DOWN

LONG HALL

LOOM

LEVEL
7M

HEMIDOME

WEST HALL

DUSKRILL

DUSK-DOOR

DARK MERE

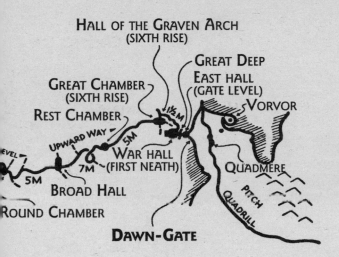

HALL OF THE GRAVEN ARCH
(SIXTH RISE)

GREAT DEEP
EAST HALL
(GATE LEVEL)

GREAT CHAMBER
(SIXTH RISE)

VORVOR

REST CHAMBER

1½M

UPWARD WAY

5M

EVEL

WAR HALL
(FIRST NEATH)

QUADMERE

7M

PITCH

5M

QUADRILL

BROAD HALL

ROUND CHAMBER

DAWN-GATE

The Brega Path

BOOK ONE

TREK TO KRAGGEN-COR

To my own Holly:
Martha Lee

"All dreams fetch with a silver call,
and to some the belling of that
treasured voice is irresistible."

Seventh Durek
December 13, 5E231

PROLOGUE

Slowly the waggon trundled westward along the Crossland Road. Ahead, the three occupants could see a great, looming, dark mass reaching up toward the sky and standing across the way, extending far beyond seeing to the north and south. Spindlethorn it was, a great tangle of massive vines rearing fifty feet or more into the air, with razor-sharp spikes clawing outward—so thickly entwined that even birds found it difficult to penetrate the thorny mass. Through this mighty barricade the road went, and overhead the tangle interlaced, forming a shadowy tunnel of thorns leading down into the river valley from which sprang the fanged barrier.

Into the tunnel rolled the waggon, and the light fell blear along the path. And long did the trio ride in the thorny dimness.

At last, ahead the wayfarers could see an arch of light, and once more into the day they came as the route crossed a bridge over the Spindle River. Beyond the bridge on the far bank again the Barrier grew, and once more a dark tunnel bored through it. Two miles the travellers had come within the thorny way to reach the bridge, and nearly three more miles beyond would they go before escaping the Thornwall.

Onto the span they rolled, and the great timbers rumbled as the waggon crossed. And the three occupants stared in amazement at the massive dike of thorns rearing upward and clawing at the slash of blue sky jagging overhead. This great spiked rampart extended all the way around the Land the wayfarers were entering, growing in the river valleys along the borders. Soon they crossed the bridge and again entered the gloom.

In all, it took nearly two hours for the trio to pass completely through the Spindlethorn Barrier, but at last they emerged into the sunlight at the far side. The countryside they could see before them was one of rolling farmland, and the road they followed ran on to the west, cresting a rise to disappear only to be seen again topping the crest beyond.

Along this way they went, and the warm Sun was pleasant. A mile or more they rode, and at last they saw workers in a nearby field harvesting grain. The driver stopped the waggon as it drew opposite the field hands.

"Hola!" hailed the waggoner. "Could you help us find our way?"

The swish of scythes fell silent as folk turned at the call to see who had hailed. But when their eyes fell upon the occupants of the waggon at roadside, the males who had been cutting stepped to the fore, while females and oldsters who had been bundling sheaves drifted to the rear, and the young ones who had been gleaning scurried to the back and peered around from behind skirts to look at the strangers. And they all stood in silence.

"We are here on the High King's business," called the driver, "and we seek the way to Sir Tuckerby's Warren."

"The King's business, you say?" piped a buccan in the fore, stepping to the side of the field and looking up in wonder at the strangers, while they in turn stared down at him in amazement. The wain riders saw before them one of the Wee Folk, a Warrow, for they had come into the Land of the Boskydells. Small he was, three and a half feet tall, yet those assembled behind him were no taller, though many were shorter, especially the wee young ones. His hair was black and cropped at the shoulder. His jerkin and breeks were the color of dusky leaves, and soft boots shod his feet. His ears were pointed like those of Elves, and there was also an Elven tilt to his bright, liquescent eyes— Utruni eyes, some would say, for the orbs of the Wee Folk resemble those of the Stone Giants. Yet, unlike the Giants, Warrow eyes are not true gems, but instead are astonishingly jewel-hued: sapphire blue; emerald green; and the third and last color, topaz gold.

"Sir Tuckerby's Warren is in Woody Hollow, some fifty miles to the west," said the Warrow, pointing down the Crossland Road. Then he turned his amber gaze back upon the strangers. "Could you use a drink of water on this warm day, or something to eat? For I know travellers build up a thirst from the dusty road . . . and get hungry, too."

"Thank you, but no, for we have food and drink with us, and our mission is urgent, else would we tarry awhile," answered the driver.

"Then fare thee well," responded the golden-eyed buccan in his piping voice, stepping back from the roadside.

With a chirk of his tongue and a flick of reins the driver urged the horses forward; and as they pulled away he waved to the Wee Folk in the field and they waved back, the tiny younglings running through the furrows amid trills of cascading laughter, keeping pace for a moment, only to turn back at sharp whistles from their sires.

"Hmph! So those are Waerans," growled one of the passengers, looking back. "I find it hard to think of such a small Folk as being legendary heroes."

"Yet heroes they are," said the driver, "and brave at that. I only hope that what we seek will be found in the journal we've come so very far to see."

"Aye, the diary of Sir Tuckerby Underbank, Hero of the Realm," grunted the other passenger. "Well do my kith honor his memory, even though his deeds lie more than two centuries in the past. Yet what my brother says is true: the iron of bravery seems to seek out this Folk; but I, too, would have deemed them too small to hold such mettle."

The driver turned to his seatmate. "Lore has it, though, that these Wee Ones—these Waerlinga—have played more than one key role in the fate of Mithgar, no matter their size—for stature alone does not measure the greatness of a heart."

Silence reigned in the waggon as legends of old tumbled through the occupants' minds, and the wain continued to roll westward on the King's business.

CHAPTER 1

THE UNEXPECTED PARTIES

"Hoy there, Mister Perry! Hoy there! Hoy there! They're com-ing to see you! Coming over from the Hall!"

Peregrin Fairhill sat in the October Sun on the stoop of his home, The Root of Woody Hollow. He looked up from the sil-ver horn that he had been diligently polishing. *What in the Seven Dells is all this racket about?* he wondered. What he saw was a young buccan—that male Warrow period betwixt the end of the teens and the coming of age at thirty—rushing up the curved pathway to The Root. Onward came the buccan, run-ning pell-mell, red-faced with effort, with two youngling War-rows capering and cartwheeling behind.

"Hold on there, Cotton! Slow down before you burst," called Perry, laughing. "And you two pinwheels stop your spin-ning."

The young buccan skidded to a halt in the path at the foot of the stoop; and the two tag-alongs, winded and panting, plopped down in the grass bordering the hedge and waited expectantly to see just exactly why it was that Cotton had been running. Pausing a moment to allow the young buccan to catch his breath, Perry finally asked, "All right now, Cotton, what's all this running about? Who wants me? Who's coming from the Hall?"

"Why, Sir, *they* want you," Cotton began, still huffing and puffing. "Hoy! Stop a minute. You two younglings"—he turned a baleful stare on the small Warrows—"this is not for your ears.

Nip along now, so's I can tell my master what this is all about. Double-quick! On your way!" The two youngsters, being well-raised and Boskydell-mannered, as are all young Warrows of Woody Hollow—and realizing that nothing was going to be said as long as they were about—scampered down the rock-lined path and out of sight around the end of the hedge.

Satisfied, Cotton began again: "Sir, I never thought as I'd see the day. Folks like them have not been seen in the Dells since the old days before Tuckerby's time. And here they are! They just come marching right into the Hall, neat as may be, and asked for the Mayor. Yes sir, there I was, sweeping the floor like I do every midmonth and they just up and ask me—*me!*—for the Mayor.

"I couldn't believe my eyes was really seeing them, and I must've looked like the witless fool I am, standing there with my mouth hanging open in pure astonishment. I guess I'd've been there still, frozen to my broom, gaping, 'cept Mayor Whit-latch chose that very instant to come rushing in.

"'Oh, Cotton,' says he, 'where's the—' Then he sees them, too, and is also struck dumb, but not for long. You can say what you want about Whitlatch's carryings-on, what with all his long-winded speechmaking and his love of ribbon-cutting cer-emonies, but I'll give him this: after the first shock, he recov-ered as steady as you please and asked them if he could do something for them.

"'We'd like to see the Mayor,' says the big one. 'I *am* the Mayor,' says Whitlatch. 'Mayor,' says the big one, 'is there some place where we can talk?' 'Follow me,' says the Mayor, and they all troop into his office.

"Well, I was just as full of curiosity as a new kitten, so I did all my sweeping right in front of the Mayor's door," Cotton continued, red-faced with embarrassment but with his jaw jut-ting out as if daring someone to call him an eavesdropper—though his gemlike emerald-green eyes did not meet the sapphire-blue ones of his master. "I couldn't hear nothing ex-cept voices murmuring so low as you can't recognize what's being said, them doors being as thick as they are. They all were in there talking low for about half an hour. Then I finally heard something more than just a mumble. It was Whitlatch. He said, 'Why, you're right! Peregrin Fairhill is the one you want to see.' And with that he flings open the door shouting, 'Cotton! Cotton!' Then he sees I'm right next to him, so he lowers his voice and says, urgent-like, 'Cotton, run up to The Root and tell your master, Mister Perry, that I'm bringing these Boskydell visitors up from Hollow Hall to see him and Tuck's diary; they need him and his book. Now hop to it, and don't be a slowcoach about it.'

"Well, I dropped my broom and ran right here as quick as I could to bring you the news, Mister Perry, that they're coming here to The Root to see you and your *Raven Book* and all— though I'll be switched if I know why."

Perry stood and wrapped the small silver horn in its polishing cloth, gathering up the green and white baldric. He turned to go through the oaken door and into The Root, where he kept his copy of Tuck's chronicle. "But, Cotton," he turned back, perplexed, "you haven't told me the most important part: Just who are they that want to see me? Who or what are they that need me? Who are they that're coming to see the Account?"

"Ninnyhammer that I am!" Cotton smote his own forehead with a sharp slap. "Why you're perfectly right, Sir. I *have* left out the most important part."

Glancing about to make sure that no one else could hear what he was going to say, Cotton completely missed the dancing, glittering eyes of the two small-fry Warrows lying on their stomachs and peering through from the other side of the hedge, where they'd got to when Cotton had commanded them to nip along. All the rest of their lives these two often would tell about the next words that Cotton would say. For as far as the Warrows of the Seven Dells in later days were concerned, this was the moment that the *real* adventure began: because what Cotton said was, "Sir, them as wants to see the *Raven Book?* Sir, well . . ." Once again he glanced around.

"Out with it, Cotton: who are they?"

"Why, Sir," he took a deep breath, then plunged on, "they're *Dwarves,* Sir! That's what they are: *Dwarves!*"

CHAPTER 2

WELCOME TO THE ROOT

"*Dwarves,* Cotton? Here in the Seven Dells? *Dwarves* to see me?*"

"And a Man, Mister Perry, two Dwarves and a Man, too."

My goodness! thought a stunned Perry. *What a piece of news this is! A Man and Dwarves, too. And they've come to see me!* He spun on his heel and rushed into the burrow with Cotton right behind.

That was indeed a piece of news, for visits by Men or Dwarves are rare in the Boskydells—Men less so than Dwarves. Why, only at one time had there been many Men on this side of the Spindlethorn, and that was way back during the Winter War—after vile Modru had sent a great gang of Ghûls to overrun the Dells. And the Evil One's Reavers had nearly succeeded, too: looting, burning, slaying, whelming the Land, nearly ruining the Bosky with their rapacious grasp of the Seven Dells.

But then came Patrel Rushlock and Danner Bramblethorn, the greatest military heroes of all Warrowdom—greater even then Abagon "Rûckslayer" Fenner over in Weiunwood. Captains Patrel and Danner had returned to the Bosky during the Great Retreat. And they began to organize the Warrows to drive the blackguards out of the Land, scouring the Boskydells free of the invaders.

And the battles were mighty, and touch and go, until at last the Men came—Vidron's Legion—and then the Ghûls were routed . . . only to be replaced by one of Modru's Hordes. Yet still, allied with the Warrows, the Men fought until the Winter War came to an end.

And after the War, again Men came, to help rebuild the Seven Dells—and rebuild they did. But rarely afterwards was a Man seen inside the Thornring, for King Galen in Pellar had declared the Boskydells a free Realm under the protection of his scepter. His edict was that no Man was to dwell in the Land of the Wee Folk. Hence, after the Winter War, those Men seen within the Barrier were usually just passing through along the Crossland Road, or the Upland Way, or down the Tineway. Oh, at rare times, Men would come to the Bosky as King's Messengers, bringing word of the King's doings; at other infrequent times, merchants would come to purchase Downdell leaf, melons, wicker works from Bigfen, or other Wee Folk trade goods. But, by Galen's edict, no Men came to stay. And when King Galen's son, Gareth, became Monarch, he reaffirmed the edict. And so it was and has been and is even unto this day that the Boskydell is a free Land in which no Men dwell, a Realm under the protection of the Kings in faraway Pellar.

But as scarce to the Dells as Men were, Dwarves were even rarer; though they were not forbidden entry into the Bosky, none had ever positively been seen by a Seven-Dells Warrow living in Perry's time. In fact, none had been sighted in such a span of time that they had become creatures of legend. Oh, an occasional Warrow travelling outside the Thornring, to Stonehill, would sometimes think that he had espied a Dwarf, but that was always a glimpse from afar so that afterwards the Warrow couldn't say absolutely that he'd actually laid eyes on one. Historically speaking, the last agreed-upon sighting of Dwarves within the Bosky itself was when several of them had passed through driving a waggon bearing weapons and armor, it was said to be used in their bitter clashes with the Rūcks. And that was way back, nearly two hundred twenty years before the Struggles, before the Winter War, before the Dragon Star—which meant that Dwarves had not been seen in the Boskydells for almost 450 years. Oh, they had been observed elsewhere, trading their Dwarf-crafted goods—just not in the Bosky. But now, if Cotton was right, both Man and Dwarf had returned.

Perry, with Cotton on his heels, rushed down the hall and

into the study. The *study:* in this The Root was peculiar, for it was one of the few Warrow homes to have such a room.

Instead of books, Warrows in general much prefer their gardens and fields and fens and woods. Oh, not to say that most Warrows aren't educated to read and write and do their sums— oh no, not at all. Many of the Wee Folk can do these things well before their second-age-name change—much pride being taken by the winner of a spelldown, or by one who can recite from memory the names of all the local heroes, such as naming those of the Struggles. However, although many Warrows are educated, most would just rather be in their vegetable patch or down at the One-Eyed Crow or Blue Bull or Thirsty Horse or any of the other Bosky taverns, with a pipe and a mug of dark beer, than to be tucked away somewhere with a dusty tome. And even when they do read books, they prefer those filled with things they already know about—such as the familiar hearth tales containing numerous stories of Warrow cleverness at outwitting Giants, Dragons, Big Folk, and other *Outsiders.* In any case, books are to be found in the *proper* places—such as in the libraries at the Cliffs or at the Great Treehouse or at Eastpoint Hall—and *not* in a private dwelling.

Thus, the study at The Root was a curiosity among Warrow homes.

It was a large, spacious room, with burrow-windows opening to the west. The floor was made of oak, but the walls and ceiling were panelled with walnut. There were many comfortable seats inside, and there were two desks and a writing table against three of the walls. There was also a low table in the center of the room, with a lounge and different-sized chairs arranged around it. There were several floor-to-ceiling bookcases with manuscripts and pamphlets and tomes and scrolls jumbled haphazardly upon the shelves. But most striking of all, there were a number of large and small glass cases in which were displayed weapons and armor, flags and pennons, and other items of a like nature—all of a suitable size to fit Warrows.

It was in this study that Tuckerby's scriveners had transcribed most of *The Raven Book,* a journal started by Tuckerby Underbank on his way to join the Thornwalkers at Spindle Ford in the year the Winter War began. Tuck was one of the most famous Warrows in all history—even more renowned than Danner and Patrel—actually being the subject of Elven songs: it was Tuckerby who loosed the Red Quarrel and destroyed the Myrkenstone, and with it Modru's power and Gyphon's threat. And his journal, *The Raven Book*—or, as it is more formally known, *Sir Tuckerby Underbank's Unfinished Diary and His Accounting of the Winter War*—contained his story and the tale of the Dimmendark.

As the buccen swiftly entered this place of History, Perry hurriedly placed the baldric and the silver horn—still wrapped in its polishing cloth—into one of the glass cases. Then he turned to the other Warrow. "Cotton, while I unpack the *Raven Book,* find Holly and tell her that there'll likely be guests at The Root tonight: three—perhaps four if the Mayor stays—extra places at the table if you please . . . and beds as well. And, Cotton, have her set a place for you, too; for you've become versed in the tales of the '*Book,* and you've met these strangers . . . and, well, stick by me; I'd just feel better if I had you at my side."

Cotton, flustered and pleased that his master wanted him at hand when these *Outsiders* came to The Root, bolted away to find young Holly Northcolt, youngest dammsel of Jayar and Dot Northcolt.

Jayar, a former postmaster and now a country gentle-warrow, was well known for the cold spring on his land suitable for chilling buttermilk and melons. A no-nonsense buccan with definite opinions, Squire Northcolt had always greatly admired the Ravenbook Scholars; and he was deeply disturbed when he learned that the new curator of The Root—a Mister Peregrin Fairhill, as it were—was not only deeply involved in scholarly pursuits but also was struggling to keep up with the cleaning and dusting and ordering of foodstuff, and no doubt probably starving on his own cooking. And so Jayar overruled Dot's weeping objections and sent young Holly driving a two-wheeled pony-cart the fifty-one miles north from Thimble to Woody Hollow to "take charge of that Scholar's welfare."

Thus it was that one day Perry answered a knock at the door, and there before him stood pretty Holly, suitcase in hand, her dappled pony munching calmly upon the lawn. "I've come to manage this burrowhold," the golden-eyed damman announced matter-of-factly; and though Perry couldn't recall having advertised for a homekeeper—for in truth, he hadn't—he welcomed her in glad relief, for he *was* practically starving on his own cooking, at least he felt so.

And so Holly's timely appearance enlarged Perry's "family" to two; and, after she'd had a chance to size up the situation, through her insistence the household grew to three by the hiring of a handywarrow: Cotton. And things got mended and the lawn trimmed, and Cotton provided an eager ear for Mister Perry's scholarly thoughts and notions.

Hence, thanks to a determined Southdell Squire and his equally determined dammsel, The Root had acquired the gentle hand of a competent young damman to steer it past the shoals of starvation and beyond the reefs of untidyness and into a haven of domesticity.

And while Cotton dashed off in search of this young damman, Perry carefully slipped *The Raven Book* out of its rich-grained Eld-wood carrying case and placed it on the writing table. Looking around, he could see nothing else to do to get ready; so as soon as Cotton rejoined him, they returned to the stoop to wait for the visitors to arrive from Woody Hollow Hall.

Meanwhile, Holly was hurriedly bustling about inside, preparing for the unexpected guests while muttering to herself: "Gracious! Guests here at The Root! And Cotton said they were a Big Man and two Dwarves! And maybe Mayor Whitlatch, too! I wonder what it is that Dwarves eat? And where in the world can the Big Man sleep? Men being so tall as they are: twice as high as an ordinary Warrow, I hear. Now the Dwarves, though it is said that they are nearly of a proper size, I don't know what they eat. Perhaps they eat mushrooms, or rabbit stew, or . . ."

Perry and Cotton had just stepped back outside when Mayor Will Whitlatch the Third and the strangers arrived. Taking Perry by the arm, the Mayor turned to the visitors and said, "Master Peregrin Fairhill, may I present Lord Kian of Dael Township, and Mastercrafters Anval Ironfist and Borin Ironfist from the Undermountain Realm of Mineholt North."

And for the first time ever, Perry set his sapphire-blue Warrow eyes upon Man: *How tall they are . . . I wonder if the ceil-*

ings in The Root are high enough; and Dwarf: *So broad and sturdy—as strong as the rock they delve.*

Lord Kian was a young Man, slender and straight and tall, almost twice the height of Perry. In his right hand he held an ash-wood stave, and he was dressed for an overland walking journey: soft boots, sturdy breeks and jerkin, and a long cloak. His clothing was an elusive grey-green color that blended equally well with leaf, limb, or stone. On his head was a bow-man's hat adorned with a single green feather. And belted over his shoulder was a plain quiver of green-fletched arrows and a curious bow—curious in that it was not a yew-wood longbow, but rather seemed to be made of strangely shaped bone, like long, curved, animal horns set into a silver handle. Kian's golden hair was cropped at his shoulders, and though his cheeks were clean-shaven, his fair countenance was graced with a well-trimmed yellow moustache which merged 'round the corners of his mouth with an equally well-trimmed yellow beard. At his waist he wore a grey belt with a silver buckle that matched the silver brooch clasping the cloak around his shoulders. The color of this metal seemed somehow to live in the grey of his sharp, piercing eyes. *Is this the way all Men are? Silver and gold? Silver-grey eyes 'neath yellow-gold brow?*

In contrast to the tall, fair Lord Kian, Anval and Borin were only three hands or so taller than Perry, but were extraordinarily wide of shoulder, even for Dwarves, seeming at least half again as broad there as the young Man. They were outfitted in dark, earthy browns for their journey, but otherwise were dressed little different from Kian. However, instead of a rude stave, they each carried a carved ash-wood staff shod with a black-iron ferrule and topped with a cunningly shaped black-iron stave head: a bear for Anval and a ram for Borin. Strapped across their shoulders by carrying thongs were sturdy Dwarf War-axes: double-bitted, oak-hafted, rune-marked, steel-edged weapons. The Dwarves themselves, though not as fair-skinned as Lord Kian, had light complexions. But their look was dominated by black: Each had a black beard, long and forked as is the fashion of Dwarves. Not only were their beards and hair as black as the roots of a mountain, the color of their eyes was that of the blackest onyx. And unlike Kian's smiling face, the look upon the Dwarves' visages was somber, dark, wary. *Gracious,*

I can't tell the one from the other, why, they are as alike as two lumps of forge coal!

Both Anval and Borin doffed the caps from their raven locks and bowed stiffly, their black eyes never leaving Perry's face. Lord Kian, too, bowed, and Perry returned the courtesy to all with a sweeping bow of his own. Mayor Whitlatch, not to be outdone and thoroughly caught up in the ceremony, bowed to each and every one there in front of The Root—except the two tagalongs, who were busily bowing to one another on the far side of the hedge.

"And this is my friend and companion, Cotton Buckleburr," announced Perry, after which there ensued a second round of bowing, including a repeat performance by the Mayor. "I understand you want me—and my *Raven Book,* too," continued Perry. "Let us all go inside, and I'll see what I can do for you."

Much to Perry's surprise, Mayor Whitlatch declined: "Oh no, Perry, I've got to get back to the Dingle. Lots to do, you know. I have to be getting down to Budgens tonight as well. A Mayor's work is never done."

Lord Kian turned to the Mayor. "Long have we journeyed to reach Sir Tuckerby's Warren. And you have guided us on the final leg so that we may speak with Master Perry . . . so that we may complete the King's business. For that we thank you, Mayor. No longer will we keep you from your pressing duties." Although Lord Kian had not said it in so many words, it was clear that Will Whitlatch was being dismissed.

Realizing that he was free to go, the Mayor, with visible relief, said his farewells and left after again bowing to them all. It is certain that Mayor Whitlatch was to a small degree disappointed, because he knew that he was going to miss one of Holly's guest meals at The Root; and since Warrows love to eat—as many as five meals a day—and since guest meals are by far the best meals, it was no small sacrifice that the Mayor was making. But on the other side of the balance scales, it *was,* after all, "King's business" that was to be discussed, and that was very tricky indeed. It was best that small Warrow Mayors of small Warrow towns keep their noses where they belong, otherwise who knows what might occur. Lawks! Look at what happened the last time Warrows got caught up with the King— why, there was all that business with the Myrkenstone. Oh no, that sort of thing was not going to happen to Will Whitlatch the Third—even if he *did* have to miss a grand meal! Will hurried faster and faster down the pathway and was soon out of sight.

"Welcome to The Root," said Perry, and he turned and opened the oakpegged door.

CHAPTER 3

THE KING'S BUSINESS

Perry need not have worried about the ceilings at The Root, for Lord Kian could stand comfortably—though he did stoop a bit when going through the doorway.

But Perry hadn't been the only one who had wondered about the room heights, for as Lord Kian remarked, "I would have guessed that Waerling homes would be smaller, not large enough to permit a Man to roam about freely without knocking his head up against the beams."

"I thought you might be bumping up against the ceiling, too," laughed Perry as the visitors removed their hats and cloaks, "but *I* at least should have known better: you see, The Root is special."

"Special?" asked Lord Kian. "How so?"

"Well, it's not like most Warrow dwellings," answered Perry, "be they the burrow holts of us Siven-Warrows, the tree flets of the Quiren-Warrows, the stilted fen-houses of the Othen, or the stone field-houses of the Paren."

"Your Folk live in four different kinds of dwellings? One for each strain?" grunted Anval, his dark scowl replaced by surprise.

"Ah," said Perry, "in the past that was true. But now many of us don't follow the old ways of the four Warrow-folk, and we live willy-nilly, skimble, skamble: burrow, flet, stilts, or stone, we lodge where we will, no matter what our lineage.

"Yet I stray . . . and, Lord Kian, you are right: The Root is extra large, as it were. Oh, it wasn't always this way." Perry gestured with a broad sweep of his hand. The visitors were being led down a wide central hallway, oak-panelled with rough-hewn beams overhead. There were many doorways issuing off to either side into unseen rooms. The hall itself contained several high-backed chairs and two small, linen-covered tables set to either side against the walls. Each of the tables bore a vase of dried flowers placed there by Holly, and here and there hung pieces of tapestry and needlepoint. At the entrance end of the hallway an umbrella stand held two bumbershoots and a cane, with a many-pegged cloak-and-coat rack on the wall above it—which the visitors did not use. The other extent of the passageway terminated in a cross-hall, and the wings of that corridor disappeared around corners: on the westward side to the kitchen, scullery, and, further on, the storage rooms; and on the eastward side to the bedrooms.

"The original Root," Perry went on, "was an ordinary Warrow-sized home, scaled to fit Warrows—and, grown up, we range from three to four feet in height. I'm rather average at three and a half feet, with Cotton here a jot taller—by an inch or so. Anyway, as I was saying, the original Root was ordinary, but it was destroyed during the War: Modru's cruel reavers— Ghûls—finding no plunder, gutted and burned it along with many other dwellings in Hollow End. But after the War, Kingsmen came, as well as others, to help rebuild the homes —but especially to work on this burrow, Tuckerby's Warren, to make it better than new. And they did, as you can see—though it's not exactly 'new' anymore, those matters being some two hundred thirty years in the past. In any event, it was at that time Sir Tuckerby asked that the new Root be dug out large enough to house any future guest who might be a Man, Tuckerby having made many friends who were Men.

"So you see, Lord Kian, the ceilings are high enough for you, and there are many sturdy—and I hope comfortable— Man-sized chairs sprinkled throughout the rooms to accommodate one of your size." (And though Perry did not yet know of it, in one of the long-unused burrow-rooms Holly had rediscovered a Man-sized four-poster, much to her surprise and delight—for now she had a proper bedroom for each of the guests, including this "Man-giant," whom she had glimpsed simply *towering* over Perry and Cotton, the Man *soaring* up to an awe-some height of six feet or so.)

"Do you mean that in any other Waerling home I would have to get about on my hands and knees?" asked Kian, reaching up and touching the oak panelling overhead.

"Not quite"—Perry smiled, warming to this tall young Lord—"though you would have to bend a bit."

Halfway down the length of the hall, Perry ushered the group through a doorway to the left and into the walnut-walled study. As they laid their hats and cloaks aside, Perry gestured at the surrounding glass cases: "The Root is special not only because of its scale; it's also special because it is a repository. You see, Warrows don't hold with memorials, the Monument at Budgens commemorating the Struggles being an exception. But this, my home, is an exception, too. Look about you; you see armor and weaponry, Elven cloaks, and many other things that are of the past. The Root is a home *and* a museum, a gallery dedicated to the Warrow heroes of the Winter War. It is a shrine, tended by the kindred of Sir Tuckerby: he who loosed the Red Quarrel; the Myrkenstone Slayer; and the last true owner of The Root. And I, Perry Fairhill, am the present curator of those glorious days."

Perry turned to one corner of the room. "Look, Anval, Borin, here's something that will surely catch your interest: a simple coat of chain mail."

"Simple coat of mail!" burst out Borin, his black eyes aglitter. He saw before him a small corselet of silver-shining armor. Amber gems were inset among the links, and a bejeweled belt—beryl and jade—was clasped about the waist. But the gemstones were not what caused Borin to cry out; he was amazed by the metal from which it was forged. "This is starsilver! A thing like this has not been crafted in centuries. It is Châkka work, and is priceless."

"Starsilver. Silveron," spoke Anval, his sturdy hand lightly brushing over the finely wrought links. "Stronger than steel, lighter than down, soft as doeskin. This was forged in the smitheries of our ancestors—it is Kraggen-cor work." Suddenly Anval smacked a clenched fist into his open palm. "Hah! I have it: this is the legendary coat given to Tuckerby by the

Princess Laurelin, as the world stood on the brink of Winter War."

"Given to Tuckerby at War's beginning and worn by him to the very top of the Iron Tower." Perry nodded, surprised that the Dwarves knew of this armor—surprised, too, by the reverence that the silveron metal brought forth from the two of them. "But I ramble. Please be seated."

As they settled comfortably, Holly bustled into the room, her pretty face smiling, her eyes twinkling like great amber gems, and she carried a tray upon which rode an enormous pitcher of dark beer and several mugs. "I was thinking the travellers would have a thirst, Mister Perry, what with their walking and all." She set the tray down on the table in the center of the room and wiped her graceful hands on her solid blue apron. "Mind you now, Mister Perry, dinner will be ready in about two hours, so don't you go nattering on beyond that time; your guests look hungry." And with that she swept from the room as abruptly as she had entered it.

"Well"—Perry smiled, a bit discomfited at being shepherded in front of strangers by the slim three-foot-tall young damman—"as you can see, I have been given my marching orders by the Lady of The Root." He began pouring beer into the mugs and passing them around. "And we have but two hours before dinner. Yet that is perhaps time enough to satisfy my curiosity, which abounds. Imagine, two Dwarves and a Man in the Bosky, here on a mission to see the *Raven Book,* and from what you said to Mayor Whitlatch, it's the King's business that brought you." He set down the pitcher and turned to get the *'Book,* but Cotton had anticipated his move and was at Perry's elbow, holding forth the grey tome.

Taking the book from Cotton, who quickly retrieved his own mug of beer and took a satisfying gulp—Warrows do love beer—Perry turned back to his guests. "Well, here it is: *Sir Tuckerby Underbank's Unfinished Diary and His Accounting of the Winter War.*" And he held it out to the visitors. Somewhat to his surprise, it was Borin and not Lord Kian who leaned forward to take the massive volume.

"So this is the famous book, eh?" Borin rumbled, turning it over and around and back again as if inspecting it for its crafting. Grunting his apparent acceptance of its outer cover and binding, the Dwarf opened the tome and, after another inspection, began avidly leafing through the pages.

"Well, not exactly," replied Perry, sipping his beer, "this is a duplicate of the original."

"*What!* Do you mean that we are not looking at the real thing?" snapped Borin, slamming the book to, his Dwarf instincts against counterfeits and copies set ajangle by Perry's words.

"*Kruk!*" spat Anval. "What good will it do to look through a *copy* when it is genuine truth we seek?"

"Hoy now," protested Cotton, his temper rising, "wait up! It may not be the original *Raven Book* you're holding there, but you can bet your last copper that it's the 'genuine truth' as you call it. I mean, well, Mister Perry made that duplicate himself, and so you know it's got to be accurate. Tell 'em, Mister Perry."

"It's as accurate as you can get!" exclaimed Perry, flustered, looking from Anval to Borin and back again. "It is an *exact* copy! It is one of several exact copies made through the years by the Scholars. It duplicates all of the original precisely, and I do mean *precisely:* even the spelling errors and the punctuation errors made in Tuck's original journal are copied faithfully. And as to the Account: places where words, phrases, sentences, even paragraphs, places where they were written in and then lined out by Tuck's scribes, even those are meticulously reproduced.

"Look, the real *Raven Book* used to be here at The Root, but no longer. Some years after the War, Tuckerby's dammsel, Raven Greylock, for whom the book is named—my great-grandam five generations removed—bore it west with her to the Cliffs, the Warrow strongholt that stood fast and did not fall during the Winter War. There, she and her husband, Willen, gathered some of Tuck's original scriveners, and others, and continued the great scribing of the History. Even now the work goes on, for history always has been and ever will be in the making. And it needs recording. But as to Tuck's original Account, the 'Book remains at the Cliffs to this day, an heirloom of the Fairhills and Greylocks, the Underbanks and Fletchers, and others of Tuck's lineage. There at the Cliffs it is revered and tended by his kindred, occasionally being added to when some bit of lore or history bearing on the Winter War comes to light, appended therein by the family scholars—but only if after due deliberation it is unanimously accepted.

"But I digress. It's from that original that the copies are made . . . and triple-, no, quadruple-checked. So, if it's truth you seek—the 'genuine truth'—then you hold it in your hands." Having given his pledge, Perry, though nettled, fell silent.

Regardless of the Warrow's passionately tendered personal guarantee of the book's accuracy, neither of the two Dwarves seemed willing to accept anything but the original. Disgruntled, they glanced at Lord Kian, and at the Man's curt nod, they reluctantly settled back and Borin resumed his search through the tome, leafing slowly through the pages. Soon his dark countenance took on a faintly baffled look. Then he stopped altogether. "Faugh! I go about this all wrong," he rumbled, at which statement Anval grunted his assent. "If what we seek is truly here, Waeran, then you must lead us to it."

"And what is that?" asked Perry, his vexation with the Dwarves yielding to a strange glow of excitement.

We've come to it now, thought Cotton, and he hardened himself as if for a blow.

"Kraggen-cor. Our ancient homeland. What you name Drimmen-deeve," answered Borin. "Durek the Deathbreaker is reborn, and we go to wrest stolen Kraggen-cor from the Foul Folk."

"Deathbreaker Durek?" asked Cotton, shivering. "Deathbreaker? That sounds right unnatural, if you ask me. Just who is this Durek? And how did he get the name Deathbreaker?" Lord Kian smiled at the directness of this small Warrow.

"He is the First, the High Leader," replied Borin, "the Father of Durek's Folk, foremost among the five Châkka kindred. Think me no fool, Waeran, for not even Durek is Death's full master, for all mortal things perish. Yet, once in a great while an heir of Durek is born so like the First that he, too, is given the name Durek. When this happens—as it has happened again—we Châkka deem that indeed the true Durek has broken the bonds of Death and once more trods the Mountain roots anew.

"And now, being reborn, Durek desires to return to his home. He has gathered many of his kith—those descended in the Durek line—be they from the Mineholt North, the Red Caves, the Quartzen Hills, wherever Durek's Folk delve. And he has raised a great army. And we are to retake Kraggen-cor, to overthrow and slay the vile Squam, usurpers of that which is ours. We are to regain our homeland, the ancient Châkka Realm under the Grimwall."

"Are there Spawn in Drimmen-deeve?" asked Perry. "The *Raven Book* tells that the mines were infested by those and other evil creatures during the War, but since then nothing has come concerning the Rūcks, Hlōks, and Ogrus that were there. Are they still in Drimmen-deeve?"

Lord Kian spoke; there was anger in his voice, and his countenance darkened. "They raid the countryside and wreak havoc with river traffic along the Great Argon."

Alarmed by the Man's seething rage, both Perry and Cotton drew back in apprehension.

Seeing the effect of his ire upon the two Waerlinga, Lord Kian struggled to master his emotion. The young Man stood and walked to the open burrow-window and stared out into the gloaming, taking a moment to quell his wrath and to collect his thoughts. Through the portal could be heard the awakening hum of twilight insects. Cotton quietly got up and lighted several tapers; their flickering glow pressed back the early evening shadows.

"Let me tell it as it happened," said Lord Kian quietly, turning from the window to face his host:

"Though I am of North Riamon," he began, "I spent some years as a Realmsman serving the High King. I won the repute of knowing the Lands as few others do. Durek heard of this, and he knew of my friendship with the King; and Durek's emissaries sought me out and bade me to meet with him in the Dwarf halls of Mineholt North. At that meeting he told me of his plans to reclaim Drimmen-deeve and to re-enter it with his kindred and make it mighty as of old. He asked that I serve as guide and advisor to Anval and Borin and to take them to Pellar so that they might make Durek's plans known to High King Darion. We were not then aware that Spawn infested the Deeves, though we had heard rumors of some dark danger along that distant edge of Riamon.

"At the court, King Darion told us of the foul Yrm. The King explained that after the fall of Gron, Modru's minions either were destroyed, or were scattered, or they surrendered. Many discovered that they had been deceived by the Evil One, and they swore fealty to the then High King, Galen, and to his line, and were forgiven and allowed to return to their homelands. Others fled or fought to the death. The Men of Hyree, the Rovers of Kistan, some fought and died, some cast down their weapons, some ran, some slew themselves in madness. But of the Spawn—Ghol, Lōkh, Rukh, Troll, Vulg, Hèlsteed—those all fought to the death, or died by the Ban, or fled into darkness; none surrendered, for they had been too long in bondage to the Evil One to yield.

"King Darion believes that many Rukha and Lōkha and mayhap some Trolls escaped to Drimmen-deeve to join those already there. They hid in the blackness for all these many years, too sorely defeated to make themselves known, too crushed by the fall of Gron to array themselves in battle.

"In the Deeves, hatred and envy gnawed at their vitals, and the worm of vengeance ate at their minds. But they were leaderless, divided into many squabbling, petty factions.

"Two years ago, belike through treachery and murder and guile, a cruel tyrant seized the whip hand. He is Gnar, one of the Lōkha, we think.

"It is he who is responsible for the renewed conflict with the Free Folk. He lusts for total power, the dominion of his will o'er all things. And to achieve that vile end, he masters his minions through fear and terror, binding them to his ruthless rule.

"Before Gnar arose, the Yrm made but limited forays from Drimmen-deeve, and then only at night, driven by their dread of the Sun and the doom of the Covenant to return to the Deeves ere daybreak. They did not range far enough to reach any homesteads, settlements, roads, or trade routes—barely coming to the foot of the mountains, reaching not beyond the eastern edge of the Pitch. But now their fear of Gnar's cruelty is such that at his command they issue forth from that mountain fastness to raid many days' journey from Drimmen-deeve, besetting Valon—the Land south of Larkenwald the Eldwood— and ranging as far as the Great Argon River.

"The Yrm lie up in black holes, caves, splits in the rock, and cracks in the hillsides when the Sun is in the sky; thus, the Ban strikes them not. But at nightfall they gang together to waylay settlers and travellers alike—slaying them and despoiling their bodies—and to attack and loot and burn the steads and holts of Riamon and Valon, or to plunder river traffic, pirating the flat-boats of the River Drummers. Gnar has decreed that there shall be no survivors from the raids, except when he orders a prisoner taken, upon whom he commits unspeakable abominations.

"All of this the King learned from a captured Rukh who boasted of it before he died when the dawn came and the Sun rose; for the Rukh was slain by High Adon's Covenant forever banning the evil Spawn to the night or to the lightless pits of the underearth when the Sun is on high.

"Upon hearing from the King that *Spaunen* held Drimmen-deeve, Anval and Borin were enraged, and pledged the Dwarf Host to the task of exterminating the Yrmish vermin from the Dwarves' ancestral home—a pledge since affirmed by Durek. This pledge was swiftly accepted by a grateful King Darion, for the Spawn present a grave problem to the Realm: the High King knows that all his cavalry and knights, his pikemen and archers, and his infantry and all other soldiery, though mighty upon any open field of battle, would be sorely pressed to fight the Yrm in the splits and cracks and other black holes under the mountains. Though he had planned to lay siege to Drimmen-deeve, the problem of routing out the *Spaunen* still remained.

"Durek's pledge solved that problem, for there is no better underground warrior than a Dwarf—and they are always eager to avenge old wrongs upon their ancient adversary, the Yrm. Thus, the Dwarves are to issue into Drimmen-deeve and vanquish the enemy. They have asked King Darion to forego his planned siege that they might more readily take the Spawn by surprise; this the King has agreed to do. During the interim, Darion sends escort with traders and travellers to protect them, and he has gathered the farmers, woodcutters, woodsmen, and other settlers into holdfasts till such time as the Dwarves smash the foe.

"Even now the Dwarf Host has mustered and, if things have gone as planned, is on the march from Mineholt North. Though Gnar's raids still go on, soon—we hope with your help, Perry—they shall be eliminated forever." Lord Kian returned from the window and settled back in his chair and fixed Perry with a keen eye.

"But how can *I* help?" queried a puzzled Perry, wondering how the Dwarf mission could possibly bear upon *The Raven Book* and him.

Borin leaned forward and pushed the *'Book* across the table to Perry. "Except for Braggi's doomed raid," Borin growled, "Châkka have not lived in Kraggen-cor for more than a thousand years—even though it is rightfully ours—for to our everlasting shame we were driven away long ago by a foe we could not withstand: the Ghath, now dead. And though our lore speaks of many things in Kraggen-cor, such as the Spiral Down or the Great Chamber, our knowledge of that eld Châkkaholt consists of legendary names and fragmentary descriptions. Our homeland is a mystery to us. We do not know the paths and halls and rooms and caverns of mighty Kraggen-cor. If we must, we will fight the foul Grg enemy upon unknown ground and chance defeat—but only if we must.

"Yet, if our information is correct, it will not come to that end. We are told by King Darion that your *Raven Book*—at least the original—holds within it a description of a journey through stolen Kraggen-cor. If so, then from that description, that route, we can glean vital knowledge of the layout of at least a part of Kraggen-cor—knowledge needed to smash the Squam and retake the caverns."

"The High King knows about Mister Perry and his book?" asked Cotton in awe, momentarily overwhelmed by the idea that High King Darion could know of someone in the Boskydells.

"Aye, he does indeed know of your *Raven Book*," answered Anval, "for he, too, has a copy in Pellar—or did have. His book was out of the Kingdom when we were there—somewhere here in the Boskydells . . . or so he told us.

"Why, if it's not at the court it must be with my grand-uncle at the Cliffs," said Perry. "He's the Master of the Ravenbook Scholars—Uncle Gerontius Fairhill, I mean—and if he's got the King's copy, then they're adding to it the marginalia collected by the Scholars over the past fifty years or so. . . . Let me see: this would be only the third time it's been updated since its making long ago—"

"Be that as it may," interrupted Borin, "King Darion told us that Sir Tuckerby's diary and the original *Raven Book* were also here in the Boskydells—perhaps at Sir Tuckerby's Warren, being tended by the Fairhills, he thought. Hence we came, and your Mayor led us to you, Master Perry.

"Heed me: The account of the journey through Kraggen-cor is vital to us. We have travelled far to see the *Raven Book*. And if the tale is here in your *copy,* we would hear it for ourselves." Borin pushed the grey book across the table toward Perry.

Somewhat taken aback by the bruskness of the Dwarves, the two Warrows glanced at one another, and then at Lord Kian. Reassured by the smile upon the Man's face, Perry reached for the tome. "Oh, the tale is here all right," replied the buccan, turning the book around, preparing to open it; but then he paused. "Only, I don't know exactly where to start. I think perhaps before I read to you of that trip through dreaded Drimmendeeve, we should speak a bit about what went before, for mayhap it will have a bearing upon your quest."

"Say on," said Borin, "for we know not what may aid." And Anval, too, nodded his agreement while Lord Kian settled back in his chair.

"Who can say where an event begins?" mused Perry, "for surely all happenings have many threads reaching deep into the past, each strand winding its way through the fabric of time to weave in the great pattern. But let me start with the first battle of the Winter War, for two of the four comrades came together in its aftermath, and went on to meet the third, and they in turn came upon the fourth:

"As Modru's forces marched from the Wastes of Gron through the Shadowlight of Winternight and down upon the northern citadel of Challerain Keep, and as women and children and the old and infirm fell back toward the havens of Pellar and Wellen, of Valon and Jugo, and of other Lands to the south, some warriors hastened north, to answer the High King's call to arms. Among those mustered was a force of Warrows, skilled in archery; and one of these Vulg-fighting Warrows was Sir Tuckerby Underbank, known then simply as Tuck.

"The iron fist of War at last fell upon Challerain Keep, and you all know the outcome of that struggle, so I'll say nothing more of it, except that the order to retreat had been given and Tuck became separated from his companions. He had spent all of his arrows, and Rûcks, Hlôks, and Ghûls were closing in. To elude Modru's forces, Tuck took refuge in an old tomb; it was the barrow of Othran the Seer. There, too, by happenstance, came Galen, then Prince of Pellar, weaponless, for his sword had shattered in battle.

"Together the two waited until the enemy passed by, and then, riding double, they struck southward through the Dimmendark, their only arms being the Red Arrow, borne by Tuck, and a long-knife of Atala, carried by Galen—both weapons having been found in the tomb.

"They had ridden to the northern marches of the Battle Downs when they came upon a scene dire, one of butchery, for the entire escort as well as the helpless innocents of the last refugee waggon train had been slaughtered. Yet neither Galen's betrothed, Princess Laurelin of Riamon, nor his brother, Prince Igon, Captain of the escort, was among the slain."

"Modru Kinstealer," said Lord Kian softly, swirling the ale in his mug.

"Just so," answered Perry with a nod. "Princess Laurelin was taken captive. The track of a large force of mounted Ghûls bore eastward, deeper into the Dimmendark, toward the Grimwall. In pursuit along this track rode Galen and Tuck, pressing into Winternight.

"At last they came unto the Weiunwood, that shaggy forest, where they learned that here, too, a mighty battle had been fought; but here the Alliance had won, using Warrow woodstrickery and Elven lore and the strength of Men. Tuck and Galen met with Arbagon, Bockleman, and Inarion—leaders of the Warrows, Men, and Elves—and Galen was told that five days past a Hèlsteed-mounted Ghûlen force had hammered by, still bearing toward the Grimwall. And afterwards a lone rider had followed slowly in their wake.

"Again, Galen and Tuck bore east, and days later came to the Hidden Refuge, Arden. There they found Galen's brother, Igon, sorely wounded. It was he who had been the lone tracker of the Kinstealer force. But his wounds, taken in the attack upon the waggon train, had at last overcome him, and he would have died but that the Elves found him lying unconscious in the Winternight and saved him.

"Even as brother spoke to brother, to the Refuge came the Elf Lord Gildor bearing word that Galen's sire, King Aurion, had been slain and that Galen was now High King of all Mithgar.

"Galen was sore beset, for his heart told him to go north and somehow deliver Laurelin out of the enemy stronghold; yet his duty told him that as King he must turn south and come unto Pellar to gather the Host to face Modru's hordes.

"The next morning, with heavy hearts, Galen and Tuck bore southward, leaving Igon behind in Arden in the care of Elvenkind. With them rode Gildor, now Elven advisor to Galen as he had been to Aurion before. The three were making for Quadran Pass and beyond to the Larkenwald, Darda Galion. Gildor sought to warn his Elven kindred, the Lian, that it was almost certain that the Larkenwald, too, soon would be under attack. The companions planned to give warning and afterward to fare onward to Pellar and the Host.

"Through the Dimmendark the trio rode, ever bearing southward. They overtook a Swarm of Modru's forces also bearing south, marching toward Black Drimmen-deeve to make it into a vile fortress whence the Spawn would launch their attack upon Darda Galion.

"Silently passing wide of the Horde, southward rode the trio of Galen, Tuck, and Gildor, in haste now, to warn the Lian of the coming enemy. Far they rode, but at last came to a defile where they heard the sound of single combat, and happened upon a lone Dwarf and a solitary Hlōk, fighting amid a great slaughter of Dwarven and Rūcken dead—"

"Brega, Bekki's son!" burst out Anval, fiercely, raising a clenched fist; and Borin cried, "Warrior, hai!"

"Yes," confirmed Perry, "it was Brega, Bekki's son; and he slew the Hlōk. Then Brega alone stood, the last of a force of forty Dwarves from the Red Caves, marching north to join in the battle against Modru. Altogether, the forty had slain nearly two hundred maggot-folk; yet at the last all had fallen but Brega."

Here Anval and Borin cast their hoods over their heads.

"Châkka shok (Dwarven axes)," rumbled Borin; *"Châkka cor (Dwarven might),"* added Anval.

In respect, Perry paused a moment, and then continued: "Now the great southward-bound force of the *Spaunen* Horde was drawing nigh, and Brega stood ready to face them alone. Yet he was at last persuaded that to gain revenge for his slain brethren he must go south with Tuck and Galen and Gildor to join the Host to battle Modru. And so, somewhat reluctantly it seems, Brega mounted up behind Lord Gildor to ride to the Larkenwald and then beyond.

"Now, at last, you see, the Wheel of Fate had turned to bring the four together, and toward Quadran Pass they rode. Cross it they did, and had come partway down Quadran Run, down the flank of Stormhelm, heading for the Pitch and the Larkenwald beyond. But here they were thwarted, for a large force of mounted Ghûls—advance eyes for the Horde—was returning over the range, coming up the Run toward them.

"The four were forced back over the Gap, ahead of the Ghûls. Yet they planned to slip aside at first chance and hide until the Ghûls were beyond them and gone. But before they could do so, Vulgs from the Horde discovered them, and ahead of Modru's riders through the Dimmendark the companions fled."

"Wouldn't you just know it!" blurted Cotton, frustrated by the turn of events even though they were more than two centuries in the past, and despite his having heard the tale many times before. Then, embarrassed by his outburst, the buccan took a sip from his mug and studiously peered at the alefroth, and avoided catching the eyes of the others.

"Southward they ran," continued Perry, "till their horses were nearly foundered, for each was carrying double. And so, out of necessity, the four at last turned east into a valley, hoping to elude the Winternight pursuit. As they neared the head of the valley, Gildor recognized the land: it was Ragad Vale—the Valley of the Door—and they were coming toward the Dusk-Door, the abandoned western entrance into Black Drimmendeeve. And the Door had been shut ages agone and had not been opened since.

"On they rode, forced ever eastward ahead of tracking Vulgs, finally to come to the great hemidome in the Loomwall of Grimspire; and a black lake was there. Along a causeway they went, till they reached a drawbridge, and it was up, raised high. While the others waited, Gildor swam across, and a great swirl in the water came nigh, for something lurked in the black depths.

"Yet the Elf safely gained the other side and began to lower the bridge; but the haul broke, and down the bascule came with a great crash. The sound boomed down the vale and brought the searching Ghûls riding at speed. The remaining comrades dashed across the bridge and joined the Elf, and all went past the sunken courtyard and to the great edifice of the Dusk-Door.

"Black water from the Dark Mere lapped at the steps rising up to the huge columns. Between these pillars the four ran, drawing the two horses behind, coming to the great portico.

"The Ghûls rode to the causeway, but then shied back, as if afraid to ride its length to get at the four.

"Brega, remembering the lore words, managed to open the Dusk-Door; yet the four were loath to enter Black Drimmen-deeve, for therein lived foul maggot-folk—but even more so, therein ruled the evil Gargon, Modru's Dread. Yet Fate offered them but two courses: to face the immediate threat of a great number of Ghûls standing athwart the path along the causeway, or to enter the Spawn-filled, Dread-ruled halls of Drimmen-deeve.

"But then all choice was snatched from them, for the lurker in the Dark Mere—the Krakenward—struck: hideous ropy arms writhed out of the black water and clutched the horses; and screaming in terror the steeds were drawn down the steps and under the dark surface. Gildor sprang forward to save Fleetfoot, but the Lian warrior was struck numb—for at that very moment, Vanidor, Gildor's twin, was slain at the Iron Tower, and Gildor felt his brother's death. A tentacle grasped Gildor as he fell, stunned, to his knees; but Galen, using the Atalar Blade, hacked at the arm, cleaving a great gash in it, and in the creature's pain it flung Gildor aside.

"Through the Dusk-Door the four fled, the enraged Monster clutching at them with slimy tentacles, lashing at them with a dead tree, pounding at the Door with a great stone, and wrenching at the gates.

"Into this nest of snakes Brega leapt and slapped his hand

against one of the hinges and cried the Wizard-word to close the portal, leaping back to avoid the Monster's clutch. And slowly the doors ground shut, all the while the creature struggling to rend them open. And as the gates swung to, Berga's last sight was of the Krakenward wrenching at one of the great columns of the edifice, grinding it away from its base.

"The Door closed—*boom!*—and the four were shut inside Drimmendeeve, in the West Hall. Brega had a lantern in his pack, and as he unshuttered it, the four heard a loud crashing; they surmised it to be the great edifice collapsing, torn down by the maddened Hèlarms.

"*Boom! Boom! Boom!* The pounding of hurled stone shook the Dusk-Door, and though Brega tried, he could not get it to reopen even a crack so that they could see what was happening.

"Now they had no choice but to attempt to traverse the Deeves and escape out the Dawn-Gate. And as they left the West Hall on that fated journey through Black Drimmen-deeve, the hammering of the enraged Monster echoed in their wake."

"*Tchaaa!*" hissed Borin, "I wonder if the foul Madûk yet lives."

"I cannot say," answered Perry, "but the *Raven Book* tells that the creature had been Dragon-borne in the black of night by the Cold-drake Skail and dropped into the old Gatemoat nearly five hundred years earlier. That was back before the Dragons began their thousand-year sleep. It is now believed that the Krakenward was a tool of Modru, placed there as part of his preparation for the coming of the Dragon Star."

"Living or no, tool or no, continue the tale," bade Anval, "for now we come to the nub of it, the part that may aid our quest."

"You are right, Anval," agreed Perry. "The time has come for me to read from the *Raven Book*." And at last Perry opened the great grey tome, turning past the part of the book that duplicated Tuck's *Unfinished Diary*—as the 'Stone Slayer had originally recorded it during his venture—and thumbing well into that part of the *'Book* Tuck later told to the scribes, recalled in full by him from his own terse journal. Finally Perry reached the proper page of the Account. "This is the tale of the four who fared Black Drimmen-deeve," he said, "the story of their flight through that dreadful place. Let me now read it to you."

And, pulling a candelabrum close, from the huge grey book he began to read of that fearful dash through Drimmen-deeve as the four sought to reach the eastern portal—Dawn-Gate—ere the Ghûls could cross back through Quadran Gap to bring word of the intruders to the dreaded Gargon and its *Spaunen* minions. Not all of Perry's words need be repeated here, for the tale is now famous and recounted elsewhere, and the full story of all the companions is long and takes many days to tell. But that evening in The Root, Perry read only that part of the story concerning the journey through Kraggen-cor, the journey of the four persons who became known as the Deevewalkers:

Perry began at the point where the four had fled from the Krakenward through the Dusk-Door and could not get back out. And from the West Hall, Gildor led them up the stairs and easterly; Gildor led, for in his youth he had gone on a trade mission through Drimmen-deeve while it was still a mighty Dwarvenholt—ere the Gargon broke free of the Lost Prison. Far they went, without encounter, for the western caverns were deserted of maggot-folk. Yet finally they had to stop to rest, the first they'd had in nearly two days.

Perry read of their pause in the Grate Room, where at last they felt a foreboding fear beating at them, and they knew then that the Ghûls had finally come to the Gargon with word of the four, and now that dreadful creature was bending its will to find them. And the halls became infested with *Spaunen* squads searching for them.

Onward they fled, deeper into fear, for they had to come nearer to the Dread in order to reach the Dawn-Gate. And as they went east, many times they eluded discovery.

Again they rested, for the way was arduous. At last they came to the Hall of the Gravenarch, and there they found the remains of Braggi's Raid, that ill-fated Dwarven mission to slay the evil Gargon.

Now the four Deevewalkers could feel the Dread approaching, for at last it could sense them—and it stalked them. Yet Brega thwarted it, for with a broken Warhammer he sundered the keystone of the Gravenarch, and the Hall collapsed, blocking the way. Through the fallen stone the Gargon's hatred beat upon them, and great waves of dread engulfed them, but the creature could not come at them. And onward they fled.

Perry read of them coming to the drawbridge over the Great Deep; and the bridge was lowered and unguarded. There, too, was oil and pitch, and they made ready to burn the wooden span and prevent pursuit. But ere they could fire it, the Gargon came upon them once more, and at last paralyzed them with its dire gaze.

And as the creature came to kill them, it made a fatal mistake, for it considered Tuck to be beneath its contempt, and the Warrow proved to be the key to the slaying of the Dread—for slay it they did.

Perry read of the fiery destruction of the bridge, and its collapse into the Deep, and the escape of the four out through the Dawn-Gate and onto the Pitch, coming at last to safe haven under the eaves of Darda Galion.

The candles were low and guttering when Perry finished reading. The room was silent as each reflected upon that which had just been recounted. Cotton got up to fetch some fresh candles to light, but at that moment Holly popped back in through the door. "Dinner is served," she announced, and led them all off to the dining room.

CHAPTER 4

THE BREGA PATH

Dinner was superb; Holly had outdone herself. Mounds of steaming mushrooms were heaped upon large platters; and she had prepared her special recipe for rabbit stew: thick and creamy and filled with delicious morsels of tender coney and chunks of tubers, parsnips, and other vegetables, all perfectly seasoned with her own blend of tangy spices and aromatic herbs. Dark ale in deep mugs sparkled in the warm, yellow lamplight, and the talk turned to things other than Rūcks and such.

"It must be a long way from Dael to Pellar to Woody Hollow," remarked Perry, popping another mushroom into his mouth. "Surely you didn't walk all the way."

"No," laughed Lord Kian. "That indeed would be a longsome stroll. Let me see, I deem we covered more than three thousand miles just going from Mineholt North to Pellar and back. Of course most of that journey was by boat on the Rissanin and Argon rivers. Then from the Mineholt to your Boskydells is nearly another thousand miles: we travelled the Landover Road to the Grimwall Mountains, where we crossed over Crestan Pass to come down near Arden, and then we followed the east-west Crossland Road to come to the Seven Dells."

"Goodness," breathed Perry, eyes aglitter. "Why, you've travelled four thousand miles in the past few months alone, and I've barely exceeded a hundred in my entire life—when I travelled from the Cliffs to here—and I am three years past my 'coming of age.' The wonderful sights you must have seen . . ." His voice trailed off in breathless speculation.

"Horses!" burst out Cotton, banging his mug of ale down on the table, some foam sloshing out. "I'll bet you rode horses to the Bosky!"

"Ride horses?" snorted Anval. "A Châk ride a horse? Hmphh! A pony, mayhap, but not a full-grown horse. We have better sense than to climb aboard one of those great lumbering beasts. Aye, Cotton, we did use horses on the roads to the Boskydells—but we *drove* them, we didn't *ride* them. We travelled sensibly—by waggon."

"Well, if you rode in a waggon, where is it now?" asked Cotton, chagrined for not remembering the idle tavern talk that occasionally turned to the subject of Dwarves, and the hearsay that Dwarves, though brave at most things, for some reason seemed to fear being borne on the back of a horse. "You didn't arrive at Woody Hollow Hall ridin' in no waggon."

"You are right, Waeran," rumbled Anval, amused by Cotton's embarrassment, "we trod the final miles on foot. The waggon is in Budgens with a rock-broken wheel being mended by one of your Waeran wheelwrights. It will be ready ere our return journey to the Landover Road Ford."

"The Landover Road Ford?" asked Perry, vaguely remembering that the ford was somewhere on the River Argon beyond the Grimwall Mountains.

"Aye, Waeran," responded Anval, "a fortnight and a week hence, King Durek and the Army arrive at the ford; so it is there that we will await them."

"It is at the ford where Durek must decide how to enter Kraggen-cor," added Lord Kian, responding to Perry's puzzled expression. "Here, let me show you: If I line up these mushroom platters . . . there, now . . . then they can represent the Grimwall Mountains, as they run down from the Steppes of Jord and on toward Valon and Gûnar in the south ere curving away westerly. Along the eastern flank of the range runs the Argon River, flowing southward toward the Avagon Sea . . . and here where I put my spoon is the ford where the Landover Road crosses the river. The road goes on up the east flank and into the mountains where it then runs through Crestan Pass, crossing over the range to come back down at Arden on the west side. Now let this saltcellar represent Mineholt North, where Durek's army started their march. . . . Mineholt goes up here—nearly three hundred fifty miles of marching to the east and north of the ford. And finally we'll put this pepper mill down here, another two hundred miles south of the ford, where lies Drimmen-deeve, with its Dawn-Gate on the east side of the mountains and the Dusk-Door on the west.

"Now you can see it is at the ford where Durek, coming down from the north and east, must choose which way to invade the Deeves: he can cross over the mountains at Crestan Pass to Arden, march down the west flank of the range, and invade by Dusk-Door; or he can stay on the east side of the mountains, tramp south along the banks of the river Argon, then come over the wold . . . about here . . . and march up the Pitch to attack into Dawn-Gate. You can also see that his choice is crucial, for these two ways lie on opposite sides of a mighty wall of mountains, and he must decide at the ford, for there is the Crestan Pass—the Army's path across the range." Lord Kian lapsed into silence, taking a long pull from his mug.

"What about Quadran Pass?" asked Perry after a moment. "It is near Drimmen-deeve. The *Raven Book* says the western reach of the pass is less than a day's march north of the Dusk-Door, and the eastern end of the pass comes down onto the Pitch itself. I repeat: what about Quadran Pass? Couldn't Durek cross over there?"

"A good question, Perry," replied Kian, "and the answer is—perhaps. Durek might be able to cross there, but he is faced with two problems: First, the gap in the Quadran, at least on the Pitch side, may be guarded by *Spaunen,* and crossing there would alert Gnar and all his forces, and our edge of surprise would be lost. Second, early winter is nearly upon us, and by the time the Army can get to that pass, Quadran Gap in all likelihood will be snowed in and impassable. No, Durek must choose at Landover Road Ford, so that the Crestan Pass can be crossed if his choice is to attack by the western door, or so that he can turn south and follow the river if he chooses to invade through the eastern gate. And our mission now is to meet him at the ford with the information gleaned from your *Raven Book,* so that he can use that knowledge in making his decision."

Again Lord Kian fell silent, and each stared at the problem laid out before him as the Man took another long pull from his mug.

"Wull, Dusk-Door or Dawn-Gate, it's a poser all right," said Cotton at last, eyeing the alignment of the mushroom platters. "But be that as it may, please pass me some of those Grimwall Mountains, and I'll have a bit of Mineholt saltcellar and Drimmen-deeve pepper mill, too, to make 'em more tasty." With a strangling cough, Lord Kian choked on his beer in laughter, and the others guffawed heartily as the Warrow piled mushrooms on his plate and salted and peppered them and began popping them into his widely grinning mouth, saying, "Mmmm, good mountains! Delicious peaks!"

The table talk continued in this fashion for two hours as the Warrows, the Dwarves, and the Man stuffed themselves with Holly's wonderful food. In time, all were satisfied, including Cotton, who had a reputation even among Warrows as an awesome trencher in spite of his slimness slim for a Warrow, that is, for they tend to roundness. But Cotton had at last met his match, for at this table Anval had surpassed the hard-eating Cotton, having put away not one but two more pieces of apple pie than the doughty Warrow. It had been a superb guest meal, with rich and wholesome food, excellent ale, and much interesting talk.

Yet though he had consumed a vast quantity of food, Borin had not been drawn into the conversation, and there was a dark, brooding look upon his face. As they each lit up a clay pipe of Downdell leaf and settled back in comfort, with Cotton blowing an occasional smoke ring, Borin growled and at last revealed what it was that troubled him. "The *Raven Book* is of little or no help to us in the coming battle: it has not the detail to lead us through the caverns. True, the book has given us news—though bitter it is—for now we know that both of Durek's choices as to the way into Kraggen-cor are even more uncertain than we had thought: The east way across Baralan— the Pitch—and on into the delf may be all but impassable because the drawbridge has burned and fallen into the Great Dēop. To cross that gulf when it is defended on the far side by an army of foul Squam would be perilous enough even with a bridge—but without it, it may be impossible. And the west way in—the Dusken Door—that way is probably blocked and may be broken beyond repair.

"But even were we to get in unscathed by either portal, still would we be at great disadvantage to the Foul Folk, for we know not the pathways of our ancient home. Hence, the slobbering Grg are given great tactical advantage, able to issue at us from byways unknown, to ambush us from coverts beyond ken.

"Aye, Master Perry, your *Raven Book* has been of some aid, for it has shown us what Durek must choose between—though a hard choice it is. But what is needed most is detailed knowledge of the passageways of Kraggen-cor: step-by-step knowledge."

"Step-by-step! The Brega Path!" cried Perry, looking swiftly to Cotton and then back again. "Why, we may have the step-by-step knowledge you seek: Brega's record! It never occurred to me that his record might be of use to you . . . that is, until you said 'step-by-step.' Cotton, run and get the Scroll."

As Cotton bolted from the room, a look of skepticism passed between Anval and Borin; yet Perry ignored this exchange as he launched into an explanation: "Put in mind, one of those four who fled through Drimmen-deeve was the Dwarf Brega, who later became the DelfLord of the Red Hills. Years after the War, he and Tuckerby were reflecting on those dark days and fell to discussing their perilous journey through the Deeves. It was during that conversation that Brega claimed he knew every twist and turn, every up and down, every hall and cavern, every detail of that path of danger. Tuckerby begged him to set it all down in writing so that it could be appended to the *Raven Book,* and Brega did so to please his old companion."

Cotton rushed back into the room carrying a yellowed parchment scroll, rolled up and tied with a green ribbon; he gave it over to Perry. "This is Brega's record of that journey," continued Perry, fumbling at the knot, "A record which soon may be added to the *Raven Book.* I have to make a few more copies to send to the Scholars to study, so that all may agree that it is authentic and belongs in the History. I've already made . . . let me think . . . ah yes, eleven copies; and Cotton and I have thoroughly checked their accuracy against this original. If it proves to be of value to your quest, you may take as many copies as you need." Finally the ribbon came off, and Perry handed the scroll to Borin.

With reservation, the Dwarves spread out the scroll upon a hurriedly cleared section of the table, holding the parchment open by placing saltcellars and pepper mills at the corners, and all gathered around to view the document. "Hah!" burst out Anval, his dubious look replaced by one of exultation, "it is signed by Brega, Bekki's son; here is his Châkka rune. And look! Here are the secret marks! And see this! Now we know that this then is no counterfeit!" To each of Anval's exclamations Borin grunted his agreement; but what the secret marks were, or what the Dwarves had seen, neither Perry, Cotton, nor Lord Kian could discern, and not Anval nor Borin would say.

Borin began to read aloud from Brega's finely wrought script: "Here begins the journey at the Dusken Door: two hundred steps up the broad stair; one and twenty and seven hundred level paces in the main passage 'round right, left, right, and right turns passing three arches on the right and two crevices on the left; fifteen and eight hundred down paces in the main passage, a gentle slope . . ."

Anval and Borin then read on silently; and as they read their elation grew, for here at last was the detail needed to invade their own ancestral homeland. Every now and again one or the other would exclaim aloud as some particular detail would confirm ancient lore: "The Long Hall . . . the Upward Way . . . Braggi's Stand . . . the Great Shelf . . ." and many more.

It was Anval who spoke first when they reached the end of the document, his look of triumph replaced by a brooding scowl. "There must be eight or nine hundred major twists and turns here, forks and splits—and twice that many minor ones," he growled, stroking his black beard.

"A good estimate, Anval," said Perry, returning to his chair, "but to be more exact, there are slightly more than a thousand major decisions—and, as you guessed, there are indeed about twice that many minor ones. That's many, many choices which must be made correctly to go from Dusk-Door to Dawn-Gate by this route. I know; I have committed it to memory. It adds up to nearly three thousand branchings and forks and splits in the trail—three thousand places to diverge from the course and lose the way. And to think, this is but one path in Drimmen-deeve; the total of your Kraggen-cor must be so vast as to defy imagination!"

Overcome at the thought of the sheer magnitude of the whole of Drimmen-deeve, Cotton plopped down in his seat, a look of wonder upon his face.

For a few silent moments the Warrows settled back in their comfortable chairs and puffed on their pipes in reflection; Cotton, with his feet up, again blew smoke rings at the ceiling. Leaving the Dwarves studying the Brega Scroll, Kian, too, returned to his seat.

After a while Perry asked a question that had been puzzling him for three years—ever since he had become Master of The Root and had discovered the Brega Scroll in the far back of a cobweb-laden pigeonhole in a long-unused desk in a dusty storeroom: "It thrills me for you to confirm that the scroll is authentic, but a thing I am curious about, Borin: The *Raven Book* says that Gildor the Elf, though he consulted Brega often, actually led the way through Drimmen-deeve, for Brega's knowledge was of little or no help. Yet here we are, ready to trust this document written years later by him; though I must say that found with the scroll was a note from that time written for Tuck by Raven where she says that Brega swiftly and easily recalled the route as if he had trod it only yesterday. How can that be?"

"He was a Châk," replied Borin, glancing up from the scroll, "and once a Châk travels a path, it is with him always, graven in his very being. But he must travel it first, for he is no better nor worse than anyone else when it comes to memorizing a route beforehand. But if a Châk trods a passage, it comes alive within him. And though Elf Gildor led that first time, had they ever travelled that way again, it would have fallen to Brega to lead.

"Hence, Master Waeran, we too could memorize the path described by this document, just as you have; yet we would be but little different at it from you. Yet, let us step it out but once, and no one except another Châk will ever equal our mastery of it." The Dwarf paused in reflection. "Without this gift, the Châkka could not dwell in the labyrinths under the Mountains."

As Borin had been speaking, a dark mood had stormed across Anval's features. Glowering at the scroll, he slammed his fist to the table, causing the dishes to rattle, startling both

Warrows, Cotton dropping his feet to the floor. *"Kruk!"* spat Anval. "Why did not Brega make such a record for the Châkka? We would have mastered it ere now! This is a long and complicated course—at least forty or more miles in length with many splits and twists." He paused a moment, again in dark thought, then once more struck the table in exasperation. "Pah! We cannot conduct a Squam-War where at every fork in the cavern we must consult a scroll!" He turned to Borin. "One or both of us must memorize this parchment and guide the Army, though mastering it will take weeks, perhaps months—time we can ill afford, for the Army is ready now." His black eyes filled with rage. "And the foul Grg raid, harass, maim, and slay each night."

Perry's heart was racing, and his face was flushed. His breathing was rapid and shallow. All during the evening a sense of destiny had been growing within him, as if a marvelous doom were about to fall. As a lad he had spent endless hours poring over his uncle's copy of *The Raven Book* and delving into other tomes of knowledge, filling his mind and heart and dreams with epic tales of grand heroism: of Egil One Eye and Arin and the Quest of the Green Stone; of Elyn and Thork and the Quest of Black Mountain; of Tuck and Danner and Patrel and the Winter War Quest; and many other eld tales of derring-do. And his daydreams had been filled with a whirl of Elves, Dwarves, Knights, Men, Wizards, Utruni, Dragons, and other peoples and creatures of legend. And in his childhood he had yearned to be a Warrow involved in another grand adventure. But quests—especially Warrow quests—never seem to happen to striplings, and so he dreamed and yearned. And his yearning had driven him to the study of the tales and records of Mithgar, and he had become a Historian, a Ravenbook Scholar.

And now Perry had heard the frustration in Borin's voice when the Dwarf had spoken of the time needed to memorize the Brega Scroll. Perry knew how to resolve the dilemma facing the Dwarves—but he was afraid. Yet even in his fear he realized that here was the chance for the adventure he'd always longed for, always dreamed of. But now the adventure was upon him and he found that he was not ready for it, not at all eager to reach out and grab it; he was unable to choose; it was too sudden.

Long moments fled, and no one said aught. And then Perry looked up into the face of the visitors, and he saw the mixture of anguish and frustration and bitterness in Borin's and Anval's and Lord Kian's eyes as they thought upon the further *Spaunen* depredations that would occur. Perry was deeply moved, and in spite of his own trepidation, in spite of the risks involved, suddenly and without conscious thought he spoke: "What you need is a guide who already knows the Brega Path. You need me, Perry Fairhill. I will go with you."

CHAPTER 5

GOODBYE, HOLLY, WE'RE OFF TO WAR

Cotton startled awake to find the late-morning Sun filling his bedroom with light. *Cotton Buckleburr,* he thought, *you slug-abed, get up and serve your master.* The buccan rolled out of bed and splashed cold water from the pitcher into the basin on the washstand and quickly scrubbed his face. Throwing on his clothes, he rushed out of the room still stuffing his shirttail into his pants; and he nearly collided with Holly, who was at that moment passing by in the hallway, her arms laden with linen. *"Oomph!"* he grunted as he twisted aside to keep from running over her, bumping into the wall instead.

"Cotton Buckleburr," Holly laughed, her soft amber-jewelled eyes atwinkle, "you big oaf, you nearly scared me to death, jumping out of the doorway at me like that. Did you hurt yourself now, runnin' into the wall and all?"

"Oh no, Miss Holly, I'm all right, and I didn't mean to scare you. But I'm late getting up, and . . . say, where's Mister Perry? Is he awake? And the visitors, are they up and about?" asked Cotton, continuing to fumble with his shirttail.

"Why they were up and gone long ago, early this morning," replied Holly.

"Gone? Oh no!" wailed Cotton. "Mister Perry can't go away without me. He needs me! Much as I don't want to go, I've got to—for Mister Perry's sake."

"Wait, Cotton"—a puzzled frown settled upon Holly's gentle features—"only the strangers left this morning. Mister Perry is still here—here at The Root. He's in the study. But what's all this about his going away somewhere and you with him? Going where for what?"

"Why he's going off to Drimmen-deeve to fight Rūcks and such," answered Cotton. "And me, well I'm going with him." And a look of wonder fell upon Cotton as he realized what he had said. "That's right, Miss Holly, I'm going with him." Cotton turned and rushed away and did not see the frightened look that sprang up behind Holly's eyes.

Well I reckon he's put both of our feet into it now, right enough, and we're in a pretty pickle if you ask me, thought Cotton as he hurried toward the study. *I wonder where the visitors went off to this morning. And are Mister Perry and me really going away from the Bosky?*

Cotton slid to a stop in the doorway of the den, and his mouth dropped open in amazement: Peregrin Fairhill stood before him, armored in the silveron mail and grasping the long Elven-knife, Bane, in his right fist. "Cotton, look!" cried Perry, holding his arms straight out from his sides and pirouetting. "The starsilver fits me as if I were born to it. And Bane, well Bane is just the proper-sized sword for a Warrow hand." The buccan swished the blade through the air with an elaborate flourish.

"Oh, Cotton," continued Perry, his sapphirine gaze upon the upraised sword, "it seems I've dreamed of this all my scholarly years. It will be an adventure of a lifetime: swords and armor, phalanxes of marching warriors, pavilions and pennons, glittering helms, shields, hauberks, pikes. Oh, how *glorious* it will be!"

Cotton looked doubtful. "But Sir, it seems to me that War is just bloody slaughter. And this War won't be no different, except the fighting and killing will be done in a great, dark hole in the ground. Many a friend will perish. Shiny swords and pretty flags there'll be aplenty, but agony and Death will be there too."

"Of course, of course, Cotton"—Perry frowned—"everyone knows that killing the enemy is part of War. And you can't have a battle without taking a few wounds." Then Perry's jewel-like eyes seemed to focus upon a distant vision of splendor. "Glorious," he breathed.

"Pardon me, Mister Perry," Cotton interrupted Perry's wool-gathering, "but just where have our visitors got off to? Holly says that they've gone away. How can we go off to Drimmen-deeve without them?"

"Oh, they'll be back. Lord Kian has just gone down to the marketplace to get supplies for our trip to the Landover Road Ford, and Anval and Borin are off to Budgens to get the wag-gon and team." Then Perry looked sharply at his friend. "What did you say, Cotton? Did you say that *we* were going to Drim-men-deeve? Do *you* mean to come too?" And when Cotton nodded dumbly, Perry shouted for joy and began capering about the room, slashing the air with Bane. "Take that and that and that, you Spawn!" He stabbed at imaginary foes. "Beware, maggot-folk, the Warrows are coming!" Then, slamming Bane home in the worn scabbard at his belt, Perry took Cotton by the arm. "We've got to get ourselves outfitted properly for this ven-ture," he declared, and began rushing about the room selecting arms and armor for himself and Cotton.

His choices, though somewhat limited, were excellent: Cot-ton was fitted with an armored shirt of gilded chain-mail; though it was light, it would turn aside all but the heaviest blades. This armor had a noble history, for during the Winter War this was the very chain corselet given over to Patrel by Laurelin from the royal armories to wear in the first great bat-tle of the Dimmendark when one of Modru's hordes swept down upon Challerain Keep. Added to the armor was a rune-marked blade about the size and shape of Bane, but which had been forged years agone by the Men of the Lost Land—and a scabbard to hold it. Each of their belts also held a dagger, and both Warrows had chosen simple leather-and-iron helms. 'Round their shoulders they had fitted Elven cloaks which blended so well with any natural background that even the keenest eyes would be deceived if the wearer covered himself and remained still.

As the two buccen had sifted through the museum cases se-lecting Cotton's apparel, the small silver horn kept turning up in one or the other's hands. And as Perry started to set it aside once more, he paused, laughing, and suddenly changed his mind: "This horn seems bound and determined to go with us,

Cotton. Here, let's hang it over your shoulder to rally friend around when faced with the foe."

It was thus that Lord Kian found them upon his return from Woody Hollow. "Ho! What's this? I go away leaving two meek Waerlinga and return to find two warriors abristle with weaponry." He smiled down at the small figures before him, accepting without speaking that Cotton, too, would accompany them to Drimmen-deeve.

Cotton squirmed under the young Man's gaze, uncomfortable in the unfamiliar golden gear, but Perry, in silver, stood proudly straighter and would have walked about except he feared—and rightly so—that he would end up strutting and preening.

"Well now, soldiers," said Lord Kian, "if I were you I'd doff that gear; it won't be required till we get to the Spawn—at least a thousand miles hence. Instead, you need to select travelling clothes: strong, sturdy, comfortable, warm travelling clothes. And good boots that will walk far and stay dry, and won't chafe your feet and will keep them warm. Remember: although it is just October now, early winter will be upon us ere we get there."

Somewhat abashed, the Warrows took off their armor and weaponry and, under Kian's critical eye, began selecting garments and other accoutrements necessary for the lengthy trip. They stopped only long enough to eat some of Holly's cold beef, cheese, fresh chewy bread, apples, and beer. After lunch they continued to choose their gear. The former Realmsman proved to be well experienced, for under his direction they selected only that which was essential for the journey. At last each Warrow had assembled the needed clothing and other travelling gear, all of it stowed in an easily manageable backpack topped off with a warm bedroll.

Late that afternoon, Borin and Anval returned, driving a small waggon drawn by a fine team of sturdy horses. The waggon had been crafted by Men of Dael, and had been chosen by Kian, Anval, and Borin as being more suitable for the journey than the available Dwarf wains, which were ponderous, made for hauling large loads of heavy cargo. The four-wheeler from Dael was made of ash wood, light but durable. There was room for two on the driver's seat, which was well padded and had a low back for support. The freight bed was short, with wooden sides and front, and had a hinged tailgate fastened with metal latches. The waggon was painted a deep red.

The Warrow wheelwright of Budgens, Ned Proudhand, had done a first-rate job on the wheel—replacing the iron rim and broken spoke, and regreasing not only the hub on the repaired wheel, but all the other hubs and the waggon-tongue pivot and the whiffletrees as well. He had painted the new spoke red to match the others. For this fine craftwork and conscientiousness, Anval grudgingly paid Ned with a tiny golden coin, the only one that Ned had ever seen, copper being his usual fare, with an occasional silver. But this coin was *gold!* Ned vowed to keep it all his life, on display, pledging never to spend it, claiming it as his Dwarf hoard, declaring that it would become an heirloom of the Proudhand clan.

Anval turned the rig over to Cotton, who drove it down to the common stables at the Pony Field on the southeastern edge of Hollow End. There he removed the harness and watered the two horses, whom he dubbed Brownie and Downy—one being all brown and the other a chestnut with an especially soft, fluffy, white mane. He rubbed them down and filled the feed bins in their stalls with an extra helping of oats. And after talking to them for a bit while combing their manes and tails, the buccan returned to The Root.

It was dusk when Cotton came up the walk toward the burrow. The autumn eve was mild, and from the open window of the study he could hear Perry's voice: ". . . paces up the gentle rise from the First Neath to the East Hall at Gate Level; then it's two hundred forty level paces across the hall and out the Daūn Gate to freedom . . ."

Why, that's the Brega Path what Mister Perry's reciting, Cotton thought. *Why in the world . . . ?* Before his mind could carry on, he heard Borin grunt and Anval reply, but what was said he could not tell. *Hoy, hold on now! Why them cheeky Dwarves are* testing *Mister Perry . . . as if they don't believe that us Warrows have good memories!* Cotton stormed toward the front entrance.

As the ired buccan stalked into the study, Borin looked up from the original Scroll; and Anval and Lord Kian glanced up from two of Perry's linen-paper copies. Empty-handed, Perry stood in room center.

"Well?" asked Perry.

"Exact," grunted Borin, a growing look of approval in his eye.

"Your duplicate, too, is letter-perfect, Waeran," rumbled Anval, turning to Lord Kian, who also nodded.

Borin stood, his black eyes aglitter in the candlelight. "Master Perry, we have seen for ourselves the exactness of your copies of the Brega Scroll; hence, because that work has proved to be unerring, we no longer doubt the accuracy of your duplicate of the *Raven Book.* You are indeed a crafter of true worth."

Borin and then Anval bowed deeply to Perry, and the buccan smiled and bowed in return. Cotton, mollified by the Dwarves' respectful behavior, completely forgot the angry words he had come to heap upon them.

"Well then," said Perry, moving to the desk, "I'd better pack some of these copies to take to King Durek." He stood undecided a moment, then mumbled to himself, "I suppose I'll just take them all. . . ." As an afterthought, he opened a desk drawer and added a small chart to the stack. ". . . as well as this sketch of mine."

That evening, once more they feasted on Holly's fine cooking. This time the meal consisted of an overlarge kettle of well-spiced green beans slow-cooked for hours with a huge ham bone and gobbets of meat and large, peeled tubers and parsnips. There was also freshly baked bread with honey, light golden beer, and cherry cobbler for dessert. Again Anval out-ate a straining Cotton. And the conversation touched upon hunting and gold, deer and gardens, delving and writing, weaponry and seeds, Wizards and Dragons, and many other things. This night Borin also joined in the talk 'round the table and proved to hold many tales of interest.

But all through the evening both Perry and Cotton would at times lapse into silence and gaze about them at their beloved Root, wondering when they would see it again.

The next morning ere dawn, Holly awakened them all, and they sat down to an enormous breakfast of scrambled eggs, hotcakes, honey, toast, and marmalade. "It is well we are leaving today," growled Anval. "Another week of this fare and I could not get into my armor."

At sunrise Lord Kian strode to the Pony Field stable and hitched up the team and drove the waggon down to the Market Square, where gaping Warrow merchants loaded the supplies the *Man* had purchased the day before. When he returned, the Dwarves and Warrows, dressed for the journey, were standing on the stoop—packs, bedrolls, armor, and weaponry ready. They placed all their goods in the waggon, and the Dwarves piled aboard with Kian. Perry and Cotton took one last long look around, reluctant to get aboard now that it had come to it. Cotton glanced at Perry and, at his nod, reached up to grasp the sideboard to climb into the wain. But before he could do so, Holly came rushing out of the door. She spun Cotton around and hugged him and whispered into his ear, "Goodbye, Cotton. Now you stay by Mister Perry, and take care of him, and keep him safe." Then she turned to Perry, and she hugged him and kissed him and then held him at arm's length and with brimming eyes looked at him as if to fill herself up with the sight of him for the long days to come. And Perry, stunned and dumbfounded, shuffled his feet and peered at the ground, unable to look again upon the anguish in Holly's face. She tried to say something, but could not and burst into tears, and with one last quick embrace she ran weeping back into The Root.

Perry stood a moment gaping at the pegged panels of the oaken door through which she had fled, and suddenly he realized how much he cared for her—in that quiet, Warrowish sort of way. Now his yen for adventure seemed somehow less important, but he glanced up into the wain where his companions were waiting; and in that instant—like countless others in all ages have found—he, too, learned the first lesson of quests: whether for good or ill, the needs of the quest overrule all else.

Curbing his confused feelings, Perry climbed into the waggon with Cotton and the others, and they drove away to the east.

CHAPTER 6

THE HORN OF THE REACH

Anval, Borin, Kian, Perry, and Cotton; they all rode away from The Root in silence, each deep in his own thoughts. In this fashion they passed down the canted road from Hollow End and on through Woody Hollow, past the mill and across the bridge over the Dingle-rill. And everywhere they passed, Warrows stood silent by the road or ran from their homes to watch the waggon roll by. This was, after all, an amazing sight, one not likely to be repeated in anyone's lifetime:

Imagine, two Dwarves and a Man, actually, right here in Woody Hollow! And Mister Perry and Cotton goin' away with them and all! Wonders never cease! It was to be the talk of the Boskydells for months, even years, to come.

A flock of chattering younglings, led by the two tagalongs, ran ahead of, beside, and behind the wain all the way to the bridge over the Dingle-rill, where the children stopped and stood watching as the waggon slowly trundled across and went on. Some tykes silently waved, others gaily piped farewells, and some seemed instantly to lose interest, for they began playing tag or wrestling or simply went wandering off. Soon the horse-drawn vehicle was around the bend and over the hill and out of sight.

Nothing was said by anyone in the wain for a mile or so, and apart from an occasional bird or an insect coming awake with the warming of the Sun, the silence was broken only by the sounds of the waggon and team: the creak of harness, the jingle of singletrees, the clip-clop of hooves, an occasional whicker or blowing, the rattle of sideboards and tailgate, and above all else the unremitting grind of iron-rimmed wheels turning against the hard-packed earthen road. In this somber mood they rode without speaking till they came to the village of Budgens.

Upon sighting the small red waggon drawing nigh, the hundred or so citizens of that village, too, turned out to watch the wayfarers pass through, taking up a position on the Monument Knoll, with Ned Proudhand in the crowd forefront showing all who would look—and there were many—his Dwarf gold piece.

As the wayfarers rolled by the Monument, Cotton, driven by an inner urge, drew the silver horn from his pack and blew it. An electrifying note rang out, clear and bell-like, its pure tones carrying far across the countryside. A great cheer went up from the small crowd, and everyone there on the knoll stood straight and tall. The gloomy mood was lifted from the occupants of the waggon, and they waved to the gathering. A youngling Warrow broke from the ranks and ran down toward the wain; others saw this and also ran down the hillside and onto the road, joining him; soon all were thronging around and keeping pace with the van.

"Where you headin', Cotton?" cried a voice from the mob.

"Out east and south, Teddy," answered Cotton, his eye falling upon the one who had called forth.

What for? shouted several at once.

"The King says there's trouble in the mountains and we're fixin' to help set it right," replied Cotton, which brought forth a great cheer; for the folks living at Budgens, being near the Monument and all, thought that Warrows were the greatest resource that the King could draw upon. Why, it was only *natural*, only *right* and *proper,* that the King call upon a Warrow or two to help settle his troubles, whatever they might be.

Persons in the crowd continued in this fashion to shout out questions or give encouragement to the travellers as the wain slowly trundled through the village. And Cotton was aglow with it all: He introduced Lord Kian and Anval and Borin to the citizens, and much to their delight the Man actually stood up in the rolling waggon and gracefully bowed 'round to all, though the Dwarves merely grunted. Then Cotton reminded the Budgens folk as to just who Mister Perry was; and the Ravenbrook

Scholar stood and bowed to the crowd, too. At each introduction, or reply to a question, or statement made by the wayfarers, the villagers cheered. And in this festive atmosphere the voyagers were escorted through Budgens. At the town limits they were given a *hip, hip, hurrah!* send-off, and soon were out of sight and hearing of the hamlet by the Rillmere.

"Well, now," said Lord Kian, white teeth smiling through yellow beard, as he turned upon the driver's seat to look back at his passengers in the van, "that was quite a lively band of citizens."

"Ever since the great battle, the folks of Budgens have had a reputation for being spirited," replied Perry. "Did you see that monument back there on the knoll? Well, that's a memorial not only to the nineteen Warrows actually killed in the Battle of Budgens in the Winter War, but also to the thirty wounded and the nearly three hundred others who took part in the fight to overthrow the reavers—evil Ghûls who were trying to usurp the Bosky, to steal our homeland during the days before the fall of Gron. And we were successful; we Warrows slew many of the corpse-foe, and later, with the help of the Men of Wellen, we drove them from the Bosky. But it was in Budgens where it really got started. Oh, the Warrows of that time had been in a lot of skirmishes with the Ghûls back when the reavers first invaded the Bosky, but it wasn't until Danner and Patrel came that the Warrows were organized properly. The first big battle of the Struggles took place in Budgens, a Warrow name of honor: *Brave as Budgens,* we say these days. The people of Budgens know that, and they see the Memorial every day, and carefully tend the garden there at the foot of the stone monument. The glory of those Warrows' bravery is with the folk of Budgens always, and they take pride for their part in history."

Borin looked at Perry. "So you Waerans have already dealt with usurpers, as we Châkka have yet to do," he rumbled, a new respect showing in his eye at the thought of these Wee Ones driving back a great gang of the reaving-foe, driving them out of Budgens—each Khōl twice Waeran size—and doing it while suffering a loss of only nineteen. "You are a small but mighty adversary."

Then Borin turned a curious eye to the other Warrow. "Cotton, show me that silver horn upon which you blew the clarion call that stirred my spirit and made hope leap into my heart."

"It's the same horn, you know," said Cotton, rummaging in his pack. "It's the one Captain Patrel used to rally the Warrows in fight after fight with Modru's Reavers. That's why I blew it; it was back to Budgens again. Usually we blow it here once a year, on the battle anniversary; but it seemed like the thing to do today also, since we're setting off on a mission." Cotton passed the small bugle to Borin.

Perry spoke up: "It's called the Horn of the Reach, and it was given over to Patrel by Vidron himself, General of the Alliance, Whelmer of Modru's Horde. The *Raven Book* says the horn was found almost twenty-six hundred years ago in the hoard of Sleeth the Orm by Elgo, Sleeth's Doom; but of its history ere then, nothing is said."

"Elgo, Sleeth's Doom, you say? Thief Elgo, Foul Elgo, treasure stealer, *I* say," snapped Borin, angrily setting the horn aside, ire flashing in his eyes. "He slew the Dragon, true, but then he foully claimed the Châk treasure for his own. But it was not his! The Dragon hoard was ours! Sleeth came to Blackstone—the Châkka Halls of the Rigga Mountains—plundering, marauding, pillaging, slaying; we were driven out. Sleeth remained, sleeping for centuries upon a bed of stolen gold. Then Thief Elgo came and slew the great Cold-drake. By trick! When we heard that Sleeth was dead, we rejoiced, and asked for that which was rightfully ours. In sneering pride, Foul Elgo came to Kachar, to the throne of Brak, then DelfLord of those halls. And False Elgo laughed at and mocked us, flinging down a great pouch made of Dragon's hide at Brak's feet, scoffing. 'A purse such as this you must make ere you can fill your treasuries with *Dracongield;* yet beware, for only the brave may pluck this cloth from its loom.'" Borin chopped the edge of one hand into the palm of the other. "Such an affront could not be borne, and we were avenged against Jeering Elgo, who japed nevermore. But nought of Sleeth's stolen hoard was ever recovered by us, the Châkka, the true owners." Borin's eyes flashed darkly, and the muscles in his jaw clenched, and he breathed heavily.

Perry had listened with growing amazement to the anger in Borin's voice, and saw that Anval, too, was grinding his teeth in suppressed rage. "But Borin, Anval," said the Warrow, baffled by the Dwarves' intense manner, "those events took place ages past, far from here, and concerned people long dead; yet it is you who seem ired, though it happened centuries and centuries before either of you were born."

"Elgo was a thief!" spat Borin. "And an insulter of my ancestors! He who seeks the wrath of the Châkka finds it! Forever!" Borin turned his face away from Perry, and his smoldering eyes stared without seeing over the passing countryside, and Anval sullenly fingered the edge of his axe.

Interminable moments passed, but at last Perry spoke: "Whether Elgo was a thief as you say, or a Dragon-slaying hero as some tell it, or both, I cannot say; but the silver horn at your side perhaps came from that disputed treasure."

And in the back of the rolling waggon, slowly and with visible effort, Borin at last mastered his Dwarvish passion; grudgingly, he began to examine the trumpet. "This was made by the Châkka," he muttered, and then he turned his attention to the engraved swift-running rider-mounted horses winding through carven runes twining 'round the flange of the horn-bell. Borin gave a start and sucked in air between his teeth, and looked hard at the clarion; and he hissed a Dwarf word . . . *"Narok!"*

Narok: Borin's taut utterance seemed to jerk Anval upright, and he stared sharply at his brother.

After a long while Borin passed the bugle to Anval, who studied it as intensely; and then, after another long while, Anval reluctantly gave the clarion back to Cotton, warning, "Beware, Waeran, this trump must be blown only in time of dire need." And about it neither Anval nor Borin would say more.

In wonder, Cotton took back the horn and looked at it with new eyes, studying it closely for the first time, driven by the Dwarves' curious behavior to seek what they had seen.

The companions had followed Woody Hollow Road to Byroad Lane, and then they had joined the Crossland Road, which would carry them all the way to the Grimwall Mountains. And the wain continued to roll eastward during the day, through Willowdell, and Tillock, and beyond, one person driving while the others lounged in conversation on the packs and bedrolls in the cargo bed. Often they changed position when some bone or joint or muscle protested at being held in one place too long or at being jounced against a hard waggon-plank by an occasional rut or rock or washboarded section in the road—not that there were many; for the most part the road was smooth and the pace was swift. Nor did the travellers engage in continuous talk; at times they lapsed into long silences and simply watched the countryside roll by, the trees beginning to change hue in the quickening autumn—many reds and yellows and a few browns starting to show amid the predominant greens.

Frequently they would stop to rest the horses and water them, and to trade off driving, and to take care of other needs. At one of these stops they saw another sign of the changing seasons: two flocks of geese flew southward overhead, high in the sky, one wedge flying above and ahead of the other. Their lornful cries were faint with distance, and Perry, as always, felt a tugging at his heart. Lord Kian shaded his eyes and looked long: "Year after year, since time immemorial, they pass to and fro, their flight locked to the seasons. Little do they care that Kingdoms and tyrants rise and fall; it is as nothing to them in their unchanging journey through time. They fly so very high above our petty squabbles and fightings and Wars and slayings. How small we must seem to them."

At another stop they fed the horses some grain while they themselves lunched on the contents of a basket provided by Holly: cold beef sandwiches and crisp Bosky apples. Anval sighed when the food was gone. "I somehow feel that may be the last I eat of Holly's cookery," he said, rubbing his stomach. "You are a fortunate Waeran, Master Perry." Perry did not answer, though he gazed thoughtfully back to the west, his mind seeing amber damman eyes brimming with tears.

It was nearly sundown when the waggon drove through Raffin, where, as in each of the other hamlets the wayfarers had passed, the citizens gathered to gawp at this strange assortment of travellers. Yet though it was late in the day, the wain did not stop, for Lord Kian planned on reaching the Happy Otter, an inn located on the western edge of Greenfields, the next town, ten or so miles east of Raffin. He and Anval and Borin previously had noted the 'Otter when the trio had passed in the opposite direction on their journey to The Root to see *The Raven Book*. Upon hearing that they were heading for the inn, Cotton perked up, for he had heard of the 'Otter's beer, and, as he said, he had a mind to try it. Anval, too, smiled with anticipation and relish at the thought.

It was night when the waggon at last came to Greenfields; the inn was dark, for the hostelkeeper, Fennerly Cotter, had gone to bed. Borin leapt down from the wain and strode to the door and hammered upon it with the butt of his fist. After a long moment a lantern-light appeared in a second-storey front window, and the shutters banged open as Fennerly looked out, and then slammed shut again. Borin continued to pound the door in exasperation as the innkeeper's light slowly bobbed down the stairs and across the common room. Fennerly, in his nightcap, at last came grumbling to the door and opened it. Raising his lantern up to see just who in the Dell this door-banger was, the innkeeper swallowed half a yawn with a gulp and stumbled a step or two backwards as his now wide-awake eyes found a fierce Dwarf warrior towering within his doorway, muttering something about Waeran innkeepers that went to bed with the chickens. But then scowling Borin was shouldered aside by smiling Anval with Cotton in tow; and he drew the Warrow to the taps, where he demanded they be served with the best ale in the house.

As Fennerly was to relate later to a rapt set of cronies, "Wull, at first I thought it were a Dwarf invasion. Gave me a right start, they did, and I was thinkin' about escapin' and soundin' the alarm bell at the Commons. Oh, I knowed that the strangers was in the Bosky, right enough, but I can't say as I was expectin' even one of them, much less all three, to come bargin' into my inn in the middle of the night—and draggin' two sleepy Warrows with 'em, no less. But in they came, the Big Man stoopin' a bit to miss the overhead beams while he and that Mister Perry was chuckling at some private joke of their own.

"Wull, let me tell you, them five drank up half my best beer and ate all the kitchen leftovers, they did. And then them two Dwarves got to arm wrestling, and they grunted and strained and fairly turned the air blue, what with them strange, blood-curdling Dwarf oaths they yelled. And each time one of 'em lost they'd take a swill of beer and change hands and go at it again. And the one was better with his right arm whilst t'other was better with his left. And the Big Man sat back and roared his laughter and puffed on his pipe. Then he arm wrestled with each, and though he finally lost, let me tell you it was a mighty struggle for them broad-shouldered Dwarves to finally put his knuckles to the wood. And all the while there was that Mister Perry sittin' there smilin' and yawnin' and blinkin' like a drowsy owl tryin' to stay awake, and Mister Cotton runnin' back and forth around the table, judgin' the contests and declarin' the victor when an arm was finally put down. But after a while the Big Man noticed that Mister Perry had fallen asleep, and so we all went to bed, and it was about time too.

"But it seemed I had no sooner got to sleep than that Dwarf, Mister Borin—the one as pounds doors—well, he were at it again, only this time it was my own bedroom door though. And he was glarin' and mutterin' something about Waeran innkeepers what *don't* get up with the chickens. I fed 'em breakfast, and they were off at the crack of dawn.

"Of course they paid me with good copper, they did, even though I hadn't got a bed large enough for the Big Man, who slept in the stable hayloft above the horses, slept right there even though they was callin' him 'Lord'—Lord Kian, that is. Don't that beat all if it's true? A Lord sleepin' in my stables! Him what is probably used to sleeping on silks and satins." Here Fennerly paused to fill the mugs and let the startling facts sink home, and sink home they did, for all the Warrows looked at each other in wonderment, and an excited buzz filled the tap-room.

"Ahem," said Fennerly, clearing his throat, announcing that he was ready to resume his tale, and silence quickly fell upon the inn's common room. "Of course, by the time anyone else in the 'Fields was up, the strangers was long gone, miles east of this village. Didn't say what they was doin' or where they was goin' or nothin'. But I'll tell you this: whatever it is they are doing, I'll bet a gold buckle that it's somethin' big." And with that pronouncement, Fennerly fell silent; and all of his cronies and listeners sighed and mulled over their ale, for they had missed the biggest event to happen in Greenfields since Tuckerby Underbank himself had passed through on his return from the Winter War. And no sooner would Fennerly finish his tale than another 'Fieldite would come into the Happy Otter, agog with the news, and the innkeeper would recount the events again, and all of the Warrows—each and every one of them—

would sit forward on the edges of their seats so as not to miss a single one of Fennerly's words—though some of the enthralled listeners were hearing the tale for the sixth or even the eighth time.

It was indeed the crack of dawn when the travellers left, after breakfast, with Cotton's head pounding but Anval seeming no less for the wear. Lord Kian was smiling and Borin scowling and Perry rubbing sleep from his eyes. Yet the road was smooth and the air crisp and fresh and soon Cotton was his normal chipper self, and all the others were wide awake and in cheerful good humor as the waggon continued to roll on toward the Boskydell border some fourteen miles to the east on the far side of the great barricade.

In late morning they drove into the thorn tunnel through the Spindlethorn Barrier, and then over the bridge above the Spindle River, passing again into the spiked barricade beyond. At last they emerged from the thorns on the far side, coming once more into the day, leaving the Boskydells behind. Looking backward, Cotton remarked to Perry: "Well now, Sir, I really do believe that we are on our way. Into what, I can't say, but on our way at last. I guess I didn't believe it till just now; but somehow, lookin' back at the Spindlethorn, well, Sir, it has smacked it home to me that we have really and truly left the Boskydells and are off to a Rūck War. And I don't know nothin' about War and fighting, that's for sure. Why I'm along at all is a mystery to me, except I somehow know I'll be needed before we're through with this. And I don't mind telling you, Mister Perry, I'm scared and that's the plain and simple truth."

"Oh piffle, Cotton!" snorted Perry, whose spirits had been on the rise all day. "That's not fear you're feeling, it's excitement! And as to why you're here, Cotton, well, you've come along to help me, and I've come along to guide the Dwarves in the great adventure of our lifetime. But you are dead right about one thing: for our own safety we've got to learn to use the weapons we brought along. You'll see, Cotton, once we can protect ourselves, nay, rather, once we can carry the fight to the Spawn, then all thoughts of fear will vanish forever. I'm sure that Lord Kian here will show us how to use our swords, and we have many days to practice before they'll become necessary."

"Well, my little friends," responded Kian, looking a bit askance at the two Waerlinga, "it isn't quite that simple. One doesn't become a master swordthane overnight. But I'll see what we can do between now and then to prepare you." Inwardly, the young Lord was relieved, for he had been about to broach the same subject to the Waerlinga. Ere now, those gentle Folk had had no need to learn the arts of War. But on this venture, like as not there would come a time when these two buccen would have to defend themselves, at least long enough for aid to reach them. The Waerlinga themselves had recognized their need to learn the rudiments of defense, thus he would not have to convince them of that; but they would have to train hard every day under deft guidance to be able to handle their long-knives by the time they reached Drimmen-deeve. Fortunately for the Warrows, Lord Kian possessed the needed skill to instruct them properly.

They drove till the westering Sun touched the rim of the Earth, and they pulled off the road to the eaves of the bordering forest, Edgewood, to camp for the night.

While Cotton and Perry made several trips to gather firewood, Lord Kian tended the horses, and Anval and Borin unloaded the evening supplies and found stones to set in a ring for the fire, which was soon crackling in the early autumn twilight. Kian refilled their leather bottles and the large waterskin from a clear freshette bubbling through the trees and running into the meadow.

As they were out gathering a final load of wood, Cotton took the opportunity to talk alone with Perry: "Mister Perry, today I took another good hard look at that silver horn of ours. After the close way they both acted yesterday and what Anval said, any ninnyhammer could see there was a lot more left unsaid by the Dwarves than all we know. Well, lookin' at it, I saw something after a long time that, well, I don't rightly know what to make of it 'cause it only adds to the mystery. But anyway, what I mean to say is that them tiny little figures of the horsemen riding like the wind and curving all around the horn, well, Sir, them riders, if you study them up close, they ain't Men riders at all. They're *Dwarves!*"

"What!" burst out Perry, astounded by this new information. "That can't be! That horn has been known too long, seen by too many people for that to have been overlooked by all eyes till now."

"I can't help it, Sir," responded Cotton stubbornly, "but them eyes just didn't look close enough. They saw what they were expecting to see, if you catch my meaning. I'm saying that them people in Valon, well, they are a Folk what lives by the horse, and they purely saw those little figures as bein' riders just like they themselves are. And since Captain Patrel got the horn as a gift from the Valon people, well he saw Valon riders, too, just like everybody else has seen 'em since that time. Beggin' your pardon, Mister Perry, but after all, it *is* called the Horn of Valon—or the Horn of the Reach—and when people hear that name they don't really look hard at the riders to see whether or not they are Men, Dwarves, Elves, or even Warrows; they only see that there are riders on galloping horses, nothing more. And with that name, naturally the people think they're Valon riders. But it isn't so. Oh, they're Dwarves right enough, but you have to look real close to see it."

"Cotton, I'm flabbergasted," said Perry, picking up another fallen branch. "If what you say is true, then it is a detail that's been overlooked by us Warrows for more than two hundred years, and by the House of Valon for twenty-four hundred years before that—since the days of Elgo and of Elyn and Thork. Of course if the riders truly are Dwarves, it'd help explain the mysterious way that Borin and Anval acted."

"Oh no, Sir, I beg to differ," said Cotton, breaking a branch in two and tucking the pieces into his bundle, "I'd say it only deepens the mystery."

"No, no, Cotton, what I mean is that the horn must have some secret meaning to the Dwarves, and that's why Borin and Anval acted as they did," Perry said. "But what do you mean, Cotton, 'deepens the mystery'? How can it get more mysterious than it already is?"

"Well, Sir," replied Cotton, "you know the old tavern talk about Dwarves not riding horses. And you remember back at The Root how Anval told me that all of his Folk had better sense than to climb aboard real horses instead of just ponies—oh, they use the big horses right enough, so that shows they aren't afraid of 'em, but they just don't *ride* 'em. Well now, I ask you, if they don't ride horses, why in the world are there figures all around the silver horn of a bunch of *Dwarves* ridin' on the backs of galloping *horses?*"

Perry, of course, had no answer for Cotton's question. He knew that the animals on the horn were horses and not ponies, but he, too, had always thought that the riders, though small in relation to the horses, were Men. Perry was eager to examine the trumpet closely for himself at the first opportunity.

Gathering the rest of the firewood in silence, they each soon had a load. On the way back, Cotton, who had collected an enormous bundle of deadwood, stepped into a low spot and fell flat on his face, throwing the branches every which way as he flung out his arms to catch himself. *"Whuff!"* he grunted as he hit the earth and seemed to disappear in the deep grass.

"Cotton!" cried Perry. "Where did you go?"

"I'm down here, Sir," answered Cotton. "I stepped in a hole. It was just like taking that extra step at the top of the stairs only to find out there weren't one . . . or rather it was like not taking a step at the bottom of the stairs only to find out there were one. Lumme! I threw wood everywhere."

And Perry, seeing that Cotton was unhurt, began laughing and describing to Cotton the cascade of limbs launched through the air. Cotton, too, began laughing, and their serious mood over the Horn of Valon was dispelled. Happily, they collected the fallen wood, this time sharing the load evenly, and returned to the camp just in time for tea.

It had been a long day, and soon both Warrows were nodding drowsily. They spread their bedrolls and shortly were fast asleep in the open air. Anval and Borin bedded down also, leaving Lord Kian sitting on a log at the edge of the firelight, whittling with his sharp-bladed knife, for the travellers had decided that a watch would be kept, though they were hundreds of miles and many days away from peril.

Perry's turn came late in the night. He was unaccustomed to sentry duty and soon found his eyes drooping. To keep himself awake he slowly strolled around and around the camp, stopping now and again to add wood to the fire. While walking his post he began to softly hum the *Song of the Nightwatch,* for at last he truly understood it:

The flames, they flicker, the shadows dance,
  Bright Stars pass overhead.
Night flies the quicker, Dawn does advance,
  For those snug in their bed.

For one on guard who walks his round
  And must remain awake,
The Night goes hard, for he is bound
  Another round to make.

In this manner he passed his vigil as the stars wheeled through the vault above, and soon he awakened Anval, whose turn had come.

Shedding his Elven-cloak and folding it as a pillow, Perry crawled sleepily back into his bed, and as he slowly fell toward slumber his thoughts drifted across Cotton's revelation about the Horn of Valon. The rest of that night Perry's dreams were filled with thousands of horses endlessly thundering across open plains, making the earth shake with the pounding of their hooves. And upon the back of each rode a Dwarf.

CHAPTER 7

HICKORY SWORDS

Just before dawn, Cotton, standing the final guard, stirred up the embers and added more wood to the fire. He fed the horses some grain and made a pot of tea. When the brew was ready he awakened the others, Lord Kian first and Perry last. As daytide crept upon the land, Perry stumped to the crystalline stream and splashed cold water on his face and hands and the back of his neck, making great whooshing sounds as the icy liquid startled him fully awake. "Hoo, that's brisk!" he called to the camp. Then he made his way back and took a bracing hot cup of tea.

Though there was not yet an autumn frost, the morning was chill, and the fire was most welcome. The five huddled around the campblaze as they sipped hot drink and breakfasted on dried venison and tough waybread, part of the supplies obtained by Kian at Woody Holly. In contrast to his overindulgence at The Root, Anval now ate adequately but sparingly, as if to conserve the supplies. Cotton, seeing the Dwarf's behavior and deeming it wise, held rein on his own voracity, too. And Borin rumbled, "Well done, Waeran Cotton, I see you learn travellers' ways quickly. Fear not, though: our short-rations fast will be broken tomorrow night when we reach Stonehill."

"With prime fare, too," reassured his fellow trencher, Anval. "Yesterweek, as we came to the Boskydells, we found that the White Unicorn sets a fine table—as good as any in the Lands."

Lord Kian downed the last of his tea, then made his way into the meadow to retrieve the hobbled horses. With Cotton's help, he hitched Brownie and Downy to the waggon, while Anval, Borin, and Perry broke camp—dousing the fire, refilling the water bottles and skin, and loading the supplies. Packs were repacked and bedrolls rolled; all were tossed into the waggon. Soon the travellers were back on the road, the wain rolling for Stonehill, with Anval at the reins.

Though Perry had wanted to examine the figures engraved on the silver horn, he did not get the chance, for the moment they got under way, Cotton turned to Lord Kian and said, "Well, Sir, seeing as how we're going off to fight Rūcks and such, it seems to me that Mister Perry and me are going to need to know something about what we'll be fighting—if you catch my drift, Sir."

"Indeed I do 'catch your drift,' Cotton," said Kian, smiling, yet looking with respect at the canny Waerling, "for to know more of your enemy than he knows of you gains vantage in battle.

"Withal, there are three of the enemy. First, the eld Rukha: foul creatures of ancient origin, of yore as numberless as worms in the earth, puff-adder-eyed, wide-gapped slit-mouthed, skinny-armed and bandy-legged, round-bellied, bat-wing-eared, small but tenacious, no taller than Dwarves, crude in the arts of battle but overwhelming in their very numbers. Second, the Lōkha: evil spawned by Gyphon, cruel masters of Rukha and Trolls, in appearance Rukh-like but tall as a Man, strong and skilled in battle, limited in number. Third and last, Trolls: enormous creatures—some say a giant Rukh—twice Man height, strong beyond belief, hard as a rock; they need have little or no skill with weaponry, depending instead upon their stone hide to turn aside blades or other arms, and upon their massive strength to crush foes; there are only rumors that any still exist.

"Rukha, Lōkha, and Trolls: all came from the Untargarda—from Neddra—and were stranded in Mithgar by the sundering of the way between the Middle and Lower planes. And they all suffer the Ban and must shun the sunlight, working instead their evil at night—though in Modru's time his malevolent will sustained them during day as well, for the Dimmendark was upon the land, and the Sun shone not."

"What about Vulgs, Ghûls, and Hèlsteeds?" asked Perry.

"Ah," responded Kian, "as to them, we think that all may have perished during the Winter War. The Wolf-like Vulgs, whose virulent fangs wreak death even though the victim is but scratched—"

"Vulg's black bite slays at night," interjected Cotton, reciting the old saw.

"Aye, Wee One," nodded Kian, "'tis true. But neither Vulgs nor the cloven-hooved, rat-tailed, horse-like Hèlsteeds have been seen among any of the *Spaunen* raiding parties that issue out from Drimmen-deeve. Hence, they may no longer exist upon Mithgar."

"And the Ghûls?" asked Perry.

"Ghola are not seen either," answered the Man. "And that is well, for they are a dreadful foe: nearly unkillable, taking dire wounds without hurt. Wood through the heart, dismemberment, fire: these are the ways to slay a Ghol.

"But as I say, neither Vulg, Ghol, nor Hèlsteed has been seen since the Winter War, and I deem we need only concern ourselves with Rukh, Lōkh, and perhaps Troll—Spawn you name Rūck, Hlōk, and Ogru: these three you must be ready for. And so, my wee fledglings, to practice your swordplay to enable you to meet these enemies we need but follow a simple plan: To learn to fight the skilled, Man-sized Lōkha you shall instead fight me; I shall play that part. And to learn to engage the small, unskilled Rukha you shall do battle with each other." Here Kian smiled.

"What about the Trolls—the giant Ogrus?" interjected Cotton.

"Though I doubt if any still exist," said Kian, "if we come upon one, then you must flee, or you will be crushed like an ant under heel."

"Flee? Flee?" protested Perry, taken aback. "Do you counsel us to flee in the midst of battle just because the foe is over-large? Some would say that is cowardice and is unworthy advice."

"Perry, Perry, green-Waerling Perry, you know not of what you speak," said Kian, shaking his head in rue. "Let me ask you this: If an avalanche were descending upon you, would you oppose it or would you flee? If a raging whirlwind were rending trees from the earth's bosom, would you slash at it with your sword or would you take shelter? Perry, Ogrus are like that: Trollish, nearly unstoppable, almost unkillable. Oh, they can be slain all right: by a great boulder dropped on them from a far height, or a fall from a mountainous precipice, to name two ways; but to slay them in battle is nigh impossible, requiring a fell weapon to be thrust just so: in the groin, or under the eyelid, or in the mouth, or in one or two other places of vulnerability. And even then the weapon may shatter against the Troll, no matter the blade's birthforge, for the Ogru is like a rock: hard and obdurate."

"Bane! Bane will sorely wound *any* foe," averred Perry in a grim voice, setting his hand to the hilt of his sword. "It was made by the Elves, and it is said that Bane's blade-jewel shines with a blue light if Rūcks or other evil things come near. Swiftly, Perry drew the sword from its scabbard and flashed it to the sky, crying, "Bane! I trust my life to you!"

"Indeed, Bane is a fell weapon of Elvish origin," said Kian, reaching out a gentle hand to touch Perry on the shoulder as the Waerling lowered the glittering blade, "and it may penetrate even the Troll-hide of the Ogrus. But, Perry, Bane is just an Elven-knife, though a long one, and may not reach an Ogru's vitals. Bitterly wounded he may be, but crush you he still will. No, you must flee and let others more able try to vanquish this foe."

Borin, sitting beside Anval on the driver's seat, twisted about and growled, "Even Châkka, as skilled in fighting as we are, give Trolls wide berth, yielding back rather than doing battle. But if we must, we will attack in strength; great numbers of axes are needed to slay an Ogru. Even then, many warriors will perish."

Somewhat disconcerted by Kian's but especially by Borin's words, grim-lipped Perry slipped Bane back into the scabbard fastened to his pack. Cotton vowed, "Well you can be sure, right enough, that if ever I see a great Trollish Ogru he won't see me: I'm going to take to my heels and fly!"

Kian smiled at Cotton's words, then grew serious once more. "Heed me now," he said. "Time is short and much needs doing. We must take advantage of every moment to train you at swords. While travelling in the waggon we will speak on the art of swords and the strategy of fighting Rukha and Lōkha—for your tactics must vary according to the size of your opponent, the weapon he is wielding, and the armor he is wearing and bearing. And at each of our stops to rest the horses we will put that art and strategy into practice, drilling at swords."

"But we've only been stopping a short while each hour," protested Cotton. "Is that enough time to learn? What I mean to ask, Sir, is, well, with such a little bit of practice, will we actually be able to fight Rūcks and Hlōks?"

Upon hearing Cotton's question, a surge of uncertainty washed through Perry, for now that it had come to the reality of beginning to learn swordplay, the buccan felt strangely reluctant to be schooled in the art of killing—as if some inner voice were saying, *Not for you, Warrow.*

Kian noted this hesitancy in Perry's eyes, and he knew that it was now or never: he had to start the training immediately, for it was vital that these gentle Waerlinga be able to defend themselves. "Let me show you, Cotton, Perry," he said, and turned to Anval, at the reins. "Anval, stop here. We must begin now."

Anval pulled off the road and into the eaves of the bordering woods. All jumped down from the waggon, Borin tending the horses. And then Kian revealed the product of his previous night's whittling: three swords made of hickory limb—two Warrow-sized and one Man-sized—blunt-tipped and dull-edged: the wood was green and supple and not apt to break. Unlike some who would have been chagrined at wielding wooden "toys," both Warrows seemed relieved at not having to practice with real weapons.

Kian allowed them each in turn to do unschooled "battle" with him, Cotton stepping back to allow Perry to "have the first go." The buccan started timidly, but the Man cried, "Ho, Waerling! Be not afraid of hurting me! Swing hard! Though I am not a real enemy, you must learn to strike with force as well as finesse!"

With this encouragement, soon Perry was slashing and hacking at Lord Kian with abandon, yet the Man fended off

the crude assaults with ease. Shortly, the Warrow began to
see that swordplay was more than just wild swinging; fur-
thermore, it came as no small surprise that no matter how
cunningly he planned a cut, Lord Kian fended it, seemingly
without effort.

When Cotton's turn came he attacked with a furious flurry,
the clack of the wooden swords clitter-clattering among the
trees of the verging forest, but he, too, could not pierce Lord
Kian's defenses. Yet, on his part, the young Man was astonished at the native quickness of this small Folk. Each Warrow
was breathless and panting in a matter of minutes; but their ex-
uberance had grown, and each had collapsed upon the ground
in laughter at the end of his turn at mock battle, whooping and
guffawing at his own ineptness. Even so, they had passed the
first hurdle; and now they were ready to begin their genuine
schooling, with its slow, step-by-step, often tedious buildup of
skill.

Much to the buccen's surprise, as breathless as they were,
only a short while had passed; even so, it was time to get under
way again. As the wain rolled back onto the road, Lord Kian
began their formal instruction: "For your swords to be effective
weapons in battle, the grip is critical: hold it too tightly and you
cannot move the weapon quickly enough; hold it too loosely
and you will forfeit your sword at first engagement. You must
grasp the weapon as if it were a small live bird, firm enough so
that it cannot escape your hand and fly away, yet gentle enough
so as not to crush its life. . . ." And thus, in the bed of a rolling
waggon, the young Lord began their first lesson, each Warrow
repeatedly grasping his sword under Kian's critical eye while
he spoke of defense against the *Spaunen*.

At their next stop, their drill followed the lesson of the wain:
the grip. Lord Kian directed the buccen to deliberately grasp the
sword too loosely, and showed that this would lead to their
being disarmed immediately; then the opposite was purposely
tried, where too hard a grip was used, so that the Warrows could
experience the limited speed of response and the swift tiring of
the wrist and forearm.

As the waggon got under way once more, Cotton exclaimed,
"Well now, not only do I understand the right way to hold a

sword, but the wrong way too! I like the way you teach, Lord Kian, and that's a fact!"

"It is the way I was taught, Cotton," replied the Man. "Not only did I learn the fit ways of fundamental swordsmanship, but the unfit ways as well, the differences between them, why some ways are superior to others, and, as it is in your case, how they all relate to fighting *Spaunen*. Yes, Cotton, my own swordmaster taught me by this means, and a good method it is."

"Tried and true," rumbled Borin, then fell silent.

"Well, in any event," interjected Perry, "if what I've learned about the grip alone is any example of how well your approach works, then I just hope that you continue it throughout our journey."

"Fear not, Wee One," responded Kian, "I plan on doing just that; in the days that follow, there'll be little or no time for aught else.

"Now, let us speak of balance: When facing a foe . . ." And again the Man took up the lessons of the sword, and the Warrows listened intently as the waggon rolled toward the next stop.

On that first day alone, by the time they reached their evening campsite on the southern slopes of the Battle Downs just after sunset, the Warrows not only knew how to grip a sword, but also the importance of balance, several stances, and how to fall and roll with a weapon in hand. And though they had not again crossed swords in mock battle, after but a single day's training, Perry and Cotton, though rank beginners, knew more about swordplay than nearly all other Warrows in the history of the Boskydells. And the two buccen were to become much more skilled in the long days ahead.

That night Cotton sat on a log near the campfire, polishing his Atalar sword with a soft red-flannel cloth. The golden runes inlaid along the silver blade glistened and sparkled in the firelight. For long moments Perry lay on his bedding and watched Cotton work, then reflected, "Your steel, Cotton, is but a long-knife to a Big Man, yet a full-sized sword to a Warrow. Recall, your blade was found north of here, in an ancient barrow, in the clutch of a long-dead seer of the Lost Land. Though nothing is known of its early years after forging, that weapon has a noble history after its finding—for it saved Gildor from the evil Krakenward."

Cotton paused in his rubbing, and his voice took on the rhythm of a chant as he recited the runes that foretold that deed:

> *"Blade shall brave vile Warder*
> *From the deep black slime."*

"Just so," replied Perry, sleepily yawning. "That is the very same long-knife Galen used to hack at the Monster when it grasped Gildor, and the Elf was saved; Gildor, of course, later saved Tuck; and Tuck at last slew the 'Stone; and so it rightly can be said that because of that keen-edged sword you hold, Modru finally met his end."

"Lor," breathed Cotton upon hearing these words. And he returned to his task with renewed vigor, the cloth in his hand fairly dancing over the golden runes; and Perry fell aslumber among the sparkling shards of glistering light.

The third day of the journey was much like the second, with sword lessons in the waggon bed and practice drills with hickory swords whenever the horses were given rest periods. The Sun climbed upward through the morning and passed overhead to begin its long fall unto the night as slowly the travellers wended their way toward the hamlet of Stonehill.

Stonehill, with its hundred or so stone houses, was a hillside village on the western fringes of the sparsely settled Wilderland. But because the hamlet was situated at the junction where the east-west Crossland Road intersected the Post Road running north and south, strangers and out-of-towners were often seen—in fact, were welcomed. Stonehill's one inn, the White Unicorn, with its many rooms, usually had at least one or two wayfarers as well as a couple of nearby settlers staying overnight: travelling crafters and traders, merchants, or a Man and his wife from a faraway farmstead. . . . But occasionally there would be some *real* strangers, such as a company of journeying Dwarves, or King's soldiers from the south, or a Realmsman or two; in which case the local folk would be sure to drop in to the common room of the inn to have a mug and hear the news from far away.

On this night, as the waggon rolled onto the causeway over the dike and into the village through the west gate of the high guard wall, there was only one guest in the 'Unicorn: a distant farmer who had come to the hillside hamlet to buy his winter supplies, and who had gone to bed with the setting of the Sun. Thus, when the two Warrows, the Man, and the two Dwarves stepped in through the front door, the proprietor, Mister Aylesworth Brewster, was pleased to see more guests for his inn; he bustled to meet them, moving his large bulk past the long-table where sat several locals who looked up from their pipes and mugs at this strangely mixed set of wayfarers. They'd seen Dwarves, of course, but not many. And Warrows were not a strange people to them, since many of the Wee Folk lived in the Weiunwood over the hill—though travelling Warrows were not very common. Men of course were not at all uncommon. However, for the three Folk—Man, Dwarf, and Warrow—to be travelling together, well, that was an event never before seen.

Lor, look there! Well that's a strange sight if ever I saw one. I wonder if they're together or just came in the door at the same time. Oh, they're together all right. See: they're talking together. Dwarves, they don't talk to just anyone, only other Dwarves, or those in their party, or those they're doin' business with. Dwarves is close people, right enough. The little uns are most likely from the Bosky, by their accent; but the Man, well he has the look of a Realmsman, if you ask me.

Ignoring the hum at the long-table, Aylesworth stepped up to Lord Kian, his ruddy features brightening. "Well now, Sir, welcome back to the White Unicorn. Will you and your party be staying overnight?" At the young Lord's nod, Aylesworth glanced out the front window at the team and wain. "Ho, Bill!" he called. Responding to the innkeeper's cry, a slender young Man popped out from behind a door. "See to these folks' waggon and horses whilst I fixes 'em up with rooms."

As Bill hurried to stable the team and house the wain, Mister Brewster led the wayfarers out of the common room and into one of the spacious wings that contained the guest quarters. The White Unicorn was accustomed to housing Men, Dwarves, and even an occasional Warrow; thus its rooms were suitable for the various sizes of the guests. Hence, Lord Kian was escorted to Man-sized quarters, and two more rooms with small-sized furnishings were shown to the others: Anval and Borin in one, Perry and Cotton in the other. As he was getting his guests situated, Aylesworth suggested, "If you want to eat, there's a lamb on the spit that Molly will have ready in two quick shakes. In any case, you're welcome to join us in the common room for a bit of ale." And, wiping his hands on his white apron, he went bustling back down the hall.

Perry and Cotton quickly stepped into their quarters and removed their cloaks and began washing the dust off their hands and faces. "I don't mind telling you, Sir, I'm hungry as a spring bear, what with all this travelling and the exercise we've been getting with the swords," announced Cotton, splashing water on the back of his neck. "And I have a need for a mug or three of old Brewster's beer to wash down some of that dry Crossland Road grit."

"Me, too, Cotton," laughed Perry, wiping his wet face with a towel. "I've been anticipating the taste of the 'Unicorn's ale ever since we sighted Stonehill. By the way, I don't think we should advertise where we're going or why. Oh, not that it's a secret, but I just feel that if anyone asks, then Borin or Anval should decide what to say about our mission."

Having made themselves presentable, the buccen eagerly left their chamber and hastened down the hall to the common room. They threaded their way among the tables and chairs and past the curious locals to a board prepared by Aylesworth. The news had travelled like lightning, and the ranks of the Stonehill folk had swelled considerably, for many had come to see for themselves the oddly mixed group of wayfarers. In fact, every now and again another local would arrive and make his way to join a friend already there to find out what was afoot.

Gratefully accepting the two frothy mugs offered by a large, cheerful Woman—Molly Brewster, the innkeeper's wife—Cotton and Perry quickly discovered that the 'Unicorn's ale was just as tasty as the rumors back in the Boskydells made it out to be. Soon Borin, then Kian, and finally Anval joined the Warrows; and after a bit they all dug into a fine meal of roast lamb while listening to the songs being sung by the people gathered 'round the longtable. And they could hear Molly's robust soprano joining in from the kitchen as harried Bill popped in and out serving lamb to those who ordered it.

Surrounded by song, and partaking of good food and fine ale, the companions passed a pleasant hour.

The five had just finished their meal when one of the locals—a Warrow, as it were—began singing, and all at the long-table joined in chorus; though rustic, the song brought Perry to the edge of his seat:

From northern wastes came Dimmendark,
It stalked down through the Land;
Behind black wall was Winternight,
Ruled by cruel Modru's hand.

> *Our Men and Elves and Warrows, all,*
> *Stood fast in Brotherhood;*
> *Left hearth and home and lofty hall*
> *To band in Weiunwood.*

The Rūcks and Ghûls reaved through the Land,
As Gron put forth its might;
Before them not a one could stand
In bitter Winternight.

> *But overhill in Weiunwood*
> *The battle plans were laid,*
> *To ply the strength of Brotherhood,*
> *And arrow, pike, and blade.*

And nearer came the Rūckish Spawn,
And closer came the Ghûl.
The Dimmendark held back the dawn,
The Land felt Modru's rule.

> *In Weiunwood—as Gron drew near—*
> *The Allies' trap was laid,*
> *With Warrow arrow, Man-borne pike,*
> *And gleaming Elven-blade.*

Into the Weiunwood Gron came,
Pursuing Elvenkind,
Who ran before them in false fear
And drew the Spawn behind.

In Weiunwood the trap was sprung
By Warrow, Elf, and Man;
They whelmed the Spawn, and it is sung
The Ghûlen rabble ran.

Old Arbagon, he killed him eight,
And Bockleman got nine.
Though Uncle Bill, he got there late,
They say he did just fine.

The Men and Warrows and the Elves,
In bravery they fought.
Though many a good friend there was killed,
They didn't die for naught.

Modru, he raged and stormed and gnashed
When Spawn came running out;
They'd entered Weiunwood in pride,
But left it in a rout!

And all throughout the Winter War
Vile Spawn again did try,
But never took the Weiunwood;
They had to pass it by.

And so, my friend, drink to War's end,
It happened long ago.
But should it ever come again,
To Weiunwood we'll go.

And Arbagon, he'll kill him eight,
While Bockleman gets nine.
And Uncle Bill, oh he'll be late,
But he will do just fine . . .
And as for me . . . I won't be late . . .
And I will do just fine—HEY!

A glad shout and a great burst of laughter rang throughout
the inn with the final *HEY!* at the end of the rustic song. And all
banged their mugs on the tables for more ale; Brewster and his
helper, Bill, rushed hither and thither topping off tankards from
large pitchers that Molly filled at the tap as the rollicking gaiety continued, cheer echoing throughout the rafters.

Amid the babble and happy chatter, Cotton burst out, "What a corking good song! Why, it's all about the Weiunwood and the Winter War and everything!"

"Weiunwood," mused Lord Kian, swirling his ale and taking a sip. "The Wilderland holt that never fell: an island of freedom deep within the clasp of Modru's Winternight—hurling back his assaults or melting away before his force only to strike unexpectedly into a weakness. And Modru's iron grip could not close on those 'puny' forest fighters, for it was like trying to clutch the wind."

"Just so, Lord Kian," responded Perry. "And even though the Stonehill song only narrowly reflects the heroic deeds done in that place, still I must record it for the *Raven Book,* for it has spirit and it is a song I've never heard before. The Scholars will want it."

Perry stood and stepped to the long-table and sat down with the buccan who had started the song.

Later that night, as he and Cotton were climbing into their beds, Perry remarked, "Isn't it strange, Cotton? Though those folks knew and enjoyed the song, they didn't know its origin or the full part that Stonehill played in the War."

"Well, Sir, it took the Boskydells to set 'em right, sure enough, what with you tellin' them the story in the *Raven Book* and all," replied Cotton, recalling with pride how Perry had enthralled the Stonehillers with a tale of Tuck and the Myrkenstone. Perry had explained how the verses in the song related to what had happened. The folks in the 'Unicorn were delighted to discover that the roles that Stonehill and Weiunwood had played in the War were actually recorded in a book. But happiest of all was Aylesworth Brewster, for Perry affirmed that the Bockleman of the song was Aylesworth's ancestor, Bockleman Brewster, owner of the inn during the War. "Mister Perry," continued Cotton, yawning sleepily, "in the song there was a part about the Rūcks and such runnin' away. Do you reckon they all ran to the Deeves?"

"Oh no, Cotton, the Spawn didn't all run straight to Drimmen-deeve, for the War went on long after—though we now know that many finally made their way there. I suppose that most of the maggot-folk perished in the War." He paused a moment; then: "Oh, that reminds me: I overheard Lord Kian talking to one of the Stonehill folk, and when he found out that we were going to Landover Road Ford, he warned Lord Kian that there were 'Yrm' south on the Great Argon River—'heard it from a trader,' he said." Perry's face took on a worried frown. "Things must be bad down there, Cotton, for people way up north here in Stonehill to hear about it. Cotton, do you think we've bitten off more than we can chew? Maybe we're just fooling ourselves by thinking we can become Rūck fighters."

Cotton did not respond to Perry's question; in fact, he had not even heard it, for he was already fast asleep. Perry sighed, blew out the lamp, and crawled under the covers of his bed. But though he was weary, slumber escaped him.

Something had been nibbling at the edge of Perry's thoughts all evening, but he couldn't bring it forth. He lay for a time watching the flickering shadows cast by the dying fire on the hearth, unable to go to sleep immediately.

Finally, after a long while, just as he was drifting away, it came to him, and he bolted upright in bed. *The horn! That's it! I must look at the horn!*

Igniting a taper from the embers in the fireplace, he relighted the lamp and turned it up full. Fetching the silver horn from Cotton's pack, he held it next to the lantern and peered closely at the riders. The clarion was ancient, and the engraving was dearly worn by the many hands that had held it through the ages. But faintly, and only faintly, upon the faces of the riders could be discerned the dim traces of forked beards—a feature throughout all history borne only by Dwarves.

CHAPTER 8

SHOOTING STARS AND TALK OF WAR

"Hammers and nails!" shouted Cotton, waking Perry from his sound sleep in time to hear the sharp rapping on the door. "Don't beat the door down! Come in, come in!" Perry opened his eyes just as the door flew open and Aylesworth Brewster, bearing a lantern, bustled across the room and threw back the drapes. Faint grey light showed that it was foredawn; the Sun had not yet crept over the horizon.

"Wake up, little masters," said Aylesworth as he lit the room lamp, "the day is adawning and the others tell me it's time you were afoot. Your bath awaits you in the bathing room, and breakfast is on Molly's griddle, so don't tarry." And with that he rushed from the room leaving the two Warrows sitting up in their beds rubbing sleep from their eyes.

"*Oooahhum,*" yawned Perry, stretching to his fullest. "Well, Cotton, it certainly isn't like living at The Root, this getting up before the Sun. But I suppose if we must, then we must." He slipped out of bed, and in his nightshirt, made for the door. Reluctantly, Cotton followed him, yawning all the way. They went down the hall to the bathing room, where they found Bill pouring hot water into a pair of large wooden tubs bound 'round with copper hoops. Soon the two Warrows were splashing and wallowing and sloshing in water and suds, occasionally splashing some over the rim and onto the stone floor. They were in a hurry and so did not loll or sing—though they chattered as gaily as ever.

"You were correct, Cotton," Perry said as they were towelling off, "the riders on the Horn of Valon are Dwarves all right, which helps to explain why no one has been able to read the runes. I think they must be written in the secret Dwarf tongue—Châkur. I wonder what they say."

"Well, whatever they say, Sir, we'll not find it out from Anval or Borin, you can bet your last penny on that," said Cotton. "When it comes to that horn, they're as closemouthed a pair as we'll ever see. Why, we'd get more out of a couple of rocks as we're likely to get out of them two."

Quickly the two buccen returned to their chamber and dressed, then snatched up their packs, blew out the lamp, and hurried to the common room. There Anval, Borin, and Lord Kian were waiting. As the Warrows entered the room Aylesworth called, "Oh ho, little sirs, you're just in time for hot sausage and eggs." And with that he began serving them Molly's fare.

Across the room sat the farmer, Aylesworth's other guest. Throughout the meal he stared curiously at the mixed group, wondering what he'd missed the evening before by going to bed at his usual time of sundown. He was later to be told by Bill that "them five knew everything there was to know about Stonehill," and that "everything in all the old songs is true," and finally that "Aylesworth's ancestor, Bockleman Brewster, and nearly everyone else that lived in Stonehill at the time, fought and practically won the Winter War single-handedly." In his later years the farmer would often tell of the time that he and the Drimmen-deeve Rūck-fighters all stayed at the White Unicorn together. But for now he merely sat at breakfast watching the others eat and prepare for the road.

Bill had hitched up Brownie and Downy, and he loaded two full burlap sacks into the waggon—grain to feed the horses on the way to Landover Road Ford. Then he drove the wain 'round front just as Cotton stepped through the door. Cotton rummaged among the waggon supplies and came up with two carrots, one for each horse, which they eagerly accepted, then nuzzled him for more—for ever since leaving The Root the buccan had been giving the horses a carrot or an apple apiece each day; and he spoke gently to them. Cotton scratched each steed between the eyes, then helped load up to be off. By this time the Sun had climbed over the rim of the world and was casting its glancing light across the countryside. Clambering into the waggon, the travellers bade goodbye to Aylesworth and Bill, and to Molly, who popped out just long enough to say farewell before popping back inside.

Mister Brewster stood at the door of the inn wiping his hands on his white apron and watched the clattering wain till it went around the turn and out of sight. "Come on, Bill, there's work to be done," he finally said, and the two of them went back into the White Unicorn.

As the waggon rolled through the gate in the east wall, leaving the cobblestones of Stonehill behind, returning to the hard-packed earth of the Crossland Road, Lord Kian began instructing the Warrows on the forehand, backhand, and over-hand sword strokes—how to deliver them and how to parry them—as he resumed their education in warfare. These lessons were to dominate every waking hour of the journey for the next fortnight or so. Oh, that is not to say that the travellers didn't speak of or do other things, or occasionally break out in song, for they did that and much else too—but only when each lesson was over: not before, not during, but after.

At the fourth or fifth stop of the day—after Perry and Cotton had absorbed in their earlier lessons some of the fundamentals of strokes, thrusts, and parries—Lord Kian again allowed them to do mock battle against him. This time, though he fended without being touched, he had a much more difficult engagement with each, for Warrows learn rapidly; and though they are not fleet, they are incredibly quick, and at times they pressed even Kian's skill to defend against their swift thrusts. Though he could have dispatched either buccan at will, the Man was well satisfied with their rapid progress. Again the Warrows whooped and laughed at the end of their engagement. Each was pleased with his own skill agrowing, and could see that the other was progressing as well. But what delighted them most was that each had not quite but almost touched Lord Kian.

"All right, my little cock-a-whoops," promised the Man above their gay braggadocio, tying his yellow hair back with a green headband, "at the next stop I will press you a bit to begin to sharpen up your defensive skills.

"Now listen, when an opponent comes at you with an over-hand stroke, you can step to the side and let the blow slide away on your own blade by . . ." And in the back of the rolling wag-gon the lessons went on, and on, and on, for the ten or so hours each day that they were on the road; and for about ten minutes in each of these hours, Cotton and Perry drilled, ingraining through practice the art of swords. And though some would say that there were not enough days left for the Warrows to become sufficiently skilled at battle, as in other times and other places the press of War left no choice.

The first evening out of Stonehill the wayfarers camped in the woods north of the Bogland Bottoms; yet the plaguey gnats of these fens were not a problem, for the nights were now too chill.

The next day the five pressed on, and the evening of the sixth day of the journey from Woody Hollow found them en-camped on the western slopes of Beacontor, a weathered mount at the southern end of the chain of the ancient Signal Moun-tains, a range so timeworn by wind and water that it was but a set of lofty hills. Beacontor had been the site of the First Watch-tower, now but a remnant of a bygone era; the ruins still could be seen on the crest of the hill; the jagged ring of tumbled stonework yet stood guard in the Wilderland between Stonehill and Arden. Neither Perry nor Cotton nor anyone else in the party climbed up the tor to see the remains. Instead, the War-rows made the most of their last short practice session, and then they helped pitch camp; by this time it was dark, so they would have seen little of the ruins anyway. As before, during the night they each took a turn at ward.

It was midwatch when Borin wakened Perry for the buc-can's stand at guard. The night was brilliant with stars, the air so crisp and clear that the Bright Veil seemed close enough to grasp, spreading its shimmering band from east to west across the star-studded sky. Perry noted that Borin seemed re-luctant to turn in, preferring instead to gaze in wonder at the countless glints scintillating above in the spangled vault.

"You seem spellbound by the heavens, Borin," remarked Perry.

"It is not often we Châkka come out from under the Mountains and see the stars, friend Perry," replied Borin. "They are special to us: more brilliant than the brightest diamonds we delve, more precious than all we have ever or will ever unearth. They are celestial gems coursing through the night above— changeless, eternal, except for the five known wanderers that slowly shift across the wheeling pattern of the others; but even these nomads, in time, cycle through the same long journeys. Aye, the stars *are* special, for they give us their light to steer by—that one yon is forever fixed in the north—and they tell us the time of season or the depth of the night or the nearness of dawn. Never can we craft anything to rival their beauty or purpose, though we have striven to do so through the ages. We believe that each star has some special meaning—though we know not what it is—and that destiny and omens are sometimes written in the glittering patterns."

Perry was filled with a sense of discovery at hearing Borin speak thus of the stars. The Warrow had seen them all his life, and till this moment he had not considered the impact that the heavenly display would have upon those who lived most of their lives under the mountains. Perry gazed with new eyes at the celestial blaze, entranced as if he had never before seen its glory. And as he watched a streak flashed across the sky, flaring and coruscating, leaving behind a trail of golden fire that slowly faded. "Borin!" he cried, pointing. "Did you see that shooting star?" His voice was full of excitement, thrilled at the display. But Borin had cast his hood over his head and was looking somberly down at the earth. "What's the matter, Borin?" asked Perry, disturbed by this dark change in his companion and wanting to help.

"When a star falls it foretells that a friend, too, will soon fall and die," replied Borin. And without uttering another word the Dwarf went to his bedroll and lay down and did not look at the sky again that night.

The next morning, as the wayfarers broke camp, Perry looked up at the ruins on the crest of Beacontor and remarked, "If ever we come this way again I'd like to see the remains of the old Watchtower; they mark an age of greatness." Anval glanced sharply at Perry and seemed troubled, but said nothing.

That day and the following were much the same as those that had gone before, and the waggon slowly rolled eastward, finally coming to the western edge of the Wilderness Hills.

Dawn of the ninth day of the journey found the skies overcast, and as the five got under way beneath the dismal glower, Lord Kian predicted rain by nightfall.

The instruction went on as always, and Anval and Borin continued to take turns driving the waggon. Though progress with the sword training was rapid, the mood of the travellers was as glum as the brooding skies. Except for Lord Kian's instructions and an occasional question from either Perry or Cotton, little was said, and no songs were sung. Even the landscape seemed unredeeming, consisting of monotonous, relatively barren, uniform hills.

To dispel this gloomy mood and restore their former high spirits, Lord Kian decided to advance one stage of the training. Looking somberly at Perry and Cotton, he announced, "It is time you each fought your first Rukh."

"Wha . . . what? Rŭck?" Perry's heart leapt to his mouth, and he looked quickly all around.

Cotton, also, scrambled to his knees and held on to a waggon sideboard, searching the empty countryside for an enemy. "Hey, now, just a moment here, it's daylight," protested Cotton, plopping back down. "Rŭcks won't be about in the daytime."

Kian broke out in laughter, and the two Dwarves smiled. Perry, realizing that Cotton was right, slumped back into the waggon in relief. "No, no," said Kian, "not real Rukha. What I meant is that at our next stop you shall cross wooden swords with one another. But wear your armor; henceforth you shall train in battle dress."

By the time they rolled to a stop in a sparse roadside glade with a thin stream running along the eastern tree line, both Warrows were armored and wore their empty scabbards—leaving their true swords in the waggon.

At first when they faced one another, neither seemed eager to strike, and they began a timid tap-tapping engagement. Lord

Kian, seeing the reluctance of two friends to confront one another, stopped them momentarily. Using blue clay from the banks of the stream, he daubed their faces, giving each a hollow-eyed, sunken-cheeked appearance, and made their mouths look broader and thinner and their eyebrows long and slanted. He turned each of their helms backwards on their heads and then had them face one another again. "There now," he said in a deep, sepulchral voice, "before you stands a Rukh." All broke out in raucous laughter, in the midst of which Cotton leapt forward with Rūck-like treachery and took a broad overhand cut at Perry; and the battle was on:

Though Cotton was stronger, Perry was more agile, and the duel between the two was an even match. During one engagement Perry maneuvered Cotton into falling backwards over a log; but on the other hand Perry was forced by Cotton into the stream bed and spent that contest splashing around in ankle-deep water trying to fight his way back onto the bank held by Cotton. They shouted battle cries and whooped and laughed, or fought long moments in grim silence. It went like this for the full practice: the buccen hacked and stabbed and parried and slashed all around the glen, each "killing" the other at least a half-dozen times. And when Kian called, "Enough!" Cotton and Perry collapsed together in laughter.

They washed away their blue-clay Rūck faces in the stream and climbed back aboard the waggon, chattering happily with Kian and the Dwarves and laughing over the pratfalls of one another. Even the usually taciturn Anval smiled at their antics, and Borin chuckled, too, as he drove the wain back onto the Crossland Road. Kian's tactic had worked: the somber mood had been broken.

The lessons went on in high spirits as Kian, using examples from the battle to illustrate his points, spoke on many things, such as the importance of holding the high ground and of knowing the obstacles behind as well as the enemy before. Every now and again the buccen broke out in broad laughter at mention of some blunder occasioned in their battle, but Kian drove home the lesson.

That evening the travellers pulled off the road next to a wooded draw. They could feel rain approaching on the wind across the Dellin Downs and over the valley of the Wilder River. The coming storm promised to be a heavy one, for as Cotton remarked, "This is sure to be a real frog strangler; why, the leaves on the trees have been turned right 'round backwards all day." All looked to the south and west and could see a dark wall of rain stalking the land and marching toward their camp-site.

Among the trees, Anval and Borin skillfully used their axes to hastily construct a large, crude lean-to out of saplings as proof against the rain, with two smaller slant-roofs to either side. The Warrows scurried thither and yon to gather a supply of dry firewood and place it under shelter. And Kian unhitched the team, leading the horses beneath the eaves of the wood and tethering them in the protection of the trees. The companions had but barely finished preparing their camp when the first drops began to fall, followed by an onslaught of water cascading from the black skies.

It rained all that night, and though the watch was kept, the guard's main duty was to tend the fire under the large lean-to, for nought could be seen or heard beyond the curtain of hard-driven rain. Kian spent his watch shaping some new wooden swords, for the old ones were badly tattered from the beatings they had received; each of the other guardians simply kept up the fire in his own turn and huddled close to the blaze to ward away the wetness.

Toward morning the rain slackened as the storm moved away to the east, and by dawn it was gone and only the leaves dripped water to the ground. The Sun rose to a freshly washed land, and the day was to be crisp and bright with a high blue October sky.

In spite of the storm-troubled sleep, spirits in the waggon were as bright and cheerful as the day itself, and after each lesson there was much singing and laughter. In the early afternoon the travellers emerged from the low foothills and saw the road falling before them, down and across a short flat to the River Caire, the waterway curving out of the north and disappearing to the south and sparkling in the midday Sun. Perry, filled with the clarity of the day, burst out in song:

The Road winds on before us—
A Path to be unwound,
A surprise around each Corner
Just waiting to be found.

> *And we, the happy travellers*
> *Who trek upon this way,*
> *Look forward in our eagerness*
> *And glance aback to say:*

The Road turns there behind us—
A path that we've unwound.
Yet sights around the Corners
Remain there to be found

> *By those who come behind us*
> *And see what we have seen;*
> *The wonders will be as fresh*
> *As if we'd never been*

Along this way before them
And gazing on this Land
With beauty spread before us all . . .
I say, oh isn't it Grand!

I say, oh isn't it Grand!

Both Perry and Cotton—who had joined in the singing—burst out in laughter. The hearts of the Man and the Dwarves were uplifted by the simple song the Warrows sang in celebration of the passing countryside. In the words of the song Lord Kian beheld two more facets of the nature of Waerlinga: *Not only do they take pleasure in seeing things of beauty, but they also take pleasure in knowing that others will share these things, too. And this gift of sharing is just one of the things that makes these small Folk special.* The Man was so moved by this knowledge that in the back of the rolling waggon he gruffly hugged Cotton to him with one arm while smiling and tousling Perry's fair hair with his free hand. Yet neither Warrow knew why.

"Ah, my wee Waerlinga," said Kian, "I think that every Kingdom, every court in every Land, needs a few of you little

ones to keep up the good spirits and the cheer of the people—
oh, not as court jesters, for I deem you too tenderhearted to fulfill that task. Instead, as a small, rustic Folk, close to the earth,
of indomitable will and gentle good sense, you would set an example for all to see and hear of living life in the spirit in which
it should be lived. You are an openhearted, cheerful, gentle,
sturdy Folk, and this old world is leagues ahead of where it
would be without you."

Somewhat embarrassed by the praise, both Cotton and Perry
said nought; yet each was pleased by the young Lord's words.

The waggon trundled across the Stone-arches Bridge over
the river and came into Rhone, the share-shaped region of land
known as the Plow, bounded on one side by the River Caire and
on the other by the River Tumble, and extending north to the
Rigga Mountains.

The road rose up again out of the river valley and wound
into the middle regions of a dark-forested hill country known as
Drearwood, in days of old a place of dire repute: Many were the
tales of lone travellers or small bands who had ridden into the
dim woods never to be seen again. From here, too, came accounts of larger, armored groups that had beaten off grim monsters half glimpsed in the night. And the Land had been
shunned by all except those who had no choice but to cross it—
or by those who sought fame. Yet no fell creatures had lived in
the area for almost three hundred years, since the time of the
Great Purging by the Lian Guardians and Men of the Wilderland. And the Crossland Road wound among the central regions
of this hill country for eighty or so miles.

At sundown the waggon had just come into the beginning
western edges of the slopes, and the travellers made camp.

That night was crystal clear, and a gibbous Moon, growing
toward fullness, shed bright light over the landscape. When not
on watch, each of the wayfarers slept extraordinarily well,
partly because their sleep during the rain of the previous night
had not been restful, but mainly because this day had gone so
well.

The order of the watch remained the same, and at the end of
Perry's duty he awakened Anval, this time with a cup of tea
ready for the Dwarf. The two sat together in silence for a while,

listening to the call of a far-off owl. Perry noted that Anval seemed more than just taciturn; the Dwarf appeared instead to be brooding. "Does something bother you, Anval?" asked Perry, sipping his own tea and huddling in his cloak.

"Aye, Small One, and it is this: although your feet are set upon one course, your thoughts trace another path; and if you do not change, you will come to great harm," growled the Dwarf. He looked with his eyes of black at the buccan, whose mouth had dropped open in astonishment at Anval's reply. But before Perry could say aught, Anval went on, "You dwell too much in past glories and not enough in the reality of today, Waeran. Heed me: we are marching off to War—not to heroism and grandeur, but to slaying and horror—and I fear what the truth of War will do to you. War is not some Noble Game. Only in time does the vile stench of War become the sweet smell of victory. Whether in ballade or ode or book, History alone looks upon War as a grand achievement; all else look upon it as a dreadful last resort. And you, Perry, seem to see the world through events and eras of the past: past Kingdoms, past glories, past deeds, past trials, past victories. But time dims the horrors of those events and magnifies the good. We Châkka have a saying:

> "The Past, the Present, the Future,
> Time's Road winds through all three.
> Live for Today, but think of Tomorrow;
> Yesterday is just Memory."

Anval's black, forked beard shone darkly in the firelight. "You must forgo the past, Perry, and live for today, and tomorrow."

"But Anval," protested Perry, disturbed by the acuity of the Dwarf's insight, "we Warrows, too, have a saying:

> "Yesterday's Seeds are Tomorrow's Trees.

"The past points toward the future. By looking into history we can at times foretell events to come. Our quest could have been foretold: Dwarves were driven from Drimmendeeve long ago and now seek to return, but Spawn were driven *into* Drimmen-deeve back when Gron fell, and War will result. So you see, Anval, yesterday's seeds *are* tomorrow's trees."

"Only if tended today do seeds grow into trees," gritted Anval. "Yesterday's deeds are but shadows of the past and are dead and gone, and tomorrow's are but visions of the future and are yet to come. The deeds of today are the images of import. Shun not the present and forfeit not the future in order to live on past glories, for that is the way of the Historian who dreams of glory and sees not horror. Your spirit will be crushed and you may even be slain if you follow the Historian's storybook way into the reality of War."

"But Anval," said Perry quietly, "I *am* a Historian."

"Oh no, little one, now you are a *warrior*." Anval turned and stared into the night, and in a low voice with driving urgency he declared, "You *must* become a warrior!" The Dwarf then strode to the perimeter and began his watch and said no more.

Perry lay down to sleep, but could not. He was disturbed by Anval's perception, and half denied, half accepted it, but thought, *How can Anval say such things? He tells me that I must forgo the past, as if he and Borin and all of Dwarfdom live that way. Yet, the mere mention of Elgo, Sleeth's Doom, drove both Anval and Borin into a frothing rage, even though Elgo won the Dragon's plunder nearly twenty-six hundred years ago. Forget the past? Hmmph! Do Dwarves? I should say not! I clearly recall Borin saying, "He who seeks the wrath of Dwarves, finds it! Forever!" That's certainly not forgoing the past.*

I think these Folk are full of contradiction: On the one hand they are suspicious; secretive; stiff-necked; proud, bellicose warriors, fierce in battle; and always ready, nay eager, to avenge old wrongs. But on the other hand they are crafters of great skill; steadfast, honorable companions; trusting enough to permit a virtual stranger to guide them in an undertaking of mortal peril; and they seem genuinely concerned over the welfare of newfound comrades. They are enthralled by the beauty of the stars, yet are afraid of their blazing omens. And, to cap it all, they appear to sincerely believe in sayings that fly directly in the face of the darker side of their own manifest na-

ture . . . *ah, but, in these things, are they different from any other Folk?*

Yet, what Anval says is *true: I* must *become a warrior!*

And as Perry lay weighing Anval's words and pondering the nature of Dwarves, he watched the bright Moon sinking behind a dark, western hill; and when the silver orb was gone, the buccan was fast asleep.

CHAPTER 9

ARDEN FORD

The early morning of the thirteenth day of their journey found the travellers back in the waggon on the east-west Crossland Road, still wending their way toward the eastern margins of the Drearwood. Earlier, they had awakened to find the glades and hills covered with bright frost and the morning air cold and crisp; and they had huddled around the fire, warming themselves with flames and tea until the Sun's rays had spilled over the hillsides and down among the trees. Then they had broken camp and resumed the trek. And as they had ridden east, the frost faded under the Sun's warmth.

The slopes rising around them for the most part provided the only view: thick-coppiced hillsides mounting up, covered with green and bronze and scarlet and yellow-gold foliage. But now and again the waggon would overtop a crest, and to the east, down on the horizon, like a jagged bank of white-tipped low-lying dark clouds, the wayfarers could see the Grimwall. Their destination, the Landover Road Ford, lay on the other side of that somber range. Though the mountains were some distance away, the comrades expected to reach the lower margins by nightfall; they anticipated crossing the River Tumble at Arden Ford by midmorning, and passing Arden by midafternoon, leaving several hours to come among the foothills by sundown. They were aiming to cross the range through the Crestan Pass, the only direct route to Landover Road Ford. Assuming no delays, Kian reckoned that they should reach the banks of the

Argon River in just six more days. There they planned to make camp and wait for Durek and the Army, due to arrive about ten days hence.

But for now, the land began falling steadily as the wain drew closer to the valley of the Tumble River. The sword training continued, and just after the fourth stop in the morning, the travellers followed the road through a dark pine forest and then into a grey-rock-walled pass cutting a lengthy slot through the saddle joining two hills.

The horses' hooves and waggon wheels echoed hollowly as they pulled through the long notch, but the echoes diminished and finally died as they emerged from the sheer-walled cleft. "Lor! Look at that!" cried Cotton, pointing ahead.

Before them the wayfarers saw the land fall steeply to a mile-wide flat running to the river where the shallow Arden Ford should have been, but was not. The valley was flooded! The river was raging: roiling water raced and plunged along the course, overspreading the banks and running far up onto the flatland. Both Anval and Borin vented bitter oaths.

"What has happened, Lord Kian?" asked Perry, looking upon the torrent. "The river looks as if it has gone quite mad, and the ford cannot be crossed."

"I do not know for certain," answered Kian, shading his eyes and gazing east and then pointing. Directly ahead in the near distance they could see the Grimwall Mountains; the jagged range marched out of the north and away to the south, a colossal barrier to cross should they ever breast the flood. "Mayhap the storm of four nights past was trapped upon the teeth of the mountains, and all its rain plunged onto the slopes and into the vales that issue into this valley, flooding it."

Cotton thought about the intensity and duration of the storm and tried to envision the enormous amount of water released on the walls of the mountains to flow down the watercourses to come to this place. He looked once more at the raging river below. "We couldn't even cross that in a boat, could we? Or a raft? No, I didn't think so. Well, Old Man Tumble has got us trapped here, right enough."

"And the problem is that there's not another way around, nor a bridge to cross, nor a ferry within hundreds of miles," said Kian, answering Borin's unspoken question. "We must cross here. Our only recourse is to wait for the waters to subside. Till then, we are blocked.

"Even so, in one way we are fortunate, for it was rain that fell everywhere and not snow, even in the high mountains; and though the ford is flooded, the Crestan Pass still seems to be open—not choked off by white. And this flood before us will eventually ebb. . . . When? I cannot say; yet ebb it will."

They camped high on the slope near the outlet of the rock-walled pass. Anval cut some stakes with his axe and walked the mile down to the edge of the rushing flood and there drove one of the wooden shafts into the earth as a marker. He then marched straight away from the water and every five paces planted another stake until there were five altogether. Cotton, who had gone with Anval, hefted a small round stone and eyed the far shore, then threw with all his might; with a splash, the stone fell short of the far bank by ten yards. He tried again with virtually identical results. Shaking his head in resignation, he trudged after Anval toward the camp.

"We will track the march of the water by using the stakes as a gauge," declared Anval to Cotton as they tramped back. "The place where I drove the markers had not yet been under flood. I deem the water is still rising." They looked back and could see that even now the first stake was being encroached upon. With a sigh from the buccan and an oath from the Dwarf, they turned and continued on toward the encampment.

Even a deluge, however, did not affect the sword instruction except to dampen somewhat the spirited play. And between lessons the five eyed the water's advance, trying to judge whether or not the river was beginning to crest. By sundown the Warrows had reached the stage where they were learning about shields and bucklers: their use, their strengths, and their weaknesses. And the water was still rising, having reached the third stake. Grumbling, Anval marched down in the twilight and drove five more markers.

That night, at each change of the watch, the guard being relieved went in the moonlight with a flaming brand to check the flood, passing the information on to the one remaining on ward. At the beginning of Perry's turn, Borin strode down to the river and looked, and the water had reached the fifth stake; at the end of Perry's watch, the buccan awakened Anval and then went to note the stage of the overflow, and it was still at the fifth marker. Perry returned to camp and reported to Anval and then fell asleep, dejected by this barrier.

It seemed that Perry had no sooner closed his eyes than he was jolted awake by Cotton whooping and laughing in the dawn: "It's goin' down! It's goin' down! It's between the fifth and fourth! Old Man Tumble is creeping back to his bed!"

Perry jumped up and ran with the others to the water's edge and saw that sometime in the night the crest had passed, and the river, though still raging and boiling, was at last receding.

All that day they watched the water's slow retreat back toward its original course. The sword training progressed at a faster pace than usual because questions or points could be illustrated instantly in false combat or in the practice drills without having to wait for a waggon-stop. This day Lord Kian showed the quick Warrows how to use a dagger in the left hand to ward an opponent's sword.

The next day an extraordinary thing occurred: Cotton "killed" Lord Kian. In mock battle the buccan actually got through Kian's defenses with a quick thrust that struck Kian above the heart. Kian was as surprised as everyone else, for he had thought that Perry, with his greater agility, would be the first to "slay" a "Lôkh." But it was Cotton who scored the first "kill." Perry looked on and was at the same time elated and frightened, for until now it had been an exciting game, but with this "kill" it suddenly became a deadly serious business. Anval tugged at his black beard and shook his head in regret, for he knew that these gentle Folk were not meant to be warriors, though necessity forced them so.

The following day the river continued to recede as the Warrows learned to combat opponents who wielded hammers, cudgels, maces, and axes. Here Anval and Borin shaped appropriate weapons out of wood and took over the teaching chores, with Borin saying, "Úkhs know not the way of these weapons, especially the axe, for they ply them as if they were hewing logs. But *this* is the true way—the Châkka way—of an axe." And, demonstrating, with two-handed grips the Dwarves grasped the oaken helves of their own runemarked axes, one hand high near the blade, the other near the haft butt. And they used the helves to parry imaginary sword blows, and stabbed forward with the cruel axe beaks, or shifted their grips to strike with power; and their axes danced and flashed in the sunlight and seemed to have a life of their own. And as for hammers, cudgels, and maces, the Dwarven way of their wielding was much the same.

The Warrows quickly learned that swords must be used differently against these massive weapons, and that agility becomes vital in waging against them, for a light sword would not halt and would but barely deflect the crushing blows. The strategy seemed to be "Get out of the way and let the ponderous Grg-swing carry past, and before the Squam can recover, use your sword." In theory it was an excellent strategy, but not against Anval and Borin—and Dwarves in general—for with their massive shoulders they had extraordinary strength; and Dwarf power when coupled with Dwarf quickness allowed them to recover almost as if they were wielding a light wand instead of an axe, hammer, mace, or cudgel. And the Dwarf way of axe battle—helve, beak, and blade—was devastating. So Perry and Cotton received by far the worst drubbings in all of their training, as there by the swollen river they engaged Anval and Borin in mock combat. Yet, toward the end of the day the buccen had improved dramatically.

That evening, beneath a Hunter's Moon, Lord Kian announced to Warrow cheers that they would attempt a crossing on the morrow, for the river was back in its banks, though still raging. "And though it will be risky," Kian added, "we must cross over soon, for Durek and his Army should be at Landover Road Ford within five or six days, and we must be there to meet them."

The seventeenth day of the journey dawned to clear skies. The travellers went together to the banks of the Arden Ford and looked upon the rushing water. It was still high and boiling, tumbling along in wild protest—a torrent. Cotton easily could throw a rock across, but it still was a good distance to have to ford, especially in these conditions. "I must set a safety line," declared Lord Kian as he shed his cloak and stripped to the waist. He tied a soft rope around his middle with the other end anchored to a tree. While Anval and Borin payed out the line, Lord Kian entered the chill rush and began wading across; and as he went he clung to great rocks thrusting up here and there through the plunging river. Kian had reached the halfway point and the water was up to his waist when he was upset by the driving current, losing his grip on one of the boulders, and was swept downstream to the end of the line, which then swung him back to the starting shore.

On the second attempt he was three quarters of the way across and nearly chest deep when again he was swept downstream, but this time his rope caught on a large up-jutting rock and he recovered near midstream.

"Third time pays for all," muttered Cotton as the Man struggled on through the race once more. This time Kian was almost to the other side when he fell, but he managed to catch hold of a low-set branch reaching out over the rapid flow, and he pulled himself to the far bank. The Warrows shouted cries of joyous relief, for they had feared for the young Lord's safety.

Kian tied his end of the rope to a tree on the far side so that the line hung low across the race, spanning from one bank to the other. Then, using the rope for a brace, he waded back to the near shore. "The water is cold and becomes deep near the far bank where the curve of the river has cut it so. It is nearly too deep for the horses pulling the waggon, for if they stumble the coursing rush may roll the wain. Yet the Waerlinga must ride." Kian turned to Perry and Cotton. "I fear your strength is not enough to cross by rope; you cannot touch the bottom for the greater part of the way, and if you tried the safety line you would have to hang on in the torrent and pull hand over hand to the other side. I would cross over by the rope twice, each time with one of you on my back, but I have fallen thrice ere now, and I think you'd each be swept away from me were I to fall again in such an attempt. I deem the waggon and surefooted horses to be a safer way to pass over. Anval and Borin, you may use the rope if you wish—I fear not for your strength in that endeavor—but for the Waerlinga I choose the waggon."

The Dwarves indicated that they, too, would trust to the horses, and the travellers returned to the fire; and as the others broke camp and hitched up Brownie and Downy, Kian warmed himself by the campblaze but did not change into dry clothes. "We may fall in while crossing," he said as he instructed them all in what to do. "We shall drive the waggon to breast the flow upstream from the rope. If you then fall overboard you will be swept to the line; merely keep your head above water and catch the rope when you come to it. If you can't pull to shore, just hang on till I get there; I'll help you. Any questions?" They all shook their heads *no* and prepared for the fording. Neither Perry nor Cotton felt it necessary to mention to Lord Kian that they could not swim a stroke—nor did the like thought occur to the Dwarves, either.

With Anval at the reins, Brownie and Downy pulled the waggon slowly into the stream while Perry and Cotton nervously peered over the sideboards at the flow. Borin and Kian sat in the far back in hopes that their weight over the rear axle would help anchor the waggon against the current. The horses seemed eager to test their strength after their nearly four-day rest, and they pulled steadily into the cold surge. The bottom was rocky, and the waggon jolted out to midstream, where the rushing water came just up to the waggon axles.

Slowly they pulled into deeper water, toward the far shore, the horses beginning to strain against the turbulent flow, and the waggon began to drift sideways, bumping and lurching on the rocky bottom. Perry started to say something when again the wain lurched sideways and passed over a deep hole and began to float, swiftly swinging in the current. With a sudden jolt the downstream rear wheel slapped laterally into a large underwater boulder, instantly halting the wain's sideways rush but pitching the waggon bed up with a lurch. And Perry was catapulted out into the boiling race. *"Mister Perry!"* cried Cotton, making a frantic grab and just missing. *"Mister Perry!"* he shouted again, and leapt in after his master.

Perry was swept away, churning and tumbling through the water with Cotton helplessly rolling and turning behind him. The icy force of the wild water was overwhelming, and neither Warrow knew up from down, being entirely at the mercy of the torrent. The mad current rolled each of them, cascading the buccen toward the safety rope. At times the raging river plunged first one then the other to the bottom; at other times it heaved them to the surface; but always it crushed their feeble efforts to breathe and to stay afloat, overturning them and smashing them under again. Perry saw the rope rushing at him and reached up, but the churning water forced him under, and he could not grasp the lifeline and was swept beyond it and away. Cotton never saw the safety line, but just as he, too, was about to pass beyond it he felt his wrist being gripped by a strong hand, and he was lifted up sputtering, and there was the rope. But he had breathed water and was coughing and had not the strength to hold on; and Kian, his rescuer, held the gasping, choking Warrow while allowing the current to press them both against the line.

Desperately, Lord Kian's sight swept downstream for some glimpse of Perry but saw no sign of the buccan among the roiling crests. Then Kian looked and there was Borin on the far shore running. Anval had managed to drive the waggon on across, and as soon as it had touched the bank Borin had leapt out and gone dashing downstream, with Anval following at a dead run, both Dwarves racing after Perry.

By this time Cotton had recovered enough to hold on to Lord Kian and ride pickaback, and the young Man used the rope and carried the Warrow toward safety. Far downstream they could see Anval and Borin splashing up to their waists in the water at a sharp bend in the river, struggling against the sweep to carry a limp burden to shore: it was Perry.

Kian scrambled up the far bank and Cotton swung down, and they sprinted to the curve, the long-legged Man far outstripping the flood-spent Warrow. When at last Cotton arrived he found the two Dwarves, their hoods cast over their bowed heads, standing above Perry's inert form, and Lord Kian on his knees beside him. "He is dead," stated Borin in a halting voice. "Drowned. The river swallowed him and killed him and swept him to shore. The star that fell was his."

Cotton burst into tears, but Lord Kian looked at Perry's pale white face and still form. "It is said among Realmsmen that the breath of the living can at times restore the breath of the drowned." And he sealed Perry's mouth with his own and breathed his breath into the Warrow. Twelve times he did this, while the Dwarves looked on in hooded silence and Cotton through his tears watched in quiet desperation. Twelve times Kian breathed into the buccan, and in between breaths he allowed Perry's chest to fall and the air to leave. Twelve times the Realmsman breathed, and the long moments seemed to stretch into forever, and Perry did not respond. But on the thirteenth breath Perry's chest suddenly heaved, and he began coughing and retching and gasping, and seemed on the verge of strangling—but at last he was breathing on his own.

"He lives!" cried Borin joyously, throwing back his hood, "He lives!" and he began leaping about and laughing and shouting in a strange tongue. Anval, too, threw back his own hood and could not contain his elation and grabbed Cotton up in a crushing embrace and swung him around and around till both were dizzy and fell to the ground.

Perry stopped retching and coughing in the midst of this gaiety and looked up at the capering Dwarves and the captive Cotton and at Lord Kian, who was on his knees and weeping into his hands, and said, "Well, hullo. What's all this fuss about?" And Lord Kian fell over on his side and began to roar with helpless laughter.

CHAPTER 10

THE CRESTAN PASS

As soon as Perry could manage it, the comrades made their way back to the waggon, stopping along the route while Lord Kian retrieved the rope, once more breasting the icy stream over and back to do so. Then they drove up out of the flood plain to the high ground where the wood was dry. There they stopped and built a large fire to warm themselves and change clothes, for they all had plunged into the icy tumult, and the October chill caused them to shiver uncontrollably and their teeth to chatter. They donned fresh garments drawn from the dry interiors of their packs, and they took time to make some hot tea and have a midmorning meal while warming by the fire.

"Let me tell you, Mister Perry," said Cotton, gingerly probing his own ribs and grimacing as he recounted his part in the venture, "the next time *I'll* be the one who recovers and *you* be the one that Anval grabs and squeezes and swings around. Why, Sir, he nearly mashed me silly!" They all laughed as Cotton looked askew at the Dwarf, with Anval roaring loudest of all.

"Well, friend Cotton, your skill had better improve ere you go splashing off on another rescue," growled Borin through his damp black beard, hefting a large rock, "for at the moment this stone floats better than you."

Again and again they burst out in laughter as each described his view of some aspect of the adventure, for the crossing had been perilous and they had but barely escaped; and as is the wont of close companions who walk on the edge of disaster and survive intact with all unharmed, their relief oft surfaces in rough jest, as if the retelling of the jeopardy in humorous account somehow lessens the past danger and reduces the future vulnerability of those involved.

Soon the five were warm and dry and had finished eating, and they could have comfortably camped for the rest of the day. But all felt an urgency to press on, for they had lost four days while waiting to cross, and the time of the rendezvous with Durek was nearly upon them. So they set out again—the waggon sideboards covered with river-drenched clothes wrung out and draped for drying—following the Crossland Road toward Arden Vale and to the Crestan Pass over the Grimwall Mountains.

It was early afternoon when they sighted the deep-cloven, concealed valley of Arden, site of the Hidden Stand, a secret Elven refuge in the north of the Land called Rell. It was here among the forested crags that many had paused during the Winter War, to rest and recover and gather strength to use against Modru. And it was said that though the Dimmendark had lain over this Land, it could not grasp the Elven Realm.

Through this narrow vale, seated between high sheer stone walls split out of the earth, ran the Tumble River, issuing out of the valley to turn west then south again. Supplied by the rains and the snows high upon the peaks of the Grimwall Mountains, this waterway fed the rich soil of Arden Gorge, and thick pine forests carpeted the valley floor. As the swift-running river emerged from the last walls of the cleft, it fell down a precipice in a wide cataract, and swirling vapors rose up and obscured the view into the canyon. It was the haze from this cascade that perpetually hid the valley from sight.

"I think I can dimly see what must be the Lone Eld Tree," said Perry, trying to pierce the mist with his gaze, "but I cannot tell if the leaves are dusky: the haze hides it. The *Raven Book* says that Eld Trees *gather* the twilight and *hold* it if Elves dwell nearby. And though it is said that the great Elven leader Talarin—Lian Guardian in Arden, Warder of the Northern Regions of Rell—no longer abides there, I thought that others did, and so I would hope to see the Eld Tree leaves be dusky." Perry turned to Lord Kian. "*Is* Arden deserted? *Are* the Elves gone?

It would become a sad day indeed to find that the Elves are gone from Mithgar."

Kian answered, looking toward the hidden dale beyond the roiling mist of the engorged waterfall: "Elves do yet walk in Mithgar, though their numbers dwindle as more ride the Twilight Path. Some Elves—the Dylvana—still dwell in the Great Greenhall, Darda Erynian, or Blackwood as it was known of old. Dwarves from the Mineholt, Men of Dael, and the Baeron converse with them now and again: trading, bartering, or simply passing the time of day.

"As to the other Elves—the Lian—I think none live any longer in Darda Galion, the Larkenwald to the south above Valon and east of Drimmen-deeve, though travellers on the River Argon say they see movement therein at times.

"But as to Arden being deserted: that I do not know. It is said that after the Winter War, Talarin and Rael went south to dwell in the Eldwood yet a while; but at last they rode the Twilight Ride to Adonar in the company of the Coron of Darda Galion; it is also said that sons and daughters and others of the Elden stayed behind. But whether they and the Lian that lived here in Arden still do, I cannot say. It seems certain that their numbers have waned—though how many remain, if any, is unknown to me."

The waggon did not enter the gap into Arden, much to Cotton's disappointment, for he wanted to meet an Elf, having heard much of these tall, fair Folk. But instead the wain rolled on up the slope of the rising land, heading into the foothills along the road to the Crestan Pass through the Grimwall.

The travellers stopped late in the evening in a russet-leaved thicket in the hills on the low shoulders of the high mountains ahead. They pitched camp, and soon all but the watch retired, for the crossing of the swollen ford had been arduous, and they were weary.

That night Perry dreamed that he was again in the river. The rushing water was tumbling him about, and he could not shout for help, for if he opened his mouth to do so the torrent would gush in and drown him. Again he passed under the safety line, and he could not reach it and he could not breathe, for the crashing river was rolling him along the bottom, smashing him into the large rocks there. He was swept into a curve where the water was less overpowering though still turbulent, but he did not know how to swim and could not get to the surface, for a great tree root had grabbed him by the shoulder and was holding him under while the river shook him and shook him. He could not breathe, but he had to, and though he held out as long as he could, finally he gasped in a great lungful of . . . air, for he awakened at that instant to find Borin kneeling above him and shaking him by the shoulder. "You were moaning, friend Perry," said the Dwarf, "and I thought it best to awaken you. Your watch is upon us at any rate, and a stand at guard should dispel evil dreams."

"Hullo, Borin. I thought you were a tree root. Thanks for getting me out of that bad dream. Once a day is more than enough to have to fight a river, much less having to do it all over again in your sleep." Perry stood, throwing his cloak over his shoulders. "That's twice today you've gotten me out of that same river, and I thank you again for it—but I do hope it's the last time we ever have to do that."

The next day was a long hard period of uphill hauling for the horses, for they had finally come upon the full mountain slopes. All day the travellers wended upward, stopping frequently to rest Brownie and Downy, and late afternoon found them in the high country, nearing the timberline. Ahead they could see tier upon tier of barren stone rising out of the earth and marching up to the sky. The snow-covered peaks were massive, towering high above, and Perry felt diminished to the size of a tiny ant slowly crawling across their looming flanks. The setting Sun threw its dying rays into the crags and onto the massifs; and as the shadows mounted, the gaunt rock took on an aspect of blood—even the high snow shone with red: it was as if the great jagged peaks were reaching up and their sharpness was wounding the sky above. *Oh! What a dreadful omen,* thought Perry, and he cast his eyes downward and did not look up at the ruddy crags again.

In the dusk, the waggon stopped in a thick pine forest—the last of the timberline—and the comrades made camp on this eighteenth day of their long journey from Woody Hollow. "Tomorrow," explained Kian as they sat around the fire, "we cross through the Crestan Pass and come down the east side, to take the Landover Road toward the ford on the Argon. We should be there three evenings hence, mayhap but one day ahead of Durek."

The next morning came, and the companions were awakened by Cotton to find it still dark; they were enwrapped in a dense, cold mist and could not see more than a few feet. "I don't know whether it's a fog that's climbed up from the bottom or a cloud that's slid down from the top," said Cotton, "but it's thick enough to cut doors and windows into, and maybe if we carved on it a bit we would let in some light. It's still dark, though I know it's time to be up and gone."

"It's dark because the Sun is rising on the other side of the mountain and we are standing in its shadow," said Lord Kian. "And this myrk makes it doubly dark. Let us hope it gets no thicker—the way is hard enough as it is without adding fog. There are many places ahead to go wrong—blind canyons, false trails, sudden precipices, blank walls, and such—and a cloaking mist we do not need. The way is before us, but I think I will not, cannot, find it till this shroud is gone."

"You forget, Lord Kian, you are with Châkka," spoke Borin Ironfist in rough pride, running his fingers through his black locks, unevenly combing out the sleep tangles, "and we trod this path on foot before—though backwards—on our way to fetch Perry. The fog is no obstacle. Were it pitch black, still could we go on, back the way we first came over this Mountain. Anval or I will lead this day til the way clears—by your leave."

"Your pardon, friend Borin"—Kian smiled—"I did indeed forget the Dwarf talent. It is new to me and wondrous. Lead on, my fellow wayfinder; here it is I who shall follow."

The road grew steep and narrow, with a sheer drop on one side and a towering wall on the other. The Warrows discovered that they and all of the party—except Anval, who drove the wain and worked the brakes—had to walk ahead of the waggon, leading the horses, for the way at times was so narrow that it was safer outside the waggon than in; further, by walking up the incline, thus lessening the load, they spared the steeds.

Slowly they made their way upward, stopping often to rest.

Yet they moved surely through the fog, Borin leading, striding purposefully forward with his walking stave clicking against the stone path, confidently guiding the fellowship past hazards and false paths and up toward the notch of the Crestan Pass. The Warrows did not realize how sheer and far the drop-off beside the road fell until the midmorning Sun began to burn away the cold mist; shortly they could see, and soon the buccen were walking next to the wall as far away from the precipice as they could manage. And though the Sun had finally pierced the icy fog, the day had gotten colder, for now the comrades were up high on the mountain in the thin air; and they all donned extra wear.

It was in the midmorn that they stopped in a wide spot, and Kian instructed all the companions to take their backpacks and bedrolls from the waggon and strap them on. "We are coming to a dangerous part," explained the young Man, looking with keen grey eyes at the slopes above, "where the smallest sound of the wrong sort can start a rock slide or a snow avalanche. If that happens, the waggon may be swept away with all in it. If we survive, with our packs we can proceed onward to the Landover Road Ford with few problems; without them, the trip would be much harder; bear your burden with that thought in mind—though it won't make the knapsack lighter, it will ease the load." He turned to the Warrows. "From here you are to make as little sound as possible. Speak if you must only in a whisper. When we reach the other side and start down, most of the danger will be past. Till then, silence is the rule. Have you any questions? Speak now, it's your final chance."

"Do you mean to tell me that sounds can cause snow or rocks to fall?" asked Cotton, peering at the solid stone walls of the mountainside with some skepticism. "Begging your pardon, but that seems like *Word from the Beyond,* if you want my opinion." Cotton, like most Boskydell Warrows, had always looked at news from outside the Seven Dells as being peculiar and suspect; thus, the saying *Word from the Beyond* indicated something which may or may not be true—something hard to accept until proven.

"Aye, Waeran," answered Anval before others could speak. "But the rock or snow does not fall for just any sound. It must be the right sound. Did you ever see and hear a wineglass sing when someone nearby struck a note on a lute, or horn, or violin, or other musical instrument? Aye, I see you have. You can feel the glass ring in response to the note. Yet other notes do not seem to affect it. It must be the right sound, the right pitch, or nothing happens: the wineglass sits there without answering. And it is not only wineglasses that jing: some sounds cause windows to rattle, others make picture frames tilt, or dishes to clatter, pots and pans to clang, and hundreds of other things to tap and drum and jump around. We Châkka believe that each thing in this world will shake or rattle or fall or even shatter apart if just the right note is sounded on the right instrument. And here in the Mountains, where the snow hangs on high and the rocks poise on the slopes, at times, when the conditions are right, certain sounds seem to cause the stone or ice or snow to shiver just as does the wineglass, and the burden can break loose to cause ruin. It must be the right sound, though: a whipcrack or shrill voice or whistle or toot—any one may or may not start the avalanche. It may be something else, like a cough or whinny. The trouble is, we do not know what will start the fall, so we must be silent in all things."

Perry and Cotton listened with growing amazement, not only at what was being said but also at who was saying it; for since leaving the 'Thorn-ringed Boskydells, but for a few rare occasions, Anval had been given to speaking only in short, terse sentences. And the Warrows had begun to think that Dwarves were about as loquacious as lumps of iron; and for either Anval or Borin to talk prolongedly had come to be a strange and rare event. The buccen could only believe that Anval thought it was important enough to speak at length so that they would understand the danger. And understand it they now did; the Mastercrafter's discourse had clearly shown them the need for silence, for they had indeed seen wineglasses sing and windows rattle at the sound of a viol or the boom of a drum. Again Cotton eyed the slopes above, this time with respect. "Mum's the word," he whispered and then made a buttoning motion on his lip, and Perry smiled and nodded without speaking.

Shouldering their packs, Lord Kian, the Warrows, and Borin went on ahead while Anval stayed back and drove the horses well to the rear. His place in line was by far the most dangerous, for the horses could not be instructed that "mum's the word."

Slowly they made their way toward the Crestan Pass, a notch through a saddle between two peaks of the Grimwall Mountains. They could see the cleft far above them silhouetted by the high morning Sun, whose light streamed through the col to glance off the rises overhead. The slopes were snow-covered, but here and there barren patches revealed a jumble of boulders, slabs, and jagged rocks balanced on the steep mountainsides. Quietly and cautiously they trudged toward the pass, making little or no sound. However, they could hear the horses' hooves calmly clip-clopping behind them and the waggon wheels grinding iron rims on flat stone. Cotton kept glancing up at the menace looking above them, thinking, *Please don't fall. Please don't fall on us or the waggon. I won't cough or sneeze, and you won't fall.*

Finally, when the Sun was standing at zenith, they at last reached the brow of the pass, and the rule of silence was over. They ate a meal and rested for a while; the path had been steep and the climb arduous in the thin air—and the pause was most welcomed. Shortly, though, they had to start down; they had to reach the lower slopes before nightfall, for they could not stay up in the peaks after duskingtide: at this time of year the dark at these heights was too cruel and bitter; the hard passage had to be made during the Sun of a single day.

They began their descent down the eastern flanks, continuing to wear their packs and lead the team and light waggon. They had gone but a mile or so when the horses began to shy and skit and pull back, and seemed reluctant to go farther. Kian stopped the party and carefully scanned the upward slopes. "I can see nothing awry," he said, "but steeds are oft wiser than Men. We shall go forth, but in caution."

Once more they started along the steep, narrow way, walking downward, again on a path caught between stone wall and sheer precipice. To the north and south they could see but little, for the flanks of the mountains on either side of the route blocked the far view; but straight ahead to the east below they could see the Landover Road wending through the foothills and out over a stretch of plains to come at last to the Great Argon River, and run on beyond into the vast Greenhall Forest—

Darda Erynian—now bedecked in bright fall foliage, whose far extent faded away beyond the silver haze in the remote distance.

They had gone another mile and were beginning to think that the skittish animals had perceived some false danger when both Brownie and Downy reared up, whinnying wildly, with nostrils flaring and blowing and eyes rolling till the whites showed in terror; they would have bolted but for Anval's strong arm. Lord Kian quickly stepped back and caught the bit reins to stop the horses from plunging. Cotton felt and heard a low rumbling from above and glanced up and saw the mountain move, its side sliding toward them. *"Look!"* he yelled and pointed, but the others had already seen the danger.

"There ahead! To the wall!" shouted Borin, leaping forward, racing toward a place where the looming mountainside partially overhung the path, providing shelter of a sort. As thick slabs and huge boulders and rocks large and small bounded and leapt and slid in a mighty avalanche toward them, the comrades ran for the concavity, with Anval driving and working the waggon brake and Kian, a bit strap in each hand, desperately pulling the rearing, plunging horses toward the cove. Even then all were being pelted by the small, round stones forerunning the vast slide, and at the last instant they lunged into shelter, Anval grabbing up his axe and pack and wildly leaping from the waggon and into the shallow depression just as a grey wall of rock sheeted down over the edge.

The ground shook and rumbled as pebbles and boulders alike cascaded down, so thick as to blot out the light, so close as to reach out and touch, racing with a speed that made them leap off the lip above and arch out over the path, some stones not striking the roadway at all in their rush to the depths below. But amid the thunder and roar, one great, thick, flat slab slowly slid down and momentarily teetered on the rim above. "Look out!" cried Perry, pointing at the giant mass, and they crowded back as far as they could.

The immense slab slowly toppled over the edge above and fell with a thunderous crash to crush the red waggon where it stood beyond the protection of the overhang; the great slab landed half on, half off the path, and slowly tilted on the edge of the precipice and began sliding over the brink, dragging the demolished waggon under it and hauling the steeds backward against their will, pulling them toward their doom. Borin leapt forward to add his strength to Anval's and Kian's to help the horses pull against the terrible weight slowly drawing them unto Death. The frightened animals at first lunged and lurched in terror at being dragged hindward, but then settled down to a hard, straining, steady pull when Cotton jumped forward and took the bit straps in hand. Perry, too, grabbed a hold and hauled with all his might along with the rest.

Tons of stone thundered past as the desperate struggle for life went on; but the giant weight gradually drew them all toward the rim; they were unable to check its ponderous drag. It seemed to pause, poised for a final plunge to carry the valiant steeds to their death below, when another great boulder slowly rolled over the edge above and dropped with an ear-splitting *crack!* onto the giant slab and then bounded on down the mountain. The waggon, though already crushed, was unable to stand more and burst asunder, releasing the slab and waggon bed to plunge over the precipice, while with a lurch the horses, Warrows, Dwarves, and Man stumbled forward into the hollow and to safety.

Cotton stroked the animals to calm them, and spoke to them even though he knew they could not hear him, for rock still thundered past. Finally the earth stopped shaking and shuddering as the slide slowly tailed off, trickling to an end with a few pebbles and an occasional rock rattling over the lip to fall below.

An immense silence beat upon their ears as they waited to see if the avalanche was truly ended. At last Borin stepped cautiously out, his boots scrutching loudly in the still. He eyed the mountain above. "It is now safe, I deem."

Slowly the others came out for a look. Perry walked through the talus to the edge of the path and carefully looked down to see where the vast quantity of stone had gone. Though he looked long, searching both down the precipice and mountain flanks below and up the slopes above, except for the rubble on the roadbed he could see no signs of the slide nor even of its passage; though to the companions the avalanche had been a momentous, desperate, life-or-death struggle, the great mountain had swallowed it up as if it were an unimportant event of

minor consequence. Shaking his head in disbelief, Perry joined
the others to help remove the waggon tongue from the horses'
harness; it had been the only part of the wain to survive. They
leaned the tongue against the mountain wall so that some passing waggoneer might salvage the beam and the whiffletrees,
and then the comrades set forth once more.

"Where do slides come from?" quietly asked Perry as they
continued on down. "I mean, well, the mountain has been here
since the birth of Mithgar, ages and ages agone. It seems that all
of the loose rock would have slid off by now."

Borin looked first at Anval then answered, his voice muted:
"The Mountains were here when the Châkka came, and they
will be here when we are gone, but even the Mountains themselves grow old and die. The water from rain and melting snows
seeps into the clefts and crevices; and when it freezes and turns
into ice it splits the stone, delving it as surely as if it were Châk
pick shattering it asunder. Over the years great quantities of rock
are broken loose, and ultimately some sound or earth shudder
causes it to slide to the margins below, and the Mountain is diminished with each rockfall. Just as we Châkka delve the inner
cores of Mountains, so do the actions of the world mine their
outer slopes. And it may be that after uncountable ages, even the
mightiest of Mountains will be humbled by this stone cracking
to become but a lowly foothill—though neither Man, Waeran,
nor Châk will exist on Mitheor long enough to see that come to
pass."

Perry felt privileged to be trusted with this glimpse of Dwarf
lore from the Mastercrafter. The buccan knew that what Borin
had revealed was true, and he looked at the mountain and was
stunned with the knowledge that such a great towering peak
would someday become just a tall hill, like Beacontor—and he
was awed by the thought that Beacontor itself might once have
been a towering peak when the world was young. And the incredible scale of time involved overwhelmed him—why, all of
recorded history was but a moment when compared to the span
of a mountain.

The companions walked downward all that afternoon and
were well below the timberline when it came time to make
camp. It had gotten dark early, for the Sun was setting on the
far side of the Grimwall, and they were in its shadow. Their last

sight of the way below showed the Landover Road running eastward, waiting for them.

They set up camp in a thick pine grove, but had nothing to eat and no tea, for all their food had been carried over the edge by the avalanche.

CHAPTER 11

MARCH TO THE ARGON

"I don't mind telling you, Mister Perry," said Cotton, leading Downy along the Landover Road, "I sure hope that Lord Kian has some luck with that silver-handled bow of his. I'm so hungry I do believe I could have eaten some of the trees right out of the ground back there in the forest where we camped—or a pine cone or two at least." Anval grunted his agreement, for they all were ravenous—stomachs rumbling and complaining—having had nothing to eat since the noon meal up in the Crestan Pass; and now it was well into the midmorning of the day after.

They had arisen just before the Sun, appetites sharp-set, and Lord Kian had put forth a proposal: "I will take Brownie and ride on ahead. Down in the foothills below I'll stop at a likely spot and with my bow I'll try for some game. You follow on foot using Downy as a pack animal; rig the traces to carry our gear. Load everything on the horse except your weapons; we have come to the stage where it is better to become accustomed to going armed. If I leave now, with luck we should break our fast this forenoon."

In considering his plan, Lord Kian had known that the two Waerlinga had never ridden a full-grown horse, and that for some reason unknown to him the Dwarves would not ride even had they the skill. He had rejected the use of sledge or travois as essentially not being any faster than walking, and some time, though brief, would be lost in the construction. And by setting out now, the rendezvous with Durek could just be made if the pace was kept brisk and no more delays were encountered. He had considered riding on alone to meet Durek at Landover Road Ford to assure him that all was well, with the rest of the comrades arriving on foot later; but he rejected that plan, for he knew to make that march without food would be an ordeal for the Waerlinga and the Dwarves.

Thus the companions settled on the scheme Lord Kian proposed, and he rode off alone with his bow. The others set off down the lower flanks of the mountain at a sharp pace, for as Lord Kian had explained, they had but two days remaining before the assembly sixty miles to the east.

The Warrows had discovered upon awakening that their muscles protested mightily at being moved, for their taxing climb up the far side of the mountain followed by the equally strenuous trek down the near side had worked little-used muscles to their limits. As Cotton said, "I'm as sore as a boil about to pop." But as they marched, the ache gradually subsided as the pain worked its way out.

And now they had come down to the foothills and were striding along the Landover Road, and it was midmorning, and Cotton was commiserating with Anval over the lack of food. Amid torturous groans of longing, they had begun describing various meals to one another: succulent roast pig and chestnuts; woodland grouse in golden honey sauce; fresh trout on a bed of mushrooms. . . . Cotton had just come to the point where he had Anval agreeing that for their next meal they would split between the two of them an entire full-grown spitted cow, when Borin, slightly in the lead, held up his hand for silence as the four of them rounded a curve.

Ahead they could see a thin wraith of smoke rising above the treetops. Borin spoke: "It cannot be a Grg fire, for the Sun is up, and in any case we are too far north for Squam. It could be a traveller, trader, or hunter, or woodsman, though it is late in the day for a breakfast fire but early for a midday meal. It may not be a cook fire at all, but an encampment instead. Be wary and speak not of our mission, for even innocent tongues if captured can betray our plans." With that admonition they again started eastward.

Soon they came to the vicinity of the smoke and found what

appeared to be a small unattended fire with four rabbits roasting above it on green-branch spits. They were looking on in wolfish hunger when Lord Kian stepped forth from behind a broad tree trunk. "What ho, boon companions!" he called with exaggerated formality as he made a low sweeping bow, "won't you partake with me this fine repast?" and then he burst out laughing as his messmates scrambled to join him.

After the meal, Cotton fetched both horses from the grassy glade where they had been tethered to graze and led them as the fellowship walked together along the Landover Road, caught up in conversation. They had gone east nearly eight more miles when they came to a stone cottage that served the Bacron as a toll station and Passwarden house.

In days of old, the Baeron, a sturdy clan of stalwart Men, had kept the Crestan Pass and the Landover Road Ford and the road in between clear of Rūcks and Hlōks and other Spawn, and safe for travellers and merchants; for this service, the Baeron charged tolls. But after the fall of Modru, the Foul Folk lived no longer in this region. The Baeron then took to keeping the road through the Crestan Pass clear of landslides and rockfalls, and to helping wayfarers and their cargoes safely through the ford in the flood season; and they continued to charge tolls.

Each year a different family came from the Baeron Holds in Darda Erynian to tend the Crestan Pass, arriving on April the first—a few weeks before the spring melt opened the col for travel—and returning to the Great Greenhall Forest in autumn, when the high snows again closed the way for the winter. This year Baru was Passwarden, and he lived with his three tall sons in the small stone cote.

The four Baeron were pleased to see Lord Kian and the two Dwarves return over the pass, for Baru had wished them well when they had gone west through the gap toward the Boskydells on their "King's business" a month and a week and a day agone. Glad though they were to once more greet the Man and the Dwarves, the passkeepers were amazed to meet Perry and Cotton, for they had never before seen Waldana, and the small Folk were creatures of legend to the Bacron—harking back to the War of the Ban and, beyond that, to the ancient time of the *Wanderjahren*—when the Wee Folk had passed over the Argon on their journey west and south and west again, searching for a homeland.

Travel was halted, and traveller and roadkeeper alike paused to pass the news over a pot of tea. The Baeron also provided the wayfarers with some delicious dark bread covered with spring-cold butter that stuck to the ribs and filled up some hollow spots.

As they took this meal together, Lord Kian told Baru of the rock slide in the pass, mentioning that now there was scree on the roadway. Baru nodded and poured more tea and passed more bread to the wayfarers; and he cocked an eye at his sons and they nodded back, realizing that a job needed doing up in the col.

Even while Perry enjoyed the drink and tea-bread along with everyone else, he noted that Baru and his sons treated Lord Kian with a deep and abiding respect, almost as if Kian were their sovereign King. *Curious,* thought Perry.

The Baeron Men seemed to know about the maggot-folk in Drimmen-deeve and the Dwarves' pledge, for they spoke of the Spawn raids and wished Anval and Borin success in their venture. No fresh news had come to Baru from the south, which was not surprising, for most of his tidings came from travelling merchants faring to cross the Crestan Pass, and it was rare for anyone to attempt to go through this late in the year. Though Baru had no news from the south, he asked that a message be carried to the southern marches: "Sire, should you meet with our kinsman, Ursor, during your quest," said Baru to Lord Kian, "we ask that you tell him that all is well at home, and trust that his vengeance against the Wrg goes to his satisfaction." Perry reasoned that one of the Baeron was off fighting Drimmen-deeve Spawn, seeking revenge for some deed committed by the maggot-folk during one of the raids; but before more was said, it was time to leave—time to continue on to the east.

"Well now, m'Lord," observed Baru, "all your supplies went over the edge with your waggon. We've not much, yet you're welcome to take what food you need to stretch over the next two or three days—till your rendezvous with King Durek."

"My thanks, Passwarden," responded Kian, knowing that Baru and his sons would require most of their own meager provisions to see them through until they were home again in Darda Erynian. The young Man hefted his bow. "I can fell

enough small game to keep us in meat, but perhaps some crue
or hardtack would go well—"

"And some tea, please," interjected Cotton, slurping the
dregs of his and setting the cup to the table, popping one last bit
of bread into his mouth.

Swiftly, Grau, the eldest son, gathered up the rations and
handed them over to Cotton, who had stepped forward to take
them.

And so they all stood and filed out of the cottage and into
the bright sunshine, Cotton packing the fare into his knapsack.
And while the comrades made ready, Baru and his sons also
prepared to go, to hike up into the pass to clear away the rubble
from the slide.

As the travellers stepped out onto the road, Rolf, the middle
son, approached Anval and respectfully said, "Sir Dwarf, you
must advise Durek to hurry if he is to go over the mountain, for
winter comes early in the high peaks; the frost is now with us
down here, which means that the first snow will soon block the
Crestan Pass." Anval nodded curtly, and then all the companions said farewell and set off again for the far rendezvous.

They started down the Road with Perry's thoughts still
dwelling on these Men. Though the visit had been short, Perry
had concluded that the Baeron would make good comrades in
time of need. The buccan also reflected on the curious, defer-
ential way the passkeepers had treated Kian, but before Perry
could ask the young Lord as to the reason, the Daelsman had
taken up his bow and remounted Brownie and galloped away to
seek their supper.

The rest of the comrades marched swiftly throughout the
day, and in the dusk an hour after sundown they once more
came to where Lord Kian was encamped. Again he had been
skillful with his bow, having downed a brace of grouse and
three more rabbits.

Cotton tethered Brownie and Downy out in the rich grass of
the wold and watched them as they began to eagerly crop their
first substantial meal since noon of the previous day, for all of
their grain had been swept away by the rockslide. Satisfied, the
buccan returned to the campsite, his stomach rumbling, for the
aroma of game on the spit filled the air.

The companions had covered some thirty-one miles that

day, and had emerged from the foothills and were well out upon the open plains—twenty-nine miles from the Argon River ford crossing. The Warrows were bone-weary, unaccustomed as they were to climbing over a mountain on one day and forcing march all the next; but though they were tired, they fell to the meal with a voracity that would have done a lion proud. Shortly they were sound asleep, and Kian, Anval, and Borin let the buccen slumber the night through without waking them to stand their turns at guard—much to the vexation of the Warrows the next morning.

All day the comrades advanced across plains that gradually fell into the valley of the Argon. Perry and Cotton and Anval and Borin tramped through a land of heather and grasses, with only an occasional hill to break the monotony of the flat, featureless country. Now and again they would flush a pheasant or covey of birds from beside the road, or surprise a fox trotting across their way, but for the most part they marched without interruption on flat, open prairie, silent except for the sigh of the chill wind that swept from the mountains and rippled low through the tall grass. Again, Kian on Brownie ranged ahead with his bow, providing meat to go with the tea and hardtack given to them by Baru. In this fashion they came to where they could see on the horizon the four-mile-wide belt of trees lining the Argon River; and they knew their journey would soon come to an end.

As their march slowly drew them nearer, they saw that there was little green left in the foliage of the river-border woodland, the fall having worked its magic to transform the leaves into yellow and gold, scarlet and russet, bronze and brown. The only green was in the evergreens: spruce, pine, cedar, yew, hemlock, and the like, clumped here and there in the river-vale forest: like living jade and emeralds among reaches of topaz and spinel and ruby 'mid burnished bronze and old leather.

In late afternoon they walked under the eaves of the river-vale forest, and then came at last to the banks of the Great River Argon. It flowed past in a wide shallow crossing—Landover Road Ford—and the companions stood and watched the river's progress, and Cotton marveled at its breadth.

Durek and the Army had not yet come, and so camp was

pitched on the verge of a grassy clearing in the woods, just a stone's throw north of where the road met the river, where the wind from the plains did not reach, though it could be heard swirling through the overhead treetops. They had made the journey from the Boskydells to the ford in twenty-one days, a time that would have been somewhat less but for the flood at Arden Ford. It was now the last day of October, and Durek was due on the morrow, the first of November.

That night the Warrows again slept deeply, for they were weary; but they stood their turn at watch, having vociferously lectured their companions on the meanings of duty, honor, and the right to stand guard. It was quite a sight to see young Cotton, hands on hips in a defiant stance, his jaw outthrust, glaring up at the towering, smiling Lord Kian and telling the Man just "where to head in" when it comes to doing a turn at watch. And so it was that they spent the night, and finally Cotton awakened them all with the coming of the Sun.

In the early morning light Lord Kian took a length of twine from his pack and caught up his bow and quiver and went through the frost to the pools in the river shallows. Shortly he was back at the campsite bearing three large trout, having shot them with an arrow tied with a retrieval line.

After the breakfast of fresh fish, again the Man and two Warrows took up the sword lessons. The buccen had not practiced since the Arden Ford crossing, and this would perhaps be their last chance: "When Durek comes we begin the long march to Drimmen-deeve," said Kian. "There will be little or no time for practice, so when next you take up weapons it will be against the foe."

A thrill of fear shot through Perry at Kian's words, and his heart beat heavily, and his face became flushed, for he thought, *This is it. It is really going to happen. War with the maggot-folk. Me! Fighting Spawn!*

All that day the buccen practiced with their true swords. They had to learn the weight and balance of their own weapons, and so new wooden swords were not made to replace the old ones that had been lost when the waggon slid off the mountain. Except for the lesson of sword against quarterstaff, they did not engage in mock battle; Lord Kian did not want to risk an accidental wound to any of them. With staves, however, Kian demonstrated how a warrior with the extraordinary reach of a staff was indeed a formidable foe. *Spaunen* were not known to use light quarterstaffs, preferring instead heavy iron poles; and the strategy against those was similar to that used when fighting a hammer. But against a good staff, the sword wielder must depend doubly upon his agility and quickness and wait for an opening to get at close quarters with the foe in order to win.

At the end of the day the Warrows had developed an excellent feel for their weapons—which were much better balanced than the swords of wood and seemed lighter—and so the already quick Warrows became even swifter. Their skill level was extraordinarily high for such a short period of training, and Kian was well pleased.

But the revelation of the day was the sharpness of Perry's sword, Bane. Its edge was bitter indeed, and the point keen beyond reckoning. The rune-jewelled Elven-blade had sheared through or mutilated several quarterstaffs wielded by Kian, and a thrust of little effort would plunge it deeply into the heart of a nearby fallen tree. "Why, it's a wonder, Sir, that it doesn't cut itself right out of its own scabbard!" exclaimed Cotton.

Finally it was sundown, and still Durek had not arrived. The comrades supped again upon Argon trout, then settled down for the eventide. When Perry's turn at guard came, Borin awakened him and growled, "Keep a sharp watch with those Utruni eyes of yours, Waeran; the horses seem restless, though I have neither heard nor seen aught. Still, Wolves may be about, so stand ready." Borin then curled up in his cloak and blanket near the fire and soon was breathing slowly and deeply as sleep overtook him.

Perry stood in the shadows high on the bank and watched the river flow past, glittering silver in the pale light streaming from the waning Moon. The wind had died, and all was still except for the low murmuring of the water. *Quiet enough to hear a pinfeather fall,* thought the buccan. He stood and watched the Moon rise slowly toward the zenith, and the water glide by, and he was content: a small figure in silveron mail with belted sword and Elven cloak; he was a helmed warrior—untested, to be sure, but warrior still, or at least so he hoped, for he had thought long on Anval's words of warning and had tried to concentrate on survival rather than glory.

His watch was just drawing to a close and he was contemplating awakening Anval when he heard . . . something. It was faint and just at the edge of perception. He could sense rather than hear it: a slow, heavy movement nearby. *Where?* He searched with his eyes and ears, trying to quell the thudding of his heart. *There! On the other side of the river!* Something vast and dark was coming through the woods and moving slowly toward the ford. Perry slipped noiselessly to the encampment and roused Anval, a finger to the Dwarf's lips. *"Shh!* Listen! Something comes!" Perry whispered.

Dwarf and Warrow listened together: there came a faint jingle of metal from afar. *"Hist,"* breathed Anval, "that was the sound of armor. We are far north of Drimmen-deeve, yet it could be foul Grg raiders. We waken our comrades—silently."

Anval awakened Borin and Kian while Perry raised up Cotton, and the five slipped quietly into the shadows, armed and armored. Perry's heart was pounding so loudly he wondered why the others did not hear its beat. The horses stamped restlessly, and Cotton started to slip away to quieten them, to prevent a whinny; but Lord Kian grasped the Waerling's shoulder and whispered that their campfire had already shouted out their presence. So the comrades lay in the dark and stared hard through the gloom at the far bank—the source of subdued noise and hidden movement. Then in the wan moonlight they could make out dark shapes of figures coming slowly down the road to the river's edge, and they heard a strong voice call out twice, *"Châkka dök! Châkka dök!"*

At this sound, with a wild neigh, one of the horses belled a challenge, or pealed a welcome; but Anval and Borin leapt up and shouted for joy and rushed for the river. They had recognized the hidden language, for it was the command "Dwarves halt! Dwarves halt!" And they knew that Durek and the Army had come at last.

CHAPTER 12

THE COUNCIL OF DUREK

Lord Kian called after Anval and Borin, his words catching them at the river's edge. "Hold!" he counseled. "Go not into the current in darkness; wait for the dawn."

And so the Dwarves waited, impatiently, and neither side crossed the river that night. They hailed greetings to one another, for the sound carried well and voices across the water could be readily understood. Durek came down to the far bank, and he and Borin spoke back and forth, with Borin indicating that the Boskydells trip had met with success, and Durek saying that the Army would ford the river at dawn to camp and rest for a day or so while the Council of Captains met to hear what had been learned and to plan the campaign accordingly. After a time the comrades wisely returned to camp to catch what sleep remained, while the Army bedded down on the far side along the flanks of the road.

At dawn Cotton awakened Perry. "Mister Perry, hurry, Sir," Cotton urged, "they're starting across." Perry bolted up, and the two buccen scrambled to join Anval, Borin, and Lord Kian on the bank where Landover Road ran up out of the river. In the dim early light they could see a group of horsemen ride into the water and come splashing across at a rapid pace.

"Vanadurin!" cried Lord Kian, pleased. "Riders of Valon! Scouts for Durek's Army." And with but a swift glance at the five companions, the horsemen charged up and out of the river,

and fanned wide as they rode into the woods beyond, their grim
sharp eyes seeming to see everything and miss nothing.

"Lor!" breathed Cotton, watching the steel-helmed, spear-
bearing, tall, fair Harlingar thunder past on their fleet steeds,
"you can't tell where the horse leaves off and the Man begins.
Why, they're all of one piece!"

"Ho! Brytta! *Hai roi!*" Kian called out to one of the riders,
who sharply wheeled his great black horse around and checked
it, seeming to stop and dismount at one and the same time.

"Lord Kian! Hail and well met!" cried the blond warrior,
Brytta, a great smile beaming upon his broad features, his quick
bright eyes dancing as he clasped the Daelsman by the forearm.
The Man of Valon was in his early middle years, and, like his
brethren, he held a spear in one hand, while a long-knife was at
his belt; the fiery black steed bore Brytta's saber in a saddle
scabbard on the left, while an unstrung bow and a quiver of arrows were affixed on the right. Brytta's helm flared darkly with
raven's wings upon each side, and he was clothed in leathern
breeks while soft brown boots shod his feet. A fleece vest covered
his mail-clad torso, and a black-oxen horn depended at his side
by a leather strap across his chest and one shoulder. Perry thought
that he had never seen anyone look quite so magnificent, for here
was a warrior bred.

"We saw your campfire early last night and knew you awaited
the Army," Brytta said, "yet my Men did not call out to you, for
they were on silent patrol—the advance scouts." Brytta paused;
then, *"Waldfolc!"* he cried out in sharp wonderment as his eyes
lighted upon Perry and Cotton. "Ai, Lord Kian, I knew you had
gone to the Land of the Waldana, yet I did not think to see one
here. My scouts thought yesternight that they were Dwarves,
perhaps from far caverns, coming back with you to carry words
to Durek. Ho! but we guessed not that *Waldfolc* came in your
train. Yet wait!" He held up a hand, forestalling introductions.
"I shall meet with each and every one later. But for now, we
must first get this Army across the river." And as Lord Kian
stepped back, Brytta sprang to his steed and with a cry of "Hai,
Nightwind!" plunged after the other riders, leaving Cotton and
Perry breathless in his thundering track.

Long moments fled, stretching out into endless minutes, and
the companions waited while the dawn sky lightened and morn-

ing crept silently upon the land. A quarter hour passed this way with nothing seeming to happen; but then they were startled to alertness by the flat *ta-roo* of a Valonian oxen horn pealing from the westerly direction the riders had gone: *Ta-roo! Ta-roo! Tan-tan, ta-roo! (All is clear! All is clear! Horsemen and allies, the way is clear!)*

A cold shiver ran up Perry's spine at this ancient call of safe passage, and he turned back toward the river and saw the first of the Dwarf Army just entering the wide ford four abreast, while stretching out in a line behind them to pass from view beyond the river-border woods was rank upon rank of tough, steadfast Dwarf warriors advancing upon the crossing. But in the forefront strode a Man, just now entering the water. The companions could not see his face in the shadowed daybreak, but Lord Kian sensed something familiar about the way the stranger carried himself. And then, as the vanguard reached midstream, Kian gave a great shout—"Rand! My Brother!"— and he ran splashing through the shallows to the center of the river and embraced the other. And arm in arm they laughed and waded their way back to the near shore where Kian presented his younger brother to the Waerlinga and Anval and Borin.

It did not take sharp eyes to see that Rand and Kian were close blood-kin: Rand, too, was slim and straight and tall, with the same grey eyes and golden hair as his elder brother; and they had much the same look about them—intense and alert, yet confident. While the younger Man was of the same height or perhaps a jot taller than Kian, Rand was the slimmer of the two, and he had a broad smile and seemed to be full of merriment just waiting to be released. But behind his quiet good humor Perry could sense a hidden strength, which was reflected in the somber manner of his dress: A grey cloak fell from his shoulders, and the gleam of light mail could be glimpsed under its cover; his breeks and boots were grey, and his hand rested casually upon the pommel of a black-handled sword. Yet 'round his head a colorful red-and-gold inlaid headband splashed gaudily across his brow, reflecting the cheer of his smiling eyes.

As Rand met the comrades he looked with intense interest at the Waerlinga, never having seen this Folk before; and to each buccan he gave a restrained bow. And as the young Man turned and greeted Anval and Borin, both Perry and Cotton detected a deep and abiding respect tendered to him by the Dwarves; the Warrows soon understood why, for the moment the formalities were over, Lord Kian spoke: "Rand, you rascal, why didn't you call across the water last night and tell me you were here? How came you to be with the Dwarves? I thought you north in Aven with the Realmsmen, but here you are at the Landover Road Ford. Did you come from Dael? Did you see Father? Mother?" Kian's words slid to a halt as Rand, laughing, held up his hands as if to ward off a blow.

"Please. One at a time, Brother," said Rand, "else I'll get lost. First, if I had called out to you in the night, then I would not have taken you unawares this morn—an opportunity too rare to forgo. Second, King Darion sent word releasing me from service in the northern provinces in order to guide King Durek's Legion to meet you—though I've since discovered that there are several Dwarves in this army who have travelled as far as Stonehill and who seem to know every tree, rock, twist, turn, and hole in the road on the way. Third, I came along because someone had to bring you your sword and mail shirt with which to fight this War, and I thought I might as well lug them about as anyone. Lastly, Father and Mother are both well, and Father sends word that he wants to step down and hand over the Crown, Scepter, and Throne to you as soon as this quest is ended, for he says he is old and deems the Kingdom needs your strong hand at the helm."

"Kingdom?" burst out Cotton, who had been listening with interest to Rand's words. "What Kingdom? What Throne?"

"Why, the Throne of North Riamon, of course," answered Rand, looking in amazement at the astonished young buccan. "Prince Kian, my brother, is to be its next King."

As rank after rank of Dwarves marched up out of the shallows and onward to the far edge of the border-forest to make camp for the day, the two Warrows looked with amazement at Lord Kian. It had not occurred to them to question why he was called "Lord," though they knew that it was a title of nobility; and now they discovered that he was not a "Lord" at all, but rather a Prince! Nay, not just a Prince, but a King-to-be! Perry at last understood why Passwarden Baru had treated Kian with such deference, for the Kingdom of North Riamon extended from the Grimwall Mountains in the west to the Land of Garia beyond the Ironwater River in the east, and from Aven over the Rimmen Mountains in the north to Larkenwald and the Greatwood in the south. The Holds of the Baeron lay near the center of this region, being in the middle-woods of Darda Erynian; and though these Baeron Men swore fealty to a Chieftain, he in turn pledged to the King of North Riamon. Thus, Baru and his sons had been speaking to their Liege Lord and future King when they had spoken to Kian. To think, all this time the Warrows had been travelling with, camping with, eating and drinking with, dueling with, and even scolding the next King of Riamon!

And in that long moment while the Warrows looked on in wonder, Kian seemed to take on a majesty: proud and tall, resolute and commanding. As Perry stood gaping, Cotton awkwardly—for Warrows know little of court manners—started to kneel before Lord Kian, but the Prince quickly stepped forward and raised him up. "Nay, Cotton, kneel not to me," enjoined the Man, "for the Waerlinga have knelt to no Sovereign for more than four thousand years—not since the Great War." Lord Kian then smiled and placed a hand on the shoulder of each buccan and said, "It changes nothing between us; just because one day I am to sit in a high seat, there shall be no bar between us. We are the same as we always have been, each of us growing and changing as circumstance and reason dictate, yet always around a central core of thoughts and ethics that makes you what you are and me what I am. Do not let a Kingship strip me of my friends."

Perry looked long at Kian and then took his hand and said, "A Kingship strip you of your friends? It cannot happen, for there is great strength in friendship, and it takes more than a mere change in station to put it aside or burst it asunder. Though you were the High King himself in Pellar, still would we be friends, for there is no more lasting a thing than the noble bond between boon companions; and this even a King must acknowledge."

"Besides," chimed in Cotton, recovering from his shock, "even a King—or for that matter a King-to-be—needs a couple of folks about who can keep him busy with something to do, like singing some rousing songs, or whacking away at each other with wooden swords; otherwise all he'd get to do is sign orders and issue edicts and inspect the army. Of course, every now and again we could jump into a flood and let you rescue us." They all laughed at Cotton's words, and smiling, turned to watch the crossing as the Dwarves continued to march by.

File after file of the forked-bearded Folk tramped past, each in a shirt of linked steel ringlets, each with an axe, each helmed with a steel cap; they made a formidable host. Dispersed along the train came trundling hued waggons bearing supplies. And occasionally, at this side of the column or that, another Valonian scout crossed; they were flank riders, drawn in for the crossing. Rand informed the companions that there were nearly four thousand one hundred warriors in the Dwarf army, and forty riders of the Valanreach—the scouts of Valon—as well as five hundred horse-drawn wains of supplies. And as they came up and out of the ford, every rider and Dwarf in the throng looked curiously at the Wee Folk, for only a few in that entire Legion had ever seen a Waeran—in the Weiunwood or Stonehill—but none had ever seen an armed or armored Waeran before, much less two of them.

"Where's this Deathbreaker Durek?" asked Cotton, peering at the marching column.

"He shall come last," announced Borin with flat certainty, his statement confirmed by a grunt from Anval and a nod from Rand. "In battle he shall be the first to the danger, but in travel he shall be the last to the comfort."

It took almost two full hours for all the Dwarves and supply waggons to cross over, but at last the comrades saw the end of the column; and bringing up the very rear was Durek. He had gone down the line from head to tail as the march across the river began, speaking to his warriors, saying a word here and giving a nod there. And when he had reached the end of the long column he simply had turned about and brought up the rear. At last he crossed the river and came to the near shore; and he stopped and looked up on the bank at Anval and Borin, Kian and Rand, and lastly at Perry and Cotton. "Hah!" he barked in a rough, gravelly voice, "if only we had some Elves, Utruni Stone Giants, and a Wizard or two from Xian, we could resurrect the Grand Alliance of old."

As Anval and Borin stepped down to greet their King, Perry and Cotton saw before them a Dwarf slightly shorter than Anval or Borin, but one with an air of command and presence unmatched by the others. His hair and forked beard were black, but shot through with silver. His eyes were an arresting dark, dark grey. He was arrayed in black and grey and silver: grey cloak over black mail; the armor was embellished with five silver studs arranged in a circlet upon his chest; grey jerkin and breeks and black boots he wore, and a silver belt was fastened around his waist, and his cloak was clasped with a silver brooch; under one arm he held a black helm; and, as with the entire Dwarf army, he was armed with an axe scribed with blackmetal runes—yet his was an axe with a silveron-edged blade.

Borin presented the Warrows, and after greeting them and Lord Kian and acknowledging Rand's presence, Durek stated, "There is more here than meets the eye: I send you on a mission to gather knowledge of the ways in Kraggen-cor, and you return with Waerans arrayed for battle." He scowled. "A tale lurks here for the telling, but first I must see that the Host is encamped for a day's rest; then we shall meet with my Captains and decide our course." And as the last of the Valonian riders—the rear scouts—rode across the river, Durek strode off to see to the Host-camp and to alert the Captains to the upcoming council, and Anval and Borin accompanied their King to speak of the mission to the Boskydells.

Rand led Kian and the Warrows to one of the cook-wains where food had been prepared, and along with many Dwarves they soon were digging into a hearty breakfast. While eating, Rand explained the Dwarf waggons to the others: "Most of them carry food. Some haul medicine and bandages. Certain ones carry hammers and tongs and forges and lanterns and other tools, and stores of firecoke and metal and wood. A few carry clothing and extra blankets, while others haul armor and extra axes—your sword and mail are in one of these, Kian. Each waggon is colored so that its hue tells what cargo is inside: green for food, white for hospital supplies, red for armor and axes, yellow for cook-waggons, blue for clothing, and black for forges and tools. On the march each color is spaced evenly among the main body of troops so that food or equipage or medicine or any other cargo is at the head, and middle, as well as at the rear of the column; thus, no type of provision is more than a few paces away from any warrior in the force. And there are nearly five hundred waggons of supplies, for this Army of four thousand must be self-sufficient for many weeks; the goal is distant and the march long. Durek has arranged with the Dwarves of the Red Caverns to be restocked from the Dwarvenholt when the waggon goods near exhaustion—but that should be well after the issue of Drimmen-deeve is decided."

After breakfast, Perry and Cotton returned to their campfire to laze around and catnap awhile, for their sleep had been interrupted with the arrival of the Dwarves, and they were yet tired from their trek over the mountains and forced march to the river. But later that morning they fashioned two swords from young alders, and Rand found them engaged in a hard-fought duel when he came to fetch them for the noon meal. He watched for a while, now and again calling out encouragement during flèches and lunges, or shouting approval at successful ripostes or when a touch was scored.

"My brother said you were becoming good swordthanes," remarked Rand as they walked toward the nearest yellow waggon, "and I now see he was right." The Warrows glowed with the praise.

The trio ate lunch, then strolled through the encampment. Everywhere, they found Dwarves sitting cross-legged on the earth industriously oiling their chain-link shirts and wiping down their double-bitted axes to prevent the formation of rust caused by the wetness of the river crossing. The Dwarves at times stopped the Warrows to finger Perry's silveron armor and to remark upon the fine crafting of Cotton's gilded mail. Several spoke to Rand, but for the most part they simply glanced up while continuing to treat their armor. While the three were sauntering thus, they were overtaken by a Dwarf runner: "King Durek sends his greetings and bids that you now attend the Council of Captains in the camp of Anval and Borin where the road joins the river."

Thus it was that when Perry and Cotton and Rand hurried back to camp, they found Durek and all this Captains sitting in a large circle, four deep, waiting for the two Warrows and the

Realmsman to appear. Lord Kian and Anval and Borin were already there as well as Brytta, Captain of the Vanadurin. A spot to Durek's right was open for the trio. As soon as they had taken their place in the circle, Durek stood and spoke, his voice raspy yet clear:

"Captains, we are here to plan our attack upon the usurping Squam who defile our Kraggen-cor. It is now that I must decide whether we issue into our ancient Realm from the west, the Dusken Door, or from the east, Daûn Gate, or perhaps both, for we stand at a fork in the Unknown Cavern: we can march west over the Crestan Pass and south aflank the Mountains to the Dusken Door; or we can tramp along the Argon south and come to Kraggen-cor up the slope of Baralan. The choice is a hard one—hard as flint—for the two ways into our ancient home lie upon opposite sides of the Grimwall. If one way is wrong and the other way right, and if I err when I choose, then to correct the mistake we will have to march an extra eight hundred miles in all: four hundred miles south to Gûnarring Gap and four hundred miles back up the other side, for it will be winter and I deem the pass over the Mountains at Kraggen-cor will be blocked with snow when first we come to the Quadran.

"Upon the chosen route depends the course of the War—and the fates of us all. Hence, we must plan and plan well, and try to divine what may befall us by either approach.

"Here among us to help with this hard choice are three you already know: Prince Kian, who guided Anval and Borin Ironfist to Pellar and back, and then west to seek knowledge of the ways in Kraggen-cor; Prince Rand, who has guided us and advised us on our journey here, and who stands ready to continue on to the caverns; and Brytta of Valon, Marshal of the North Reach, and Captain of the Harlingar, who are the wide-ranging eyes of this army. There are also two here you do not know: Two Waerans—Masters Peregrin Fairhill and Cotton Buckleburr of the Boskydells, western Land of legendary heroes, who stand ready to guide us through the passages of our ancient homeland."

A low murmur broke out among the Captains at this last statement: *Waerans guide Dwarves? In Kraggen-cor?*

Durek held up his hand for silence, then continued: "It is a long tale that has brought us to this place, a tale rooted in the past yet growing through the present toward the future. Some of you have heard parts of this story, others have heard other parts; none of us has heard it all. But now, I propose we hear the whole of it ere I seek your counsel, for the decision I must make is one to be made in the fullest knowledge available."

Durek called first upon Lord Kian, who spoke of the journey to Pellar and King Darion, telling in full about the outbreak of the *Spaunen* raids under the new Yrm leader, Gnar the Cruel. He recounted the pledge of Anval and Borin, in Durek's name, to eliminate the Spawn and reoccupy Drimmen-deeve. Then Kian told of the trip to the Boskydells to seek *The Raven Book* and to glean from it whatever detail of Drimmen-deeve it held. He related that the knowledge had been found, telling of Perry's offer to guide the Dwarves through the caverns. He then spoke briefly of the return journey, barely mentioning the sword training, the flood, and the avalanche—much to Cotton's disappointment, for the buccan would have made a very long, thrilling tale out of their two narrow escapes. Lord Kian was interrupted only twice during his narration: once when a Captain wanted to verify that King Darion had called off his planned siege of Kraggen-cor in order to give the Dwarves the element of surprise; and once more when Durek asked about the condition of the Crestan Pass. At the end of the tale Lord Kian resumed his seat.

Durek then asked Anval and Borin if there was aught they would add. After a long silence Anval stood and announced, "We Ironfists have named both Waerans *Châk-Sol (Dwarf-Friend)*." Then he sat down amid a hubbub of surprised conversation among the Dwarf Captains.

Durek held up his hand, and when silence fell he said to Perry and Cotton, "You have each been named *Châk-Sol* before the Council of Captains. So it was said; so shall it be." And Durek called a herald to the Council circle and proclaimed, "Let all the Hosts know that henceforth Peregrin Fairhill and Cotton Buckleburr, Waerans of the Boskydells, are each *Châk-Sol*. I, Durek, King of the Host, declare it so."

Again the Council circle was filled with a low murmur, with the somber Dwarvish scowls of most Captains being replaced by brief smiles and curt nods to the Warrows. Though neither Perry nor Cotton knew it, to be named Dwarf-Friend was a sig-

nal honor shared by a rare few in past ages, and it was tanta-
mount to being adopted as Dwarf-kith. It meant that the Warrows were privy to the secrets, councils, and counsels of all
Dwarves of Durek's Kin.

Again Durek held up his hand for quiet; then he spoke to
Perry: "Our campaign ahead is filled with many unknowns, but
you can bring light into much of this darkness, for you have the
knowledge of the last trek through lost Kraggen-cor. Only those
of you who journeyed from the Boskydells have heard the full
account of the Deevewalkers' flight through the caverns; none
of the rest of us here know other than fragments of that tale. Tell
us of the journey through the Châkkaholt of our ancestors, and
then tell of the Brega Path."

Perry had not known that he would be speaking before the
assembly, but though he was taken by surprise, he was un-
daunted, for he had narrated that tale to Bosky folk many times
and knew it well. Perry started at the point where the Four had
failed in their attempt to cross the Quadran at Mount Coron,
known as Rávenor by the Dwarves and Stormhelm by Men;
and Perry's tale ended with the escape of the Deevewalkers
onto the Pitch. Though he told it from memory, it was nearly as
accurate as if he had been reading it from *The Raven Book* itself. The Dwarves sat enthralled, for Perry was a natural story-
teller: they growled at mention of the Warder in the Dark Mere;
and bitterly shook their heads at the blocking of Dusk-Door;
they grunted at each mention of some legendary feature of
Kraggen-cor; and cast hoods over their heads at the telling
of the finding of Braggi's Stand; they groaned at the collapse
of the Gravenarch; and scowled at the naming of the Gargon;
and muttered at the burning of the bridge over the Great
Deep.

After telling of the flight of the survivors onto the Pitch,
Perry spoke on the important meeting between Tuckerby and
Brega, and the recording of the Brega Scroll. Cotton had
fetched Perry's pack from the nearby campsite, and from it
Perry took copies of the Scroll out of a waterproof pouch; they
had been wrapped around a section of broomstick and tied with
a ribbon; each copy was made on fine linen paper, and all of
them together took up little space. Perry passed one copy to
Durek, and the others to the Captains, and Borin assured the

Council of the accuracy of the duplicates. They all studied the scrolls carefully, those in the back rows peering over the shoulders of those in front. The scrolls were passed from Captain to Captain till all had seen Brega's record.

Then Perry again addressed the Council: "The Brega Path is long and complex, being some six and forty miles from Dusk-Door to Dawn-Gate, with thousands of places to go wrong." Agreement muttered throughout the circle. "But I am prepared to guide you through, for I know the Brega Path by heart. It seems to me, however, that you will be able to plan the War more easily by seeing an overall picture of the Brega Path." And Perry again rummaged in his pack and then drew forth another paper. "This map is only my crude representation of that tortuous path and leaves out much, in fact most, of the detail of Brega's instructions, but it may be of aid in planning your strategy." And Perry passed the sketch to Durek.

Durek eagerly accepted the drawing and studied it long and hard, and then passed it to the Captains, who also scanned it carefully. A low swell of commentary rose up among the Dwarves as the map slowly made its way around the Council circle.

Neither Anval nor Borin nor Kian had seen this map till now. Perry had only remembered it the evening he had been tested by Anval and Borin, and the buccan had brought it along only as an afterthought. In truth he had not thought that the map was very useful, for it contained only the broadest detail of the Brega Scroll, and Perry had made it only to amuse himself some time after he had discovered the Scroll. But he could see that here, in the Council of Captains, the map could be of some use in planning the broad strategy of the coming campaign; and so, what originally had been a scholar's diversion became an important tool in the planning of a War.

The Sun moved slowly down the sky while all in turn looked on this unique chart, studying it with care, seeing for the first time a plan showing some of the arrangement of the halls and chambers of mighty Kraggen-cor. After a long while the map came full circle back before Durek to lie alongside the copies of Brega's complex instructions. Durek held up his hand and gradually the babble died down.

"Now we have all heard the full tale and have seen the

record of Brega, Bekki's son, and have looked upon the map of Friend Perry. Are there questions on these or upon the tale of the Four Who Strode Kraggen-cor, or upon Lord Kian's account? For on this evidence we must base our strategy."

To Durek's right, up stood a red-bearded Dwarf: Barak Hammerhand, doormaker and Gatemaster, Mastercrafter of the secret stone doorways and Dwarf portals into the mountain strongholds, one of Durek's Chief Captains. "Friend Perry, was the Dusken Door destroyed by the Monster of the Mere?" His question brought grunts of approval from the assembly, for it was a crucial point: if the Army was to invade by the western door, they must pass through the portal, and its condition would count heavily in any plan.

Perry answered: "The *Raven Book* says only that the creature had enormous strength and wrenched at the doors; Brega closed them and guessed from the sounds he heard that the Krakenward had torn down the great flanking pillars, and that the edifice collapsed, blocking the Door. They could all hear thunderous booming, as if the Monster were hurling great rocks against the Loom. In any event, the portal would not reopen, though when Brega attempted it, the doors seemed to tremble as if trying; on the other hand, the doors could have been trembling from the impact of stone being hurled by the Krakenward. Hence, the Door either may be blocked, or broken, or both. No one to my knowledge has actually seen the portal since that time, so I know not whether it can be reopened."

Barak was still standing at the end of Perry's answer, and again Durek nodded at the Gatemaster. "Friend Perry," Barak spoke up, "say again what your *Raven Book* tells us of the Great Dēop at the eastern gate." Once more Barak's question brought forth a low mutter of comment, for the state of that entrance would bear heavily in any invasion plan. Barak had put his finger on the two most critical points.

"The gulf is virtually bottomless," answered Perry, "and at least fifty feet across. The only span, the drawbridge, was destroyed—burned—and fell into the depths, leaving no way to pass over."

Barak sat down and a white-bearded Dwarf across the circle stood. It was Turin Stonesplitter, Minemaster, delf shaper, chief of the tunnelmakers. "I also have two questions: Does the Krakenward still live? What know we of the foul Grg numbers now in stolen Kraggen-cor?"

Again Perry spoke: "As to your first question, I do not know if the Dusk-Door is still warded by the creature, for the *Raven Book* says nothing more of it. And since we are not certain of the Monster's origins, we have little to go on, little that might indicate its subsequent fate. Yet this we know: Gildor said that five hundred years before the Winter War, the Lian Guardians for weeks watched two mighty Trolls mine great stone slabs from the top of the Loom and cast them down into the vale below. And the Ogrus used these slabs to dam up the Duskrill, and slowly a black lake came into being.

"And when the Dark Mere had formed behind the Troll-dam, the Dragon Skail winged through the dark night, *bearing a writhing burden,* and dropped it in the old Gatemoat at the Dusk-Door. We now know that it was the Krakenward, a creature of power; but though the Krakenward had power, and the Dragon had power, just think of the hideously overwhelming force Modru need have wielded to cause such an evil thing to occur! Yet occur it did.

"The next day the Elves saw that the Dusk-Door had been sealed shut, by *Spaunen* hand, for now the Dark Mere with its Monster warded the west entrance.

"It was only after the Monster's attack upon the four Deeve-walkers that Gildor pieced together all of the story, deducing that it was Modru's handiwork, preparing for the coming of the Winter War—*five hundred years in advance. . . . Nay! more than a thousand years, for the Evil One had previously used his art to have the Gargon set free long before!* For you see, Drimmen-deeve was to be the fortress from which would be launched Modru's conquest of Darda Galion.

"Yet I stray from your question: whence came the Monster of the Dark Mere, none can say, though Gildor did guess that it was a Hèlarms from the Great Maelstrom in the Boreal Sea."

Hèlarms? Maelstrom? A muttering again swelled up around the Council circle, but slowly subsided as Durek held up a hand for silence and Perry continued: "But as for now, the creature may still live and be in the lake, or may live elsewhere, or it may have perished with the lifting of the Dimmendark. I cannot say."

Lord Kian answered Turin's second question: "Little is known of the number of *Spaunen* dwelling in Drimmen-deeve, but there must be many, for the raids are frequent and in force. The captured Rukh questioned by King Darion said that his people were as numberless as the midges of the Great Swamp—the Gwasp—but that claim may have been spurred by false bravado to put fear into our hearts. The Rukh also spoke of Trolls in Drimmen-deeve, but that, too, may be a falsehood."

At the naming of Ogrus, fell looks came over the faces of the Captains, for they knew that the presence of these dire creatures would seriously affect the outcome of any battle. The Captains spoke in low, hushed voices at this revelation; many grimly fingered their axes. After a while Durek again held up his hand for silence. "War not with the Trolls until they stand before you, for to do otherwise is to battle with phantoms of rumor."

Brytta of Valon then spoke up: "I know not how to deal with Ogrus, but spies and ambushes along the way are my concern: what of the lands between here and the Black Hole; do enemies lurk therein?"

"As to that, I cannot say for certain," answered Lord Kian. "The Yrm raid east and south of the Pitch, along the rivers Rothro and Quadrill and Cellener to the banks of the Argon; they ravage my countrymen's holts in that southwest limit of Riamon, and raid beyond the River Nith and down the Great Escarpment into the camps and settlements of the North Reach in your Land of Valon, Brytta, as you well know, for it is your demesne they despoil.

"Yet I think the Spawn are not north of Darda Galion—the Larkenwald—for the land twixt here and there is nearly deserted, thus empty of plunder; and so, if we journey down this eastern side of the Grimwall Mountains, perhaps we will be unobserved and safe until we are nigh upon the Pitch, where we must at last encounter the Yrm raiders and patrols.

"As to the west side of the range, *Spaunen* may have crossed through Quadran Gap—yet we have no news of ravers in the Land of Rell, for that realm, too, is nearly abandoned, and Yrm would find little to carry back to Gnar's coffers. Hence, I think they come not down the western slopes; and should we march through the Crestan Pass and down that side of the mountains, we should reach unseen the very Doors of Dusk, the western gate.

"Even so, Brytta, by either route your scouts must ever be on the alert for signs of Spawn passage or spying eyes or ambush—even here in the north, especially in and near the mountains—for we know not for certain how far this *canker* has spread."

Again there was a mutter of agreement within the circle, and Durek let it run its course. Then he asked, "Are there other questions concerning the *Raven Book,* the Brega Path, or King Darion's information? No? Then let us consider our courses of action."

In the hours that followed much was said and many clever and not-so-clever courses were proposed, examined, and accepted or rejected. Often the map was referred to, and many actions were proffered based on distances between chambers and the sizes of halls. Nearly all was debated, and the Sun sank low and disappeared. A fire was kindled and still the deliberations continued. Many plans and counterplans were settled on, all depending upon the way the Host entered Kraggen-cor and the numbers and kinds of enemy encountered. Finally Durek rose to speak:

"We have before us two strike-plans which seem sound, but both abound with unknown risks, and by these risks may fail:

"First, we can invade by the eastern Daūn Gate and try to cross over the bottomless gulf. The thieving Grg must now have some sort of bridge over the chasm, for they issue in force from the Daūn Gate and withdraw through that same portal, and thus must have a way of passing over the Great Dēop. But it is certain that this bridge is constructed to foil invaders: perchance it is a drawbridge; for all one knows it could be a span set to fall if the Squam vermin take certain actions. So we cannot count on capturing this overcrossing. Hence, to attack through this entrance we need construct invasion bridges of great span—mayhap building them in Blackwood—and haul them through the Daūn Gate and to the Dēop. This portal is certain to be heavily guarded, and Grg parties crawl all over the land betwixt Kraggen-cor and the Argon River—to launch an unexpected attack this way is unlikely. Aye, we can expect the entire Squam army to be waiting for us on the far side of the gulf; and to cross that rift in the teeth of a prepared enemy will be hard—perchance impossible—for no assailing force has ever won across the Great Dēop in a War, though many have tried.

"Our second course is to invade by the western Dusken Door. Here, mayhap there is a huge creature of great strength barring the way. And perchance the portal itself is buried under tons of rock. The very gates may be broken and no longer act— and Barak believes that such gates can be repaired only from the inside. Yet the chambers and passageways at that end are likely unguarded; and if we can gain entry through the western doors, we will take Gnar and all of his forces unaware. Our chances for success are much higher—if we can get in."

Durek stood in thought for a while, and silence reigned in the ring. All the Council waited. Cotton thought, *It's as plain as a pikestaff. The only sure way to get in is through the Dawn-Gate and over the gulf—but not if the Spawn army is there; and the only safe way to get in is past the Dark Mere and through Dusk-Door—but not if the Krakenward is there, and only if the door can be opened.*

At last Durek spoke: "This, then, I choose: we shall go by the Dusken Door." At these words, pent breaths were released; many in the Council relaxed: Durek had made his choice. The Dwarf King spoke on: "If we cannot get by the Warder, if it still lives and is there, or if we cannot open the doors, mayhap we can fare over the Quadran Gap and down the Quadran Run and invade by Daūn Gate—though I deem that snow will have barred that way across the Mountains. If the Gap is closed, then we must march south, through Gūnar Slot and the Gūnarring Gap, passing near the Red Hills, where we may winter. If so, then we launch our Daūn Gate invasion in the spring. Yet it is too soon to speak of failure, for we know not what awaits us at the Dusken Door." Durek then fell silent.

Anval had spoken little for most of the council, only grunting now and again his approval or disapproval as the plans had been put forth. He had listened to Durek's decision, and he knew as well as all the others that success hinged upon whether or not the portals at the Dusken Door could be opened. If they were damaged, then repairs could be made only from the inside. When Durek fell silent, Anval stood and was recognized. "King Durek, that we can defeat a monster warding the Dusken Door, I do not doubt. And a Châkka army can clear tons of rubble with ease. But, as has been said here, if the doors do not open, then breaking them down or delving a new tunnel will cause enough sound to echo through the passages to alert the Grg forces, and they simply will pull the hidden linchpins—if the Squam have discovered that secret—and collapse the old tunnels, or at least delve and collapse them; and we will have to dig up an entire Mountain to get in: years of effort. Though we could then come at the eastern gate, all surprise would have been lost and the way well defended; and if we attack into an alerted enemy, it will be into their strength, and we will suffer high losses—perhaps too high. We could lay siege, but again that would take years of effort. Hence, what we need is a way to make certain that we can open the western doors; and for that I have a plan which, though it does not guarantee success, will give us a good chance at it:

"What I now propose is that a small sneak force slip through the Daūn Gate and follow the Brega Path backwards to the Dusken Door. A small force of no more than six or eight has a chance to reach the east entrance unseen and then pass undetected through the Mines and gain the western doors without alerting the Squam. Even if alerted, the foul usurpers would not connect the presence of such a small force to an impending invasion. But if undetected, we could put a crafter of Barak's skill at the Dusken Door, on the inside, to repair any damage and ensure that the doors will open to let the Army within. The gamble is great, but the stakes are high; yet he who dares, wins." And with these words, Anval sat back down.

A rising tide of agreement swelled throughout the circle of Captains: Brytta approved of this planned swift stroke, for it suited his bold spirit to cleave straight through the core of the enemy; Kian and Rand saw it as a brilliant yet dangerous strategy to tip Fortune's scales in their favor; the Châkka agreed, for it was an unexpected masterstroke to surprise and whelm an ancient, hated enemy; even the Warrows admired its Dwarvish nature: bold, clever, perilous, secret. But Durek cut through to the heart of the plan and found waiting there the sharp-pointed horns of yet another dilemma—and Perry was deeply shaken by Durek's next words: "Well thought, Anval—but here is the rub of it: to succeed in this assay, Friend Perry would need guide you through the Mines along the Brega Path; and if he were delayed, captured, or slain, then there would be no guide for the Army if the Dusken Door is unbroken and we enter. Yet if the portal *is* broken, then you are right: to put Barak at the inside of the doors would all but assure victory." Durek then fell into deep thought, balancing the alternatives.

A dead silence fell over the Council as Durek considered the proposal. Only the crackle of the fire in the center of the circle broke the quiet. Perry felt a great foreboding, as if impending doom were about to strike; for to go into battle surrounded by an entire army is one thing, but to go among the teeming enemy with only six or seven allies is quite a different prospect. To penetrate Drimmen-deeve would mean passing through miles of lightless caverns infested with swarms of maggot-folk, avoiding detection in a place where a Rūck squad could be lurking around every turn, passing through tunnels with no side passages to bolt into if trapped between groups of Spawn, and travelling along passageways with many side tunnels out of which Rūcken forces could issue unexpectedly. Perry had visions of hiding furtively while maggot-folk marched past, and of being lost in a black labyrinth, fleeing hordes of slavering Spawn through an endless maze, and of being trapped facing an evil army of advancing Rūcks and Hlōks. And these visions made the buccan tremble in fear. But he could also visualize the Dusk-Door swinging open and the Dwarf Army marching through. The thought of passing undetected through the center of the Rūcken forces terrified Perry, but he understood the need only too well. The risk was incalculable, but so, too, was the reward.

Shakily, Perry got to his feet and said in a small voice, "King Durek, I will go with Anval and Barak if you approve the plan."

In frustration, Durek slammed his clenched fist into his palm. "*Kruk!* Had we known of the Brega Scroll but six months ere now we could have trained another guide . . . nay, *many* other guides for this thrust! But as it is, we have but one pathfinder where two are needed. Dare I send our only wayleader on a mission of high risk? The reward for success may be victory, but the penalty for failure may be defeat. Oh, had I but another guide for my Army, then we would take this gamble for victory."

Again the silence stretched out, drumming on the ears. All were looking with downcast eyes at the ground, waiting for Durek to decide. Thus, few saw a small figure stand, but all heard his words: "I know the way. I can guide the Army along the Brega Path, even though it means I'll be separated from my master." And Perry looked up in astonishment, *for the speaker was Cotton!*

CHAPTER 13

THE STAVES OF NAROK

"Cotton!" exclaimed Perry, "Wha—Are you saying that *you* know the Brega Path?"

"Yes Sir," declared Cotton, "I memorized it when we were checking all those copies of the Brega Scroll you made for the Ravenbook Scholars. Riddle and reason, Mister Perry! After all, we did go over every one of them time after time till my eyes were falling out. Anybody would have learned the Brega Path if he had done what we did."

"Why, that's true, Cotton!" exclaimed Perry. "Oh, dunce that I am: I should have known that you, too, had learned the path by heart."

"Oh, Sir, you're not a dunce," asserted Cotton. "I would have told you earlier, but, you see, before the Council met, I just didn't think it was important. But after Anval told us his plan, well, I knew then that it was a matter of life and death; but there was my promise to your Miss Holly to think about: 'Goodbye, Cotton,' she said. 'Now you stay by Mister Perry, and take care of him, and keep him safe.' And I nodded *yes,* and that's a promise. I had to think of whether she'd ask me to keep it or not, knowing, as it were, how desperately these Folk need our help. And the only way we can give that help is for us to separate. I know Miss Holly would not hold me to a promise made in ignorance.

"Oh, Sir, I don't want to go away from you, but one of us must stay with Durek's Army—though that could be you as well as me. What I mean, Sir, is, well, you could guide the Army and let me go with them as is headed to the inside of the doors." Cotton hoped that Perry would accept the offer, for Cotton was thinking, *That will be a perilous trip, and I did promise Miss Holly to keep him safe.*

"Cotton, I thank you for the offer, but still I think it is mine to do. Besides, those who go through the caverns to the inside of the doors will travel the path backwards. That means the guide must be able to follow the Brega Scroll instructions in reverse: every 'up' will become a 'down,' every 'left' will then be a 'right,' every 'split' will become a 'join,' and so on. I've thought about it, and I am certain that still I can guide the penetrators—even though it is backwards on the Brega Path—for going backwards through the instructions with my mind is almost as easy as going forwards, even though I have to turn lefts into rights and make the other changes too." Perry looked searchingly at Cotton. "Knowing that everything will be all turned around in reverse, do you think you could guide the squad to the doors?"

Cotton appeared surprised. "I never thought of that, Mister Perry, but you are as right as rain: everything *will* be all backwards for them going through to the inside." Cotton then paused in inward concentration: he closed his emerald-green eyes, and a frown of intense effort crossed his countenance. After a short while, "Plague and pox!" he exclaimed, nettled, "this is worse even than trying to say the alphabet backwards after an ale night at the One-Eyed Crow! Seems like I have to start at the front most of the time and run to the place I want before I can back it up. Going forwards is easy. Going backwards is hard."

"Well, that settles it then," declared Perry. "If Durek chooses this course then I will go with the squad, and you will go with the Army."

Durek and the Council had heard all that Perry and Cotton had said, and a murmur rippled throughout the circle. Durek held up his hand for silence. "Friend Cotton, that you are certain the steps of the Brega Path are carved upon the tablets of your mind, I do not doubt, for you have been named *Châk-sol.* Even so, I cannot gamble the fate of mine Host upon skills untested—"

"Here begins the journey at the Dusken Door," interrupted Cotton, picking up one of the copies of the Brega Scroll and handing it to Durek. When the Dwarf King found the place, Cotton took a chin-up, chest-out, hands-behind-the-back, school-recitation stance and continued: "Two hundred steps up the broad stair; one and twenty and seven hundred level paces in the main passage 'round right . . ." And as Cotton recited from memory the words on the Scroll, Perry followed along in the mirror of his own mind while the Captains of the Council waited expectantly.

". . . then it's two hundred forty level paces across the hall and out the Daūn Gate to freedom." Cotton sat back down and for the first time looked at Mister Perry; and a great beaming smile was spread upon Perry's face.

Durek set the Brega Scroll aside and said simply, "We have our guide." And a rumble of approval rose up from the seated Captains as Cotton flushed in pleased embarrassment.

When silence fell, Durek turned to Anval Ironfist: "Yours is a perilous scheme for those who attempt it, but our need is dire and your plan worthy. The force must be kept small to avoid detection, yet large enough to include all the skills needed to reach the far doors and to repair the arcane hinges, if they are broken. This squad I must choose wisely, for success depends upon having the right skill at the right time." And Durek fell silent, thinking upon the problems likely to be faced.

"King Durek," said Kian, "first the force must reach Dawn-Gate. For that task a guide is needed who knows the way from here to the Pitch and thence to the east portal, a guide who is wise in the ways of woodcraftiness—to slip by Yrm parties— and one who is wise in the way of weaponry in the event of mischance and discovery. I am that guide." And Durek nodded his acceptance.

Borin stood. "In the caverns the squad will need speed and stealth, yet also strength and fury should the force be discovered: fighters to hold the way while others reach the doors and repairs are made; fighters to mislead the thieving Grg should the need arise. Warriors are wanted in this task, for which I propose myself and Anval." Durek again nodded his acceptance, for the Ironfists were the greatest of all his champions.

Red-bearded Barak spoke: "The doors of the west are known only in legend to me, yet I believe I can divine the way of their working. Two doorcrafters may be needed if repair is required, but in this I ask that three be sent, for one may be slain. For this task I propose myself and Delk and Tobin." Two other Dwarves stood in the Council circle: Delk Steelshank, brown-bearded and black-eyed, stern-visaged and strong-bodied; and Tobin Forgefire, fair beard and hair, smooth-faced, blue-eyed, slender for a Dwarf.

"And thus the Squad of Kraggen-cor is chosen," proclaimed Durek in his gravelly voice. "Seven strong: Barak, Delk, Tobin, Anval, and Borin, and their guides and advisors: under the sky, Prince Kian, and in the caverns, Friend Perry. May success go with you."

Then Durek took his axe by the haft at the blade and smote the earth with the butt of the handle and cried, *"Shok Châkka amonu! (The axes of the Dwarves are with you!)"* and all the Council of Captains took then their axes and together struck the haft butts hard to the ground and called out, *Shok Châkka amonu!* And the shout rang through the forest and across the river and beyond; and everywhere that Dwarf warriors of the encamped Army heard it, they knew that some of their comrades faced a grim mission.

Durek then spoke to his Captains: "Gather your warriors on the morrow and tell them what has passed here in the Council tonight. Tomorrow, one hour after sunrise, the Chief Captains are to return here for the detailed march planning." With that he dismissed the Council. The Dwarf King then summoned a scribe and gave over Perry's map with instructions to gather other scribes and make enough duplicates for the Chief Captains. And finally he turned to the Waerans and invited them to sup with him, and the three of them headed for the yellow waggon serving the Captains a late meal.

"Beggin' your pardon, King Durek," said Cotton as they sat on a log under the stars and ate by the light of the still-burning Council fire, "but just how are we going to get to this Dusk-Door?"

"Prince Rand tells me that after we cross over the Crestan Pass we will follow the Old Rell Way down from Arden along the west side of the Grimwall Mountains; it will take us to the Quadran and the Door," answered Durek, licking hot gravy from his fingers. "I am told that the Old Way is grown over and gone in many places, and all that remains are ancient pathways—sometimes wide, sometimes narrow. In places some of the old stonework even yet can be seen. The trek at times will be swift, and at other times slow, the wains holding us back. But in all, with no delays we could arrive at the western doors in a fortnight and four days, it being nearly sixty and one hundred leagues distant by that route. But we must start soon—tomorrow or the next day—for it is already the second of November, and the high snows are due to fly; we must be over the Crestan Pass ere that occurs."

"The second of November?" mused Perry. "Why, yes, it *is* already that date. I had forgotten. Today is the anniversary of when Tuck became a Thornwalker. And the ninth will be the anniversary of when Tuck and the others set out from Woody Hollow to join the Eastdell Fourth on Beyonder Guard and Wolf Patrol. The folks back home are probably angry at us, Cotton, for we have taken the Horn of the Reach with us, and they won't be able to sound it a week from now at dawn at the Commons to celebrate the beginning of what turned out to be Modru's downfall."

"Well, Sir, I'll just give it a toot right here and now, and that'll just have to do." And Cotton set his mess kit aside and jumped up and ran to his pack and pulled out the silver horn.

"Wait!" cried Perry. "Remember Anval's warning. He said to blow it only at dire need."

"Narok!" hissed Durek, and his face blenched at the sight of the trumpet. "Aie! The Ironfists told me that you had borne this token into our midst. And now I see that they spoke true. It *is* the harbinger of *Narok.*"

"That's what Borin said: *'Narok.'* Then he closed up tighter than a clam!" exclaimed Cotton, carrying the horn back to the log. "What in the world does *Narok* mean, anyhow?"

Durek looked long at Perry and Cotton and the bugle. Then he set his own mess kit down and spoke, for the Warrows had each been named Dwarf-Friend:

"Narok. I do not know what it apprehends, but it is terrible."

Durek paused, and a chill ran down Perry's spine. The Dwarf continued: "The word '*Narok*' itself means 'Death-War.' But the legend of *Narok* is an enigma handed down from the time of First Durek. It was he who brought the silver horn to the Châkka, having crafted it himself, or mayhap he received it from some unknown crafter—we know not the which of it. It bears the unmistakable stamp of being Châk-made, yet its creator we do not know.

"Even in those elden days the horn was an object of fear, and was sent north to be hidden away forever. And it was shut away in a secret trove for thousands of years. But it was lost to the Dwarves when Sleeth the Orm—great Dragon of the Gronfang Mountains—came to the Châkkaholt of Blackstone under the Rigga Mountains, slaying Châkka and taking their home for his lair and their treasure for his hoard.

"When Sleeth at last was slain and we heard not that the horn was recovered, we thought mayhap it was gone forever, perchance having been unmade by the Dragon spew, or even destroyed in the fire of Black Kalgalath's ruin. And we rejoiced! But we knew not for certain; thus we feared it still, for its Doom is dreadful, though we know not its meaning."

"*Doom?* It has a *Doom* upon it?" asked Perry. "Why, we have sounded it many, many times without harm. *Doom?* I say nay! For oft times it rallied the Boskydells in time of great need. It is not doomed; it is blessed. And were you to hear its clarion call, you would know of its power."

"That it has power, I have no doubt. And others may sound it without hurt, for its Doom is not for them," answered Durek. "Châkka alone must face its destiny—though when, I cannot foretell."

"We knew it had something to do with Dwarves," interjected Cotton, holding the horn in the firelight so that Durek could see the riders and runes. "These riders are Dwarves, yet Dwarves don't ride horses, if you catch my meaning."

"I had not seen the horn till now, yet I have known always the detail of its semblance. It is *because* of this horn, and the legend, that Dwarves do not ride horses," answered Durek.

"But Brega, Bekki's son, rode horseback," said Perry. "The *Raven Book* tells how he rode double with Gildor the Elf on the horse Fleetfoot, a steed of Arden—why, to the very doors of

Drimmen-deeve, they rode. And later, Brega rode other horses, though he seemed to fear them: to Gûnarring Gap, to Gron, to Arden. So says *The Raven Book*."

"Brega was not afraid of horses," responded Durek. "He only feared the consequences of a Châk *riding* a horse, perhaps fulfilling a prophecy that would lead to the Death-War. Yet, in his time the need was great, for the world was coming to an end—impelled by the Enemy in Gron—and had Brega not been borne by steeds into battle the outcome may have been different, and that is why he rode.

"Even so, the Châkka on horses graven on this horn are known to all of Durek's Folk. And because of the legend we do not ride horses in hope that the Doom of Narok will not fall. Though we know not its meaning, we fear it."

"What is the legend? What do these runes of power mean?" asked Perry, shaken by the dread in Durek's look.

Durek paused, collecting his thoughts; then he spoke: "Translated, the runes say:

> *"Answer to*
> *The Silver Call.*

"That is but half of one couplet from the *Rime of Narok,* an ancient foretoken of the Doom from the age of First Durek. The complete rime is:

> *"Trump shall blow,*
> *Ground will pound*
> *As Dwarves on horses*
> *Riding 'round.*
>
> *"Stone shall rumble,*
> *Mountain tremble,*
> *In the battle*
> *Dwarves assemble.*
>
> *"Answer to*
> *The Silver Call.*
> *Death shall deem*
> *The vault to fall.*

"Many perish,
Death the Master.
Dwarves shall mourn
Forever after.

"These staves are known to all of Durek's Folk. They fore-tell a great sorrow to befall. Whence came these stanzas, none knows—perhaps from the crafter of the horn. And yet, the words of the staves do not rime in Châkur, only in Common. And its rhythm is strange to my ear; were this verse Châkka-written, it would have a different beat. Hence, we deem the crafter of this time to be of a race other than my Folk. Horn and verse, they are a mystery. And though the stanza has been known and argued for ages, we are no closer to knowing the Doom than when the horn was first seen by Eld Durek. But we do know that the trump of the ode is the silver trumpet Friend Cotton holds. And we do not ride horses because of the rime and because of the graven images on the bugle. Aye, we believe that this small, silver horn will signal the Death-War—*Narok*—and I deem it bodes ill that it has come to us at this time."

Cotton looked at the bugle as if it were an alien thing. Always he had known that during the Winter War this trumpet had helped save the Bosky, and he believed that it was an instru-ment of good. Yet to the Dwarves it was a feared token of doom, foretelling of some great sorrow to come. They had re-joiced when it was lost with Sleeth, but now it was come among them again, to haunt them and to threaten their future.

Perry and Cotton and Durek sat in the flickering firelight and said nothing, each plunged deep in his own thoughts. Over-head the bright stars scintillated in black skies and wheeled through the heavens: remote, glittering, silent. At last Perry stood and took up the horn and spoke: "King Durek, we know not how to aid you against the ominous prophecy, for we know not its meaning either. But if possession of the horn will help you, then here, it is yours." And he held out the silver trumpet to Durek.

But Durek shook his head and said, "Nay. I do not want it. Though you offer me this thing in compassion for our unknown fate, I must refuse, for we are safer with it in hands other than our own."

And as he spoke Durek raised his hand to push the gift away. But at the very instant that his fingers touched the cold, silver metal, an awful portent befell! The skies aloft blazed with hundreds upon hundreds of incandescent, fiery shooting stars, streaking upon golden tails across the startled heavens. Their very numbers seemed uncountable as blaze after blaze sped to its doom. The coruscating barrage silently flared directly overhead and the land was illumed brightly as legions of burning points swept across the firmament to score the vault above.

Durek fell back in horror, his eyes wide and fixed upon the streaking fires aloft, the back of the hand that had touched the horn pressed against his mouth as air hissed in through his clenched teeth in a prolonged gasp. And a great moan of dismay rose up from the encamped Army.

And as the myriad incandescent trails faded and were gone and the land fell into darkness, Durek cast his hood over his head and walked away into the night.

CHAPTER 14

THE PARTING

It was an hour after sunrise, and the Chief Captains had gathered again at the Council fire. Spirits were subdued, for last night's awful portent, the shower of stars, had dismayed the Dwarves; they truly believed that each falling star signalled the death of a friend. But they had mastered their fear, if not their misgivings, and plans were being made for the march of the Army to the Dusk-Door and of the Squad to the Dawn-Gate:

Barak held the Council's attention: "The Dusken Door was crafted in the First Era by the greatest Gatemaster of all, Valki. He was aided in this one effort, though, by the Wizard Grevan, who cast the hidden theen signs on the portal. The lore words of vision cause the Wizard-metal runes and other markings to appear: pale in the daylight, brighter in the moonlight or starlight or on a darkling day, but brightest of all in the black of deep night. And when the markings become visible, then a wayfarer need only say the Wizard-word *Gaard,* meaning, we deem, *move,* and the doors will open—or rather, now, they may or may not open, depending upon the state of repair." Barak shook his head in regret. "Today we craft no Châk doors that open by word alone; their construction is a lost art. Yet I trust that the skill and loreknowledge that Tobin, Delk, and I hold will be equal to the challenge."

Barak paused, tugging on his red beard, and then spoke on: "But herein lies a problem: if the Army tries to open the doors from without ere the inside repairs are finished, it may create further damage. I know not for certain how long it will take Delk, Tobin, and me to set the doors aright, but time must be allowed for this task.

"On the other hand, if the Squad tries to open the doors from within while still blocked without by broken stonework—as Brega tested—it could also worsen the damage. So time must be set aside to allow the Army to remove the blockage.

"It is my meaning that neither the Squad on the inside nor the Army on the outside should attempt to open the portal until both sides have completed their work. Yet how will each know that the other is ready? We must not signal through by tapping on the rock, for the rap may alert the Squam; the sound of hinge repair or rubble removal mayhap will do that in any event, but we must avoid hammer-signalling through the stone.

"As has been said, we must work to matched schedules, each side giving the other time to come to the doors and do the work, with some allowance for unknown mischance. I propose now that our separate march schedules be drawn up, and the work time allocated, and that we select the moment when King Durek speaks the words of power." Barak's counsel brought nods of approval from the Chief Captains. He continued, "King Durek, when you say the words of opening, if the portal does not swing wide, then it either will be because mischance has delayed us or because repairs are beyond our skill. If they do not open, say then *Gaard* once more, and the attempt to open will cease. In the event that perhaps we are delayed, I ask that you try again under the stars each mid of night for a sevenday. If after that time they still remain shut, then we will never come.

"I have but one more thing to say, and it is this: for our part at the Dusken Door, Delk, Tobin, and I will need no more than one day's time after we reach our goal; if we cannot repair it in a day, we cannot repair it at all."

Barak sat down and white-bearded Tunnelmaster Turin Stonesplitter stood and was recognized. "King Durek, I can only guess at the amount of rubble blocking the doors, but if necessary we have more than four thousand Châkka to remove it, whatever the quantity." Turin thought for a moment. "Give me four days—in four days we Châkka can move a small Mountain."

Prince Rand then spoke: "By the roads and paths that lie ahead of us it will take eighteen days to march to Dusk-Door: two days and one half to reach the Grimwall Mountains, one day to cross through the Crestan Pass, one day to reach the Old Way below Arden, and the remainder to march to the western portal."

"By my reckoning, then," calculated Durek, "by leaving here at noon today, the Army will be in position and ready to open the Dusken Door the evening of the twenty-fifth of November, two and twenty days hence. Will the Squad be ready by then?"

Lord Kian answered first: "If we use a raft by day to go down the River Argon to the wold above Darda Galion, and thence walk west across the land to the Pitch and on into the Dawn-Gate, then that will take twelve days in all: three days are needed to build the float, and at the rate the river flows, four more to raft to the point where we start overland; then, with four days of westward trek, we should reach the hills bordering the Pitch; finally, with but one more day of marching up the Pitch, we will come to the east portal."

Perry sat huddled with Anval, Borin, Barak, Delk, and Tobin. The six of them were closely studying one of the scribe-copies of Perry's map and muttering about distances and chambers and halls and stairs. At last Perry spoke up: "King Durek, the Brega Path is six and forty miles long, and two days should suffice for the passage. However, we cannot say how often we may have to hide from Spawn within the Deeves, or be delayed for other reasons yet unknown. Thus, we set aside one more day for delay. Hence, to reach the doors, we must allow three days to traverse Drimmen-deeve."

"And so," responded Durek, "twelve days to the Daūn Gate, three days to the Dusken Door, and one day for repairs: sixteen days in all for the Squad to complete the task. Since less time is needed for this venture than for the Army to be ready at the Door, you seven must delay along the way so that the completion of your task coincides with the completion of ours: start late, hold along the river, camp on the wold—do what must be done, but stay out of the danger of Kraggen-cor until it becomes necessary. The twenty-fifth of November is the appointed day that both sides must be ready.

"And now, Prince Kian, I have consulted with all of your squadmates, and they are agreed: you are delegated as leader of the Squad of Kraggen-cor. In times of hard choice, yours shall be the final decision; I have but meager advice for you, and that is to draw upon your companions' knowledge and wisdom, listen closely to their counsel, and choose wisely.

"My Chief Captains and I have but to make final our plans for the march, and the Army shall embark at noon. You, too, must now gather the Squad together, and you must collect from the waggons the supplies you need to fulfill your task."

The seven penetrators withdrew twenty yards or so to the comrades' encampment and began discussing what was needed to carry out the mission. They spoke of food—such as crue—and water for their journey; tools to build the raft; heavy rope to bind the logs; light rope for other needs; hooded Dwarf-lanterns to light the way along dark paths; special tools—such as a small-forge and bellows and special firecoke, and augers and awls and hammers—to repair the hinges; clothing and armor and weaponry; and many other things. They did not take all they spoke of, but they considered well, and in the contemplation made firm some plans that required detailed thought.

Perry was surprised at how much yet needed to be decided and at how thorough the planning was, and he paid close heed to the deliberations. But every now and again he glanced up to see Cotton sitting in the other circle engaged in Army march planning. *Oh Cotton,* Perry thought, *you said you did not want to leave me, and in truth I, too, do not want to go away from you. But the need is great, and there is no other choice. It ever must be so in War: that best friends are separated by the circumstance of the moment. How often, I wonder, do they part never to meet again? Will we, Cotton, greet each other after today? Will either of us ever see the other, or the Boskydells, or The Root again?*

Soon the Squad completed its initial planning, and Perry went with the others to gather the needed supplies. Perry did not see the stricken look on Cotton's face as Cotton looked up and saw Perry leave; for Cotton, too, was dreading the impend-

ing separation, feeling as if he were about to be cast adrift, or
abandoned, or as if he were somehow forsaking his "Mister
Perry."

Anval and Borin, Barak and Delk and Tobin, Kian and
Perry, all made repeated trips to the various, hued waggons, se-
lecting supplies. At times they enlisted some local aid from
Dwarves lounging in the vicinity of whatever waggon they
were drawing from to help carry part of the provisions. The
pile grew, and Perry wondered if all of this could actually be
used by the seven of them between now and November
twenty-fifth. *Oh, well,* he thought, *what we don't use we can
cache,* and the buccan continued collecting items under Kian's
directions. Finally they were finished—and just in time, for the
Army began the initial preparations necessary to start the long
march.

The cook-waggons then served an early lunch, and the
seven were joined by Durek, Cotton, and Rand for their last
meal together before the parting. Their spirits were exceed-
ingly glum, and for the greater part of the meal, no one said
aught. Finally Durek broke the silence: "I know not what to
advise, for I know not what you will meet on your mission—we are faced with too many imponderables. Still,
stealth and secrecy seem called for, yet there may come
times when dash and boldness will serve better. Only you
can judge what will be necessary to pierce the caverns from
Daūn Gate to the Dusken Door, and then only at the time
you are doing it, for much of the journey cannot be foreplanned since it depends upon what the foul Grg adversary
is doing. Yet this we know: You may travel under the Sun
with impunity—though you must guard against Squam
deadfalls and hidden traps—so make the most of daylight.
At night, keep a good watch and burn not encampment fires
once you are within the reach of Grg raiders. This too: enter
Kraggen-cor in the morning Sun, for the east light of the
dayrise will reach far into the portal, driving the Squam
back, and it will be less well guarded; but the Sun will not
protect you deep in the caverns, for there it does not penetrate except at the stone window-shafts; even in that light
you are not safe since black-shafted poison Grg arrows can

be loosed at you from the depths of the surrounding darkness. And so, take care."

And then Durek stood and said in his gravelly voice: "Brega, Bekki's son, strode into legend along a steadfast course of honor. May the span of all our strides match his—for that is the true Brega path."

Durek then fell silent a moment, looking intently upon each member of the Squad as if to pierce the veil of the future and see their fate, but he could not; and at last he said, "May the eye of Adon watch over you, and His hand shield you from harm." And he bowed low to each of the seven. "And now we must part, for I have a far rendezvous to keep with seven trusted Friends at the mid of night on November the twenty-fifth." And the Dwarf King then turned and strode away.

At that moment Brytta rode to them on his black steed, Nightwind, and leaned down and clasped Lord Kian's forearm. "My Lord, fare you well. Eanor, King of all Valon, would bid you safe journey were he here, but he is not, so I speak for all of my countrymen: Good fortune to you all, each and every one!" And with a waving salute to the members of the Squad, the Man from Valon called out to his mount, and they thundered away.

Cotton went to Perry and they embraced. "Now, Sir, you are part of the Secret Seven, so don't go giving yourself away to no Rūcks. And stay out of trouble for your Miss Holly's sake."

"I don't envy you going back over the Crestan Pass again, Cotton, but say 'hullo' to Baru and his sons for us," responded Perry, attempting to be casual; but then: "Cotton, old friend, I'm going to miss you, but we shall meet again at the Dusk-Door."

Rand and Kian also embraced and looked long at one another. "The Kingdom needs your hand, Kian," said Rand. "Keep safe; wear that chain mail we hauled all the way from Dael."

"Rand, when this is over," pledged Kian, "you and I shall take the time to go on a long hunt as in days past: ahorse, with falcon, hawk, and dog. Till we meet at the west portal, fare thee well, my brother."

The Seven stood at the edge of the woods and watched as

Brytta's mounted scouts of Valon—acting upon Rand's description of the lay of the land and the planned Dwarf Army march route—rode off in different directions out upon the grassy plains, while the Dwarf column formed up on the road: Dwarves four abreast in march order, waggons pulling into their assigned places in line, spare horses tethered to the tailgates of the black waggons. The Sun stood at the zenith when at last all was ready. Durek's voice rasped out, *"Châkka!"* There was a long pause while like a dying echo the order was repeated down the line by Captain after Captain. *"Hauk!"* And the Army began to move.

Like some vast multilegged creature, the Legion surged out onto the plains: Dwarf boots tramping on hard-packed road; hued waggons rolling slowly forward: the slap of sideboard, the creak of harness, the grind of iron rims rolling; the jingle of armor; the clop of hooves: all these sounds and more the four-mile-long column made as it undulated slowly out over the prairie. As Durek strode by at the head of the force, he and Rand saluted the Seven with an upraised right hand, and so did the Captains as each of them passed by. Rank after rank tramped past with tinted waggons spaced along the line: white, green, black, red, blue, and yellow. At last the Squad saw the end of the train approaching them, and at the very last came a yellow cook-waggon being drawn by Brownie and Downy, and beside the grey-bearded driver sat Cotton.

As this last waggon rolled by, Cotton, though distressed, smiled at his "Secret Seven" and waved. The wain slowly trundled past and moved out onto the prairie. Cotton stood and faced back toward the Seven and drew his sword and held it to the sky, the golden runes on silver blade burning in the sunlight, his gilded armor blazing as well. *"Shok Châkka amonu!"* he cried out, "and the swords of the Bosky, too!" And he quickly faced about and sat down, for he did not want them to see that he was weeping.

Perry stood by a birch tree and leaned his head against the smooth white bark as he watched the column march toward the Grimwall Mountains, dimly visible low on the horizon. The plains were flat, covered only by tall waving grass and heather, and so he watched for a long, long time as the Host moved out across the wold. The Sun had fallen past the zenith to midafternoon when the buccan at last turned away and trudged toward the campsite, unable to see the yellow waggon any longer.

CHAPTER 15

WAROO

"It ought not to be this way, Bomar," said Cotton to the grey-bearded Dwarf on the seat beside him, and then the buccan turned around again to look far back over the grassland toward the distant border-forest. "No sir, it just ought not to be this way. When you say goodbye to your best friend, you just ought to disappear with a flash and a bang and maybe a puff of smoke, and get the goodbye over with all at once. Instead, we said goodbye almost three hours ago, and here I can still see the silver glint of his armor in the Sun, and maybe he can still see the gold of mine. It just makes the parting last longer."

Cotton once more faced the mountains, but he could not remain that way for long, and again he turned to look back over the plains toward the river. "Oh," he said in a small, dismayed voice, for the argent glint was gone, and Cotton felt as if he had somehow betrayed Perry by not seeing the glimmer disappear. Glumly he faced forward along the direction of march.

Stretching out before him was the long Dwarf column, feet tramping and wheels rolling toward the mountains ahead. Except for the Army, and an occasional distant scout, Cotton could detect nothing else moving across the prairie, not even the wind. With little to distract him, the Warrow rode along in silence, feeling all alone amid an army of strangers, paying scant heed to anything except his own wretchedness.

"Put your sorrow behind you, Friend Cotton," advised Bomar after a while, flicking the reins lightly to edge Brownie and Downy a bit closer to the ranks ahead. "Though you have parted from a boon comrade, do not dwell upon the woe of separation; think instead upon the cheer of reunion, for you will have a tale to tell that he knows not and will hear from him an adventure new to you.

"But Bomar," protested Cotton, "if it's tales and adventures we're living, well then I'd rather be in the same story with my master than in a different one."

Bomar tugged on his grey beard and scowled. "Friend Cotton, you are not in a different venture from your 'Mister Perry.' Aye, you are now separated from him, yet the tale is the same—separate or together, we are all of us living in the same story: it is a tale that was started before the beginning, before the world was made; and it will go on after the end, when even the stars are unmade again. And in any tale such as this there are those whose accounts seem always to touch, and those who weave in and out of the tales of others, and many more whose narratives touch but once or never. Even twins, or brothers, or kindred, or just good companions will have times of separateness. We must savor the times we are together; and store up the times we are apart. Let not the sadness of separation dull these jewels, but instead look with joy toward your reunion so that they will brightly sparkle."

"Why, you've hit the nail right square, Bomar!" exclaimed Cotton in surprise, seeing the separation in a different light. "We *are* still in the same story together. And I've got to start living my part of it, looking at things through happy eyes, not sad ones, so that when we get together again, well, I'll have some of them bright jewels to show him."

Had it been an overcast day, perhaps Cotton's somber mood would have clung longer, but the Sun was shining in a high blue sky, and the Warrow's spirits rose with every turn of the waggon wheel, until they were as bright as the day. "Bomar," added the Warrow after a long while, "I do hope that Mister Perry has someone as wise as you to set him right about being apart from a friend." A smile flickered over Bomar's face, but he said nought; and the waggon rolled on.

The column moved across the prairie all that afternoon, finally coming to a halt at dusk. They had covered some fourteen miles, and in the distance before them they could see the foothills rising up to meet the mountains—though where the column had stopped was still well out on the plains.

The cook-waggon rolled off the road and into the bordering grass and heather, parking beside a green food-waggon. Bomar and Cotton jumped down and were joined by eight bustling Dwarves, each of whom began to work at tasks under Bomar's directions: Nare made three fires using wood brought in the waggon from the river-border forest, for Bomar as well as the other cook-wain drivers had known the column would stop on the open treeless prairie, and each had cut, loaded, and hauled a supply of firewood from the margins of the Argon to use in preparing the evening meal. Caddor and Belor filled great teakettles with water from the barrels, while Naral set up hearth-arms to hang the kettles over the fires; and Oris, Crau, Funda, and Littor began preparing a vat of stew.

Cotton unhitched Brownie and Downy and led them a short way out into the lush prairie grass where he fed them some grain, then hobbled them to graze. He stood and talked to each horse awhile, stroking them, and then went back to the waggon.

When he arrived at the cook-site, the pots and kettles were bubbling and boiling merrily, and supper was on its way. Cotton pitched in and helped with the chores that remained. In about an hour the meal was ready, and the cook-crew served stew and honey-sweetened tea to one hundred or so hungry warriors, and to one lone scout who rode in after dark. Before sitting down to a meal of their own, Bomar's crew set a pair of large kettles of water to boil over two of the fires; they would be used by the warriors to wash and rinse their mess kits.

Cotton was just dishing up some stew for himself when Durck and Rand strode into the circle of firelight. "Well, Friend Cotton," rasped Durek, "though in your case it will not be critical till we reach the Dusken Door, the tail end of the train is a strange place for one of my pathfinders to be." Laughing, they sat down for a meal together.

When Cotton went to bed that night, after helping Bomar's crew clean up, he noted that the Dwarf Army had set up a picket of sentries; the buccan felt a twinge of regret that he wouldn't be standing his turn at ward; he had come to enjoy seeing the dawn sky slowly change from black to grey to purple to pink and orange, joyously heralding the arrival of the Sun.

The next morning Cotton was awakened by the sound of Bomar and his crew rattling pans and kettles, preparing the breakfast meal. Cotton jumped up and discovered that he had not missed dawn after all, for it was still dark; and as the buccan was to learn in the days to come, Bomar's day started early and ended late. The Warrow helped Bomar with the work, and watched the sky celebrate the coming of the golden orb; and the buccan served warriors as the Sun tipped over the rim of the world.

Following breakfast, Cotton went to Brownie and Downy. After greeting them with an apple treat, he removed their hobbles and led them back to the waggon and fed and watered them. Then he hitched them to the yellow wain while Bomar's crew loaded the utensils aboard. Soon the command to march came echoing down the line, and the cook-waggon pulled back onto the road.

In midmorning the Army entered the foothills and began slowly climbing higher as they moved up the shallow slopes of the lower flanks of the mountains. Cotton noted that in these uplands the leaves for the most part had lost their bright colors and had become a uniform rich brown, with just a few reds and yellows stubbornly remaining. And many of the leaves had fallen, to crackle and crunch and swirl 'neath tramping feet.

The march continued on through this umber woodland for the rest of the day, stopping a few moments each hour for a brief rest. During these stops Cotton would finger his sword and think of other days. It was early dusk when the Legion came to their final stop; they had marched some twenty-nine miles since dawn.

That evening Cotton again took a meal with Durek and Rand, but the Man and Dwarf brought with them three surprise guests—Grau, Rolf, and Wrall: Baru's sons; the head of the column had stopped at the Passwarden's stone cottage. As they ate, their conversation turned to the Crestan Pass. "Father says you have come just in time," said Rolf, "for he feels snow deep in his bones—has felt it these past five days, ever since we were up in the pass clearing away the scree from the slide our Lord Kian told us of. And Father says each day the feeling grows stronger: the weather must soon break."

Durek squinted through the dark in the direction of the pass. "In days agone we did not concern ourselves with the snows; the Mountain tops could be covered with ten fathoms or a hundred of snow, but that affected us not—for then we knew the way under."

"Under?" asked Grau. "Do you speak of the mythical pass beneath the mountain? Why, that's just a tale to amuse children."

"Nay," replied Durek, "the way is there. Though it is lost, it remains there still, hidden behind secret Châkka doors. These Mountains have many hidden entrances and exits which lead to the tunnels below. And here as in Kraggen cor the caverns reach from one side of the range to the other."

"Hey!" exclaimed Cotton, "speaking of secret doors, I just remembered: Bosky legends warn about Rūck-doors under the Grimwall. They say Modru's Mines are down there, behind hidden Rūck gates. I wonder if any of those Spawn-doors are nearabout."

"The Rutch-doors onto these slopes were destroyed by my forefathers," responded Grau. "We are told that the Baeron fought the Rutcha and Drōkha and Ogru-Trolls in the hills and mountains above Arden and Delon for many years. At last all of the Wrg-doors into the passes also were found and destroyed; that I have always believed to be true; but never did I deem the tale of the way under the mountain to be true till now."

"Even if we knew where it was, it'd be trouble, wouldn't it?" asked Cotton. "I mean, well, what about the maggot-folk? Aren't they still down there waiting?"

"No," replied Wrall. "The last of the Spawn were driven away by my forebears in the time of the Winter War."

"Then why don't we just hunt up the Dwarf-doors to the way under and go that way, instead of worrying about snow?" asked Cotton.

"I am told that the secret doors of the Dwarven Folk are hidden too cunningly," answered Rand. "Unless you know exactly where they are, you'll never find them; they look just like unbroken rock walls, or large boulders, or even great slabs lying on the slopes. So, Cotton, it isn't just a matter of simply hunting up the doors, for we don't even know where these portals are or what they look like; and we can't pry up every rock and boulder on the mountainside, or tap with hammers on every rock wall for hollow sounds. We'd be here till the mountains were gone before we'd find even one door."

"Aye. Prince Rand has the right of it," growled Durek. "Once the way is lost, it is usually lost forever. Without guidance, the entrances remain hidden. Even with instructions, sometimes the way cannot be found. Even so, were we to stumble accidentally onto a door, still we would not pass under the Mountain, for we have no 'Brega Scroll' here to guide the way through."

"Say!" exclaimed Cotton, "I just thought of something: are we going to have trouble finding the Dusk-Door? Oh, I know the *Raven Book* says the Door had steps and columns and such, but, if Dwarf-doors are impossible to find, what about the door we're going to?"

"Worry not, Friend Cotton," replied Durek, "the Dusken Door was meant to be found. It was made as part of an old trade route, and the way to it is well marked. It is not hidden, except perhaps now by stonework rubble."

"Well that's good," said Cotton, "'cause I'd hate knocking on stone walls with hammers and prying up slabs with crowbars for the rest of my life." They all enjoyed a hearty laugh at Cotton's words, especially Durek, who found the image of a Waeran scrambling over stone with hammers and pry bars hilarious.

Though the talk was lively and the company pleasant, at last Durek and Rand had to leave to see to the roadside encampment and to plan the morrow's march. Reluctantly, Grau, Rolf, and Wrall also left, for they knew that it had been a long day's journey for their friends, and rest was needed for the upcoming trek. After the visitors were gone, Cotton pitched in to help Bomar and the rest of the crew clean up the utensils, and he bedded down about an hour later.

*   *   *

The Army got under way again shortly after sunrise. Soon Cotton's waggon rolled past the stone cottage, and he waved goodbye to Baru, Grau, Rolf, and Wrall, who called, "Good fortune!" And the Baeron watched as the column disappeared from sight in the wooded hills.

The march twined through the uplands, winding higher and higher upslope. The mountains now towered above the Host, the stone ramparts impervious to the many-legged creature crawling up the flanks. The Sun, too, climbed up the mountain, warming the escarpment above. The Army tramped upward along the road, which wove back and forth through the mountain forests. As the column climbed higher, the woods slowly changed from the lowland trees, such as oak and maple, to upland wood, such as aspen and other poplars, and at last to the evergreens of the high country.

It was midafternoon when the Army came to the last thick stand below the timberline, and the Legion was called to a halt. They had covered eighteen miles of upward march, and though there was daylight still, the trek was halted, for from here it was twenty miles of open mountain before timber would be reached again; and the nights of November were too bitter upon the open crests to permit travel after dark, and so camp was made early.

With a cry of horns, all of Brytta's scouts, too—point, flank, and rear—were called in to join the column at camp; all, that is, except for the Army's advance eyes: four Vanadurin outriders: a lead scout named Hogon—who had journeyed this way a year or so earlier—and three others, all of whom had ridden ahead and were even then crossing the range.

Cotton tethered the horses in the pines and returned to help build the fires. The Sun had passed behind the peaks, and a chill shadow lay over the land; but the encampment was much colder than the shadow would account for: a frigid iciness seeped down from the heights; borne on a raw drift of air that spilled from the summits and slid to the borders below. As evening approached, the drift became a breeze blowing downward. Cotton and others donned warmer clothes from their packs, but still the chill bit through, and the fires were built higher to provide more warmth.

An hour after sundown, the warriors had been fed and the supper cleanup was finished, though kettles of hot tea still remained over the cookfires as proof against the frigid cold. Cotton was just filling his cup when a Dwarf picket rang out a call—"Someone comes!"—and Cotton heard footsteps trotting up the road. As they sounded closer, Cotton could see in the firelight that it was a Man—it was Rolf!

"Rolf!" Cotton called. "Over here!" And the youth came winded to the fire.

Without speaking further, Cotton offered the panting young Man a cup of tea, but Rolf waved it away and croaked, "Water!" Far from being cold like those huddled around the campblaze, the youth was drenched with sweat from his run. Swiftly, Cotton dipped a cup into a water barrel and passed it to Rolf. The Man gulped the drink, gasping for air between draughts. After another cup and a few moments to catch his breath, he asked, "Where's Durek? A blizzard is coming, and he must be warned."

"Why, he's up front somewhere," answered Cotton, waving a hand up the road toward the mountain, and he watched as Rolf trotted away.

It was not quite an hour later that a Dwarf herald came through the night to each fire, finally arriving at Cotton's. "King Durek summons all Chief Captains and all who have travelled through the pass on other journeys to counsel him at midtrain," he announced to the group. And so Cotton, who had been through the Crestan Pass, stood to go—as did Bomar and Littor, both of whom had been over the mountains to Stonehill. Together the three walked toward the front of the long encampment, going nearly two miles to the midpoint of the column. There Durek had formed a Council circle.

Durek spoke to the gathering: "Rolf brings word from Baru. You must all hear, and prepare for what comes." And he indicated to Rolf—now wrapped in a blanket—that he was to speak.

"My father, Baru, says that a blizzard will be in the peaks ere noon tomorrow," announced the youth in a clear voice. He wetted a finger and held it up in the chill breeze. "That wind you feel is known as the breath of Waroo. To the Baeron children the story of Waroo is a hearthtale of a great white bear from the north with very cold breath who claws over the tops of the mountains to bring hard winters down onto the land. But upon growing older we find that Waroo the Blizzard is much more deadly than any white bear—for when a bear stalks it can be fled from or, at last resort, it can be slain, but a blizzard at best can only be endured, never killed. And when Waroo approaches, his breath flows coldly adown the Grimwall, and it signals the first blizzard. When Father felt Waroo blowing down below, we knew we had to warn you, and I came, for I am the swiftest.

"If you are to pass over the mountain, you, too, must move swiftly, for you have twenty miles of barren high rock to cross before the shelter of timber is reached. You cannot go in the night, for it is too cold, yet you cannot delay overlong, for the storm will strike sometime tomorrow.

"Father advises that you do not go at all, for he is afraid you will perish in any attempt; yet he realizes that you feel you must. His next advice then is that you prepare tonight, dress in your warmest winter clothes, and start just before dawn. Still, it will be bitter that early, but leaving then at a quick step may get you across ere the snow flies—though he doubts it.

"I offered to guide you, but Father laughed and said, 'The only time you may guide a Dwarf is when he's not been there before. Durek needs not our guidance across the mountain, for he has Dwarves in his company who have crossed over ere now.' Father did say that he has felt this storm coming for a week or more, and he expects it to be an ill one." Rolf hitched his blanket around himself and sat down.

"How many here have walked the Crestan Pass?" asked Durek, pausing while he counted upraised hands. "I tally three and twenty Châkka. This then is what I propose: Gaynor, you shall head the column at Prince Rand's side; Berez, you shall walk with me along the train; Bomar, you shall hold your position at the last; let the rest count off and evenly space along the line—ten with the ten red waggons, the other ten with the black. If the storm strikes while we are yet upon the open stone and our sight is limited by the snow, let each guide lead a segment of the train to come down into the thick pines above Arden. Stragglers are to follow the red and black wains; Bomar, you sweep up any who fall all the way to the rear. Marshal Brytta, hold your scouts with the column, spaced along the train with the white waggons. All in the Host shall wear their down-filled clothing on the march tomorrow, or tonight if needs dictate. We will leave one hour before sunrise, which will give us six hours to go the twenty miles if the snow does not come til midday. With a quick-march we may yet succeed in outstepping the storm. Any additions to the plan? Questions? No? Then, Captains, instruct your warriors; guides, count off and find your waggons."

Durek turned to Rolf: "Baru's son, your warning may save our quest, for without it we surely would have started on our march tomorrow at a later hour, and we would have gone at a slower pace. Though your sire would have us turn back from this danger, we cannot, for delay of our mission means the evil in Kraggen-cor will live longer and more innocents will die. And though Baru holds us in concern, he knows we must go on.

"We welcome you to rest this eve with us, for you are weary from your gallant run. Stay the night, and bid us farewell in the morning, and carry the word to your father; he will see that it is borne to those who should hear tidings of the Host."

Durek stood. "And now we must rest, for tomorrow promises to be a hard task. Oh, Waeran"—he looked across at Cotton—"if you have no goose-down winter suit in your pack, draw one from a blue waggon." Without further word, the Dwarf King turned and walked off toward the front of the column.

Accompanied by Brytta, Cotton and Bomar made their way back toward the rear of the train. There was a dark brooding upon the face of the Man from Valon. "You look like a storm about to burst, Brytta," said Cotton. "What's gnawing at you?"

"My far outriders, the advance scouts," Brytta replied grimly. "Hogon, Eddra, Arl, and Wylf, they are some leagues ahead of us, beyond the Crestan Pass. If there is a blizzard, it will strike them first. I would that they were among us rather than . . ." His voice trailed off, but Cotton and Bomar knew his feelings.

They soon came to the scouts' fires, and Brytta turned aside to join the Harlingar. Cotton and Bomar strode on, stopping only long enough at a blue wain to draw warm winter Dwarf-clothing; Cotton was given the smallest goose-down-filled quilted coat and quilted pants that the driver could find; they were still overlarge on the Warrow, but would have to serve.

It was yet black night when Cotton was awakened. The raw wind was blowing harder, but the down-filled clothes kept the Warrow warm. Bomar had shown him how to fasten the hood so that his face was protected, and the Warrow could peer out at the world through a fur-rimmed tunnel; Bomar had also given him some mittens, fastened together by a long cord that ran up one sleeve and down the other to prevent loss.

Cotton hitched the horses to the waggon, and after a cup of tea and a crue biscuit, he was ready to start. Upon command, warriors quenched the fires, and Dwarf-lanterns were un-hooded along the column to bathe the train with their lambent soft blue-green light while all waited. Finally the order came, and the Dwarf column moved out at a quick-step pace. Shortly Cotton's waggon passed Rolf standing huddled in a cloak next to the only remaining campfire. Cotton's hood was back, and by the firelight Rolf recognized him and waved. Cotton called, "Goodbye, Rolf. And oh, by the by, say 'hullo' to Baru, and Grau and Wrall, too. Say, 'hullo' for Mister Perry, also. Or maybe instead of saying 'hullo' you ought to say 'good-bye' for us. . . . Whatever."

And Rolf called back, "I'll untangle the greetings from the farewells, Cotton. Good fortune. Take care. And beware of Waroo, the White Bear." And the young Man watched as the last of the train moved away in the cold darkness, a long line of blue-green lanterns swinging and bobbing up the windy slopes.

The Legion marched swiftly, and after a while Cotton could tell by the sound of the waggon wheels and see by the glow of the lanterns that they were no longer in the woods. The strength of the wind increased, and it groaned and wailed through the crags and moaned down the side of the mountain, and the higher they went the more bodeful it sounded.

When daylight finally came it was dim, and fell through an

overcast; and they could see an ominous blowing whiteness streaming from the crests, like enormous ragged clinging grey pennons slowly whipping and flowing in the wind that howled over the range from the far side. Cotton could see that the white streamings came from the old high snow as part of it was blown from the peaks and whipped about and carried up and far, far out to disappear—perhaps to sift down onto the foothills or plains far below, he could not tell which. The Host was about six miles from the Crestan Pass, and the cold was oppressive; and with the overcast the Sun would not warm the journey at all.

The nearer the Army came to the pass, the stronger grew the wind, for on the far slope whence the gale blew, the mountain flanks on either side of the route acted as a huge funnel, and the wide wind was channeled to blow through and over the constricted slot in the saddle. The shrieking gale frightened many of the teams on the narrow way, and they had to be led by those on foot, or even blindfolded and pulled against the screaming blast. Thus it was that as the column entered the pass, a howling gale-force tramontane pummeled and buffeted the Dwarves, and slammed at them, and tried to blow them and their horses and waggons away. The blast was so strong that Dwarves on foot had to lean and struggle to get through the gap, and most of the teams and waggons had to be pulled and pushed by warriors just to make it up the last slope. The wind took Cotton's breath away, and he had to struggle and gasp just to get air. Finally the column was through, past the neck of the funnel, though the wind tore and howled at them still, and voices could not be heard. With his elbow, Bomar jostled Cotton, getting the Warrow's attention and pointing ahead. With wind-watered eyes Cotton squinted out through his hood to see a roiling wall of white advancing up the reaches on the wind: the blizzard, Waroo, the White Bear, had come, and they were still ten miles from safety.

Driven by the yawling blast, the snow hurtled over the train, enveloping it in white obscurity. Signing Cotton to work the brake, Bomar climbed down and made his way to the horses; he took one of the bit reins in hand and began leading the team and waggon through the howling wind and slinging snow. The wind-whipped whiteness whistled up the precipice and along the wall, through crags and canyons, around bends and corners, and lashed into Cotton's face. He drew his hood tighter to fend the blast; still, he had to duck his head to keep the snow from driving through the fur tunnel and into his eyes. Now and again the Warrow glanced up to get a quick look at where they were going, but all that Cotton could see clearly were the Dwarves on foot directly in front, and the next waggon ahead; he could make out the vague shape of the waggon beyond, but could see no farther. He noted that at every side canyon and false trail, Bomar would move across to scan for stragglers, but so far had found none—though if they were more than twenty or thirty yards distant, an entire army could have been lost.

Slowly, for what seemed like days, the buffeted Legion moved down the raging mountainside. And the snow grew thicker until Cotton could but barely make out Bomar leading the horses. At first the driving wind did not allow the snow to collect on the path, whipping it off as fast as it tried to accumulate. But then at corners and crevices it began to gather in drifts. The train came to a complete halt at times; Cotton believed that the head of the column had come to a drift that had to be cleared before they could go on. In these places the braking was slippery, and often the waggon lurched perilously close to the edge of the precipice, with Cotton's heart hammering wildly.

The white wind howled and screamed and pummeled horse, Dwarf, Man, and Warrow alike, and it seemed to suck the heat right out of the body and dash it against the looming stone walls to be consumed without effect on those frigid surfaces. Sitting up high on the waggon seat, Cotton was chilled to the marrow, but as cold as he was, he worried more about Brownie and Downy: even though they were toiling, active with the labor of working the wain downward, moving against the storm, there was no doubt that if they did not reach shelter soon the horses would perish in the freezing shriek.

Bomar not only realized the plight of the horses, but he knew Cotton's condition, too, and the Dwarf arranged for one of the walking warriors to spell the buccan, who then helped lead the team. And even though the white wind raged and blasted him with snow, Cotton warmed a bit in the effort of walking, though he was still miserably cold.

They continued down the treacherous slopes, trapped on a howling trail, caught between a sheer wall and a steep precipice, passing by yawning canyons in the wall, trudging beyond forks in the path. At one false trail Bomar found a squad of lost Dwarves who had somehow become separated from the column in the obscuring whiteness. They had struggled down a wrong split but had realized that they were alone and had just fought their way back to the main route when the waggon rolled by. A long rope was tied to the tailgate, and the Dwarves gripped it and trailed along behind as the party pushed on for the unseen pines somewhere below.

Cotton had lost all sense of time and place and direction, stumbling along through the white blindness and into the teeth of the screaming blizzard. He was wretchedly cold—freezing—and wanted nothing more than to be in front of a blazing fire at The Root, or no, not even that, just to be warm *anywhere* would be enough. Numbly Cotton looked at the whistling whiteness flinging past and was thankful he was with Bomar, for without the sturdy Dwarf, Cotton knew that he and the others would not know the way and would die among the frozen crags.

They had collected another squad of stragglers, this time with a green waggon, and were pressing on into the icy blast. Cotton and several of the Dwarves took turns driving the two waggons, working the brakes while others led. And Cotton was on the seat of the yellow waggon when he discovered that they had just come among a few sparse trees. "Hurrah!" he hoarsely shouted. "We've made it!" But the wind whipped away his words and shredded them asunder, the fragments to be lost in the vast whiteness, and no one heard him.

Grimly, Bomar pressed on, for they had two miles to go to reach the thick pines, and in the blasting white gale it took another hour. But at last they came to the sheltering forest: Bomar leading and Cotton up on the yellow wain with nineteen lost Dwarves holding onto a rope trailing behind followed by a green waggon.

As Bomar and Cotton and the tagtails emerged from the swirling snow, Durek, who had been standing in the eaves of the wood, stepped forward and directed them into one of the shielded glens where lean-tos were being constructed and many fires blazed. And as the stragglers passed, Durek smiled, for they were the last.

There among the trees the wind was not as fierce, for the thick pine boughs held it aloft and warded the Host. Still the snow swirled and flew within the glens and collected heavily on the branches; and so the fires were kindled out from under the limbs—otherwise, the heat would melt the snow to come crashing down.

Cotton drove the waggon to the place indicated and numbly crawled down to accept a hot cup of tea from Rand, who was waiting; and the shivering Warrow diddered, "W—well, we m—m—made it. The w—worst is over."

"Not yet, Cotton," replied Rand grimly, gauging the snowfall. "We must move on again as soon as possible, for to stay here will trap us in deep drifts."

Night was falling, but the need to press on was urgent. Durek called his Chief Captains together, and their tallies showed that thanks to Bomar and the other guides, miraculously no one had been lost, though three waggons had slid over the edge, pulling the doomed horses with them—yet the drivers had each managed to leap to safety. Thus, all were accounted for except Brytta's four advance scouts, of which there was no sign. It was hoped that the quartet of Valonian riders had forged ahead to the low country ere the blizzard struck; yet Brytta fretted, though nothing could be done to aid his missing Men.

The Host was exhausted, chilled to the bone, and so Durek decided that the Army would rest in the pines until the snowfall became deep enough to be worrisome—judged by Rand to be about four or five hours hence. The Chief Captains made plans for a risky lantern-lit trek through the blizzard, should the need to move onward become imperative.

But they had reckoned not upon the course of the storm, for it doubled its fury within the next half hour; and the driven snow thickened, and the blizzard could not be endured out of the shelter of the pines; and so the planned night march was abandoned.

Later that night a drained Cotton wearily leaned his head against a pine tree trunk as he sat on a carpet of fallen needles and stared through the low, sheltering boughs at the fluttering fire under the nearby lean-to. The wind moaned aloft, and the snow thickly eddied and swirled down. Tired though he was, anxiety gnawed at Cotton's vitals, for all he could think of was, *What if we're trapped here? What if we don't get to Dusk-Door on time? The twenty-fifth will come and go, and Mister Perry and the others will be trapped down in the Rück pits.*

Overhead, Waroo, the White Bear, raged and groaned and moaned and growled, and stalked about and clawed at the mountains and doubled his fury again.

CHAPTER 16

RIVER RIDE

Perry walked back into the campsite where the other members of the Squad were gathered. "Well, they've gone," he announced. "I stood and watched and could see them for three hours before the last waggon passed beyond my view on the flat prairie. Oh—I shall miss Cotton dearly, but we will meet again at the far door."

"Three hours?" questioned young Tobin Forgefire. "You watched them go away for all that time? Hmph! That was a long goodbye. In the caverns of Mineholt North—or in any Châkka cavern for that matter—goodbyes can last but a moment, for that is all it takes before the one who is leaving turns a corner or passes through a door and is lost to sight. On the other hand, hellos can last a goodly while, since those who are meeting can stand together and talk for as long as they wish. Hah! That is the way it should be: short goodbyes and long hellos."

Lord Kian looked up from the smooth bare ground in front of him. "Dwarves have the right idea when it comes to partings and meetings," he agreed. "You and I, Perry, can learn much from these Folk." Then Kian began scratching marks in the smooth earth with a short stick.

Perry watched for a while, puzzled, but just as he started to ask about it, Lord Kian called the Squad together. "When I was a lad in Dael," he began, smoothing over the loam, "often Rand and I would construct a raft out of tall, straight trees and float down the River Ironwater to the Inner Sea and visit the city of Rhondor." A faraway look came into Kian's eyes. "There we would sell the raft for a silver penny or two, for Rhondor is a city of fire-clay tile built on the coastal plain along the shores of the great bay, and wood is always in short supply and welcomed by the townspeople. And Rand and I would take our coins and tour that city of merchants, where the market-stalls had items of wonder from Pellar and Hurn and even faraway Hyree. Ah, but it was glorious, running from place to place, agonizing over what things of marvel to buy: pastries and strange fruit; trinkets and bangles and turtle-shell combs for Mother; curved knives and exotically feathered falcon hoods for Father; horns made of seashells; mysterious boxes—it was a place of endless fascination. After spending our money on the singled-out items, winnowed from the bedazzle, we would trek home to bestow the largess upon Mother and Father, and to think upon another raft."

Kian smiled in fond remembrance, but then sobered and drew with his stick in the smoothed earth. "This is the way of their construction," he said, and began outlining the procedure for building a raft, indicating that they would use white oak from the thick stand below the ford, where the trees grew tall and straight and had no limbs for more than half their length. The Dwarves listened intently, for though they were crafters all, they never before had constructed a raft.

The next morning, just after breakfast, using woodcutters' axes they had taken from one of the black waggons, Anval and Borin began felling the trees marked by Kian the day previous. The rest of the Squad trimmed and topped the fallen trees, then dragged the logs to a work site at the edge of the river. It took a full day of hard labor by each of the Seven to accomplish the task, and as dusk approached, Lord Kian called a halt to the work.

Wearily they returned to camp and ate a supper meal, then all bedded down except the guard. When Perry's turn at watch came, he made slow rounds and wondered if Cotton, too, was standing ward.

* * *

The following dawn, Perry groaned awake with sore arms, neck, back, and legs; hewing and hauling is hard labor, and once again the Warrow had called into play little-used muscles. The others smiled sympathetically at him and shook their heads in commiseration as he groaningly stumped toward the fire. Aching, he hunkered down next to the warmth and moved as little as possible to avoid additional twinges while he took his breakfast.

Over the course of the day, however, Perry worked out the soreness as under Kian's directions the Seven toiled to construct the bed of the raft from the felled trees: Perry was sent to fetch rope while the other six comrades hoisted up the long straight timbers and laid them side by side upon two, shorter, crossways logs. And as the wee buccan struggled to drag each of the large coils of thick line to the work site, Anval and Borin notched the logs so that a long, sturdy, young tree—trimmed of branches and cut to length by the other three—could be laid completely across the raft in a groove that went from log to log; three times they did this: at each end of the raft and across the center. At each end, Barak and Delk bound the logs to one another with the heavy rope; and as the two went they lashed each of the three cross-members to each long raft log in turn. In the meantime, Kian, Anval, and Borin used augers to drill holes through the cross-members and through the raft logs below, while Perry helped fashion wooden pegs that he and Tobin then drove with mallets into the auger holes to pin the structure together. This work took all of the second day to complete, and again the Squad wearily retired to the campsite.

The next morning dawned dull and overcast, and there was a chill wind blowing from the mountains. A rain of leaves whirled down, covering the woodland floor with a brown, crackling carpet. Glumly the Seven huddled around the campfire and breakfasted, each keeping an eye to the bleak sky for sign of cold rain.

That day began with the Squad constructing a platform in the center of the raft as a place to stow the supplies away from the water plashing upward, and they fashioned a simple lean-to as part of the platform in case of rain. To pole the raft, they cut and trimmed long saplings. Then they made two sculling sweeps, and crafted oarlocks, placing them at each end of the raft, fore and aft; the sweeps would be used to position the craft in the river current. Kian took time to instruct the others in the plying of these oars, as well as the poles.

Lord Kian and Perry went searching for boughs for the roof of the lean-to. Spying the color of evergreen through partially barren branches of the fall woodland, they climbed up a slope and emerged at last from the shelter of the trees to find themselves upon a clear knoll near a small stand of red pine. On the exposed hillock the chill wind from the mountains blew stronger, cutting sharply through their clothes. Lord Kian drew his cloak closely around himself and stared long over the forest and beyond the open grassland at the faraway peaks, the crests of which were shrouded by roiling white clouds under the higher overcast. "The White Bear stalks the mountains," he observed.

"Bear?" asked Perry, who had been half listening. "Did you just say something about a bear?"

"It is just an old tale told to children in Riamon," answered Kian, "about a white bear that brings cold wind and snow to the mountains."

"We have a legend like that in the Bosky," responded Perry, "except it isn't a bear, but a great white Wolf instead. The Wolf only comes with dire storms though, for that is the only time you can hear him howling outside the homes. The story may have come from the time of the Winter War, two hundred thirty-odd years ago—though as for me, I believe the tale is older than that. During the War, however, white Wolves came down from the north and pushed through the Spindlethorn Barrier and into the Boskydells. It was touch and go for many families, but the Gammer and others organized Wolf patrols—they went with bows and arrows and hunted the creatures, and finally the Wolves came to fear the sight of Warrows.

"But what about the bear? Does he, too, signal fierce weather? In the mountains? Oh, I hope the Army is down out of the high country." And thereafter Perry took to glancing often toward the mountains far to the west; he looked in that direction even after he and Kian returned to the raft site and the forest trees blocked the view.

The Squad laid log rollers down the bank from the raft to the river to launch the float, and they tied ropes to the craft to pull it over the rollers. By the time they had completed this work, night was drawing upon the land, but at last the raft was finished. "Tomorrow will be soon enough to load the supplies and launch our 'ship,'" announced Kian. "We've done enough for today. Let's bed down." And so the Seven returned to camp.

That evening there began a cold, thin drizzle, and though they stayed under the campsite lean-tos, the night became miserable for the comrades, and they got little rest.

The icy rain continued, and the next morning, as the Seven huddled under the shelters, Kian surveyed the group: "How many here can swim? None? None other than myself?"

"That should not surprise you, Prince Kian," grunted Barak, "for though there is water aplenty under the Mountains—pools and streams, and even lakes and rivers—we Châkka have no desire to plunge into the black depths merely for pleasure. Swimming is a sport of clear water and warm sunshine and open air, or it is a necessity for those who ply boats, but it is not an activity of stone delvers."

Borin nodded in agreement with Barak's words, then added, "Among the Châkka in this company, I deem that only Anval and I have ever spent much time on water, using the skills you taught us, Prince Kian, as you well know, to ply a boat on our journey to Pellar and back. Even so, we did not learn to swim."

Tobin lifted an eyebrow at Perry, and the Buccan responded: "As to Warrows, of the four strains, only the fen-dwelling Othen know much of boating and swimming—although some of the Siven strain, notably those living in Eastpoint, occasionally take up the sport. I was not one who did—as Lord Kian already knows."

"So be it," said the Man. "I was going to instruct you to leave off your mail, not only to take away its tiring burden, but also so that it would not weigh you down in the event you fall in. I think now not only will we forgo our armor, but also we will attach a safety line between each of us and the raft to haul us back aboard if we fall off.

"And now, since you have not ridden a raft before, remember, it is best if we do not all crowd together at times on one side or the other of the float, for it will tip; and although rafts seldom overturn—and do not sink as sometimes boats with heavy ballast or cargoes do—still it will be better if we keep the craft floating on the level." Kian stood. "Are there any questions?" he asked. "Then let us stow the cargo and armor and launch our raft, and be on our way."

They made several trips from the campsite to the float, loading their supplies and packs and armor onto the platform in the center of the craft, covering it all around with a waterproof canvas and lashing it in place. Finally, all was ready for the launching. Anval and Borin knocked the wedges from beneath the logs the raft was resting on, and with the other five pulling on the launching ropes, the massive craft slowly began rolling onto and over the hewed trunks laid down the bank; and the raft ponderously trundled down with gathering speed to enter the river with a great splash. It floated out, but was snubbed short by a mooring line cinched to a tree, and cumbrously it swung in the current back to the shore.

Lord Kian and Anval carried the two sweeps to the craft and set them in the oarlocks while the others took the raft poles aboard. Soon the Dwarves and Warrow had secured safety lines around their waists and were pronounced ready. With a last look around, Lord Kian untied the mooring line from the tree and ran down the bank and jumped aboard. Borin and Tobin and Delk poled away from shore, then Kian and Anval used the sweeps to pull the float into the swift current in midriver. Perry watched the shore slide by and knew that they were on their way at last.

The icy rain continued, and the raft riders sat on the supply tarpaulin, huddling under the on-board shelter, as the craft floated through the drizzle. Occasionally, two would use the sweeps to correct the raft's position in the current, but for the most part the oars were shipped aboard out of the water. The Squad travelled thusly all day, with little change except occasionally one or another would stand and stretch his legs.

The river continued to flow between bordering woods. In places, the trees were thickset but slender; at other places, old huge trees, set far apart, marched away to either side for as far as the eye could see; still elsewhere, the margins seemed to be nothing but dense thicketry. Most of the foliage had turned brown, and at times sudden gusts of wind caused the forest to shower down swirling, wet leaves; here and there all that was left behind were stark, barren branches clawing up toward the leaden skies. The Squad saw little animal life on the land, and only a few birds, mostly ravens.

That first day, the Seven floated for just over eight hours and covered nearly fifty miles, coming south from the ford to a point five miles above Great Isle. There they used the sweeps and poles to land on the west bank, where they tied up for the night.

Early the next day, ere dawn, the drizzle stopped and the wind died, and by midmorning the overcast was riven by great swaths of blue sky slashing overhead, and later on there were towering white clouds aloft, serenely moving to the east.

That day the raft drifted past Great Isle with its steep rocky banks and large gnarled trees of ancient age. The island was nearly twelve miles long, and it took two hours for the craft to float its length. At its northern end in ancient days there had been a fortress where guardians of the river dwelled. But they had been corrupted by the Evil One, and had begun marauding and harassing river trade, plundering merchants and pirating cargoes. Finally, the woodsmen of the Argon vales banded together to destroy the looters and lay the fortress to such great waste that nothing remains of it to this day—not even its name is remembered. Past this island the float drifted down the western side to come at last to the southern end, where the cloven river came together again.

Although the craft was large, still it was confining, and there was little to do. Even so, now that the raft was once more in midstream of the wide river and needed only minor corrections, Perry replaced Anval at the aft sweep. The Dwarves gathered in the center of the float just forward of the cargo, and fell to talking about the ways the Dusk-Door might be constructed; the red-bearded Gatemaster Barak did most of the talking while the others, including Anval and Borin, listened closely. The Dwarves sat up away from the lapping plash, each on a short section of log split in twain lengthwise and placed on the craft with the flat side up while the round side was down, trapped from rolling, lodged in the long clefts between raft logs. Thus

the Châkka sat and debated while the craft was borne south
by the River Argon.

Slowly the land changed, and the farther south they drifted,
the sparser became the woods that lined the shores, until late
in the afternoon they were floating between open plains with
only an occasional thicket or a willow or two to break the view.
They had come to the far northern reaches of the Dalgor March,
and they camped that evening in a thicket at the edge of that land.

The next day the raft floated down past the point where the
Dalgor River issued into the Great Argon River. The open Dalgor March had become more and more fenlike as they neared
the tributary, and a breeze blew rattling through the tall, waving
reeds, now brown with winter approaching. The sky was bright
and the day clear, and Perry looked on this area with interest. It
was here in this region that the Othen strain of the Wee Folk
had settled and later fled, for here it was that savage battles
were fought in the Great War with Gyphon, and heroes were
slain, and the Dawn Sword vanished. It was an area steeped in
the epic happenings of History, though now it was deserted of
all but the wild things.

The float continued on past the southern reaches of the Dalgor March, and the land became less marshy and began to rise
around them. Thickets began to reappear, and isolated large
trees too; and by evening the Seven were again drifting between river-valley woodlands.

All during the morning of the next day, the land gently rose
until it was well above the level of the river. The raft swept
downstream at an ever-increasing pace, for as the land had
risen, the watercourse had narrowed.

In the early afternoon the float approached a long, strait,
high-walled canyon known as the Race; and the closer the raft
drew to the gorge, the louder came the roar of crashing water
within. The Race was the narrowest point on the Argon below
Landover Road Ford, and the current was swift and strong; here
river traffic going north had to travel overland along the
portage-way on top of the eastern bluffs; but river traffic going
south needed only to stay in the rushing center of the river,
away from the jagged rocks at each side.

Lord Kian and Anval used the sweeps to position the rude craft as close to dead center as they could judge, and then shipped the oars on board. Kian shouted the command to "Hold fast!" and the raft plunged into the bellowing gap.

The uproar in the ravine shook Perry's small frame, for the river thundered between the high stone palisades, the deafening sound trapped betwixt the high walls to reverberate and roar and shout and rend the air with the thunder of water plunging apace along the ramparts, cresting and rolling and breaking over hidden barriers, smashing around great rocks to leap and fall crashing back only to drive into the next barrier and the next and the next. And amid the crests and troughs and rolling swells came the raft: out in midstream and turning slowly, beyond the control of the two sweeps.

Perry and the others tightly clung to the cargo frame as the craft pumped and smashed over roiling, roaring billows; and the cold river water crashed again and again up through the gaps between the logs to spray and drench them all with the icy splash.

Again and again the raft leapt up, to pause, and then to plummet back to the water; and Perry caught his breath each time the craft fell; he and the others were jolted and jarred each time the timbers smacked down; and once Perry was knocked to his knees, but he held on tightly with both hands and lifted himself up again before the next plummet. The turning, pitching float bucked and plunged downriver, racing toward a place where the canyon walls drew inward. As Perry saw the notch rapidly loom closer, he fleetingly pictured the cliffs pinching together to crush these insignificant intruders; but then they passed up a swell and through the constriction and slid down a long ramp into a deep trough, to spin and plummet onward.

Suddenly the walls began to diminish and recede as the land sloped downward and the watercourse grew wide. The thundering roar became a rumble, and the plunging crests smoothed to long, undulating rolls; and then they were back on the broad, smooth river curving between quiet, brown, riverborder woodlands, with the din just a faint, dying echo behind.

"Whew!" exclaimed Perry, his voice seeming unnaturally loud on the rewon stillness, "that was quite a wild ride. I could not hear my own thoughts back there, it was so deafening."

"Aye, Friend Perry," agreed Delk, "mayhap it is the loudest spot in the known Kingdoms." And he dug a little finger into one ear and yawned and swallowed to try to regain his full hearing.

"One would think so," said Kian, untying the canvas so that all could change into dry clothes, "but the river itself has a place of even more roar: it is Bellon, the great cataract to the south. Its voice shouts endlessly as it plunges down the Great Escarpment and into the Cauldron. It is a sound that not only assaults the ears but also thunders into your entire being to shake and rattle your very essence. Ah yes, the Race is thunderous—but Bellon is whelming."

Anval and Borin grunted their agreement, for twice within Ctor's shout they had walked the Over Stair, an ancient portage-way across the Great Escarpment to pass around Bellon. There, too—five miles to the west—could be seen the silvery Falls of Vanil, where the River Nith plummets down the Escarpment and into the Cauldron to join the mighty Argon.

Late in the afternoon Barak and Delk used the sweeps to bring the craft to the western shore, and the Squad made their final landing, for it was the sunset of the fourth day of travel, and they had come to the wold above Darda Galion. The Pitch, Dawn-Gate, Drimmen-deeve, all lay directly to the west: a march of five days would bring the Seven to the eastern entrance of Kraggen-cor.

CHAPTER 17

WARRIORS ON THE WOLD

That same evening, as the Squad sat around the campfire and took supper together, Kian announced, "Now comes the long wait: here we must tarry for six full days, and start west on the seventh, for we must pace our arrival to fit with Durek's plan. Once we start overland we will burn no more fires; but here in this uninhabited realm we are far north of the raiders' range; for as I have said before, the Yrm harass the people in the regions south of Darda Galion, down the Great Escarpment and beyond into the North Reach of Valon, and they strike southeastward at the river traffic along the Argon above and below Bellon Falls. Hence they come not into this empty region, and here we will wait.

"While we wait, we will lay our final plans, and study Perry's map, and think closely upon what we must do to aid our chances at success. For one thing, Perry, we must do something about that bright silver armor of yours—mayhap blacken it—so it will not shine like a lost gem in the *Spaunen* torchlight within the caverns of Drimmen-deeve."

Perry held up a silver-clad arm and turned it slowly and saw that it glittered in the firelight. "I simply could wear a long-sleeved jerkin over it," he suggested, seeing that something indeed had to be done to hide its glint. The Warrow stepped toward his belongings. "What about our faces? We should blacken them, too, else they'll show in the torchlight. Perhaps we should use charred wood—or mud, as Cotton and I did in the Wilderness Hills when we were 'Rūcks.' " Perry began rummaging through his pack.

"Châkka armor is already black iron," grunted Delk. "And we have with us the Châkka blackener for hands and face, and so our Squad need not use ashes or dirt. As to how to spend the next six days, I deem we need to discuss further the way the Dusken Door is perhaps made, for I have had some new thoughts concerning it."

"There," interrupted Perry, "how's this?" He had slipped a dark green shirt over his starsilver armor; it brought nods of approval from all the company, for no longer did he gleam like a minor beacon: the shimmering corselet was completely hidden.

"We must also select which of these things we mean to carry to the Dusken Door," said Tobin, waving a hand toward the pile of supplies. "What I would wish is that we carry only our axes to caress Squam necks. But, alas, we must eat, and drink, and work on the Door as well." Tobin's remark brought grim smiles of agreement from the other Dwarves.

The discussion continued as each proposed ways of using the six-day waiting period. They spoke of maps, and of making alternate plans for crossing the Great Deep should there be no Spawnish bridge for them to sneak over, and of the need to deal with sentries and patrols; those and many other topics were debated far into the night. Finally they all felt the need for sleep and so bedded down, except for the one to watch. They maintained the same order of guard duty that they had been using since the ford—Kian, Anval, Tobin, Perry, Barak, Borin, Delk—each in turn patrolling the perimeter, heeding Lord Kian's reminder to keep their eyes off the fire, the better to see into the dark.

That night, after Perry had awakened Barak for his turn, as was their custom they talked while the Warrow stoked the campblaze and the Dwarf stood looking into the night and sipped upon a cup of tea. Perry looked forward to these nighttime conversations with Barak, for the red-bearded Dwarf spoke intensely of many things not heretofore known to the Warrow. "Barak," asked Perry, "what do you plan to do after this is all over?"

"When it is over? Pah! Waeran, you know not these Squam. War with the Grg will never be over—not until the last of them

are slain or are driven from this world, from Mitheor," growled
Barak. The Dwarf held up a hand to forestall Perry's interruption. "Yet, Friend Perry, I *do* understand your question. As to
what I plan when we have driven the Squam from our homeland: I shall search out all the other doorways of Kraggen-cor
and discover each of their ways of working, and put them in
order."

"Other doorways?" asked Perry, puzzled. "What other doorways?"

"Hah! Kraggen-cor has many other doors, some hidden,
some plain. But it is the secret doors I would discover: there are
those within the caverns to hidden rooms; and those that issue
out, to the east, west, north, south, and points in between. There
are high doors and low doors, many openings onto the slopes of
the Quadran, onto the four great Mountains: Uchan, Ghatan,
Aggarath, and Rávenor. Heed: the Dusken Door and Daūn Gate
are not the only ways in and out, they are just the only *known*
ways; the others are lost. But once inside the caverns, the doors
can be found again: at what looks to be dead ends of passageways; under arches against blank walls; behind uncommon
slabs in chambers; and near special, secret marks.

"When found again, I aspire to divine their means of opening: Some doors open by keys, some by secret levers hidden behind intricate carvings or simple blocks; other doors are opened
by pressing special places on the stone. Some Châkka portals
are fashioned after the way of the Lian, an ancient Elf race of
Mastercrafters from whom we learned much; these doors usually are opened by Elven-made things, such as carven jewels
that fit in special crevices, or a glamoured key, a spellbound
blade, or an ensorcelled ring; or they are opened by speaking
the correct word or phrase, such as is the fashion of the Dusken
Door.

"As to why I seek these hidden doors . . . Hai! It is to discover what they conceal! Some doors lead to secret treasure
rooms, or secret weapons rooms, or secret hideaways. My
heart hammers to think of these doors, for they will open into
chambers that contain things hidden away for hundreds, even
thousands of years. Yet such rooms must be entered with caution, for once inside, the door may close and vanish, trapping
the unwary in a sealed vault—it is a defence against looters

and other evil beings. Yet all delved chambers have ways in and ways out, if you can find the secrets of the doors and have the keys. The trick is first to find where each portal might be and then to divine the means required to open it. Without the key, even a Wizard or an evil Vûlk cannot pass through some hidden doors.

"Aye, Perry, I shall search out the lost portals of Kraggen-cor. And when I locate them and deduce the ways of their opening, I shall pass through those doors and tread where no Châk has trod for centuries . . . and I shall *discover.*" Barak paused, staring out into the darkness beyond the campblaze, lost in thought. After a moment he roused himself as Perry threw another log on the dying fire. "That is my dream. What is yours?"

"Mine? My dream? Well now, I haven't thought of what I'll do. Go back to my studies at The Root, I suppose. Or maybe write this adventure up as another chapter to be added to the *Raven Book,* since our tale does have its roots in the War and all." Perry sighed. "Of course, it seems to me that all we've done is wait, and then we rush to some other place just to wait again. I mean, well, it isn't much of an adventure that has its principal characters just sitting around waiting for something to happen."

Barak momentarily turned away from his vigil of the dark beyond the limits of the firelight and looked hard into Perry's jewel-like, sapphirine eyes. "I would that this were all the action any of us *ever* sees," he said sharply. "That Kraggen-cor were totally deserted would be best for us all. But we know that is not so. Let us next hope that the Squam are few and the fighting short."

Perry was taken aback by the sudden intensity of Barak's manner, but he did not know what caused it or what to say. After a while he said good night and went to his bedroll. He lay and watched the stars, and just before he drifted off he saw one fall, and then another, and then two more. *How can such a wondrous thing be the awful portent to the Dwarves that it is?* he mused drowsily. *Falling stars always seem to come this time of year. And besides, when two or more strangers far, far apart see the same falling star, for which is it meant? And what about when a star falls which no one sees? I must ask Borin about this; it seems that* . . . But Perry fell asleep before he could complete his thought.

Morning came, and Perry awakened late. But he was not alone in his slugabed manners: the only ones up and about were Delk and Lord Kian, who had decided that there was no need to disturb the others since no journey or immediate project was at hand. Perry arose and took breakfast and watched as one by one the others awakened and joined the circle around the fire.

That day they considered several of the courses of action they had spoken of last night: The Dwarves continued to debate the manner of the Dusk-Door. Ways of crossing the Great Deep were discussed. Methods of dealing with sentries and patrols were explored. The map was studied by all. That night again they slept and stood guard in turn.

Resting and discussing: that was the pattern the Seven followed for two days. On the third full day at the campsite a wind blew up from the south, and it rained; little was done that day. The next two days were spent as before. And as the plans materialized, the comrades began to select from among the supplies those things that they would need: The only food they would take was crue, a waybread prepared by bakers throughout Mithgar, though that which the Seven took was oven-made in Mincholt North; each of the tough, easy-to-carry, nutritious biscuits would sustain a traveller over many hours, the single disadvantage being that the waybread was relatively tasteless. In addition to the crue, each of the Squad members would carry a leather water bottle, to be filled from streams along the way. Barak selected tools for the Dusk-Door. And the Squad chose miscellaneous all-purpose items, such as rope, to add to the packs. Each of the comrades took up one of the small, hooded Dwarf-lanterns; these were finely wrought of metal and crystal, and glowed with a soft blue-green light; the hood could be adjusted to allow no light, or a tiny gleam, or a widespread lambent glow, or any level in between; Perry could not divine the way of their working, for no fire needed to be kindled and no fuel seemed consumed. Slowly the Squad came to decide upon their final plans, to lay out alternative courses of action, and to select needed items. Thus passed five days in the campsite on the edge of the wold.

The night of the fifth day came with a chill cold; it was the eventide of the fifteenth of November, and winter was at hand. The Squad would start for Dawn-Gate on the morning of the seventeenth, but for now they slept around a fire built higher to press back the bite; they would lose this luxury when they started for Drimmen-deeve.

Tobin had awakened Perry to stand his turn at guard. They spoke briefly, and then the Dwarf went to his bedroll as the Warrow cast two more logs on the fire. It blazed up and cracked and popped a few times and then settled back. Perry stood and began to pace his rounds out on the perimeter.

He had walked slowly around the camp several times when he heard another *pop!* and thought, *The fire . . . but no! Wait! That sound came from the darkness!* And he stared into the deep blackness in the direction of the noise. *Snap!* Perry's head jerked toward the point of the crack. *There! Another sound!* He unsheathed Bane, *and a blue fire was streaming from the blade-jewel and running along the sword's bitter edges!*

Perry stared dumbly at the cobalt flame a moment, his wit having fled him, and then he shouted with all the force he could muster, "Spawn! Awake! The Spawn foe is—" But at the same moment, with a great cry of snarls and grating shouts, a howling, Hlōk-led force of Rūcks crashed into the camp, iron cudgels flailing, curved scimitars swinging.

Perry was overborne in the charge, knocked sprawling backwards into the campsite, Bane flying from his grip to land in the dirt near the fire. The Dwarves started up at Perry's cry, hands instinctively grasping for axes. Lord Kian leapt forward with sword in hand to slash at the forefront and blunt the hoarse charge just enough for the Dwarves to orient themselves to the rush.

Perry was stepped on and kicked by scuffling feet. He crawled and scuttled for Bane, but was smashed to the ground by a falling dead Rūck. He could not reach his blade, and several of the enemy swooped toward him. At the last moment, red-bearded Barak leapt to his defense and swung his bloody axe, mortally cleaving two of the Squam.

Lord Kian slashed his sword in a wide, two-handed arc and gutted another of the foe. Tobin and Delk stood back to back, both bleeding from wounds, but their deadly axes lashed out as they swung at and chopped and slew the archenemy. And Anval and Borin, those mighty warriors, venting oaths and howling War cries, smashed aside cudgels and scimitars alike and sundered Grg with every swing. But the Rūck numbers were many and the Squad but seven strong, and it would be only a matter of moments till the comrades would be overwhelmed.

Perry was still on the ground amid dead Spawn, grasping in the dirt for Bane; and Barak, above him, fought for both of their lives.

The Hlōk leader jumped forward with his curved scimitar slashing, and Barak engaged the larger foe. There was a clanging of axe on blade, and Perry was kicked aside. The Warrow glanced up and saw that Barak was pressing the Hlōk back; yet a Rūck from behind smashed a long iron cudgel into the Dwarf's skull, and Barak fell. The Hlōk leapt over Barak's still form and grabbed Perry by the front of his tunic, jerking him up off the ground, feet flailing and kicking. And with a slobbering, leering laugh, the huge Hlōk drew back his scimitar, preparing to backhandedly lop off the Warrow's head.

Just then a loud, venomous oath barked from the dimness beyond the firelight: *"Hai, Rûpt!"* At this cry the Hlōk's head snapped up, and with fear in his eyes he looked frantically into the gloom for the source of the challenge, the Warrow dangling from his grip momentarily forgotten.

At the moment the Rūcken leader jerked up to see—*Sssthok!*—an arrow hissed out of the blackness and struck the creature between the eyes, the shaft seeming to spring full-grown from his forehead as it crashed into his brain. Black blood splattered Perry full in the face, and the Hlōk pitched over backwards, dead before he hit the earth, his hairy fist still locked onto Perry's jerkin. With a *whoof!* Perry smashed into the Hlōk's chest as they struck the ground, and his face was pressed against the foul, scratchy jaw of the dead Rūck leader. Hammered by panic, Perry jerked and twisted, lunging backwards, wrenching sideways, frantic to be free of this dead thing that held him clenched in its final grip. Tearing loose at last, he rolled away and sprang to his feet, his breath whistling in and out of his constricted throat; and he stared in horror at the dead Hlōk, for its feet were spasmodically drumming the ground.

"Down, Waerling!" came a cry from the night. *"Down, fool! You block my arrow shot!"*

Perry did not even hear the warning cry, for he was frozen in horror, his eyes locked upon the dead but jerking Hlōk, and he was unable to tear his gaze away. He did not see the Rūck behind racing toward his unprotected back, spiked iron cudgel upraised to crash through Perry's skull. But then in that instant a huge, bearlike Man silently hurtled out of the writhing shadows beyond the guttering firelight, and a massive forearm smashed Perry aside, while at the same time the Man swung a great, black mace overhand and with a looping blow crushed the Rūck like a bloated spider under heel.

Perry again had been knocked to the ground, but this time his hand fell near the hilt of Bane, cobalt flames blazing forth from the blade-jewel and down the fiery edge. He grasped the weapon and looked up. Straight ahead, Tobin and a Rūck with an iron War-hammer were locked in furious battle. Tobin stumbled backward over the corpse of a fallen foe, and the Rūck swung at the off-balance Dwarf. Though falling, Tobin warded with his axe, and the great hammer struck the blade with a *clang!* But the sledge was only deflected, and it cracked into the Dwarf's leg, and Tobin fell with a cry. The Rūck drew back his mallet for the final blow, but instead screamed in agony, blood bursting forth from his throat as he tumbled forward—for Perry had leapt up and plunged Bane into the Rūck's back.

"'Ware, Waldan!" the huge Man shouted, and Perry turned in time to see another Rūck leaping on bandy legs at him; and without thinking, Perry lunged full-length under the other's guard to pierce him through. As the dead Rūck fell, another took his place. Perry stared across Bane's blue flame into the swart, snarling face and glaring, viperous, yellow eyes of the enemy; and the Warrow attacked with a running flèche. Perry's backhanded slash hewed the foe across his free hand, shearing off the knobby thumb and first two fingers. The Rūck screamed, and threw his scimitar at Perry, and ran off shrieking, only to be hewn down in passing by Anval.

Arrows flew from the darkness, hissing into the campsite to fell Rūck after Rūck, and the huge stranger crushed the foe with his great black mace. Kian, Anval, Borin, and Delk still stood and clove Squam with sword and axes, and now at last Perry, too, with blue-flamed Bane slashed and felled the enemy. Even so, the battle would have gone to the Rūcks, for there were too many of them; but at that moment, with cries of *Hai, Rucha!* a new force of green-clad warriors with bright long-knives and glimmering swords charged out of the night to beset the maggot-folk. There ensued a fierce, short skirmish, and with wails of dismay the Rūcks were routed, their new assailants and the huge Man with the black mace in deadly pursuit.

As the din and cry of battle receded, Perry ran to Tobin's side and dragged the dead Rūck from the Dwarf's chest. Tobin was barely conscious and covered with gore, most of it foe's blood. He was in agony, and his leg was twisted at an odd angle: the hammer had broken it above the knee. Perry was joined over Tobin's form by a bow-carrying, green-clad warrior who directed, "Move him not until I can splint the leg." And before Perry could say aught, the warrior vanished into the dark, returning shortly with cut saplings.

Lord Kian and Delk joined them, and under the stranger's guidance they examined Tobin's leg to see if the bone had pierced through to cause bleeding; it had not, and so the leg was pulled straight and bound in splints. "We must get him across the river to my people in Darda Erynian," said the newcomer, "for his own thews will soon twist the bone out of line again unless it is given constant pull using rope and weight."

Tobin looked up at the stranger and gritted through his pain, "You and your companions saved our lives, and now you treat my injury. For that I am grateful, and I thank you for us all. I am called Tobin Forgefire. May I have your name, good Elf?"

Elf? Perry looked at this warrior in amazement. He saw before him what looked to be a lean-limbed youth with golden hair cropped at the shoulder and tied back with a simple leather headband. He had a fair face with grey eyes atilt, and his ears were pointed like those of Warrows. His hands were long and slender and deft. He carried a bow and an empty quiver, having spent all his arrows killing *Spaunen*. He was clad in green and wore a golden belt which held a long-knife. His feet were shod in soft leather. His slim height fell short of Lord Kian's by a hand.

"I am called Shannon by some in Darda Erynian, and Silverleaf by Men, though my Elden-name is Vanidar," replied the Elf softly. "Now rest, Drimm Tobin. Your strength is needed, for you have ahead of you a journey of several days to reach a place of peace and healing." And he placed his hand on the Dwarf's forehead, and *lo!* Tobin closed his eyes and fell into a deep sleep.

"Barak!" cried Perry, suddenly remembering, and he turned toward where the red-bearded Gatemaster had fallen. But he saw a sight that filled him with dread: Anval and Borin were standing above the Dwarf's still form with their hoods cast over their heads. Barak was dead, his skull crushed by the Rūck cudgel while he fought, defending the fallen Warrow.

That night Kian, Anval, Borin, Delk, and Perry washed the blood from themselves and treated their wounds, taking extra care that the cuts they had taken, though slight, were clean—for Spawn often poison their blades, and death could befall a warrior days after taking but a minor hurt from one of these evil edges. Afterward, Kian and Shannon spoke together softly, while Perry sat alone and stared numbly into the darkness.

As the next day was dawning, the force of green-clad Elves and the bearlike Man returned and quietly spoke with Shannon. Then, while the Elven company dragged the dead foe out into the sunlight where Adon's Ban turned the corpses into dust, Shannon came forward with the big Man, and the two sat down with the Dwarves and Kian and Perry. "This is Ursor, the Baeran," said Silverleaf. "He has deep grievance against the *Rûpt.*"

Ursor was a giant of a Man, almost two hands taller than Lord Kian. He had brown hair with a reddish cast, but it was lighter colored on the tips, giving it a silvery, grizzled appearance; his full, close-cropped beard was the same grizzled brown; and his eyes were a dark amber. He was dressed in deep umber with a dark brown boiled-leather breastplate. At his side depended the great black mace. "There were no survivors among the Wrg raiders," Ursor grunted fiercely, striking a fist into an open palm.

Shannon looked into the drawn faces of each member of the

Squad. Then the Elf spoke: "We had been tracking, pursuing, that band for four nights from the glens below the River Nith in Darda Galion. Without knowing, we drove them toward your party, and that I regret, for I grieve with you in your loss. An hour before the battle, we had lost them, and they would have escaped, except they unwisely chose to assault your seemingly defenseless group. We were spread wide, searching, when we each heard the clamor of combat and came. I was nearest and arrived first, with Ursor coming shortly after. Then the rest of my force arrived."

"In the nick of time for most of us," said Kian softly, "but too late for Barak." And they regarded the Dwarf's still form, now enfolded in a blanket.

"You must tend to him, for he fought bravely and deserves a hero's burial," said Shannon.

"Stone or fire," came Anval's gruff voice from within his hood. "He must be laid to rest in stone, or be placed on a fitting pyre. Nought else will serve. It is the way of the Châkka."

And so Anval carried Barak Hammerhand to the raft, while Borin and Delk followed. And they laid the slain warrior to rest on the central platform on a soft bed of pine boughs. And they washed the blood from him, and combed his hair and beard, and placed his helm upon his head. At his side they placed his axe, and they crossed his hands upon his breast. The weapons of the fallen Squam were laid at his feet, and more pine boughs were heaped all around him. And then Anval and Borin and Delk stood near him and spoke in the hidden tongue, while the company of Elves stood upon the shore and looked on in sorrow. Ursor and Kian had borne wounded Tobin on a litter to the shore, and he, too, spoke the words in unison with his brethren. And Perry took Barak's hand in his own and bowed his head and wept. "Oh, Barak," he cried, "you fought to save me, and now you will never get to pursue your dream and search out the hidden doors of Kraggen-cor."

Then Lord Kian stripped to his breeks and stepped on board with a flaming brand in hand. Perry was led weeping from the craft by Delk and Anval and Borin, and Shannon cast loose the mooring line, Kian poled a short way to the edge of the swift current, and set the pine boughs ablaze; and he dived into the river and swam back to shore, where he was wrapped in a blanket.

The flaming craft was caught in the wide current and slowly borne away as all the company and Squad watched, and many wept. Shannon Silverleaf stepped to the water's edge and sang, his clear voice rising unto the sky:

> *"From mountain snows of its birth*
> *The River runs down toward the Deep,*
> *Now added to by clear cold rain*
> *That flows by stream from lush green land,*
> *To rush at last into the Sea,*
> *Great Mother of the rains that fall*
> *And snows upon the mountains high,*
> *Take our Brother into your arms*
> *And cradle him in final sleep."*

The flames blazed up furiously as the burning raft swept somberly around a bend, the pyre gradually disappearing from view. But still the smoke rising above the bordering trees marked its passage, until at last that, too, was gone.

Later that morning, as planned by Lord Kian and Shannon Silverleaf ere dawn, the company of Elves set off to the south, bearing Tobin's litter. As they were leaving, Tobin rose up on his elbows and gritted through his pain to Kian: "Go on. Complete the mission. King Durek needs you." And he fell back in a swoon and was borne away. The Elves were just a short march from a hidden cache of Elven-boats; they would ply them down the river and to the other side, taking Tobin with them to a place of refuge in Darda Erynian, near the ruins of Caer Lindor. But Shannon and giant Ursor remained behind: Kian had asked that they sit in council with the Squad.

The small assembly gathered around the fire, and Kian told the Elf and the Baeran of the mission to Kraggen-cor. Durek's Army, the Brega Path, the Dusk-Door, the Squad's mission: Kian spoke of it all; and the Sun rose high during his words. And when he was finished with the telling, he spoke of that which now troubled him: "This is our dilemma," Kian declared. "We have lost two of our Gatemasters to the ill fortunes of War;

only one, Delk, remains, where we started with three. Yet, at the Council of Durek, it was said that two were needed to work on the Door; and though two are needed, we have but one. I now seek counsel on how to proceed."

Delk responded, his voice a low growl: "Tobin spoke my mind: we must go on with our mission, for King Durek needs our aid. Grievous is the loss of Barak . . . and Tobin too; yet still we must try to succeed. Heed me: Anval and Borin have both taken part in the debates of how the Dusken Door may be repaired. They are both Mastercrafters, and though their skill has not heretofore been used on gates, still their aptness when joined with mine will be considerable. We *must* try to repair the Door! We *must* go on!"

"But then," growled Borin, "who will defend the way? Who will mislead the Squam if we are discovered? That was the charge Anval and I accepted from Durek when we joined the Squad."

"Regardless as to what your duty was then," responded Delk, "our larger responsibility is to get to the Door and repair it so that Durek can lead the Army through."

"I can mislead the Yrm," interjected Kian. "Once we reach the Deeves, my task as guide is ended and Perry's begins. I had always planned on becoming a decoy, or holding the way with Anval and Borin as it became necessary; but now if we are discovered, I will mislead the *Spaunen* alone."

Shannon glanced up at Ursor, who nodded in unspoken agreement. "What of us?" asked the Elf. "We are indirectly responsible for your predicament. Had we not driven the *Rûpt* north, they would not have fallen upon your band. King Durek's plan is sound, yet it is a plan weakened by your unexpected losses here on the banks of the Argon. Hence, let the two of us—a Baeron and an Elf—go with you to act as warrior escort, to hold the way in time of need, for in this we have a debt and an obligation and a duty."

Ursor looked at Lord Kian. "Durek's mission, Sire, must succeed," rumbled the giant, and his hand went to his mace, "for with this one blow the Wrg will be crushed from the Black Hole forever."

Lord Kian nodded and glanced around the circle, receiving nods of assent from each of the others. "So be it!" he declared.

"Once we were seven strong, and so we are again. And though we cannot replace Barak or Tobin, still we can complete our mission."

He stood and bade them all, "Let us now break our fast, and then speak of that which we have planned, for tomorrow we start for Kraggen-cor, and our new companions must be prepared."

Perry spoke little that day. He had said nothing at council, and later responded only to questions put directly to him. And he did not seem to want to be with the others, preferring instead to sit alone on a log down by the river near the point where Barak's funeral barge had been cast free. At the campsite Shannon glanced away toward the water's edge and the Warrow, and Lord Kian quietly said, "It is his first brush with War. He is numb with the realization of what killing and slaughter and battle are truly like. But there is a sturdy spirit inside of him. I think that he and his gentle people are capable of withstanding much and contributing greatly in times of terror and distress. He will soon come to grips with his pain, and will emerge whole and sound from this shell he is in."

Later the Elf went to the riverside to cleanse the smùt from the arrows retrieved from the dead Rück bodies. He squatted at the shore a step or two away from the Warrow and laved the shafts.

"It was so confused," said Perry without preamble. "Nothing was as the tales and songs would have you believe. There were no long duels of sword-play or axe wielding. There were no glorious stands where one lone hero held an army of villains at bay with his flashing weaponry to emerge victorious over all. There were only sudden rushes and quick, grim slaughter, only slashing and hacking and friends being maimed; hurtling bodies, shoving, grunting, wild swinging and stumbling, and people falling down and being trampled . . . and Death." Perry buried his face in his hands only to see Hlōk heels drumming against the ground.

Shannon Silverleaf gazed with softness upon the weeping Waerling. "War is never glorious," quietly said the Elf. "Nay, glory has no part in it. Instead, it is a tedious, chaotic, repugnant chore: It is tedious because most of the time warriors are waiting for something to happen, or are days on the march, or are encamped and unengaged. It is chaotic, for during combat there is only slaying and struggle and confusion. And it is repugnant because the killing even of *Spaunen* and other fell creatures in time of battle is still the slaughter of living beings. Yes, War against the *Rûpt* is abhorrent, but think how much more hideous it would be if it were Waerling against Waerling, or Man against Man. In this be grateful you are fighting a real and present evil that must be destroyed—for there have been times when the only evil was in the minds of the opposing leaders of innocent, trusting followers." Shannon, his task completed, stood and turned to the buccan. "Master Perry, all War is terrible—even those that are Just—but though terrible and horrifying, this War must be fought and the foul wickedness in Black Drimmen-deeve eliminated, for to do anything less will allow the vileness to fester and grow and wreak more death upon the defenseless." Shannon touched his hand to that of the Waerling, and then turned and walked away; and with brimming eyes, Perry watched him go.

That night Perry sat on sentry duty, staring without seeing into the darkness beyond the campsite; Bane had been drawn and was at hand, embedded in a log, sticking upright: a silent sentinel whose blue flame would blaze if Rück or other Spawn came near, now shining with nought but reflected firelight.

Huge Ursor came and eased his bulk down to sit beside the Warrow. In silence they watched the night flow by. Finally Perry spoke: "All the time I was making my copy of *The Raven Book,* my mind was filled with the sweep of glorious battles and visions of heroic deeds against dark forces. I thought, 'Oh, wouldn't it be wonderful if I, too, could be caught up in such an adventure.' Well now I am in a like venture, and the reality of it is nearly more than I can bear.

"I did not stop to think that a great battle is nothing more than large-scale butchery. But even in battle what it really boils down to is that someone with a weapon is trying to slash, hack, smash, or pierce someone else while at the same time trying to keep from being maimed or killed in return. And the incredible thing is that though the battle involves entire armies, each fight is just one against one, one against one a thousand or ten thousand times over: thousands of desperate pairs locked in combat. And in each pair one will fall and the other one will go on to find another and do it all over again until it is ended.

"I never thought of it being that way. I never thought that someone I could see and hear and smell and touch would be trying to kill me, striving to snuff out my life, while I would be struggling to kill him in return." Perry's eyes widened in remembered horror and filled with tears, and he stared down unseeing at a point within the earth as remote as the stars, and his voice rose and trembled in distress. "But that's the way it really is: the enemy right there in front of you, face to face, grunting, sweating, straining, gasping for breath, trying to break your guard, and trying to keep from being hurt. It doesn't really matter whether you're in a battle, or in a skirmish, or are all alone when you meet your foe, it's all the same: just one against one. Even if you are outnumbered, still each is fleetingly met one at a time.

"And none of my visions included staring across a sword blade directly into the eyes of an enemy. I always dreamed that battle would be clean and heroic and remote; but I've found that it is anything but heroic: the first Rūck I slew, I stabbed him in the back—that's how noble it is. It isn't pure and gallant and distant at all; instead, it is dirty and desperate and suffocatingly close.

"And I'm frightened. I know nothing of weaponry. This company needs warriors, not dreamers and scholars. I don't belong here: I belong back at The Root or at the Cliffs locked away someplace among books, tediously copying ancient tomes. My Scholar's dream was to go awarring—to be a hero— but in reality I am only a frightened Scribe.

"I am a terrible, worthless liability to this company. Barak died because of me. He tried to save me, and instead he is dead." Perry began to weep silently, his mind filled with chaotic visions of the desperate stand that red-bearded Barak had made above him while he scuffled ineffectually in the dirt below, and how Barak had finally fallen, crushed from behind by a Rūck cudgel.

Giant Ursor shifted his weight on the log where he sat. "You are right, Waldan," he rumbled, "and you are wrong. You are right in your assessment of the reality of battle. You are wrong in the valuation of your worth. You are a warrior, for you slew a foe who was about to slay a companion. And though overwhelmed, you engaged the enemy when you gained your feet, with weapon in hand, until the enemy was routed. In your fear and revulsion, you are no different from any other warrior. Yet I believe if you think on it, you will find you suffered no fear during each engagement, only afterward; for while locked in a duel there is only time to act and to react and no time to quail.

"As to your worth to the company: the mission cannot go on without you; if others fall, it will go on, but not if you fall. Only you can guide this group through the caverns; only you can deliver a Crafter to the Dusk-Door. Barak knew this. Of all those beset, he chose to fight by your side, for not only were you his friend, you are also the hope of this mission.

"And this mission *must* succeed, for the growing evil in the Black Hole must be *crushed*"—Ursor's great hands made grasping, strangling motions, and his voice gritted out between clenched teeth—"for they slay the innocent and unprotected. My bride of two summers, Grael, and my newborn . . ." but Ursor could say no more, and he stood and stalked to the edge of the darkness.

Wiping his eyes on his sleeve, Perry watched the big Man walk to the distant limit of the light and halt. At last the buccan knew why the giant was at war with the Spawn; and Perry was crushed with the knowledge of the other's pain, the Warrow's own anguish diminished in the light of the Baeran's grief. "Ursor," he called, "I'm so sorry. I didn't know . . ." Perry fell silent, his thoughts awhirl. How long he sat thus, he did not know.

Finally the buccan rose and took up Bane—for he was still on guard—and walked to the side of his newfound friend, not knowing what to say, his heart reaching out to Ursor. Long the Warrow stood in silence beside the Man, peering out into the darkness at the vague black shapes of barren trees sleeping in the early-winter night. Then at last Perry spoke, his voice falling softly in the quiet: "Ursor, I feel your pain, and I grieve with you. But I do not know . . ." Again Perry lapsed into silence.

After a moment Ursor placed a huge hand on Perry's small shoulder. "It is enough, Wee One. It is enough."

Again they stood quietly and looked out upon the night. Then once more Perry spoke, and firm resolve filled his voice: "You are right, Ursor, you are right about everything. The evil in Drimmen-deeve must be crushed—and our mission will see to that." The Warrow looked grimly to the west, as if willing his sight to fly far overland and pierce the darkness and see deep into the heart of the Black Deeves. "Tomorrow we start the final leg to Kraggen-cor, and beginnings are often times of oath-takings and predictions. Yet I'll not make a prediction, though I do have something to say. I said it once before when I knew nothing, but now I say it again: Beware, maggot-folk."

CHAPTER 18

SNOWBOUND

Cotton thrust his head from beneath the squat, snow-covered shelter and out into the howling grey morning. Still the blizzard moaned up the mountain slopes and toward the Crestan Pass, and the driven snow hid all but the nearby view. The Warrow peered but could see no movement of anyone, and there was little sign of the Host; only three other shelters were visible to him—small mounds in the snow.

Last night, when the storm had worsened and the cold had become cruelly bitter, Durek had issued the order for warriors to pair up and spread out and gather pine boughs to make shelters. The entire Army of four thousand had then moved into the forest in couplets to collect the branches, to return and construct the tiny bowers—a form of snow refuge known to those who dwell on and within the mountains. Bomar had selected Cotton as his shelter-mate simply by grunting, "Come with me"; and they had taken up a lantern and some rope and had moved out through the drifts and into the woods.

When Cotton had glimpsed through the flying snow that the Army was spreading out and separating during a blizzard, the buccan had protested: "Bomar, this is madness!" he had cried above the shrieking wind. "We'll all be lost in the storm; the Army will be destroyed, split apart. We'll never find the others again—and they won't ever find us, neither."

"Remember, Friend Cotton," Bomar had shouted back, "you are with Châkka, and although we often do not know where we are going, we always know exactly where we have been—even in a blizzard at night." And Cotton and Bomar had waded onward through the swirling, moaning wind and knee-deep snow.

They had cut boughs, and lashed them together using the rope; they had dragged the bundle like a sledge back to the glen; and Bomar had made their shelter: First he had fashioned a frame of bent branches, and had pegged it to the ground with iron spikes he called "rock-nails." Then he had lashed boughs thickly to the frame, so close that when he and Cotton had piled snow on, none sifted through the matting.

Then the two had crawled inside, and there was just enough room for both of them. They had thus spent the night in snug warmth.

And now it was morning, and still the blizzard enveloped them. "What's going to happen now, Bomar?" asked Cotton as he pulled his head back into the bower.

Bomar reached for the lantern filling the refuge with a blue-green radiance, and dropped the hood so that the glow was extinguished; and grey morning light filtered down through the flying snow and into the shelter opening. "Nothing," he rumbled. "We do nothing till the storm abates."

"I wonder when that will be," fretted Cotton in the dimness. "I mean, well, I don't know much about blizzards—especially mountain blizzards. In the Bosky we seldom get real mean snowstorms. Why, let me see, there's only been one bad storm that I can remember; only once has the White Wolf howled around Hollow End and The Root since I've been there. And it lasted for two days, and it put almost two foot of snow on the ground. But I hear mountain blizzards can last for weeks. . . .

"Oh, Bomar, I don't know why I'm nattering on about that. What I'm really afraid of is that we're going to get caught here, and we won't reach the Dusk-Door in time for Mister Perry, and they'll be trapped in that black puzzle with all the Rūcks and Hlōks and Ogru-Trolls after them—"

"Hush, Waeran," growled Bomar. "It does no good to a warrior's heart to think of his comrades in need of aid when that aid cannot be given. We have no choice but to wait for the blizzard to slacken. We cannot go on, for I have seen this kind of storm before: here in the protection of the thick forest it is not too severe; but out in the open the snow fills the air with whiteness—

nothing can be seen more than a yard or two distant. And the cold wind is a terrible enemy: it sucks the heat away with its icy blast, and an animal will fall in midstride, to freeze in moments. We cannot go forth into that. We must wait."

"Animals? Freeze? What about Brownie and Downy?" asked Cotton anxiously. "For that matter, what about *all* the horses? Are they going to drop in their tracks and freeze? We can't let that happen! We've got to do something!" And Cotton started to crawl out, but was stopped by Bomar.

"Hold, Cotton!" demanded the Dwarf, gripping the Warrow by the shoulder. "The horses are all right. Aye, they are chilled, but they are not freezing. Only in the open blast would they be in danger; but here in the pines they are well protected from the wind."

"Well let's go see anyway," insisted Cotton. "My legs need the stretch."

Bomar saw how concerned the buccan was; and with a shrug of his shoulders he pulled his hood up snug, motioning the Waeran to do likewise. They crawled from the shelter and struck out for the pen where Brownie and Downy were held, Bomar leading the way.

The snow came to Cotton's midthigh, though in places the drifts were deeper, but the sturdy Dwarf broke the path, and the smaller Warrow followed in his wake. They struggled through the swirling white, stopping frequently to rest, while the wind moaned aloft in the treetops. A blinding sheet of whiteness raced by overhead on its flight to the mountain crests, and only a portion of the howling fling fell swirling through the boughs to coldly blanket the forest below. But even the small part that came down was enough to curb vision and pile snow deeply, to be driven into larger drifts.

At last Cotton and Bomar reached a thick grove of low pines; a large group of horses stood huddled within its protection where the snow was less deep and the wind did not cut. The animals seemed glad to see the two; and eagerly they pressed forward for a smell and a look, for they had seen no person since the previous night, when each had been fed a small portion of grain and then had been driven with the others to cluster in the simple rope pens among the thick, low, sheltering pines near the encampment glens.

Cotton and Bomar spent a good while walking among the animals, patting their flanks and rubbing their necks and muzzles. Though they spoke to the horses, the wind drowned out their words; but their very presence seemed to reassure the steeds that all was well. Cotton finally located Downy and later Brownie, and they each nuzzled him; and thus Cotton, too, felt assured that the horses were faring well.

The Warrow and Dwarf had worked their way through the herd when Cotton leaned over and called above the wind moan, "What we need is a hot cup of tea, but we'll never get one in this storm."

Bomar snorted and declared, "Come with me; we will go make some."

Breasting the snow, they toiled back to the glen, where they located a black waggon; from it they took a small-forge and a supply of black firecoke, and carried it to the lean-to beside their yellow waggon. Shortly they had a hot blaze going in the forge, and they melted snow in the large kettle to brew the tea. Leaving Cotton to tend the pot and make the drink, Bomar trudged out into the swirl and located other shelters and invited those within to join them. Soon Dwarves straggled to the fire, and Cotton served hot tea to go with their crue biscuits.

Thus the Warrow and Bomar passed the day—tending the kettle on the forge in the lean-to, brewing hot tea, and serving grateful Dwarves—while all around the snow spun and the wind groaned. Busy as he was, Cotton still fretted and worried, vexed by the storm but helpless to do anything about it. *Stranded!* he thought. *Stranded here on the mountainside. Rolf said, "Beware of Waroo," and he was right: the White Bear has us trapped like bugs on a board. Oh, Mister Perry, what's to become of you?*

The next morning, before dawn, Cotton bolted upright in the shelter thinking, *What's that?* but he struck his head against a thick branch in the shelter roof and flinched back down, rubbing his crown through his hood. *What did I hear that made me bump my noggin?* he wondered, and he listened intently, but heard only Bomar's quiet breathing in the still night. Excitedly, he grabbed Bomar's shoulder and shook him. "Bomar! Bomar, listen! What do you hear?" he cried. Bomar came groggily awake and cracked open the lantern hood, and blinked and rolled his eyes in the phosphorescent light. "Listen, Bomar, what do you hear?" repeated Cotton.

Bomar listened quietly and then exclaimed with fierce exultation, "Nothing! I hear nothing!"

"That's just it!" chortled Cotton. "Nothing! No sound at all! No wind! No howl! The storm is over!" And he grabbed the lantern and scrambled from the shelter with Bomar right behind. And the buccan was correct: the wind that had howled and moaned and groaned and shrieked for two days was gone; the blizzard had blown itself out; all that remained was a light snow falling gently through the pines. And the Warrow laughed and danced and capered in the deep snow by the blue-green radiance of the lantern, while the usually somber Dwarf looked on with a great grin upon his face.

As dawn broke, Bomar and his crew again had prepared a hot breakfast, and had served storm-weary but grimly smiling warriors. The light fall had stopped, and the skies had begun to clear. Now the meal was over and the utensils cleaned and stored, and still the command to prepare for the march did not come. Two more hours passed and yet no orders came and nothing was heard. Finally a Chief Captain arrived and called the warriors of the glen together. "The way is blocked by great drifts," he announced—and Cotton's high spirits plummeted into despair—"but three miles downslope they diminish, and the snow on the road beyond is not deep, and it can be travelled. Hence, we must dig a path to freedom.

"There are four thousand Châkka to open the way, yet we have but a limited number of shovels. Heed: use any scoop to move the snow—spare pots and pans and kettles from the cookwaggons, the beds from the smallforges, and aught else that works.

"Our first task is to clear a route from here to the road; let lie any snow that is less than knee deep, for the horses can broach that. When we reach the road we are to work in shifts with other companies.

"We are already delayed, and the Seven depend upon us to be at the Dusken Door and ready to enter on the twenty-fifth"— and the Chief Captain raised his voice in a shout—"so let us work as only Durek's Folk can!" And the squadron gave a great yell, and Dwarves rushed out to be at the task, while Cotton, Bomar, and the cook-waggon crew remained behind to prepare hot food and drink for the road workers.

The snowbound Army inched a clear path down the mountain as the bright Sun climbed up in the sky to shine down on the white slopes. Each Dwarf pulled his hood tight and peered out through the resulting fur tunnel, using it to screen out the intense glare and ward off snowblindness. And they scooped snow with shovels, pots, pans, forgebeds, boards, helms—anything that could be used. And slowly they crept downward.

Company relieved company, and the toil continued. Weary Dwarves trudged back to their campsites to grab a hot bite to eat and drink, and then to cast themselves down in their shelters for a short rest—which ended all too quickly, for in due time they were called upon to relieve yet another company. The cycle went on and on. And at one of the busy yellow waggons—Bomar's—Cotton helped with the work. And it seemed to the Waeran that no sooner did he finish feeding one crew than another would line up for a meal.

Progress down the mountain was measured in tens of feet. Cotton spoke to the returning crews and got reports on the headway: a giant wide drift at the quarter-mile mark slowed progress to a creep. The Dwarves finally broke through just before noon, and the advance went more swiftly.

It was not long after when there came the flat *Tan-ta-ra* of a Valonian black-oxen horn faintly bugling up over the snow from the slopes far below. Instantly, it was answered from a nearby glen by Brytta's great ebon horn. Again and again they called to one another, at times in short bursts of but a few notes, at other times with long flourishes . . . and finally they fell still.

Cotton wondered at the signals, and when Brytta eventually came, searching for the Warrow to speak with him and to take a meal, there was a huge grin upon the face of the Marshal of the Valanreach. "It is Hogon!" he exulted. "And Eddra and Arl and Wylf! My advance scouts. They are safe! They spent the blizzard with their horses, out of the blast—in a cave five or six miles downslope. Aye, I should have known that Wylf would have one eye out for comfort. Arl claims that at first flake-fall Wylf declared 'twas time for snug shelter, and led them on a line no bee could have flown straighter nor swifter directly to the hole; Eddra and Hogon checked it for the bears that were not there, and in they went, horses and all, two steps ahead of the white wind. And this morning they kicked and clawed and dug their way out through the snow that had drifted over the cave mouth. Ah, but they are safe! And they wait below for us to break through."

"You learned all that just from tootling horns across a snow-field at one another?" Cotton asked, and at Brytta's pleased nod the Warrow marveled at this, to him, heretofore unrealized potential of horn calls. And though Cotton had not met the advance scouts, he felt eased that they had come to no harm. Yet his relief was tempered by the realization that time was slipping away from the Army, and Mister Perry and the Squad depended upon them to be ready on schedule at the Dusk-Door; and here they were—drift-trapped.

In the early afternoon the army of digging Dwarves passed the half-mile point, but then the snow deepened, slowing the forward way. At sundown the road had been cleared for a mile, and work went on by lantern-glow and by the light of the stars. At midnight, the mile-and-a-half point was reached.

Bomar urged Cotton to take to his shelter for a rest. The buccan had been working nonstop all day, and was bone weary. Yet he was frustrated, for he had the irrational feeling that if only he were *out there shoveling rather than back here cooking, well, the road would just get cleared a whole lot faster. What can be taking so long? I mean a whole army ought to be able to do this job in just an hour or two.* Not only was Cotton frustrated by the snail's pace of the progress, he was angry with himself for being frustrated in the first place, for he knew that the Dwarves were advancing downslope as quickly as possible, and he could make his best contribution to the effort by working with the cook-crew and *not* with the road crew.

After only five hours of sleep, the Warrow awakened and trudged back to the cook-waggon. He took a bite to eat and drank a cup of hot tea, and then relieved Bomar. It was false dawn, and the sky was pale grey. A thin crescent of a waning Moon rode low over the mountaintops. Cotton and three of the cook-crew were on duty, and soon another shift came to be fed. Cotton discovered that the road crews had just passed the two-mile point.

Dawn came, followed by another bright morning. The exhausting, backbreaking job went on, and again the Sun marched up the sky. Word came that the road gangs had encountered another giant drift, and the advance was stalled just a half mile from the end. Cotton felt both helpless rage and unremitting despair at the news, and he threw himself more than ever into his work.

Before noon, Bomar and the other five Dwarves rejoined the cook-crew, and the discouraged Warrow took a mug of hot tea and wandered to the edge of the glen where it was quiet and he could rest a moment. The Sun was just reaching the zenith when from far off something rumbled low and long, like distant thunder among the crests. Cotton stared in the direction from which the roll had come, but the trees obscured his vision, and he could see nothing to indicate the source of this unknown, far-off roar. A few moments later the buccan returned to the cook-waggon and asked Bomar, "What would make a great rumble up in the high peaks?"

"Snow avalanche," replied Bomar. "That was a distant avalanche. Something caused a Mountainside of snow to give way and cascade down; it comes as a giant wall and carries all things before it, snapping off trees both large and small and rolling great boulders along under it, causing other snow to cataract down too. Sometimes it slides for miles, a great wave growing wider and higher as it thunders down to wreak its destruction and bury its victims."

"Lawks!" responded Cotton. "I thought the rock slide was bad, but this sounds worse. I hope no snow avalanche decides to slip this way."

About two hours before sundown a ragged distant cheer echoed up over the quiet snow to those in the glen; the road crews had broken through the last drift, and the way before them held only diminishing snow. The word came to harness up the teams and prepare to move out; no more time was to be spent in the high country; the Army was to trek down to the foothills, marching part of the night.

And so, even though they were weary, the Host gladly

shouldered their packs or hitched up the horses or otherwise prepared to travel. Just as the Sun disappeared, the trek began, and lanterns were carried to illuminate the way.

The Host moved slowly out of the glens and onto the road. Cotton and Bomar in the yellow waggon again brought up the rear, and often they would come to a complete halt, to stand and wait for long minutes while the leading teams and wains struggled through places still deep in snow, with Dwarves pushing and pulling and straining to roll the stuck vehicles forward by grasping and turning the wooden-spoked wheels. Then the column would move ahead once more until the next deep place was encountered and the horses again needed help.

And thus the train moved down the mountain, sometimes easily, sometimes struggling. It proceeded like a great undulating caterpillar, bunching up behind barriers and lengthening out beyond them. At the rear of the column, the only trouble Cotton and Bomar encountered was that of the waggon oft' sliding where the snow had been packed unto ice by the four thousand warriors and nearly five hundred waggons ahead of them: here, Brownie and Downy found the footing treacherous, and the wain brake was of little help. Even so, still they managed to work the waggon past these slick stretches to come to safer purchase.

In places the wain went between high, close walls cloven through the long, deep drifts. At times the snow ramparts were well over the heads of the Warrow and Dwarf sitting up high on the waggon seat; and at last Cotton could envision the massive effort required to clear the road, and he was humbled.

The long line of swaying, bobbing lanterns wended slowly along the carven track set within the snow. In harness again, the horses seemed eager to press forward, and their breath blew white from flaring nostrils in the cold night air as they worked the waggons downward through the drifts, following after the leaders as repeatedly they emerged from one long, narrow, deep channel and into the open, only to enter another long notch.

Thus they passed the three miles from the glens and down through the deep snow to come at last to the shallow fall. It had taken the Army a day and a night and yet another day of incredible labor to dig the three-mile path, and now Cotton and Bomar had driven its length in less than two hours.

The Host continued the march for six hours, and came down out of the high country and into the foothills above Arden, covering some fifteen miles in all. The lower they came, the less snow there was, until it but barely covered the rim of a waggon wheel where it touched the ground. At last Durek called a halt to the march; the Captains posted a picket of warders as Dwarves made campfires; and weary warriors fell asleep wherever they found themselves.

Just as Cotton was preparing to lie down, Durek and Rand came walking to his fire. The buccan had not seen either for three days, but they said little to one another, for all were spent; this night neither King nor Prince returned to the head of the column; this night they bedded down by the last fire instead of the first.

And as Cotton was drifting off he heard another long, low rumble of distant thunder, and he knew that somewhere a white avalanche had cascaded down the mountainside. He wondered if their old, high-country camps and glens had been buried, and if the backbreaking work of days had been covered in mere moments by masses of slipping snow; but before he could speculate more, he fell fast asleep.

CHAPTER 19

WRATH AT THE DOOR

The next morning, Durek, Rand, and Cotton broke fast together. Each felt the pressing need to get under way, for the snowstorm had trapped the Host for three days, and their rendezvous with the Seven was now in serious jeopardy.

"We are late and the Legion is weary," rasped Durek, "and the goal is far south down a ruined road through rough, inhospitable land. Yet we must somehow recapture the days lost to the storm but not expend the whole of the strength of the Host in a race for the Dusken Door; we must not be exhausted when we enter Kraggen-cor, for there we must be strong to meet the foe. I have thought long as to how we might gain back the time without losing our strength, but no good plan comes to mind except a forced march, where our brawn will wane with each day of the pace. We cannot ride the waggons, for there are too many of us—and the wains may be too slow in any case. Prince Rand, a question: Can we float down the River Tumble on rafts? Dwarves know not the skill of swimming nor the art of these craft; yet we would go that way if it would regain the lost time and husband our strength."

"Nay, not the Tumble," answered Rand, shaking his head. "Oh, as to the rafts, though I could teach you the way of their making—and the manner of poling and steering them is simple—still we could not use them down the Tumble, for the river is truly named: there are many rapids and falls between Arden and the place south where the watercourse turns west to join the

Caire, where we would strike for Drimmen-deeve overland. . . .
Nay, the Tumble is no river for a raft.

"And since the Army can ride neither water not wain, I, too,
believe we have no choice but to force march down Rell Way.
There is no other means, and we cannot be late to the rendezvous with my brother and the others."

"On that we agree," gritted the Dwarf, vexed, "yet such a
course will but weary our Legion more. We do not want to arrive too spent to swing Châkka axes at Grg necks." Frustration
loomed in his eyes.

"King Durek, if we can force march but a week or so, we
can draw almost even with our first plan," said Rand, "and that
will leave us five days at normal pace to regain strength before
reaching the Dusk-Door. And at the Door, only those removing
the rubble will be working; all others will rest until it is their
turn at that task."

"Again our thoughts agree," growled Durek, "but for an
army going into battle, a long rapid march is a heavy burden to
bear."

"Speaking of heavy burdens," piped up Cotton, "why don't
we give the armor a ride? What I mean is, well, we can't very
well give every warrior a ride, but armor is a different thing.
Most of the food waggons are now only partly full and so
there's room; and the horses can pull the extra weight. Chain
mail is a burden, right enough, and warriors would march
lighter and faster without that load of iron."

Durek and Rand turned to one another in surprise. That simple suggestion was completely obvious to one unaccustomed to
wearing mail—such as the Warrow—but Dwarves made light
of heavy burdens, and a Dwarf going to War *always* wore his
mail shirt; neither Durek nor Rand had ever considered it being
any other way. This mail had in fact been worn all the way from
Mineholt North, and thus the idea simply had not occurred to
either. Durek roared with laughter and clapped his hands together, for Cotton, of course, was right.

Thus it was that when the Army began its march, nearly all
the armor rode in the green waggons, and the Dwarves marched
"lighter and faster without that load of iron," though each
Dwarf still bore his pack and his beloved axe.

The Riders of the Valanreach swiftly ranged far to the fore

and aft and out on the flanks of the Host as down out of the last
of the snow they came at a forced pace, down from the high
foothills; and ere they came nigh the southern reach of the
cloven vale of Arden, southward they turned onto an eld abandoned roadbed: the long-disused Old Rell Way, grown over
with weeds now dead in the winter cold.

The land the Legion entered was tough, and the trees sparse,
there being only barren thickets or lone giants with empty
branches clutching at the sky. In the folds of the land grew
brush and brambles, but for the most part the region was one of
open high moors and heather. Into these uplands they forced
march south on the ancient way—and though they did not
know it, they were paralleling the path taken by Tuck, Galen,
and Gildor more than two hundred and thirty years past; those
three, however, had gone secretly in the Dimmendark and had
not taken to the Old Way until they were nearly fifty leagues
south of the Hidden Vale, for in those days the Way near Arden
was patrolled by Ghûls—Modru's Reavers.

At times the ancient road was blocked by thicket growth or
fallen stones, or by a washout that cut the track; but the waggons were guided around the blockage, or many Dwarves gathered and removed the barrier. Twice the roadbed completely
disappeared, but Rand led the train along pathways that soon
rejoined the Old Way.

The day was bright and the pace was swift, and the Host
stopped but once for a rest and a quick noon meal of crue and
water. They marched all day at the same hard stride, always
bearing southward with the Grimwall Mountains towering off
to their left. And when they stopped that night they had covered
twenty-nine miles, and Rand and Durek were well pleased.

They continued this swift pace for two more days, going
some sixty miles more. But on the next day it rained, slowing
progress, for the roadbed was ancient and did not drain well,
and by the time the latter part of the train came, the pathway
was a sea of mud, churned to muck by all the tramping Dwarf
boots and turning waggon wheels and driving horse hooves that
had gone before. At times the late wains became mired beyond
the strength of the horses to pull them free, and Dwarves and
spare horses would then help wrest the waggons out.

Being at the very last of the train, Cotton and Bomar's yellow cook-waggon was often bogged down, and their usual good tempers suffered as a result. "You know, Bomar," complained Cotton, nettled, "the trouble with being at the tail end of things is not only do we get stuck a lot, but also we're the last ones to find out what's going on. I mean, here we are, just as important as anyone else in this army, but we never seem to know what's going on. It's either stand around and wait, or rush to get ready, and we never find out what's happening till we fall in a hole, or get stuck, or what have you. I don't much like it, Bomar, this not knowing, and I don't like all of this hurry up and wait either."

"Hah! Friend Cotton," laughed Bomar, "now I know that you are at last a true campaigner, for you have just voiced the warrior's eternal plaint. It has ever been so in armies since time began and shall be so for as long as they exist. It is the soldier's lot to 'never know' and to 'hurry up and wait.'" Dwarf and Warrow, they both laughed long, and thereafter their spirits were high, even though the waggon often mired and one or the other had then to jump down to help roll it free.

The column stretched out in length for nearly eight miles as the front of the train made good time while the last did not. Thus it was that when it came time to stop, although the front halted, the rear was far behind and had to keep travelling to close up the line; and Cotton and Bomar did not arrive until three more hours had elapsed.

That day the column moved only twenty-two miles.

The next day was clear, and as the Legion marched, the roadbed dried out, and so good progress was made. Far ahead they could see an arm of the mountains standing across the land to block their way, but as they drew nearer, the Old Rell Way swung out on a southwesterly course to go around this spur. They forced march this direction for three more days, and on the fourth day the Way again swung back to the south and east as they rounded the side-chain and at last headed on a line for the Quadran and Drimmen-deeve. It was the sixteenth day since they had left Landover Road Ford and the ninth day of march from the Crestan Pass; the Host was weary, yet on this day

Rand dropped back the pace, for he reasoned that they had drawn nearly even with their original plan.

The way began rising up again through the foothills as the Army tramped toward the Quadran; and finally there hove into view the four great mountains under which Kraggen-cor was delved: Greytower, Loftcrag, Grimspire, and mighty Stormhelm. The Legion's goal, the Dusk-Door, was carved in the Loom of Grimspire, a hard day's trek south of Stormhelm's flanks. Yet now that the four soaring peaks were in sight, all of those striding south along Old Rell Way felt that they could nearly see their destination; their spirits lifted and new vigor coursed through their veins.

That night, Rand estimated that four more days on the march would bring them to the Door.

Two days later, just at sundown, the column pitched camp at an old fork in the road. Rand and Durek and Brytta looked at the ways before them. "The left-hand course—Quadran Road—goes up to Quadran Pass," said Rand, "to climb over the Grimwall and come down the Quadran Run to the Pitch below. We can no longer cross over; the entire saddle is white; the way is barred by snow. The right-hand course bears south to the Dusk-Door; it is the continuation of the old trade route between the Elves of Lianion—called Rell by Men—and your ancestors in Kraggen-cor, King Durek. By this route—the Old Rell Way—we will come to the Door in a half and one day."

"It is as I feared back at the ford," rasped Durek, his sight leaping up the stone ramparts to the snowbound gap above. "The way over the Mountain is blocked. The blizzard that nearly thwarted us at the Crestan Pass had wide wings, and here the slot is closed. Yet but had we the knowledge of the Elden, even now the col might still afford entry into Kraggen-cor: Châkka lore has it that a secret High Gate opens into the Quadran Gap. Yet in these latter days we know not where it lies— whether this side or that, or in between, in the clear or buried under snow, we know it not. But, though we here are ignorant, perhaps it has been discovered by the foul Squam since their occupation of Kraggen-cor; and even now hostile eyes may be upon us, spying out our every move." At these words Brytta's hand strayed to his spear, and Durek grimly smiled at the warrior's reaction. "Yet I think not, Reachmarshal, for the High Gate was secret, and even Gatemaster Barak may find it hard to discover its location, much less the manner of its working."

Durek's words did not soothe Marshal Brytta, for his sharp eyes continued to search the upward slopes.

"And so," continued Durek, "with the pass closed, if we fail to open the Dusken Door, then we must go far south through Gûnar Slot to the Gûnarring Gap to come to the other side of the Mountains. But let us not speak of failure; instead, let us go to sit with Friend Cotton at the last fire." And they strode to the far yellow waggon, arriving in time to eat.

The waxing Moon had risen in the early afternoon and passed overhead two hours after supper. Speculatively, Cotton gazed up at the silver orb. "I wonder what Mister Perry and Lord Kian and Anval and Borin and the others are doing right now. Do you think they're looking up at the same Moon and wondering what we're doing?"

"Pehaps, Cotton, perhaps," answered Rand. "If I have reckoned correctly, this is the twentieth day of November, and they are drawing nigh to the Pitch. Tomorrow they should fare up the slope and arrive at Dawn-Gate. And the next day, they enter the Deeves."

At these words Cotton's heart gave a lurch, for with the Quadran at hand the dire mission of the Squad took on grim reality.

"If all has gone aright with them, they will be in the caverns and on the Brega Path when first we come to the Door," said Durek, and Cotton's heart sank even further. "It is we who are late—by one day," growled the Dwarf King, a dark look upon his face. "Let us hope that there is enough time to uncover the portal, once we arrive."

"We are not a full day behind, King Durek," amended Rand, "but only one half a day instead. We should arrive by mid of day the day after tomorrow."

Still, even with these words, the Dwarf King's heart did not seem eased, and the conversation dwindled to a halt. At last, Brytta, Durek, and Rand bade good night to Cotton and returned to the front of the train to settle down for the eventide.

Yet, for much of the rest of that night, Brytta's thoughts dwelled upon the ancient, secret High Gate somewhere in

Quadran Pass, a Gate lost by the Dwarves in eld times, but perhaps now known to the Wrg. And he could not banish the specter of skulking Rutcha slipping in and out of that hidden portal, of treacherous Drōken eyes spying out their every move, of sly Wrg mouths whispering to Cruel Gnar word of the Dwarves' mission. And by the light of the westering Moon and the wheeling stars overhead, Brytta's own gaze turned ever and again toward Quadran Col, searching up the high slopes for sign of the enemy but seeing none; and sleep was a long time coming.

Thus it was that at dawn, as the column came awake and plans were made for the day's march, the Reachmarshal called Eddra, Arl, and Wylf to him to confer with Prince Rand. Acting upon Brytta's wary suspicions, those three riders were to set watch upon the Gap. As Brytta explained, "I would rather set a ward against a danger that never comes than to pay in blood for an unseen thrust." And so, Rand described the lay of the land between the col and Dusk-Door, and plans were made to light a balefire at the top of Redguard—one of the lesser mountains overlooking the road to the gap—as a warning beacon to the Legion should an army of Spawn issue from the secret High Gate to fall upon the Dwarves' back. Hence, as the column got under way, tramping to the south toward the Dusk-Door, three silent riders of the Valanreach detached themselves from the Host and cantered to the east toward Mount Redguard.

Cotton had looked forward to another day of swift march; but early in the morning the Legion came to a place where the old road had been washed away over the years by heavy rains and melting snows, and a narrow but deep ravine blocked the route. Brytta's mounted scouts rode east and west and soon a way was found around the channel; yet the detour took several hours to negotiate because of the roughness of the trail.

The next day, the Army finally came along the ancient Rell Way to the deep channel through which the Duskrill once flowed; but not even a thin trickle could be seen down among the stained rocks, though a few standing pools showed the glimmer of water. Here the way forked, and the Host took the leftward path—the Spur—following a route that wound along the edge of the empty stream bed for several miles.

As they marched now to the east, the land around them rose, and soon they were travelling in a deep valley—the Ragad— that shut off their view of all but the highest peaks of the mountains ahead. At last, as heralded by the black-oxen horns of the Valonian point scouts, the fore of the column wound to journey's end; the Old Way Spur rounded a foothill near the head of the valley to turn eastward again where the road cut upward along the face of a high stone cliff, a cliff down which the Duskrill had once tumbled in a graceful waterfall to drop into a wide basin in the deep ravine beside the Spur. Here the Host ground to a halt, facing the bluff.

Carved in the jut of the cliff was a steep stairway leading up beyond the rim, continuing on up to a sentinel stand atop a high spire overlooking the valley where in days of old Châkka warders had stood watch o'er the vale. And beyond the rampart and dwarfing it was a great massif of the Grimspire mountain rising into the sky.

Up the stairs Durek, Rand, and Turin Stonesplitter climbed. As they mounted upward they began to see before them a stonework dam across the width of a ravine above the lip of the linn and blocking the Duskrill. "The *Raven Book* may be right, for this dam is not Châkka-made," noted Turin, looking at the bulwark. "Nor does it look Ükkish. The stones are too great; powerful energy was needed for this: it is the vile work of Trollfolk, I deem."

On up the stairway they continued, and above them, hovering over, was the great natural hemidome of the Loomwall. Up beside the dam they mounted, till they came to the top of the bluff, and behind the dam and embraced by the cavernous Loom lay a long, narrow, black lakelet, running a half mile to the north and nearly two miles to the south. The massive stone flank of the hemidome sprang up along the distant shore to arch upward and overhead; and delved somewhere along this massif was the Dusk-Door, ancient trade entrance and way into Grimspire and the caverns of Kraggen-cor.

"Across this foul black lake and south of the old Sentinel Falls shall be the Dusken Door carven in the Loom," declared Durek, peering over the still, dark mere at the great flank.

"Look!" cried Turin. "There is the old bridge! And see, below!" And he pointed at a place a short distance southward along the base of the hemidome and beyond the ruins of an old drawbridge; and there rubble, boulders, and other debris were piled high against the Loom. "That must be it. If so, the *Raven Book* is right, and the way is blocked. I must cross over to see what needs to be done to uncover the portal. It does not appear to be more than two days' labor, from here; but ere I say for certain, I must give it close scrutiny, for we are some distance away."

"I judge it to be slightly more than a quarter mile across this dark tarn," said Rand, gauging the distance by eye, "but we must walk around the north end to come to the pile, and that is a trek of more than a mile but less than two."

Durek called down to one of the Valonian scouts and bade him to ride back along the train and tell the Host that they had arrived at the long-sought goal and to make camp along the north flank of the valley. He also instructed the scout to herald the Chief Captains to the Sentinel Falls to see the Loom and await a Council. Finally, he bade the scout to ask Friend Cotton to gather his belongings and move to the head of the train and then to join the Council.

As the rider sped away, Durek, Rand, and Turin tramped northward along the barren shoreline. They crossed the place where the Spur wound on upward; here the road topped the bluff and started across the swale toward the Door, only to plunge under the ebon surface of the Dark Mere, blocked by the black lake in the desolate, water-filled valley. Neither bird nor beast nor small furry thing did they see in the tangles of the brush and stunted bushes and brown grass on the slopes; and no fish or frog or watersnake or creature of any sort was seen in the dismal water under the ocherous scum that lapped the shore, nor among the brown strands of dead waterplants reaching up from the unseen depths to clutch at the dull lake surface. But it was winter, and much life elsewhere had gone to warmer climes, or had denned to sleep through the cold, and plants had browned and lost leaves and would not green again until spring; thus the lack of living things was not remarkable. Yet this lifeless vale was somehow . . . ominous.

Hundreds of feet overhead arched the Great Loom, and the

two Dwarves and the Man strode below the black granite burden. Soon they reached the far north end of the Dark Mere, where they stepped through shallow, weed-infested, stagnant water that barred the way; the torpid swash of their passage sluggishly seeped through dead reeds, and the bottom sucked at their boots with slime-laden silt. The trio crossed over and walked south on the narrow strip of rocky land trapped between the water, dark and forbidding to their right, and the Loom, stern and towering to their left. They came to the Spur again, now a causeway, sundered by time; here the shattered roadway lay along the Loom and ran south to an ancient drawbridge, ageworn and weatherbeaten. The bridge was lowered and could not be raised, for its haul was broken.

"This bridge was once a Kraggen-cor defence," stated Durek. "It was raised in time of trouble. It is said that once the span remained up for three years, never lowered. Ah, but it is down now, and ancient. Yet look! Still it will bear the weight of an army." Durek stamped his foot on the bed, proud of his ancestors' crafting. Then he peered over the side at the nearby black water. "Lore tells us that here should begin an arc of a moat, hemming in a courtyard—a *moat*, not this . . . this dark blot."

Across the bridge they strode and south, finally to come to the steps rising up from a drowned courtyard, and to the pile ramped high against the Loom face. Up close they saw that the rubble consisted of large broken stone columns, and the work of a great edifice, cracked and split in shards; and among the rock were huge uptorn trees with broken roots and splintered trunks.

"Aie!" moaned Turin. "The destruction of such a work." And he fell into silent, anguished study.

"Some of these stones are larger than I gauged from the far shore; moving them will be a chore, indeed," reflected Turin after a time, his manner now that of a Crafter with a task. "Yet I deem we can remove all of this in one half and two days."

"*Kala!*" replied Durek, pleased, "for it is now the afternoon of the twenty-second of November; you will finish on the twenty-fifth, exactly on time to meet the Seven." He turned and looked at Rand, who was studying the ramp with a brooding look. "Something disturbs you, Prince Rand?"

"These stones, King Durek, these broken columns," replied the Man, his manner intense. "Look at how huge they are, and at how they are split and cracked—as if flung by some awful power, to shatter in the smash of their impact. The strength of the Krakenward was greater than I imagined; to hurl stones this enormous, even in hatred, takes incredible power."

At mention of the monster's name, the two Dwarves uneasily eyed the dark expanse of motionless water just a few paces away.

When word came down the line that they had arrived, like a wave a cheer washed along the column. Thus, Cotton suspected the news even before the herald came to confirm it. But when the horseman also informed the Warrow of Durek's request that Cotton move to the head of the column, the buccan felt both eager to be there and reluctant to go: he was eager because he was anxious to get the Door open and see Perry again, and reluctant because he would be leaving his friend, Bomar. But Bomar put things in perspective for Cotton by clapping him on the shoulder and rumbling, "Aye, Friend Cotton, I would that you could stay with me and be at my side when we take on the thieving Grg; but your mission is up front, guiding the Host into the ancient homeland, whereas my duty is at the hind as part of the trailing rearguard. Set forth, Pathfinder, for King Durek needs you to point the way."

Cotton leapt down from the waggon and hurriedly donned his armor and buckled on his sword and dagger and gathered up his pack. "Well, Bomar," he said, "we've come a good long way together, and I expect to chat with you after this is all over. So, as you said to me that first day, store up the memories of the time we're apart, and I'll store up mine, and when we get together again we'll have some tales to tell."

Then Cotton stepped to the horses and patted them; they nuzzled him, and he gave them each a carrot. The buccan called to Bomar, "Take good care of Brownie and Downy," then turned and started for the head of the column.

As Cotton walked up the line, horses were pulling waggons off the Spur, and warriors bustled to prepare campsites upon the slopes. Dwarves were retrieving their iron-mail corselets from their temporary storage in the green wains and armoring themselves again. Cotton nodded to many as he strode by, and they smiled or nodded back, some hailing this doughty golden warrior who was to lead them through the caverns.

Cotton reached the head of the column where were assembled the Chief Captains. They gazed up at the linn high above them, now just a stark rock precipice over which no stream tumbled. As they looked, Durek stepped into view on the edge and motioned for them to mount up the steps.

When Cotton arrived at the top with the others, he stared uneasily at the flat, still, dark waters and thought, *Well, now, there's something about this lake that isn't right. It's like the water itself is dead.* And then he saw that neither cloud nor sky nor the towering Loom was mirrored in its depths; not even light itself seemed to reflect back from the dull surface. And as if to underscore the unpleasantness generated by this dark pool, several large bubbles rose to the surface nearby to burst with soft plopping sounds and release a foul-smelling reek of rotted matter, while the dark rings of passage writhed and intertwined and spread outward and quickly died to leave the sullen surface without motion once more.

"Over there," Durek rasped, pointing, "lies the Dusken Door. That pile of rock against the Loom holds within it the shattered edifice and columns spoken of in the *Raven Book*. We can see the facings whence they were sundered, shallow with age but still sign of where it all once stood flanking and capping the portal—a massive work, now destroyed. There, too, are uptorn trees, rent from the drowned courtyard. Yet, even with all the stone and wood, Turin estimates that but one half and two days are needed to clear the way, which will put us at the Door on the twenty-fifth, as planned."

There was a general murmur of approval, and Cotton's heart leapt for joy; he had been worried about being late, and now his anxiety fled with the news.

"Turin has a plan," continued King Durek, "of how to array the stone workers to make short shrift of this labor."

Durek stepped down from the large stone upon which he had stood to address the Council, and Turin Stonesplitter, Masterdelver, mounted up in the Dwarf King's stead. "First, we shall divide ourselves into the same shifts as were used against the snow," he began, and then went on to describe how the pile would be reduced and what tools were needed.

And though Cotton tried to pay attention, his eye was irresistibly drawn to the darkling mere, its ominous surface lying dead and dull. And Turin's voice faded from the Warrow's consciousness as he swept the length of the lake with his sight, to see . . . nothing.

The westering Sun was low and the Great Loom bloomed orange with its setting, yet the tarn showed only dismal gloom in its bodeful murk. And as the Council came to an end, the planning over, and the Captains made their way down the stairs in the dusk, Cotton took a last look at the lake as he brought up the rear; he heard a soft plopping and saw out in the center large rings rippling shoreward, and he wondered if they, too, were caused by bubbles.

Work began early the next morning as hundreds of delvers lined along the base of the Loom on either side of the ramped rubble while many more scrambled up the face of the heap. With picks and mattocks and sledges and spikes and levers and ropes, they began loosening and breaking up the pile, freeing stone and tumbling it down for the others to carry or horses to drag away. As Rand had noted the day before, much of the rock was already split and shattered, and great shards were toppled to slither down to those waiting below. Yet there were large fragments requiring many Dwarves hauling upon strong ropes to nudge them, grinding, away from the ramp. Slowly the workers uncovered one of the great trees, and they brought into play axes and saws to hew the branches and sever the trunk, and Dwarves dragged and rolled the hacked and sawn timber aside.

Amid all this activity, directing the work forces, white-bearded Turin Stonesplitter climbed and pointed and gesticulated—in command. The laboring Dwarves set to with great energy: shoving, rolling, pulling, hauling, pushing, and, with horses, dragging the great stones and timbers away, while others hammered and pried and tied and chopped and sawed, tumbling the wood and rock down. Shifts changed, but the toil ceased not.

Across the lakelet, Cotton sat atop the dam and watched the work proceed; he was far enough away so that he marveled at how much like an anthill the activity seemed. All day he looked on, only taking time away for a quick lunch, watching the pile slowly diminish, measuring its fall by its height on the Loom.

It was nearly sundown when Rand, Durek, and Brytta mounted up the carven steps. "Ho, Cotton!" hailed Rand, "we are going around to see the progress made on this day. Care to join us?"

Would he? Yes indeed! Cotton eagerly jumped to his feet. He had been itching to go take a look, yet had not wanted to be in the way; but now it was an altogether different prospect, for he had an excuse: he was going with the King to inspect the work.

As they trudged through the sere grass and brown weeds, and around the clots of thorny, woodlike, dried brambles tangling through the stunted, twisted, withered trees along the scum-laden shore of the dull pool, making their way toward the north end of the Dark Mere, Durek spoke: "This vale seems utterly dead, unlike the tales of old when it was said that lush grass and slender green trees and fruit-laden bushes carpeted the land and stood upon the slopes; and the dell was a verdant emerald set among the towering Mountains. But now it is Death-struck, as if this dark lake were a great strangling cesspool of choking black poison, and it seems as if the very earth of this once beautiful Ragad Vale has been slain by this evil."

Cotton looked around and shuddered at Durek's imagery; and Brytta added, "Aye, this vale indeed seems cursed, for Nightwind and the other steeds will not touch this foul pasturage. Yet there is not enough grain nor clear water to long support the herd, for there are more than a thousand of your horses, and forty-four of ours. We must move the steeds, and so I have sent a scout looking; shortly we will drive them south to the great winter grasslands of the western vales—that is, as soon as you succeed in uncovering the Door and enter the caverns."

Durek nodded and sighed. "Just so, Brytta, though I had hoped we would not have to take this step as you foresaw we might; for I have come to depend heavily upon the eyes of the Vanadurin, and the loss will be greatly felt—though we have little or no choice."

"Even so," Brytta growled, "it rowels me to know that we

will not be with you at the Wrg-slaughter, avenging the victims of North Reach and elsewhere. But we Sons of Harl are better suited to deal with the horses, and to watch the Quadran Col should Spawn come that way—though the high snows blocking the gap would seem to bar that event.

"Yet, the Rutcha and Drōkha may have found the High Gate you spoke of, and may now have a way to march from that direction. But even though it is more likely that the Spawn will come at you through the dark passages of the Black Maze, I swear that they shall not strike at your back by coming down from the Quadran Pass and through this valley, for we shall keep sentinels posted at the gap, and they shall light a signal fire should the Wrg come; and we will abandon the herd and harass the Spawn to draw them aside and keep them from falling upon you from behind.

"And when you enter the caverns and the battle begins, should any flee your axes and escape through this west Door, ere they can debouch Ragad Vale, another of my guards posted here will strike a signal fire and summon the Harlingar from herd duty, and the craven Spawn will fall prey to our lances."

Here, Brytta flourished his spear, thrusting it forward as if he were lancing from horseback. "Perhaps we shall see some fighting yet—though it seems likely that it will not come to pass, and some of us will merely watch in vain for Rutcha and Drōkha, while the rest of us keep the drove.

"Nay, galling or not, we must tend the herd and guard the vale, for it is better we do these necessary things we know than to flounder about in a dark crack in the earth, more a hindrance than an aid, for the Black Hole is no warring place for a plainsman bred."

"Hah!" cried Durek, clapping the Man of Valon upon the shoulder. "Plainsman bred you are and plainsmen bred we need: to be our eyes, and to guard our flanks, and to speed tidings of our fortunes along the margins of Valon where lies the mineholt of my kindred in the Red Hills, and thence to your King Eanor in Vanar; and to ride beyond Valon to Pellar and bear the news to High King Darion at Caer Pendwyr. And aye, we need you to ward horses, as Vanadurin have done throughout the centuries. And further, we need you to stand fast at our backs and guard against unseen assault. Yet think not that these are but small tasks, Brytta of the Valanreach, for without the Riders of Valon, much would go amiss."

And Durek clasped the forearm of the Reachmarshal, and the blond warrior smiled down upon the Dwarf King; and Prince Rand and Cotton the Waerling witnessed the final healing of the ancient rift between the Men of Valon and the Line of Durek, and they were glad.

The four strode up to the north end of the black pool and crossed over the torpid water, there to turn south along the Loom. Cotton did not like wading through the skirt of the stagnated mere, his boots sliding and sucking through the muck; and the clinging slime and yellowed scum made his feet feel befouled even though they were shod, as if something evil and unclean had defiled him. He tried to shake off this impression but did not succeed, and still his jewel-like viridian eyes strayed over the menace of the dull black waters. He felt certain that the Krakenward was gone, for surely by now it would have attacked the workers; yet somehow the dark mere seemed to bode an ominous doom—a threat he felt growing with the coming of darkness.

The four of them crossed the bridge and came to the northern arm of the work force, and Durek nodded and smiled at the workers as he passed, saying words to a few. And then they came to the pile, and Turin jumped down to speak to his King. To Cotton and Brytta the remaining heap looked enormous at hand, but to Rand and Durek, who had seen it before, it was greatly diminished.

"We are doing better than I gauged," said Turin. "We may finish earlier than expected."

Durek smiled and said something in return, but Cotton did not hear it.

A great feeling of dread overwhelmed the buccan and he turned to look at the lake, the hair on the nape of his neck standing erect. He could see nothing, yet fear coursed through him and his heart pounded. The Sun was low and sinking, and work had been called to a halt and the horses had been led away. The Dwarves were retrieving their mail from the base of the Loom and donning it, slipping their broad-bladed axes back into their carrying thongs. Again voices around Cotton seemed to become muffled, and he felt an impending doom approaching.

The Sun sank lower, and now its rays crept up and away from the black mere until they struck only the Great Arch of the Loom. And at the moment that the last ray left the lake and its leaden surface fell into shadow, Cotton's searching eyes saw a huge ominous wave flowing out of the dim recesses of the southernmost end—as if something large and fast were speeding just below the surface . . .

"Look!" Cotton shouted and pointed. "The Warder comes!"

Durek spun and saw the fast-flowing wake, a hurtling wedge of water, its point aimed at the Dwarves. *"Châkka shok!"* he barked, and all the Dwarves grimly drew their axes, and Cotton and Rand unsheathed their swords, while Brytta gripped his spear.

On came the great wave, a massive flowing heave in the ebon waters, a foaming black wake churning behind, hard-driven by some hidden leviathan menace. Onward rushed the dark billow, toward the grim-faced Warrow and Men and Dwarves, sword and axes at the ready. And Cotton trembled to see how swiftly it came. Onward the crest of the huge wedge sped, straight toward the Door, nearer and nearer, the wave at last surging and boiling over the strand.

And then a hideous creature was upon them:

Great ropy tentacles writhed out of the water to grasp at the intruders on the shore. Dwarves coiled back and cries of dismay rent the air. Brytta set his black-oxen horn to his lips, but ere he could sound it a huge tendril slapped him aside, and he was whelmed against the Great Loom and fell senseless to the ground at its base.

Then a Dwarf was snared, and another, and another, and drawn struggling in vain back across the strand and pulled beneath the water. Other Dwarves hewed at the slimy arms, but the axes did not cut through the thick, unyielding hide. And Durek was grasped about the waist, a great tendril wrapped about him several times, and he was thrown to his knees and his axe flew forward, lost to his grip; he was slowly dragged toward the foul black water, as if a malevolent evil intelligence was toying with a helpless small thing—torturing it, slowly drawing it toward a horrid death.

Rand sprang forward and drove his black-handled sword down onto the arm, but the blade merely bounced from the vile hide; again and again he struck, but to no avail, and Durek was drawn onward.

Rand flung his own useless sword aside and caught up Durek's silveron-edged axe; but ere the Man could use it, Cotton brought his weapon of the Men of the Lost Land to bear— this Atalar blade had been forged to battle against powers of evil, and its golden runes flashed bright in the dying sunlight. Cotton dropped to one knee and slashed the blade downward in a great overhead two-handed stroke which landed athwart the snaky arm and clove a deep gash in it. Instantly Rand hewed the glittering axe into the opening made by Cotton's weapon; the end of the tentacle was shorn off, to drop from Durek's waist and flop and writhe and coil and lash out with a life of its own. The main tentacle gushed forth black blood and was whipped back into the water as Durek stumbled hindward to the Loomwall.

And the creature went mad, for only once before had it ever felt pain, and that was when it had been dealt a wound *by the very same Atalar Blade,* a blade wielded long ago by yet another who sought to enter the Door; but that pain then was as nothing compared to now, for golden-runed sword and silveron-edged axe together had maimed it dearly.

The foul water roiled with the creature's anger, and a great stench filled the air as twenty or more tentacles boiled forth to lash out and grab Dwarves and fling them against the Loom, and to wrench others into the black lake, swiftly now in rage and no longer slowly in calculated cruelty. The creature grasped a huge boulder and pounded it like a great stone maul, smashing with dreadful effect into the helpless Dwarves. It snatched up several of the Châkka and rolled them in tentacles to squeeze them lifeless; the dead were flung down and others caught up; thus did Turin Stonesplitter die.

Durek looked on with horrified eyes at the havoc being wrought as tens and twenties of his kindred were destroyed. "Flee!" he cried. "Back!" And Rand, calling upon a reserve of hidden strength unexpected in one of his slim build, hoisted unconscious Brytta over his shoulder and carried the stunned warrior as they all scrambled and fled northward, trapped within the creature's reach on the narrow strand between the Loom and the water.

Cotton ran in terror, stumbling and scuttling over the rocks and slabs as the creature's great tentacles lashed and flailed all around him, grasping and smashing and slaying. A huge tendril whipped into the rocks just ahead of him, but the Warrow leapt over it and ran on as it snatched empty air inches behind him. A Dwarf was grabbed up from beside him and hurled into the Loom. A ropy arm cracked the great rock hammer to smash into the ground to miss Cotton again. Another tentacle shot out to bar the way, but the buccan slashed it with his sword of Atala, and again the bitter blade gashed the creature; the cut arm lashed back and forth, but Cotton fell flat and it swept overhead.

The frightened Warrow scrambled up and fled onward, across the bridge and along the sundered causeway. And all around him, before and after, others ran and fell and scuttled and fled and died as the Hèlarms pursued, still under the black surface, with only its huge tentacles worming and writhing and grasping and smashing fleeing victims, until the quarry came to the north end where the water was too shallow for the creature to follow. Even then its great bulk flanked the shore as the survivors made for the dam, but they stayed well up out of the Monster's reach as, weeping and defeated, they came stumbling down the hill to the Host.

An hour passed and the dusk deepened, and still Durek sat on a rock, unmoving, with his hood cast over his head. The gathered Legion waited in silence, even those who wept. Brytta had regained his senses, and he, too, sat grim and silent as Hogon bandaged the Reachmarshal's right hand, broken by the Krakenward's slap. Rand stood with his own hands tightly clasped behind his back, his face stern, staring at the fading violet sky to the west as dusk yielded to night and the vale gradually fell into darkness. Cotton sat nearby on the slopes in the twilight as slowly his horror and grief gave way to a dull red hate. And then from across the lake there sounded a great clatter of rock, and a sentry came down from the top of the hill and said to Durek, "Sire, the Madûk heaps more stone upon the Door."

Durek sat a moment without moving; then he cast back his hood, and there was a fell look upon his face. "This cannot be borne," his voice grated. "We shall slay that spawn of evil. Get Gaynor to me, and Berez, and Bomar. Bring Tror and his Hammerers and Felor with his Drillers. Before this night is over, it shall be done."

As Cotton watched, the message went forth, and Dwarves arrived, bearing with them tools from the black waggons. Lanterns were unhooded and carried up the stairs to the face of the dam. Gaynor, Berez, and Bomar were all accounted Masterdelvers and had been second only to dead Turin. With King Durek they crawled over the stone face of the dam, studying the fissures in the rock, judging its faults. Then Tror with twelve other Dwarves carrying sledge hammers, and Felor with as many carrying tongs and pointed iron rods and wedges, climbed up to the sites indicated by the Delvers; and they set the rods and irons in place and began hammering them and wedging them into the cracks and crevices. The Host and waggons and animals were gathered up out of the valley and moved to high ground. And by the blue-green light of the Dwarf-lanterns the pounding and delving went on.

They were going to break the dam.

They had hammered but a short time when suddenly a great tentacle looped over the top of the barrier and wrapped about the neck of a Driller, snapping it and then flinging the Dwarf aside. With cries of terror, the others fled downward as more arms writhed and slithered over, reaching and grasping, clutching two more ere the others escaped.

A moan of dismay rose up from the watching Legion as the creature slew their kin and then wrenched loose the drills to throw them aside. The arms lashed and whipped menacingly, then sinuously withdrew as the creature lurked on the far side of the dam. Many Dwarves tore at their beards in rage, but Durek's look became more resolute than ever, and he called the Chief Captains to him. "Fire," he ordered in a grim voice. "Build me a fire on the dam above the drilling site. Make it as fierce, as hot as the heart of a crucible, or an iron forge. Spread it along the top above the work point farther than the Madûk can reach."

Wood was gathered and brands lit; oil was spread on the tinder. It was quietly carried up to the stonework and placed on top and fired. More timber was added, and the flames shot high. When the heat became nearly unbearable the drilling work resumed under the blazing barrier. Drillers and Hammerers were spelled often, for it was like working in a furnace; sweat poured off even those watching from the vale sides, and cloaks and jerkins were removed.

When the pounding began again, the creature once more reached a tentacle out of the water, but the flames repelled it; and it moved to a place where the fire was not and groped over a dam but could not reach the workers. There was a great beating and lashing of the water as the frustrated Krakenward whipped the surface in its fury. Then it raced to the other end of the flames, but there, too, it was thwarted; and the water boiled and foamed in the Monster's rage; a malodorous reek rose up, and an ominous hissing could be heard, as if from some reptilian source. But the work went on.

The nearly full Moon slowly came over the mountains and added its silver radiance to the firelight and the lantern-glow. And still the work continued.

Clang! Clang! Chink! Clank! The great sledges drove home the drills and wedges under the roar of the fire. Mighty thews swung the mallets with Dwarf-driven force, and each Driller held the rods with the tongs until they were wedged deeply; then they placed longer ones in the crevices when the shorter ones had been driven home. And the stone split slowly along the weakened fissures as many teams cracked the rock in two separate vertical lines some twenty feet apart.

Chank! Clank! Thunk! Chang! The crews nearest the top of the wall—nearest the fire—had to be relieved most often, but those at the bottom required spelling, too. And on the vale sides, Dwarves gathered wood and placed it at the disposal of the fire teams, who kept the blaze going. The entire Host now worked to slay the creature: many who had never drilled took shifts and handled the tongs and irons; others swung the sledges; still others placed wedges to be driven in; wood gatherers and fire teams rotated. Cotton, Rand, Brytta and his Men from Valon, and all the Dwarves were struggling to destroy a creature that alone could slay the entire Army.

And slowly the fissures were widened and deepened. Gaynor went up into the heat and examined the splits, and then he ordered everyone out except four teams—two on each breech—for the fissures now seeped water and would soon give way.

Bang! Clank! Dlang! Chunk! The pounding resumed. But then a great wave smashed into the dam, quenching part of the fire. The creature had found a weapon! Water! Another great dark surge slammed into the dam, and more of the flames were drowned.

Bang! Chank! Fire teams ran with dry wood to start new blazes in the gaps, but sinuous tentacles reached up to smash the Dwarves aside.

Chank! Clang! Blang! Now began a desperate race between stone delvers and a cunning evil monster. Once more the creature used its great bulk and raced toward the dam, pushing the water in a high crest ahead of it. With a great *whoosh,* a last large wave washed over the top and extinguished the remainder of the fire directly above the workers.

Bang! Clank! Chunk! By the luminous phosphorescence of the Dwarf-lanterns and the pale radiance of the bright Moon overhead, the Host saw slimy wet tendrils slowly snake over the top, to find the flames gone. Then the tentacles plunged toward the now-fleeing Dwarves, catching up one: Gaynor. It held the Dwarf high and reached up a second hideous arm to grasp him also, and then it exerted its terrible strength and tore him in two and flung the remains down.

Many Dwarves wept and gnashed their teeth and tore at their hair in helpless rage, for the Monster had won. And they watched as the great slimy tendrils groped for more of these small creatures to fling to their deaths, and to smash with rocks, and to squeeze to pulp, and to drown struggling, and to rend in twain. It reached down, but found only more rods to rip out and fling away. It had triumphed! It raised up its hideous tentacles, seeming to celebrate its victory. Cotton wept, while King Durek looked on grimly. Berez raged, and Brytta clenched even his broken fist, while Rand closed his eyes in silent grief. Bomar gazed at the failed delving in . . . but wait! He stared hard and saw . . . "King Durek!" he shouted. "Look! Look at the fissures!"

Slowly the great long cracks were widening, and water was beginning to gush forth, faster and faster. Almost imperceptibly the ponderous slab began to tilt outward; a splitting and cracking rent the air, and a deep heavy grinding of massive stone upon stone sounded. Then, with a thunderous crash that shook the vale, the giant slab toppled over to smash into the stone of the Sentinel Falls precipice; and then it fell onward, tumbling down the linn to shatter at the bottom. Right behind came a great roar of water, freed at last from its centuries-old trap to blast outward in a great torrent and leap to freedom over the cliff, to plunge toward the Ragad Valley in a massive wall of water that carried giant boulders bouncing and smashing along the ravine and rent great trees from the earth to lash and tumble and splinter in the deluge.

When the slab toppled and the water thundered out, the Krakenward was caught directly in front of the gap. Impelled by a force it had never felt before, the evil creature was hurled toward the gaping space, borne outward by the massive surge. Yet as the Monster passed into the roaring slot, it flung out all of its malignant tentacles to grasp the walls of the dam and throw all of its evil power into a mighty pull to propel it back into the depths. But the Madûk reckoned not with the whelming dint of the escaping flood, for the creature's bulk was inexorably drawn through the gap. With a malevolent surge of power it slowly drew back inward, yet all the malefic energy coiled within the great ropy arms could draw it but partway back through the slot. And for the first time within its evil memory, the Madûk felt something more powerful than itself.

Fear drove into its malignant core, and it frantically redoubled its effort. But then the dam, unable to withstand the force of the rush of the water, broke again—first on one side of the gap and then on the other. And the Krakenward was hurled down the falls still clutching the great slabs that had been the flanks of the slot. The Monster smashed into the stone basin below; and the creature's pain was great as it was flung into the walls and shoulders of the ravine and boulders ground over it.

The Host had watched the mighty struggle by the light of the waxing Moon, and when the Madûk was carried over the brink to smash into the darkness below, a great shout of victory rose up.

The dark waters of the black mere continued to pour out. Great masses of foetid rot from the lake bottom were borne forth by the roaring flood, and a putrid fetor swept over the vale. The Army reeled back from this foul stink, and many gagged and retched in the charnel rank. More of the dam crumbled. Giant slabs of stone fell to the falls precipice, and the torrent widened and blasted through the huge rocks to rush over the lip and cascade down.

Hours passed. The Moon set. The water level in the lake sank as it emptied, and the strength of the flood ebbed. What had been a torrent became a rush and then a broad outflow; slowly it continued to wane until it reduced to a wide stream runneling between the huge chunks of fragmented dam up on the precipice to fall in several separate streams to the basin below.

It was now dawn, for the breaking of the dam and the Krakenward's struggle and the emptying of the lake had taken all night. The gloom in the vale of the Sentinel Falls was slowly driven back as the day came; but the Sun rose on the east side of the mountains and the vale was on the west side, and thus it stood in the shadow of the range. Yet the dark retreated and the stars winked out as day broke on the land. As the sky lightened, still the Host watched, looking toward the dark ravine down which the water and rocks and creature and the tons of sludge and filth and rot had all disappeared.

Cotton sat leaning back against a rock, his eyes closed, drained of energy. Exhausted, he was drifting off to sleep when he heard a shouting of voices and a clamor of disbelief and fear. The Warrow snapped open his eyes to see what the commotion was about just as a warrior stepped to Durek's side and pointed to the face of the Sentinel Falls precipice. "Sire, the Madûk, it lives," he announced grimly.

Cotton looked and saw in the early morning light first one tentacle and then another groping upward through the falling water along the cliff face, straining to reach the top of the precipice but falling short.

Durek stood and stared, his eyes filled with rage. His teeth ground together and his hands clenched into fists. His face turned black as anger shook his frame, and his voice rose in a hoarse cry—"To me! To me! Châkka to me!"—and he sprang down the hill. Cotton and Rand, Brytta and Bomar, Berez, Tror, Felor, all leapt after him with Drillers and Hammerers and Delvers close behind.

Plunging down the slope, they charged onto the top of the linn, splashing through the flow to come to the head of the falls and look over the lip through the streams of cascading water and down into the basin below. There in the blackness Cotton could dimly see a huge mass in a bed of runny sludge and black filth and foetid rot; it flopped and writhed with sucking noises as it heaved and hitched its horrid bulk through the muck and churn at the base of the precipice. Though he could not see it clearly in the darkness, Cotton could discern that the Monster was bloated and blotched, slimy and foul, repulsive and horrifying. Long was its swollen body, and from one end a roiling nest of suckered tendrils writhed. Some of these tentacles had been crushed by rock, and one of the creature's eyes had been torn open; but the other baleful red eye glared malignantly up, and a wave of evil incarnate beat at them. The Madûk could see the people limned against the pale morning sky, and a dozen huge tentacles boiled up out of the blackness and lashed at the wall. A hissing was heard and a great stench rose up. But the Monster could not reach them, and the light of the day bore hurtfully through its one good eye and blazed into its brain. In an earlier age, before the Ban, ere it had been borne here, its own malevolence had driven it even unto the sunlight to wreak havoc upon ships plying the lanes near the Great Maelstrom. But now the coming of the Sun meant that it must hide away, and it was frantic to be back in its dark den at the bottom of the black water; and it clutched and grasped futilely at the linn-wall.

Durek glowered down in hatred at the malignant creature, then he turned and gritted, "We shall slay it with stone."

He called Dwarves to him, and with Cotton and Rand and broken-hand Brytta helping, they struggled and strained, pushing and pulling, as from the shattered dam they levered a massive granite block that ground and grated and slowly slid to the lip of the precipice. Gradually it edged out above the Monster, to tip and balance on the rim. Then with a final heave it was prized up to ponderously slide with a rush over the edge to fall silently, slowly turning, to come down upon the Monster and land with a great squashing *splat!*—smashing into and through the bulk. Many of the huge tentacles fell lifeless, and others plucked feebly at the massive stone.

A triumphant shout burst forth from the Host, and Durek looked down and grunted in grim satisfaction. Then he stepped back and raised up a clenched fist and hoarsely called out in a loud voice, "Let all the Companies each in turn cast a block down upon this spawn of evil so that every Châk in the Legion can share in this revenge." And as one body the Dwarf Army wrathfully surged forward, silent and grim, each warrior chafing to extract personal retribution for his fallen brethren.

And Brytta of Valon stood fast and raised his great black-oxen horn to his lips and winded it, summoning the company of the Vanadurin to him to avenge their slain allies, as Durek, Cotton, Rand, and Bomar turned and walked back up the hill in the morning light of a new day.

"Bomar," rasped Durek, "we must go see how much is to be done—how much rubble is to be removed from over the Door—for the Madûk heaped more on. I fear we may now have more work to do than there is time to do it. Tomorrow is the day set for the rendezvous, and the Seven are now within the caverns and may already be at work on the hinges. We cannot fail them; we *must* succeed."

And as the four walked around the foetid rotting black crater where once stood the lake, the Host of Dwarves of Kraggen-cor dragged great slabs of rock from the broken dam to the precipice and cast them down to crush the Monster. They had fought the Madûk with axe and sword and Atalar blade, and hammer and tong and wedge and drill, and fire and water, and at last they slew it with stone. They had finally won, but barely.

"Brega, Bekki's son, strode into legend along a steadfast course of honor. May the span of our strides match his—for that is the true Brega path."

Seventh Durek
November 3, 5E231

BOOK TWO

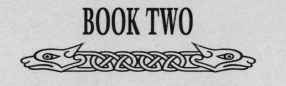

THE BREGA PATH

To the memory of my father:
Burton Edward McKiernan

"I have walked in Kraggen-cor, a bygone Realm of might;
but its light is gone, and dread now stalks the halls."

Brega, Bekki's son
January 18, 4E2019

CHAPTER 1

THE GREAT DEEP

Perry was awakened at dawn by Delk, who had the last watch. Before joining the others for breakfast, the Warrow retrieved Bane from the log beside him; the Elven-blade had been embedded in the bark point down, the long-knife left standing upright through the night as a silent sentinel for all the company to see. And as each member of the Squad had taken his ward tour, he had kept a close eye on the sword, watching for the flickering blue flame that would gleam from the blade-jewel if *Spaunen* drew near.

Shannon Silverleaf, whose turn at guard had come after Perry's, had been especially interested in the blade, and had plucked it out and held it with reverence. "This was crafted long ago in the city of Duellin, in the bygone Land of Atala," the Elf had said to Perry after long study, "and the way of its making is lost. This blade speaks of the Elden Days, when it was one of many weapons fashioned to engage the evil forces of the Great Enemy, Gyphon—the High Vûlk. In a way, we are fighting Him still, for it is He who bred the Rucha, Loka, and Ogruthi—as well as other evil beings—in Neddra, in the Untargarda. My forefathers in the House of Aurinor made these blades to fight that spawn.

"Alas, though many of these poniards were forged in those Elden Days, few remain in Mithgar, and fewer still are yet in use—most lie in rest in ancient graves or upon dusty tombs." Silverleaf had then flourished the blade. "But this pick still serves. I think the name for this edge, Bane, is well chosen, and one which imparts honor to the weapon. This is a great token to carry into Black Drimmen-deeve, and it bodes well for our mission." The Elf then had plunged its point back into the log and replaced Perry at guard.

But now it was dawn, and any maggot-folk abroad would have taken cover from the coming Sun, so Perry sheathed Bane and hunkered down for the morning meal.

"Enjoy your hot tea," said Kian, "for there'll be no fires after this one until our mission is done; this is the last pot we'll brew till then. But we'll not be without tea for long: Today we start overland. At sunrise on the sixth day hence we should be entering Dawn-Gate. At midnight of the ninth day we should see Durek with Cotton and my brother, Rand, enter the Dusk-Door with the Army right behind. Then, after another day or three and many dead Spawn, we will at last build us a fire and enjoy some more hot brew."

"It will give me much pleasure removing the uninvited Wrg 'guests' from our upcoming tea party," grunted giant Ursor, and the others nodded and smiled grimly.

Soon breakfast was finished, and all the spare supplies were cached. The Sun had risen, and it was time to go. Delk quenched the fire, and all shouldered their packs. Perry took one last look at the Great River Argon in the direction the blazing funeral raft had swept. "Farewell, Barak," he whispered, and turned to join the others.

They started west over the land, walking in single file: Lord Kian led the way, the young Man armored in mail and a plain iron-and-leather helm, and armed with his silver-handled bow and arrows, and a sword and dagger; behind Kian marched Anval, the Dwarf warrior mail-shirted, iron-helmed, axe-armed; Ursor the Baeran came next, wearing a dark-brown boiled-leather breastplate and carrying his great black mace; Perry was silveron-mailed under his shirt, with Bane and a dagger at his belt, and on his head he wore a simple steel-and-leather helmet; lithe Shannon Silverleaf strode next, without armor but armed with a bow and arrows and a knife the length of Bane; Borin and Delk brought up the rear, these two Dwarves each armed and armored like Anval, with axes and helms and black-iron mail. All wore green or grey or brown travelling clothes that blended with earth and stone, leaf and branch; and they bore packs containing the needed tools, food, and other supplies for their mission; each carried a leather water bottle at his hip. Their bedrolls and cloaks were fastened in rolls on top of the packs. Thus did they trek in file toward Kraggen-cor, leaving the Argon behind.

Soon the Seven emerged from the river-border forest and came to the wold, a treeless rolling plain that slowly rose up toward the far mountains. Occasionally a thicket stood barren in the winter Sun, and heather and gorse grew on the land. The slopes were gentle and the growth was low, and so they walked in a line straight to the west; only now and then would they make a detour to pass around an outcropping or a tangle of briars or other minor hindrance. Only twice did they come to major obstructions: The first was a deep, wide ravine across their path, running out of the northwest and down to the southeast. They clambered down one steep side and into the wooded bottom where a wide stream bubbled and danced through mossy rocks; the company took the opportunity to replenish their canteens in its clear, sparkling depths. Crossing over, they scrambled up the other side and back out onto the wold. The second obstacle was a minor bluff that jumped up out of the land to steeply bar the way. They walked north three miles before finding a cut that they could walk up through to pass beyond this high rampart.

The second day was much like the first: Even though it was mid-November, the day stayed mild and the air was calm, and so the trek was made in good weather. The course the comrades took was over gentle land, and they made good time. The wold continued to rise slowly as they marched westward toward the mountains.

That evening the Seven bedded down on the lee slope of a hill, sheltered from the light vesper breeze by a massive rock outcropping. Perry sorely missed the cheery campfire, though the Moon waxed overhead, shedding enough light to see out upon the open wold.

That night Perry was awakened by Anval, who pressed a finger to the Warrow's lips and whispered, "Bane glimmers." Perry looked in silence and saw that the guardian blade had a faint blue glint that dimly flickered deep within the rune-jewel.

All the company was now awake, crouched in the shadows of the outcropping, each facing outward, scanning the moonlit land, weapons drawn, senses alert. Shannon Silverleaf whispered to Kian and then silently withdrew and made his way noiselessly to the crest of the hill, where his keener sight and sharper hearing could be used to advantage.

Perry knelt without breathing for long intervals, straining his own hearing to detect the enemy, but he neither heard nor saw movement. Bane had been resheathed so that its werelight would not shine across the wold to give them away, but occasionally Perry would carefully draw it but a small way—an inch or so—cupping his hand to shield the glimmer, checking the faint blue flame. The flicker persisted for about an hour but slowly died away until once more Bane shone only with pale moonlight, the distant danger past.

And then Shannon came back down. "Though I saw nothing," he said quietly, "I felt the presence of evil to the south, toward Darda Galion. Mayhap my kindred will soon engage the foul despoilers on the borders of that abandoned forest."

The following day they marched swiftly across the uplands, and the wold continued to rise. They could now see the mountains, and before them was the Quadran, four peaks taller than the rest; and one of the four towered above the other three. "That is mighty Rávenor," answered Borin to a question from Perry, "the greatest Mountain in the known ranges. Even from here you can see that it looms over the others. My people call it the Hammer because of the sudden storms that maul its slopes, to the ill of those caught in its blasts." Borin gazed with admiration at its dull red sides. "Even though it now houses Squam, still I am eager to walk the halls and chambers within. And when we have routed the foul foe, and cleaned their stench from the stone, we shall make it into a mighty homeland as of old."

The next day the companions entered a low range of foothills that jutted out across the way. In the lead, Lord Kian struck for an old footway in the north of the spur, and soon they were on a narrow path wending up through the hill-chain. As they climbed to the ridge, low on the horizon far to the south they could see a darkling green. "Look," said Perry, pointing, an unspoken question in his eyes.

"That is Darda Galion, the Larkenwald," Shannon informed the buccan, "the last true home of the Lian here in Mithgar. Most have now ridden the Twilight Ride, but a few of us remain, scattered to the four winds, living in other forests with our kindred, the Dylvana, while Darda Galion lies empty."

"Lord Kian told us he thought the Larkenwald was deserted," said Perry, looking southward at the shaded green far away.

"Yes, it is so," responded Shannon with regret. "We no longer dwell there. Many left in the ancient days when the *Vani-lērihha*—the Silverlarks—disappeared. Others fled when once more the power of Gron arose and the *Draedan*—the Gargon—was loosed. Still more went when the Mistress—Dara Faeon—rode the Twilight Path to plead with Adon for succor. And when she was gone, the light seemed to go out of the forest. After the Winter War, many followed her to Adonar, while others lingered in Mithgar, not ready to ride to the High One's Lands. Even Coron Eiron was unready to follow her, and dwelt yet a while in Mithgar among the mortal Lands. But he grew weary of living without her brightness and now is gone too. And when all the Lian had gone from the Eldwood forest, the Dylvana, too, went away, crossing the Argon to come into Darda Erynian and the Greatwood to live with their brethren. And then Darda Galion stood empty, but for a small force of Dylvana warders."

Perry stopped, pausing a moment, gazing in sadness at the now-empty realm. Then he turned and hurried to catch up with Shannon. As they tramped onward, Perry remarked, "Lord Kian said that travellers at times catch a glimpse of movement in the forest—as if Elves were still there. And I see that the green *holds dusk,* as of a Land in twilight, though the Sun yet rides the day."

"Ah yes, the trees do now hold the foredark, for again my kindred are there. We learned that Rucha and Loka—Gyphon *Spaunen*—were stirring in Black Drimmen-deeve," said Shannon grimly, "and raiding south through the Larkenwold. A company of us returned, to bar the way and stop their passage through Darda Galion. But there are many companies of them, and we are but one, and thus the foul despoilers yet win through, though now we give them pause."

"How came Ursor, a Man, to be with a company of Elves?" asked Perry.

"Ah," replied Shannon, "that is a mystery: One night, we beset a company of *Rûpt,* and in the midst of battle, there he appeared, swinging that black iron mace with great effect. He has been with us ever since; his woodcraft nearly equals an Elf's. He talks seldom of his past, but this we now know: He was hunting *Spaunen* alone, wreaking vengeance for his wife and child, slain on a journey to far Valon. Before joining us he would lie in wait for a Ruch or three to become separated from their bands, and then he would strike. He also set snares and deadfalls and spiked pits on the paths Rucha and Loka alone travelled. Now that he is with us, he need no longer wait for mischance on the part of just one or two *Rûpt*; as you have seen, he attacks with us in fury to lay many victims by the heels. He says his revenge now goes swifter."

Perry looked ahead at the big Man and almost pitied the maggot-folk. Then something that had been nagging at the back of his mind sprang to the fore, and Perry called, "Ursor, wait!" And the Warrow rushed to catch up with the Baeran.

As the two of them strode side by side, Perry said, "Ursor, I just now remembered, your kinsman Baru, warden of the Crestan Pass, and his three sons send greetings. Baru says that all is well at home. He also trusts that your vengeance against the 'Wrg' goes to your satisfaction."

The Squad tramped onward in silence, two of the buccan's strides matching one of the Baeran's. Finally Ursor replied, "Thank you, Wee One. Long has it been since I've had word from my kith."

The Seven marched swiftly along the path and came through the hillpass and started down the far slopes. Spread out before them was a great tilt of land trapped between the eastern spur they had just crossed and the Grimwall Mountains on the western side. The slope rose up to the west and into the flanks of the Quadran: Rávenor, Aggarath, Ghatan, and Uchan. These four mountains were known to Man as Stormhelm, Grimspire,

Loftcrag, and Greytower, and to Elves as Coron, Aevor, Chagor, and Gralon. Each held stone of a different hue: ruddy Stormhelm, sable Grimspire, azurine Loftcrag, ashen Greytower. Beneath this quartet of mighty peaks was delved Kraggen-cor; and cupped within their embrace was a wide, cambered valley: the Pitch.

When the slant came into view, the company paused, and the Dwarves eagerly crowded forward to see down into the land. With a wide sweep of hand, Lord Kian gestured at the great acclivity hemmed by the mountains. "There lies the land the Dwarves call Baralan," he said to Perry, "and the Elves name Falanith; it is the Pitch." Kian then pointed toward the upward end of the long slant. "And up there at the far brim and looking down upon this slope is our next goal: Dawn-Gate. On the morrow we march to the portal, in sunlight. But now evening draws nigh, and we must camp away from this path, for its sign shows that heavy-shod feet have marched by recently: Yrm boot, I think. It would not do to be discovered by a chance patrol."

The Seven moved out of the path and to the cover of a thicket in a swale on the slope. The Sun had dropped beyond the mountains, and they made camp in the deep shadows of the peaks.

That night, early in Kian's watch, Perry was awakened by Delk to see Bane's blade-jewel flickering again with a cobalt gleam. As before, Perry slipped the blade into its sheath so that the blue light would not be seen by the enemy. Periodically he would shield it with a cupped hand and draw it an inch or two, then slide it back into the scabbard to hide its luminance. This time the light slowly grew to a strong blue flame that ran along the blade, and they heard heavy boots stamping up the path, and armor jingling. The waxing Moon was over half full, and the companions watched as a large company of maggot-folk tramped up the path and passed in the night. And within his bosom Perry's heart hammered as if it were a caged bird wild to escape.

Slowly the flame subsided as the danger marched away, until it was but a faint glimmer. Slowly, too, did Perry return to calmness, and then only by pushing aside all thought of maggot-folk and sinking deep within his memories of Woody

Hollow and The Root and the sound of Holly quietly humming as she tended her flower garden.

Twice more that night the flame flickered lightly within the jewel of the Elven-blade, but the Seven saw no other Spawn.

The next morning, in early sunlight, the Squad started on the last leg of their overland journey. They came down out of the hillspur and headed west up the long Pitch. As the Seven moved onto the slope, the margins became steeper on the sides of the valley, and here and there they were covered with runs of birch and fir trees; and heather and furze grew on the land. Down below, the comrades could see a sparkling stream dashing down out of the vale: it was the Quadrill, a river fed by many mountain streams to grow wide on its run through Darda Galion, where it was joined by the Cellener and the Rothro to flow onward and come at last to the Argon.

In the early afternoon the Seven moved deeply into the Pitch, flanked on three sides by mountains. Perry could see to the north end, where a glittering rill cascaded in many falls down from the snows of Stormhelm. The stream and the path it fell beside were named the Quadran Run; the pathway led up over Quadran Pass to come down in the land called Rell. "How close are we to Durek's Army and Cotton and your brother Rand?" Perry asked Lord Kian, peering at the snowbound pass.

"If my reckoning is right and nothing has delayed their course, the Army should now be coming to the Dusk-Door. And we are two days of swift march from here to that portal—if we could cross through yon blocked gap and then follow the Old Way. But, Perry, could you fly like an eagle, you are but forty miles, or so, over the mountain from there." Lord Kian looked down at the Waerling. "Of course, we cannot soar like the hawk, but must instead go to ground like the badger, for the route we follow is under the mountain, with many twists and turns—six and forty miles by your Brega Path."

On they marched until they came to the Quadmere, a clear, blue lakelet less than a mile from the east portal, Dawn-Gate. They went down the sward to the cold water to replenish their canteens. Anval, Borin, and Delk looked upon the still mere with a sense of wonder, for there began the realm of Kraggen-cor. On the far side of the azure pool a stone embankment fell sheer into the water; up on the level top of that shore stood a broken pillar, like a maimed finger pointing at the sky: it was a Realmstone, marking this place as being a Dwarvenholt. And runes upon the stone bade all who desired, to drink deep of the pure cold water from the depths of Châk-alon, the Dwarves' name for this quiet tarn.

Lord Kian's eyes swept the flanks of the mountain, and then his look became fell. "There, I think. There lies the Dawn-Gate," he said in a grim voice, and he pointed up the slope.

Perry's heart jumped to his mouth, for there before him, high up on the west wing of the Pitch, stood their destination: like a gaping black wound, the east entrance into Kraggen-cor yawned mute, a dark and forbidding portal into a Spawn-filled maze. His heart thudded and his hands shook, and a thrill of fear coursed through him, for with the coming of the early morning Sun on the morrow, they would begin their desperate dash through this black hole to the far Dusk-Door. And he would be their guide, for it was his task to lead them without flaw on the tortuous way to that distant goal; and the full responsibility of his role now began to crush down on him.

Perry tore his eyes away from the black hole and let his gaze follow the broken stonework of an ancient wide roadway winding down from the entrance and into the valley below, where it was lost among the heather and gorse on the west side of the lake. But try as he might to not look, his vision was drawn again and again to that jet-black slot, and each time he looked his heart flopped over and he drew in his breath.

Ursor leaned down and said in a low voice that only Perry could hear, "Don't worry, Wee One; once we start we'll be too busy to think about it." Perry gave the large, understanding Man a flicker of a smile but said nought in return.

Lord Kian chose a thick grove of pine trees for the Squad to camp in that night. The wood stood high on the slope a mile north of the Dawn-Gate. He reasoned that Yrm forces would issue out of the gate and go east and south toward Darda Galion—away from the chosen coppice—and that any return-

ing forces would come from that way too. Hence, well before
daylight faded, the Seven were comfortably ensconced among
the whin and pine, hidden from prying eyes.

As they lay in the evergreens, Perry became aware of the
distant gurge of a great churn of tumbling water, and when he
asked about it, Delk replied, "It is Durek's Wheel, the Vorvor."
But the Dwarf did not say on, for night had fallen upon the
Spawn-laden land, and they spoke no more.

Darkness overspread the valley, and shortly they saw Hlōk-
led Rūcks, bearing torches, issue out of the gate. And once
again Perry's heart quickened its pace. Amid the clangor of
armor and weaponry, a force was assembled, and then it
marched away to the east along the old, broken road. Sentries
were left guarding the portal, and guttering torchlight shone
forth out of the cavern. And for an hour or two the only movement was that of Rūck guards shuffling around or slouching beside the entrance.

The silvery Moon overhead cast a pale radiance down into
the valley and upon the mountainsides. By its light the companions continued to watch the entrance.

A time passed, and then, tramping up out of the vale, came
a company of *Spaunen* bearing bales of unknown goods;
whether they carried meat, grain, bolts of cloth, or other kinds
of loot and plunder, the Seven could not tell, for they were too
far removed from the Gate to see the nature of the freight. The
Rūcken company bore the burdens into the cavern, disappearing from view.

Another long while passed, and Perry fell asleep watching.
When he was awakened, several hours had elapsed, for the
Moon had set beyond the mountains. The buccan had been
roused by Ursor and cautioned to quietness; a squad of torch-
bearing maggot-folk had marched out of the gate and had
turned north! They were coming toward the hiding place!

In ragged ranks, the maggot-folk tramped right at the pine
grove; and the Seven flattened themselves, peering from con-
cealment, hardly daring to breathe. Carefully, quietly, all but
Perry took a weapon in hand, preparing for battle. The Warrow
found his palms were wet with tension, and he wiped his hand
on his breeks ere taking hold of his sword. But though Perry
grasped Bane's hilt, he did not draw the long-knife, for he knew

its werelight blazed, hidden by the scabbard. And the comrades lay in wait as the Spawn came onward.

Closer drew the maggot-folk, and now Perry could hear them speaking, but he could not make out what was being said; they were still too far away. As they came on, he found that although he could discern the individual voices and words, he could not understand their meaning at all; the words were harsh, somehow foul-sounding, as if made up of acrimonious snarls and discordant curses and grating oaths. There were guttural growls and slobbering drool sounds. The Spawn were speaking in Slûk, an argot first spoken by the Hlōks; but long ago in Neddra, Gyphon had declared it a common language for all of Spawndom.

Perry shuddered at the sound of this festering tongue, but otherwise lay still as the Rūcks tramped along an unseen path, only to turn and march past the grove and away to the north, toward the Quadran Run.

About an hour before dawn, the *Spaunen* patrol returned from the north, scuttling in haste to be in the Gate before the Sun rose. This time, though, there were more maggot-folk in the group. When they scurried near the grove, Perry was surprised to realize that he could now understand what was being said: they were no longer using the Slûk but instead were mouthing words in a polyglot akin to Pellarion, the Common Tongue of Mithgar, a polyglot often used by Hlōks when they did not want their words to be well understood by their underlings, the Rūcks:

"Gorbash's scummy company brought in a lot of loot tonight," whined one of the Hlōks as they scrambled across the slope. "Maybe Gnar'll be pleased and lay off the whip."

"Not rat-mouth Gnar," snarled another. "That big pusbag ain't pleased with nothin' these nights. Ever since them bloody-handed Elves started cuttin' down his Nibs's minions, he ain't been pleased."

"I hear there's another whole company missing, overdue by three days—Gushdug's bunch."

"Blast that rotskull Gushdug! If you ain't lyin' that means stinkthroat Gnar'll be layin' about with his cat-o'-tails more than ever; I'll ram this iron bar up his snot if he cracks those thongs my way. It's bad enough he had me and my bunch guarding this side of that stupid path over the scabby mountain, when he knows that slime-nose Stoog's gang alone is plenty; and they can watch from shelter, whereas we can't, burn their gob-covered hides. And Gnar deliberately left me there in the cold two extra weeks after the snows closed the way. I'll rip his throat out if he even looks sideways at me."

"You, Crotbone? Ha! You've got a big mouth, maggot brain. I know you: you'll be groveling in the dirt at his stinkin' feet like the rest of us when we report in, lickin' his boots and calling him 'O Mighty One,' and all the time, just like the rest of us, you'll be wishing you could catch him from behind down in a dark hole alone, without Goth and Mog watchdogging him, then . . ."

Perry heard no more, for they had moved beyond earshot.

As the rising Sun glanced over the horizon, Delk rubbed face blackener on Perry's cheeks and forehead and directed him to put some on his hands. The other members of the company were also darkening their hands and faces and checking each other for light spots. "Remember," Delk warned Perry, "when we are hiding, do not look directly at a Grg—your eyes will catch the torchlight and shine at him like two hot coals, and we will be discovered. Look to one side, or shield your eyes tightly with your hand and look through the cracks of your fingers; especially keep those jewel-like Utruni eyes of yours covered, Waeran, for they will glow like sapphires. Also, lest its light give us away, it would be better to keep Bane sheathed unless there is no other choice."

Perry nodded and rubbed a bit more of the sooty salve on Delk's exposed cheek. Satisfied, Perry stepped back and looked around at the others, seeing darkened faces and smudged hands. "My, what a ragtag bunch," he declared. "I'd always envisioned warriors as being bright and shining, but here we stand, the 'Secret Seven,' as motley a crowd as you'd ever ask to see." Perry at first just smiled, but the more he gazed at his companions the funnier it seemed. And suddenly he broke out in quiet laughter, and he could not seem to stop. And the others stared at him amazed, and still he laughed. And then its infectious quality caught Shannon, and he began chuckling too. Soon all had joined in, looking at each other's besmudged features and finding them comical.

"Well, my wee Waldan," growled Ursor with a grin, "I hope you don't get to giggling down in the Wrg pits; we'll be discovered for certes, all of us sitting around in a circle laughing our fool heads off." Again the company broke into hushed laughter.

"I never thought I would set forth on a sneak mission with a group of court jesters," growled Delk. "Yet, mayhap it is a new way of outwitting the foul Grg: I doubt that japes and buffoonery have ever been used against thieving Squam before. If we meet any, we will just fall on our prats, and while they are screaming in merriment, blinded with tears of joy, we will slip away and pop open the Dusken Door and bring in the Army for an encore."

Lord Kian laughed quietly with the others, but he knew that their fey mood concealed a tension within, for they were about to set forth on a dire mission, and as is the wont of warriors everywhere in every age, rude jests are bandied about before sallying into an ordeal. Aye, Kian laughed too, yet a grim look crept o'er his features . . . and then: "Let us go now," he said, squinting at the half-risen Sun, and all smiles vanished. "By the time we get there the light will be shining full into the East Hall."

They started off down the slope and toward the gate. Perry's heart was racing, for they were about to step out of the kettle and into the coals. He mentally reviewed what he had told the others countless times during the overland journey about what to expect in the way of halls and chambers, especially on their initial penetration through Dawn-Gate. They had closely studied the map and reviewed every applicable bit of knowledge and lore known to Perry, Anval, Borin, and Delk. And now the Warrow nearly had to bite his tongue to keep from repeating it aloud as an outlet to relieve the enormous pressure growing within him as they strode cross-slope toward the Gate.

And then they were there.

* * *

Cautiously, bow fitted with arrow, Kian peered around one of the great gateposts and down the sunlit hall: it was empty. At the young Lord's signal, each of the comrades in turn stepped across the entryway and crept in past the great doors, torn from their hinges ages agone and flung down on the stone floor, where they still lay. Standing in the shadows, the Seven could see before them a huge room delved out of the stone, with a single outlet two hundred yards away leading down a corridor. The direct rays of the Sun shone through the Gate and struck the farthermost wall just to the right of that distant portal yawning darkly at the remote end of the chamber, that corridor which led down into the interior of Kraggen-cor. In rapid file, the Squad hastened across the room—the East Hall—keeping to the south side and out of the direct sunlight so that their own shadows were not cast down the far passageway to betray them.

The Dwarves looked around in wonder, for at last they had come into their ancient homeland. Perry saw little, for he was busy counting paces, and when they reached the distant outlet and the broad road that led down toward the Great Deep, he was relieved to find that his measure reasonably agreed with that of Brega's of long ago.

They entered the corridor and sidled along the south wall, which was deepest in shadow. The farther they went, the darker it got, but their eyes adjusted to the dim light reaching down the passageway. Down a gentle slope they crept, another furlong or so, stepping quietly, down from Gate Level toward First Neath. And the light continued to fade as they went, but ahead there began to glimmer the dim flicker of far-off torchlight. The Seven edged to the limit of the corridor and paused ere creeping out upon a landing at the top of a short flight of wide stairs; the steps led down to the Broad Shelf.

The Shelf in turn came to an abrupt end, scissured by the Great Deep, black and yawning, the ebon gape splitting out of the high rock walls to jag across the expansive stone floor and bar the way. Beyond the mighty fissure the wide stone floor continued, lit by guttering torches, and on farther the Squad could see the beginnings of the vast Mustering Chamber—the War Hall—receding beyond the flickering light into impenetrable blackness, the distant ceiling supported by four

rows of giant Dragon Pillars marching away into the vast
dark. Across the Great Deep a spidery rope bridge with
wooden footboards was suspended. The span was narrow;
those using it would have to cross the wide gulf in single file.
It was anchored on the near side by two huge iron rings on
iron posts driven into the stone; and it was held on the far
side by a winch set far back from the lip of the rift—the
winch a remnant of the ancient drawbridge destroyed in the
Winter War. Guarding the hoist on the distant side were two
Rūcks, squatting on the stone floor, casting knucklebones and
muttering curses at each other.

Lord Kian motioned Shannon Silverleaf forward. "Can you
fell the Rukh on the left with an arrow from here?" Kian whispered.

Shannon eyed the distance; it was a far shot. "It would be
surer from the bottom of the steps." He motioned downward
into the shadows.

Lord Kian gave a curt nod, and signalling the others to remain, the Man and the Elf crept down the broad stairway. At the
bottom, Kian knelt to one knee while Shannon stood straight,
and each drew his bow to the full. The Rūcks continued their
quarrel, unaware of their danger; one, enraged at the turn of the
dice, jumped up with a snarling oath and clouted the other behind the ear. The second Ruck kicked out at the first and with a
curse sprang to his feet, and they both drew their scimitars, bent
on murder. But before they could close with one another in battle, *Th-thunn!* two arrows were loosed and sped hissing through
the air to lodge deeply into the Rūcks. One fell instantly dead,
pierced through the heart. The other stared in astonishment at
the point emerging from his stomach, but ere he could draw
breath to scream, *Th-thock!* two more arrows thudded into him,
and he pitched forward on his face, dead before striking the
stone floor.

Perry and Delk dashed down the steps, with Anval, Borin,
and Ursor right behind. "Now!" barked Kian. "Across the
bridge. Hurry!" But Shannon, in the lead, had just stepped onto
the span when out of the first side tunnel on the left came
tramping a Hlōk-led company of Rūcks. It was the change of
the guard.

For an instant in time, the Rūcks stopped, frozen in amazement at the sight of these intruders. Then, with snarls of rage, the maggot-folk leapt forward, scimitars raised.

"Wait!" Kian called to his companions. "There are too many of them to meet on the open floor. We'll make our stand on this side of the bridge where they can only come at us one at a time. Ursor, to the bridge. Anval, Borin, flank Ursor. Shannon, with your bow stand thwartwise to the span from me; we'll catch them in our cross-fire. Perry, Delk, take those who get past the first rank. Yield no quarter."

Across the bridge charged the maggot-folk, the span bouncing and swaying under their rushing feet. On they came, right into Ursor's devastating mace, and Anval's and Borin's lethal axes, and the first to fall was the Hlōk leader.

His heart hammering, Perry had drawn Bane, and its blue flame blazed; the Warrow and Delk stood ready, but as of yet no Spawn had won past the front rank. Kian's bow hummed as arrow after arrow hissed into the Rūcks at the rear, and Shannon's aim was just as deadly, the bolts slashing into the foe from right and left.

The Rucks were single file on the narrow bridge and jammed closely together; those in the fore fell screeching into the Deep, hurled there by mace or axe, while those in the rear plummeted into the black depths with quarrels through them. Many in the span center turned to flee, elbowing, pushing, wildly clawing, jolting into each other and shoving one another off in their mad bid to escape; yet some at the distant end regained the far side only to be dropped by deadly arrows before they could reach the sanctuary of the far tunnels.

But one fleeing Rūck ran to the windlass, where he grabbed up a mallet and with a wild swing knocked the brake-wedge loose just as an arrow sprang full from his chest and he fell dead. Yet the winch was free and spinning as the anchor ropes ran loose. And the bridge, now held only at one end by the large iron rings, rucketted down to crash into the side of the abyss, and the remaining Spawn fell screaming to their doom. And Perry's blood ran chill as he unwillingly listened in frozen horror to the shrieks and wails of the plunging Rūcks—screams that dwindled and faded, to be lost at last in the black silence as the maggot-folk plummeted beyond hearing down into the dreadful depths.

A quick check showed that none of the Seven had received so much as a minor wound, though there was a long scimitar scar on Ursor's leather breastplate. Albeit free from injury and successful in battle, still the Squad may have lost the campaign, for they had yet to cross the gulf; and the span was down, dangling from the iron rings on the near side, creaking and swinging slowly like a great long pendulum as it hung down the sheer undercut wall of the Deep.

"Did any of the Rutcha escape to warn the others?" asked Ursor. "I could not tell, for I was busy at the fore."

"I think not," answered Shannon, gesturing toward the many dead on the far shelf. "Our arrows dropped all who tried to flee."

"Though none escaped," declared Kian, "we must be across and gone ere any more come. If that was the changing of the guard, we have at most six or eight hours—likely less—before others arrive."

They went to the lip of the gulf and searched for a way across. The chasm was wide: the far rim at the narrowest point was some fifty feet away, and in many places the width exceeded one hundred feet.

Anval, Borin, and Delk unhooded three Dwarf-lanterns, and with Perry they lay on their stomachs on the lip of the rift and examined the depths for as far as the light shone. They could see the bridge dangling down the wall, swaying slowly, but they found no way to span the abyss, for below the undercut the sides were smooth and sheer, dropping straight for as far as the eye could see, vanishing into the unguessable depths beyond. Perry quailed at the sight of the endless fall, and pushed back from the rim.

Finding no way to cross down below, the buccan and the Dwarves strode out to the sides where the great ebon crack disappeared into the stone walls of the mountain, but the rift was even wider at those points. Lord Kian, Shannon, and Ursor spoke quietly together and eyed the distance to the winch; they saw that it was covered with a grapnel-shelter whose rounded edges and turned-under sides were cunningly contrived to resist hooks; in any event, the cast was a long one to carry a rope of any consequence. The rest of the far-side shelf was barren and smooth, flattened ages agone by Dwarven adze and stone chisel to resist invaders' grapnels.

"Our mission has failed before it ever got properly under way," groaned Perry in despair. "We are stopped here at the Great Deep. All of our hopes and plans have fallen into its black depths just as the burning Gargon fell long ago."

"Speak not the name of the Dread needlessly"—Shannon's voice held a sharp edge—"for it portends evil in Black Drimmen-deeve. And do not despair too soon, for I believe our Drimm friends will yet show us the way."

"*Kruk!*" spat Anval. "We cannot throw a hook to cross over, and we cannot go around the ends, and we cannot climb down and across. Borin, it will be slow, yet all that is left to us is a climb up and over on the roof."

"Roof? Climb?" asked Perry, looking upward, dumbfounded. "How can we cross over on the roof? It must be eighty or a hundred feet up to there, and we are not flies to walk upside down on that stone ceiling. Do you propose an enchantment, a miracle?"

"Nay," growled Borin, rummaging in his pack, "not a miracle, nor spell, but this instead." From his pack Borin extracted a leather harness laden with crafted metal snap-rings and thin-bladed spikes, each spike with an eyelet on the side of the thick end; also affixed to the belting were many different-sized, small, irregular iron cubes, each hollowed out by a hole through the center.

"What is that?" asked Perry, puzzled.

"A climbing harness," replied Borin.

"And what are those things fastened to it?" Perry pointed to the metal objects.

"Rock-nails. Rings. Jams," answered Borin, unfastening one each of the three types of devices and handing them to the Warrow, who held them in the lantern light to examine them closely. Borin spoke on: "Heed: with the nail, you drive the spike into a thin crevice in the stone, then snap a ring through the eyelet; one of several leather straps is then clipped between the climbing harness and the ring. You haul yourself up and along as you go, suspended by strap on a trail of driven rock-nails and attached rings. When you come to a place where the crevices are wider, you wedge a proper-sized jam in place, slipping a snap-ring through the hole, using it instead of a nail."

Borin turned to Lord Kian. "I will make the climb, and once across I will let myself down; and then we will fix a rope over the Great Dēop for the rest to use; or we will haul the bridge back up, and all can stride above the dark depths on its broad span."

Perry examined the devices while Borin prepared himself for the climb, putting on the tackle, buckling the cross straps of the harness and cinching tight the wide belt burdened with the rings, nails, and jams. The Dwarf also attached hanks of rope to the belt; and he tied a small hammer by a thong to his wrist.

"Here," rasped Anval, fastening a thick leather pad to the hammer face, "it will deaden the sound of each strike." Borin nodded but said nought, for his gaze was sweeping up and across the roof.

"It is a long reach," growled Borin to his brother as they surveyed the intended route. "Should I need more climbware, I will drop a line to you." Anval merely grunted in reply.

The Ironfists selected a place to start, and Perry gave Borin back the nail, jam, and ring. The Dwarf reached up high on the wall beside the stairs and with muffled blows drove the rock-nail into a thin crack; then began the perilous climb.

Quickly, Borin drove nail after nail into the stone, clipping and adjusting an appropriate harness anchor strap to each new nail as he went, unclipping the hindmost strap and retrieving the free snap-ring as he left each embedded nail behind; and up like a fly he clambered. At times there were handholds, and he did not use the rock-nails as he ascended. At other times, however, long still study was needed before he drove a nail or wedged a jam and moved onward. At last he topped the wall and started across the ceiling, the Dwarf now totally dependent upon the leather belting, rings, nails, jams, and harness. Perry was glad that it was not he who had to climb so high and dangle like a Yule decoration, and he was amazed by Borin's ability. "How surely he goes," breathed the Warrow, looking up, knowing that were their places exchanged he would be frozen with fear.

"Aye," answered Delk. "Borin is accounted a master stone climber—even among the Châkka."

"You speak as if all Dwarves climb like that," said Perry.

"Aye," responded Delk, "for the inside of a Mountain needs climbing more than its outside ever does. And the Châkka have been climbing Mountains since we and they were created—yet we more often climb within the living stone than without. Even so, mayhap Borin is the best of us all."

Once again Perry turned his sight toward the Dwarf above. Yet Borin's progress had slowed markedly, for he was now on the most difficult, the most hazardous reach.

Bit by bit, the Dwarf inched across the ceiling as precious time eked beyond recall into the past. And Perry fretted that the climb had already taken too long, and that more time would be spent ere the task came to an end; for the buccan knew that at any moment a Rücken band could swarm into the War Hall. These thoughts were on Lord Kian's mind too, for the young Man said to Shannon, "It is now that Borin is most vulnerable to Yrm arrow; if *Spaunen* come, we must slay any archers first." Perry's heart sank at these dismaying words, and his eyes once again turned to the exposed climber.

And up above, the Dwarf crept onward as the sands of time ran swiftly down.

Hours later, it seemed, Borin, now well out over the chasm, called down to the companions below, pitching his voice so that it would not carry into the caverns to be heard by hostile ears: *"Ziggurt!"*

"What did he say?" asked Perry.

"Ziggurt," replied Delk. "It is one of the many Châk words describing the condition of rock. Borin says the roof stone where he is, is *ziggurt*. That means it is not completely sound; perhaps when the Great Dēop first split upward, reaching into the Mountain from below, the stone was stressed so."

"Does that mean it's going to fall?" asked the Warrow, yielding back.

"Nay," Delk assured him. "*Ziggurt* is not rotten stone, yet it may give way, but only if stressed more. *Ziggurt* means that the rock is crazed, that it has many small cracks and large, and fissures running widely through it. The rock is untrustworthy for bearing weight: small chunks may fall if pulled upon; large slabs can shatter down if stressed just so. No, *ziggurt* does not mean weak stone; it can be very strong and stand forever. But long careful study is necessary beforehand when working the stone, to prevent mishap. Yet *ziggurt* is more than I have just told you. Pah! The Common Tongue is not suited to any better description than that; it is not capable of shading the meanings of stone as is the Châk Speech."

"Time, Delk?" asked Kian. "There is the rub: you have said that time is needed to work *ziggurt* rock to prevent mishap; yet I deem that our time is nigh gone. Other Yrm patrols will come, and we must be away ere then with no trace of our passage remaining. If Gnar suspects that his enemies are within these caverns, he will turn out all of his forces to search for us. And we do not want a *Spaunen* Swarm hunting through the halls, seeking our party. No, our only hope to help Durek is to win through without alerting the entire Yrm army." In a muted voice, Kian called up to Borin, "Can you go on?"

"It is *ziggurt* for as far as the eye can see," Borin called back down, waving a hand across the gulf and toward the Mustering Chamber. "But I must try, though it will be a gamble, for the way is obscured by soot from the time the ancient bridge burned, and long study is needed, yet we have not the time. I must chance a hasty crossing."

"Wait!" softly called Shannon, cupping his hands about his mouth so that his voice would reach the Dwarf above. "There is this: if you can lower a rope to me, I can swing across—if the stone and iron rock-nails will bear my weight." The Elf looked at Lord Kian. "Except for Perry, I am the least heavy, and you cannot risk him on this scheme." Lord Kian nodded his assent.

Borin hammered in another rock-nail, and then like a swaying spider strand a thin, strong line came snaking and swinging down out of the overhead gloom. Borin had tied his hammer to the end to give the rope a pendulum weight, and he swung it as he payed it out. Shannon nimbly caught the line on one of the long arcs, and as soon as Borin called down that all was ready, the Elf gave the company a rakish grin and sprang off the edge of the Deep.

Shannon's first long swing was not far enough, and he rose to the end of his arc, seemed to pause, and then hurtled back across the yawning gulf. On the second swing he pumped hard over the bottomless pit and carried farther still, though it was not yet enough. On the third pass he almost gained the far lip of the chasm, but not quite.

Only Borin, clenched against the ceiling by the short anchor straps, did not see the Elf come closer and closer with each plunge; instead, the Dwarf kept his eye riveted to the rock-nail. The swings were placing heavy stress on the eyeletted spike, and Borin intensely watched the crevice the nail blade was riven into. On the third arc, a stone chip flaked from the crack: the nail was coming loose! Quickly, Borin jammed his right forearm up into a large *ziggurt* cleft and made a fist, wedging his clenched hand tightly in the rift; he wrapped the loose end of the pendulum rope around his left arm and forcefully gripped it. No sooner had the Dwarf caught hold than the nail tore loose, and the weight of the plummeting Elf jolted through Borin's arms and shoulders.

Silverleaf was swinging back from the far lip when he felt the rope give then catch again, and the jar nearly shook his grip loose, the line slipping in his grasp ere he caught tight. His grip firm again, he continued his arc and pumped hard on the next plunge across.

Borin strained desperately to hold on, gritting his teeth and closing his eyes with the effort, his great arm and shoulder muscles cracking with the stress, for he was the anchoring link between the stone overhead and the taut rope to the Elf hurtling the abyss below. The greatest strain came when Shannon hurtled through the bottom of the arc, and Borin strove to hold on: his right fist, jammed in the crack, felt as if the bones in his hand were breaking, and the rope wrapped around his left arm seemed as if it were cutting through the elbow, and his shoulders felt as if his arms were being plucked from the sockets. Yet grimly he held on as Shannon hurled up in a rising arc out of the depths and to the far lip. The Elf cast loose from the line and plunged forward to the stone, falling with a roll and then springing nimbly to his feet.

Aloft, Borin gave a grunt of relief, and, dangling by the leather straps between his climbing harness and the embedded rock-nails, he extracted his skinned-knuckled hand from the jam-crack and massaged his shoulders, neck, and arms. After a moment, he began coiling the pendulum rope, drawing it upward into the shadows, preparatory to starting back the way he had come.

Shannon called for a hammer and a rock-nail, and they were tossed over the abyss to him; the Elf drove the spike into a thin chink in the floor. At Silverleaf's command, Perry attached his soft and pliable ancient Elven-rope to a grapnel and threw it across to the Elf, who then wedged a tine of the hook into the eyelet of the nail, while the other end of the line was anchored to one of the iron post rings. At a gesture from Shannon, huge Ursor swung hand over hand and joined the Elf; though he was a giant, the Baeran was deft and graceful.

Perry gasped at Ursor's deed, for the line was so slender and the Man so huge, and the Warrow feared that the rope would snap; but it was Elven-made, and Silverleaf had known that it would hold ten like Ursor.

Again Perry caught his breath and gritted his teeth in fear for a companion's safety, for Lord Kian clambered down into the black abyss on the dangling bridge; while it swayed and jolted against the sheer wall, the Man hauled the far loose ends of the anchor ropes up out of the darkness and secured a light line to them. That done, he then climbed back up and out, bringing the line with him. Once out, he used another of their grapnels to pitch the slender cord over to Ursor, who fetched the heavy anchor ropes up to the far side where he and Shannon ran them onto the ancient winch. Then, with a grinding clatter of gears, Ursor began hoisting the bridge up out of the chasm, back toward its original position.

Up on the ceiling, Borin had worked his way to a place where, once again, he was above the Broad Shelf. Fixing a jam and ring in a crack, the Dwarf payed out a line; and slipping it through the snap-ring, he used the rope to free-rappel to the wide stone floor. With a flip of the wrist, he pulled the free end of the line through the ring above to come piling down. And as Anval coiled the rope, Borin removed the tackle with the remainder of the rock-nails and jams and snap rings and restored them all to his pack along with his ropes. As Borin closed his backpack, Ursor finished his task at the hoist: the bridge was once again in position, with the brake wedge in place. All the extra lines were untied and repacked. Then the rest of the Seven queued up to cross the gulf.

When Perry's turn came he clutched the hand ropes with all his might, for the Great Deep fell sheer and bottomless below him, and a cold chill rose up around him from out of its depths. He felt that the bouncing bridge would collapse again, and its swaying frightened him. He had been amazed at how casually Lord Kian had climbed down the bridge when it was dangling free and swinging beneath the undercut. He also felt that Ursor's hand-over-hand trip above the yawning chasm had taken unimaginable bravery and dexterity. And Borin up on the ceiling, hanging by narrow straps from small iron cubes or thin iron blades driven into crevices, or Shannon swinging by a slender line over those dreadful depths, well, it was all quite beyond Perry's courage and skill to do. And now he was having trouble just putting one foot in front of another on a bouncing, swaying, narrow rope-and-board span above an endless fall into a gaping, black depth; and in his mind's eye he once again saw the Rūcks plunging to their doom. *Hey! This won't do,* he thought, *now don't you freeze in fear out here; after what all the others did, you've just got to cross over this awful black pit.* And cross it he did, trembling and clutching, but moving ahead all the time. He was greatly relieved when he stumbled onto the other side, nearly falling to his knees when his feet came off the bounding span and met the hard, unyielding stone.

Last to cross was Delk, who strolled over as if the narrow bridge were a broad highway.

After retrieving the arrows from the dead Rūcks, the Seven dragged the corpses to the lip and flung them into the Deep, pitching the Rūck weapons after. Perry threw a fallen torch into the gulf, and as it fell, a smoldering spark caught, and it burst into flame; and Perry watched its guttering light as it tumbled end over end. His sight followed it for what seemed to be an endless time as it slowly became a tiny speck of luminance plummeting down and down, until it disappeared; whether it plunged beyond an outcropping to be seen no more, or fell at last into a stream at the bottom, or blew out, or simply became too small to see, Perry could not tell. He shuddered at the awful depths involved, unable to imagine their limits and not wanting to know. Again he drew back from the edge in fear.

With one last sweeping look, Lord Kian saw that all overt

evidence of the battle was gone. "I think no one will discover that we were here. Even the blood is cleaned up well enough so that only close inspection will show that any was spilled. The Spawn simply will be presented with the mystery of a missing company, and some guards that disappeared. Gnar may think that they deserted. The main evidence of our passage lies in the unguessed depths of the Great Deep."

"Not all," grunted Borin. "The rock-nails and jams are in place on the wall and roof. But they are small and dark and should go unnoticed. Even if discovered, mayhap the Squam will think them an old dead end, for they go nowhere."

"Let us be gone, then," declared Lord Kian, "for we can do no more here, and we must away ere we are discovered.—Perry."

With the Warrow in the lead next to Anval, they started at a jog trot toward the black gape of the second tunnel on the right. Dwarf-lanterns were slightly unhooded and cast narrow phosphorescent beams to dimly light the way. The Seven entered the dark passage and started up the first of several flights of stairs that would lead to the Hall of the Gravenarch. Suddenly Shannon hissed, "*Quiet!* Shield the lights. *Rûpt* below." The Elf's sharper hearing had detected the tramp of Rūcken boots.

The lanterns were hooded and the company stood quietly, poised on the steps. Down at the entrance of the corridor, they saw reflected torchlight flicker by, and they heard the heavy tread of Spawn heading for the bridge. The companions had started just in time; it had taken seven full hours to get from Dawn-Gate to these steps, but fortunately for the Squad the band of maggot-folk now tramping to the bridge had come too late to thwart this initial thrust.

After the *Spaunen* passed, the companions started up the stairway once again, coming quickly to the top and continuing down the passageway. They ignored the side corridors and went on for nearly a mile and a half, climbing six flights of steps separated by long stretches of level cavern. They came to the base of the seventh flight, but the way was barred by large blocks of broken stone amid piles of rubble. "It is as I feared," said Perry. "*The Raven Book* tells that the roof collapsed when Brega sundered the keystone of the Gravenarch and nearly lost his life. We must now attempt to find a way up to the Sixth Rise above

Gate Level and come to a place where I again recognize the way. In this search a Dwarf should lead."

Delk Steelshank was chosen to go first, for in his youth he had apprenticed to a Tunnelmaster before he finally turned to the craft of gatemaking. He studied Perry's map with Anval and Borin, and then led them down two flights of steps to the first westbound tunnel; they strode along it for a half mile, coming to a corridor to the right with steps bearing upward. They climbed up the flight, and a level cross-passage bored away in both directions. Ahead they could see another flight of stairs going on up. They mounted these, then went ahead and up another flight. "Here, we are on the Sixth Rise, and near to the point where we were blocked," announced Delk, and Anval and Borin grunted in agreement. "Now it is merely a matter of closing the course to come to the other side of the blockage—or of coming upon something Friend Perry can reconcile with the Brega Path."

"*Hsst!*" shushed Shannon, whose keen hearing again proved sharper than that of Dwarf, Man, or Warrow. "I hear another company of *Rûpt*. They tramp nigh."

The comrades looked back down the way they had come and could see the faint flicker of far-off torchlight bearing in their direction.

"This way—quickly," whispered Delk, and they bolted down a side corridor curving 'round to the east and south. Quietly they went, as swiftly as they could, the faint glow of their lanterns showing the way. They came to an opening on their left. They were about to pass it by when more torchlight could be seen ahead of them. "We have no choice," hissed Delk. "There are Squam before us and Squam behind. Into this room."

Hurriedly, they stepped into a narrow, long chamber. A great pile of fallen stone blocked most of the room, ramping upward from the center to the unseen, distant wall, and there was no way out except the one door they had come through. They were trapped!

The Seven ranged themselves along the near wall as the boots tramped closer. The Dwarf-lanterns were closed and the room plunged into darkness. All weapons save Bane were drawn and readied. They could now see the torchlight flickering up the passage and through the broken door.

Tramp! Tramp! The Spawn came onward.

Perry's heart thudded, and he grasped Bane's hilt, preparing to draw the blade should the maggot-folk come through the door.

Tramp! Tramp! They were now close enough for the Seven to hear the snarling and cursing in the Rūcken ranks.

Tramp! Tramp! Perry steeled himself.

And then the *Spaunen* marched by the door and headed on up the passage.

Perry discovered that he had been holding his breath, and he let it out in a sigh of relief. But in alarm he immediately caught it again as from the corridor there came a great cursing and shouting: the Rūcken band going up the passage had met the band coming down, and they jostled and jolted and elbowed one another as they passed. Then the second band, still grumbling, marched past the room where the Seven were hiding.

When the tramp of *Spaunen* boot became but a faint echo, Perry slid shakily down the wall and sat on the floor. That had been entirely too close. They had narrowly escaped being caught between Rūcken forces, and their mission had nearly ended after it had just begun. Perry's hands trembled and his breath seemed to whistle hoarsely in and out of his throat. But none of the others said anything and did not seem to notice.

Soon Delk cracked the hood of his lantern, and a faint glow lit up the ruined room. They sat awhile without speaking.

Perry was taking a careful sip of water when he noted a portion of a dark rune-mark on the side wall, hidden by rubble. Picking up the lantern, he stepped over to look at the ebon glyph. It was neither Common nor Elvish but, rather, it was Dwarvish. The buccan pushed some of the shattered rubble away from the top of the pile, revealing the whole of the runes written in some black ichor, now dried: ᚠᚱᚢᛏᛟᛁ

Perry looked on for a moment, puzzled. These glyphs were familiar. They were in *The Raven Book* somewhere. The Warrow frowned in concentration. It was . . . it was . . . "Hoy!" Perry exclaimed, "This is Braggi's Rune! I know where we are!"

CHAPTER 2

⟨❧⟩

FLIGHT UNDER THE MOUNTAIN

Perry's announcement brought Lord Kian to his feet. The Man stepped to the wall and took a Brega-Path map from his jerkin and spread it on the floor before the Warrow. "Where?" asked Kian. Perry squatted and adjusted the lantern to illuminate the chart as all the comrades gathered 'round.

"Right here!" proclaimed the buccan jubilantly, stabbing his forefinger to the map. "This room is the Hall of the Gravenarch, Braggi's Stand. See? Here is Braggi's Rune." Perry touched a glyph on the wall beside him, then gestured about. "And this rubble around us, it is where the ceiling collapsed when Brega broke the keystone." Perry peered through the dimness at what could be seen of the extent of the room. "Somewhere should be sign of Braggi's ancient battle: broken weapons, shattered armor, the long-dead remains of the combatants; but I guess it is now buried 'neath the fallen rock."

The Warrow looked 'round at the faces of the other members of the company, eerily shadowed by the lantern on the floor. "Yonder, under that wreckage, lies the eastern hall-door," he continued, "and beyond it lie the blocked stairs where we were turned aside by the fallen stone. We've come a long way to be standing only a couple-hundred paces from where we started."

"Aye. I knew we had come nearly full circle," grunted Delk, and Anval and Borin nodded silently in agreement, "but the foul Squam drew my attention elsewhere."

"Since now you know where we stand, Perry, it must mean we can set forth," growled Borin.

"Yes," replied Perry, "for here we are past all the fallen rock, and once more we are upon the Brega Path. Our way to Dusk-Door lies there." Perry pointed to the broken portal and through to the hallway they had fled.

In two strides Ursor stepped to the door and cautiously looked out into the corridor, then turned to the comrades. "The way is clear," he rumbled.

"Then let us go forth at once," urged Lord Kian. "Crossing the Great Deep, finding our way to this Rise, and eluding the Yrm has caused great delay, precious time we can ill afford."

The Seven stepped out through the portal and took the left-hand way, travelling the Brega Path in reverse. Swiftly they went south through the passage and soon came to the Great Chamber, a huge room in the Drimmen-deeve. They peered out of the corridor and into the vast delving. No Rūcken torchlight was seen; the chamber was dark and empty. "To the right," whispered Perry, "across the wide floor and out the passage at the west end, nearly one-half mile away."

In haste they sped across the stone floor to the far west end and sallied into the passageway there—and none too soon, for as they entered the shaft, Shannon, bringing up the rear, again whispered, "*Hsst!* The lanterns." The lamps were quickly shuttered. As the companions stood in blackness, far behind them in the huge chamber a *Rūpt* company bearing burning brands marched out of the south corridor, across the wide floor, and entered the north passage. When the torchlight disappeared, the Seven resumed their trek.

The corridor gently sloped downward as they went. The way before them was broad and swift, and there were no side passages. Perry knew that this would be one of the most dangerous traverses along the Brega Path: over the next five miles this passage had no side corridors to bolt into should Spawn come. But in this passage Perry unsheathed his Elven sword. "Here I will carry Bane in the open," the Warrow declared, "to warn of approaching maggot-folk if its blaze grows." The blade-jewel flickered a faint blue, telling of distant danger. And the companions strode on.

Quickly they marched, and the road gently curved right and

left and right again as they walked downward. They trod between vertical walls beneath an arched roof. Occasionally they saw runes carved along the passageway but took no time to examine the glyphs for their message. Again the corridor curved left. As Delk had informed Perry some time back, Dwarves often shaped a natural passage into a delved road, and this corridor with its many gentle curves seemed to be one of those. Brega had called this path the Upward Way, but of course to the Seven it was a downward way, for Brega had gone in the opposite direction.

At last they came to another huge cavern. "This is the Rest Chamber, so named by Brega because of the stone blocks like seats scattered across the floor," said Perry, pointing at one of the square-cut giant stones. "Yet I think we should not pause here, for our goal is distant and our need to press on is urgent. Yon lies our course: to the west side and out we go. Ahead, about seven miles hence, is a chamber where we may rest."

Again they resumed the trek, and soon passed out of the room and back into a corridor. Perry spoke once more: "From here on we will have side fissures and passageways to hide in should *Spaunen* come; but by the same token, there are more places from which maggot-folk might fall upon us. So stay ready." Bane's rune-jewel still flickered faintly, but the danger was too distant to concern them, and they marched secure in that knowledge.

This time the corridor was less delved, more like a natural cavern: though the floor was smooth, the walls and ceiling were but lightly worked by Dwarf tool and had a rough look. The broad shaft continued to wind downward, and there were many lateral splits cleaving off into the darkness.

They marched down to the west for nearly three more hours, coming at last to the chamber foretold of by Perry. "Brega called this the Broad Hall," stated the Warrow, "but I say it is a dining hall, for I am hungry—and weary. Lord Kian, I suggest we eat and rest. It has been a long day, though I don't know exactly how far we've come nor what time it is."

"We have walked nearly sixteen miles in the caverns," declared Delk, "fourteen on the Brega Path and two to bypass the fallen stone at the Hall of the Gravenarch." Anval and Borin nodded their agreement, for the distances and directions were emblazoned in their Dwarf memories.

"Though I am not certain," rumbled Ursor, "I think the day outside has fled, and the Moon rides the eventide. It is my guess that it is now near the mid of night."

"It is two hours beyond midnight, and the Moon sinks low in the west," corrected Shannon with a certainty the others did not doubt, for though days, weeks, months, and even years seem to mean little to Elves, and they appear to note only the seasons, still they know at any moment where stand the Sun, Moon, and stars.

"Well, no wonder I'm hungry and tired," sighed Perry.

"So are we all," agreed Lord Kian. "Perry is right. Here we will eat, drink, and rest. We stand the same order of watch as before. Bane shall be our silent sentinel."

Perry hungrily consumed three crue biscuits and drank a small amount of water; on their next long march they should reach the "safe" stream that flowed through the Bottom Chamber, seventeen miles to the west, but till they did, water was to be conserved. The Warrow then plumped his pack into a pillow and, settling back, fell instantly into slumber. Bane, leaning against a block of stone, softly glinted, whispering of far-off enemies.

Four hours later, Ursor awakened Perry for his turn at guard. Again, to stay awake, the Warrow slowly paced back and forth in the dim light cast by the barely cracked Dwarf-lantern. He watched Bane, but it changed not. Finally, his tour over, he went to rouse Shannon Silverleaf.

The Elf sat quietly with his back against a wall, and his tilted eyes glittered in the lantern light, for the sleep of Elves is strange and wholly different from that of Dwarf, Man, or Warrow—if indeed Elves sleep a genuine sleep at all. It is said that in their Lands twilight rules, and the days pass not, and slumber never visits. Legend would have it that some mortals have become ensnared in this timeless existence. Yet these legends of Lands where time's hands stand still, these legends would seem to fly in the face of the Elves' "knowing" where stand the Sun, Moon, and stars. On the other hand, many would say that Elves' "power" over time *proves* that they live in twilight and sleep not. Still, it is recorded in *The Raven Book* that Lord Gildor said that though Elves could go for many days without true slumber, even they must sleep at last.

But when Perry approached the resting Elf, Silverleaf stood ere the Warrow came nigh and indicated to the buccan that he should sleep.

In all, the company had rested for some eight hours when Delk finally roused the others. They ate a quick meal and sipped water, and then they struck out once more. Perry continued to carry Bane unsheathed, and still the faint blue flame spoke only of distant danger.

The farther west they went the less finished the passageway became. Now they occasionally came upon splits and fissures in the floor; most could be stepped over, but at times Perry had to spring across, though none of the others did, being taller than the wee buccan. At one point they passed a broad tunnel merging from the right. Its worn floor bespoke heavy travel throughout the ages, yet whether it was smoothed by Rūcken feet or by the Dwarves before, they could not tell. The timeworn track continued on in the passage the Seven followed, and once again their speed was considerable.

They had gone this way for a time when Perry noted that Bane's jewel was beginning to glitter more strongly; but whether the danger was before them, or overtaking from behind, or coming from the side, they knew not. "Ahead lies the Round Chamber," announced Perry. "It has many entrances and exits to hide us. It is not far. Let us make for it."

Swiftly they strode forward at a pace set by the Warrow. Bane's flame continued to grow. Finally they came to the gallery Perry had spoken of: it was another huge room, as most of the chambers in Kraggen-cor seemed to be; this one was circular, and there were many portals along its perimeter, some delved, some natural clefts. The chamber was empty, but Bane's blade-jewel now glittered brightly. "We know not which way the danger comes," said Kian, "but chances are it will issue from one of the delved ways and leave by another. Let us choose one of these unworked cracks to slip into to remain undetected. Perry, be prepared to sheath Bane's blue light."

The Seven found a natural fissure with undisturbed dust carpeting its level floor; they slipped into the cleft and waited with lanterns tightly hooded. Bane's glow grew to a cobalt flame that ran along the bitter edge, and Perry sheathed the blade. The Squad could see torchlight bobbing up the south passage they had just come from: the danger had been overtaking them from behind. A large company of Rūcks jog-trotted out of the tunnel and into the great, round room. They loped to the center of the huge chamber. A command was snarled by the Hlōk leader, and the company halted. Another command, and the Rūcks broke from their ragged ranks and flopped to the stone floor. They were staying.

Lord Kian drew back from the cleft entrance and turned to the companions he could now dimly see by reflected torchlight. Before Kian could speak softly, Borin stepped out of the darkness at the back of the split and motioned Kian to him. "This crack is a dead end," the Dwarf whispered. "We cannot get out."

They watched the Rūcks for six taut yet somehow dreary hours. During that time the maggot-folk had quarreled, cursed, and snarled; several fights had broken out among them, only to be stopped by the raging Hlōk lashing the squabbling Rūcks and anyone nearby with a great, cracking whip. The maggot-folk had gluttonously eaten a grisly meal of some unknown flesh: hunkered down, slobbering and drooling, and throwing splintered bones into the darkness beyond the torchlight after cracking them open and tonguing out the marrow. At last, however, the Spawn had finished their gruesome repast and then had resumed quarreling and cursing, casting lots, shoving one another, bickering.

"This is awful," whispered Perry to Lord Kian. "We have got to get out of here. We've lost too many hours as it is, and we must be on our way. Can't we slip through the shadows and out the far north door?"

Lord Kian, sitting on the floor with his back to the wall, grimly shook his head. "Look closely," he breathed, "they are athwart all our paths, both to the west and around the chamber to the east and north. We have no choice but to wait them out."

Another hour went by; then there was a great hubbub in the chamber as a second Hlōk-led, torch-bearing company of

Rūcks loped through one of the west portals and into the vast room, halting aflank the first band. "Where've you been, Plooshgnak, you slime?" snarled the first Hlōk, cracking his whip. "We've been stuck here waiting for your snot-wart hides too long. I ought to run some maggot holes into your stinking guts with a hot iron."

"Aw, shut your snag trap, Boshlub," snarled the Hlōk leader of the second band. "We're not the last: Gushmot's not here, blast his pus-rot teeth."

The two Hlōks were cursing each other and arguing violently when, moments later, a third company of Rūcks galloped into the chamber. The Hlōk leader of this band seemed enraged with the other two quarreling Hlōks. *"Ngash batang lûktah glog graktal doosh spturrskrank azg!"* he howled in the foul, harsh Slûk tongue. *"Gnar skrike!"* At mention of Gnar's name, Plooshgnak kicked a seated Rūck, and Boshlub cracked his whip onto the back of another and snarled orders. The first two Rūck companies fell into ragged ranks, jostling and elbowing and grumbling. With a crack of Boshlub's lash, all the Rūcks loped out through the northeast corridor. And the Round Chamber was left in dark silence.

After a moment, Perry unsheathed Bane. The blue light coldly flamed from the jewel and down the blade, but as the Seven watched, it grew dimmer. "Let's go now," urged Perry, "before any more maggot-folk come to this way station."

A glance around the great room revealed only utter blackness; no light of torch could be seen flickering through any portal. The Seven eased open the hoods of their Dwarf-lanterns a bit, to let narrow shafts of radiance illuminate the way. Swiftly the companions crossed to the north tunnel and entered the passage.

The way became narrow in places, and at times chasms bore off to the right or left, and the company would walk along the shelved precipices. Fissures opened to either side, and Perry continued to make the choices dictated by Brega's instructions. The Warrow had found no surprises in the path, for the Brega Scroll was accurate and detailed. Yet though he had not been surprised, he was astounded by the sizes of the chambers they had passed through: the East Hall at Dawn-Gate had been two hundred yards in length, two hundred in width; the Mustering

Hall at the Deep was a mile long and half that wide—according to Brega, who had seen its extent by the light of raging flames as the drawbridge over the Great Deep burned by Elf-set fire; the Great Chamber was a half-mile long and a quarter-mile wide. Enormous, the rooms were enormous. And the number of halls, tunnels, fissures, cracks, and additional passages leading away to other reaches of Drimmen-deeve indicated that the delvings of Kraggen-cor were intricate beyond imagination, for what the comrades had seen was incredibly complex and colossal—and they had seen but a minuscule portion of the whole.

Again the way sloped downward, and wide cracks appeared in the floor. Now Perry had to leap over three- and four-foot-wide crevices; considerable jumps for one who was only three and a half feet tall. The Squad came to a narrow shelf on the face of a precipice; a chasm yawned bottomless to their right. They edged for scores of paces along the wall above the rift before coming again to a wide ledge. The chasm narrowed as they walked onward, and soon they were once again striding through an arched tunnel.

They had walked, leapt, scrambled, and sidled for three hours since leaving the Round Chamber, covering some six miles. At last they came to the Grate Room, a small round chamber to the north side of the main passage. Behind them the cavern split four ways: the left-hand way was wide and led down; the two middle ways were narrow and twisting—one up, one down; and the right-hand way was the one whence they had just come down. Before them the passage ran on downward, heading for the still-distant Dusk-Door.

"We are yet one and twenty miles from our goal," announced Perry, "but I think we must rest and eat before going on. Let us tarry in the Grate Room for a while."

Lord Kian and the others agreed; they were indeed weary, for hiding in a crevice from squabbling Rūcks had been nearly as tiresome as would running from a pursuing *Spaunen* Swarm. "Take care not to step onto the old grillework," cautioned Perry as they stepped through the door, "for it is corroded and may crumble, and you would fall into the shaft it covers, said by *The Raven Book* to be in the center of the chamber floor."

The room they entered was perhaps twenty feet square with a low ceiling—certainly the smallest chamber they had seen in

Kraggen-cor. Centered in the room, a huge rust-stained chain dangled down from a narrow, grate-covered square shaft set in the ceiling, and passed through a like grate placed in the floor, the mighty links appearing out of the constricting blackness above and disappearing into the darkness of the straight shaft below. Avoiding the rust-worn grille covering the ebon hole, Perry, along with the others, flung his pack down to be rid of the burden. He took some crue, and leaned back against his soft bedroll and sighed. After a bit he asked, "What is the hour, Shannon?"

"It is nearly the middle of the night," answered the Elf. "We have just eight and forty hours before Durek tries the Door."

"Two full days," stated Kian. "One to get there, and one to work on the Door. It is well that at Durek's Council we put aside a day in our plan to account for delay, for we have used it, and used it all. Now let us hope we meet with no further mischance, else we will not arrive in time to aid Durek."

Borin snorted in exasperation, "Had we come to the Round Chamber just a quarter hour sooner we would not have been forced to sit in that dark crack for seven hours listening to stupid Ûkhs bicker. May such mishaps elude us in the future."

"Ah, but there is the rub," smiled Shannon. "Perhaps all mishaps, accidents, or calamities could be avoided if only we knew when, where, or how they were to come about. Then we simply could be at a place a moment earlier or later or not at all; or we could change the how of things by moving the rock that otherwise would be stumbled over; or we could turn the blade a different way so that a finger would not be nicked; or we could do a multitude of other things to avoid all problems. But alas! it is not ours to know the morrow, and so only reasonable steps can be taken to turn aside misfortune. Of course, if we did know the future, life would be safe—but unspeakably dull."

"Mayhap the next time there will not be so many Grg," growled Delk, running his thumb along the blade of his axe, "and we can solve the problem with a few quick strokes, disposing of the evidence in nearby cracks and crevices." Anval and Borin grunted in agreement.

"Let us rest an hour or so," suggested Lord Kian, whose thoughts were focused on their mission, "then press on westerly toward Dusk-Door. While we tarry, we will again use Bane as an early beacon of danger."

At the mention of Bane, Perry sat up, startled: he had unconsciously sheathed the sword when he had taken off his pack. Quickly he pulled the blade free—and its jewel was silently shrieking, *Spawn!* the cobalt blaze blasting throughout the room as all the company started up. At that same moment the stone door of the chamber swung wide, and a torch-bearing Rūck poked his head through the opening and looked in upon the Squad. *"Waugh!"* he squalled and jumped backwards and fled down the western passageway.

Lord Kian sprang to the portal and looked along the corridor. "The foe is upon us!" he barked, swiftly stepping to his pack. "We must fly from here!"

The Seven scooped up their weapons and packs and bolted through the door. They could hear the Rūck skreeking and see the bobbing firebrand as he ran to meet the distant torchlight coming up the west way. Kian quickly turned and scanned the four eastern passages. "There! See! Torchlight also comes down the corridor from the Round Chamber!"

Once again they were caught between Rūcken forces; this time, though, the Seven had been detected. There were three ways left to flee.

"Swift!" barked Kian, "is there any reason why we should not take the left-hand way? It is wider and we can go faster." He looked at each of the companions, and they said nothing. "So be it! Delk, you lead, for again we must leave the Brega Path. Let us fly!"

They sprang into the left-hand tunnel and fled downward along the sloping floor; deeper they went under the mountain. The way was broad, but there were no side passages, and so they had no choice but to flee onward.

They had run but a short way when from behind they heard a raucous horncall, its blat echoed down the passage after them. There was an answering call, as if one *Rūpt* force were signalling the other. Perry felt like a hunted fox, with braying horns and snarling dogs driving after him.

As they ran, Perry became aware of an unwholesome odor hanging faintly on the air. "Lord Kian," he panted, "I just remembered. *The Raven Book.* Gildor. When the Deevewalkers came through Kraggen-cor, Gildor said he did not like this left-hand way, for it had the smell of a great viper pit, and so they turned back and instead took the other of his two choices. Now I smell something, something unpleasant—as if we are running toward a foul place."

"We cannot turn back, or even aside yet," rasped Kian, "for surely the Yrm are now on our trail, and there have been no side passages."

On they scrambled, downward, ever downward, down to the very roots of the mountain and beyond, and Perry felt as if he could hear the burden of the stone groaning above. At last they came to a cross-junction: The main path went straight, but within one hundred feet the corridor plunged under water. The fissure to the right bore upward. The crack to the left had a level floor. Neither the fissure nor the crack showed any sign of being delved. Delk turned down the left way. "It bears westward, where lies the Door," he stated, and onward they fled.

The crack under the mountain twisted, turned, rose, and plunged. Perry lost all sense of direction, and he felt as if they had been fleeing for hours. A wide ravine had been following along on their right, bordering their way from the moment they had entered this tunnel; up from its depths rose the churning sound of tumbling water. On they ran along this rough path, scrambling up ledges, leaping wide cracks, sidling along narrow shelves, sliding down rock-strewn slopes. Behind, they could hear horn blats, at times faint, at other times loud and echoing. Bane continued to blaze with a bright blue flame. Shannon estimated that the *Spaunen* were no more than a half mile behind, and gaining.

They had fled for more than five hours, covering just nine miles, for the way was difficult, when at last they came to another junction in the cavern; it was only the second one they had encountered since their flight began. At this junction the water ravine ran on straight, but there was no footpath to follow; a cross-shaft confronted them: the right-hand tunnel passed over the ravine on a natural stone arch and ran on upward, disappearing around a curve; the left-hand way ran straight and down a gentle slope. Again Delk chose the left-hand passage. "It turns back towards the Brega Path," he said simply.

Though it was not an arched, smooth corridor, the chosen way was delved, for the walls and floor bore the marks of chisels, picks, and mattocks. "This is an old mine shaft," grunted Anval as he scurried over a large boulder blocking the way, "one delved deeper than any I have ever known; and from the smell, something was uncovered that would have better remained buried." All the time they had been running, the foetid odor hanging on the air had become stronger; each of the companions was now aware of the stench, though none knew what it was. But, odor or not, along the shaft they scrambled, for Rūcken horns were sounding and faint torchlight could be seen shuttering down the passageway behind them: the maggot-folk were drawing nearer.

The Seven fled down this shaft for something under an hour, going some four miles on a downward but more or less straight course. Abruptly the delved shaft narrowed, becoming a slot only wide enough to travel single file. In the notch the malodor became almost overwhelming, causing Perry to gag and catch his breath; he did not want to come into this stink, but the Spawn gaining behind left him no choice.

As they edged along the cleft, Delk exclaimed, "Starsilver! Look! See the ore vein! This delving is a silveron shaft!"

Perry could see the soft glimmer of silvery metal twinkling in the lantern light and running on ahead. And even though they were being pursued, the Dwarves paused long enough to reach out and touch the precious lode, for they had never before seen silveron in its native state. This was the wealth of Kraggen-cor; in only two other places in Mithgar was silveron known to exist.

Suddenly they came to what had been the last extent of the silveron shaft; but they could see that the end wall had been burst through from the far side: the stone was splintered as if some enormous force had blasted into the delf from beyond the wall.

They clambered over the shards of rock and came into a carven chamber. This room was the source of the foul reek, but they could see nothing to cause the stench; it was as if the fetor exuded from the very stone itself.

The chamber was long and rectangular; its far end was lost beyond the shadows. In the center was a raised stone slab, a huge block with a smooth top and carvings on the side. Here, too, were scrawled serpentine signs. Shannon Silverleaf held up a lantern and quickly scanned the glyphs. They writhed across the stone and looked somehow evil and foul, recorded in a long-lost tongue; yet the Elf was skilled at runes and rapidly deciphered the words: "*'Thuuth Uthor.'* Ai!" Shannon sucked in a gasp of air. "This is the Lost Prison. The *Draedan*'s Lair. No wonder the stone is imbued with a foul reek, for here, trapped for ages, was the Dread of Drimmen-deeve—the Gargon— trapped till the Drimma were deceived by Modru's vile gramarye and delved too deeply and set the *Draedan* free."

"*Trapped?*" exclaimed Kian. "Trapped in this chamber? Is there no way out?"

All the lanterns were opened wide, and light sprang to the far end and filled the room. No archways were discerned, no black tunnel mouths gaped in the walls; only smooth stone, blank and stern, could be seen. No outlet, no portal of escape stood open before them, and behind, a horn blared loudly and they could hear the slap of running Rūcken feet.

CHAPTER 3

THE WORDS OF BARAK

"Quickly, Ursor, Anval, to the cleft!" barked Kian. "Borin, Delk, flank them. Let no Spawn through. If we are trapped, then let it cost them dear to pluck us forth."

Ursor sprang to the notch, shifting to one side, with Borin warding his flank. Anval leapt thwartwise the notch from Ursor, Delk at hand. Shannon and Kian quickly stepped to the third rank, and Perry took a place at Shannon's side. They could see torchlight wavering down the slot, and suddenly a Rūck burst forth from the breach, to be felled by Ursor's great black mace. A second Spawn came on the heels of the first, and Anval's axe clove him from helm to breastplate. A third Rūck Ursor crushed, and a fourth. The next Rūck threw down his iron bar and turned to flee but was pushed shrieking and gibbering into the chamber by those behind who did not yet know that anything was amiss, and Anval smote him and the next with his blade. The maggot-folk finally stopped coming in as enough of those in the front ranks at last turned and shoved back through the press in the notch.

A time passed, and the Seven could hear the *Spaunen* snarling and cursing, but the Slûk speech was being used, and so the comrades did not understand what was being said. For a moment it became still, and then a spate of black-shafted Rūcken arrows hissed through the cleft to strike the far chamber wall and splinter on the stone. Then there came a great shout from the maggot-folk and a rush of booted feet: they were mounting a charge. One leapt in, only to be dropped by Ursor's mace. Three more hurtled through and were slain by Anval, Borin, and Delk. More charged forward but stumbled over the dead bodies of the slain Rūcks and were themselves dispatched. Once more the Rūcks withdrew.

Just as it had been at the rope bridge over the Great Deep, the Spawn could only come at the Seven single file, and thus the *Rûpt* could not bring their greater numbers to bear to their advantage. No Rūck had yet reached the third rank of the defenders. Four warders alone could hold off an entire Rūcken army, especially since the comrades flung the dead *Spaunen* one atop another to clog the entrance, forming a grisly but effective barricade.

An hour went by, and again the maggot-folk charged. Once more the defenders slew all that entered. This time the second rank killed but one Rūck; all the others were slain by Ursor and Anval. The bulwark of dead Spawn grew higher.

Borin and Delk then stepped to the first rank, relieving Ursor and Anval, who stepped back. Lord Kian and Shannon took over the second file. Perry, who had yet to engage the foe, felt useless, but he realized that in this battle the others were larger and more effective than a Warrow would be.

But it was not only a sense of uselessness that disturbed the buccan: most of all, Perry felt a deep sense of guilt over the turn of events. "Lord Kian," the Warrow quietly declared, "I have failed you and my other comrades here; I have failed Durek and all those with him; and I have failed myself." At the Man's questioning look, the buccan continued: "Back at the Gate Room I did not keep Bane in the open, and we were discovered. Our mission is in dire jeopardy, and I am to blame."

"Perry, Friend Perry," sighed Lord Kian, "had Bane been left unsheathed, mayhap we would not have been discovered just then. Yet I think we would have fled west on the Brega Path when Bane's flame cried *'Rûpt!'* And we would have run into the band of Yrm coming up that way. Of course we could have run east on the Path and into the arms of the other Spawn back that way. Perry, Bane is a wondrous Elven-blade, yet it does not tell us where the danger lies, only that it is near or far or not at all. Let me say this: as we came to the Grate Room you remarked that there were no side passages off the Brega Path for the next mile; and the last mile we travelled to that place also had no corridors or crevices off to the side. True?"

"Yes, there are only those passages right at the Grate Room," replied Perry, "four eastward, one westward."

"And of those ways," continued Kian, "two had Yrm forces in them: one behind us on the path, and one ahead. Heed me: we would have seen Bane's glimmer and run along the Path into one *Rûptish* band or the other, with no place to hide; and we would have been trapped between the two gangs, overwhelmed by their very numbers in those broad halls." Lord Kian fell silent, and though Perry had to agree with the Man's reasoning, still he felt somehow guilty that the Seven had been discovered.

"Lord Kian is right," said Shannon to Perry, softly. "He has the wisdom to see that what has befallen would have done so one way or another no matter the circumstance, for we were already trapped yet did not know it. Some who call themselves leaders would have leapt at the chance to fix the blame on you, Perry, deserved or not; to them, finding fault is more important than finding solutions to their dilemmas. With them it is more important to punish in the name of justice than it is to right a wrong.

"But I stray far afield. Lord Kian knows that our task is to somehow rescue our quest from the jaws of adversity, and it is not our concern to blame one small Waerling for all the *Spaunen* that teem in these caverns—" Suddenly, with a screeching howl a large, spear-bearing Hlōk leapt onto the dead-Rūck barricade, only to be gutted by Delk's axe. Three more Rūcks were slain by Delk and Borin. Again the attack was shorn off short, the Rūcks fleeing back up the notch.

Two more hours passed without attack, except now and again a black shaft or two would hiss into the chamber to fall with a clatter at the far wall. The guard on the cleft had been rotated, and in turn each of the Seven had walked the chamber—staying out of line of the black arrows, looking for a hidden door or passage—but none had been found, for this was indeed the Lost Prison, the Gargon's Lair: that terrible creature had been sealed in this chamber from the overthrow of Gyphon, at the end of the Ban War, to the year 780 of the Fourth Era: nearly three thousand years in all. The Dwarves had inadvertently set it free while mining silveron, led this way by Modru's evil art; it could be seen that the Dwarves had delved up to the wall of the chamber, but from all appearances, the Gargon had blasted through the weakened wall—whether by spell or by sheer strength, the Squad could not say.

The old tales told that the Gargon had slain many Dwarves, including a Dwarf King and his son: Third Glain fell in 4E780, and with him Orn was killed. After they and others were slaughtered in a bloody day of great butchery, the Dwarves fled Kraggen-cor. Yet Dwarves were not the only ones driven from this region: great numbers of Elves of the bordering Realm of Darda Galion fled from the Dread, as well as steaders of Riamon. The Gargon ruled Black Drimmen-deeve for more than one thousand years, till slain by Tuck, Galen, Gildor, and Brega in a fiery doom. It took all of their efforts to vanquish this terrible foe, and even then it was but by chance circumstance that they slew the Dread, for it was a mighty creature.

Yet, as mighty as it had been, still it had not been able to break out of this prison until a wall had been weakened by delvers. The Seven were dismayed by this knowledge, for it meant that this chamber was a dungeon of extraordinary strength: it had defied the power of a mighty Gargon for nearly three millennia. Hence, how could the comrades even hope to break free in a matter of mere hours in order to aid Durek—especially in the teeth of a force of Spawn?

"What is the hour, Shannon?" asked Perry, for he was bone weary.

"It is midmorn of the twenty-fourth of November," answered the Elf.

Lord Kian's face took on a grim look at Silverleaf's words, for the time was perilously short, and they were yet trapped. Lord Kian knew, however, that for whatever plan—if any—they devised for winning free, rested warriors were needed. They also needed water, for theirs was nearly gone. He did not know what mischief the Yrm were devising, but it was certain that they would attack sooner or later. "The Rukha seem to have fallen quiet," said Kian, "planning some deviltry. They can afford to wait for reinforcements, for we are trapped. We must use this time to recover our own spent strength: While we are under siege, we will take turns resting. Two will hold the way while the others rest, perhaps even sleep. Keep nearby to aid in the event of attack. Stay out of arrow flight from the cleft. Think on ways that we may escape—though Adon knows how that may be."

Perry lay down off to one side. He was exhausted: the flight had taken much of his strength, for the way had been hard and he was of small stature. He rested his head against his pack, and his thoughts were awhirl. He felt something tugging and nagging at the back of his mind, but he could not bring it to the fore. He believed that something was being overlooked, yet he knew not what. He gazed at the smooth cavern walls, ceiling, and floor of the chamber. The silveron vein came through the guarded broken wall and ran on across the floor to vanish into the shadows. The argent line had many offshoots, running short distances, tapering off into thinner and thinner veins, to finally disappear. One such seam zigged across the ceiling, to end in a whorl. Another seam ran to the large stone block in the center of the chamber and up the side, to come to an end among the writhing runes set thereupon by the Gargon. Yet another silver line shot up a side wall, to crash back to the floor. Perry lay there letting his gaze follow the precious seams, and even though the Rūcken enemy was but a few paces away, he gradually drifted into slumber as his eyes roamed along glittering pathways streaking across the prison.

Perry slept for five hours without moving, exhausted, exempted from guard duty by the others; but then he began to dream: He was back on the Argon, riding the raft. But the river wasn't water; instead it was flowing silveron. The argent stream rushed into a roaring gap, and the raft was borne into a tunnel. Perry looked about and saw that he was riding with the other companions, yet there was a hooded Dwarf sitting on the far end of the float whom Perry did not recognize, for he could not see the Dwarf's face.

The starsilver river rushed through dark caverns, carrying the raft along, and Rūcks sprang up to give chase. Onward the raft whirled, to come to many Dwarves delving stone and scooping up treasured water into sacks, which they bore away. The float sped toward a stone wall, but just before the craft crashed into it, the wall burst outward and a dark Gargon jumped forth with four warriors in pursuit. The raft whirled into the chamber and sped on the silveron vein out the other side, but all the companions were tumbled off by the far stone wall, even though the float somehow went on through. The wall became transparent, and Perry could see that the raft was caught in an eddy of silveron, and the mysterious Dwarf was still aboard in spite of the invisible wall. Perry looked at the Dwarf and called, "Help us. Help us get through. You got out; how can we get out too?"

The Dwarf turned and threw back his hood. It was Barak! The dead Gatemaster! Slain by the Rūcks far away on the shores of the Argon River! *"All delved chambers have ways in,"* Barak intoned in a sepulchral voice, *"and ways out, if you can find the secret of the door and have the key. Without the key even a Wizard or an evil Vûlk cannot pass through some doors."* The raft burst into flames, and Barak lay down on the platform and uttered one more word: *"Glâr!"*

The burning raft whirled off on the swift-running silveron vein, and Perry woke up calling out, "Barak! Barak! Come back!"

When Perry opened his eyes, Shannon Silverleaf was bending over the Warrow shaking him by the shoulder. "Wake up, Friend Perry," urged the Elf, "your slumber disturbs you."

"Oh, Shannon, I had the strangest dream," declared the Warrow, rubbing his eyes and squinting at the far wall to see if it was truly transparent; but he saw only solid stone. "It was all mixed up with rivers of silveron, the Rūcks, this chamber, the Dread, and a conversation I had with Barak long ago in our last camp by the Great River Argon, where he was slain."

"Though Elves do not sleep as Men, Drimma, and Waerlinga do," stated Shannon, "still I believe I can understand the way of some dreams. Though many are strange and appear to make little sense, now and again darktide visions do seem to have significance; mayhap yours is one of those."

"Maybe it is," agreed Perry. "I've got to talk to Delk. He's a Gatemaster, as was Barak." The Warrow rose and went to the brown-bearded Dwarf who was standing guard at the notch with Ursor. "Delk," began Perry, "Barak and I often chatted at night. Once he told me that all delved chambers had doors, some secret; and for those what is needed is to divine each secret and to have the key it calls for. Delk, this Gargon's Lair is a delved chamber. Surely there must be a way out other than through a hole in a broken wall. Barak must be right."

"Were this chamber Châk-delved, I would agree," grunted Delk, "but it is not. The work is more like that of . . . of . . ." Delk fell silent in thought, then continued. "Old beyond measure, I deem, like the work of an ancient Folk called the Lianion-Elves—though but traces of their craft remain that I have seen."

"Lianion-Elves?" exclaimed Shannon. "The Lianion-Elves are my Folk, the Lian!" Now it was Silverleaf's turn to fall silent and study the chamber. "You are correct, Drimm Delk: this chamber *does* resemble the work of my ancestors, though it is different in some ways. I knew that my Folk had known of the Lost Prison, but that we delved it would be news to me. And if delved by the Lian, I doubt that originally it was meant to house such a guest as a Gargon—though as to its initial intent, I cannot say."

"Well, if Barak was right," said Perry, "there is a secret way out strong enough to defy even an evil Vûlk. And if we can find it, maybe we can divine the way to open it. You are a Gatemaster, Delk; surely you can locate a hidden door. And you, Shannon, your Folk perhaps made this place; maybe you can find the secret way. We've got to try."

"Ah, but Friend Perry," protested Delk, "we all have searched every square inch—walls and floor alike—and we have found nought." Delk looked from the cleft to the far wall and finally at the slain Rûcks; then he growled thoughtfully, "Nay, not all; we have not searched it all. We have not searched where the Grg arrows can reach. But the dead-Ûkh barricade is now high enough that if we stay low we can safely examine the stone block in the center of the chamber."

Delk awakened Borin to take his place at the cleft, and then Gatemaster, Elf, and Warrow crawled to the central platform and began the search.

Perry watched as the other two carefully inspected the stone, but his mind kept spinning back to his dream of Barak: the Dwarf had said, *"Glâr!"* yet Perry knew as a Ravenbook Scholar that *glâr* was the Slûk word for "fire." Though the raft in the dream had burst into flames, why would he dream that Barak had said a Slûk word? How did fire bear on their problem? Maybe it meant nothing. Perry watched as the search continued.

Delk had begun to examine the silveron seam running up the side of the block, and suddenly he gave a start. "This vein is not native to the stone," he muttered after long study, "it is *crafted!*—made to look like a natural branching of the starsilver offshoot. And see! Here the silveron is shaped strangely, like two runes—though I cannot fathom their message."

Shannon crawled around to join Delk, staying well below the Rūck arrow line, and peered at the silver thread. "These are vaguely like ancient Lian runes, made to look like odd whorls of silveron in the stone. This rune, I would guess it to say 'west,' and the other rune says 'point'—or mayhap 'pick' is more accurate, I'm not sure. West-point or west-pick, that is the best I can guess these odd runes to mean."

"Hola!" exclaimed Delk, "here is a thin slot in the stone at the end of the crafted vein, as if the silveron had run its course but the crack ran on a bit. Mayhap—"

"The Wrg are up to something," rumbled Ursor at the notch, interrupting Delk. "They may be preparing another rush. They are chittering like rats, and again I can hear them calling, *'glâr!'*"

"*Glâr!*" exclaimed Perry, startled. "That's what Barak . . . Ah yes, I see: I heard it in my sleep. Ursor, *glâr* is a Slûk word for fire." The three crawled away from the stone block and out of arrow flight, and stood beside Ursor. "What can they be up to?" asked Perry, listening to the Slûk jabber.

"I have my suspicions," growled Ursor. "We've been trapped here many hours. Time enough for them to devise some terrible plot and secure the means to carry it out."

"Look!" cried Delk, pointing to the floor at the cleft. In through the entrance a dark liquid flowed. They could hear a wooden barrel being broken, and a surge of fluid gushed in through the notch. "It is lamp oil," growled Delk, testing it with his finger and smelling it. Then his eyes widened—"They seek to flood the chamber with oil and set it afire!"

Shannon fitted an arrow to his bow and quickly stepped across the entrance, loosing the bolt as he went. A scream came from the dark notch as the hard-driven shaft found a victim. Delk awakened Anval and Lord Kian. The young Man joined Shannon, and they sped missiles into the cleft, and the Spawn answered with bolts of their own. In spite of the arrows, oil continued to gush forth from the notch to overspread the chamber floor.

Perry watched in desperation, for he knew that the maggot-folk were nearly ready to transform this prison into a burning tomb. *We have to get out!* thought the Warrow frantically, on the edge of panic. But then with a conscious force of will he wrenched his terrified mind toward the paths of reason. *Now settle down. Don't bolt. And above all, use your scholar's brains to think!* The buccan believed that there was a hidden door, and he felt that the secret and its solution was within his grasp if he could only get the time to think it through. What had Barak said that night long ago on the banks of the River? Something about Lian Crafters. *"These doors are usually opened by Elven-made things,"* Barak had said, *"carven jewels, glamoured keys, ensorcelled rings,"* and something else, but what? What did the runes on the stone block mean, "west-point"? Perry glanced up at the Elf.

"Lord Kian," urged Silverleaf, "before they put the torch to this oil, let us rush them. At least we will take some of that evil spawn with us." Ursor grunted his agreement, Delk thumbed the blade of his axe, and Anval and Borin nodded. Shannon drew his long-knife, shaped much the same as Bane. "This edge of the Lian, forged in Lost Duellin—the Land of the West—will taste *Rûpt* blood for perhaps the last time; yet this pick, though it has not the power bound into the blade as that of the Waerling's pick, will—"

"I've got it!" shouted Perry. "I know the way out!" He flashed Bane from its scabbard, and its edges blazed with flaming blue light streaming from the rune-carven jewel. Perry held the sword high and laughed. "Here, as Barak would have said, is a spellbound blade. The key! Made by the Elves in the Land of the West. In your words, Shannon Silverleaf—and in those of the silveron runes on yon block—it is a west-pick. No wonder the Gargon couldn't get out: he hadn't a key. If I am right, then this blade—or any like it—will do with a simple thrust

what the Gargon in all his awesome power could not do in three thousand years."

Crouching low, the small Warrow stepped through the in-flowing oil to the stone block and plunged the blade into the slot at the end of the silver line. The Elven-knife went in to the hilt. There was a low rumble of massive stone grating upon stone, and a great slab ponderously swung away from the far wall; a black opening yawned before them where solid stone had been.

Shouts of astonishment burst forth from the Squad, yet Gatemaster Delk had the wit to call out above their cries, "Withdraw the sword and do not plunge it in again, else the portal will close once more!"

Heeding Delk's words, Perry immediately withdrew the dazzling blade, and the door remained open; but the Warrow's thoughts were upon another Gatemaster, now dead: the one who had shown him the way. "Barak, you were right," whispered the Warrow quietly. "Thank you."

A Rūcken horn blared from the notch and a stentorian voice snarled, *"Glâr!"* They were bringing a torch to fire the oil.

"Quickly!" shouted Kian, catching up his pack. "We must fly!" Each of the companions took up his own bundle and headed for the open door: Kian in the lead, Delk last. The oil made the stone floor as slippery as ice, and the footing was dif-ficult; haste was needed yet could not be afforded. "Hurry!" Kian urged as he reached the door and stood by the open por-tal.

Just then there was a great *Whoosh!* as the oil was fired and flames ran into the chamber, lighting it a lurid red. The dark shadows were driven from the far recesses of the room, and through the blaze the *Spaunen* could see for the first time the opened, secret door. They snarled and howled in rage—their victims were escaping!—and their own Spawn-set fire would cut off pursuit!

As the companions tumbled across the doorsill, inches ahead of the flames, a burst of black arrows whined across the room, most to splinter against the stone wall; but one shaft took Delk through the neck, and he fell dead at the threshold. Lord Kian reached for the fallen Dwarf, but a hot blast of fire drove the Man backwards through the door as the last of the oil ignited.

The portal had opened into an undelved cavern leading away from the chamber. The companions were waiting just around a corner when Kian stumbled into their midst, singed and gasping. "Delk is dead. *Rûpt* arrow." Anval and Borin cast their hoods over their heads, and Perry bit his lower lip and tears sprang into his sapphire-jewelled eyes.

The raging flames behind them pitched writhing shadows on the walls of the cavern, and the grotto was illuminated a dull red. Towering stark stones stared silently at the group huddled below, and the sound of weeping was lost in the roar of the blaze. Massive blocks and ramped ledges stood across the cave, barring the way for as far as the firelight shone, and the rock yielded not to the grief.

Lord Kian looked at the group standing numbly before him. "He is wreathed in flame," said Kian above the sound of the fire, "and his funeral chamber contains the weapons of the foes he slew. Thus he goes on in honor on his final journey. Delk will be missed; he will be remembered. But he would urge us to mourn not, and to go on—for Durek needs us, and we are late."

For long moments no one spoke, and the only sound heard was the brawl of the fire. Then finally:

"You speak true, Lord Kian," concurred Anval, casting back his hood with effort. "There will come a time when we will mourn the loss of Delk Steelshank, but now we must go on to the Dusken Door—though how we will repair it without his aid, I cannot say. Our Gatemaster has fallen, and there is little hope for our mission without his gifted hand."

"But we must try," interjected Perry, choking back his grief, "else all this has been in vain. We must get back to the Brega Path and on to the western portal—though whether there is yet time to do so, I know not."

"It is sunset of the twenty-fourth of November," announced Shannon. "There remains but one and thirty hours until Durek is to attempt the opening of the Door."

"Now that Delk has fallen, I will lead," stated Borin, casting his own hood from his head, "though I cannot take his place.

And I shall try to hew to his plan, turning always back toward the Brega Path when fortune allows me the choice."

"Then let us go away from this bitter place now," urged Perry. Lord Kian nodded, and Borin set forth, climbing up the ramps and across the looming stones to an exit on high. And they entered a rough-floored cavern that led them generally south and west.

The way was slow and difficult, for they had to clamber up and down steep slopes and over great obstacles. Giant Ursor often lifted Perry up to ledges just out of the Warrow's reach, or lowered him down drop-offs just a bit too far for the buccan to jump. Without the big Man's help, the journey would have been beyond Perry's abilities. Even the Dwarves were hard pressed to negotiate this passage. Only nimble Shannon seemed at ease on the rugged way. There were no offshoots from the cavern, and so a smoother way was not a matter of choice. It took them three hours to traverse just four miles of this arduous cave; and their thirst had grown beyond measure, for their water was gone.

But then they were brought up short by both a welcome and at the same time a disheartening sight: the cavern dead-ended at an underground river. The water rushed out of the stone on the right side of the cave, and plunged under the wall on the left side. The far bank was a narrow ledge of rock, shelving out from a sheer stone wall that ran to the ceiling with no outlet. Though he was desperately thirsty, and water was within reach, Perry flung down his pack and broke into tears of frustration. "If this doesn't beat all," he vented bitterly. "Trapped again. Stone and water before us, and Rūcks and fire behind us."

And then, from far off, faintly echoing down the cavern, came a discordant horn blare. "I fear the fire is no longer burning," declared Lord Kian, "and the *Spaunen* are once more in pursuit."

CHAPTER 4

WIZARD WORD

Two Dwarves, a Warrow, and a Man threaded their way along the Great Loom of Aggarath as they walked toward the pile of stone covering Dusk-Door. Everywhere they stepped, it seemed, they came to another fallen Dwarf warrior, slain by the monstrous Krakenward during the fearful retreat along the causeway. Durek and Bomar had cast their hoods over their heads, as is the manner of Dwarven grief; tears silently coursed down Cotton's cheeks as the Warrow passed the broken bodies; and Rand's countenance was bleak. But they did not stop to mourn, for as Durek had said, "There will come a time to lament, but now we must think of the living. Our companions in the halls of Kraggen-cor depend upon us; we must not fail them."

Where the lake once stood, a black crater now scarred the land. Of the Dwarves drawn underwater by the malevolent creature, there was no sign. Along the sundered causeway the four strode, and over the ancient bridge. Far below in the muck-laden bed of the drained lake they could see the ancient stonework of the old Gatemoat at last revealed to the light of day after long, dark ages. With the Troll-dam destroyed, water once again flowed through an unseen fissure under the Loomwall and into the moat, filling it to spill over a formed lip in the massive bulwark, shaping the beginning of a stream. After centuries of silence, the Duskrill once more fell asplash to meander across the upper vale—now a black crater—to come to the linn of the Sentinel Falls and cascade down into the stream bed below to flow onward through the ravine of Ragad Vale.

Onward strode Cotton, Durek, Bomar, and Rand. Now they could see, here and there, the pave of the ancient courtyard before the Dusken Door, a courtyard no longer drowned, yet one burdened with mire and silt. There, too, they could see the ancient remnants of great trees that had once grown before the western portal.

The four finally came to the bank of rubble over the Door; it was immense: the evil creature not only had put back all the stone removed by the Dwarves; it had heaped even more rock on the pile.

Cotton looked at the great mound in dismay, for the buccan did not see how even a Dwarf army could move this mass of stone in a week—much less in the scant hours remaining before the appointed rendezvous. Rand retrieved Brytta's spear, and picked up his own sword from where he had dropped it and had caught up Durek's axe during the Krakenward's attack. Grey Bomar stood and surveyed the ramped heap. "King Durek," rumbled the Masterdelver, "I know not whether we can move all this stone twixt now and mid of night tomorrow." Bomar glanced at the forenoon sky. "Already I judge it to be drawing upon midmorn, and whether there are enough hours for this labor is questionable. Yet we must try. Berez and I will set the shifts and oversee the work: one of us will guide the delving by day, the other will lead the toil at night, for we must work nonstop by lantern light throughout the eventide, too, if we are to succeed by tomorrow night."

Durek nodded, and the foursome turned and walked back along the causeway, and around the north end, to come to the broken dam and the Sentinel Falls.

Still the Dwarf companies were in turn casting stone blocks down on the now-lifeless carcass of the Monster. The mound had grown large in the basin below the precipice, and the Duskrill plunged over the linn to cataract down onto the jagged heap; and only here and there could the mottled green hide of the hideous creature be discerned. Cotton looked on and shuddered in revulsion, for even though only slight glimpses of the

Krakenward were visible, that which could be seen was repulsive to behold.

Durek summoned Berez and called his Captains together; and the Dwarves gathered in a great circle, along with Cotton the Warrow and two Men: Prince Rand and Reachmarshal Brytta. As soon as the Council was seated, the Dwarf King spoke: "The broken stones over the Door are piled yet higher. The task of uncovering the portal by midnight tomorrow may prove impossible, but Bomar has a plan for working day and darktide, too. But ere he speaks, I would say this:

"First, there are many fallen kindred on the sundered causeway. We cannot stop to mourn the slain, although they deserve the honor. Even though we shall not mourn, let those who sorrow work with hooded heads, and use stone from over the Door to build cairns against the Great Loom for the dead to rest within. After we have defeated the Squam, we shall decide whether to let the cairns stand for all time, or instead to delve stone tombs or set funeral pyres for all those the Madûk slew.

"Second, there are those among the Host wounded by the Monster of the Dark Mere. The injured will not issue into the caverns to fight the Grg, but will stay behind. Those among them who can, will help the healers with the more severely afflicted and prepare them for a short waggon trip south; all wounded will go with the Vanadurin when they drive the horses to better pasturage.

"Third, as Bomar will explain, we will toil in shifts. But only those removing the rubble will be working; all others must rest until it is their turn at the labor. The one exception to this rule of rest will be you, the Captains: Friend Cotton will meet with you on the morrow to describe the major features of the Brega Path, so that we will be better prepared for the War. The Chief Captains will gather here midmorning tomorrow, and all other Captains as their work shift permits that same afternoon.

"Finally, I have faith that the Host shall succeed in this task of removing the stone, for they are staunch and have the will to overcome even this. And remember, at this very moment seven of our comrades and kindred are within, and they depend upon us. *We must not fail!*" Durek then gave the Council over to Bomar, who began outlining the shifts and the way of working.

Cotton tried to pay heed, but his mind simply could not concentrate upon Bomar's words. Had the Dwarf been speaking of growing a garden, or of shaping wood, or of treating an animal or a bird, then the buccan's attention would have been riveted to every syllable Bomar uttered. But the Masterdelver was speaking of stone and levers, of slings and prybars, of work shifts and horses and duties; and even though these words were vital to the mission and vital to the rescue of Mister Perry and the others, Cotton's thoughts purely would not stay focused upon Bomar's work plan.

Instead, the Warrow again fretted about Mister Perry, wondering where the Squad was, and whether they had met with mischief: how had they fared? And his thoughts scurried along these endless paths to nowhere, for how long he did not know.

But suddenly, he became aware that he was listening intently, not to Bomar, but to the valley, for it seemed as if, above the shush of Sentinel Falls, he had heard a faint cry; yet it was so dim, so far away—just on the edge of perception—that he wasn't at all certain whether he had actually heard it, or had merely imagined it.

The Warrow swept his emeraldine eyes around the circle; no Dwarf there appeared to have noted anything other than Bomar's words; yet both Rand and Brytta seemed to be listening intently for a distant call—especially Brytta, who had risen to his knees and turned his face toward the west.

There! It came again! To Cotton the call had the sound of a far-off horncry. Brytta cocked his head and held up his broken hand. "Quiet!" he barked. A hush fell upon the Council, and only the cascade of the falling water failed to heed Brytta's sharp command.

Once more! Again! It *was* a horncall! Now all heard it, and it grew stronger:

A-raw, a-rahn! A-raw, a-rahn! A-raw, a-rahn! Over and again it belled, growing louder, and Marshal Brytta leapt to his feet. "A foe! Alert!" he cried, his good left hand gripping his spear as he sprang to the rock in circle center, his sharp gaze piercing the length of the valley to the west.

"A horseman comes!" cried down a Dwarf lookout from atop the Sentinel Stand.

A-raw, a-rahn! came the call again; and at last bursting into sight along the valley floor came a rider flying at full gallop; clots of flood-dampened earth were flung behind from plunging hooves as the horse thundered down the vale and toward the Host along the Old Rell Spur. "It's Arl!" cried Brytta. "From Redguard Mountain! From Quadran Gap!" Couching his spear, Brytta blew a signal upon his own black-oxen horn—*Hahn! Hahn! (Here! Here!)*—and he sprang toward the stairs beside the linn and plunged down them to meet the flying scout.

No sooner, it seemed, had Brytta reached the bottom of the steps than Arl pounded up, hauling his lathered mount short as he leapt to the ground. Quickly the two Men spoke in Valur—the warrior tongue of Valon—with Arl gesticulating fiercely, his hands and spear describing numbers, directions, and actions. In but a moment Marshal Brytta brought him up to the Council circle as all eyes followed them, and Cotton discovered his heart was racing. Brytta spoke: "It's Wrg! Some know we are here! *They go to warn Gnar!*"

Angry shouts burst forth from many in the circle, while others spat oaths and gripped their axes. Durek held up his hand, and when silence returned he motioned for Brytta to continue. "It seems as though the secret High Gate is known to the Spawn after all, and we are revealed. But here, let Arl tell it."

The tall young rider of Valon stood before them. As with all the Harlingar, he was clothed in leathern breeks and soft brown boots, while a fleece vest covered his mail-clad torso. Arl's steel helm sported a flowing black horse-tail crest, and his flaxen locks fell to his shoulder. He bore a spear in his left hand, while a long-knife was at his belt, and a bow and arrows could be seen at his horse's saddle, as well as a scabbarded saber. At his side depended a black-oxen horn, taken from the wild kine of the south—the mark of a Son of Harl.

It could be seen that the youth was weary; yet his manner belied the fatigue, for he stood warrior straight. With a quick sweep of his eyes, Arl's intense gaze took in the Council circle, and in a firm voice he spoke, his scout's report stripped starkly bare of all but the essential facts: "For those here who know it not, three nights past, Eddra, Wylf, and I were left atop Redguard Mountain to watch for a Wrg army should they come to attack from Quadran Col.

"Last night a torch-lit Rutchen band of thirty or so scuttled down from the Gap and turned south toward this valley.

"Leaving Wylf behind to watch for a larger force, Eddra and I rode from Redguard and trailed the Spawn at a distance. Our plan was to divert them were they nigh to discovering the Host; or, should we fail to deflect them, our plan was to warn the Legion if the Wrg espied you here in this place.

"We followed them south for some leagues, when the band we trailed met up with a like number coming north from the direction of this vale.

"They joined forces and turned back for Quadran Gap. *Yet heed!* As they loped past where we were hidden, we overheard them cursing: '. . . *we tell Gnar of the lake-draining army of foul-beards at the buried door!*'"

"*Kruk!*" burst out Durek, slamming fist into palm, his face dark with rage. "They know who we are, where we are, our exact numbers, and our very goal!"

Again angry shouts swept forth from the Council circle, and many pounded the flats of their axes to the ground while venting oaths. Durek struggled to master his own passion, and held up his hands for silence; and Dwarves swallowed their rage and clenched their jaws. And when quiet returned the Dwarf King motioned for Arl to continue.

"Eddra is tracking them yet, or did so till dawn," the young rider spoke on, "leaving sign along the Grg path, marking their dash for the hidden High Gate. I came as quickly as I could to warn of the danger."

Arl turned to Brytta. "Sire," he spoke urgently now to his commander, "there are perhaps seventy of them, and they are swift. Yet I think they have not now reached the pass, for dawn was nigh and first light of day will find them holed up until sunset, when once again they will take up the race for the Black Hole. They must be intercepted ere they can carry word to Gnar, else we are foredone; and the riders of the Valanreach are the only ones fleet enough to overhaul their track." The youth, pale and harried from his all-night venture, looked into the drawn, tired faces of Brytta and the Council, weary, too, from their night-long struggle with the Krakenward.

Durek, rubbing his eyes with the heels of his hands, rasped,

"Marshal Brytta, Warrior Arl is right. Only the Vanadurin can thwart this threat." As the Dwarf King looked up at the Reach commander, others in the Council grunted and nodded their agreement, for it was clear that only the horse-borne Harlingar would be swift enough to overtake the fleeing Squam. No one there knew just how far the two bands of maggot-folk had gotten before dawn broke, the oncoming dayrise forcing the Spawn to take cover in the splits and cracks of the western side of the range to await the onset of night and the final dash for the High Gate. Indeed, perhaps some had already reached that goal and even now were on their way to Gnar with news of the Dwarves at Dusk-Door.

Brytta's voice was grim: "Arl, get a fresh mount; you will lead us back to Eddra. If they have not yet done so, these Wrg must not escape to alert Gnar. Go now; and bring Nightwind to me." And as Arl sprang down the steps, the Reachmarshal glanced at the morning sky. "Prince Rand, by the straightest horse route, how far lies the road to Quadran Gap?"

"Nine leagues, perhaps ten, through the foothills by horseback will set you upon the way to the pass," answered Rand after some thought. Both Brytta and Durek grunted in agreement, for the estimate confirmed their own. Rand continued: "The route through the margins will be rock strewn and slow, rugged, broken, though I can see no swifter way to cut off the Yrm." Rand then turned to the Dwarf King. "Even so, King Durek, when the Vanadurin reach the road, how far upwards should they ride? Where lies the secret High Gate?"

Durek shook his head. "Lore only tells us that it is somewhere within the pass. Yet it cannot be more than a league or three upslope, for we now know that it is this side of the high snow, the deep snow, else the Grg could not have used it. How they found it and discovered the way of its working, we may never learn, though they have had more than a thousand years to know of it."

"Oh, no sir," spoke up Cotton. "Beggin' your pardon, King Durek, but I think they've not known about it all that time. Why, if they knew of that High Gate just as recent as Tuck's time—two hundred thirty or so years past—well then, Sir, you can stake your last copper on the fact that they'd've used the High Gate to get at him and the other three when those four tried to cross over Stormhelm during the Winter War." Cotton looked around and saw nods of agreement. "So, as I'd say, since they didn't grab at Tuck in the pass, well, they must have got that secret door open since then."

Brytta glanced down into the vale and saw Arl riding a fresh mount and leading Nightwind to the Sentinel Falls. "Regardless as to when it was discovered by the Wrg, they know of it now. No more time can be spent in speculation. It is time for deeds, not talk." And Brytta raised his black-oxen horn to his lips to signal the Harlingar.

"Wait, Sir!" cried Cotton. "What about the wounded? What about those hurt in the fight with the Monster? Who will take them south? And, for that matter, what about the horses? We can't just leave them here in this dead place; how will they live?"

"Cotton, my gentle friend, unforeseen events are running roughshod o'er us, trampling our careful stratagems," declared Brytta. "Hence, for those things you name—and perhaps more—other plans must needs be made; for, wounded or not, horses or not, still the Spawn must be stopped ere they reach the High Gate; and none else can do that but the Vanadurin. We must ride now!"

Astride a fresh mount and leading the Reachmarshal's steed, Arl had come to the foot of the linn; and Nightwind reared and his forelegs pawed the air, sharp hooves flashing. Brytta glanced down, and then spoke to all in Council: "Fare you well, Lords. May each of you succeed in your mission, and we in ours."

And Brytta again raised the black-oxen horn to his lips, and this time an imperative call split the air. Nightwind belled a challenge, and other notes rang forth as Brytta's call was answered in kind by each of the Harlingar; and horn after horn resounded, which set the echoes to ringing, and the Ragad Vale pealed with the fierce calls of the untamed horns of Valon.

'Mid the Vanadurin horncries to battle, Brytta sprang down the steps and vaulted to Nightwind's back. And with yet another blast upon his horn, the Reachmarshal spurred his dark steed to the west toward the mouth of the valley, and at his side rode Arl on a grey. High upon Arl's upright spear flew the War-banner of the House of Valon: a white horse rampant upon a field of green, an ancient sigil ever borne into battle by the Harlingar. And as Brytta and Arl went swiftly past each of the other riders, they, too, spurred in behind. Soon all the Vanadurin were in the column, riding at a fast pace, in pairs, a forest of spears bristling at the morning sky: thirty-seven grim warriors upon whom the hopes of the Dwarf Army rested.

And as the Valanreach column rode forth, Cotton turned to Prince Rand. "Sir, what about Marshal Brytta's broken hand?" asked the Warrow, fretting. "How can he fight? How can he defend himself?"

Rand did not take his eyes from the distant riders, and his answer was a long time coming: "Fear not, Cotton, for he shall manage," said the Prince finally; yet Cotton was not comforted by the words.

Slowly the day crept forward, and Cotton's weary mind continued to churn with worry: over Perry and the Squad; over Brytta and the Vanadurin; over the vast amount of rubble covering the Door; and over the mission in general. Realizing at last the state he was in, he decided to try to break this darkling mood with a trip to see Brownie and Downy, and to visit with the cook-crew of the last waggon.

Tiredly the buccan trudged along the Old Spur back to where the rear of the train was encamped upon the vale sides. All along the way there was torn landscape where the loosed water had whelmed the ravine. Most of the black rot from the lake bottom had been washed away by the Duskrill flowing once more along the ravine, yet some of the decay still clung here and there to the rocks and crevices of the valley floor. And where the rot was, an unclean odor emanated; but there was a cool breeze blowing along the vale and toward the mountain and up, and the reek of centuries of accumulated foulness, though prevalent, did not overpower those at the wains.

After visiting the horses, Cotton ate a meal with Bomar's cook-crew. They seemed pleased to see the small, gold-clad Warrow; yet at the same time, *something* about the buccan's presence unsettled them. Uneasily, they sat in a circle; and what conversation there was turned again and again toward Brytta's mission, and toward the upcoming invasion of Kraggen-cor. And in the fashion of Dwarves, the talk went from Dwarf to Dwarf around the circle:

"Just how did the foul Squam discover the High Gate into Quadran Pass?" growled Nare.

"If a thieving Grg found it, then it has to be easily done—no doubt from the inside," answered Caddor. "It is, after all, a secret door, Châkmade. Yet, in this, I think it is concealed only on the outside."

"Let us hope the Vanadurin can intercept them before they regain the High Gate," said Belor, to a general murmur of agreement.

"Why were the Foul Folk on this side of the Mountains anyway?" snapped Naral. "There are no homesteads nearby, nor villages, no one to ravage or plunder."

"For aught we know, they were trailing us," responded Oris. "We marched by the pass. In open view."

Crau leaned forward, poking the fire. "Aye, Oris, mayhap. Yet there were two bands."

"One band trailing us and another band trailing them? Spies watching spies?" queried Funda, scratching his head.

"Who knows?" growled Littor, exasperated. "Ravers, scouts, trackers, spies: the only thing that matters is they have seen us and must be stopped!"

"Wull," chimed in Cotton, "if anyone can stop 'em, it's Marshal Brytta and his horse riders!"

Shifting edgily at Cotton's words about horse riders, most of the Dwarves glanced at the silver horn the Warrow bore and then quickly away, and a strained silence fell upon the group. Finally, after a time, with visible effort, Nare again took up the conversation, and soon all were engaged:

"It is an ancient dream, the retaking of Kraggen-cor," observed Nare. "We of Durek's Folk have dreamed this dream for many a long age."

"Aye," responded Caddor. "An ancient dream of an elder race. It is a dream yearned for by many: bethink! we here do not fight just for ourselves; we also fight for our kith who remained behind in Mineholt—and in the Quartzen Caves, too."

"Not to mention those down in the Red Hills," added Belor, pouring himself a cup of tea.

"For that matter," spoke up Naral, "some of Durek's Folk dwell in the far western Sky Mountains and in the rewon halls of the Rigga Mountains to the north."

"But it is not only Durek's Folk we fight for," said Oris thoughtfully, "or just the Châkka. The foul Squam raid the Lands of Valon and Riamon, where they maim and slaughter the innocent and plunder that which others' labors won."

"I have heard the Elves of Blackwood and the Baeron think on action against the raiders," declared Crau as he threw a log on the cook fire.

"I know the Men of Pellar stand ready to aid us if we call," added Funda.

"It means that our Captain has the right of it," stated Littor. "We must strike and strike hard in the coming conflict. Dwarves, Men, Elves: all will gain from our victory."

"Hey!" exclaimed Cotton, "What about us Warrows? I mean, we'll benefit too. You left us out, Littor."

"Ho, my Friend Cotton," laughed Littor, standing up and bowing low to the buccan. "Waerans, too. I did not intend to exclude you, though it is not likely that Grg would bother the Boskydells—or the Waerans of Weiunwood near Stonehill, for that matter."

"Wull, that's where you might be wrong, Littor," asserted Cotton. "I mean, we fought the Spawn in the Bosky during the Winter War . . . and over in Weiunwood the maggot-folk tried more than once to invade—but the Rückslayer drove 'em out, he did."

"Rückslayer?" asked Caddor.

"That's what he was called," answered Cotton. "His real name was Arbagon Fenner. He led the Warrow force in the Battle of Weiunwood and drove the Rücks and such out; that was back in the time of the Winter War too. The Rückslayer must have been quite a buccan: why, they say he once even rode a horse into battle—and I don't mean a pony, I mean a real horse."

At this second mention of horse riding, all the Dwarves again uneasily glanced at and then hastily looked away from the silent horn that Cotton now carried in plain view—a horn no longer stowed out of sight in the Warrow's pack. An irre-

deemable pall fell upon the conversation, and Cotton soon
started back toward the head of the column.

The Dwarves at Dusk-Door toiled without pause, and
slowly the great rock pile diminished. The stone itself was
used to build cairns for the fallen against the Great Loom. All
Dwarves worked hooded out of respect for their dead kindred,
but they took not the time for formal mourning, though grief-
stricken they were. Several cairns also were made near the
broken dam for those killed by the Krakenward during the
drilling. Gaynor's remains were recovered and put to rest, as
well as were the slain Drillers and Hammerers and the members of the fireteam broken by the clutch and slap of great tentacles. The Monster itself had been crushed by stone, and now
it, too, was completely covered by rock, all Dwarf companies
and Brytta's scouts having tumbled blocks down upon it.

Late in the afternoon, Farlon, a Valonian scout, rode in
from the south. Not finding Brytta, he located Prince Rand to
report that good pasturage with hearty grass and sparkling
water lay in a wide vale but eleven miles downchain. After
giving his report to the Prince, Farlon swept his eyes about the
flood-whelmed valley and noted, "Much seems to have happened here since yesternoon, when last I saw this vale—as if
a great stroke has hammered this land. The stream that was
dry now flows again. The falls that were not, now tumble free.
The dam that was whole is now shattered. A foulness lingers
on the air. And gone are my comrades, and Marshal Brytta.
Where are they? Where are the Vanadurin? And what has befallen this vale?"

Rand now realized that Farlon had ridden south at noon
the day before to look for fair pastures for the horses. Hence, the
scout knew nought of the events concerning the battle with the
Monster, nor of the discovery of the Host by the spying bands
of maggot-folk. And so the Prince told the horseman of the
struggle with the Warder of the Dark Mere, while Farlon stared
with eyes wide with wonder at the broken dam and the black
crater, at the Duskrill and the Sentinel Falls, at the Great Loom
of Aggarath and the pile of rubble over the Door, at the toiling
Dwarves and horses, and at the cascade-shrouded mound of
stone covering the creature's carcass.

Then Rand spoke of the prying *Spaunen* and explained Brytta's mission, and Farlon railed at the Fates for separating him from his brethren on this thrust to intercept the Rūck spies. Even then Farlon would have ridden to join the Vanadurin, and he strode resolutely to his horse. But ere he could mount, "Hold!" commanded Rand. "Your fellow horsemen are by now too far toward the pass for you to overtake ere nightfall, when the Yrm begin to stir. And a lone rider running at speed in the dark or by moonlight perchance would spoil any ambush set for the Foul Folk."

Farlon began to protest, but his words were cut short by Rand: "Horse rider, think! Would you gamble our quest 'gainst your desire to join your comrades in battle?" At Farlon's sullen silence, Rand spoke on: "In sooth, horseman, we have more need of you here than there, for someone must lead the wounded south to the haven you have found."

"Garn!" growled Farlon, "I'm a warrior, not a nurse-maiden."

Cotton, who had been listening to the exchange, flushed with anger. "Warrior? Nursemaiden?" he cried, stepping in front of the scout. "Those words have no meaning in this! Ally! Helper! Friend! That's what's needed now! Come with me, *warrior,* and look!" And the small enraged Warrow grasped the Man by the wrist and stormed off toward the white waggons standing nearby, hauling the astonished rider in tow.

Long minutes fled, till nearly an hour had passed. Yet finally the two returned to Rand's side. And Farlon was most subdued, for he had seen and spoken with many Dwarves lamed and broken by the evil Monster's might in the long battle with that hideous creature. "Sire," said the rider to Rand, "I am much shamed by my unthinking words. I do humbly place my service at your command, to succor the needs of the *Dwarvenfolc* wounded in that dire struggle."

And Farlon turned to Cotton. "Little friend, you spoke truth: neither warrior nor nursemaiden are words to be bandied here; rather ally, helper, or friend best describes the need." And Cotton shuffled his feet and peered at the ground, all too embarrassed by his own temperamental outburst.

Rand clapped the horseman on the shoulder, and the awkward moment was dispelled. "Good! Now we must think upon how best to move the injured south; in this we must seek the advice of a healer. As to when to move them: *if* the Door opens at the mid of night on the twenty-fifth, and *if* the Host enters Kraggen-cor, then you *must* move them no later than the morn of the twenty-sixth, perhaps e'en sooner, to get them out of harm's way should Spawn flee the battle and come forth through this vale."

"Aye," answered Farlon, "there is that to think on. And there are the horses, too. My original mission was to find them good pasturage, which I have done. Yet how will I get them south? Drovers are needed, but all my brethren are gone, and the wounded cannot move the herd. Yet the steeds cannot be left here."

"You can do nought but loose them and hope that most will follow behind your waggons bearing the hurt Dwarves," stated Rand. "They are horses of Riamon, more tame than the fiery steeds of your Land, more likely to follow. Even so, if they do not come with you, I think they will stay together in a great herd and wander to other pastures upon the western wold, to be found again once the issue of Drimmen-deeve is over and done with."

"Mayhap we should leave some of the horses behind, here near the Door; perchance there will be a need," suggested Farlon. "Come, let us see how that might be done. And, too, let us find a healer and speak upon the move south."

And the scout and the Prince strode away, leaving Cotton behind. And the Warrow watched across the black crater as the work at Dusk-Door went on. The Sun set and darkness fell, yet the toil at the distant Loom continued by lamplight. Shifts changed and fresh workers replaced weary ones. Dwarves not working slept, as Cotton finally did, succumbing at last to his fatigue.

The next morning, Cotton awakened to find that more than half the stone had been removed from the Door, and he was overjoyed until he tallied up the hours to find that more than half the work time also was gone. He breakfasted with Rand, who said, "It is going to be close. Whether we reach the portal by mid of night depends upon whether any more great stones are found like the one last eventide that took more than an hour to move." No sooner had he said that than word came that another massive block barred the way.

After breakfast, Cotton went to the remnants of the dam above the falls and sat and once again watched the work. Time passed, yet by midmorn the pile did not seem to have diminished. The Warrow let his sight stray up along the reaches of the massif and down into the black crater. And then his jewel-like eyes swept to the Sentinel Stand. He could see someone—Farlon it was—carrying a bundle of wood up the steps to the top of the spire. Now why would the rider be carrying a fagot up there? But ere Cotton could puzzle it through, Durek brought his Chief Captains to the buccan, and Cotton began to describe the main features that the Army would see along the Brega Path, starting at the Dusk-Door.

Using copies of Perry's map, Cotton began by telling of the stairs leading up behind the western doors, and he went on to speak of the halls and chambers and passageways they would encounter within Kraggen-cor. The Captains were especially interested in places where there would be bottlenecks, or where maggot-folk could lie in ambush. Cotton had to draw upon all of his knowledge of the Brega Scroll to answer their enquiries, particularly those of Felor the Driller, who asked many penetrating questions, dwelling almost exclusively upon the first several miles of the Brega Path. Cotton was later to discover that Felor's companies were to be in the forefront of the invasion—the spearhead of the Dwarf Army.

Though he couldn't answer all their queries, Cotton had done well, and the Chief Captains thanked him for the review, and at noon they withdrew. But shortly thereafter, Cotton went over the same information with another group of Captains. Three more times, meetings were held at which the Warrow spoke of the Brega Path in terms of bottlenecks, ambuscades, deployments, and other tactical features. It was sundown when he finished, and at last all the Captains had heard his words.

During the time Cotton was speaking, the work at Dusk-Door continued. At times it went swiftly, at other times slowly, yet progress was being made. More than three quarters of the stone was now out of the way, yet only seven hours remained until midnight. Lanterns were again unshielded, and the toil went on.

Cotton ate his evening meal, then sat once more atop the broken dam and watched the labor at the far wall. The stars began to shine in the vault above, and still the effort went forth. Time passed, and Rand joined the Warrow. "In just three hours night will be at its deepest," remarked the Man, peering at the starfield.

They continued to watch the work in silence, each immersed in his own thoughts. Farlon came and joined them, but said nothing as he, too, regarded the sky and judged the depth of the night. Shortly, however, there came a cheer from the Great Loom, and Cotton sprang to his feet. "They're done!" he shouted. "They must be! See, the light shows only a few rocks remain, and they are being rolled into the black crater even now."

The three watched, and soon the lanterns began bobbing northward as the workers and horses returned to the encampment. Word finally came: the task was indeed finished—the massive job done with. Durek, smiling, came carrying a lantern to the top of the falls. "Well, Friend Cotton," he rumbled, "we have succeeded, and with yet two hours to spare."

Durek summoned a herald to him and spoke a word or two. The herald stepped to the edge of the falls precipice and raised a golden horn to his lips, and blew a blast that echoed throughout the vale, causing all who heard it to leap to their feet with hands flying to axe hafts. And even though Cotton was standing next to King Durek, still the Warrow found himself reaching for the hilt of the Atalar Blade, so compelling was the hight to arms of the War Horn.

At this sound, Farlon raised his own black-oxen horn to his lips, and an imperative call split the air. Again Cotton felt his heart thud and his blood surge, and his gaze leapt in wonder from Durek's golden War Horn to Farlon's black-oxen horn. And he glanced to the silver Horn of the Reach hanging by the green and white baldric over his own shoulder, recalling its heartlifting voice. The peals of these three clarions seemed, somehow, irresistibly compelling, though their calls were different: the golden horn was resonant and commanding; the black, flat and challenging; the silver, sharp and calling.

Cotton, too, felt the urge to sound the trumpet he carried—the silver Horn of the Reach—and his hand grasped the bugle; yet he did not set the wind to it, for he knew the dread this token held for the Dwarves; and so he let it fall back to his side unvoiced.

Yet other sounds pealed forth as Durek's and Farlon's calls were answered by the shouts of Dwarf warriors and by the clack of axe upon buckler, a sonance which soon became a great rhythmic pounding of steel upon bronze.

And Cotton's heart pounded too, and his blood surged and his spirit flamed as the Ragad Vale rang with the great hammering and with the roar of the fierce War calls of the Châkka. And above this din pealed the wild cry of a horn of Valon, but above all belled the great golden command of Durek's mighty War Horn.

And the Dwarves of the Army came to the golden call, for it was the summons of their King. Their blood was up and their hearts aflame, and as they came they shouted and flourished their weapons to the sky, and their Dwarvish passions blazed. And when the clamoring Host had gathered on the sides of the vale near the Sentinel Falls, a great proud cry burst forth from the Legion entire as above them Durek stepped to the edge of the linn and stood.

The light of the lanterns filled the valley before the Dwarf King, and he was wreathed in the blue-green phosphorescence. The Moon was full and shone down on him, and the circlet of stars on his black mail-shirt glittered silver in the moonlight. And at his side the water tumbling o'er the linn shimmered brightly. His black and silver locks fell from his helm, and his forked beard shone with luster. He grasped his silveron-edged axe in his right hand, and the blade sparkled. And he looked somehow greater than his stature, for he was King.

Durek raised his arms, and when quiet fell, he spoke; and though he did not seem to raise his gravelly voice, still all the Host heard him: "We stand ready to issue into our rightful homeland and drive the foul usurpers out. This ancient foe we have met in battle many times, and never yet have we suffered defeat at their hands. But heed me: My meaning is not that the

Grg is a soft, easy opponent. To the contrary, the Squam are evil and cunning, and in every battle the struggle has been mighty and the outcome uncertain. Yet we defeated the Foul Folk in the Wars of Vengeance; we defeated them again in the Battle of the Vorvor; and we again defeated Squam in the Great War, as well as in the Winter War. And now, once more we go to fight the Grg, and this time the victory may be yet harder to grasp, for this time they shall be in their strength, for the battle will take place underground, where the Sun threatens them not. But we, too, shall be strengthened, for we shall be in our rightful homeland. And when this War is done with, Kraggen-cor shall again be ours!"

There was a great roar of voices, and a pounding of axe haft upon stone, and the black and golden horns blew wildly.

After a time, Durek once more held up his arms for quiet, and slowly the swell of voices and horncalls and clatter of axes subsided, till only the susurration of the tumbling glitter of the Sentinel Falls remained. And above the shush Durek spoke: "We have conquered much that has stood in our way to come to this moment: we outfought the blizzard in the Crestan Pass; we overcame the deep snow on the Mountainside; we quick-marched long to defeat time and distance; we slew the vile Monster of the Dark Mere; and we moved a great mass of stone to uncover the Dusken Door. There is but one thing more that stands in our way, and that is the Grg Swarm. But as we have done before, so shall we do again: we shall meet them in battle and crush them! Victory shall be ours!"

Again there was a mighty shouting and a wild pealing of the black and golden horns, and the strike of axe haft on stone became a great rhythmic beat, and four thousand voices chanted, *Khana-Durek! Khana-Durek! Khana-Durek! [Breakdeath-Durek!]* over and over and over.

At last Durek held up his hands for quiet, but it was a long time coming. "I go now to the Dusken Door to speak the words of power at that portal. If the Squad of Kraggen-cor has won through the caverns to the goal, then at the mid of this night we shall set foot into our ancient homeland. Yet hearken: it may not be the Squad we meet at the Door but, rather, the Squam army, for we know not the success or failure of Marshal Brytta's mission, and the Grg spies may have slipped past the Vanadurin and borne to Gnar word of our Army here at the Dusken Door. Regardless, if it is the Grg Swam we meet, then we will begin the War just that much sooner and regain our ancient homeland all the quicker. Heed: We all know our battle assignments. Form into your Companies, for the hour is nearly arrived. And may Elwydd smile upon each of us, and Adon strengthen our arms."

Then Durek flashed his axe up to the moonlit sky and cried the ancient battle challenge of the Dwarves: *"Châkka shok! Châkka cor! [Dwarven axes! Dwarven might!]"*

And thrice a mighty shout went up from all the Host: *Châkka shok! Châkka cor!* and Cotton felt his heart leap and his blood surge. The Warrow stabbed his sword to the sky and he, too, shouted with all the Legion the battle cry of the Dwarves. And he turned to see that Rand, also, had his Riamon blade upraised in solemn pledge; and Farlon stood with the butt of his spear grounded to the earth of the Valley Ragad as a steadfast vow that he would lead the wounded to the south, out of harm's way.

Then Durek spun on his heel and started for the Door with Cotton and Rand at his side; and the Dwarf Legion surged along the Old Rell Spur and up the cliff to follow after, while Farlon of the Valanreach stood firm.

As the warriors strode around the crater and by the cairns along the Great Loom, desperate thoughts whirled through Cotton's mind: *Oh, please let Mister Perry be at the Door. He's just got to be there. It won't be right if he ain't.* But then he thought, *Whoa now, Cotton Buckleburr, why are you thinkin' he might not be there? You know he'll make it. Nothing can stop him, not even a black mine full of maggot-folk. It'll sure be good to see him again—if he's there. If he ain't there, well, then, I'll just lead the Dwarves down the Brega Path till we find him and the others, even if Marshal Brytta didn't stop those spies and we have to go through a whole Spawn Horde. But I won't have to do that, 'cause Mister Perry'll be there and the maggot-folk won't be . . . I hope. Then he'll lead and I'll follow. But if I do have to lead then it's: two hundred steps up the broad stair; one and twenty and seven hundred level paces in the main passage 'round right, left, right, and right turns passing three arches . . .*

And as Cotton strode with the others toward the Door, through his mind marched the beginning steps of the Brega Path.

At last they halted at the place of the Dusk-Door. Blank stone loomed where the portal should appear. It was not quite midnight, and so they stood and waited. Behind them the Host moved into position: Felor's companies were first, standing ready with axes, and some sported small bucklers on their left arms. Cotton could see rank after rank of Dwarves stretching back around the black crater toward the Sentinel Falls. Lanterns glowed softly, carried by the warriors. Cotton's eyes followed the lights all the way to the last group of lanterns: Bomar's company: the rear guard.

Atop the Sentinel Stand stood Farlon and a head-bandaged Dwarven observer, peering at the stars overhead and at the bright Moon riding high. At last the two looked to one another and nodded; and the Dwarf took up his lantern and threw the shutter wide, and a beam sprang toward the Door, toward those under the great hemidome who could not see the whole of the spangled heavens wheeling through the ebon sky. And as the lantern flashed its signal, Rand drew his sword, and Durek gripped his axe. Hastily, Cotton, too, drew his blade. It was midnight, the appointed hour—time to attempt the opening. They did not know whether the doors would swing wide; and if the portal opened, would the Host be met by friend or foe?

King Durek stepped to the towering Loom and set his axe down, leaning it against the massif, and placed his hands upon the surface of the blank stone, muttering strange words under his breath. *And springing forth from where his hands pressed, there spread outward upon the stone a silvery weft that shone brightly in the lantern glow and by the moonlight and starlight. And as the tracery grew, it took form. And suddenly there was the Door!* At last they could see its outline shining on the smooth stone, and they could see within the glittering web three runes set thereupon, wrought of theen, the Wizard metal: a glowing circle in the center of the Door; and under the circle and off to the right, the Wizard Grevan's rune *G,* and to the left, Gatemaster Valki's glyph *V.*

Durek caught up his weapon by the helve and stepped back from the high portal; all that remained was for him to say the Wizard-word for "move," and the Door, if able, would open.

The Dwarf turned to Cotton, Rand, and Felor. "Stand ready," he warned, "for we know not whom we meet."

Cotton gripped his sword and felt the great pressure of the moment rising inside him. The tension was nearly unbearable, and he felt as if he needed to shout, but instead he thought, *Let Mister Perry be at the Door and not no Rūck.*

Durek turned back to the Door and gripped his axe; he placed his free hand within the glittering rune circle; then his voice rang out strongly as he spoke the Wizard word of opening: *"Gaard!"*

CHAPTER 5

SPEARS OF VALON

Forty hours before Durek spoke the words of opening at the Dusk-Door, the horse column of the Harlingar quickly moved out of the Ragad Valley. The warriors rode two abreast with spears bristling to the sky; favors fluttered from the hafts, while in the lead the War-banner of Valon snapped and cracked in the breeze. The dark helms of the Vanadurin threw back no glints, yet gauds of horsehair and wings and horns flared from the steel. Swiftly they passed, yet not at full gallop, for they had far to go and must needs save their mounts. And the earth trembled at their passage.

Brytta rode in the fore with Arl at his side, and all cantered at the steady ground-devouring pace of a Valanreach long-ride. And no rider spoke as their grim eyes swept the bleak high wold for sign of movement but saw none. The column rode thus as the Sun clambered up through the winter sky, and miles fell away beneath hooves. Slowly the land changed as they went, the rolling western wold yielding to rugged hills, which in turn gave way to a rough, broken region of shattered rock and deep defiles, of high stone walls and jagged slopes, and of flint-hard paths twisting through a splintered land, as if the world's crust had been thrust asunder by the towering mountains bursting forth from the fettering rock below.

Brytta's force rode with relentless determination to succeed in this desperate mission to intercept the two bands of spying Wrg ere they could reach the hidden High Gate in Quadran

Pass, for the Spawn were carrying to Gnar word of the Dwarf
Army at the western Door. And but a bare four hours of daylight remained; and then the Sun would set and the Foul Folk
would again take up their dash for the Gate. And the riders had
yet some leagues to go to reach their goal: the road to the Gap.

The land now consisted of huge upjuttings of red granite,
striated in places with hued bands of layered stone. It would
have taken great skill for the Harlingar to track the Rutcha
through this tangle of rock, yet early on Arl had unerringly led
the column to find Eddra's wake: Eddra, who had trailed the
Spawn throughout the previous night, leaving clear Valanreach
signs indicating the Wrg path for the pursuers to follow. And
the Vanadurin had followed that track for hours.

'Mid the red crags and rudden bluffs wended the riders,
strung out in their long column of twos, their gait slowed to a
mere picking walk through the tumble of shattered stone. As
Nightwind stepped through the broken rock, Brytta, seeking
some tactical advantage over the foe, reflected back upon the
tale Arl had told him during other slow passages such as this, a
tale not stripped bare as would be a scout's terse report but,
rather, one told in full:

"Three days agone, after the Legion marched away from the
fork in the road toward that . . . that dead vale back there"—
Arl gestured toward the Ragad Valley—"Eddra, Wylf, and I
took the other fork and rode like the wind to the small watch-
mountain, Redguard, where we set vigil o'er the pass. We huddled atop that cold stone peak for what seemed an endless time,
wood for the balefire ready but unlit, awaiting the coming of a
Wrg army. And we burned no campfire at night, for that would
signal our presence to enemy eyes.

"And cold we were, so cold. . . . A bitter, rimed grip was
upon the land; and the very stone cracked under heel—frost-
riven, broken by that dread clime's grasp. Even Wylf's luck at
finding comfort failed, and we lurked there among the icy rock
in the long, bitter nights; and the cruel wind cut like sharp
knives as we huddled shivering, urging on the morn so that we
could then light a small campblaze for its feeble warmth. At
times we even japed that should a Rutchen army come, we then

could kindle the balefire and warm by its flames; yet it did not happen. For two nights nothing happened.

"But, on the third night—last night—thirty or so Rutcha bearing torches came marching down from Quadran Col just after sunset."

"Hold!" interrupted Brytta. "Whence came they? How far up were they? Did you see them come from the High Gate?"

"I have thought long upon that," answered Arl, his brow furrowing, "and this is the way of it: the first we saw of their torches, they were nearly at the snow line, high up on the roadway o'er the Gap."

Brytta grunted, then motioned for the young rider to continue his tale, and so Arl did: "Though we had hoped for some action to fire our blood, when the Spawn came all thoughts of discomfort, all longing for warmth fled in our dismay, for we knew that here could spell the doom of the quest. There were only thirty or so of them, but still it could mean discovery of the Host. Yet down the flanks of Stormhelm they tramped, and turned south. And while they marched, we considered our course.

"Because there were so few, we did not light the balefire, for that signal was meant to warn the Legion of the coming of a full Wrg army, not just a mere squad. Too, a beacon would only serve to warn the Spawn that something was stirring on this side of the mountains. Yet it seemed likely that their spying eyes had seen our Army bear south along the Old Rell Way, and this force had come to see what was afoot.

"They marched for two hours, or a bit more, going perhaps six or eight miles, down from the snow line and passing below us on the east flank of Redguard. Yet suddenly they stopped, seeming to mill about in fear or confusion, and we wondered at the cause. Then we, too, saw what had affrighted the Foul Folk, and we ourselves were taken aback, for it was indeed a bodeful sight: that great cusp of a stone wall at the head of the Valley of the Door . . ." Arl turned and swept his hand back toward the hemidome of the Great Loom, which, through the granite crags behind, could be seen towering up the side of Grimspire, "that wall was flaring and blooming red and orange and yellow in the night, like the very forge of Hèl, and great dark shadows were guttering and twisting and writhing up the mountain flank and into the blackness, as if some vast fire was ablaze in Ragad Vale."

"Indeed, 'twas a great conflagration," verified Brytta, turning Nightwind through the jumble of rock, "set ablaze atop the dam last night to thwart the evil Warder as the Dwarves strove to break the stone and loose the lake. But that is a tale to be told later, after yours is finished. Speak on."

But at that moment the land opened somewhat, calling for a faster pace. Arl shifted the banner spear from the left stirrup to the right, couching the haft butt in the cup there, and spurred his horse to a swift canter. They rode thus for a time before coming again to shattered land where the column had to slow. And when the pace dropped back, Arl continued as if there had been no break in his narrative: "We were filled with foreboding, whelmed by the unknown yet dire portent of the flaring upon the Loomwall. It seemed as if some great battle perchance raged in the Valley of the Door while we three on Redguard stood mayhap a less necessary duty. We argued whether or not to ride to the vale to help; yet we knew not the cause of the flaming, thus could not easily decide upon our course: at hand directly below us was the given threat of a small, perhaps unimportant, force of Wrg; while far off was the sign of a great raging effort of some unknown action, which for aught we knew could be entirely peaceful, though we three thought elsewise."

"*Arn!*" snorted Brytta. "'Twas anything but peaceful. Yet I interrupt. Go on."

"In the end," continued Arl, "we chose to hew to our original duty—to watch the Gap for a Rutchen army—but also to watch the track of this Wrg band below us. In any event, in spite of the fact that we would rather be at our comrades' sides in any conflict, we knew that surely the Host could face any foe and fare as well without us as with us, though it goes against the grain to admit so. On the other hand, we alone knew of this squad of ravers. We knew, too, that should they espy the Host at the Dusk-Door, then Gnar would be alerted, to the ill of our quest."

"You chose aright," commented Brytta, "though difficult it is to forbear rushing to the aid of arms-mates."

"After a time," Arl went on, "the Spawn once again started south, toward the valley, and we came to the decision that one of us should ride to warn the Host, mayhap to set a trap or to divert the Foul Folk if it seemed they were near to discovering the Army. Yet, to set a trap, we needed to know their goal; and to divert them, if that became necessary, we needed to be on their track. The ravers had just passed beyond sight within the foothills, and we were not certain as to their course.

"In haste, we drew lots. Wylf lost, pulling the short twig, and was left atop that cold Redguard Mountain while Eddra and I rode down to trail the Spawn. I had drawn the long stick and would be the messenger to warn the Host should the need arise.

"Ahorse, we followed their path along a rocky trace, and in the full moonlight we set a goodly pace. Soon we came to where we could again see their torches, and we lagged far behind, trailing their slow march southward. After the mid of night, as if a vast fire had been drowned, the Great Loomwall suddenly went dark, and again the Wrg milled about in confusion or fright, as if they were undecided as to what course to follow. And both Eddra and I were sore beset with doubt, for we knew not the meaning either, but we guessed yet again that something dire was happening south in the Ragad Valley. But we knew our duty was to follow the Spawn, as we had planned.

"Once more the Wrg started toward the Ragad Vale, and again we trailed them. Some time passed, and we covered two leagues or so. They drew nigh to the Valley of the Door, and Eddra and I knew we had to decide soon on how we would act: to ride among them, shouting, and then away to draw them off; or to wait to see their goal, and then warn the Host. But ere we could act, a *second* torch-bearing gang of thirty *more* came through the night—but *they* came *from* the direction of the *valley*. The two bands clotted together and shouted and snarled and cursed one another, and the two leaders argued; but then with a lashing about of thongs, the Drōken leaders turned the Rutcha back toward Quadran Pass.

"Moving quickly now, no longer uncertain, loping at Rutch-pace, they began running toward the Quadran Gap, coming straight at Eddra and me. We quickly stepped our mounts off the path and into the surrounding dark scrub and rock, and we dismounted, holding our steeds' muzzles to prevent a challenge. The returning Wrg loped past without seeing us, and among their words both Eddra and I heard one of them snarl something about '. . . *we tell Gnar of the dam-breaking lake-draining army of foul-beards at the buried door!'* Though we knew not what all overheard meant, we did know that the Host had been discovered by these Spawn now on their way to the High Gate to warn Gnar.

"As soon as they were beyond hearing, Eddra told me to ride to warn the Legion while he stayed behind to trail the Wrg and leave Valanreach signs along their track for pursuers to follow. And we parted, Eddra following Rutcha and Drōkha north while I hastened south.

"Swiftly I rode, and the Moon was bright; yet I could not fly apace until the coming of first light, and then at last Firemane could see to run in full. And as I rode, I knew that only the Vanadurin would be fleet enough to intercept the two bands of Wrg ere they reached the pass—if they have not yet attained that goal. But I think the dayrise will have found them short of the Gap, and they will be holed up awaiting nightfall—at least I hope their Wrg-lope was not fast enough to carry them to Stormhelm before the coming of the Sun.

"And you know the rest of the tale, Sire." Arl fell silent, and onward they rode, following Eddra's well-placed markers.

Thus had Arl told his full tale; and now, miles later, Brytta reflected upon the scout's words for some shred, some scant fact, that would give the Vanadurin added advantage over the foe—but beyond knowing their number and their goal, the Reachmarshal found nought he could use.

Once more the column of Valanreach riders came upon an open flat, and again the pace quickened as swiftly they coursed north, and the high stone of the flanking mountain ramparts flung back the thunder of their passage, and the plateau drummed beneath the driving hooves.

Ahead they could see a towering scarp rear up from the land and stand athwart their path, and a great dark crack jagged upward into its flank. And toward this yawning split, Eddra's signs pointed. Black it looked, dark though the Sun still rode the sky. And the closer they came, the more dreadful it seemed. And into this fissure, Eddra's track plunged.

The column rode into the forbidding cleft, now single file, for the walls were close upon them. Though it was daytime still, a shadowy muffled murk clutched at them, and the rays of the Sun fell dim and feeble into the cold depths. Splits and cracks radiated away into the flanks, their ends beyond seeing, lost in darkness. Horses shied and started at the black gapings, sensing the disquiet of the riders they bore as they passed these holes. Ancient Vanadurin legends told of the haunted Realm of the Underworld, where dwelled the living dead; and ever in these hearthtales, heroes came to woe and grief and unending agony. And always these paladins had entered into the halls of the dead through caves and rifts and clefts in the land, ignoring the warnings of a loved one to stay clear of these fissures. Hence, for those accustomed to open skies and grassy plains, these dark legends gave rise to inchoate yet palpable feelings of dread whenever a dark pit yawned before them. And the Vanadurin column now rode through the dim light at the bottom of a black abyss while splits and cracks and holes without number leapt at them from the looming stone walls; and the pits cast back shattered echoes, reverberating hollowly like laughter from Hèl.

These dim legends scuttled on spider claws through Brytta's mind as he felt his hackles rise, but he dismissed them, for warriors believe they have long since cast aside the hearthtales of youth. Still, the thought of being underground was dire, and the prospect of fighting a War below earth—as the Dwarves were wont to do—caused Brytta to marvel at the Dwarves' staunch courage, and unformed feelings of apprehension rose within his own heart. But uneasy or not, the column rode ahead, as Brytta fleetingly thought of Hèl. And his sight darted from hole to hole. And it seemed as if he could feel the presence of hundreds of malevolent Rutchen eyes glaring out at the passing horsemen—if not the Spawn they were pursuing, then perhaps others; for despite Durek's assurances to the contrary, the Valanreach Marshal was more than convinced that the walls of this region were riddled with a thousand secret bolt holes to the great Black Hole of Drimmen-deeve—a thousand places for sudden assault or surreptitious spying or swift escape. Yet even if there were not here secret shafts boring away to the Black Maze, still Brytta felt watched. Were the eyes of the undead staring out from the blackness? Hèl's spawn?

Shaking his head to dispel these fey thoughts, Brytta squinted up the looming walls to the jagged rift of sky far above, knowing that if foul Wrg or aught else lurked in the splits of this dreadful crack, the wan light of day dimly reaching these depths was not enough to keep the creatures pressed back into the dark shadows at the deep roots of the riven fissures.

The walls of the cleft twisted tortuously, and the long path before the line of horsemen began to rise. Slowly they rode up out of the stifling narrow crack, to come at last to another open plateau. And as they came out upon the high plain, out into the cold crisp air of day, the sense of cloying suffocation left Brytta and he breathed freely again. And the wisps of fables and lurking Wrg fled Brytta's mind, though he still marveled at the courage of the *Dwarvenfolc*.

"Sire!" Arl exclaimed and pointed. Far ahead they could see a dun horse standing near several huge boulders where yet another bluff lunged upward, and again a great split fissured away into blackness.

"It's Eddra's mount," growled Brytta, and his heels clapped into Nightwind's flanks and the great black horse sprang swiftly forward. "Sound no horns," Brytta ordered as the column matched his stride.

As they rode toward the towering cliff, Eddra stepped out from the shadow of a boulder and hand-signalled that all was well. The Marshal felt a surge of relief that his scout was alive, for Brytta, seeing what appeared to be a riderless, abandoned horse, had fleetingly feared the worst. Yet Eddra was hale, in fact was less weary than his brethren, for he had dozed under the Sun while awaiting the Harlingar, whereas none of them had rested for nearly two days: Arl had ridden throughout the preceding night, while Brytta and the others had struggled without letup in the battle with the Krakenward.

"*Hál!*" cried Eddra, pleasure upon his features, as the riders wheeled 'round him in a semicircle and brought their steeds to a halt, half to the left of Brytta, half to the right.

Brytta dismounted and signed to the others to do the same, for they had been long in the saddle. "*Hál,* rider! Clear was your track and long have our eyes sought you. How fares your mission? Where be the Spawn?"

"The Wrg spies lie up in yon crack," answered Eddra, gesturing at the dark split in the face of the bluff, "waiting for the westering orb to fall." Many glanced at the late-afternoon Sun, and but two hours or less remained before it would set. "Far did they run through this broken land, and weary was I with the chase. Yet there they lurk in the deep black shadows, soon to fly out the crack's far side.

"Still we may head them, for to the west but a ways lies a path around this dark cranny, where we may pass beyond them without their knowledge. North, too, is water for the horses. A short ride, then, will bring us to a deep stony defile through which they must pass, for it is upon the road to the Quadran Gap and the secret High Gate, a defile with steep walls where we may entrap them and they cannot escape our spears."

"Hai!" cried Brytta, and his dour features broke into a wide smile, and he clapped Eddra upon the shoulder; for his warrior had scouted the lay of the land and had found a snare for the foe, a place where at last the Harlingar could stand athwart the fleeing Spawn's path. "Let us spend no more time in idle chatter," he grinned. "I would as lief be on our way. Lead, fair Eddra, and we shall follow."

Once again the warriors mounted, and this time their hearts sang, for now they had the knowledge that they were not on a shadow-mission—a mission of little or no hope—for each had secretly feared that they would be too late, and now they knew they were not.

Following Eddra, swiftly they rode to a narrow path pitching shallowly up the face of the bluff. Along this slant the horses went, steeds and riders seemingly oblivious to the steep fall on their left. And at the top they came out upon the last plateau. In the distance before them they could see the road leading up to the Gap of Stormhelm. To the west lay Redguard Mountain, and they knew that even now Wylf, at its crest, watched them ride forth into the open and toward the col. They pressed ahead and at last came to the side of the road, and here and there an ancient pave-stone could be seen, though most were buried and a few were thrust aside by weed and hidden in the tangle. And at roadside, a spring thinly crusted with ice bubbled down from the snows in the pass; and they paused long enough to water the steeds and to refresh their canteens.

Slowly the Sun sank, and just as it lipped the earth, they came to the defile spoken of by Eddra. The sides were steep and

the canyon long; Quadran Road wended upward through its
flanks, to pass beyond sight at a far turn, rising toward the Gap.
Up to the turn they rode, there to lay their trap for the Wrg.

Brytta gathered his riders about him, and in the dimming
dusk he set forth his plan. And when he was done, each knew
his assignment and was pleased, for Brytta was a mighty Captain, and his strategy suited their nature. He spoke in Valur, the
enduring Battle-tongue of the Valanreach, which hearkened
back even unto the ancient days when their forebearers had ridden free on the high northern steppes, a time long before any
had come south to the grassy plains of Valon. And as darkness
fell, Brytta repeated an elder benediction of the Vanadurin:

> "Arise, Harlingar, to Arms!
> Fortune's three faces now turn our way:
> One smiling, one grim, one secret;
> May the never-seen face remain always hidden.
>
> Hál, Warriors of the Spear and Saber!
> Hál, Warriors of the Knife and Arrow!
> Hál, Warriors of the Horn and Horse!
> Ride forth, Harlingar, ride forth!"

And in the gathering darkness, the fierce Valanreach warriors, their hearts pounding and spirits surging, mounted and
rode to take up their battle positions to await the coming of the
Spawn.

Brytta, far up the defile, sat his horse and stared down the
dark road rising up to meet him. Riders four abreast formed a
long column behind their Marshal. And as they held, the horses
were calm, occasionally shifting their weight; and saddle
leather creaked and the thicket of upright spears stirred to and
fro.

The night deepened and the stars shone forth. To the east beyond the range, the bright Moon climbed up the star-studded
sky, and at last the silver rays spilled through the gap between
Grimspire and mighty Stormhelm, bathing the defile with pale,
glancing light. And sharp-edged blackness clung to boulders

and crags and streamed darkly away. To the west, Redguard's peak jutted up out of the shadows of the range and into the moonlight, and past Redguard lay the western wold stretching beyond sight to the River Caire. The air was cold and crystalline, and the night was still, and the breath of horses and warriors alike rose in white plumes.

And the spears of Valon waited.

Ppfaa! Nightwind suddenly snorted and tossed his head, and Brytta listened sharply. At first he heard nothing; then dimly came a sound, faint: a scrabbling, like a chitinous scuttling. Stronger it grew, resolving at last into the distant slap of iron-shod Rutch boot.

"*Stel! [Steel!]*" hissed Brytta, reining to the side, and the lances in the first row dropped level, held steady by firm grips; and clear eyes watched the far turn. Louder came the sound of running, and now all could hear the clack of harsh voices, cursing and snarling, whining, panting, grating, the speech foul. Louder it came, and louder still, nearly upon them. Suddenly, a ragged loping column of torch-bearing Rutcha burst into view, scrambling around the turn below, and they jostled and jolted and elbowed and railed at one another as they swarmed up the road.

"*Tovit! [Ready!]*" Brytta hissed a second command in the Valonian Battle-tongue, and the horse-column seemed to bunch itself, as a tautly drawn bow ere the arrow is loosed. Yet tense and quivering, still they held their places; and onward came the Spawn, as yet unaware of the danger ahead.

And when it seemed that the Wrg must at last see the Harlingar, a flat horncry sounded from below, from behind the Foul Folk, as the Vanadurin posted there took station upon the road when the last of the Rutchen column passed by.

And the trap sprang shut!

"*V'ttacku! [Attack!]*" barked Brytta, and swift as an arrow loosed at last, the first four riders charged forth, spears leveled, thundering death.

"*Stel!*" called Brytta, and the lances of the second row

dropped level. *"Tovit!"* His voice was sharp and clear, and he paused but a moment; then: *"V'ttacku!"* And another line charged forth, havoc upon four horses, ten running strides behind the first.

"Stel!" the command came again, and again, and again, and rows paced forward, and lances lowered, and file after file of swift-running doom was launched down the road, down from the high ground.

At first the Spawn did not realize their plight, and when the Valonian horncall sounded from behind them they quickened their pace, fleeing unknown pursuit. And it was not until the last moment that those in the fore saw by moonlight and torch flare the first strike swooping down upon them, and then it was too late as wave after wave of lethal spears, hard driven by full-running horses, shocked into and through and over the Rutchen column. And screams rent the air as victims fell underfoot to be trampled, and lances impaled others, some spears to shatter in the impact. Sabers were drawn and slashed to and fro, felling foes, and Valanreach battle cries burst forth:

> *Hál Vanareich! [Hail Valon!]*
> *B'reit Harlingar! [Ready, Sons of Harl!]*
> *Kop'yo V'ttacku Rutcha! [Now whelm the goblins!]*

A few Rutcha tried to flee, but the walls of the defile were too steep to clamber, and the dreaded horsefolk were both before and behind them. Yet most of the foul breed, though taken by surprise, fought with feral savagery, for they were cornered: Torches were thrown in the faces of horses, and steeds shied and reared. Iron bars were swung with cunning force to crack across the forelegs of several charging coursers, and they fell screaming among the enemy, and the riders were set upon by the Wrg. Yet other horses, riderless, trained for War by the Vanadurin, lashed out with sharp hooves, felling Rutcha with their crushing blows. And warriors rose up out of piles of Spawn and cast the foe aside, and many Harlingar sang as they slew, a terrible burning light in their eyes.

Into the fray came Brytta, hewing left-handed with his saber, slashing Death borne upon Nightwind's back. And it was a mighty slaughter, and Brytta's arm grew weary with the reaping of Rutcha. Yet the battle raged on, for the Foul Folk were savage. And lance pierced, and saber slashed, cudgel smashed, and hammer crushed. Scimitar clashed with long-knife, and flashing hooves struck o'er iron bar. Grunts and screams and oaths and cries filled the air, and so, too, did the harsh clang of steel upon steel. And the struggle swept to and fro. Yet slowly the Vanadurin prevailed, and the Wrg numbers dwindled.

All Rutchen torches had been flung aside, or at riders, or at their steeds, and now only the bright Moon illumed the battle-ground, though here and there a brand sputtered on the road. Surviving Spawn flicked in and out of dark shadows, striking quickly then leaping back into blackness.

And slowly the fight became a grim stalking, as the Vanadurin dismounted and took up torches and spread across the road and searched each cleft and shadow. And the Foul Folk were found, sometimes singly, sometimes clotted together in pockets. And no quarter was given.

Brytta sat upon Nightwind, looking down the defile; he watched as the Harlingar sought living Spawn in the blackness, and made certain that those lying upon the ground were dead and not feigning. It was long-knife work, and saber, too; and struggles were short and fierce. And as he looked, a stone rattled down from above.

On the wall! A Drōkh! No, two! Flitting through the shadows above Brytta were two Drōkha who had managed to scale up a cranny to a high path along the south wall of the defile, a path running to the top. And now they were fleeing along it, escaping the defile, fleeing for the High Gate.

With effort, Brytta strung his bow, cursing the pain and clumsiness of his broken right hand. Another rider was nearby; "Didion! To me!" cried Brytta. "Wrg! On the wall! Your bow!" And as Didion rode to him, Brytta set an arrow to string and tried to draw the weapon with his broken hand. A low agonized groan hissed between his clenched teeth, and with the bow but half drawn the arrow fell from the weapon and clattered to the ground. *"Rach!"* Brytta cursed, and changed hands, shifting the bow to his clumsy right, reaching for arrow with his left. The Drōkha now scrambled the last few steps toward the top of the wall, an open plateau—and if they reached it, they were free!

Again Brytta set arrow to string, this time drawing the bow against the heel of his shattered right hand and gritting against the grinding pain while beads of sweat burst forth upon his brow. "Take the right, Didion, I'll take the left," he gasped, and as the Drōkha momentarily reappeared from the shadows, two arrows hissed through the air, one well aimed, the other less so. Now at the top and just entering the shadow again, one of the enemy flung up his hands and a piercing scream rent the air as he plunged backward down the defile wall to land with a sodden thud in the roadbed. The other Drōkh pitched forward into the blackness, and if he was arrow-struck, they did not see.

"Didion, after him! He must not escape!" Brytta barked. "Ged!" he called to another rider coming nigh. "Go with Didion! Drōkh on the height!" And Ged leapt from his horse and scrambled up a cleft behind Didion, finding the steep climbing no easy task.

And the search for Rutchen survivors went on.

Night passed and the Moon set, and dawn crept upon the land to find stricken Harlingar: exhausted, for they had spent two nights without sleep; wearied by struggle, first with the Krakenward, then with Wrg; drained, for some, weeping, had had to slay their own steeds, legs broken in battle; afflicted, for nearly half the warriors bore wounds, some serious, some minor, now bandaged; filled with heartgrief, for five of the Vanadurin would never again answer horncall. Thusly did the dayrise find the riders of the Valanreach.

Earlier, a count showed that three and seventy Rutcha and one Drōkh had fallen to the riders; and in the predawn the carrion were dragged down out of the defile and flung into a ravine, where the coming of the Sun would shrivel them to dust, as Adon's Ban decreed. The Wrg weapons were gathered, and in dull rage the riders snapped the blades and shattered the hafts and bent the iron bars beyond repair, and these, too, were cast into the ravine.

In midmorn, Didion and Ged returned to the defile and sought out Brytta. "Sire," said Didion, drawn and weary, "long we hunted, and this we found." He held up an arrow, broken in twain, covered with dried black Wrg gore. Brytta examined it closely and grunted: it was his. "Yet," Didion went on, "no Drōkh did we find, not near nor far; and by dawn's light we searched even unto the snow line. At the first, a spotted trail we followed, and quickly found the arrow. Soon the trail diminished, at last to disappear on the edge of a deep crevasse with a black still pool at bottom. Ged, here, climbed down while I cast about, but neither he nor I found aught else."

"*Skut!*" spat Brytta, flinging the fractured arrow from him and looking bitterly at his broken hand. "The Drōkh may have been but fleshwounded, snapping the arrow in twain and pulling it through himself. As to the Wrg's fate thereafter, we know not whether he pitched off into the crevasse by accident, or while dying, or not at all. He may have escaped entirely; if so, then even now word goes forth to Gnar.

"Yet you have done all I could ask, and though no Drōkh was found, feel no blame; the hand that failed was mine." And Brytta dismissed the two and cast himself to the ground. And he sat with his back to the wall, and his brooding stare bore into the stone opposite him. His mood was black and bitter, and in his eyes lurked fault.

Yet after a long while of smoldering thought, he again stood and gathered his warriors to him: "Vanadurin," he spoke, "I deem we must remain on guard in this defile, for other bands of ravers may be about the land. Yet all must come through this slot to reach the secret High Gate. And though this is the night appointed when King Durek will attempt the Dusk-Door, still it may not open, for the Squad of Seven may be delayed.

And it is in my mind that other trials may come, and we stand at guard here at the Dwarf Army's back. Even now, word may be going forth to Gnar, and he may set a Rutchen army on the inside of the Door to await the Dwarves. And in that event, if the Squad be delayed, then likely they will not be able to penetrate Gnar's waiting Swarm to reach the Door hinges. And if the Squad cannot reach him inside of the Door, then who will let Durek's Legion within?

"Too, there may be other doors, other gates, through which Gnar may launch an attack upon the Host. Yet the secret Gate in yon Quadron Gap is the only one we are certain of. And if an army marches down this way, then we with quick, slashing strikes must bait and harass and divert their energies aside for as long as our War-skill permits, to give the Squad and the Legion precious time to ope the Door.

"And so, here we must stay, both foreguarding and hindguarding the Dwarf Army. And a long wait it may be, for we know not when the Door may yield: tonight, tomorrow, in a seven-night, or never.

"Yet even though we wait, there is still much to do: Place our slain comrades 'neath stone cairns, until proper burial. Tend your steeds. Then rest, for you are weary. Go now, and know you stand a vital duty."

And the warriors saluted Brytta—*Hál!*—and turned to take up their tasks.

"Hogon," Brytta called, "set forth a ward of eight: four upslope, four down, two-hour watches."

And while Hogon selected the guard, Brytta turned to a flaxen-haired youth: Brath, Brytta's bloodkith. "Brath, sister's son, to me," he said wearily as he sat down upon a small boulder.

The younger Man, his left arm bound in splints and held in a sling, stepped to his kinsman's side. "Sire?"

"Your arm is shivered and your leg gashed," observed the Marshal, a fierce pride in his eyes, for Brath had accounted for many of the Rutchen slain. "Were we in other times or other places, I would send you to the hearth." Brytta held up both hands, forestalling the protests leaping to the young warrior's lips. "Instead, I would have you go to yon mountain"—he pointed to Redguard—"and relieve Wylf, for he is hale and we need his strong arm. In this, go with honor, for we must have one to tend the balefire, to signal the Host if need be. Take an extra overgarment, for Arl said it is cold; his cloak will do, for he needs it not and would give it gladly could he say."

And Brath went forth, and Gannon went with him, for both of wounded Gannon's hands were shattered, and he could no longer bear arms, though his vision was sharp and he could set watch.

And temporary cairns were made for the slain riders, to shelter them until they could be brought forth to the wide grasslands below and laid to rest 'neath turves. The Vanadurin withheld show of their grief for their fallen brethren—though it cut to the quick—for it is the custom of the Harlingar to mourn not until the final burial.

The Sun climbed high and passed overhead, and warriors rested. Two hours ere sunset, Wylf rode into the quiet encampment. He sat in the afternoon Sun, basking in its warmth as Brytta slept. Wylf spoke to one of the warders, and in the Valonian War-tongue the companion told the tale of the Kraken-ward, the Rutchen spies, and the battle in the defile; and Wylf listened grimly, and his eyes took on a steely glint.

In foredusk, the camp awakened, and a quick meal of way-bread and dried venison was taken, and the horses were gathered from the sward downslope. And warriors girded themselves for what the eventide would bring.

Night fell, and again the devastating trap was set, ready to spring shut should Spawn come. This time the Vanadurin posted a bowman upon each wall of the defile, to stop Wrg from fleeing that way; yet Brytta thought that this was latching the stable after the stallion has fled, for it yet burned within him that perhaps a Drōkh had escaped to carry word to Gnar, to the great ill of the quest—a Drōkh that he, Brytta, should have slain; and the Marshal again glanced with bitterness at his broken hand.

The darktide deepened, and stars wheeled above. Again the Moon shone silvery, full and bright. And the warriors spoke quietly of the Dusk-Door and wondered if it would open, for this was the night.

Time crept by at a slow-moving gait, and each moment seemed frozen in stillness.

Yet of a sudden the twelfth hour was upon the land. Now was the time for King Durek to say the words of opening. Silent moments fled and mid of night passed, and Brytta yearned to know what befell at the Door, and his heart felt taut with foreboding. And again time plodded.

Suddenly the bowman upon the south steep shouted in wonderment: "Ai-oi!" he cried, his voice loud in the hush. "Sire!" he called to Brytta, "at the Great Loomwall in the Valley of the Door, a balefire flares!"

"What? Balefire? At the Dusk-Door?" cried Brytta. "A recall beacon! Spawn! Or does it mean the Door opened? If so, was the Host met by friend or foe? Or have the Wrg fallen upon them from another gate? Fie! Whether or not we knew the which of it, it is of no moment, for we must ride!"

And Brytta sprang to Nightwind's back and raised his horn to his lips and blew a mighty blast that rent the air. And Nightwind reared and pranced and curvetted with side-steps, eager to answer the Valonian hight to arms. And Brytta called to the Vanadurin: "Mount up, Harlingar, and ride! Ride to the Dusk-Door! Let any who fall behind come at their own pace, for we are summoned! Forth, Harlingar, ride!"

And he clapped his heels into Nightwind's flanks, and down the shadowed road they sprang, hooves thundering, horn pealing, racing through the moonlit night. And so went all the Vanadurin, bursting forth from Stormhelm Defile, sparks flying from steel-shod hooves. And the fierce horns of Valon blew wildly.

CHAPTER 6

TRAPPED AGAIN

A day earlier, with the Squad lost at a dead-end passage and with no Gatemaster, and but twenty-eight hours remaining ere the appointed time of the rendezvous at the Dusk-Door, Perry drank his fill from the clear cold water of the underground river and refilled his leather water bottle. He was putting in the stopper when another faint hornblat echoed down the cave behind them. "Oh, why didn't we search for a way to close the secret door to the Gargon's Lair?" he asked. "Then the Rūcks wouldn't have been able to follow us."

"We were fortunate just to have found the way out," rumbled Borin, "and we had not the time to spare to look for the way of closing the portal; it is not our mission to discover the workings of all hidden gates in Kraggen-cor; our goal is to reach the Dusken Door and set it right."

"Well, we've got to get out of here," responded Perry. "The Spawn will be upon us shortly."

"I judge they are only about an hour or so behind us in that hard passage," said Shannon. "In the meanwhile, I urge that we look for another hidden door. The secret way at the Lost Prison opened onto this passage, and so there must be another door in and out of this cave."

"But that hidden door could be anywhere over the miles we just travelled!" cried Perry. "There's no reason to believe that it's here, near this dead end. Besides, we don't even know what we are looking for: it could be another slot for a west-pick, like

Bane, or a stone that gets pressed, or a special word that must be said, a glamoured key, or a hundred other things. And our Gatemaster is dead."

"But we must try, Friend Perry," insisted the Elf softly, "we must try."

"Oh, Vanidar Silverleaf, you are right, of course," admitted the Warrow, abashed at his own behavior. "I am just bitterly disappointed at this setback."

"So are we all," said Lord Kian. Above the gurge of the river came another faint horn sound. "Ursor, can you swim? Good. Doff your clothes and cross the river with me, and we will search the far wall for slots, runes, hidden levers, and other such devices. Anval, Shannon, take the right-hand wall. Borin, Perry, search the left side. Let us see if we can locate a way out."

Long and hard they searched by lantern light. Anval and Shannon found only one strange-looking rock, which, when they twisted it, merely came loose from the wall. Borin and Perry ranged along the left side, and Bane was thrust into several crevices to no avail. Kian and Ursor disrobed, then cast a grappling hook to the opposite bank of the river; it caught between two rocks, and when they tugged, it remained well anchored; after tying the line to a boulder on the near shore, they pulled themselves across the swift current and over to the far bank. But after a careful search, the sheer end-wall proved to be a blank. All the while the Squad looked, the Rūcken horn sounded closer and closer. Finally the comrades also examined the rough floor of the cavern for sign of an exit from the cave; but that, too, proved fruitless. "We must have passed it," called Kian from the far bank, waving a hand toward the Gargon's Lair as he prepared to cross back over.

The Squad came back together on the bank of the river, Ursor coming last, casting loose the grapnel and grasping the boulder-tied rope to ride the swift current and swing to the near shore. The Rūcken horn echoed again, and Bane blazed fiery blue. "We'll make our last stand there," decided Lord Kian as the Baeran came out of the water and into the group; Kian pointed at a high ledge running athwart the cavern. "That stone wall will be our rampart, and we will give good account of ourselves before their very numbers overcome us."

"Sire," spoke up Ursor, "there is but one other thing I'd like to try first. If I fail, it may mean you will be without my strength in the final battle. But if I succeed, then we will yet escape the Spawn."

"Escape?" exploded Perry in astonishment. "How can we escape? There is no way out!"

"There may be one, little friend," answered Ursor. "The river. As I was crossing back over I was swept toward the left wall, and I wondered where the river goes on the other side of it, if indeed there *is* another side; it occurred to me that the river may run into another cavern."

"It may," rumbled Anval, "but then again it may not, and you may drown finding out."

"He also may succeed," countered Borin.

The Rūcken horn blatted again, and Kian looked back the way they had come. "The gamble is worth the risk," he said after a short moment. "Our mission is to reach Dusk-Door, not to engage Yrm. If Ursor does not try, we will die fighting *Spaunen.* If he tries and fails, again we will perish. But if he succeeds, then we will go on. Yet hurry, for not much time remains."

Their longest line was swiftly fixed to Ursor's waist, and he took a Dwarf-lantern for light, for they are unaffected by water. "Let Wee Perry count one hundred heartbeats," Ursor instructed, "then pull me back."

"But my heart is racing," protested Perry as the Rūcken horn sounded again. "One hundred frightened-Warrow heartbeats will take but a moment. Let Shannon count instead."

Shannon nodded; and after four deep breaths, the giant Man ducked under, the lantern around his neck casting a rippling glow through the crystal-clear water as his powerful strokes and the current carried him under the wall. The others watched the glow recede and payed out the line. In spite of the fact that Shannon was counting, Perry also kept track of his own racing heart. The Warrow's count was nearing two hundred and Perry was feeling frantic when Shannon called, "Time!" and they began hauling in the rope.

At last the glow of light appeared and became brighter as they pulled strongly, and then Ursor emerged from beneath the wall and surfaced, blowing and gasping. "Nothing," he panted after a bit, "not even an air pocket."

Perry's hopes were dashed, but then Ursor spoke: "I'll try the opposite side."

The echo of a Rūcken horn sounded down the cavern.

"They come," gritted Kian.

The giant moved to the upstream wall and again entered the water. Once more the Baeran breathed deeply, and on the fourth breath he dived under and swam now against the strong current and slowly passed out of sight beneath the wall. Again Perry's racing heart passed the count of two hundred, and once more the blat of Rūcken horn clamored along rock walls. The raucous blare was much closer, and Borin ran to the rampart and looked down the length of the dark tunnel. "Their torchlight is faint but growing swiftly," he called back. "They will overtop this ledge in less than a quarter hour."

Lord Kian, who was tending Ursor's line, announced, "He's taking no more rope. He's stopped."

A moment later, Shannon called, "Time!" and Anval and Kian hauled on the line.

"It will not budge!" shouted the Dwarf. "He must be caught on something!"

Shannon and Perry sprang to the line and pulled also, but still it would not haul in. "We've got to do something!" cried Perry. "He'll drown!" But the rope stubbornly refused to be drawn in and only grew iron-rod taut under the strain.

Then Shannon cried, "Look! A light!"

And a faint glimmer appeared in the water and swiftly grew to a bright glow, and then Ursor came under the wall and burst to the surface. "It's there. Another cavern," he gasped. "I tied the line to a boulder. We can use it to hale ourselves against the swift current."

"Quickly!" cried Kian, beginning to don his clothes in haste and motioning Ursor to do likewise. "Shannon, you go first. Perry, you second. Then Anval and Borin. Pull yourselves hard hand over hand along the line. Leave your packs, but carry your weapons, and wear your armor. Don't let go of the rope. Here, Shannon, carry this lamp at your waist. Go now, swiftly. The Spawn draw near." As if to spur them on, a discordant bugle blatted loudly.

Shannon hurriedly tied the lantern to his waist and entered the flow. He took a deep breath and disappeared under the wall. Perry was frightened, but he knew he had to move quickly or all would die. His thoughts had returned to the terror-fraught time he tumbled helplessly under the floodwaters at Arden. Oh! he did not want to go into the rush; but in spite of his fear, he plucked up his courage and entered the underground river. The water was icy, and he gasped in the coldness. He grasped the rope and took four deep breaths as he had seen Ursor do, and on the fourth one he plunged beneath the surface, his eyes tightly shut. The last thing he heard as he went under was a loud horncall.

Hand over hand the Warrow desperately hauled himself; and he gripped to the limit of his strength, for he knew that if he let go of the line he would be swept to his doom under the opposite wall. The current was swift and buffeted him. Bane slapped against his legs, and his armor for the first time felt heavy. Hand over hand he pulled, and he needed air. *Oh, don't let me breathe water again,* he thought in dread, and hauled with all his might. Just as he was certain his lungs would burst, his head broke through the surface, and he explosively gulped sweet breaths of air and opened his eyes for the first time since starting.

By the light of Shannon's lantern the buccan could see the Elf reaching out to help him, and he took Silverleaf's hand and stumbled up to the shore in the cave. No sooner had he reached the bank than Anval and then Borin came. After a moment, giant Ursor surfaced, closely followed by Lord Kian. As soon as Kian reached the bank he called to the company to reel in the line, and tied to the end were knapsacks and lanterns.

"Well," declared Kian, "that'll give the *Spaunen* a riddle to read. Let us hope they believe we went through another secret door."

The companions stripped off their sodden clothes and searched through their packs for drier garments. Although the backpacks were not made to be submerged, still they were to a degree waterproof, and the clothing inside, though wet in places, was for the most part relatively dry. The bedrolls were not so fortunate, and, at Lord Kian's suggestion, were abandoned along with the drenched garments they had removed. Perry's warm Elven-cloak, however, seémed to shed water as effectively as a duck's back, and he rescued it from his roll. All ropes and tools were retained, but most of the food had been ruined by the underwater jaunt, and the waterlogged crue as well as the mian—a tasty, Elven waybread carried by Shannon and Ursor—were discarded. Perry's map and his copy of the Brega Scroll were preserved in their waterproof wrappings. The weapons, armor, and lanterns were no worse for the trip.

Borin wrung water from his black forked beard and then caught up a lamp and went exploring. An undelved cavern ran down out of the north, swung west over the river, and curved away to the south. As in the last cavern, the river itself issued from one wall, cut across the cavern, and dived back under the other wall. Borin crossed over the water on a ledge along the northwest wall, and soon his lantern light disappeared around the curve to the south; but shortly he returned. "The way looks open, but this cavern, too, is arduous, with many shelves and slabs and cracks on our path. I deem we are walking in channels never before trod by Châkka, paths as old as the Mountains themselves. Yet the southern way should lead us back toward the Brega Path, and we must begin."

Once more the Squad took up the trek, and as Borin had said, the way *was* arduous: ledges, splits, ramps, boulders, and ravines stood across their path. Twice they edged along a lengthy narrow path etched on the face of a sheer precipice. At one place they walked under a roaring cataract that leapt from a distant hole in a high wall to fall into a churning black pool far below the wet, slippery path they trod along a narrow stone ledge. But most of all they clambered: up, down, over, and across. Once Borin had to drive rock-nails and tie a rope so that the company could ascend a sheer precipice. Another time they thought that they would have to do just the opposite, sliding down a steep cliff on a rope tied at the top; but Anval lay on his stomach and dangled his lantern over the edge to espy a ledge aslant down the face of the bluff; and they followed this shelf to the cavern floor.

They had struggled for six hours and had gone only five miles when the cavern came to an end at a high wall with great boulders strewn at the base or canted against the end wall. "Oh, no!" cried Perry, distressed, "we've come all this hard way only to find another dead end!"

* * *

Dejectedly, the Squad slumped to the cavern floor, weary and bitter. Suddenly, Shannon called, "*Hsst!* I hear *Spaunen* boots."

The lanterns were shuttered, and Perry drew Bane; the blade was blazing, and quickly the Warrow resheathed it to hide its light. Now they all heard the Spawn, yet where could the foe be? This cavern had no side passages.

Quietly, facing the way they had come, the Squad knelt in readiness, all weapons save Bane in hand, but the comrades could see no enemy. At Perry's side was Anval, who turned his head this way and that, searching for the Squam in the darkness; after a moment he leaned toward the buccan and whispered, "Look to the end wall."

Perry turned and saw a dim glimmer of torchlight shining through the base of the wall, faintly backlighting one of the huge slabs leaning against a fold. Perry whispered to the Dwarf, "I'm going to take a look." And before Anval could object, Perry was gone, slipping noiselessly toward the great rock.

Behind the stone was a cleft, blocked completely except for a small opening at the base. The torchlight came glimmering through that crack. It was a way out! But the hole was barely large enough for the Warrow to crawl through. Cautiously, he poked his head and shoulders into the opening. The crevice curved away, and from around the bend came the far-off flicker of burning brands and the faint sound of maggot-folk. The buccan wriggled through and into the cleft, where he could stand. Beyond the turns, the slot widened and issued out into a huge, delved chamber. Remembering the words that Delk had said back at the pine grove outside Dawn-Gate, Perry shielded his tilted, jewel-like eyes with his hand and, standing behind a rock outjutting, he peered through the cracks between his fingers and cautiously looked around the corner and toward the firelight in the chamber.

In the center of the floor, sprawled all about, was a Hlōk-led band of Rūcks, nearly one hundred strong. By the light of their torches, Perry looked at the features of the chamber: It was nearly circular. From one end he could hear the sound of running water, and he saw a natural stone arch crossing a wide stream. His heart leapt for joy, for once again he knew where he was: this was the Bottom Chamber, a watering spot on the Brega Path. Dusk-Door was yet fifteen miles away, Rūcks and a huge slab barred the route, and there were only twenty hours remaining till Durek was to try the words of opening, but Perry again felt hope, for he was no longer lost.

As Perry watched, he saw one of the Rūcks slink secretively away from the others and come straight toward the cleft and the Warrow. Perry drew back. *What could the Rūck be coming this way for? Did my eyes catch the light in spite of looking through the cracks of my fingers?* Then Perry saw that his right sleeve was unbuttoned—perhaps had never been buttoned from the time he had changed out of the wet shirt back at the underground river. And the cuff had fallen away from his wrist as he'd held his hand over his eyes, and the firelight had reflected on his silveron armor; the Rūck was coming to claim for himself what he believed to be a long-lost gem gleaming in the dark. Perry scurried back along the cleft and popped through the opening and into the other cavern.

"What did you see?" whispered Anval from the darkness beside the great slab.

"There's a Rūck coming this way," hissed Perry, "and a lot more are sprawled in the chamber on the other side of this barrier."

Ursor's great hand drew the Warrow into the darkness along the wall. "Fear not," breathed the Baeran, "I'll handle the Rutch."

Perry could hear the Rūck scuffling down the cleft, cursing and muttering. It reached the end and stopped. Then the Warrow heard the Rūck drop to its hands and knees; the faint glow of torchfire reflected from the stone was blotted out as, grunting and swearing, the Rūck started squeezing through the opening. The cave was too black to see what happened next, but Perry heard a choked-off intake of breath and the thrashing of limbs and a scuffling sound that was quickly repressed. Then there came a *snap!* and all was quiet. "It's done," Ursor hissed, and Perry was glad that he had not seen what had just occurred.

In the darkness the Warrow gathered the Squad together. "The Brega Path is just beyond the end wall," he said quietly. "We are at the Bottom Chamber, fifteen miles from Dusk-Door.

There is a Rücken company barring the way; but even if the Rücks weren't there, the way into the Chamber is blocked with that great slab of stone, and unless we get rid of it, I am the only one here small enough to get through the hole."

"Perhaps we can topple the stone," conjectured Anval. "But the crash will bring all the Grg rushing."

"Then let us decoy them," said Shannon. "After all, that is one of my purposes for being here: to draw off the *Rûpt* if there is no other choice. Here is what I propose: We locate three places nearby to hide. Then we topple the stone. When it falls, Perry, Anval, and Borin get to the hiding places while Lord Kian, Ursor, and I hie back the way we came, lanterns brightly lit, drawing the *Spaunen* behind. As soon as the way is clear, you three will make for the Door while we three will escape underwater."

"But there are maggot-folk back that way, too," protested Perry. "You'll just be running from one Spawn force to another. Why don't we simply wait for this Rück company to move on?"

"The Wrg back at the underground river are likely gone by now," responded Ursor, "and we know not when this company will move. No, Shannon is right: we must draw them off."

"But Perry speaks true too," countered Borin. "If the Squam move soon, there is no need to take this risk."

"These are my thoughts," announced Anval: "Borin and I can do but a limited amount at the Door without the guidance of a Gatemaster. If the trouble is simple, we may be able to set it aright. If not, then we could work for weeks and still not succeed. Hence, I deem it will matter little if we get there with ten hours to work, or with but one. With that in mind, let us set the toppling ropes on the slab now and get everything in readiness. Then we wait. If the Grg have not moved in good time—say, four hours—then we go ahead with Silverleaf's plan; on the other hand, if they *do* move on, we can all proceed to the Dusken Door together."

"That plan, though well thought, may just lose us four hours," pointed out Shannon.

"Aye. But it may also save us from dividing our strength," retorted Borin.

The Squad fell silent while Lord Kian weighed the alternatives. Finally he chose: "Set the lines, seek out the hiding places; as soon as all is ready, we topple the stone; we shall not wait. Our mission now is for Perry to deliver Anval and Borin to the Door as quickly as possible; we must not delay any longer, for the time may be needed for other tasks, as yet unseen, between here and Dusk-Door."

Quietly the Squad set about to carry out Shannon's plan. The hole was covered with Perry's cloak, and lanterns were dimly unhooded. Ursor cast the dead Rūck into one of the wide cracks in the floor as the rest of the Squad searched for and located three places to take cover: one on a ledge high on the west wall, the other two behind boulders along the east wall. And Perry, Anval, and Borin made sure that they could quickly get concealed in their selected hiding places: Borin on the ledge, Anval and Perry behind the boulders. Then a trio of toppling ropes were tied to the great slab up high, Borin clambering to do it. That done, the lanterns were hooded, and Perry made one more trip through the hole and down the cleft, this time with his sleeve well buttoned. When he returned he reported that the maggot-folk showed no sign of moving on.

"Then we must delay no longer," declared Lord Kian, and he turned to Anval and Borin. "We have come far together, and it saddens me that we are to be sundered. Yet the mission is our first concern and makes this separation necessary. In my heart I believe we will meet again."

Then Lord Kian knelt on one knee before Perry and placed a hand on each of the buccan's shoulders. "Friend Waerling, though we have known one another but a brief time, I value your friendship. Take care and guide well." He embraced the Warrow and then stood.

Shannon and Ursor in turn said a simple "Tarc you well" to the Dwarves and the Warrow. Perry was too overburdened with emotion to say anything, and Anval and Borin managed to say only, *"Shok Châkka amonu."*

Lord Kian stepped forward and took up one of the toppling lines, and so did they all: Borin assumed a stance behind Kian on that line; Ursor, and behind him Shannon, took up the second line; and Anval with Perry grasped the third and last line. At Kian's quiet command, they all hauled back; the ropes grew taut as the Squad pulled, yet the stone yielded not. Again Kian gave the command, and all put forth maximum effort: grips tightened, arms knotted, backs straightened, and legs strained; still the rock remained stubborn and did not move. "Enough," panted Kian, and released his grip.

Dejectedly, Perry dropped his end of the rope and sat down with the others, rubbing his forearms. "Now what do we do?" asked the Warrow.

Borin glanced at the top of the slab. "When I fastened the lines," he recalled, "I saw a notch high up behind the rock. I deem a Châk could climb into it and use his legs to lever the stone. Anval, you are strongest. Climb to the cleft, brace between the rock and the wall, and give it enough more of a push with us pulling to o'erbalance it."

No sooner did Borin speak than Anval swarmed up the slab and into the notch. He then placed his feet on the rock and braced his back against the stone wall. The rest of the Squad took up the ropes: Borin, Kian, and Ursor on the three separate lines, Shannon behind Kian, and Perry behind Borin.

At Kian's soft command, again they pulled: Perry leaned into the rope with all his might, straining to his uttermost limits. Borin's great shoulders knotted, the muscles becoming iron hard as he hauled on the rope. Kian and Shannon threw all their weight and strength into their line, their arms rigid and their legs trembling with the effort. Giant Ursor had braced his feet against a fissure in the floor, and his body leaned almost level, his mighty thews drawing down hard on his rope.

But it was Anval who proved to be the key: He summoned all of his power into pushing against the slab; perspiration beaded his brow; ligaments and tendons and blood vessels stood out in bold relief on his arms, neck, and forehead; his teeth ground together; and his face distorted with effort. His fingers clawed into their hold on the stone of the notch, and his arm muscles knotted. His back and shoulders braced hard against the wall, and his thigh muscles trembled with the strain. He emitted a low moan as the stress became nearly unbearable, and then slowly, slowly his legs began to straighten as the massive slab inched away from the cleft.

Ursor's great legs, too, began to uncoil as the slab gradually stood upright, and the Baeran's mighty back straightened. Perry's foot slipped, and he fell to one knee, but he quickly recovered and threw his strength back into the struggle. Borin,

Kian, and Shannon felt the rock pulling away from the wall and strained mightily to haul with all their strength for just a moment longer.

And then the rock passed over center to fall to the cavern floor with a thunderous *CRACK!*

And the black fissure into the Bottom Chamber stood open before the Squad, lighted by a lantern at this end and by far-off burning brands at the other.

Momentarily the Squad slumped back, drained of all energy. Then Kian struggled upright. "Quickly!" he gasped, "we must act now."

As Perry retrieved his cloak, Anval dropped down from the cleft, and he and the Warrow limped to the crannies behind the boulders while Borin wearily scaled up to the high ledge. Kian, Shannon, and Ursor, their strength returning, unhooded three lanterns and fled back down the cavern. A shout came from the chamber, and the slap of running Rücken boots could be heard. Perry scuttled behind his boulder. He could see through a crack between rocks. Torchlight shuttered down the notch, and a large Hlōk-led band of Rücks burst through the mouth of the cleft and into the cave. From far off Perry heard Shannon Silverlead call, "Hai, Rucha!" and two arrows whined into the enemy, felling two Rücks. Then two more arrows hissed through the air to thud into another pair.

The Rücks quailed back, but the Hlōk snarled, *"Ptang glush! Sklurr!"* and cracked the thongs of a cat-of-tails. Most of the Rücks leapt forward in pursuit, but the Hlōk shouted more orders, and ten of the maggot-folk stayed behind while the leader sprang after the others, torches pursuing lanterns. Soon the sound of the chase was remote, and the notch-warding Rücks fell to squabbling among themselves.

Perry was dismayed. *This is awful,* he thought. *They've left behind a rear guard, to the ruin of our plan. Now we can't get through. Oh, why did this have to happen? Hey! that's a fair question. Why would a rear guard be left behind? Are they waiting for something? If so, what?*

As Perry pondered the questions, he glimpsed Anval behind the other boulder; and the Dwarf made shushing, stay-where-you-are hand signals at the Warrow. Perry nodded his understanding and leaned back against the stone wall behind, waiting.

An hour went by, then another, and another. Perry cautiously shifted about uncomfortably; it seemed, no matter where he moved, there was always a rock or a hump or a lump in the wrong place, and it ground into his back or thigh or seat. He wondered what Anval's plan was, and then he could see that the Rūcks were nodding off, one by one. *How did Anval know that they would sleep?* Perry wondered; then: *Perhaps it is the nature of the maggot-folk to shirk duty at every opportunity.*

In another hour all the Rūcks were asleep, including the one who was supposed to be standing guard.

Anval cautiously signalled Perry, *Go quietly*—and they slowly and soundlessly crept from behind their boulders as Borin silently descended from the ledge. Both Dwarves held their axes in readiness, and Perry unsheathed blazing Bane. On tiptoe they threaded their way among the sleeping Spawn. As they passed the guard, Borin's foot rolled a pebble that went clattering toward a crevice in the floor, sounding to Perry as loud as thunder itself. The three froze, and Perry held Bane ready to slay the slumbering watch, the sword point poised steadily over the Rūck's heart. Restlessly, the sleeping guard moaned and shifted his weight, while the pebble rattled to a stop down in the crack to leave silence behind, broken only by the snoring of the maggot-folk. None of the Rūcks awakened, and the Dwarves and the Warrow passed into the cleft.

As they emerged into the Bottom Chamber, Perry sheathed Bane's light and led the way toward the arch over the stream. Swiftly they crossed the floor, passing over the bridge and beyond the running water. But before they could reach the west corridor, they saw light coming down the passageway toward them.

Quickly the trio dived behind a low parapet of delved stone off to one side. A large company of Spawn loped into the Chamber. *This is why ten Rūcks were left behind: to meet this gang,* thought Perry, and he watched them lope to the center of the Chamber and halt. "We got out just in time," the Warrow breathed to Borin. "They've got the way we came stopped up like a cork in a bottle."

As the three looked on, several of the notch-warding Rūcks trotted out of the crevice and spoke with the newly arrived Hlōk leader, but Perry and the Dwarves were too far away to hear what was being said. To the dismay of the three, however, the Hlōk snarled orders, and Rūcks jumped up and ran to guard each of the entrances and exits of the Bottom Chamber, including the west portal. Then runners were dispatched: one east, one west, and one south. "He sends messages to other Hrōken leaders," hissed Anval. "No doubt, Gnar also will be informed as to the 'intruders' in this part of the caverns. *Kruk!* This will make it even more difficult for us to reach the Dusken Door."

"How do we get past the guard at the west corridor without raising the alarm?" whispered Perry. Borin touched his finger to his lips for quiet, and silently crawled off into the dimness.

Perry and Anval watched the guard slouching against the wall beneath a torch lodged in an ancient lantern bracket on the delved wall, a bracket put there in elden times by the Dwarves. Minutes fled by and nothing happened. As the two watched, time seemed to stretch out endlessly, and the Warrow could see no sign of Borin. Still they waited. Suddenly it seemed as if one of the shadows behind the guard detached itself from the wall and soundlessly engulfed the Rūck. Perry heard a quiet thump, and then Anval was pulling on the Warrow's arm and hissing, "Now!"

Swiftly they flitted along the wall and into the corridor; Borin carried the dead Rūck over one shoulder, and hid the body at the first wall crevice. The three then fled down the passageway. Behind them, all was still; their escape had not been noted.

The next four miles was a nightmare of hide and run. Repeatedly, the companions dived into crevices, notches, and side passages, to remain hidden as Hlōks and Rūcks came loping eastward. Many small squads and large companies passed by. Perry guessed—rightly—that the news of a few "intruders" had spread, and the Spawn were flocking to the sport of hunt and slaughter.

At last the threesome approached a room called the Oval Chamber in the Brega Scroll. Once more the trio found the way blocked by maggotfolk, but Anval motioned, *Follow me,* and taking an enormous gamble they began crawling from shadow to shadow along the north wall.

At times they lay without moving for long minutes as one or more Rūcks in the chamber came near. At other times they crawled swiftly from rock to pillar to crevice, only to find that again they had to remain motionless in the darkness with Spawn barring the way. Finally they came to the passage leading on toward Dusk-Door, and after a long wait they managed to slip out of the chamber and into the corridor.

Though they met no maggot-folk, the three found the next few miles arduous, for there were cracks in the floor that yawned unexpectedly. Yet, one crevice that they came to was foreknown to Perry, and dreaded by him: it was the Drawing Dark, so named because of the awful *sucking* sound that could be heard in its lost depths, thought by the Deevewalkers to be a slurking whirl of water in an underground river at the bottom of the crack; but to Perry this explanation was of no comfort, for it sounded as if *something* below were *alive* and questing for victims.

Although Perry had been expecting this rent—for it had been mentioned both in *The Raven Book* and in the Brega Scroll—still he found it difficult to summon up the courage to leap it, for it was fully eight feet across, and he could not banish the specter of being sucked down into the deep crack, drawn down into an unseen maw ravening in the black depths. But at last he took three running steps and sprang with all his might and cleared it by a good three feet.

The trio pressed on for the Long Hall, and as they neared it, Bane's fire grew. Soon Perry sheathed the sword, for its flame was bright. Yet when they came to the chamber, they could see neither torchlight nor *Spaunen.* "Let us cross the floor quickly, before the Rūcks arrive and block our way again," urged Perry, and they started across the Hall.

As they reached midchamber they heard shouts and snarls, and looked around to see a company of maggot-folk issue out of a corridor behind them. The trio had been detected!

"Fly!" cried Perry, and the three ran toward the west corridor; but as they approached they could see light reflected around a bend moving swiftly *toward* them from the passage ahead. Perry darted a look over his shoulder: the other exits were already cut off by the howling Spawn closing behind. *Trapped!*

At a glance, Anval took in the situation. "The force before us is as yet unaware of us, and there may be only a few. Let us charge through if we can. If not, then we will slay many before we fall."

Borin brandished his axe. *"Châkka shok! Châkka cor!"* he cried. Anval, too, gripped his double-bitted weapon and vented the ancient battle cry. Perry whipped out flaming Bane, determined to sell his life dearly.

Forward they charged, running toward the oncoming force. Behind them the yawling Rūcks pursued, weapons and armor clattering, boots slapping against stone. Ahead and toward them came the others, suddenly rounding a corner and bursting into view. And Perry's racing heart leapt to his throat, and he gave a great shout, for at the forefront of the oncoming force ran a small form in golden armor with a bright sword. *It was Cotton! And Durek! And Rand! And four thousand others! The Dwarf Army was within the Halls of Kraggen-cor!*

CHAPTER 7

INTO THE BLACK HOLE

Three hours earlier, the Host had stood before the Dusk-Door, and Durek had said the words of power, and by moonlight and starshine and Dwarf lantern the theen tracery and runes and sigils had appeared.

Durek caught up his weapon by the helve and stepped back from the high portal; all that remained was for him to say the Wizard-word for "move," and the Door, if able, would open. The Dwarf turned to Cotton, Rand, and Felor. "Stand ready," he warned, "for we know not whom we meet."

Cotton gripped his sword and felt the great pressure of the moment rising inside him and he felt as if he needed to shout, but instead he thought, Let Mister Perry be at the Door and not no Rück.

Durek turned back to the Door and gripped his axe; he placed his free hand within the glittering rune-circle; then his voice rang out strongly as he spoke the Wizard-word of opening: "Gaard!"

The glowing web of Wizard-metal flashed brightly, and then—*as if being drawn back into Durek's hand*—all the lines, sigils, and glyphs began to retract, fading in sparkles as they withdrew, until once again the dark granite was blank and stern. And Durek stepped back and away. And slowly the stone seemed to split in twain as two great doors appeared and soundlessly swung outward, arcing slowly, the black slot between them growing wider and wider, becoming a great ebon gape as the doors wheeled in silence, till at last they came to rest against the Great Loom.

A dark opening yawned before the vanguard of the Legion, and they could see the beginnings of the West Hall receding into blackness; to the right a steep stairwell mounted up into the ebon shadows. And those in the fore of the Host—weapons gripped, thews tensed, hearts thudding, hackles up—stared with chary eyes at the empty darkness looming mutely before them.

And they were astonished and baffled, for no one was there, neither friend nor foe, only silent dark stone!

And of all those in the vanguard, only one did not seem rooted in place: "Mister Perry!" shouted Cotton, and before any could stop him, he sprang through the doorway and bolted up the stairs, holding his lantern high and calling as he ran: "Mister Perry! Mister Perry!" he cried, but his voice was answered only by mocking echoes: *Mister . . . ister . . . Perry . . . erry . . . erry . . . ister . . . erry . . . erry . . . y . . .*

"Cotton! Wait!" shouted Rand, breaking the grip of his bedazement. "'Ware *Spuunen!*" And he and Durek and Felor and the forefront of the Host leapt forward after the Warrow. And they could see the light of Cotton's lantern dashing up the steps far above them to disappear from sight over the top.

"Fool!" Prince Rand cursed the Waerling's rashness, and sprang up the steps two at a time, his long shanks outdistancing the Dwarves behind. The steps were many, and soon he was breathing deeply, for the climb was strenuous; but in a trice he o'ertopped the last one. Ahead and around a bend he found Cotton at the first side passage, his lantern held high, peering through the arch and into the dark. Several swift strides brought the Prince to the Warrow's side. "Cotton," he gritted through clenched teeth, angered by the Waerling's thoughtless actions.

"He . . . he's not here, Prince Rand," stammered the Warrow, turning in anguish to the Man. "Mister Perry's not here."

"Cotton, you are our only guide. The Yrm . . ." but ere Rand could say on, he saw that the Waerling was weeping quietly.

"I know, Sir. I know," sobbed Cotton, miserably. "I've acted the fool, rushing in like I did, and all. But Mister Perry wasn't there, and I couldn't stand it. I just had to see, had to see for myself. But he's not here at all. He's not here; the Squad's not here;

the Rūcks are not here; nobody's here. But the Door opened. It *opened!*"

There was a clatter of weaponry and a slap of boots and a jingle of armor as Durek and Felor and the vanguard of the Host topped the stairs and started forward, their sharp eyes sweeping the shadows.

"As you say, Cotton, the Door opened," replied Rand, "yet no one met us. Mayhap the Squad was here, for the Door worked."

"Wull, if they were here, where are they now?" Cotton demanded.

"I know not," replied Rand, his voice grim. "Perhaps Spawn . . ." His words trailed off.

"Spawn!" cried Cotton, bitterly, turning as Durek strode up.

King Durek stood before the Warrow, an angry glim in his eyes. "Cotton," he gritted, "the fate of this quest lies in your hands, for where you lead, we must follow. Without you, we are lost. Henceforth, stay at hand where our axes may protect you; never again dash off into the dark alone." The Dwarf King's voice held the bite of command that brooked no disobedience, and the Waeran nodded meekly. "As to these empty halls," continued Durek, his flinty eyes sweeping the passage, "we can only press forward and hope to find the Squad of Kraggen-cor safe, and not Grg-endangered, or worse."

"Grg-endangered? Worse?" blurted out Cotton. Then his viridian eyes became fell and resolute. "Let's go," he said sternly. "We've got to find Mister Perry and the others."

And at a nod from Durek, the Warrow went forth, with Rand at one side, Durek and Felor at the other, and four thousand axes behind. And along the Brega Path they strode.

A mile went by, and another, and yet one more, and still they saw no sign of life, friendly or otherwise. Only dark splits and black fissures and delved tunnels did they see, boring off into the ebon depths. Through this shadowy maze, Cotton unerringly led. And the axes of the Dwarves stood ready, but no foe appeared. Another mile, and another, and still more; and time trod on silent feet at their side. An hour had passed, no, two, then a third; and swiftly they marched into the depths of Drimmen-deeve.

Suddenly: *"Hist!"* warned Felor, and held up his hand, and

the command quickly passed back-chain and the Army ground to a silent halt.

In the quiet they could hear the far-off yammering of many voices—yelling and howling—yet they could make out no words. Ahead in the curving tunnel they could see a glimmer of distant light dimly reflected around the bend.

"They know not that we are here," hissed Durek. "Weapons ready! Forward!"

And the Host moved swiftly, running now to catch the foe unaware and suddenly fall upon them. Forward they dashed, toward the Long Hall just ahead. And as they ran they could hear more shouts—battle cries, it seemed—their meaning lost in reverberating echoes. Ahead the light grew brighter as the oncoming force neared. And suddenly bursting into view came three forms running.

CHAPTER 8

THE SILVER CALL

At first Cotton thought that these three figures plunging head-long at him and the Army were Rūcks, for the faces of Perry, Anval, and Borin were covered with blackener, and Perry's starsilver armor was hidden beneath his shirt; and so this charging trio did not at all look like the friends and companions that Cotton had last seen by the Argon River. But as the three ran toward the vanguard, Cotton saw the flaming sword borne by the one and the Dwarf axes of the other two and the Dwarf-lanterns the trio carried, and by these tokens alone he knew that they were not Rūcks. And suddenly there came a voice he recognized, a voice calling his name: "Cotton! Cotton!"

"It's Mister Perry!" cried Cotton, and he leapt forward, running to meet his master.

"Mister Perry! Mister Perry!" he shouted and wept at one and the same time, for when the portals of Dusk-Door had silently swung outward and none of the Squad of Kraggen-cor had been waiting inside, Cotton had feared the worst. But he had led the Army along the Brega Path in spite of his fears. And here were Mister Perry and two Dwarves seven miles from the Door, alive after all.

As the two Warrows ran together and embraced one another, Anval shouted, "King Durek, Squam pursue us! A hundred fly at our heels!"

"Felor!" barked Durek, "Axes! Forward!" And the spearhead of the Host sprang around the curve and into the Long Hall.

The onrushing maggot-folk wailed in dismay as hundreds of Dwarves issued into the chamber. Some Spawn stood and fought and died, some turned and ran and were overhauled from behind and felled, others escaped. The skirmish was over quickly, and the Dwarves were overwhelmingly victorious in this opening engagement of the War of Kraggen-cor.

After the battle and before resuming the northeastward march, Durek called the trio to him; and Cotton for the first time saw that these two blackened Dwarves were actually Anval and Borin. Prince Rand and Felor joined the circle of the small council kneeling on the stone floor of Long Hall. "Tell me not your entire tale," Durek bade the three, "but for now speak of the Grg along the route before us; tell me of any problems with the Brega Path for which we must change our battle strategy; tell me where Prince Kian, Barak, Delk, and Tobin are; and finally, speak on any other thing of importance to our campaign that you think pertinent but about which I know not enough to ask."

Anval spoke first: "As to the Grg, our suspicions were correct: there are great numbers of the vile enemy in Kraggen-cor, for often we had to hide or flee from large bands within the passageways and chambers. We saw many of the foul foe on our journey, at least ten or twelve companies—a total of more than a thousand Squam—and that just on the path we trod. I have no count of the true number of thieving Grg in Kraggen-cor, but I gauge it to be many times more than we saw."

"The Brega Path we trod," added Borin, "posed no special unforeseen problems, but we did not see it all; we left the Path twice. Perry, give me your map." Ere Perry could act, Felor quickly pulled a copy from his own jerkin and gave it to Borin, who spread the map before Durek.

"Here at Braggi's Stand, the way at the Fifth Rise is blocked. We went around it by going west at the Third Rise to the first north passage, from there to the Sixth Rise, and thence east and south to the Great Chamber, coming back to the Path at this point." Borin traced the route they had taken, a sturdy finger moving through part of the blank area on the map. "We left the Path a second time here, at the Grate Room; we were discovered by Squam and fled thusly"—again Borin traced their route—"passing down a tortuous path to emerge in the Bottom Chamber. And so, we know not the Brega Path between the Grate Room and the Bottom Chamber; but the Path is nearly certain to be better than the hard way we ran." Borin fell silent.

King Durek turned to Perry. "And the others, where are the others? Where is Barak?"

"Dead," answered Perry, his eyes brimming, "slain by Spawn on the banks of the Argon." Durek, Anval, Borin, and Felor cast their hoods over their heads.

"Tobin, and Delk, where are they?" demanded Durek from his cowl.

"Tobin is with the Elves in Darda Erynian, wounded in the same battle at the Great Argon River," replied Perry. "Delk was slain by Rūck arrow as we fled the Gargon's Lair here in Kraggen-cor." Perry pointed at the approximate location of the Lair on the map.

"*Gargon?*" blurted Durek, his voice filled with surprise and dread.

"The Ghath slain by Brega and the others in the time of the Winter War," responded Anval. "We found its ancient prison when we fled. There, too, is a vein of starsilver."

"And my brother," asked Prince Rand, his face bleak, "where is Kian?"

"We don't know," said Perry, anguish in his voice. "He and the Elf Vanidar Shannon Silverleaf, and Ursor the Baeran— new companions who joined us at the Argon—those three decoyed a company of Rūcks so that we three could reach Dusk-Door. They fled back from the Bottom Chamber toward the Lair, drawing the maggot-folk behind them. But I fear for their safety, for later we saw many Spawn moving—we think to join the hunt. The three may escape by the underwater path we found, but I fear they may be trapped between Rūcken forces. And the terrible truth is, their decoy strategy went for nought, for we didn't even reach Dusk-Door."

"You didn't?!" burst out Cotton. "Well then, who fixed 'em? I mean, they opened just as slick as a whistle."

"It seems," replied Durek, "that no one repaired them. Hence, the Warder did not damage them when he wrenched and hammered at the doors centuries agone. Valki builded them well, for they withstood the awesome might of even that dreadful Monster."

"You speak as if you saw it," spoke up Perry, "the Krakenward, I mean. Did you see it? Was it there?"

"We slew it," growled Durek, "but it nearly proved our undoing, for it killed many of us and buried the Door under yet more rock ere we succeeded." The Dwarf King fell silent for a moment. "Where best to array the Host?" he then asked Anval.

"The Mustering Chamber, the War Hall of Kraggen-cor," replied Anval; and Borin nodded his agreement. "It is vast, and will be a good location to meet the Squam Swarm—or to sortie from."

"But that's all the way back to the Great Deep!" cried Perry, weary and exasperated. "Nearly to Dawn-Gate!"

"Naytheless," insisted Borin, "it is the best battleground for our Legion, for though it was delved long ago as an assembly chamber to array the Host against invaders coming over the Great Deop, it will serve equally well to array the Army against the Grg within the caverns. We must go there quickly to gain the advantage of a superior formation."

"But what about Lord Kian, and Shannon, and Ursor?" demanded Perry, fearing the answer. "What are we going to do about them?"

"Nothing," replied Prince Rand, his voice trembling in helpless agony. "We can do nothing, for we must race to the battleground to arrive first and array in the strongest formation, which will force the Spawn to take a weaker one, if they come. We cannot jeopardize the entire Host for the sake of three; nor can we send a small force to search for them, for as you say, the Yrm flock in great numbers to hunt the trio, and a small force of Dwarves would be o'erwhelmed in that mission. No, we must make haste to the Mustering Chamber, and hope against all hope that the three somehow elude the enemy until we are victorious." Prince Rand turned his face away, and his hands were trembling.

At Prince Rand's words a great leaden weight seemed to crush down upon Perry's heart, and he despaired. "You are saying we must abandon them. Surely there is some other choice."

"Choice?" barked Durek, his face shadowed by his hood in the lantern light, his voice tinged with grim irony. "Nay, we have no choice. And we will get no further choices till the issue of Kraggen-cor is settled. As with the very act of living, there are but few true times of choosing, for most of life's so-named *choices* are instead but reflections of circumstance. And now is not a time of choosing; nay, our last time of choosing was at my Captain's Council at Landover Road Ford. Since then, Destiny alone has impelled each of us along that selected path. Yet, Friend Perry, we all knew our course would lead us into harm's way, and that some of us would cast lots with Death and lose, for that is one of War's chiefest fortunes. Nay, Waeran, we cannot send aid to that trio of comrades now, for their lot, too, is cast, and their future is as immutable as ours."

"But to abandon them all but assures their doom, if it is not yet upon them," Perry said bitterly. "By doing nothing we might as well have sentenced them to death. And there's been too much needless death already: first Barak and then Delk, and now Kian, Shannon, and Ursor." The buccan's eyes filled with tears of frustration, and he hammered his fist against his leg. "And all for nothing! All for a door that wasn't even broken! All for a needless mission!"

"Yes!" Rand gritted angrily through clenched teeth at Perry, for the Warrow had not yet admitted to the reality of their strait plight. And the Prince sprang to his feet and paced to and fro in agitation. "Yes!" he spat, "all for a *needless mission!* But one that had to be assayed at all costs, for we knew it not that the Dusk-Door had survived the wrenching of that dire creature. The Door was not broken, but we were ignorant of that knowledge. It is ever so in warfare that *needless missions* are undertaken in ignorance.

"Ignorance! Pah! That, too, is one of the conditions of War. And good Men and Dwarves and others die because of it. This time our ignorance may have cost me my brother; but worse yet, it may have cost my people a *King!* So prate not to me about *needless missions,* Waerling, for it is time you realized to the uttermost what being a warrior means, and the necessity of the cruel decisions of War, for you seem to think that we do not grasp the fullness of our course.

"But we *do* know! *Yes,* it is abandonment! *Yes,* it spells doom! *Yes,* we *know!* But it is *you* who does not seem to grasp what it means to do otherwise! This Army *must* be held together to meet the strength of the Yrm, and must *not* be fragmented into splinter parties searching for a mere three; for in that foolish action lies the seeds of the destruction of our quest—and the needs of the quest gainsay all else, no matter who is abandoned."

Like crystal shards, the jagged truth of Rand's angry words tore at Perry's heart, and the Warrow paled with their import.

"Hold on there, now!" Cotton protested sharply, starting to rise to defend his master, upset not by the meaning of Rand's words but rather at the angry manner in which Rand had spat them at Perry, "there's no cause to—" but Cotton's words were cut short by a curt gesture from Borin. And Cotton reluctantly fell silent, unsaid words battering at his grimly clamped lips as he tensely settled back, ready to speak up for Perry if need be.

But then the Prince halted his caged pacing and for the first time looked and saw how utterly stunned Perry was. And Rand's own heart softened, and his voice lost its edge of wrath as he turned and reached out to the buccan. "Ah, needless missions, times of no choice. There is no choice, Perry, no choice; and in that I grieve with you, for it is *my brother* we abandon to War's lot. I would that it were otherwise, yet we can do nought but hope, for instead we must set forth at once to array the Host against the foul Spawn."

Anval had listened to the Prince speak sharply to Perry, but in spite of the harshness, the Dwarf was in accord with Rand's meaning; yet at the same time Anval also had seen the anguish in the Waeran's eyes. The Dwarf leaned forward and gently placed a gnarled hand upon Perry's forearm and spoke: "Aye, Friend Perry, you, I—the Squad—we all went on a necessary yet needless mission; and now you despair, for our staunch companions are missing, facing dangers unknown, fates dire; and you have said that their sacrifice has gone for nought, for it claws at you that we did not even reach the unbroken Dusken Door, the sought-for goal, our mission's end. Yet, take heed: *missions fail!* Only in the faery-scapes of children's hearthtales do all goodly quests succeed. But in this world many a desperate undertaking has fallen full victim to dark evil, or has been thwarted: turned back or shunted aside or delayed, not reaching the planned end, costing the coursing lifeblood of steadfast comrades. Such thwart fell upon our mission. Yet heed me again: all warriors who encounter such calamities and who live on must learn to accept these truths and go forth in spite of unforeseen setbacks.

"Once I said unto you that you must become a warrior; and you have. But times as these test a warrior's very mettle, and he must be as stern as hammered iron. We live, and so might our lost comrades; but in any case, we must now go forth and war upon the thieving Grg, for that is our prime reason for being here ready for battle." Anval fell silent and turned and looked expectantly at his King.

With effort, Durek cast his hood back and reluctantly agreed: "Though I am loath to abandon our comrades to the Grg's hunt, Prince Rand is correct, and so too is Anval: we must hasten to the War Hall at the Great Dēop to meet the Squam Swarm. Gnar soon will know that we are within the corridors, and he will muster to meet us. We must needs be arrayed in our strength, for the numbers of his force may be great indeed. But hearken to me, Friend Perry: after our victory, I will send search parties for any of the three who still may live. Yet now the Host must hie forth to the War Hall and array in our strongest formation."

And Perry's heart at last admitted to the grim truth, and he nodded bleakly as Durek issued the commands; and once again the Army began to move deeper into Kraggen-cor, striding to the northeast at a forced-march pace.

Borin led the way back toward the Bottom Chamber. Once more, when they came to the Drawing Dark—the eight-foot-wide crack in the tunnel floor—Perry overcame his fear and made the running leap over the fissure, this time with less hesitation; but Cotton delayed long, while others passed over, mustering his courage for the hurdle above the sucking depths, the leap a long one for a Warrow. At last the buccan stepped into the line of warriors and took his turn, and cleared the wide crack easily; Perry had waited for him, and together they ran to catch up with the head of the column.

At the Oval Chamber, as signalled by Bane's jewel-flame, a force of Rūcks was arrayed to meet the Dwarves: some of the enemy who earlier had escaped had told of the Dwarves' coming, and the Spawn did not yet know that it was an entire army they faced, believing instead that they were meeting, at most, a company-sized troop. And so, once again the Dwarves issued against the maggot-folk in overwhelming force, and the skirmish was short and decisive.

Durek had ordered Cotton and Perry to remain out of the fray, saying that although Anval and Borin knew most of the Path now, he wanted to hold the Waerans in reserve, at least until the Great Dēop was reached—then he would have an entire legion of guides. And so Cotton and Perry remained back in the corridor until the engagement was over.

The march toward the Mustering Chamber continued, and as they tramped, Cotton, who was happy simply to be reunited with Perry, chatted about the Army's trek from Landover Road Ford to Dusk-Door. In spite of his low spirits, Perry soon found himself becoming more and more interested in Cotton's venture; and Perry was slowly drawn out of his black mood by the tale he was told. Cotton spoke of: the shrieking, clawing wind at the Crestan Pass; Waroo the Blizzard and the blind guides and lost Dwarves; being snowbound and the great dig-out; the forced march down the Old Rell Way, and the mud mires; the arrival at Dusk Door; the battle with the Krakenward and the breaking of the dam and slaying of the Monster of the Dark Mere; the discovery of the Host by the Rücken spies and Brytta's troop riding from the valley to intercept them; and the removal of the mountain of rubble and the opening of the Door at midnight.

Perry was fascinated by the story. "Why, Cotton," he declared when the other was finished, "you have lived an epic adventure, one as exciting as even some of the old tales."

"Wull, I don't know about that, Mister Perry." Cotton shrugged doubtfully. "It seems to me that most of it was just a bother, if you catch my meaning."

"Oh, it's an adventure, alright," assured Perry, "and when we're through with all this, I'll want to set it down in a journal for others to see." He began asking questions, seeking more detail about Cotton's venture, and Perry's bleak mood ebbed as he and the other Warrow marched north and east with the Host.

And both Warrows soon fell to speculating as to the outcome of Brytta's mission. Each worried that the Harlingar had met up with a Swarm; yet Cotton surmised, "Oh, I believe the Valonners did their job, Sir, 'cause Gnar's army wasn't waiting at the Dusk-Door when it opened. In fact, nobody was. Not even you. But I knew you'd be all right. And since the maggot-folk weren't there, well, that means Gnar hadn't got the word, so as the Valonners must have succeeded in stopping the Rūcken spies."

"I'm not sure of that, Cotton," mused Perry, "not sure at all. I mean, I'm not sure that some Spawn didn't get through to Gnar. After all, if they did get through, there would have been only a bit more than a day for Gnar to muster his forces. And perhaps he has—has mustered them, that is. Perhaps there's a great ambush awaiting us ahead and we're walking into an enormous trap."

Cotton's heart gave a lurch at these ominous words. "Wull, if that's true, Sir, then that means that Marshal Brytta may have met up with more than he bargained for; and that would be news I'd rather not know about." Yet, in spite of his remarks, Cotton fretted over the fate of the riders of the Valanreach, and would have given much to know their state of health and their whereabouts.

At that very moment, it was early morning in the Ragad Valley, and Brytta, at the fore of the Harlingar, had just ridden in to find the vale empty of all but his kinsman Farlon and the Dwarven wounded, preparing to embark on the journey south to the grassy valley.

Farlon was overjoyed to see the Vanadurin arrive, for he had longed to know their lot; and now he could see that most were safe, though his searching eyes failed to find some of his comrades in the column. Too, he felt relief, for now he would have escort in moving the wounded. And now, also, the herd could be driven south, and not left to wander the wold. The horses had been loosed, yet in their tameness had not gone from the valley.

At Brytta's query, Farlon explained that it was he who had fired the recall beacon atop the great spire of the Sentinel Stand after the Door had opened and the Host had entered. Brytta then ordered that more wood for yet another signal fire be laid high upon the towering spike to call the riders back should Wrg come fleeing out of the Dusk-Door; the top of the spire was the best place for the beacon, for, as reported by Farlon, a fire upon the tall spire should clearly be visible from the southern pasture. Three scouts, Trell, Egon, and Wylf, were named to this balefire duty. Taking turns, one of the trio always would be atop the stand to set the beacon ablaze if the Rutcha came. As Brytta said when he gave over the guard duty to the three, "I'm certain you would rather ward against a danger that never comes, than to wait with the rest of us in a pasture watching horses crop grass."

Then Brytta and the Harlingar rounded up the horses and waggons bearing the wounded and began the drive west and then south, following Farlon's lead. And Farlon was pleased, for not only was he reunited with his fellow Vanadurin, he also was fulfilling the pledge he had made to Prince Rand and to that fiery little Waldan, Cotton: a pledge to guide the wounded Dwarves to safe haven.

But neither Perry nor Cotton knew of those events then occurring in the Ragad Valley, and so they fretted over the unknown fate of the Harlingar; yet in spite of this uncertainty, Perry had nearly regained his former pluck. Even so, when they came to the Bottom Chamber, where last he had seen the missing trio of companions, Perry's high spirits crashed.

The Chamber was empty of Spawn; the word of a Dwarf army had passed ahead of the Host, and the Rūcks and Hlōks had fled before them. As the Legion marched across the arch over the stream and into the huge round room, Perry looked toward the notch in the north wall; no light came through it from the cavern beyond. "There, Prince Rand," said the Warrow, pointing, "there's where Lord Kian, Shannon Silverleaf, and Ursor the Baeran misled the Rūcks."

Rand looked on bleakly as they tramped by. Suddenly the Prince ran to the cleft and down its length, and peered into the black cave beyond, and whistled a shrill call that echoed and shocked along the cavern to be lost in its dark distance. Twice more he whistled, and each time at echo's death he was answered only by ebon silence. When he returned to the column, his face bore a stricken look, and he spoke not. Perry, too, fell into mute despair. And the Army marched on.

Here Cotton took over the guide chores from Borin; the Host now began moving into the corridors between the Bottom Chamber and the Grate Room, a part of the Brega Path not yet trod by Borin, for the Squad had fled through the Gargon's Lair instead.

Bane's blade-jewel spoke only of distant danger, and the long column soon reached the Side Hall, where the floor of the corridor began its long, gentle upward slope out of the lower Neaths and toward the upper Rises. During this part of the trek, Cotton chatted gaily, trying mightily to draw Perry out of his black mood, but to no avail.

As they marched away from the Side Hall, Bane began to glimmer more strongly, and word was passed that Squam were coming nigh. They tramped for two more miles and Bane's light slowly faded; but then a great hubbub washed over the Legion from the rear of the column. "Hey," questioned Cotton, "what's all this commotion about?" But no one there could answer him.

Finally, word was passed up-column to Durek that a large force of Rücks had boiled out of the Side Hall and had attacked the rear guard of the Host. A savage battle had ensued, and the Spawn were once again routed, but this time some Dwarves had fallen in the fight.

"So it begins at last," rasped Durek. "The foul Grg will harass and ambush us from coverts until Gnar musters his forces for battle. Pass the word that the War has begun. Henceforth, the slain shall lie where they are felled, and we shall remain unhooded until the last battle is done."

The march began again, and now Cotton fell into a black mood too, for he knew not the lot of Bomar, Captain of the Rear Guard, nor the fate of his friends of the cook-waggon crew. But though the Warrow fretted, he continued to guide well, and the Legion made good time in their trek toward the Grate Room. Again Bane's rune-jewel began to glow brighter as they marched east; and the nearer they came to the Room, the more luminous became the blue flame. They trod swiftly, and the vanguard of Felor's forces gripped their axes in readiness as they quickstepped up the passageway. And then from ahead they heard a great shouting of maggot-folk and a clatter of weapons.

Felor's companies sprang forward, and they raced toward the last turn before the Grate Room. As they rounded the curve, up a long straight corridor they could see torchlight, and there were Spawn clamoring and milling about the door of the Room, battering it with hammers and a ram. Momentarily, the Rūcken band did not see the Dwarves; and Felor's Companies made many running strides toward the enemy before the Host was detected; and then it was too late, for the Rūcks had not enough time to array themselves to meet the rush.

There was a clash of axes on scimitars, and the Spawn were borne backwards by the charge. Again the battle was swift and savage: the Dwarves hewed the Squam, and black Rūcken gore splashed the stone as the maggot-folk were felled.

And in the midst of the fray, Perry saw the Grate Room door fly open, and out sprang two tall, face-blackened figures ready to join the fight. It was Lord Kian! And Shannon Silverleaf! They were alive!

From a distance, Prince Rand, too, saw his besmudged brother and gave a shrill whistle, and he and Kian looked upon one another, and they were glad. Then Rand raised his sword and inclined his head toward the retreating Spawn, and they both plunged after the Dwarves to join the battle against the foe.

Perry shouted in his glee. His friends were safe! But, wait . . . where was Ursor? As the battle receded before him, Perry made his way to the Grate Room and stepped in. The Warrow saw that two of the iron stone-wedges, tools carried for work on the gate, had been used to jam the door of the Room against the maggot-folk. Perry could see the corroded grille had been wrenched away from the square shaft, and the dark hole gaped at him; cautiously looking into it, he could see nought but the massive, rust-stained chain dropping down sheer, straight walls into the blackness below. Shuddering, Perry turned away and found Kian's and Shannon's backpacks. But of the Baeran, the room was empty of all sign. Fearing the worst, Perry scooped up the wedges and packs and stepped back into the corridor, to find Cotton searching for him.

The engagement had ended, the Rūcks had been slain or had fled, and the head of the column was forming up again when Rand, Kian, and Shannon finally came to where Perry and Cotton were waiting. Kian embraced both of the Warrows, and Shannon greeted Perry with a grin and a hug. "You came barely in time, Friend Perry," said the Elf. "We were just preparing to start down the dark square shaft to who-knows-where when you led the Drimma to our rescue."

"Oh, but it wasn't me," protested Perry, "my good friend here, Cotton Buckleburr, was leading." Perry then introduced a self-conscious Cotton to Shannon; at first Cotton felt somehow clumsy and awkward in the presence of the lithe Elf, but Shannon's lighthearted manner soon put the Waerling at his ease. "Lord Kian," asked Perry, his apprehension growing, "Ursor, where is Ursor?"

A troubled look came over the Man's face. "We do not know where he is," answered Kian. "We led the *Spaunen* on a desperate chase back to the underground river. When we got there, we debated whether to go on up the north passage or to swim under the wall and go through the Gargon's Lair and on to await the Host at the five corridors by the Grate Room. Ursor asked us to stand ready while he swam to see if the Yrm were gone from the cave leading to the Lair. He tied a rope to a boulder and let the swift current carry him under the wall. When he returned, he said all was black in the other cavern—those Rukha were no longer there. He had lashed the line securely on the far side, and he asked us to go ahead of him in the water. By this time the pursuing Yrm were nearly upon us. Shannon and I plunged in and pulled under to the opposite tunnel. Almost as soon as we got there, the rope went slack, and we hauled it in, and tied to the end were our backpacks. But Ursor never came. We tried to go back, but neither Shannon nor I was a powerful enough swimmer to battle back through the rush without the aid of the line, and we could not get to the other side to find him and aid him. We know not his fate, though I fear it was grim." Lord Kian stopped speaking, a pained look in his eyes.

"We took a long rest," said Shannon after a moment, taking up the rest of their tale, "and then we made our way back through the Lost Prison, up the silveron delving, and finally through the tunnels to the Grate Room. Again we rested, this time in the upward middle corridor of the four eastern ways. But it was not our lot to idle our time away until the Drimm army arrived, for *Rûpt* forces came at nearly one and the same time along all passageways, including the west one. We were revealed and fled into the Grate Room, where we drove wedges under the door to jam it shut. We indeed were about to try to escape down the shaft when we heard the ancient *Châkka shok! Châkka cor!* battle cry of the Drimma and were saved that perilous descent."

Shannon fell silent, but before Perry or Cotton could ask any questions, Durek, Anval, and Borin returned, and once more the march resumed, Borin again in the lead, for the Legion now marched in passageways he had trodden before.

The Host halted for a rest in the great Round Chamber. Patrols were maintained along the corridors, and Bane was posted in the center of the gallery as a ward for all to see. Perry fell instantly into slumber, for he was exhausted, having had no sleep since he had rested in the Gargon's Lair. Cotton, on the other hand, before settling down made certain that his friend Bomar was unhurt, for the Warrow had been deeply concerned ever since the Legion had marched past the Side Hall and the Spawn had attacked the rear guard. Bomar laughed and told Cotton it would take more than a Grg or two to do him and the cook-waggon crew in, and not to worry. Relieved, Cotton returned to where Perry slept and lay down nearby. Cotton, too, quickly went to sleep, and his and Perry's slumber was undisturbed.

But all too soon it was time to move on; and so, after but six hours of respite, the Army again headed east along the Brega Path, Borin still in the lead.

As they marched, Cotton seemed withdrawn, as if bemused by some deep thought. Finally, when Perry sounded him out, Cotton grasped the Horn of Valon and held it for Perry to see and said, "Well, Sir, I mean, look here: ever since we've come into Kraggen-cor, the Horn of the Reach has ... changed. It seems more polished, or, well, as if it were somehow shinier. I don't know what it is exactly that's different but it seems to be, as it were, more ... more *alive!*"

Perry looked closely at the bugle, and he, too, sensed that it had changed. The metal appeared to have more depth, the racing figures seemed to have taken on greater dimension, the carven runes higher luster. Yet Perry could not say whether this silvery *life* was due to an actual change in the horn or, rather, a change in the way he himself viewed it. "Perhaps, Cotton, it only *seems* to glisten more because this cavern is dull and dark and provides great contrast to the shining silver; or perhaps it glimmers more because it now is illumed only by the light of Dwarf lanterns."

As if in response to Perry's words, the bugle glinted and flashed in the blue-green phosphorescent glow; yet, deep within, it seemed to burn with a light of its own.

"That may be, Sir," replied Cotton, looking with perplexed wonderment at the glittering metal, "but I think it's got more *life* because it's back to its home again, back to its birthing place, back to where it's meant to be."

About the horn, Cotton said no more, and the buccen strode onward in silence, each deep in his own thoughts, as the Army pressed on through Kraggen-cor.

The Host covered the remaining twenty miles in six hours, and they were attacked twice: The first time was a minor assault: arrows hissed at them out of the side passages of Broad Hall; Felor's companies rushed the corridors, and the maggot-folk scuttled away in the darkness, and the attack was over. The second time was a major engagement: a force of nearly four hundred maggot-folk had lain waiting in ambuscade in the Great Chamber; but Bane had alerted the Legion that Spawn were near, and the Army avoided the concealed assault and fell upon the enemy in fury, driving them out of the chamber. In both engagements, Dwarves died, though the number was small.

The Legion then made its way along the two-mile detour around the wreckage of the Hall of the Gravenarch and then marched the final mile to come down at last to their chosen battleground: the vast Mustering Chamber, the War Hall of the First Neath.

Dwarf lanterns were affixed to each of the ancient cressets, and the hall was brightly lighted. Patrols were again posted in the corridors, and the Host was arrayed to meet Gnar's Swarm. But the *Spaunen* did not come. Dwarves were sent over the rope bridge to Quadmere to fetch its cool clear water, and the Army rested. Again Perry and Cotton slept.

Upon awakening, both Warrows were well rested but famished. Unfortunately, the only food at hand was the crue Cotton had brought in his pack. And so they ate the tasteless waybread and drank water for their meal. Rested, with his stomach full, and in the spacious, bright Hall, Perry's spirits began to recover at last. He had washed his face clean of the face blackener, and had removed the shirt hiding his armor; now he was a resplendent silver warrior. And though he was troubled by Ursor's unknown fate, still he started joining in conversation with Cotton.

Before he realized it, Perry began telling the other buccan all about the journey down the river, across the wold, and through the caverns. The words came tumbling out, his voice hesitating only when he painfully spoke of Barak's death and funeral, and of Delk felled by Rūck arrow in the Lair fire. When Perry fell silent at the end, his tale told, Cotton leaned back in wonderment, his jewel like green eyes wide. "Why, Mister Perry," declared Cotton, "*you're* the one that's had a real adventure, not me. That's the story you've been wanting to write: not *my* adventure, but *yours*."

Perry shook his head in disagreement, for as it is with many a neophyte adventurer, his own story seems insignificant alongside others'. Cotton, seeing the self-doubt in Perry's eyes, then added, "Wull, maybe you just ought to write 'em both up, and we'll have a contest and vote on 'em, and then we'll see which one is the more adventuresome."

Perry laughed outright at the absurdity of the suggestion, and Cotton joined him, and it was the first time mirth had visited either in a long, long while. Before they could say more, a Council of Captains was called, and the two Warrows were summoned to attend.

As soon as all had gathered, Durek spoke: "Cruel Gnar seems too timid to bring his forces to face ours; and so we must draw him out. We must lure him into battle here in the great Mustering Chamber." Durek gestured at the mighty War Hall. This enormous gallery was more than two thousand Dwarf-strides long, and half that wide, its ceiling a hundred feet high. A fourfold row of huge delved pillars marched down its length, carven to resemble great Dragons coiling up fluted columns, each graven monster glaring in a different direction, some with stone flame or spew splashing against the roof. Along the walls were lesser sculptings of bears, eagles, owls, Wolves, and other creatures of rock perched on interior cornices, looking down from the high shadows cast by the hundreds upon hundreds of Dwarf-lanterns that brightly illuminated the Hall.

"This chamber shall become the center of our forays into the passages to destroy the Squam," Durek rasped, then paused; but what he was going to say next shall forever remain a mystery, for it was at that moment that Gnar announced that the Foul Folk were indeed coming to fight: A great rolling *Doom!* of a huge drum thundered into the cavern; so vast and loud was the beat that Perry's small frame shook in its echo.

Boom! Doom! came the beats again, and the very stone itself seemed to rattle and sound with their call.

Boom! Doom! Doom! The mighty vibrations caused rock dust to sift out of cracks and drift to the floor.

"To your Squadrons! Array the Host!" shouted Durek. "Gnar comes at last!" And the Captains sprang to their feet and sped to their Companies.

Boom! Doom! Perry's heart leapt in terror at the great booming sounds, and the blood drained from his face. *Hold on, bucco,* he thought, *settle down. You know what that is: it's a great marching drum of a Rūcken Horde*—The Raven Book *speaks of them.* Perry looked at Cotton, and the other buccan's features were drawn, his lips pressed into a thin white line.

Perry reached out and squeezed his comrade's hand, and Cotton cast Perry a fleeting smile from his stricken face.

Boom! Boom! beat the great pulse, as if the mountain itself were being struck by a mighty hammer to ring in response. And then clamant, discordant hornblats sounded, and there came echoing horns from each of the passageways leading into the vast chamber, followed by a shattering volley of harsh clashing of scimitar and tulwar upon dhal and sipar.

Boom! Doom!

As foreplanned, the Dwarf Legion formed up in the center of the great floor, all warriors facing outward with axes and bucklers at the ready. On three sides of the Host stood the stone of the chamber walls, with many dark holes showing where passageways bored off into the black reaches of Drimmendeeve. It was these portals that the elements of the Army watched, for through these ways would come Gnar's forces. On the fourth side was the Great Deep, and only a few of the Host looked thereupon, for it guarded the Army's back better than another Legion could. Across the floor from sidewall to sidewall and through the Host ran several wide fissures—great cracks in the stone; here and there, huge slabs spanned the fissures, footbridges placed there ages agone by the Dwarven Folk.

Doom! Boom!

Both Perry and Cotton were too short to see over the warriors' heads, and so they mounted up on the base of one of the pillars and watched; Perry drew Bane, and Cotton the Atalar Blade, and Bane's flame was nearly bright enough to hurt the eyes, while the golden runes on the sword of Atala glinted in the phosphorescent glow of the Dwarf-lanterns.

DOOM! DOOM! whelmed the vast pulse, and then fell silent. There was one more bray of horns, as one raucous blare was answered from all corridors by other blats. From afar the Host could hear the sound of running Rūcken boots slapping against the stone. Louder and louder the footsteps sounded, until they became a veritable thunder of feet.

And then Rūcks began to issue into the Hall out of every corridor, every orifice, like black ants vomited from a thousand holes. And among the Rūcks scuttled armored Hlōk leaders. Still the maggot-folk poured through the portals and into the chamber. And they deployed themselves along the walls and around the Host.

The Dwarves stood their ground in silence, though many faces were grim to see the awful flood of Squam. And then at last the Spawn were arrayed, and they shouted and clamored in a thunderous din, brandishing their weapons and threatening the Dwarves by making menacing swipes and swirls and starts. But though they raised a great outcry, they attacked not, for they were awaiting the coming of Gnar.

And then he came; the supreme Man-sized Hlōk came. Into the far end of the chamber he strode, and through the massed ranks of Rūcks. When he reached the forefront of his Horde, he stopped and stood on widespread legs with his fists on his hips: cruel and proud, swart and yellow-eyed, armored in black scale mail and a high-peaked helm, and armed with a great long scimitar. And the shouting voices of his Swarm proclaimed him to the Dwarven Army. Gnar stood 'midst the clamorous roar; then he raised up a clenched fist, and the ranks of his Horde abruptly fell silent, as if their very breath had been choked off. And Gnar laughed in the sudden stillness, for there were ten thousand Rūcks to but four thousand Dwarves.

"What slime comes into my kingdom?" Gnar bellowed across the distance that separated the two armies. "Who is the stupid fool leading this paltry group of foul-beards? Why have you of little wit blundered into my caverns?" And a great derisive shout went up from the Rūcken Swarm, as if Gnar had somehow scored a victory with insults alone. Yet the Dwarves stood grim and silent, facing the gibing enemy, not responding, waiting for this *noise* to subside. At last Gnar again raised his fist, and once more the Horde's voice chopped shut.

Still the Dwarf Legion stood fast; and when the cavernous echoing died, Durek spoke: He did not seem to raise his voice, yet he was plainly heard by all in the Hall: "I, the Seventh Durek, and mine host have come to take back that which is rightfully ours. And we have come to avenge old wrongs and hurts. And more, we have come to stop your rape of the land around. But above all, we have come because you are Squam and we are Châkka." And the Dwarf King fell silent, but with a deafening clap of axe on buckler and with a single great voice, the entire Army shouted once only: *CHÂKKA SHOK!*

At this thunderous call the Rūcken Horde cringed, but seeing the Dwarves stand fast, blustered up again. Gnar glared at his craven Swarm and then turned to the Legion and laughed derisively. "Do you rabble *truly* expect to evict us? Look about you, imbeciles! You are doomed, for we are nearly thrice your numbers. Even so, we could conquer you weaklings with less, in fact, perhaps with but two of us." And Gnar turned and shouted, "Goth! Mog!"

And as the Horde howled in evil glee, from the dark shadows of the end-cavern ponderously came two great, hulking creatures: nearly fourteen feet tall, swart, greenish, scaled, red-eyed, each monster clutching a massive iron pole in one thick hand, each brutish face filled with a vile, malignant leer. They were Cave Ogrus. They lumbered through the massed Rūcken ranks to stand aflank of Gnar. And Gnar threw back his head and laughed in derision.

The Dwarf Army blenched, for even though there were a full ten thousand Rūcks surrounding them, till this moment the

Dwarves had not truly felt fear. But now their eyes were drawn irresistibly to the great Cave Trolls, and the massive strength of rock-hard flesh seemed to spell doom, for they were an awful enemy. At last Perry knew why Ogru-Trolls were so feared: they were direful behemoths of crushing power, and they looked unstoppable. Perry tried to remember the places of Ogru vulnerability, but his wit fled in his fright, and he could only recall that a sword thrust under the eyelid and into the brain would kill one.

Holding up his fist to stop the jeering of his Swarm, Gnar sneered from between the massive Trolls, "I will give you but one chance to surrender, fools. All I ask in tribute are your inferior weapons and pitiable supplies, and eternal bondage as my groveling slaves." Raucous laughter swelled up from the Horde, and they jittered in revelment. But their shrill gaiety was cut short by another dinning clash of axe on buckler, again followed by a single thunderous shout bursting forth from the entire Legion: *CHÂKKA COR!*

And quickly upon the ensuing silence, Durek roared in wrath, "We did not come to parley with a foul usurper! We are here to fight to the death!" And the Dwarf King signalled his herald, who raised the great War Horn to his lips and blew a blast that sprang from pillar to post to wall and roof. The Hall seemed to tremble and shudder with its sound, and all the Host took heart. An answering blare came from the *Spaunen* horns, and the two mighty armies came rushing together with hoarse shouts and a great resounding crash of weapons.

Perry and Cotton sprang down from the base of the pillar and rushed to the fray. Faced by the Rūcken Horde, the Dwarves had formed a wall of flashing axes, and the maggot-folk could not break through the phalanx. Likewise, neither Warrow could reach the Rūcks; the two ran up and down the lines, but to no avail. The axes hewed and slashed and cut the foe with dreadful effect. Dwarves also were felled, but the ranks somehow closed, and still the Spawn failed to penetrate.

Gnar had withheld the great Ogru-Trolls, for they were the last in Drimmen-deeve, and the secret of his power; and the prowess of Dwarf Troll-squads was legendary. Hence, only shouting Rūcks and snarling Hlōks clashed with the Dwarves in this first charge.

Blood and gore splashed the stone of the hall, and screams rent the air, and corpses littered the floor! The Dwarves' compact deployment defied the enemy attack, and at last the Horde withdrew! Dwarf wounded were drawn into the center, and fresher warriors stepped to the fore.

Twice more the Spawn charged, only to suffer dismaying losses, for twice more the Dwarves' formation held, and the Horde was beaten back; the Rūcks could not break through to bring their greater numbers to bear! Many of the Chȃkka, however, were felled, and the Dwarves yielded back a bit to consolidate their perimeter.

Gnar knew that he would have to use the great Trolls, even though he could not replace them, even though were they to fall, his rule in Drimmen-deeve might fall with them, for other Hlōks could then challenge him without fear. Yet without the Ogrus, the Hlōk-led Rūcks could not break the Dwarf array, and unless the array were broken, Gnar would suffer defeat at the hands of the Chȃkka.

Hence, once again Gnar ordered a charge, but this time he loosed the Cave Trolls! These mighty engines of destruction waded into the forefront of the Dwarves, their great iron Warbars swinging to and fro to crush all before them. The Dwarves gave back, and there stood a gap in the wall of axes. Hordes of Rūcks streamed into the center, and the Dwarves' mighty phalanx disintegrated: the formation was broken and the Dwarf defence was sundered into companies, squads, pairs, and single Dwarves fighting against desperate odds.

In the center, fifty or more Dwarves surrounded each Ogru, hewing and hacking at their vitals and great legs; but Gnar ordered Rūcks to attack the Troll-squads, and whether the Dwarves would have succeeded in felling the giants will never be known, for the Rūcks assaulted the squads and turned the Dwarves' energies aside.

Perry and Cotton found themselves facing the foe at last, and the relentless hours of Kian's sword-instructions now showed their worth, for the Warrows' blades wove swift nets of death upon the enemy!

Perry lunged under a hammer, and blazing Bane drank black Rūck's blood, the foe fell, but another foe took his place, and Elven-blade clashed against Rūcken-scimitar. A parry, riposte,

and thrust ended that duel, but another Rūck lashed a bar at the
Warrow. And amid snarling Rūcks and cursing Dwarves and the
clash and clangor of War, Perry dodged and whirled and darted,
and hacked and stabbed and cut, felling Rūck after Rūck in the
swirling battle.

Cotton, too, was pressed by a great number of the maggot-
folk: they seemed to come at him from all points. Twisting
among ally and foe alike, Cotton hewed and clove and pierced
with his Atalar sword; and Rūcks fell about the Warrow like
grain before the scythe.

And as circumstances would have it, the two Warrows found
themselves battling back to back near the lip of the Great Deep,
hindguarding one another while dealing death to the foe at
hand.

Soon the assailants fell back, for these small warriors were
much more skilled than they, and the two in glittering silver and
shining golden armor seemed bright and invincible.

But then a great Hlōk jumped forward to challenge Cotton.
Even as the Hlōk engaged Cotton's sword, a Rūck tried to take
the buccan from the rear; but Perry and Bane cut down the foe,
the Rūck's death scream to be lost among the shouts filling the
War Hall. And with Perry guarding his back, Cotton fought the
enemy before him. *Clang!* went sword on scimitar, and the clash
and skirl of steel upon steel rang out. Cotton was pressed hard,
for the Hlōk was skilled, but at last the Warrow turned a thrust
aside and slashed his blade through the throat of the Hlōk.
Blood flew wide, and the enemy fell.

Ai! wailed the Rūcks and drew back; but one set an arrow to
his bow and drew it full to the cruel barb and let the black shaft
fly at point-blank range. But Perry had seen the danger, and
with a warning shout he leapt forward to knock Cotton aside.
And the arrow slammed into Perry, its force so great that it pen-
etrated even the silveron mail, bursting through a chink high on
the chest where an amber gem was inset among the links. And
the Warrow slammed backwards against the base of one of the
great Dragon Pillars, and crumpled to the stone, the buccan
pierced through. Cotton sprang forward with a cry of rage, and
his blade mortally clove the Rūck from helm to breast. The remaining Rūcks fled from the small enraged warrior in the

golden mail. And Cotton's wrath turned to dismay as he fell to his knees beside Perry's still form.

"Mister Perry! Mister Perry!" wailed Cotton, hugging the fallen Warrow to his breast. And then Perry moaned, and Cotton saw that he wasn't dead. "Oh, Mister Perry, you're alive! Oh, don't die, Mister Perry. I couldn't bear it if you died."

With chaos and confusion and slaughter all around, and with a savage and desperate battle raging back and forth above them, Cotton knelt at the edge of the Great Deep and held on to Perry and wept and rocked back and forth in torment.

Perry opened his eyes, his vision swimming in a sea of pain, and looked to see Cotton's face dimly before him. "Oh, Cotton, Cotton, what have I done?" whispered Perry. "I have dragged you off into a quest where neither one of us belongs. And you may be slain. Oh, Cotton, when I reached for this adventure, I did not stop to consider anyone's feelings but my own. The only thing that mattered was my own lust for excitement. I did not stop to think how you felt, or Holly . . . poor Holly . . . Did you see how she cried, Cotton? I didn't know. I didn't think. That's it! I didn't think. Me, the bright scholar, the glorious Fairhill Scholar, and I can't think my way past a foolish dream of bold achievement.

"It was all foredoomed anyway. My whole witless venture was unnecessary. No single part of it was necessary. Look at our mission: We tried to sneak through Drimmen-deeve, and the Dusk-Door wasn't even broken. Barak died for nought. Tobin suffered needlessly. Delk died for nought. And Ursor. And what for? . . . What for? . . . What for?"

Cotton looked into Perry's sapphirine eyes. "Oh, no, Mister Perry," he protested, "you've got it all wrong. That's not the way of it at all. They *needed* us. Without us the raids of the maggot-folk would go on. Without us the Dwarves might not have gone to Dusk-Door and would have died in the Great Deep." Cotton gestured at the nearby gulf. "Without us the Dwarves wouldn't have stood a chance."

A grimace of pain crossed Perry's features, and he gasped through clenched teeth. "Leastwise now, leastwise now . . ." A shuddering sigh racked the wounded buccan, and unconsciousness mercifully washed over him.

"Mister Perry!" cried Cotton, fearing the worst, but before

he could press his ear to Perry's breast, one of the huge Cave Trolls, seeing two small, helpless targets hidden in the shadow of a Dragon Pillar, lumbered toward the Warrows.

Cotton saw the Ogru coming, and gently eased Perry to the floor. Catching up his sword, Cotton sprang between the Troll and the wounded buccan. And as he ran into the path of the dire creature, the story from *The Raven Book* of Patrel and the Ogru on the bridge flashed into Cotton's mind, and he shouted, "*Hai!* Troll! You great clumsy oaf! Look at me! I am the golden warrior!" And the buccan held his arms wide and danced to one side, drawing the Troll's full attention. The huge Ogru stared stupidly at the small creature in the shining gilded mail; then he raised his great iron bar and struck.

Crack! The bar smashed to the stone, but the nimble Warrow was not there. Cotton sprang to the side and forward, and hewed with his Atalar sword, hacking just above the great Ogru's knee, for that was the highest the small Warrow could reach with his blade. But the edge clanged into the Troll's armor-like hide and glanced down.

Crack! The great iron bar missed again, and once more Cotton's blade failed to cut the stone skin. As the Warrow dodged away, he knew that sooner or later the Troll would make contact, and the fight would end then and there. Cotton knew he needed help; and in that moment he glimpsed from the corner of his eye Bane's blue flame burning on the stone where the sword had skidded when Perry had been felled.

Crack! The Ogru missed again, and Cotton darted to the side and scooped up the blazing Elven-blade. Yet the monster shouted in vile gloat, for it now had Cotton trapped: to get at Bane, the Warrow had dashed beyond the Troll to the precipitous edge of the Great Deep; and the only way to freedom led back past the great foe. To cut off escape, the Ogru spread its arms wide and took a ponderous stride forward.

Cotton, his eyes locked upon the massive War-bar, stepped back, and his foot came down upon the edge of the great split. He teetered and gasped in fear, his arms windmilling. And the vast dark gulf gaped blackly, and waited. Yet with a twisting motion, the Warrow managed to fall forward. And as he had been trained, Cotton rolled as he landed, to come back to his feet in a balanced stance with sword in hand to again face the foe. The great Cave Troll snarled in anger, yet its eyes took on a look of evil cunning, for it still had the wee Warrow trapped; and the monster swooshed the bar in a feint followed by a swift overhand stroke.

Crack! The iron pole just missed the dodging Warrow, so close it ticked a golden scale.

Again Cotton leapt to one side and then lunged forward; and the blazing rune-jeweled Troll's Bane flashed up as Cotton plunged it into the Ogru's kneecap: the stone-like skin that easily turned aside axes and swords yielded like soft butter to the flaming Elven-blade; the point sank through the cap and into the knee joint, plunging nearly to the sinews at the back of the leg. Cotton jerked Bane out and twisted aside; black blood dropped from the bitter blade to the stone floor, and where it fell a reeking smoke coiled up from the hard rock.

The great Troll roared in agony and clutched at its pierced knee, and stumbled with a sliding crash to the stone at the lip of the great black abyss, to slip over the edge, grasping frantically but in vain at the smooth floor. And with a bellow of terror and its eyes wide in fear, and still gripping the massive War-bar, the huge Ogru fell howling beyond the rim and down into the bottomless black depths.

Cotton stared for a moment at the place where the Troll had gone over the edge; then the Warrow scooped up the Atalar Blade and ran back to Perry, who was conscious again. Once more Cotton cradled the wounded buccan.

As Cotton watched the hideous battle, Perry gazed up into the shadows on the ceiling. The War was going badly for the Dwarves: the Spawn now controlled the center of the chamber and the Dwarves were at the perimeter. The great numbers of the Rūcken forces and the strength of their position weighed the battle heavily in their favor; though much more skillful, the Dwarves were in weak array, and by the hundreds they had fallen to Gnar's Swarm. As Cotton looked on in dismay, Perry whispered, "That's where Borin climbed."

"Wha . . . what, Mister Perry?" asked Cotton.

"That's where Borin climbed over the ceiling. When we crossed the gulf, I mean," rambled Perry, lying on his back, looking upward above the chasm. "Over there. Above the bridge."

"You said he didn't make it all the way. The ceiling was all cracked, *zig . . . zig* something," wept Cotton, crying for the Dwarf dead as he tried to comfort his wounded master.

"*Ziggurt.* The roof is *ziggurt.* As far as the eye can see. Borin told us." Perry's blurred gaze roamed down the Hall along the roof above the pillars.

Though he was weeping, Cotton felt strangely at peace—sitting here, holding his friend, chatting about inconsequential things—as the mighty clash and clangor of weapons and War swirled back in the main chamber just a stone's throw away.

"Rocks, stone, that's all the eye can see," muttered Perry. "No green growing things, no soft comfortable things, just hard rock and stone. I had enough of rocks when the slide nearly got us back in the Crestan Pass, oh so long ago. Those were the days. Just you and me, and Anval, Borin, and Kian."

"True," answered Cotton, "those were the days. They taught us a lot, Lord Kian and the Dwarves." And Cotton again looked at the black shaft standing out from Perry's shoulder. "I just wish they'd taught me about healing instead of about swords, and rock slides, and snow avalanches, and—"

A startled look had come over Perry's face, and a fierce energy suffused his pained lineament, and he urgently interrupted Cotton: "That's it! Cotton, that's it!" he gasped through his pain. "You've solved the riddle! We've got to get to Durek! We can win the War yet! Get me to Durek. Get me to Durek." And he clutched desperately at Cotton's arm, and struggled to rise. "Get me to Durek."

Cotton helped Perry to stand, and the wounded buccan fought to keep from swooning. His good arm was over Cotton's shoulders, and he absently clutched Bane in his other hand, having grasped it when Cotton had laid it aside. Slowly they started along the south wall; Cotton didn't know why, but his master urgently needed to get to Durek.

As they crept forward, Cotton's emeraldine eyes cast about for the Dwarf King. Perry's eyes, too, sought Durek as the Warrows limped slowly along the perimeter, the black shaft standing full neath Perry's left collarbone. Cotton saw Dwarves striving desperately with two, three, or four Rūcks at once. He also glimpsed Kian and Rand in a small force battling the remaining Ogru:

Only a handful hewed at the Troll where fifty were needed, yet at bay they held the creature. Of those facing the Ogru, it was Prince Rand who had harassed and baited the fell beast into a foaming rage; for after the two Trolls had burst through the Dwarves' defense, Rand had seen that these great monsters if unchecked would assure a Yrm victory. And he had run before one of them, shouting and waving his arms, leaping away from the crashing iron bar, drawing the Ogru out of the general mêlée in the creature's rage to smash this puny Man-thing that it couldn't quite seem to hit. Again and again Rand had leapt aside, and again and again the great iron pole had smashed to empty stone where Rand had stood but an instant before. But the Prince was growing weary, for he had baited the beast long, and the great bar was becoming more difficult to dodge.

Then Lord Kian saw his brother and the Ogru, and he ran to aid Prince Rand. Kian fell upon the Troll from the rear and lashed his sword in a mighty arc, but the blade crashed into the stone hide and glanced away notched. Three Dwarves joined the fray, but their axes proved no better. "His heel!" cried Prince Rand. "Go for his heel when I draw him forth!" And Rand stood motionless at a long reach for the Troll.

The monster lunged forward, swinging his bar in a wide sweep; and as he extended his body, the creature's ankle bent sharply and one of the scaled plates of his greenish hide lifted away from his heel. Lord Kian stepped up, and using two hands he swung his sword of Riamon with all the strength he could muster. The blade sped true, and the keen edge flashed under the scale and into the flesh to sever the heel tendon and chop to the bone and lodge in the joint. Kian's sword was wrenched from his grasp to shatter in twain upon impact as, with a great bellow, the Ogru crashed forward onto the stone, to roll and clutch at his ankle; the great beast was now out of the battle and would aid the Rūcks no more, for it could not stand.

"Rand, we did it!" Kian shouted, elated, and looked up and saw to his horror that his brother had stood fast so that the Troll could be felled, and Rand had been smashed to the wall by the cruel iron bar.

And as he saw his brother's crumpled form, and the howling Ogru rolling in agony upon the stone, a madness of fury possessed Lord Kian. Weaponless, he seized hold of the Troll's great War-bar which had been flung from the monster's clutch, *and even though the mass of the bar was beyond the strength of two Men to heft, in his wrath Lord Kian raised up the huge pole and violently smote it down upon the thrashing Troll.* The Ogru saw the strike coming and warded with his forearm, but the force of the blow was so great that the rock-hard limb was broken as if it were a twig, and the War-bar drove on to smash into the Troll's thick neck, crushing its throat; and the great creature's eyes bulged out as it tried to breathe but could not, and its limbs flailed about in desperation. And though the monster was mortally struck and falling swiftly unto Death, Lord Kian tried to raise up the War-pole for yet another blow, but could not, for with that one strike the towering fury had been spent and the bar was now far beyond his power to wield.

Catching up a fallen axe from the lax hand of a slain Dwarf, Lord Kian turned from this heel-chopped, throat-crushed monster, and made his way toward Prince Rand's fallen form.

Slowly the Warrows went forth, and they both saw Anval: he was battling Gnar! There was a great clanging as axe and scimitar clashed together. Anval drove the great Hlōk back, but then the tide turned as more Rūcks joined Gnar to attack the Dwarf. "Get back! Get back!" cried Perry, feebly, but his whisper was lost in the shouts and screams of others and in the din of steel upon steel. Suddenly a Rūck behind Anval hurled a War-hammer, and it struck the Dwarf on the back of his helm! And Anval staggered! And Gnar's great scimitar flashed up and back down, and clove into the Dwarf, blood flying wide, and Gnar threw back his head in wild laughter as Anval fell dead.

Cotton and Perry both gasped in horror, and their minds fell numb with shock. Then they heard a raging scream above all others, and they saw Borin rush at Gnar roaring, "For Anval! For Anval! Death! Death!" And he fell to with a rage unmatched by any. The Rūcks shielding Gnar were cut down by Borin's bloody axe like wheat before a reaper, and then the Dwarf and Hlōk rushed together in savage combat.

Cotton tore his eyes away from Borin and Gnar, and at last

he saw Durek. The Dwarf King and Shannon Silverleaf stood back to back, battling Rūcks, besieged near one of the entrances into the War Hall. Cotton drew Perry as close to the fracas as he dared, and sat the wounded buccan to the floor, his back to the wall. "Don't move!" Cotton cried, and then he drew his blade of the Lost Land and attacked the Rūcks from behind.

Cotton felled three before the enemy realized that another foe had joined the fray. Two more dropped, but then the Warrow's foot skidded in gore, and the buccan fell. A scimitar came slashing down and Cotton started to roll to one side, but he was not quick enough to avoid the cut. Another blade seemed to flash out of nowhere to slash with the descending curved edge: it was Shannon's long Elf-knife, and it turned the scimitar aside to crash with a sheet of sparks into the stone floor. Then Shannon cut upward, and the Rūck fell dead. Cotton sprang to his feet to see the remaining Rūcks flee screaming from this deadly trio.

"King Durek!" cried Cotton, "Mister Perry calls you to him. He is wounded and says you must come. Here, this way." And he led the Dwarf King to Perry's side. Perry had swooned again, but he opened his eyes when Durek knelt at his side and called his name.

As Shannon and Cotton stood guard, Perry spoke: *"Narok,"* whispered Perry, and Durek leaned closer to hear. *"Narok!"* Perry said more strongly. "The roof is *ziggurt.* The slide in the mountains—Anval told us about the rock slides and how they are started. But Anval is dead." Perry began to weep. "Borin fights on for him. But the sounds . . . you must make the right sounds."

Durek looked upon the weeping, incoherent Waeran. The Dwarf had no idea what it was that Perry was trying to tell him. With an arrow standing forth from high on his chest, the small warrior sat against the wall: wounded, crying, looking up with pain in his eyes, bloody Bane blazing, held in the hand of his hurt arm. "Friend Cotton," asked Durek, "do you fathom what Friend Perry is trying to tell me?"

Cotton shook his head in anguish. "No, Sir, I don't, but whatever it is, he's got a good reason."

Durek turned back to Perry, but the Warrow was staring

through his tears at the mighty battle between Cruel Gnar and raging Borin. "Friend Perry," rumbled Durek, "you are sorely wounded and I grieve for you, but I must return to the fight." And he started to rise to his feet.

But Perry desperately clutched him by the wrist. "*No!* No! It's time that Dwarves come on horses, King Durek," pled Perry. "You must sound the Horn of Narok. Sound assembly! *Now!* Before all is lost! It is our only hope!"

The Dwarf looked doubtfully away at Cotton, and then again at Perry, who was struggling to reach the trumpet on Cotton's shoulder. Cotton quickly removed the bright horn and handed it to Perry who, in turn, held it out with trembling hand toward King Durek. "Believe me . . . oh, please believe me," begged the Warrow.

In an agony of indecision, Durek looked at the fearful token and then away to the savage mêlée in the Hall and back to Perry again. And the Dwarf dreaded touching the glittering silver. "We are at our uttermost extremity. More than half of my warriors have fallen, and it seems certain that the Grg will have the victory. This trump we Châkka have feared all of our days, yet you say it is our only hope—but I do not know why. Yet I deem I must believe you, though I do not understand. You may be right, Friend Perry: perhaps the wind of *Narok* is our last hope. Perhaps the Châkka must at last ride the horses." The Dwarf King looked away from the dreadful clarion and into Perry's wide, tilted, gemlike eyes. Tears glittered in the sapphire-blue gaze, and desperate urgency welled up from the jewelled depths. "Aye, I believe you, Friend Perry. Quickly now, before I change my mind, before I lose my courage, give me the trumpet; I will sound it ere all is lost."

And Durek, full of apprehension, accepted the brilliant horn from Perry's trembling fingers. And *lo!* at Durek's touch the metal shimmered with light, and sparkling glints shattered outward; and the Dwarf King set the dazzling horn to his lips and began to blow:

The silver call electrified the air. Its clarion notes rang up to the roof and sprang from the walls and sounded throughout the great War Hall. Everywhere, Dwarves' hearts were lifted; and the Rūcks and Hlōks quailed back in fear. Again and again the call resounded as Durek blew the signal to assemble; and the sound leapt into the Great Deep, falling to its depths and running out into the vast rift in the walls; and then it seemed to spring back from the nether parts of that great split, magnified by the sheer stone faces of the mighty fissure. Durek blew the shining horn again and again, and the whole of the War Hall appeared to tremble in response to the silver notes.

Imperceptibly at first, but swiftly growing, the floor began to resonate as a crescendo of sound mounted up from the depths of the Great Deep and the echoes piled one upon the other; and still the Dwarf King winded the sparkling trumpet. Stronger and stronger came the vibrations, racking through the floor in continuous waves. And then the entire Chamber began to quiver, and rock dust drifted down from the cracks above. And still the echoes and vibrations grew as Durek sounded the bright horn and the stone shook. The Rücks huddled together, screaming in fear in the center of the thrumming floor, the place of strength they had won. All battle and fighting had ceased in the shivering Hall *Nay!* Not all! For mighty Borin yet raged against Cruel Gnar to avenge fallen Anval.

Durek blew, and still the echoes grew. Now all of the War Hall wrenched: the floor rattled, the walls groaned, the pillars lurched, and the roof pitched. *And there came from the stone a sound like that of an endless herd of horses wildly thundering by in racing stampede.* Cotton became aware that Perry was chanting, and Cotton listened in wonder:

> *"Trump shall blow,*
> *Ground will pound*
> *As Dwarves on Horses*
> *Riding 'round."*

It was the Staves of Narok! Perry chanted the Staves of Narok as Borin's axe and Gnar's scimitar clashed together again and again, and sparks flew up from their collisions. The two fought on as the Hall groaned and rumbled and shook, as if an earthquake strove within the mountain.

And Cotton looked at Durek. Now the horn seemed to be blazing, flaming with a bright internal fire; and the figures, riders and horses, *were they moving?* Galloping through runes 'round horn-bell? Or was it just a judder-caused illusion? Cotton squeezed his eyes tightly shut and rubbed them with his fists and then looked again, but he could not tell, for the quake jolting through the Hall blurred his vision.

Still the Dwarf King blew, and except for Borin, all the surviving Dwarves, their numbers now less than a thousand, flocked to Durek's signal and arrayed themselves along the southern wall. The Rūcks wailed with dread, for they knew not what was coming to pass. And Perry chanted on:

> *"Stone shall rumble,*
> *Mountain tremble*
> *In the battle*
> *Dwarves assemble.*
>
> *Answer to*
> *The Silver Call."*

And still Durek continued to sound the flaring trumpet, and the silver notes grew, and the mountain shook. Pebbles fell from the *ziggurt* ceiling, and rocks, and slabs. And great clots of Rūcks and Hlōks jerked this way and that as the stone smashed into their ranks.

Borin pressed Gnar back to one of the huge shuddering pillars. A great slab of rock crashed down from above to land beside the battling pair, but they gave it no heed. Now they grappled, and Borin's great shoulders bunched, and he forced the Hlōk back against the quaking stone support. Gnar screamed hoarsely in terror, and Borin's axe flashed as stone fell all around. Up went the double-bitted blade, and then down it fell with a meaty smack, *and Gnar's head was shorn from his thrashing body.* Borin laughed wildly as rocks and slabs, summoned by the Silver Call, crashed from the ceiling to the floor and giant pillars toppled with thunderous wrack; and the Dwarf held up the grisly trophy by the hair, shouting, "For Anval!" And he flung it bouncing and skidding across the wide stone floor as the entire roof of *ziggurt* rock at last ripped completely away from the cavernous vault above, and the great, invincible, rushing mass fell with a cataclysmic roar to smash across all of the broad center of the vast War Hall.

> *"Death shall deem*
> *The vault to fall."*

And as the rock thundered down, the surviving remnants of the Dwarf Army reeled back aghast against the southern wall, their eyes locked in awe upon the crashing mass, their hands clapped over their ears. Durek desperately held the Horn of Narok in his white-knuckled grip, and he winded it a few notes more, but its silver echoes were lost in the deafening roar of thundering stone.

Tons upon unnumbered tons shattered down, crashing into the Hall, a great, bellowing, endless, rolling roar. Rock smashed upon rock, hammering, shattering, pulverizing, destroying. It seemed as if the vast collapse would never stop . . .

But suddenly it was over: the thundering rockfall ended. Slowly the rolling echoes of cracking stone and cleaving rock died away. Billowing stone dust whirled and settled, and the survivors gazed stunned across the wreckage. Volume upon volume of stone had crashed down into the chamber. Only along the walls had the roof been sound, and the Dwarves who had assembled there had, for the most part, escaped the carnage, although here and there a few huge rocks had bounded and crashed to crush some unfortunate Dwarves. But in the center of the chamber, all living things had perished: All the myriad Rūcks and Hlōks. And Borin.

The battle was finished, the War over. Four fifths of the Dwarves had been slain in battle; ten thousand *Spaunen* had died, two thirds at the hand of the Host, the rest by falling stone. Perry looked out across the wreckage:

> *"Many perish,*
> *Death the Master,*
> *Dwarves shall mourn*
> *Forever after."*

Durek had taken the silent bugle from his lips. Stunned, he looked across the shattered sea of stone. He turned to Cotton and gave him the Horn of the Reach, now softly glowing with but the gentle sheen of fine silver and no longer flaring with glitterbright fire. Cotton took it with numb fingers and unconsciously hung it over his shoulder.

At last Cotton had seen the connection between Perry's pain-driven, rambling speech and the crashing down of the ceiling. Cotton, too, now remembered Anval's warning in the Crestan Pass of just how the right sound would cause rock to jink and come roaring in avalanche. And he remembered Anval's exact words: *"We Châkka believe that each thing in this world will shake or rattle or fall or even shatter apart if just the right note is sounded on the right instrument."* And the Horn of the Reach—the Horn of Narok, the Death-War—crafted ages ago by an unknown hand, had been created for just this event: created against the day when Dwarves, driven to their uttermost limits, would have to bring the vast *ziggurt* roof of the immense War Hall down upon some great horde of enemies. The Staves of Narok were not made to warn Dwarves against riding on horseback. No, for that line in the ode spoke only of the drumming sound the rock would make in the event the horn was winded. And to Cotton it was now plain that the vault referred to in the rede was the wide ceiling of this huge stone chamber; till now, Cotton had suspected that the vault of the poem was the sky above and that somehow the Staves were related to the Dwarves' belief that falling stars foretold of Death's coming. But Mister Perry had figured it all out, and just barely in time, too.

Cotton was wrenched from his stunned thoughts and back to the here and now by an anguished cry from Perry, who was staring toward the center of the chamber. "Oh, Borin, Anval, we loved you and now you are gone." And the wounded buccan began weeping as, slowly, the healers started moving among the Host, tending the injured. And Shannon came to Perry and examined the arrow standing forth from the juncture between the Waerling's chest and shoulder.

As the Elf prepared to extract the barb, with Cotton hovering nearby, ready to aid, King Durek began to make his way along the wall, at the edge of the wrack, seeing but too benumbed to fathom the total destruction wrought in the War of Kraggen-cor: The great War Hall was destroyed. Tons unnumbered of fallen *ziggurt* ramped upward toward the center of the chamber; like a vast cairn, it covered the crushed bodies of all the Úkhs and Hrōks, all the Châkka slain in battle, the Troll felled by Rand and Kian, and Gnar's slayer, Borin Ironfist. Here and there a broken Dragon Pillar jutted upward through the great heap, a jagged reminder of the ancient rows of columns, now collapsed and part of the rubble. Durek also made his way past many of the eight hundred or so surviving Châkka quietly and methodically binding up each other's wounds. All were stunned by the cataclysmic ruin, and had not yet realized the staggering cost of their victory.

King Durek saw the devastation, but he, too, did not comprehend, until at last he came upon Lord Kian. Nearby lay the axe Kian had carried back into battle: one bit broken, the other blade chipped and jagged, the helve cracked, the iron and oak now awash with black Grg-blood; Lord Kian had wielded it beyond its endurance, for his vengeance had been mighty. Kian was also drenched, some of it Squam gore, some of it his own blood, for he, too, was wounded—by spear thrust and scimitar cut—although not mortally; but Prince Rand was dead, slain by Troll War-bar. And Lord Kian huddled on the stone floor, hugging his brother's lifeless body to his breast, and he wept and rocked in distress.

Durek gazed on in sorrow, and Lord Kian looked up through his tears at the Dwarf. "When we were but lads," wept Kian, "we were in the market, and Rand took up a turtle-shell comb in his hand. And he laughed happily over the raft we had made and ridden to Rhondor and sold for two silver pennies. And Rand bought that comb for Mother, and we went home and gave it to her, and Rand glowed in the pleasure of her delight. We began planning a new raft: two children rejoicing in the flush of youth, as close in life as two brothers who loved one another could ever be. But now he is dead and nevermore will we laugh together, for the lad who plied rafts with me to Rhondor has now sailed without me on his final journey." And Lord Kian rocked and keened in his grief.

It was in this poignant moment of kin-death lamentation that at last the cost of the victory came clear to Durek. And the overwhelming despair of the War-loss uncontrollably welled up in the Dwarf King; and he quickly pulled his hood over his head, and his face fell into shadow, for no one should see the heart-grief of Dwarves—for to look upon Dwarf bale is to gaze upon sorrow beyond measure. And the Dwarf King sank to his knees and choked upon his own woe. His glistening tears fell to splash upon the stone, and great sobs racked his frame as he and Lord Kian and uncounted others grieved in deep despair along the wall behind the jumble and scree of fallen *ziggurt*. But the slain of the Death-War heeded them not.

CHAPTER 9

❧❧❧

THE JOURNEY BACK

Two weeks passed, and Perry's wound steadily healed. The black shaft had driven through muscle, all vital parts having been missed, and the barb had not been poisoned. Both Warrows' spirits, however, were greatly injured, for four out of every five of the Host had fallen, and nearly all of their comrades had perished. Cotton was often seen searching, looking for some sign of Bomar and the cook-waggon crew; but he found them not, for they had been slain in combat and were buried under tons of stone in the ruined War Hall; and he wept for them and for Rand and for all the others lost. And Perry, too, spent long days in anguish, remembering Delk and gruff Barak, and huge Ursor, and the Ironfist brothers, Anval and Borin. And the Warrows thought upon all the times that were, and they grieved for all the times that might have been but now would never be. Of their close companions, only Durek, Shannon, and Kian remained, and a desolate mood haunted them as well as each of those of the Host who had survived: King Durek looked upon his won Kingdom, but felt only grief. Lord Kian stood for long moments and stared without seeing into the dark corners of Kraggen-cor. Often someone—anyone—would be seen with his face buried in his hands. All were stunned by the overwhelming losses of their victory. And their heartgrief filled them.

On the seventh day after the battle, word came from the Dusk-Door of Brytta's safety and that of the Vanadurin; yet this good news caused no celebration, only quiet relief. Even the arrival on the tenth day of a force of Dylvana Elves from Darda Galion stirred little excitement. How the Elves had become aware of the victory, none knew—or would say—although Cotton did overhear an Elf Captain speaking to Silverleaf, asserting, "We came at your summons, Alor Vanidar." But the buccan did not see how Shannon could have sent a message, and thus dismissed it from his mind.

At last Perry came to King Durek and said, "I can stand this sorrow no longer. My physical wound is well enough to travel"—and the Warrow flexed his fingers and turned his hand over and again, and then stiffly he eased his arm from the sling and set the cloth aside—"but my very being is sorely injured. I must go to a place of quiet and solitude, a place far removed from the reflections of War and evil memories, a place where pleasures are simple and time goes slowly. King Durek, I am returning home to the Bosky, for The Root calls me with an irresistible voice, and I must answer, and rest, and be drawn forth from this bleak place where my heart and spirit have been driven."

And Durek saw that the Warrow was indeed injured far beyond what the eye could see. "Come with me," Durek rasped, and they strode forth from the Great Chamber, where the remnants of the Host were now quartered. Out through the north entrance they went, and up within the mountain. High they climbed, and higher still, mounting up stair upon stair delved within the stone of Stormhelm, passing through Rise after Rise; many times they rested, yet still they ascended, and the stair was ancient, but lightly trod. Once more they rested and then pressed on, and finally they entered a carven hall. But the Dwarf held his lantern high and led the Warrow into a dark, twisting crack with shoots branching off in many directions.

At last they came to a small but massy bronze door, and the rune-laden surface flung brazon glints back unto the eye. The Dwarf King took hold of the handle—a great ring of brass—and muttered strange words under his breath; and then he turned his wrist, twisting the ring post, and pushed the door outward.

Bright light streamed in through the open portal, and blue sky could be seen beyond. The Dwarf King crossed over the bronze doorsill and bade Perry to follow. And blinking his watering eyes in the brilliance, his hand shading his sight, the Warrow stepped through into the light.

And Perry found he was upon a windswept ledge on a towering vertical face of stone on the outer flanks of Rávenor—of Stormhelm. High up he was, yet still the mountain reared above him, rising toward the snow-laden crest. A low parapet was before him, and there King Durek stood, leaning forward upon both hands and looking down into the land. But Perry shrank back from such a view, for the drop was sheer and awesome. Yet Durek turned and held out his hand, and in spite of his fright, Perry stepped forward and took it; and strength seemed to flow from Dwarf to Warrow, and never again was Perry to fear heights.

It was a rare day upon Rávenor, for no storm hammered its peak. The cold thin air was crystalline, and the endless sky was calm, and a few serene clouds drifted past. To the north and south the great backbone of the Grimwall marched off into the distance. The other three peaks of the Quadran—Aggarath and Uchan, south and southeast, and Ghatan, east—shouldered up nearby. The clear-eyed Warrow could see far and away: to Darda Galion and beyond; to the Great Argon River; even unto the eaves of Darda Erynian. Perry's vision swept outward, over the southwest borders of Riamon and into the North Reach of Valon, where perhaps horses thundered across the plains. And it seemed to Perry as if the very rim of Mithgar itself might be seen from here.

And Durek directed the Warrow's eyes down onto the Pitch, and like tiny specks, a work crew of Dwarven Folk could be seen fetching water from the Quadmere. And Durek and Perry looked deeper down into the Quadran, and there in a great fold of stone on Ghatan's flank stood the Vorvor, a whirling churning gurge deeply entwined in Dwarven legend: There a secret river burst forth from the underearth to rage around a great stone basin and plunge down into the dark again; and a great gaping whirlpool raved endlessly and sucked at the sky and funneled deep into the black depths below. Dwarves tell that when the world was young and First Durek trod its margins, he came unto this place. And vile Úkhs, shouting in glee, captured him and from a high stone ledge they flung him into the spin, and the sucking maw drew him down. According to the legend, none else had e'er survived that fate; yet First Durek did, though how, it is not said. To the very edge of the Realm of Death, and perhaps beyond, he was taken, yet Life at last found him on a rocky shore within a vast, undelved, undermountain realm; and First Durek strode where none else had gone before—treading through that Kingdom which was to become Kraggen-cor. How he came again unto the light of day, it is not told; yet it is said that Daūn Gate stands upon the very spot where he walked out through the mountainside; but how he crossed the Great Dēop remains an enigma, though some believe that he was aided by the Utruni—the Stone Giants. And the enmity with Squam began here too, more deadly than the ravening whirl of the roaring Vorvor.

Yet none of this legend did Perry and Durek speak upon at length, for the violence of the Vorvor was remote down within the Quadran; and the distant whirling waters seemed to twist around in silence, for only a winking glitter of the far-off wheeling funnel reached up into the lofty aerie.

Durek glanced at the sky, gauging where stood the Sun. "Here, Friend Perry," the Dwarf King counseled, "sit here." And he led the Warrow to an unworked quartzen outcrop, in part naturally shaped much the same as the bench of a massive throne. "Look east to the peak of Ghatan, just there where the high cleft and grey crag meet. And wait, for the time is nearly upon us."

And so they waited in silence, Perry's gaze locked upon the place Durek had directed. Slowly the Sun came unto the zenith, and lo! a circlet of light bejewelled with five stars sprang forth from deep within the crags. Perry looked in wonder at the Dwarf King and saw that the studded circlet and stars on Seventh Durek's armor were arrayed in the same number and fashion as those reflected from the spire of Ghatan.

"You see before you the Châkkacyth Ryng—the Dwarvenkith Ring," declared the Dwarf, "spangled with a star for each Line of the Châkka Kindred. Ever has the Ryng lived in our legends. Ever has it signified the unity of our Folk. And I came to Kraggen-cor to claim the Ryng for myself and my kith. But alas! I did not know the terrible cost that such a sigil would bear.

"I now feel that I will be the last King of Durek's Folk, and that after me we shall be no more. Oh, we shall not die, nor leave Mitheor; but instead, I deem we must come together with others of our Race to merge our blood with theirs, and the pure line of Durek will vanish. For if we do not meet and merge with others of our kind, Durek's Folk will fall into weakness and futility; our losses were staggering, and alone, we who were the mightiest cannot recover.

"Already Châkkadom is spread thinly, and our numbers gradually dwindle, for we are slow to bear young. I think that this War has sounded the death knell of the separate Châkka Kindred, and to survive, the Five Kith must become but one. Accordingly, I have sent out the word of our . . . victory—not only to Mineholt North, where my trothmate Rith and the families of my warriors even now prepare to join us, but also to the other Châk Kindred both near and distant, asking any who would come to do so.

"I brought you here, Friend Perry, to show you that Ryng, to show you that symbol of our dream: five stars upon a perfect circle. But I also wished to show you the cost of that dream—for as it can be with each great dream, sometimes the cost to the dreamer is staggering.

"All dreams fetch with a silver call, and to some the belling of that treasured voice is irresistible. And in many quests, the silver turns to dross, while in others, it remains precious; but in the harsh crucibles of some quests, the silver is transformed into ruthless metal. Such was the case with both of our dreams, Waeran, yours and mine: we answered to the lure of a silver call, but found instead cruel iron at quest's end. Yet what is done is done, and we cannot call it back, we cannot flee into yesterday.

"That does not mean that it is wrong to dream, nor does it mean that one should not reach for a dream. But it does mean that all dreams exact a price: sometimes trivial, sometimes more than can be borne.

"Some dreams are small: a garden patch, a rosebush, the crafting of a simple thing. Some dreams are grand: a great journey, a dangerous feat, the winning of a Kingdom. And the greater the dream, the greater the reward—yet the greater can be the cost. One cannot reach for a dream and remain unchanged, and that change is part of the cost of the dream. But when events go awry and disaster strikes, each of us who dreams must not let his spirit be crushed by the outcome.

"A person can be safe and never reach for his dream, never risk failure, never expose his spirit to the dangers inherent, but then he will never reap the rewards of a dream realized, and he might never truly live.

"Friend Perry, you reached for your dream, you grasped it, and held on to the very end. You found that the cost was high—higher than any of us had anticipated. And now you would go and rest and be at peace, and I believe you should. But do not hide away and brood, and fester, and become small in spirit; instead, rest, and reflect, and grow."

Durek then fell silent. And as the Sun passed beyond the zenith, Perry and the Dwarven King sat upon the Mountain Throne, and together they watched the Ring fade from sight—and as the glitter dimmed, the grasping bitterness gently fell away from the Warrow's heart, though the deep sadness remained. After a while, they stood and walked in silence back into Kraggen-cor, closing the bronze door behind.

The next morning, Cotton and Perry prepared to leave. They would head back through Kraggen-cor to Dusk-Door, and Silverleaf would go with them: Shannon was to be their guide through Lianion to the place called Luren. And as the Warrows prepared, so did Lord Kian; in the company of the Elves of Darda Erynian he would go east to the Rissanin River and then northeasterly to Dael, returning to Riamon and his Kingdom.

At last all was ready. Perry and Cotton, Shannon and Kian, all stood with Durek in the Great Chamber of the Sixth Rise. None knew what to say, for it was a sad moment. The Man looked to the center of the hall, to a white stone tomb—a tomb upon which lay an unadorned blackhandled sword of Riamon—a tomb wherein Prince Rand had been laid to rest in honor. And tears sprang into Kian's eyes Durek followed the young Lord's gaze and said, "Your brother died in glory and is the only Man ever to be so honored by the Châkka."

Tears coursed down the cheeks of the Warrows, and Kian turned to them and pledged, "I shall come to the Boskydells after a time, and we'll have a pipe and speak of better things.

Look for me in the spring, summer, or fall, not the next but perhaps the ones after; but do not look for me in the winter, for it will be bleak and stir up too many painful memories. I will come when the grief has faded to but an old sadness." He embraced the Waerlinga and clasped the forearm of Shannon and Durek, and without another word, turned and walked swiftly away through the lantern light, striding toward the Dawn-Gate, where awaited his escort of Elves.

"Fare you well," called Cotton after him, but Perry could say nought.

Then Perry and Cotton in turn took the hand of Durek and said goodbye. And Durek gave Cotton a small bag of silver pennies to see to their expenses on the way home, and a small silver cask, locked with a key, that they were not to open until they had returned to The Root—and what was inside was for the both of them. He returned to Perry the silveron armor; and the quarrel hole had been repaired by Durek himself, the arrow-shattered amber gem now replaced by a red jewel, and all the gems were now reinforced behind by starsilver links. And Durek bade him to put the armor on. Perry donned the mail but vowed, "I have had enough of fighting and War, and though I wear this armor, I will fight no more."

The Warrows and Shannon turned and began trudging west across the floor, along the Brega Path. Durek watched them go, and before they entered the west corridor he called out after them, "Perhaps I, too, will come to your Land of the Bosky."

And only silence followed.

The trio spent that night in the Grate Room, and the next morning they went on. When they came to the Bottom Chamber, Perry did not look at the cleft in the wall where Ursor had gone, but instead he hurried past with his eyes downcast to the stone floor. They came to the eight-foot-wide fissure and found that the Dwarves had constructed a wooden bridge over it to carry the supplies across, and the Warrows were relieved that they didn't have to leap above the dreadful depths of the Drawing Dark. Onward they went until they came to the stairs leading down to Dusk-Door, and at the bottom they found the gates standing wide and two Dwarves guarding the portal.

"This is where the Dark Mere was," said Cotton, pointing at

the black crater, "and all that rock down there is what used to cover the Door." Perry looked at the tons of debris strewn over the ancient courtyard, and wondered how the Dwarven Army had ever managed to move all that mass.

In silence they passed the cairns along the Great Loom, and only the sound of the free-flowing Duskrill intruded upon their thoughts. As they came to the vale, Cotton called Perry's attention to the Sentinel Falls, now a silver cascade, falling asplash upon a great mound of rock. "There stood the dam that was broken, and down under that heap of stone is the dead Monster." Perry looked on and shuddered.

That night they talked with members of the Dwarf Company at Dusk-Door and with two Valonian riders, messengers. They were told that most of the waggons now stood empty, the supplies having been taken into Kraggen-cor. Messages had been borne by rider south to Valon and Pellar and the Red Hills, and Dwarven kindred would be coming north to bring more supplies and to gather the wain horses from the Vanadurin and to take the surplus waggons and teams south. And some Dwarves would be coming north to remain in Drimmen-deeve.

Durek had sent word to the Company of the Dusken Door that Cotton, Perry, and Shannon would be coming, and a waggon with a team had been prepared with the provisions needed for the trip to Luren and to the Boskydells beyond.

The trio ate a short meal and then retired for the night.

The next morning, waving goodbye to the Dusk-Door Company, the trio in the wain started west down the Spur, Cotton at the reins. They emerged along the foothills and turned south, following the Old Rell Way toward the River Hâth. The Old Way wended toward Gûnar, and slowly the waggon rolled along its overgrown, abandoned bed. Shannon spoke of the days when there was trade between the Realms of Drimmen-deeve and Lianion—called Rell by Men—and the city of Old Luren, now destroyed. The roadbed they followed would lead to the new settlement on the site of those ancient ruins.

In late morning they crested a ridge and looked down into a wide grassy valley, where they saw a great herd of a thousand horses grazing beside a glittering stream in the winter pasture. Soon they came to the camp of the Harlingar, and there they were hailed by raven-helmed Brytta. And the riders were pleased to look once more upon the *Waldfolc,* and they treated the Elf with the utmost respect. And the three travellers took a meal with the Vanadurin; and Brytta ate with his left hand while he loosed an occasional oath at the awkwardness caused by his tender bandaged right. And in his oath-saying, he was joined by his bloodkith, Brath, whose left arm was broken, and by Gannon with the shattered fingers, who was fed by both of them, much to his disgust and their amusement.

They spoke on the War, and talked of the final battle, and then Cotton asked the Valanreach Marshal to tell his tale.

Brytta told them of the desperate ride to Quadran Pass in pursuit of the foul Rutchen spies, and the ambush and battle with the ravagers. Brytta's voice dropped low when he spoke of the Drōkh who may have escaped, for the Marshal yet held himself at fault in this, even though it was now clear that whether or not the Drōkh had reached the High Gate to warn Gnar, it had had no bearing on the outcome. Brytta then spoke of the long dash back to the Ragad Valley, summoned by Farlon's recall beacon, only to find the vale empty of the Dwarf Army, the Host having entered the Black Hole. And he told of bringing the wounded and the herd south, and of setting the guard atop the Sentinel Stand to signal should the Wrg flee the Dwarves' axes out through the Dusk-Door: "But the Spawn never came. . . ." His tale done, his voice dwindled to silence.

"Just so!" groused Wylf in the lull, his countenance chapfallen. "The Wrg never came . . . not while I was near. For during the battle of Stormhelm Defile, I was stuck atop Redguard Mount. And they came not the next night when I sat ambush on the road to Quadran Col. Nor did they flee out of the Door while I warded atop the Sentinel Stand. They never came to me, or to Farlon. We alone of all the brethren did not get to share in the great vermin-slaughter. Yet I suppose we served as well by watching for the enemy—though he never stood before us— and by tending the wounded and the herd. Even so, it seems that fortune could have thrown at least one or two Wrg our way."

"It was not ill fortune that kept the Spawn from you," declared Perry. "Rather, it was to your good, for War is bitter luck indeed." And the small Warrow fell silent and said no more, and Brytta looked at him with surprised eyes.

The Sun was bright and the air still, and in the grassy vale a gentle warmth o'erspread the land. All was quiet. But then the startling sound of sharp fife and tapping timbrel floated through the calm, and Perry saw nearby a loose circle of Brytta's Men sitting upon the earth. And from this circle came the pipe and tap. One by one the Men joined in the music, their hands clapping time to the air. Soon all there were sounding the beat, and some gave over their long-knives to comrades, who added the iron tocsin of blade on blade to the rhythm. Quickly the tune became more barbaric, wild fife and drum and steel on steel and strong hands clapping. And as Perry watched, a young warrior sprang to circle center and whirled 'round the fire, his feet stamping the earth, joining the savage beat. He spun and gyred and leapt high, and fierce shouts burst forth from his companions as the wild dancer whirled and tumbled and cartwheeled over the flames.

Perry's heart was tugged two ways, and he turned to Brytta: "How can they be so festive?" he asked, and his silent thoughts went on to add, *when so many have perished.*

Brytta's gaze strayed far away to a coppice of silver birch at the distant high eastern reach of the grassy vale. A great curving stone upjut on the mountain flanks cupped the grove, sheltering the clean-limbed trees from harsh mountain winds. Beyond Brytta's sight, but nevertheless seen by him, there, too, were five fresh mounds in the sward; five barrow mounds where five warriors slept the eternal sleep 'neath green turves: Arl, Dalen, Haddor, Luthen, and Raech, forever standing guard o'er the sheltered glen. And this dale became known in later years as the Valley of the Five Riders. It was said that weary, riderless horses often made their way to this place, to rest and heal and become strong again, to eat of the green grass and drink of the crystalline water springing forth from the stone bluff and flowing out and down through the peaceful land. And it was also said that at times in the dim twilight shadows or misty early dawn, the faint sound of distant oxen horns hovered on the edge of hearing.

Brytta's eyes rested momentarily upon the far wooded dell, and his sight misted over, and then he answered Perry: "It is not a gay dance, not a happy tune my scouts tap to. No, not festive; they are not festive. Yet in time they will be. For life continues, and grief fades."

Of a sudden, the wild piping and stamping dance, the tattoo beat and steely claque, and fierce clapping and savage shouts, all stopped; silence fell heavily down upon the still vale, and not an echo or whisper of the frenzied music remained. And Perry looked and saw that deep dolor pressed a heavy hand down upon them all.

At that moment, Hogon rode up leading two horses, and Cotton shouted in glee, "Brownie! Downy!" And he leapt up and ran to greet them as Hogon and Brytta smiled widely.

"We thought you would come hence," explained Hogon, "so we have kept them nearby."

"Oh, thank you, Hogon; thank you, Brytta," bubbled Cotton, and his face was aglow. "They are a sight for sore eyes." Then he turned to the horses, and they nuzzled and nudged the War-row. "Why, you rascals, you've grown fat and frisky in these parts! Wull, we're just going to have to work some o' that stoutness off of you."

And so, when Perry, Cotton, and Shannon said goodbye to the Men of Valon, it was Brownie and Downy in harness pulling the waggon toward the south. And as they at last crested the austral rim of the valley, the trio paused and looked far back into the vale, and waved to the distant Harlingar. And floating up to them on the breeze came the lornly cry of Brytta's black-oxen horn: *Taaa-tan, tan-taaa, tan-taaa! [Til we meet again, fare you well, fare you well!]* And with that faint call echoing in their hearts, Cotton flicked the reins and they passed from the sight of the Vanadurin.

The waggon rolled southward for two days, and just before sunset of the second day, they reached the River Hâth. The ford was shallow, and they made the crossing with ease. The aban-doned Old Way turned westward, and they followed its course. They drove by day and camped at night, and because it was winter they found the days short and blustery and the nights long and cold. They dressed as warmly as they could, donning the quilted down-suits given to them by the Dwarves; at night they camped in sheltered ravines and built warm fires. Still, by night and day alike, the icy chill drove a dull ache deeply into Perry's tender shoulder; and each morning when he awakened, his arm was stiff and could be moved but gingerly.

On the evening of the sixth day from the Dusk-Door, they arrived at the Ford of New Luren. Here, the abandoned way they followed joined the Ralo Road, and when that track passed north of New Luren, it became known as the North Route by some and as the South Route by others, yet most called it the Post Road. Just above Luren, the rivers Hâth and Caire joined, and the ever-changing swirl of the waters of their meeting was named the Rivermix. From that point on down to the sea, the river was called Isleborne by all except the Elves, who named it the Fainen. At Luren crossed the trade routes between Rell, Gûnar, Harth, and Trellinath, for here was the only ford in the region. And on the west bank of the ford was the site of Luren.

Old Luren had been a city of free trade serving river traffic and road commerce from all the regions around. It had suffered mightily during the ancient Dark Plague—more than half its populace had died—but slowly it had recovered, and though it did not reach its former heights of commerce, still it was a city of importance. But then a great fire raged throughout the city, and Luren was devastated and abandoned.

It was not until about fifty years ago that New Luren sprang up on the site, mainly serving travellers going up and down the Post Road and the Ralo Road. New Luren was but a small village surrounded by the great Riverwood Forest, yet it had an inn—the Red Boar—where the food was plentiful, the beer drinkable, and the rooms snug and cozy. Cotton drove the waggon across the ford and into the village.

When the three travellers stepped across the threshold and into the Red Boar, all conversation among the locals came to a halt as they craned their necks to get a look at these strangers. At first the Lurenites thought a fair youth and two boys had entered the inn; but then Perry and Cotton doffed their warm jackets, and there before the patrons stood two small warriors in silver and golden armor—and the fair youth in green was suddenly recognized to be one of the legendary Elf Lords. And a murmur washed throughout the common room:

Lor! Look at that. One of the Eld Ones. A Lian! If these are

*people out of legend, then the two small ones must be Waer-
linga, the Wee Folk.*

The proprietor, Mister Hoxley Housman, stepped forth.
"Well now, sirs, welcome to the Red Boar," he boomed, drawing them toward the cheery fireplace, and unlooked-for tears
sprang up in Cotton's eyes, for it was the first "proper place"
he'd been in since that night, oh so long ago, at the White Unicorn in Stonehill.

The next morning was one of sadness, especially for Perry,
for Shannon Silverleaf was turning back to Drimmen-deeve
and then going beyond to Darda Galion. Three ponies had been
purchased from innkeeper Housman, one for each of the Warrows to ride and one to carry their goods. Shannon would return
the horses and waggon to the Dwarves.

Cotton stood outside saying goodbye to Brownie and
Downy, while inside the Red Boar, Shannon looked at Perry
and smiled. "Friend Perry, I, too, think I'll visit you in the
Bosky—in summer, when the leaves are green and the flowers
bloom and your gardens begin putting forth their fruit. Not this
coming summer, but the next one instead, for I deem it will be
that long ere all will be ready for that encounter. But fear not, I
shall come, and I think others will too."

Together the Elf and the Warrow stepped out of the Red
Boar to join Cotton; and the pair of buccen said their goodbyes
to Shannon, and the Elf climbed up on the waggon and flicked
the reins, and drove back in the direction of Luren Ford as the
Warrows watched. Finally Perry and Cotton turned and clambered aboard their ponies and began the journey north and west,
up the Post Road toward the Boskydells, their pack pony trailing behind.

On the fourth day along the route, the Warrows came to a
fork in the road: the Post Road turned northwards, heading for
Stonehill; the left-hand road, the Tineway, swung westerly,
making for Tine Ford on the Spindle River, and the Boskydells
beyond. Along this way the buccen turned, and in the afternoon
of the next day they came to the great Spindlethorn Barrier. Into
the towering bramble they rode, following the way through the
vast tangle. It was late afternoon when they crossed over Tine

Ford and again entered the long thorny tunnel on the far side. Another hour or so they rode, and it was dusk when they finally emerged from the Barrier and came into the region known as Downdell. At last they were back in the Boskydells.

On the west side of the Spindlethorn they stopped the ponies and dismounted and stood looking out upon the land. Cotton peered through the twilight to the north and west, and filled his lungs with air. "It sure does feel good to be back in the Bosky," he observed, "back from them *Foreign Parts*. Why, here even the air has the right smell to it, though it's winter and the fields are waiting for the spring tilling, if you take my meaning. But though we're back in the Dells, we've still got a good bit left to go before we're back to The Root—about fifty leagues or so. Right, Mister Perry?" And Cotton turned to Perry, awaiting his answer.

But Perry was gazing back toward the thorny growth, along the dark road that they had come, looking in the direction of faraway Kraggen-cor, and his eyes brimmed with tears. "What . . . what, Cotton? Oh yes, another fifty leagues and we'll be home." And he quickly brushed his eyes with his sleeve and began fumbling with his pony's cinch strap.

The way from the Spindle River toward Eastwood and beyond to Woody Hollow, though long, was not arduous. And the Warrows rode during the day and camped at night, as they had throughout their journeys. On the fourth morning after entering the Boskydells they awakened to a light snowfall. They had camped south of Brackenboro on the eastern side of a trace of a road in the eaves of the Eastwood standing near. After breakfast they prepared to cut cross-country, striking directly for Byroad Lane through Budgens to Woody Hollow.

As they rode, the snow thickened, but there was little wind and the flakes fell gently. And for the first time in a long, long while, Cotton burst into song, and soon he was joined by Perry:

> *The snowflakes fall unto the ground,*
> *In crystal dresses turning 'round,*
> *Each one so white,*
> *Their touch so light,*
> *And falling down upon the mound.*

Yo ho! Yo ho! On sleighs we go,
To slip and slide on a wild ride.
Yo ho! Yo ho! Around the bend,
I wish this ride would never end.

The snow lies all across the land
And packs and shapes unto the hand,
Rolls into balls,
Shapes into walls,
Makes better forts than those of sand.

Yo ho! Yo ho! Let's throw the snow,
From bright fort walls sling white snowballs.
Yo ho! Yo ho! Here comes a hat,
Let fly the snow, knock it kersplat!

Let fly the snow, knock it:
Kersplat!

And both Warrows found themselves laughing in glee.

They rode all through the daylight hours and came to By-road Lane at dark. By then the snow was nearly a foot deep, and their ponies chuffed with the effort. Still the flakes swirled down thickly, but there was only a slight breeze, and neither Warrow was uncomfortable.

The ponies plodded through Budgens and past the Blue Bull. Yellow light shone out through the inn windows and across the white snow. Singing came from within; and as the two rode by, someone stepped through the door, and the song burst forth loudly, only to be muffled again when the door swung shut.

The Warrows rode on, and finally crossed the bridge over the Dingle-rill and passed beyond the mill. Their ponies plodded up into Hollow End, and they came at last to the curved hedge along the snow-covered stone walkway to The Root.

They had dismounted and were tethering the ponies to the hedge fence when the oaken door burst open, and out flew Holly. She hugged them both and kissed Perry. And Perry held her tightly and tears coursed down his cheeks, but he said nothing. And she held him close for a moment, and then drew them both inside. And there they found waiting a rich meal of roast goose and *three* places set at the table, for as Holly explained through her tears of happiness, "It's Year's End Eve, and I've been expecting you all day."

CHAPTER 10

THE HEROES

A year and a half had passed since Mister Perry and Cotton had come home, and the Bosky was bubbling with excitement. For on this day—Year's Long Day—there was to be a Ceremony. Oh, not just an *ordinary* Ceremony—with Mayor Whitlatch giving a speech and cutting a ribbon—but a real *King's* Ceremony. In fact, it was even better than that, for it was to be a *High King's Ceremony:* High King Darion *himself* had come with a great retinue to the Boskydells. But it wasn't only the High King that had come: it seemed as if every King in Mithgar was in the Dells . . . well, maybe not *every* King, but all the *important* ones had come; and the gossips and the tittle-tattles were having a field day:

There is that King from North Riamon, Kian, the one as what fought the Rūcks and such; there's that King Eanor from Valon and his Man Brytta, the ones as what came with all those horse riders; and lawks! there's even a Dwarf King, Durek, the one as what gave Mister Perry and Cotton that box of jools! Yes, and he's got that Dwarf with him the one as limps, Tobin something-or-other, and all his Company of Dwarf warriors what came in riding ponies, wouldn't you know, except for them two Dwarf striplings, them as what came riding on horses, just grinning and lording it as if they were doing something really special. But more, there's that Company of Elves with the Elf Lord, Vanidar Shannon Silverleaf, and if he ain't the King of the Elves, I'll eat my hat! And who knows what other Folks might come, what with more Outsiders *arriving all the time. Why, another whole bunch of them big Kingsguards rode in from Dael just this morning. Oh, it's a big day in the Bosky, all right, one that'll be remembered when it's long past.*

Yes, the Boskydells were all aflutter, because the *important* thing about the Ceremony was that all those Kings had come to honor two Warrows: Peregrin Fairhill and Cotton Buckleburr.

It's like the folks down to Budgens always say, "Whenever them Kings get into trouble they allus find they got to call on a Warrow *or two to settle them troubles, whatever they might be."*

But the folks of the Boskydells thought that the very *best* thing about the Ceremony was that right afterward there was going to be a big free meal down at the Hollow Commons, and everybody—I mean *everybody*—was invited.

And inside The Root, Holly fluttered about her husband of one year, getting him ready for the Ceremony. "I'm so proud of you, Perry, and Cotton, too," she chatted as she straightened his cloak collar and brushed back a stray curl, thinking how splendid her buccaran looked in his starsilver armor. "Imagine, you're to be named a Hero of the Realm."

"Oh, piffle," protested Perry, uncomfortably, "I'm not a hero. Anyone who's read my journal knows that I'm just an ordinary Warrow and not some great warrior." On the table by his bedside was his journal; it was open, and on the first page, in Perry's fine script, was written:

The Silver Call

*A Tale of Quest and War as
Seen by Two Warrows*

*The Journal of
Peregrin Fairhill*

"Well, I've read your journal," said Holly, "and a lot of others have too: the Ravenbrook Scholars, to name a few. And we all think that your story, and Cotton's, well, it's a tale of a noble quest."

"Ah, but my dammia, that's just it," sighed Perry. "My tale

wasn't meant to be noble; it was meant to tell of the horror of War. I wanted to tell of War as it *really* is. In so many tales, none of the heroes ever get killed or even hurt."

Perry paused, raising his hand to touch the blood-red jewel that marked the armor where the Rūck-arrow had pierced through. "Oh, some hearthtale heroes now and then have been slightly wounded, nothing more. But in most tales, only the villains die. And the heroes never suffer the pangs of fear or doubt, and the villains can't seem to do anything right. Well, that isn't what War is really like. In *real* War, many, many heroes are slaughtered, and feel fear, and make blunders. And the villains are victorious . . . oh, so often.

"And as to it being noble: this War, well, it was just fleeing and fighting and killing down in a great, dark hole in the earth. We slew living beings, Holly, without warning when we could—Rūcks and Hlōks to be sure, and an Ogru or two, but living things all the same."

"But it was necessary," insisted Holly. "Cotton says it was necessary; Kian says it was necessary; Shannon says it was necessary; Durek says so, and so does High King Darion, and all the Dwarves, Elves, and Big Men that have come to honor you."

"Necessary, yes; still it was abhorrent," said Perry. "And so many comrades, who didn't deserve to die, fell in battle. So who am I to be singled out with Cotton to be a hero? I'm just an insignificant character in the role of the world."

"Why, Mister Peregrin Fairhill, don't you go saying such a thing!" protested Holly, golden fire flashing deep in her great amber eyes. "If it weren't for you and Cotton, the maggot-folk would have won. They'd still be raiding and killing in the Lands around; and more: Shannon Silverleaf told me that if the Spawn had won, they would have started spreading out in the Grimwall Mountains again, and that would have spelled trouble for everyone. Why, they might even have tried to invade the Bosky after a time. But thanks to you and Cotton, that won't happen. You *are* Heroes of the Realm: Cotton's sword saved Durek from the Monster of the Mere, and Cotton was a Brega-Path guide, and he killed the Troll, and he carried the Horn of Narok; without Cotton doing those things, the quest would have failed. And you, Perry, you carried Bane that warned of maggot-folk, and you were a Brega-Path guide, and you found the key to the Gargon's Lair, and you solved the riddle of Narok; without you the Spawn would have won.

"Oh, you're heroes all right, but you just don't see that you are. Instead you say you are just some 'insignificant' character in the world. Well, don't you see that it is just the ones that you seem to think 'insignificant' that are truly important? It's on folks like you and Cotton that major events turn. Without you 'insignificant' ones, the world would fall before the cruel and evil.

"Now don't you go downplaying yourself just because you're a Warrow and not a King or a Big Man or a high Elf, or even a clever Dwarf. You're a Warrow, the best there is, and a Hero of the Realm, and that's why all the Kings are here to honor you and Cotton: King Eanor's Land of Valon is no longer being plundered; King Kian's subjects in Riamon no longer live in fear of Rūcks and Hlōks; and Shannon Silverleaf, Elf Lord of Darda Erynian, his Land of Galion is free of spoilers; the Halls of Kraggen-cor are once more filled with Dwarves, and King Durek reigns; and High King Darion, well, all is at peace in his Kingdoms again. And without you it would not have happened, and they've all come to pay you the highest homage because of it."

Not quite convinced, yet unwilling to argue further with his dammia, Perry stood still while Holly fastened the silver brooch at his collar. Again he fingered the blood-red jewel inset among the links of his armor; and deep within his shoulder there pulsed a dull ache, and he knew that within two days the weather would change. But he said nought and instead wished that these *formalities* would just get over and done with.

Holly, flicking one last invisible speck from Perry's cloak, stepped back and appraised her buccaran with a critical eye. "Well," she said at last, pride shining in her face, "it looks like you're ready. Now there's a Big Man waiting in the study with Cotton to escort you both before the assembled Kings. You'd better hurry on now before you're late."

Perry sighed and stepped out of the bedroom, and went down the hall and around the corner toward the study. As he approached that chamber, he saw an object on the table outside the study door. And his heart leapt, for it was a great black mace!

"Ursor!" he shouted, and ran into the room just as the great bear of a Baeran was getting to his feet. "Ursor!" cried Perry, and he wept and laughed, and the Big Man smiled, and Cotton grinned from ear to ear.

"Well, little one," huge Ursor rumbled, "we meet again." And he caught up the wee Warrow and embraced him with a *whoof!* and then sat him down on the edge of a table like a small child, the buccan's feet dangling and swinging.

"Ursor, we thought you were dead!" exclaimed Perry, an incredulous look on his face. "What happened? How did you escape? Tell me before I burst with perplexity!"

"It's a long tale, and we can't be late before the Kings," smiled the Baeran, fingering a deep scar that ran down his left cheek from the corner of his eye to his jaw. "I'll tell it in full after the Ceremony. Let me just say that I decided to mislead the Spawn up the north passage from the underground river, to make certain that they didn't follow my Liege Lord, Kian, now King of North Riamon. My running battle with that company of Wrg in the undelved halls of the Black Hole lasted long, and I did nearly die, but it was of starvation and not by Rutchen hand. I was lost, but at last found my way to the Dwarves—or they to me, for Durek had sent them searching right after the great battle. And they finally found me, and I was saved, three days after you had gone.

"But we will speak of the full story later, for I want to hear your tale from your own lips too," declared Ursor, Commander of the Kingsguard of Riamon. "But now the Kingdom awaits its Heroes."

And so they stood and stepped into the hall, where Ursor took up his great black mace and hung it from his belt; and they strode to the oaken door of The Root. Ursor opened the portal, and the sunshine outside was bright.

Through the doorway Perry could see, to his wonder, the Kings of Pellar, Valon, Riamon, and Kraggen-cor, and an Elf Lord of Darda Erynian: each down upon one knee, paying high homage to him and Cotton. Beyond the Kings, all the knights and warriors and attendants—Men, Dwarves, and Elves—of all the retinues also knelt on one knee. And beyond them it seemed as if every Warrow of the Boskydells stood quietly in End Field, waiting.

Perry looked up at Ursor, and over at Cotton, and last of all to Holly, and she beamed and inclined her head toward the open door. And Perry and Cotton, smiling, stepped forth into the sunshine, resplendent in their sparkling silver and glittering golden armor; and from the waiting multitude a mighty roar flew up to the sky.

". . . stature alone does not measure the greatness of a heart."

Lord Kian
October 7, 5E231

APPENDICES

A WORD ABOUT WARROWS

Common among the many races of Man throughout the world are the persistent legends of Little People: Wee Folk, pixies, leprechauns, sidhe, pwcas, gremlins, cluricaunes, peris, and so forth. There is little doubt that many of these tales come from Man's true memories of the Eld Days . . . memories of Dwarves, Elves, and others, harking back to the ancient times before The Separation. Yet, some of these legends *must* spring from Man's memory of a small Folk called Warrows.

Supporting this thesis, a few fragmentary records are unearthed once in a great age, records that give us glimpses of the truth behind the legends. But to the unending loss of Mankind, some of these records have been destroyed, while others languish unrecognized—even if stumbled across—for they require tedious examination by a scholar versed in strange tongues—tongues such as Pellarion—ere a glimmering of their true significance is seen.

One such record that has survived—and was stumbled across by an appropriately versed scholar—is *The Raven Book;* another is *The Fairhill Journal*. From these two chronicles, as well as from a meager few other sources, a factual picture of the Wee Folk can be pieced together, and deductions then can be made concerning Warrows:

They are a small Folk, the adults ranging in height from three to four feet. Some scholars argue that there seems to be little doubt that their root stock is Man, since Warrows are human in all respects—i.e., no wings, horns, tails, etc.—and they come in all the assorted shapes and colors that the Big Folk, the Men, do, only on a smaller scale. However, to the contrary, other scholars argue that the shape of Warrow ears—pointed—the tilt of their bright, strange eyes, and their longer life span indicates that some Elven blood is mingled in their veins. Yet their eyes do set them apart from Elvenkind: canted they are, and in that the two Folk are alike; but Warrow eyes are bright and liquescent, and the iris is large and strangely colored: amber like gold, the deep blue of sapphire, or pale emerald green.

In any case, Warrows are deft and quick in their smallness, and their mode of living makes them wood-crafty and nature-wise. And they are wary, tending to slip aside when an *Outsider* comes near, until the stranger's intentions can be ascertained. Yet they do not always yield to intruders: should one of the Big Folk come unannounced upon a group of Warrows—such as a large family gathering of Othens splashing noisily in the waters of the fen—the *Outsider* would note that suddenly all the Warrows were silently watching him, the dammen (females) and oldsters quietly drifting to the rear with the younglings clinging to them or peering around from behind, and the buccen (males) in the fore facing the stranger in the abrupt quiet. But it is not often that Warrows are taken by surprise, and so they are seldom seen in the forests and fens and wilds unless they choose to be; yet in their hamlets and dwellings they are little different from "commonplace" Folk, for they treat with *Outsiders* in a friendly manner, unless given reason to do otherwise.

Because of their wary nature, Warrows usually tend to dress in clothing that blends into the background: greys, greens, browns. And the shoes, boots, and slippers they wear are soft and quiet upon the land. Yet, during Fair Time, or at other Celebrations, they dress in bright splashes of gay, gaudy colors: scarlets, oranges, yellows, blues, purples; and they love to blow horns and strike drum, gong, and cymbal, and in general be raucous.

Some of the gayest times, the most raucous, are those which celebrate the passing from one Warrow age to another, not only the "ordinary" birthday parties, but in particular those when an "age-name" changes: Children, both male and female, up to the age of ten are called "younglings." From age ten to twenty, the males are called "striplings," and the females, "maidens." From age twenty to thirty, males and females are called respectively "young buccen" and "young dammen." It is at age thirty that Warrows reach majority—come of age, as it were—and until sixty are then called "buccen," or "dammen," which are also the general names for male or female Warrows. (The terms "buccen" and "dammen" are plurals; by changing the "e" to an "a", "buccan" and "damman" refer to just one male or female Warrow.) After sixty, Warrows become "eld buccen" and "eld dammen," and beyond the age eighty-five are called respectively "granthers" and "grandams." And at each of these "special" birthday parties, drums tattoo, horns blare, cymbals clash, and bells ring; gaudy colors adorn the celebrants; and annually, on Year's Long Day, during Fair Time, bright fireworks light up the sky for all who have had a birthday or birthday anniversary in the past year—which, of course, includes everyone—but especially for those who have passed from one age-name to the next.

Once past their youth, Warrows tend to roundness, for ordinarily they eat four meals a day, and on feast days, five. As the elders tell it: "Warrows are small, and small things take a heap of food to keep 'em going. Look at your birds and mice, and look especially at your shrews: they're all busy gulping down food most of the time that they're awake. So us Wee Folk need at least four meals a day just to keep a body alive!"

Warrow home and village life is one of pastoral calm. The Wee Folk often come together to pass the day: the dammen klatch at sewings or cannings; the buccen and dammen gather at the field plantings and harvests, or at the raising or digging of a dwelling, or at picnics and reunions—noisy affairs, for Warrows typically have large families.

Within the home, at "normal" mealtimes all members of a household—be they master, mistress, brood, or servantry—flock 'round the table in one large gathering to share the food and drink, and to speak upon the events of the day. But at "guest" meals, customarily only the holtmaster, his family, and the guests come to the master's table to share the repast; rarely are other members of the holt included at that board, and then only when specifically invited by the head of the house. At meal's end, especially when "official business" is to be discussed, the younger offspring politely excuse themselves, leaving the elders alone with the visitors to deal with their "weighty matters."

Concerning the "hub" of village life, every hamlet has at least one inn, usually with good beer—some inns have the reputation of having better beer than the average—and here gather the buccen, especially the granthers, some daily, others weekly, and still others less frequently; and they mull over old news, and listen to new happenings, and speculate upon the High King's doings down in Pellar, and talk about the state that things have come to.

There are four strains of northern Warrows: Siven, Othen, Quiren, and Paren, dwelling respectively in burrows, fen stilt-houses, tree flets, and stone field-houses. (Perhaps the enduring legends concerning intelligent badgers, otters, squirrels, and hares, as well as other animals, come from the lodging habits of the Wee Folk.) And Warrows live, or have lived, in practically every country in the world, though at any given time some Lands host many Warrows while other Lands host few or none. The Wee Folk seem to have a history of migration, yet in those days of the *Wanderjahren* many other Folk also drifted across the face of the world.

In the time of the writing of both *The Raven Book* and *The Fairhill Journal,* most northern Warrows resided in one of two places: the Weiunwood, a shaggy forest in the Wilderland north of Harth and south of Rian; or in the Boskydells, a Land of fens, forests, and fields west of the Spindle River and north of the Wenden.

The Boskydells, by and far the largest of these two Warrow-lands, is protected from *Outsiders* by a formidable barrier of thorns—Spindlethorns—growing in the river valleys around the Land. This maze of living stilettoes forms an effective shield surrounding the Boskydells, turning aside all but the most determined. There are a few roads within long thorn tunnels passing through the barrier, and during times of crisis, within these tunnels Warrow archers stand guard behind movable barricades made of the Spindlethorn, to keep ruffians and other unsavory characters outside while permitting ingress to those with legitimate business. In generally peaceful times, however, these ways are left unguarded, and any who want to enter may do so.

In that warm October of 5E231, when this tale begins, it was a time of peace.

An Abbreviated Family Tree
of Peregrin Fairhill

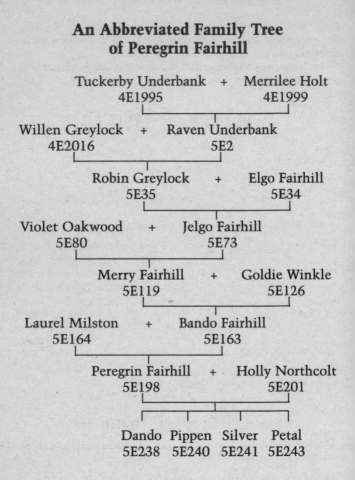

Tuckerby Underbank   +   Merrilee Holt
4E1995   4E1999

Willen Greylock   +   Raven Underbank
4E2016   5E2

Robin Greylock   +   Elgo Fairhill
5E35   5E34

Violet Oakwood   +   Jelgo Fairhill
5E80   5E73

Merry Fairhill   +   Goldie Winkle
5E119   5E126

Laurel Milston   +   Bando Fairhill
5E164   5E163

Peregrin Fairhill   +   Holly Northcolt
5E198   5E201

Dando   Pippen   Silver   Petal
5E238   5E240   5E241   5E243

CALENDAR OF THE SILVER CALL

Some Events of the Second Era

In the final days of the Second Era, the Great War of the Ban is fought. On the High Plane, Adon prevails over the Great Evil, Gyphon; on the Middle Plane, by an unexpected stroke the Grand Alliance is victorious and vile Modru is defeated upon Mithgar. Adon sets His Ban upon the creatures of the Untargarda, who aided Gyphon in the War: they are forever banished from the light of Mithgar's Sun, and henceforth those who would defy the Ban suffer the Withering Death. Gyphon, swearing vengeance, is exiled beyond the Spheres. Thus does the Second Era end and the Third Era begin . . . and so matters stand for some four thousand years, until the Fourth Era is some two millennia old.

Some Events of the Fourth Era

4E1995: Tuckerby Underbank born in Woody Hollow, Eastdell, the Boskydells.

4E2013: Comet Dragon Star flashes through the heavens of Mithgar, nearly striking the world. Great flaming, gouting chunks score the night skies, some pieces hurtling to earth. Many see this hairy star as a harbinger of doom.

4E2018: Tuckerby Underbank, Danner Bramblethorn, Patrel Rushlock, and other Thornwalkers set out from Woody Hollow to join the Eastdell Fourth Company to walk Wolf Patrol and stand Beyonder Guard. This mission ultimately will become the quest that will culminate in Modru's downfall. In this year the Winter War begins.

4E2019: The Deevewalkers pass through Drimmen-deeve from Dusk-Door to Dawn-Gate; the Dwarf Brega is one of the Four. Also in this year, the Winter War ends as Modru is destroyed and Gyphon's Gate is closed. Rūcks, Hlōks, and Ogrus are slain or flee, and over the next few years many Spawn come to Drimmen-deeve to join the Horde there.

Some Events of the Fifth Era

October 15, 5E2: Raven Underbank is born in Woody Hollow, Eastdell, the Boskydells.

Circa 5E7: Tuckerby Underbank is commissioned by the High King to gather and record the history of the Winter War, a work that is to take his lifetime and will be called *Sir Tuckerby Underbank's Unfinished Diary and His Acounting of the Winter War.* In the work, Tuck will be assisted by many scholars and scribes, but mainly by his daughter Raven. In later years, Tuck will refer to the work as *The Raven Book.*

5E26: Brega the Dwarf, DelfLord of the Red Hills, at the urging of Tuckerby Underbank, records the Brega Scroll, detailing the path taken by the Deevewalkers through Kraggen-cor.

5E31: Raven Underbank marries Willen Greylock. They move to the Cliffs, Westdell, the Boskydells, where Willen founds the Ravenbook Scholars.

Circa 5E40: Tuckerby's Warren, The Root, becomes a museum housing artifacts of the Winter War.

Circa 5E47: Rumors abound of many Elves passing to Adonar upon the High Plane, leaving Mithgar behind.

December 31, 5E73: Eleventh Yule: Year's End Day: Tuckerby Underbank, Bearer of the Red Quarrel, 'Stone Slayer, Hero of the Realm, dies at the age of 97.

5E193: Brega, Bekki's son, DelfLord of the Red Hills, dies at the age of 242. Thus passes away the last of the mortal Heroes of the Winter War.

5E198: Peregrin (Perry) Fairhill born at the Cliffs.

5E205: Cotton Buckleburr born in Brackenboro, the Boskydells.

5E222: Perry makes his copy of *The Raven Book.*

5E228: Perry comes of age and moves to Woody Hollow as the new Scholar of The Root. Holly becomes housekeeper of The Root. Cotton is hired as general handywarrow of The Root, where he becomes Perry's friend and companion. Perry discovers the Brega Scroll.

5E229: Gnar the Cruel arises as supreme leader of all Rūcks, Hlōks, and Ogrus in Drimmen-deeve; Raids in Riamon and Valon begin.

5E230: Seventh Durek, Dwarf King in Mineholt North, asks Lord Kian to guide Anval and Borin Ironfist, Dwarf warriors and Mastercrafters, to High King Darion in Pellar to advise him of the Dwarves' plans to reoccupy Drimmen-deeve. At court, the two Dwarves learn of the Spawn in Drimmen-deeve and pledge to cleanse the caverns of that evil. King Darion informs the Dwarves that the tale of the Deevewalkers, told in *The Raven Book,* in the Boskydells, may reveal detail of Drimmen-deeve's halls and passageways, detail useful in any War conducted in the caverns.

The Quest of Kraggen-cor
5E231

October 9: Lord Kian, Anval, and Borin arrive in Woody Hollow and come to The Root. Perry's copy of *The Raven Book* is examined, and the tale of the Deevewalkers is told. Perry shows the visitors the Brega Scroll, which has the detail the Dwarves seek. Perry has memorized the complicated Brega Scroll and volunteers to guide the Dwarves along the Brega Path.

October 10: Cotton decides to go with Perry on the quest.

October 11–12: Perry, Cotton, Anval, Borin, and Lord Kian leave The Root and Woody Hollow by waggon, heading for the rendezvous with Durek's Army at Landover Road Ford, beyond the Grimwall Mountains. Cotton sounds the Horn of the Reach in Budgens; the Dwarves examine the horn and regard it as a token of fear, muttering the word *Narok*. Travelling by the east-west Crossland Road, they stay at the Happy Otter Inn in Greenfields the first night out. Travel the next day carries them out of the Boskydells, and they camp in the eaves of Edge-wood.

October 13–23: Travel eastward continues, and sword training begins. Nights are spent encamped on the southern slopes of the Battle Downs, at the White Unicorn Inn in Stonehill, and in encampments north of the Bogland Bottoms, at Beacontor, within the Wilderness Hills, along the margins of the Drear-wood, and then at Arden Ford. The ford is flooded and they cannot cross.

October 24–26: Arden Ford floodwaters slowly recede. (Full Moon, October 26)

October 27–28: Arden Ford is crossed. Perry and Cotton are swept downriver by the floodwaters, but they are rescued. That night the comrades camp in the foothills of the Grimwall Mountains, and the next night up in the high country.

October 29: The travellers cross through the Crestan Pass, over the Grimwall Mountains. The waggon is destroyed by a rock-slide.

October 30–31: The companions continue on foot toward the Landover Road Ford. In the foothills they meet Passwarden Baru and his sons. Marching onward, the travellers follow the Landover Road beyond the foothills and across the plains to come at last to the river-border forest along the Argon River, ar-riving at the ford to await Durek and the Dwarf Army.

November 1: Durek and the Army arrive at Landover Road Ford at midnight.

November 2: The Dwarf Army crosses the river. They are ac-companied by forty riders of Valon who act as scouts, led by

Brytta, Marshal of the North Reach. Also, Lord Kian's brother, Rand, is with Durek. The Warrows discover that Lord Kian is heir to the Throne of North Riamon. The Council of Durek is held. It is decided that the Army will march over the mountains and south to Dusk-Door and try to enter; it is also decided that a small squad will not cross the mountains, but instead will go south down the Argon River and then west across the wold and attempt to sneak through Dawn-Gate and penetrate the length of the Spawn-infested caverns and, from the inside, repair the hinges of Dusk-Door, if they are broken. Cotton is to go with Rand, Durek, Brytta, and the Army as their Brega-Path guide; Perry is to go with the squad, consisting of Lord Kian and the Dwarves Anval, Borin, Barak, Delk, and Tobin. That night, Durek tells Perry and Cotton the Legend of Narok, a riddle of the silver horn foretelling a doom of sorrow to befall the Dwarves.

November 3: The Army and Cotton leave the ford and march toward the Crestan Pass, heading over the Grimwall Mountains toward Dusk-Door, on the west side of the range.

The Squad and Perry stay at the ford, and Kian outlines how to build a raft.

November 4: The army arrives at the Passwarden's cottage in the foothills.

The Squad cuts logs for the raft.

November 5: The Army marches to the edge of the timberline below the Crestan Pass. Late at night, Rolf, Baru's son, arrives and warns that the cold wind blowing down means that a blizzard is on the way.

The Squad fashions the log bed of the raft.

November 6: The Army crosses the Crestan Pass in a blizzard and struggles to a sheltering pine forest on the far side of the mountains.

The Squad completes the raft, and a cold rain begins that evening.

November 7: The blizzard continues, trapping the Army in the shelter of the pines.

The Squad embarks downriver and arrives at Great Isle by nightfall; the cold rain continues.

November 8: The blizzard ends, but the Army is snowbound; the dig-out begins.

The rain ends and the river brings the Squad to the far northern reaches of the Dalgor March.

November 9: The dig-out ends at sundown, and the Army moves down out of the snow.

The Squad floats past the mouth of the Dalgor River and comes to the far southern reaches of the Dalgor March.

November 10: The Army begins a forced march to Dusk-Door; they are three days behind schedule because of the blizzard.

The Squad rides the raft through the Race, and at nightfall they come to the final campsite on the river; Drimmen-deeve and Dawn-Gate lie five days' march overland to the west.

November 11–14: The Army forced march continues; rain on the thirteenth causes waggons to mire and the march is slowed.

The Squad makes final plans while waiting to set out for Dawn-Gate.

November 15: The Army forced march continues.

A Rūcken raiding party falls upon the Squad: Barak is slain; Tobin is wounded; the Squad is saved by the Elf Shannon Silverleaf, Ursor the Baeran, and a company of Elf warriors.

November 16: The Army forced march continues.

Barak's funeral is held. Tobin is borne toward Darda Erynian by the Elf Company. Shannon and Ursor join the Squad.

November 17–21: The Army's forced march ends on the eighteenth as they draw nearly even with their schedule, and they continue at a normal pace toward Dusk-Door, passing beyond the old road that leads up toward Quadran Pass on the twentieth. Brytta learns of a legendary but lost High Gate in the Pass and posts a guard to watch for Spawn should they come from that way.

The Squad marches over the wold toward Dawn-Gate. On the twentieth they arrive at the foothills that border the valley leading onto the Pitch. The Squad arrives at Drimmen-deeve on the twenty-first.

November 22: The Army arrives at Dusk-Door, one day late.

The Squad enters Drimmen-deeve through Dawn-Gate and slays the guards and a large number of *Spaunen*. The Squad crosses the Great Deep and finds a way around the collapsed Hall of the Gravenarch.

November 23: The Army begins removal of the rubble blocking the way into Dusk-Door. At sunset the Krakenward attacks. The battle between the Army and the Monster rages all night.

The Squad sneaks to the Grate Room, about halfway to Dusk-Door, where they are discovered by *Spaunen* and flee to the Gargon's Lair and are trapped.

November 24: The Krakenward is finally slain by the Army at dawn. A short while later, one of the Valonian scouts left at Quadran Pass arrives bearing news that the Dwarf Army has been discovered by Rūcken spies now fleeing for the High Gate in Quadran Gap. Brytta's riders depart on a desperate mission to intercept the Spawn. At Dusk-Door, rubble removal begins again; cairns are built for the many Dwarf dead.

That night, Brytta's force springs a trap on the Rūcken spies, slaying all, they think, but one Hlōk, who may have escaped to warn Gnar.

The Squad free themselves from the Gargon's Lair, but Delk, the last Gatemaster, is slain. Later, the Squad finds the underwater path to again elude the Spawn.

November 25: The stone rubble covering Dusk-Door is finally removed; the Dwarf Army enters Kraggen-cor at midnight. (Full Moon)

Just after midnight, a Valanreach recall beacon in Ragad Valley is lit, and Brytta's force, not knowing the reason for the balefire, begins a race from Stormhelm Defile to the vale.

The Squad topples the stone blocking the way into the Bottom Chamber. Kian, Shannon, and Ursor mislead the *Rûpt* while Perry, Anval, and Borin press on toward Dusk-Door through Spawn-infested passages. Kian and Shannon are separated from Ursor.

November 26: The Army rescues Perry, Anval, and Borin from a company of Spawn. The Host marches toward the Second Hall. Kian and Shannon are rescued at the Grate Room.

Brytta's force arrives back at the Valley of the Door to find the Dwarves have entered Kraggen-cor. The Vanadurin withdraw to a grassy vale to tend the wounded and to put the Dwarves' great herd of horses to pasture.

November 27: The Army arrives at the War Hall.

November 28: The final battle is fought between the Spawn and the Dwarves in Kraggen-cor; Perry is wounded. Many comrades are slain. The Horn of Narok is sounded and the *Spaunen* Horde is destroyed.

November 29 to December 13: Perry sufficiently recovers from his wound so that on the thirteenth he decides to return to The Root.

December 14–15: Perry, Cotton, and Shannon travel the Brega Path to Dusk-Door and leave Drimmen-deeve.

December 16–21: Perry, Cotton, and Shannon travel from Drimmen-deeve to New Luren. On the sixteenth they pass through the valley where the Vanadurin tend the herd, and they bid farewell to Brytta and his Men. On the twenty-first the three come to New Luren, where they stay overnight in the Red Boar Inn.

On the seventeenth, a Dwarf search party finds Ursor alive but starving in the caverns.

December 22: Shannon turns back from New Luren, heading for Drimmen-deeve and beyond to Darda Erynian. Perry and Cotton, riding ponies, leave New Luren for the Boskydells.

December 23–29: Perry and Cotton follow the Post Road to the Tineway, crossing Tine Ford and entering the Boskydells on the twenty-sixth. (Full Moon, December 25)

December 30: Year's End Eve. Snow. Perry and Cotton arrive in the evening at The Root. End of Quest.

Three Later Events

5E232: Perry writes *The Silver Call,* a journal of the quest.
June 5: Perry marries Holly Northcolt.

5E233: June 21: Year's Long Day: Perry and Cotton are named Heroes of the Realm by High King Darion. The Ceremony is attended by High King Darion of Pellar, King Kian of Riamon, King Eanor of Valon, King Durek of Kraggen-cor, Elf Lord Vanidar Shannon Silverleaf of Darda Erynian, Ursor the Baeran, Brytta of the Valanreach, Tobin Forgefire, and many Elves, Dwarves, and Men of the Realm, and by a great number of Boskydell Warrows.

Songs, Inscriptions, and Redes

[Listed by: type; title; first line; volume and chapter(s) of appearance]

Warrow saying: Brave as Budgens (Vol. I, Chap. 6)

Warrow song: "Song of the Night Watch": The flames, they flicker, the shadows dance (Vol. I, Chap. 6)

Free Folk saying: Vulg's black bite slays at night (Vol. I, Chap. 7)

Inscription on the Tomb of Othran: Blade shall brave vile Warder (Vol. I, Chap. 7)

Stonehill song: "The Battle of Weiunwood": From northern wastes came Dimmendark (Vol. I, Chap. 7)

Warrow song: "The Road Winds On": The Road winds on before us—(Vol. I, Chap. 8)

Dwarf rhyme: "Time's Road": The Past, the Present, the Future (Vol. I, Chap. 8)

Warrow saying: Yesterday's Seeds are Tomorrow's Trees (Vol. I, Chap. 8)

Warrow saying: Word from the Beyond (Vol. I, Chap. 10)

Dwarf pledge: *Shok Châkka amonu!* (Vol. I, Chaps. 13, 14; Vol. II, Chap. 6)

Dwarven inscription on the Horn of Narok: Answer to/The Silver Call (Vol. I, Chap. 13)

Dwarven (?) staves: *The Rime of Narok:* Trump shall blow (Vol. I, Chap. 13; Vol. II, Chap. 8)

Elven dirge: From mountain snows of its birth (Vol. I, Chap 17)

Dwarf War cry: *Châkka shok! Châkka cor!* (Vol. I, Chap. 3; Vol. II, Chaps. 4, 6, 7)

Vanadurin benediction: Arise, Harlingar, to Arms! (Vol. II, Chap. 5)

Valonian Battle cries: Hál Vanareich! (Vol. II, Chap. 5)

Warrow song: "Yo Ho! Yo Ho! Here Comes the Snow!": The snowflakes fall unto the ground (Vol. II, Chap. 9)

Translations of Words and Phrases

Throughout *The Fairhill Journal* appear many words and phrases in languages other than the Common Tongue, Pellarion. For scholars interested in such things, these words and phrases are collected in this appendix. A number of tongues are involved:

Châkur	=	Dwarven tongue
OHR	=	Old High tongue of Riamon
OP	=	Old tongue of Pellar
Slûk	=	Spawn tongue
Sylva	=	Elven tongue
Twyll	=	ancient Warrow tongue
Valur	=	ancient War-tongue of Valon

The following table is a cross-check list of the most common terms found in various tongues in *The Raven Book* and *The Fairhill Journal*.

————Men————

Warrow (Twyll)	Valon (Valur)	Pellar (Pellarion)	Elf (Sylva)	Dwarf (Châkur)
Rūck	Rutch	Rukh	Ruch	Úkh
Rūcks	Rutcha	Rukha	Rucha	Úkhs
Rūcken	Rutchen	Rukken	Ruchen	Úkken
Hlōk	Drōkh	Lōkh	Lok	Hrōk
Hlōks	Drōkha	Lōkha	Loka	Hrōks
Hlōken	Drōken	Lōkken	Loken	Hrōken
Ghūl	Guul	Ghol	Ghūlk	Khōl
Ghûls	Guula	Ghola	Ghūlka	Khōls
Ghūlen	Guulen	Gholen	Ghûlken	Khōlen
Dread	Dread	Dread	Dread/ Draedan	Dread
Gargon	Gargon	Gargon	Gargon	Ghath
Gargons	Gargons	Gargons	Gargoni	Ghaths
Ogru	Ogru	Troll	Troll	Troll
Kraken	Kraken	Kraken	Hèlarms	Madûk
maggot-folk	Wrg	Yrm	Rûpt	Grg
Spawn	Spawn	Spawn; Spaunen	Spaunen	Squam
Dwarf	Dwarf	Dwarf	Drimm	Châk
Dwarves	Dwarves	Dwarves	Drimma	Châkka
Dwarven	Dwarven	Dwarven	Drimmen	Châkka
Elf	Deva	Elf	Lian;* Dylvan	Elf
Elves	Deva'a	Elves	Lian; Dylvana	Elves
Elven	Deven	Elven	Lianen; Dylvanen	Elven
Giant	Giant	Utrun	Utrun	Utrun
Giants	Giants	Utruni	Utruni	Utruni
Warrow	Walden	Waerling	Waerling	Waeran
Warrows	Waldana	Waerlinga	Waerlinga	Waerans
Wee Folk	Waldfolc	Wee Folk	—	—

*The Elves consist of two strains: (1) the Lian, the First Elves, and (2) the Dylvana, the Wood Elves.

In the following text, words and phrases are listed under the tongue of origin. Where possible, direct translations () are provided; in other cases, the translation is inferred from the context {} of *The Fairhill Chronicle* or *The Raven Book*. Also listed is the more common name [], where applicable.

Châkur
(Dwarven Tongue)

Aggarath {stone-loom} [Grimspire]

Baralan {sloping land} [the Pitch]

Châk (Dwarf)

Châk-alon {Dwarf pure-spirit}

Châkkacyth Ryng (Dwarvenkith Ring)

Châka dök! (Dwarves halt!)

Châkka shok! Châkka cor! (Dwarven axes! Dwarven might!)

Châk-Sol (Dwarf-Friend)

Ctor (shouter) [Bellon Falls]

Daūn {sunrise} [Dawn]

DelfLord {Lord of the delvings}

Dēop {deep}

Dusken {sundown}

Faugh! {untranslated exclamation of contempt or disgust}

Gaard! {a Wizard-word perhaps meaning Move!; Act!}

Ghatan {ringmount = Mountain of the (Châkkacyth) Ring} [Loftcrag]

Ghath (horror) [Gargon]

Hauk! (Advance!)

Hola! {Untranslated exclamation used to express surprise or to call attention}

Kala! (Good!)

Khana (Breakdeath)

Khana Durek! (Breakdeath Durek!)

Kraggen-cor {Mountain-might} [Drimmen-deeve]

Kruk! {untranslated expletive of frustration or rage}

Madûk {evil monster} [Hèlarms, Kraken, Krakenward, Monster]

Mitheor {mid-earth} [Mithgar]

Mountain {living stone} [living stone, mountain]

Narok (Death-War)

Rávenor {storm hammer} [Stormhelm; the Hammer]

Shok Châkka amonu! (The axes of the Dwarves are with you!)

trothmate {true-pledged mate}

Uchan {anvil} [Greytower]

Vorvor {wheel} [Durek's Wheel]

ziggurt {shatter-rock}

OHR
(Old High Tongue of Riamon)

myrk {murk}
swordthane {sword warrior}

OP
(Old Tongue of Pellar)

Larkenwald {lark wood} [Darda Galion; Eldwood]
Rach! {untranslated expletive expressing frustration}
Untargarda {Under Worlds}
Weiunwood {wee-one-forest}

Slûk
(Spawn Tongue)

Glâr! (fire)
Gnar skrike! {Gnar commands!}
Ngash batang lûktah glog graktal doosh spturrskrank azg!
{untranslated invective}
Ptang glush! {After them!}
Sklurr! {Now!}
Tuuth Uthor {dread striker; fear lash}
Waugh! {untranslated exclamation expressing startled fright}

Sylva
(Elven Tongue)

Aevor {wind-dark = Darkwind Mountain} [Grimspire]
Alor (Lord)
Chagor {jag-top} [Loftcrag]
Coron (king/ruler) [Stormhelm]
Dara {Lady}
Darda Erynian {leaf-tree hall-of-green = Greenhall Forest}
[Greenhall Forest; the Great Greenhall; Blackwood (of old)]
Darda Galion {leaf-tree land-of-larks = Forest of the Silver-
larks} [Larkenwald; Eldwood]
Draedan (Dread One) [Gargon]
Drimm (Dwarf)
Drimmen-deeve (Dwarven-delvings) [Kraggen-corr]

Dylvana {wood-Elves}
Falanith {valley rising} [the Pitch]
Gralon {grey stone} [Greytower]
gramarye {spell-casting} [sorcery]
Hèlarms {hell arms} [Kraken, Krakenward, Madûk, Monster]
Lian {First Elves}
Lianion {first land}
mian {waybread}
Mithgar {mid-earth}
Ogruthi {Trollfolk}
Vanidar (vani = silver; dar = leaf) [Silverleaf]
Vanil (silvery)
Vani-lērihha (Silverlarks)

Twyll
(ancient Warrow Tongue)

Cor! {untranslated exclamation used to express wonderment}
Hoy! {untranslated exclamation used to express surprise or to call attention}
Lawks! {Lord!; Mercy!; Lord of mercy!; Lord have mercy!}
Lor! {Lord!}
Lumme! {Love me!}
Wanderjahren (wandering days)

Valur
(ancient Battle-tongue of Valon)

A-raw, a-rahn! (A foe, alert!) [Valonian horncall]
Ai-oi! {untranslated exclamation to express astonishment or to call attention}
Arn! {untranslated interjection used to express ironic reversal}
B'reit, Harlingar! (Ready, Sons of Harl!)
Dracongield {Dragon-gold}
Dwarvenfolc {Dwarvenfolk}
Garn! {untranslated expletive used to express disappointment or frustration}
Hahn! (Here!) [Valonian horncall]
Hai roi! {untranslated exclamation, an enthusiastic call of greeting}
Hál! (Hail!)

Hál Vanareich! (Hail Valon!) {Hail our nation!}

Harlingar (Sons of Harl) [Men of Valon]

Hèl {Hell}

Hola! {untranslated exclamation used to express surprise or a greeting}

Kop'yo V'ttacku Rutcha! (Now whelm the goblins!)

Rach! {untranslated exclamation used to express frustration}

Skut! {untranslated exclamation used to express rage or frustration}

Stel! (Steel!)

Ta-roo! Ta-roo! Tan-tan, ta-roo! (All is clear! All is clear! Horsemen and allies, the way is clear!) [Valonian horncall]

Taaa-tan, tan-taaa, tan-taaa! (Till we meet again, fare you well, fare you well!) [Valonian horncall]

Tan-ta-ra {Answer me} [Valonian horncall]

Tovit! (Ready!)

Valanreach {Valon-reich}

Vanadurin {bond-lasting = our lasting bond}

V'ttacku! (Attack!)

Waldfolc {wood-folk = folk of the woods} [Warrows]

A Note on the Lost Prison

As to the Gargon's Lair: It remains uncertain to this day whether or not the chamber was delved specifically to be a prison for the Gargon. It seems more likely that the room was delved as a treasure store, and the Gargon, fleeing Adon's Ban, became trapped when the door closed behind it, and the creature had not the means or the power to escape. But then we are left with the mystery of whom the room belonged to, and why they did not inadvertently release the Dread when visiting the chamber.

Concerning this second point—why they did not accidentally free the creature—perhaps the unknown delvers knew the Gargon was trapped inside the room; in fact, they might have sprung the trap knowing the evil Vûlk would be captured in the chamber.

As to who delved the room, that, too, is a mystery; the work was both like and yet unlike that of the Lian (see Volume II, Chapter 3); but we know from Dwarven lore that the Châkka believe that the Eld Durek was the first to stride Kraggen-cor when he survived the Vorvor (see Volume II, Chapter 9); and then he brought his folk to make it into a mighty Kingdom, and that was ere the Ban War; which leads to the following dilemma: Would the Dwarves permit the Lian to delve a Vûlk prison or a treasure store within the Dwarven Realm? On the other hand, had the Dwarves known of the chamber, would they later have forgotten and delved the starsilver shaft toward the prison? Perhaps they knew of the chamber but not that the Gargon could burst through stone walls and layers of mineral-veined rock.

The runes "west-pick" were vaguely similar to those of the Lian. The chamber was like yet unlike Lian work. Dwarves learned much craft from the Lian, according to Delk (see Volume II, Chapter 3). Yet whether the chamber was Dwarven-delved, Elven-delved, or Other-delved, many questions remain unanswered.

Elven lore spoke of the Lost Prison, and maintained that great evil was entrapped beneath the Grimwall; yet how they knew of it is not told. It was further believed by the Elves that Modru, preparing for the coming of the Dragon Star, somehow used his evil art to cause the Dwarves to drive a silveron shaft toward the Gargon's Lair, according to Silverleaf (see Volume II, Chapter 3). And thus it was Modru who caused the Gargon to be freed.

If not Dwarf-delved, or Lian-delved, then who made the chamber? Ravenbook Scholars continue to debate the issue. Most believe the room was delved as a treasure store by a group of Dwarves with Lian help. The Scholars further believe that all those who knew of it, and of the silveron lode, were later slain in the Great War of the Ban, and thus the secret of the chamber died with them, though rumors of the chamber's existence persisted. It is also the general belief that the Gargon accidentally trapped itself within the chamber as it was fleeing from Adon's Covenant, but that somehow this became known to the Lian Guardians, who then told of the vile creature trapped in the legendary Lost Prison.

Recall the words of Barak (see Volume I, Chapter 17): "Some doors lead to secret treasure rooms, or secret weapons rooms, or secret hideaways . . . Yet such rooms must be entered with caution, for once inside the door may close and vanish, trapping the unwary in a sealed vault—it is a defence against looters and other evil beings . . . without the key, even a Wizard or evil Vûlk cannot pass through some hidden doors." Ravenbook Scholars believe that Barak essentially described how the Gargon came to be entrapped in that chamber, but none profess to know how the chamber itself came into being.

Glossary

	In this glossary:	
Châkur	=	**Dwarven tongue**
OHR	=	**Old High tongue of Riamon**
OP	=	**Old tongue of Pellar**
Slûk	=	**Spawn tongue**
Sylva	=	**Elven tongue**
Twyll	=	**ancient Warrow tongue**
Valur	=	**ancient War-tongue of Valon**

(the) Account: Tuckerby Underbank's accounting of the Winter War as told to the scriveners of *The Raven Book*. Also the accounts of others recorded in the same book.

Adon: the high deity of Mithgar. Also known as High Adon, the High One, The One.

Adonar: the world on the High Plane, where Adon dwells. Also known as the High World.

Adon's Covenant. See (the) Ban.

Aevor (Sylva: wind-dark): Elven name for Grimspire (q.v.) meaning Darkwind Mountain.

age-names: names used by Warrows to indicate their general ages. These names change as Warrows grow older (see Appendix: A Word About Warrows).

Aggarath (Châkur: stone-loom). See Grimspire.

Ai-oi: an exclamation of surprise or to call attention.

ale-night: Cotton's term for a drinking bout.

(the) Alliance: the forces of Men, Elves, Dwarves, and Warrows opposed to Modru's forces in the Winter War. Also the name by which the Weiunwood Alliance was at times known.

(the) Allies: Folk of the Alliance. Also a general term given to any alliance of Free Folk.

Alor (Sylva: Lord): an Elven word meaning Lord.

Alor Vanidar (Sylva: Lord Silverleaf). See Vanidar.

amonu (Châkur: are with you): Dwarven term meaning "are with you."

Anval Ironfist: a Dwarf of Durek's Folk. Brother of Borin Ironfist. Masterwarrior. Mastercrafter. Member of the Squad of Kraggen-cor. Hero of the War of Kraggen-cor. Slain by Gnar in the Battle of Kraggen-cor.

Arbagon Fenner: a buccan Warrow of the Weiunwood. Leader of the Wee Folk in Weiunwood during the Winter War.

Arden. See Arden Valley.

Arden Falls: a cataract between high canyon walls at the narrow mouth of Arden Valley. The mist from this waterfall hides the valley from the view of outsiders.

Arden Ford: a ford along the Crossland Road where it crosses the Tumble River near Arden Valley.

Arden Gorge. See Arden Valley.

Arden Vale. See Arden Valley.

Arden Valley: a forested valley of crags in the north of Rell. Home of Talarin's band of Lian Guardians. Perhaps deserted in the time of the War of Kraggen-cor. Site of the Hidden Stand. The Hidden Refuge. Two hidden entrances lead into the Vale: the one in the north is a tunnel-like cavern through Arden Bluff; the one in the south is a road beneath and behind Arden Falls. Also known as Arden, Arden Gorge, Arden Refuge, Arden Vale, the Hidden Stand, the Hidden Vale, the Refuge.

(the) Argon River: a major river in Mithgar, running along the eastern flank of the Grimwall Mountains and emptying into the Avagon Sea. Also known as the Great Argon River and as the Great River Argon.

Arin: an Elfess. Companion of Egil One Eye in the Quest of the Green Stone of Xian.

Arl: A Man of Valon. One of the riders in Brytta's force. Slain at the Battle of Stormhelm Defile. One of the Five Riders (q.v.).

(the) Army: generally taken to mean any Army of the Free Folk.

Arn (Valur: untranslated interjection): an oathword of Valon used to express ironic reversal.

(the) Arrow Bearer. See Tuckerby Underbank.

Atala: an island that cataclysmically drowned beneath the sea. Also known as the Lost Land.

(the) Atalar Blade: a long-knife of the Lost Land, found in the tomb of Othran the Seer by Tuck. Borne by Galen, who used the blade against the Krakenward to save Gildor. Borne by Patrel during the Battle of Challerain Keep. Placed on display at Tuckerby's Warren after the Winter War. Borne to the War of Kraggen-cor by Cotton, where it was used again to wound the Krakenward to help save Durek.

Aurion: a Man of Pellar. High King of Mithgar. Slain at the Battle of Challerain Keep during the Winter War. Known as Aurion Redeye because of a scarlet eye-patch worn over an eye blinded in combat against the Rovers of Kistan when he was a young Man. Also known as King Redeye and as Redeye.

(the) Avagon Sea: a sea bordering upon the southern flanks of Garia, Pellar, Jugo, Hoven, Tugal, and Vancha; on the eastern flanks of Alban, Hurn, and Sarain; and on the northern flanks of Chabba, Karoo, and Hyree. The great island of Kistan is in the western Avagon Sea.

Aven: a Realm of Mithgar. Bounded on the north by the Grimwall and on the south by North Riamon.

Aylesworth Brewster: a Man of Stonehill. Husband of Molly. Owner of the White Unicorn Inn.

Baeron (singular: Baeran): Men of great strength living in the northern vales of the River Argon and in the forest of Darda Erynian. This branch of Mankind fought with the Alliance against Modru's Hordes during the Winter War. Also known as the woodsmen of the Argon vales.

Baeron Holds: dwelling places of the Baeron.

balefire: a signal fire used to summon help or to communicate disaster.

(the) Ban: Adon's banishment of all the creatures of the Untargarda from the light of Mithgar's Sun as punishment for aiding Gyphon during the Great War. Daylight strikes dead any who defy the Ban: their bodies shrivel into dry husks and blow away like dust; this is called the Withering Death. Some creatures of Mithgar, such as some Dragons, also suffer the Ban—but in the case of Dragons, although they die, they do not suffer the Withering Death. Also known as Adon's Covenant, the Covenant, the Eternal Ban, High Adon's Ban, High Adon's Covenant.

Bane: an Elven-blade forged in the House of Aurinor in the Land of Duellin for use in the Great War. Bane, a long-knife, is one of several Lian sharp-edged weapons equipped with a blade-jewel that shines with a werelight when Evil is near; the light of Bane is blue. Bane was borne by Gildor and Tuck during the Winter War. Tuck used the blade to wound the Gargon. Bane was placed on display in Tuckerby's Warren after the Winter War. Bane was borne on the Quest of Kraggen-cor by Peregrin Fairhill and aided the Squad of Kraggen-cor on their mission. Used by Cotton to cause the death of one of the Cave Trolls during the Battle of Kraggen-cor. Also known as Troll's Bane.

(the) Ban War. See (the) Great War.

Barak Hammerhand: a Dwarf of Durek's Folk. Gatemaster. A member of the Squad of Kraggen-cor. Slain by Rūcks on the banks of the Argon during the Battle of the Last River Camp.

Baralan (Châkur: sloping land). See (the) Pitch.

(the) Barrier. See (the) Spindlethorn Barrier.

(the) barrow of Othran the Seer. See Othran's Tomb.

Baru: a Baeran Man. Warden of the Crestan Pass in 5E231.

(the) Battle Downs: a Wilderland range of hills to the west of the Weiunwood. Here was fought a mighty series of battles during the Great War.

(the) Battle of Budgens: a Winter-War battle at the village of Budgens, where Warrows trapped Ghûlen reavers in an ambush. The first battle of the Struggles (q.v.)

(the) Battle of Kraggen-cor: the last great battle of the War of Kraggen-cor. Fought between Gnar's Horde and Durek's Legion in the vast War Hall. Many perished. The Dwarves were barely victorious as the Doom of Narok befell.

(the) Battle of the Last River Camp: the skirmish between the Squad of Kraggen-cor and a Hlōk-led band of Rūcks, fought on the west bank of the Argon River. Here Barak was slain and Tobin severely wounded. The Squad was rescued by Ursor the Baeran, Shannon Silverleaf, and Shannon's Company of Elves.

(the) Battle of the Vorvor: a battle between Dwarves and Spawn. Fought in the Ravine of the Vorvor.

(the) Battle of Weiunwood: generally refers to the first battle fought between elements of Modru's Horde and an alliance made up of Warrows (from Weiunwood), Men (from Stonehill), and Elves (from Arden). The three-day battle was fought during the opening days of the Winter War. The alliance set many ambuscades and defeated the Horde.

(the) Battle-tongue of the Valanreach. See Valur.

Beacontor: the southernmost of the Signal Mountains. The Crossland Road passes near its flanks.

Bekki: Brega's sire.

Bellon Falls: a great cataract where the Argon River plunges over the Great Escarpment to fall into the Cauldron. Also known as Ctor (Châkur).

Belor: a Dwarf of Durek's Folk. One of Bomar's cooking crew. Slain in the Battle of Kraggen-cor.

Berez: a Dwarf of Durek's Folk. Masterdelver. One of the guides in Crestan Pass during the blizzard.

(the) Beyond: a term used by Boskydell Warrows to indicate any place outside the Thornwall.

Beyonder Guard: warders posted along the entrances into the Boskydells to guard against unsavory *Outsiders*. Also known as the 'Guard, the Thornwalker Guard.

Bigfen: a great marshland in Centerdell.

Big Folks: a Warrow term meaning Mankind.

Big Men: a Warrow term meaning Mankind.

Bill: a Man of Stonehill. Aylesworth's helper in the time of the War of Kraggen-cor.

(the) black crater: the black lake bed left behind when the Troll-dam was broken and the Dark Mere drained.

(the) Black Deeves. See Drimmen-deeve.

Black Drimmen-deeve. See Drimmen-deeve.

blackener. See Dwarf blackener.

(the) Black Hole: a name given to Drimmen-deeve by Men.

Black Kalgalath: the Fire-drake that captured Elgo's hoard.

Kalgalath was so mighty that only the Kammerling could slay him.

(the) Black Maze: a name given to Drimmen-deeve by Men.

(the) Black Mere: See (the) Dark Mere.

Black Mountain: a great dark mountain in the Land of Xian. Home of Wizards.

black oxen: wild black kine living in the Lands of Hoven, Jugo, Tugal, Valon, and Vancha. Source of the black-oxen horns. Also known as the wild kine of the south.

black-oxen horns: War horns used for signalling and borne by the Men of Valon. These horns, coming from the black oxen (q.v.), are much prized by the Vanadurin.

Blackstone: the Dwarvenholt in the Rigga Mountains invaded by Sleeth the Orm. Also known as the Châkka Halls of the Rigga Mountains.

Blackwood: the eld name for Darda Erynian (q.v.).

blade-gem. See blade-jewel.

blade-jewel: a special gem set in the blade of an Elven weapon that emits light when Evil is near—specifically when creatures of the Untargarda are in proximity, although some Mithgarian beings (such as the Krakenward) also cause the jewel to glow. The brighter the light, the nearer the Evil. Also known as a blade-gem.

(the) Blue Bull: a Boskydell inn in Budgens.

Bockleman Brewster: a Man of Stonehill. Owner of the White Unicorn Inn during the Winter War. Hero and leader of the Men of the Weiunwood Alliance. Also known as Squire Brewster.

Bogland Bottoms: a large boggy region south of the Crossland Road and thirty or so miles east of Stonehill.

Bomar: a Dwarf of Durek's Folk. Bossed a cooking crew on the way to Kraggen-cor. Also known as Grey Bomar.

(the) 'Book. See *(The) Raven Book*.

(the) Boreal Sea: a frigid sea north of the Dalara Plains, Rian, Gron, and other Lands, and bordering on the Northern Wastes.

Borin Ironfist: a Dwarf of Durek's Folk. Brother of Anval Ironfist. Masterwarrior. Mastercrafter. Member of the Squad of Kraggen-cor. Hero of the War of Kraggen-cor. Gnar's slayer. Killed as the Doom of Narok befell.

Boshlub: a Hlōk of Gnar's Horde.

(the) Bosky. See (the) Boskydells.

(the) Boskydells: a Warrow homeland surrounded by the Spindlethorn Barrier. Bounded to the north by Rian, to the east by Harth, to the south by Trellinath, and to the west by Wellen. Also known as the Bosky, the Dells, the Land of the Waldana (Valur), the Land of the Wee Folk, the Seven Dells.

(the) Bottom Chamber: one of the chambers in Kraggen-cor along the Brega Path.

bower shelter: a tiny form of shelter made from evergreen boughs; their way of making is known to mountain dwellers.

Brackenboro: a Boskydell village south of the Corssland Road and inside the western edge of Eastdell. Here was fought the Battle of Brackenboro during the Winter War. Also known as the 'Boro.

ᚠᚱᚢᛜᛚᛁ: Châkka runes meaning Braggi. (See Braggi's Rune.)

Braggi: a Dwarf warrior. Leader of a doomed mission into Kraggen-cor to slay the Ghath.

Braggi's doomed raid: Braggi's doomed mission.

Braggi's Raid: Braggi's doomed mission.

Braggi's Rune: Braggi's name written in large letters of Squam blood on the wall of the Hall of the Gravenarch.

Braggi's Stand: the place in Kraggen-cor—the Hall of the Gravenarch—where Braggi and his Raiders fought their last battle against the Squam. The Dwarves were overcome by the Ghath and slain.

Brak: DelfLord of Kachar during Elgo's time.

Brath: a Man of Valon. One of the Riders in Brytta's force. Brytta's sister's son.

Brave as Budgens: a Warrow saying indicating great courage, harking back to the time of the Winter War when a force of Warrow archers overcame a company of Ghûlen reavers in the Battle of Budgens.

Breakdeath Durek: a name given to Durek (q.v.) by the Dwarven Folk, who believed that Durek now and again broke the bonds of Death to be reborn among his Folk. Also known as Deathbreaker Durek, Khana (Châkur) Durek.

(the) breath of Waroo: a cold, transmountain wind indicating the onset of a blizzard. (See Waroo.)

Brega: a Dwarf of the Red Caves. Bekki's son. Hero of the Winter War. One of the Deevewalkers. Leader of the squad to lower the drawbridge and open the gate of the Iron Tower on the Darkest Day. Scriber of the Brega Scroll. DelfLord of the Red Caves after Borta. Also called Axe-thrower and Warrior Brega.

Brega, Bekki's son. See Brega.

(the) Brega Path: the route through Kraggen-cor taken by the Deevewalkers during the Winter War. Because of the Brega Scroll, this route became known as the Brega Path. Also known as the Path.

(the) Brega Scroll: Brega's record of the route taken by the Deevewalkers through Kraggen-cor. The scroll was found by Peregrin Fairhill years after its making. Also known as Brega's record and as the Scroll.

Brega's record. See (the) Brega Scroll.

B'reit (Valur: ready): a Valonian word meaning ready.

(the) bridge: the Warrow name for the bridge along the Crossland Road over the Spindle River.

(the) Bright Veil: a haze of stars in an east-west band across the skies of Mithgar. (Thought to be the Milky Way.)

(the) Broad Hall: one of the chambers in Kraggen-cor along the Brega Path.

(the) Broad Shelf: the name given to the wide stone floor on the east side of the Great Deep of Kraggen-cor. Also known as the Great Shelf and as the Shelf.

Brownie: a workhorse used by Cotton and others during the Quest of Kraggen-cor.

Brytta: a Man of Valon. Warder of the North Reach. Valanreach Marshal. Captain of the forty horse-borne Vanadurin scouts who accompanied Seventh Durek on the march to Kraggen-cor. Fought in the Battle of Stormhelm Defile.

buccan (plural: buccen): the general name given to a male Warrow. Also the specific age-name given to male Warrows between thirty and sixty years old.

buccaran: a Warrow term of endearment used by dammen Warrows when speaking to or about their husbands or sweethearts.

bucco: a Warrow term meaning son.

Budgens: a Boskydell hamlet. Site of the first battle of the Struggles during the Winter War.

(the) buried door: the name used by Hlōks to mean Dusk-Door.

burrow: an underground Warrow dwelling.

Buttermilk Springs: a Boskydell spring near Thimble, cold enough to keep melons and buttermilk cool in the summer. Owned by Jayar Northcolt.

Byroad Lane: the road running south from Budgens to the Crossland Road.

Caddor: A Dwarf of Durek's Folk. One of Bomar's cooking crew. Slain in the Battle of Kraggen-cor.

Caer Lindor: an Elvenholt on an island in the River Rissanin between Darda Erynian and the Greatwood. Destroyed in the Great War.

Caer Pendwyr: southern strongholt, winter home and Court of the High King. Situated on Pendwyr Isle, Pellar, between Hile Bay and the Avagon Sea.

(the) Caire River: a river with northern origins in the west side of the Rigga Mountains and running south to the Rivermix at Luren.

Captain: a rank or position of authority among the Free Folk. Typically, Captains commanded up to one hundred warriors.

Captain Patrel. See Patrel Rushlock.

(the) Cauldron: a great churn of water where Vanil Falls and Bellon Falls plunge down the face of the Great Escarpment to thunder into the River Argon.

Cave Ogru. See Ogrus.

Cave Troll. See Ogrus.

(the) Cellener River: a river flowing into the Quadrill in Darda Galion in southwestern Riamon.

(a) Ceremony: a public gathering of Warrows at which both formal and informal speeches are made.

Chagor (Sylva: jag-top). See Loftcrag.

Châk (plural: Châkka) (Châkur: Dwarf): Dwarven word meaning Dwarf.

Châk-alon (Châkur: Dwarf pure-spirit): the Dwarven name for the Quadmere (q.v.).

Châkka (Châkur: Dwarves; of the Dwarves): Dwarven word meaning "Dwarves" and "of the Dwarves."

Châkkacyth Ryng (Châkur: Dwarvenkith Ring): a sigil shining forth from Ghatan Mountain, seen from the Mountain Throne on Rávenor. The Ryng, a circlet of light studded with five stars, one for each of the five Châkka kindred, only appears as the Sun passes through the zenith. Also known as the Dwarvenkith Ring, the Ring, and the Ryng.

Châkkadom (Châkur: Dwarfdom): the totality of Dwarven Folk.

Châkka doors (Châkur: Dwarven doors): doors, usually concealed, made by Dwarves. Also known as Dwarf doors.

Châkka Halls of the Rigga Mountains. See Blackstone.

Châkkaholt (Châkur: Dwarvenholt). See Dwarvenholt.

Châkka Kindred: the five branches of the Dwarven Folk. Also known as the Kindred.

Châk-Sol (Châkur: Dwarf-Friend): an honorary rank of Dwarf Kith given to a rare few non-Dwarves throughout the history of Mitheor. Perry and Cotton each were named Châk-Sol—Dwarf-Friend—by Anval and Borin. Also known as Dwarf-Friend, Friend.

Châk Speech. See Châkur.

Châkur (Châkur: our tongue): the secret language of the Dwarves. Also known as Châk Speech, the Dwarf speech, Dwarf tongue, the hidden language, and the hidden tongue. (For various Châkur words and phrases, see Appendix: Translations of Words and Phrases.)

Challerain Keep: northern strongholt, summer home and Court of the High King. Situated in Rian. Also known as the Keep.

(the) Chamber: a term applicable to many rooms in Kraggencor: e.g., the Bottom Chamber, the Oval Chamber.

Chief Captain: a rank above Captain in Dwarf armies.

(the) Chieftain: the leader of the Baeron (q.v.).

(the) Cliffs: a western Boskydell Warrowholt. A honeycomb of Warrow dwellings in a limestone cliff along the Wenden River in Westdell.

Cold-drakes. See Dragons.

(the) Cold Iron Tower. See (the) Iron Tower.

Common: a term meaning "of the Common Tongue" (q.v.).

(the) common room: a large public room at an inn where both guests and locals gather to eat, drink, and talk.

(the) Commons: a town square generally without buildings other than a pavilion or two for entertainment or speechmaking purposes.

(the) common stables: a public barn or corral for keeping horses and ponies.

(the) Common Tongue: q.v., Pellarion.

(the) Company of the Dusken Door: a Dwarven Company set to ward the Dusken Door. Also known as the Dusk-Door Company.

(a) copper. See copper penny.

copper coin. See copper penny.

copper penny: one of three types of coins used for commerce in Mithgar (silver and gold being the other two types). Also known as a copper, a copper coin, and a copper piece.

cor (Châkur: might): a Dwarven term meaning might (power). Also, a Warrow exclamation used to express wonderment.

Coron (Sylva: King/Ruler): Elven name for Coron Mountain (King of the Mountains) (see Stormhelm). Also the Elven name for their own Elven King (see Eiron).

(the) corpse-foe. See Ghûls.

cot. See cote.

cote: a small dwelling (cottage); usually a small, stone field-house or a tiny house in the woods. Also known as a cot.

Cotton Buckleburr: a buccan Warrow of the Boskydells. Handywarrow at Sir Tuckerby's Warren. Member of the Quest of Kraggen-cor. Bearer of the Horn of Narok. Member of Durek's Army. Brega-Path guide. Wielder of the Atalar Blade. Drimmen-deeve Rück-fighter. Hero of the Realm. Also known as Friend Cotton, Master Cotton, Mister Cotton, Pathfinder.

(the) Council of Durek: a council held at Landover Road Ford to plan the strategy of the invasion and War of Kraggen-cor.

(the) Council of Captains: a gathering of Dwarf Captains to advise a Dwarf King.

(the) Covenant. See (the) Ban.

(a) Crafter: one who takes up a crafting skill. Among Dwarves, there are Gatecrafters, Tunnelcrafters, Minecrafters, Doorcrafters, etc.

Crau: a Dwarf of Durek's Folk. One of Bomar's cooking crew. Slain in the Battle of Kraggen-cor.

Crestan Pass: a pass above Arden Valley, crossing the Grimwall Mountains, connecting the Crossland Road with the Landover Road.

(the) Crossland Road: a major east-west road of Mithgar, west of the Grimwall Mountains.

Crotbone: a Hlōk of Gnar's Horde.

crue: a tasteless but nutritious waybread.

Cruel Gnar. See Gnar.

Ctor (Châkur: shouter): Dwarven name for Bellon Falls (q.v.).

Dael: the capital city of North Riamon. Also known as Dael Township.

Daelsman: a Man from the vicinity of Dael.

Dael Township. See Dael.

Daelwood: a forest in Riamon within the ring of the Rimmen Mountains.

Dalen: a Man of Valon. One of the riders in Brytta's force. Slain in the Battle of Stormhelm Defile. One of the Five Riders (q.v.).

(the) Dalgor March(es): a region of Riamon west of the Argon River and east of the Grimwall, through which the Dalgor River flows.

(the) Dalgor River: a river flowing eastward from the Grimwall into the Argon River.

damman (plural: dammen): the general name given to a female Warrow. Also the specific age-name given to female Warrows between thirty and sixty years old.

dammia: a Warrow term of endearment used by buccen Warrows when speaking to or about their wives or sweethearts.

dammsel: a Warrow term meaning daughter.

Danner Bramblethorn: a buccan Warrow of the Boskydells. Hero of the Winter War. Leader of the Struggles. One of Tuck's companions. Thornwalker. A member of Brega's squad. Slain at the Kinstealer's holt. Also known as Captain Danner, Sir Danner, and the King of the Rillrock.

Dara (Sylva: Lady): an Elven title for an Elfess consort.

Darda (Sylva: leaf-tree): Elven word meaning forest.

Darda Erynian (Sylva: leaf-tree hall-of-green): Elven name meaning Greenhall Forest. A great forest east of the Argon River in Riamon. Also known as Blackwood of old, and as the Great Greenhall.

Darda Galion (Slyva: leaf-tree land-of-larks): Elven name meaning Forest of the Silverlarks. A great forest of Eld Trees in southwestern Riamon, west of the River Argon. Last true home of the Lian in Mithgar. Also known as Eldwood and as Larkenwald.

Darion: the High King of Mithgar during the time of the Quest of Kraggen-cor.

(the) Dark Mere: a black lakelet under the Loom at the Dusk-Door. Abode of the Krakenward. Also known as the Black Mere.

(the) Dark Plague: a ravaging plague that swept Mithgar in days of yore and slew as much as one third of the total population. Commonly believed to be a sending of Gyphon or Modru.

darktide: night

(the) Daūn Gate (Châkur: Sunrise Gate). See Dawn-Gate.

(the) Dawn-Gate: the great eastern entrance into Kraggen-cor. Situated on the southeastern flank of Stormhelm Mountain. Opening onto the Pitch less than a mile from the Quadmere. Also known as Daūn (Châkur) Gate, the Gate, and Quad Gate.

(the) Dawn Sword: a special sword said to have the power to slay the High Vûlk, Himself. This weapon disappeared in the region of Dalgor March.

dayrise: sunrise.

daytide: daytime.

Deathbreaker Durek: an appellation of Durek. The Dwarves believe that, after death, spirits are reborn to walk the earth again, some more often than others. They believe that the spirit of First Durek is one that breaks the bonds of Death often; hence the name Deathbreaker Durek. (See Durek, First Durek.)

(the) Death-War. See Narok.

(the) Deep. See (the) Great Deep.

(the) Deeves. See Drimmen-deeve.

(the) Deevewalkers: the name given to the four companions who strode through Drimmen-deeve during the Winter War: Brega (Dwarf), Galen (Man), Gildor (Elf), and Tuck (Warrow). Slayers of the Gargon. Also known as the Dread Slayers, the Four, the four heroes, the Four Who Strode Drimmen-deeve, the Four Who Strode Kraggen-cor, the Four Who Strode the Deeves, and the Walkers of the Deeves.

delf: a common Mithgarian term meaning a digging of some sort, such as a quarry or a mine.

DelfLord: a title given to Dwarf Lords of outlying mineholts. Second in power only to Dwarven Kings.

Delk Steelshank: a Dwarf of Durek's Folk. Gatemaster. Member of the Squad of Kraggen-cor. Slain by Rūck arrow in the Gargon's Lair.

(the) Dellin Downs: a low range of hills central to Harth.

(the) Dells. See (the) Boskydells.

Delon: an island in the Argon River, north of Landover Road Ford.

Delver: a Dwarf whose craft is delving, generally in or through stone.

(the) Dēop (Châkur: Dēop = Deep): a Dwarven name for the Great Deep.

dhal: a Rūcken shield similar to a sipar in construction but slightly smaller. See sipar.

(the) diary of Sir Tuckerby Underbank: Tuckerby Underbank's original diary of his adventures during the Winter War.

Didion: a Man of Valon. One of the riders in Brytta's force. With Ged, vainly pursued the Drōkh that escaped the Battle of Stormhelm Defile.

(the) Dimmendark: a spectral dark over the land, cast by Modru using the power of the Myrkenstone during the Winter War to negate Adon's Ban. Also known as the 'Dark, Modru's myrk, the murk of the Evil One.

(the) Dingle: a term generally taken to mean the Dingle-rill (q.v.), but also can indicate all of the hollow bottom through which the Dingle-rill flows in the vicinity of Woody Hollow.

(the) Dingle-rill: a Boskydell river flowing from Bigfen eastward to empty at last into the Spindle River. Also known as the Dingle.

dök (Châkur: halt): a Dwarven word meaning halt.

(the) Doom of Narok. See (the) Staves of Narok.

(the) Doomed Raid of Braggi. See Braggi's Raid.

(the) Door. See (the) Dusk-Door.

(the) Doors of Dusk. See (the) Dusk-Door.

Dot Northcolt: a damman Warrow of the Boskydells. Wife of Jayar Northcolt. Holly's dam (mother).

Downdell: the southeasternmost of the Seven Dells of the Boskydells. Noted for its leaf.

Downdell leaf: apparently tobacco. Downdell leaf is reputed to be the best.

Downy: a workhorse used by Cotton and others during the Quest of Kraggen-cor.

Dracongield (Valur: Dragon-gold): a Valonian word meaning Dragon-gold.

Draedan (Sylva: Dread One). See (the) Gargon.

(the) Draedon's Lair [Sylva: (the) Dread One's lair]. See (the) Lost Prison.

(the) Dragon Pillars: four rows of great pillars in the War Hall of Kraggen-cor. The pillars are carved to resemble Dragons twining up around the columns.

Dragons: one of the Folk of Mithgar. Comprising two strains: Fire-drakes and Cold-drakes. Dragons are mighty creatures capable of speech. Most have wings and the power of flight. Generally they live in remote caves and ravage the nearby land. They sleep for one thousand years and remain awake for two thousand. Often they seek treasure, which they hoard. Fire-drakes spew flame. Cold-drakes spew acid but no flame, for they once were Fire-drakes but sided with Gyphon in the Great War and their fire was taken from them by Adon as punishment. Cold-drakes suffer the Ban—yet though they are slain by the Sun, the Withering Death strikes them not (i.e., when Sun-slain, they do not wither to dust in its rays). No female Dragons are known, and it is said by the Dwarves that Dragons mate with Madûks (Krakens). Dragons named in *The Raven Book* and in *The Fairhill Journal* are Black Kalgalath, Ebonskaith, Skail, and Sleeth the Orm. Also known as Orms (Worms).

Dragon spew: generally refers to the acid spat forth by Cold-drakes, but also can mean the flame of a Fire-drake.

(the) Dragon Star: a comet that nearly collided with Mithgar. Sent by Gyphon, it bore the Myrkenstone to the world, to be used by Modru.

(the) Drawbridge at Dusk-Door: a span across the Dusk-Moat at Dusk-Door.

(the) Drawbridge at the Great Deep: a span across the Great Deep near the Dawn-Gate.

(the) Drawing Dark: a deep, eight-foot-wide fissure in Kraggen-cor from which emanates a hideous sucking noise (possibly a whirlpool down within the crack). So named by

Tuck because it seemed as if the crevice were trying to draw one down into the darkness. Also known as the eight-foot-wide crack, the eight-foot-wide crevice.

(the) Dread. See (the) Gargon.

(the) Dread of Drimmen-deeve. See (the) Gargon.

Drearwood: a forest in Rhone through which wends the Crossland Road. In this wood in days of yore were said to dwell dreadful creatures, creatures driven out by the Elves of Arden and Men of the Wilderland during the Purging. Also known as the 'Wood.

Driller: a Dwarf whose craft is drilling, one of the skills of stone delving.

Drimm (plural: Drimma) (Sylva: Dwarf): Elven name meaning Dwarf.

Drimmen-deeve (Sylva: Dwarven-delvings; Dwarven-mines): Elven name for Kraggen-cor (q.v.). Also known as the Black Deeves, Black Drimmen-deeve, the Black Hole, the Black Maze, and the Deeves.

(the) Drimmen-deeve Rūck-fighters: the name in Stonehill by which Anval, Borin, Cotton, Kian, and Perry became known after the Quest of Kraggen-cor.

Drōken: a term meaning "of the Drōkha."

Drōkha (singular: Drōkh) (Valur: vile-filth). See Hlōks.

(the) drowned courtyard: the ancient courtyard before the Dusk-Door, inundated when the Duskrill was dammed by Trolls.

Duellin: a city of Atala. Also known as Lost Duellin when Atala sank.

Durek: a recurring name within the line of Dwarven Kings of Durek's Folk. Durek was thought to be reborn often throughout the Eras and thus was given the name Breakdeath Durek, Deathbreaker Durek, Durek the Deathbreaker, the High Leader.

Durek's Army. See (the) Dwarf Host.

Durek's Folk: one of the five strains of the Dwarven Folk. Also known as Durek's Kin.

Durek's Kin. See Durek's Folk.

Durek's Legion. See (the) Dwarf Host.

Durek's Wheel. See (the) Vorvor.

Durek the Deathbreaker. See Durek.

(the) Dusk-Door: the western trade entrance into Kraggen-cor.

Situated under the cavernous hemidome at the base of the Great
Loom on the western flank of Grimspire Mountain. Crafted by
the Dwarf Valki and by the Wizard Grevan. After arcane words
are spoken, the Dusk-Door can be opened and closed by
Dwarves using the Wizard-word Gaard. And just inside the
West Hall, a chain also can be used to close (and perhaps open)
the portal. Also known as the Door, the Doors of Dusk, the
Dusken (Châkur) Door.

(the) Dusk-Door Company. See (the) Company of the Dusken
Door.

(the) Dusken Door (Châkur: Sundown Door). See Dusk-Door.

duskingtide: the march of evening, from its onset until full
night falls.

(the) Dusk-Moat: a moat surrounding the courtyard before the
Dusk-Door. A Dwarven defence at the Dusken Door. During
the time of the Troll-dam, the moat was submerged under the
Dark Mere. Also known as the Gatemoat.

(the) Duskrill: a stream flowing from Grimspire through
Ragad Valley. Used to create the Dusk-Moat. Blocked for centuries by the Troll-made dam.

Dwarf blackener: a salve used by Dwarves to darken their features when going into combat at night or underground. Also
known as blackener, face blackener.

Dwarf doors. See Châkka doors.

Dwarf-Friend. See Châk-Sol.

(the) Dwarf Host: generally taken to mean the Army that accompanied Seventh Durek to Kraggen-cor. Also known as
Durek's Army and Durek's Legion.

Dwarf-lantern. See Dwarven lantern.

Dwarf Speech. See Châkur.

(the) Dwarf tongue. See Châkur.

Dwarf Troll-squad: a force of fifty or more Dwarves especially trained to do battle with Trolls.

Dwarven: a term meaning "of the Dwarves."

Dwarvenfolc (Valur: Dwarven Folk): a Valonian word meaning Dwarves.

Dwarvenholt: a Dwarven stronghold. Also known as Châkkaholt.

(the) Dwarvenkith Ring. See (the) Châkkacyth Ryng.

Dwarven lantern: a small hooded lantern wrought of brass and crystal, glowing with a soft blue-green light. No fire need be kindled, no fuel seems consumed. Also known as Dwarf-lantern.

Dwarves (singular: Dwarf): one of the Folk of Mithgar. Comprising five strains. The adults range in height from four to five feet. Broad-shouldered. Aggressive. Secretive. Clever. Mine dwellers. Crafters. Also known as Châk(ka) (Châkur), Drimma (Sylva), Dwarven Folk, *Dwarvenfolc* (Valur), forked beards, and the forked-bearded Folk.

Dwarvish: a term meaning "of the Dwarves."

Dylvana (Sylva: Wood Elves): one of the two strains of Elves upon Mithgar.

Eanor: a Man of Valon. King of the Vanadurin at the time of the Quest of Kraggen-cor.

Eastdell: one of the Seven Dells of the Boskydells.

Eastdell Fourth: a Thornwalker Company of Eastdell. Also known by Tuck and his comrades as the Thornwalker Fourth.

(the) East Hall: one of the chambers in Kraggen-cor, just inside the Dawn-Gate, along the Brega Path.

Eastpoint: a Boskydell village in Eastdell, south of the Crossland Road, near the Spindle River.

Eastpoint Hall: a large warren in Eastdell. Here lived Tuck's cousins, the Bendels. Here, too, was housed one of the libraries of the Boskydells.

Eastwood: a large forest in Eastdell, in the Boskydells. Also known as the 'Wood.

Eddra: a Man of Valon. One of the riders in Brytta's force.

Edgewood: a large forest in Harth, on the eastern border of the Boskydells.

(the) edifice of the Dusk-Door. See (the) great portico (of the Dusk-Door).

Egil One Eye: a Man of Mithgar. Companion of Arin in the Quest of the Green Stone of Xian.

Egon: a Man of Valon. One of the riders in Brytta's force.

(the) eight-foot-wide crack. See (the) Drawing Dark.

(the) eight-foot-wide crevice. See (the) Drawing Dark.

Eiron: a Lian Elf. Coron (Sylva) of the Elves in Mithgar during the Winter War. Consort of Faeon.

eld buccan (plural: eld buccen): the age-name given to a buccan Warrow between sixty and eighty-five years old.

eld damman (plural: eld dammen): the age-name given to a damman Warrow between sixty and eighty-five years old.

Eld Days/eld days: old days.

Eld Durek. See First Durek.

Elden/elden: a term used to mean ancient, old, olden.

Elden Days: olden days.

Eld Ones: beings of ancient legend; e.g., Lian Elves were also known as Eld Ones.

Eld Trees: great trees, hundreds of feet tall, said to have the special property of gathering and holding the twilight if Elves live nearby.

Eld wood: The precious wood of an Eld Tree. Used to make things of great worth; e.g., Perry had an Eld-wood carrying case for his copy of *The Raven Book*.

Eldwood. See Darda Galion.

Elf Lord: a title given to all Elves by common Folk.

Elgo: a Man of Valon. The hero who slew the Cold-drake Sleeth by tricking it into the sunlight, thus winning the Dragon's hoard. Also known as Sleeth's Doom.

Elven: a term meaning "of the Elves."

Elven cloak: a cloak of the Elves; of a color said to blend into a background of limb, leaf, or stone. Danner, Patrel, and Tuck were given Elven cloaks by Laurelin; Patrel's and Tuck's ended up on display in The Root. Cotton and Perry wore these cloaks in the Quest of Kraggen-cor.

Elvenholt: an Elven stronghold.

Elven rope: a soft, pliable, strong, lightweight rope made by the Elves.

Elves (Singular: Elf): one of the Folk of Adonar, some of whom dwell in Mithgar. Comprising two strains: the Lian and the Dylvana. The adults range in height from four and one-half to five and one-half feet. Slim, Agile, Swift. Sharp-sensed. Reserved. Forest dwellers. Artisans.

Elves of the West: Elves who dwelled in the Land of the West ere it sank beneath the sea.

Elvish: a term meaning "of the Elves."

Elwydd: daughter of Adon. Held in special reverence by the Dwarves.

Elyn: a Woman of Jord. Companion of the Dwarf Thork in the Quest of Black Mountain.

(the) End Field: a large open field in Hollow End, in Woody Hollow.

(the) Enemy in Gron. See Modru.

Era: a historical age of Mithgar. These ages are determined by world-shaking events, which bring each Era to a close and begin the following Era. At the time of the beginning of the Winter War it was the Fourth Era (4E), the year 2018: 4E2018. The Winter War ended in 4E2019. The Fifth Era (5E) began on the next Year's Start Day. The Quest of Kraggen-cor took place in 5E231.

eventide: generally taken to mean the march of dusk, from its onset until full night falls; however, it also can mean all of the time between sunset and sunrise.

(the) Evil One. See Modru.

(the) Evil One's Reavers: generally taken to mean Ghûls (q.v.).

face blackener. See Dwarf blackener.

Faeon: Elfess. Mistress of Darda Galion. Consort of Eiron. Daughter of Talarin and Rael. Sister of Gildor and Vanidor. After Vanidor's death, Faeon rode the Twilight Ride to Adonar to plead with the High One to intercede in the Winter War.

(the) Fainen River (Sylva: Fainen = Fair): Elven name (Fair River) for the Isleborn River (q.v.).

(The) Fairhill Journal: the chronicle written by Peregrin Fairhill to describe the Quest of Kraggen-cor. Also known as *The Silver Call.*

(the) Fairhills: the Fairhill lineage.

(the) Fairhill Scholar: a title given by the Ravenbook Scholars to an outstanding student among them of the Fairhill lineage.

Falanith (Sylva: valley rising): the Elven name for the Pitch (q.v.).

(the) Falls of Vanil. See Vanil Falls.

False Elgo: a name given Elgo by the Dwarves after their dispute over Sleeth's hoard.

Farlon: a Man of Valon. One of the riders in Brytta's force. The scout who first found the Valley of the Five Riders.

(the) farmer: a Man of the Wilderland near Stonehill. Unnamed guest of the White Unicorn Inn when the Drimmendeevc Rûck-fighters were also guests.

(the) Fates: the spinners of the skeins of the world; the personification of the ancient belief of the Men of Valon that unseen forces weave the fortunes of all peoples.

(the) Father of Durek's Folk. See First Durek.

Faugh: a Free Folk exclamation of contempt or disgust.

Felor: a Dwarf of Durek's Folk. Masterdriller. Chief Captain of the Spearhead of the Dwarf Army in the War of Kraggen-cor. Felor and his drillers helped break the Troll-made dam to empty the Dark Mere during the battle with the Madûk.

Fennerly Cotter: a buccan Warrow of the Boskydells. Owner of the Happy Otter Inn in Greenfields at the time of the Quest of Kraggen-cor.

'Fieldites: citizens of Greenfields.

(the) 'Fields. See Greenfields.

firecoke: a special charcoal uscd by the Dwarves in their forges.

Fire-drakes. See Dragons.

Firemane: a horse of Valon. Arl's mount.

First Durek: a Dwarf King and founder of Durek's Folk in the First Era. Discoverer of Kraggen-cor. Also known as Eld Durek and as the Father of Durek's Folk. (Scc Breakdeath Durek, Durek).

(the) First Watchtower: an ancient sentry tower, now ruins, on the crest of Beacontor.

(the) five Châkka kindred: the five strains of Dwarves. Also known as the Five Kith.

(the) Five Kith. See (the) five Châkka kindred.

(the) Five Riders: the five riders of Valon slain in the battle of Stormhelm Defile: Arl, Dalen, Haddor, Luthen, Raech.

(the) flatboats (of the River Drummers): barges, trade boats, used by river merchants.

flet: a tree house or tree platform used as a dwelling, notably by the Quiren strain of Warrows.

Fleetfoot: Gildor's horse. Slain by the Hèlarms during the Winter War.

(the) Fletchers: the Fletcher lineage.

Folk: a branch of the Free Folk (q.v.) or of the Foul Folk (q.v.). Also known as a Race.

(the) Ford of New Luren: the ford across the Isleborne River at the hamlet of New Luren.

forebears: ancestors.

Foreign Parts: a Warrow term meaning anywhere beyond the borders of the Boskydells.

(the) forge of Hèl: Hell's smithery. A term used to mean a harsh or hellish experience or place.

(the) forked-bearded Folk: a term generally taken to mean Dwarves. In Mithgar, only Dwarves sported forked beards.

forked beards: a term generally taken to mean Dwarves. [See (the) forked-bearded Folk.]

Fortune's three faces: the three aspects of chance. The Valonians believed that Fortune had three faces: one fair, signifying good luck; one scowling, signifying bad luck; and one unseen, signifying not only Death's visage, but also misfortunes too terrible to contemplate.

foul-beards: a term used by Hlōks in general, and Gnar in particular, to mean Dwarves.

Foul Elgo: a name given to Elgo by the Dwarves after their dispute over Sleeth's hoard.

(the) Foul Folk: any or all of the Folk allied with Modru or Gyphon, the most notable of which are Cold-drakes, Ghûls, Hèlsteeds, Hlōks, Ogrus, Rūcks, and some Men (e.g., in the past, the Rovers of Kistan, the Lakh of Hyree).

(the) Four. See (the) Deevewalkers.

(the) Four Who Strode Drimmen-deeve. See the Deevewalkers.

(the) Four Who Strode Kraggen-cor. See the Deevewalkers.

(the) Free Folk: any or all of the Folk allied with Adon, the most notable of which are Dwarves, Elves, Man, Utruni, Warrows, Wizards. Also known as the High Folk.

Friend: abbreviated form of Dwarf-Friend. (See Châk-Sol.)

Funda: a Dwarf of Durek's Folk. One of Bomar's cooking crew. Slain in the Battle of Kraggen-cor.

Gaard: a Wizard-word perhaps meaning move, or act. Used by Dwarves to both open and close the Dusk-Door.

Galen: a Man of Pellar. Eldest son of Aurion. A Lord and

Prince who became High King during the Winter War. Deeve-walker. Hero. Founder of the Realmsmen. Husband of Laurelin. Sire of Gareth. Also known as Shatter-sword. Died at age 71 during a storm at Caer Pendwyr.

(the) Gammer (Alderbuc): a buccan Warrow of the Bosky-dells. A granther Warrow and past Captain of the Thornwalkers at the time of the Winter War. Organizer of the Wolf Patrols at the onset of the cold winter heralding the Winter War.

Gannon: a Man of Valon. One of the riders in Brytta's force.

(the) Gap. See (the) Gap of Stormhelm, Gûnarring Gap, Quadran Gap.

(the) Gap of Stormhelm. See Quadran Pass.

Gareth: firstborn of Galen and Laurelin. Gareth became King in 5E46.

(the) Gargon (plural: Gargons, Gargoni): a Vûlk aiding Gyphon in the Great War. Trapped in the Lost Prison by Lian Guardians. Freed by Modru's art. Ruler of Drimmen-deeve for more than a thousand years. Slain by the Deevewalkers. Also known as the *Draedan* (Sylva), the Dread, the Dread of Drimmen-deeve, the Dread of the Black Hole, the Evil, the Fear to the North (of Darda Galion), the Ghath (Châkur), the Horror, the Mandrak (Twyll), Modru's Dread, and the Negus (Slûk) of Terror.

(the) Gargon's Lair. See (the) Lost Prison.

Garia: a Land of Mithgar bounded on the north by Aven, on the east by Alban, on the south by the Avagon Sea, and on the west by the Inner Sea and Riamon.

Garn (Valur: untranslated interjection): oathword of Valon, used to express disappointment or frustration.

(the) Gate. See Dawn-Gate, (the) High Gate.

Gate Level: the level at the Dawn-Gate to which all other levels in Kraggen-cor are referenced: Deeper chambers have "Neaths" as their level designations (i.e., First Neath, Second Neath, etc.), whereas higher chambers have "Rises" as their level designations (i.e., First Rise, Second Rise, etc.); those chambers in Kraggen-cor at the same level as the Dawn-Gate are said to be at "Gate Level."

Gatemaster: one who has mastered the Dwarven craft of gate making.

Gatemaster Valki. See Valki.

Gatemaster Valki's glyph: a rune *V* inscribed in theen upon the Dusken Door.

(the) Gatemoat. See (the) Dusk-Moat.

Gaynor: a Dwarf of Durek's Folk. Masterdelver. One of the guides through Crestan Pass during the blizzard. Slain by the Krakenward.

Ged: a Man of Valon. One of the riders in Brytta's force. With Didion, vainly pursued the Drōkh that escaped the Battle of Stormhelm Defile.

Gerontius Fairhill: a buccan Warrow of the Boskydells. Peregrin Fairhill's uncle. A Master of the Ravenbook Scholars.

Ghatan (Châkur: ringmount); the Dwarven name for Loftcrag (q.v.), meaning Mountain of the Ryng. So named because the Châkkacyth Ryng shone forth from the crags of Ghatan.

(the) Ghath (Châkur: horror): Dwarven name for the Gargon (q.v.).

Ghola (singular: Ghol): Pellarion for Ghûls (q.v.).

Ghûlen: a term meaning "of the Ghûls."

Ghûls (singular: Ghûl): minor Vûlks. Savage. Hèlsteed-borne reavers. Very difficult to slay. All perhaps perished in the Winter War. Also known as the corpse-foe, the corpse-folk, the corpse-people, Ghola (OP), Ghûlka (Sylva), Guula (Valur), Khōls (Châkur), Modru's Reavers, reaving-foe, reavers.

Giants: the Warrow and Valonian name for Utruni (q.v.).

(the) gilded armor. See (the) golden armor.

(the) gilded mail. See (the) golden armor.

Gildor (Sylva: gold-branch): an Elf. Lian warrior. Elf Lord. Son of Talarin and Rael. Twin brother of Vanidor, brother of Faeon. Hero. One of the Deevewalkers. Also known as Alor Gildor, Gildor Goldbranch, Goldbranch, Lord Gildor, Torchflinger.

Glain. See Third Glain.

Glâr (Slûk: fire): a Spaunen word meaning fire.

Gnar: a Hlōk. Leader of the Spawn in Drimmen-deeve. Anval's slayer. Slain by Borin in the War of Kraggen-cor. Also known as Cruel Gnar, Gnar the Cruel, his Nibs, and O Mighty One.

Gnar's Horde: the Horde of maggot-folk living in Kraggencor during the time of the Quest of Kraggen-cor.

Gnar the Cruel. See Gnar.

(the) golden armor: armor originally made by the Dwarves of the Red Caves for young Galen. The mail was given to Patrel by Laurelin to wear at her birthday feast and was worn by him throughout the Winter War. The armor was ultimately placed on display at Tuckerby's Warren, where it was to be left in possession of the Warrows until recalled by the shade of Aurion. Worn by Cotton in the Quest of Kraggen-cor. Also known as the golden mail, the gilded mail, and the gilded armor.

golden coin. See gold penny.

(the) golden mail. See (the) golden armor.

(the) golden War Horn: a golden horn of Durek's Folk used to summon Dwarves to battle. Also known as the War Horn.

gold penny: one of three types of coins used for commerce in Mithgar (silver and copper being the other two types). Also known as a gold, a gold coin, and a gold piece.

Gorbash: a Hlōk of Gnar's Horde.

Goth: a Cave Ogru of Kraggen-cor. A Troll in Gnar's Horde.

Grael: a Baeran Woman. Ursor's wife. Slain by Spawn on a trip to Valon.

Gralon (Sylva: grey-stone). See Greytower.

gramarye: the art of sorcery.

(the) Grand Alliance: the alliance of Dwarves, Elves, Men, Utruni, Warrows, and Wizards who fought on the side of Adon in the Great War against Gyphon, Modru, and the Foul Folk.

grandam (plural: grandams): the age-name given to a damman Warrow eighty-five years old and beyond.

granther (plural: granthers): the age-name given to a buccan Warrow eighty-five years old and beyond.

(the) Grate Room: a small chamber in Kraggen-cor along the Brega Path. Also known as the Room.

Grau: a Bacran Man. Eldest son of Baru, the Passwarden of the Crestan Pass in 5E231.

(the) Gravenarch: a Dwarf-crafted arch in Kraggen-cor in the Hall of the Gravenarch. Destroyed by Brega during the Winter War.

(the) Great Arch of the Loom. See (the) hemidome.

(the) Great Argon River. See (the) Argon River.

(the) Great Barrier. See (the) Spindlethorn Barrier.

(the) Great Chamber (of the Sixth Rise): one of the chambers in Kraggen-cor along the Brega Path.

(the) Great Deep: an unplumbed abyss in Kraggen-cor near the Dawn-Gate. Also known as the Deep, the Dēop (Châkur), and the Great Dēop.

(the) Great Dēop: (Châkur: Dēop = Deep): Dwarven name for the Great Deep (q.v.).

(the) Great Enemy. See Gyphon.

(the) Great Escarpment: a great uplift in the land running east from the Grimwall Mountains and curving south along Greatwood. Bellon Falls marks the place where the Argon River plunges down the Escarpment, just as Vanil Falls marks where the River Nith cascades.

(the) great flank. See (the) Loom.

(the) Great Greenhall (Forest). See Darda Erynian.

(the) great hemidome. See (the) hemidome.

Great Isle: an island in the Argon River some fifty miles south of the Landover Road Ford. Site of an ancient fort whose guardians were corrupted by Gyphon; the fort was subsequently destroyed by the Baeron.

(the) Great Loom (of Aggarath). See (the) Loom.

(the) Great Loomwall. See (the) Loom.

(the) Great Maelstrom: a giant whirlpool in the Boreal Sea between Gron and the Seabane Islands, where it is said that Krakens dwell. Also called the Maelstrom.

(the) great portico (of the Dusk-Door): an edifice of marble columns supporting a marble roof against the Loom at the Dusk-Door. Destroyed by the Krakenward during the Winter War. Also known as the edifice of the Dusk-Door.

(the) Great Purging. See (the) Purging.

(the) Great Retreat: the retreat of all Free Folk from the forces of Modru during the early stages of the Winter War.

(the) Great River Argon. See (the) Argon River.

(the) Great Shelf. See (the) Broad Shelf.

(the) Great Swamp. See (the) Gwasp.

(the) Great Treehouse: a huge treehouse in the Boskydells containing a library.

(the) Great War: the part of the War between Gyphon and Adon that was fought in Mithgar. Also known as the Ban War, the Great War of the Ban, and the War of the Banning.

(the) Great War of the Ban. See (the) Great War.

(the) Greatwood: a vast forest in South Riamon stretching from the River Rissanin to the Glave Hills.

(the) green-and-white of Valon: the colors of the flag of Valon. [See (the) War-banner of Valon.]

Greenfields: a Boskydell hamlet on the Crossland Road east of Woody Hollow. Also known as the 'Fields.

Greenhall Forest. See Darda Erynian.

(the) Green Stone (of Xian): a jade egg. Said to hold the spirit of the Dragon-King.

Grevan: a Wizard of Mithgar who helped Valki construct the Dusk-Door. Also known as Grevan the Wizard, the Wizard Grevan.

Grevan the Wizard. See Grevan.

Grey Bomar. See Bomar.

(the) Greylocks: the Greylock lineage.

Greytower: the southeasternmost of the four mountains of the Quadran beneath which Kraggen-cor is delved. Greytower was so named because of the grey stone of its composition. Also known as Gralon (Sylva), and Uchan (Châkur).

Grg (Châkur: worms of rot): the Dwarven name for the maggot-folk.

Grimspire: the southwesternmost of the four mountains of the Quadran beneath which Kraggen-cor is delved. Grimspire is a mountain of black stone, and along its west face is the Great Loom in which the Dusk-Door is delved, opening into the mountain. Also known as Aevor (Sylva), the Aggarath (Châkur).

(the) Grimwall. See Grimwall Mountains.

(the) Grimwall Mountains: a great chain of mountains in Mithgar generally running in a northeasterly-southwesterly direction. Also known as the Grimwall.

Gron: Modru's evil Realm. Barren and bleak, it is a great wedge of land between the Gronfang Mountains to the east, the Rigga Mountains to the west, and the Boreal Sea to the north. Also known as the angle of Gron, the Northern Wastes (of Gron), and the Wastes of Gron.

(the) Gronfang Mountains: a north-south chain of mountains running from the Boreal Sea to the Grimwall. Also known as the Gronfangs.

(the) Gronfangs. See (the) Gronfang Mountains.

Guardian(s). See (the) Lian Guardian(s).

Gûnar: an abandoned Realm in Mithgar bounded on the north by the Grimwall and on the east, south, and west by the arc of the Gûnarring.

Gûnarring Gap: a pass through the Gûnarring (Mountains) joining Gûnar to Valon. Also known as the Gap.

Gûnar Slot: a great wide slot through the Grimwall connecting Gûnar to Rell.

Gushdug: a Hlōk of Gnar's Horde. Probably the leader of the company of Rucks slain by the Squad of Kraggen-cor, Ursor, and Shannon Silverleaf's Elven Company in the Battle of the Last River Camp. If so, Gushdug was killed by arrow from Silverleaf's bow.

Gushmot: a Hlōk of Gnar's Horde.

(the) Gwasp: a vast swamp in Gron. Also known as the Great Swamp.

Gyphon: The High Vûlk, whose struggle with Adon for control of the Spheres spilled over into Mithgar as the Great War. Gyphon lost and was banished beyond the Spheres. Gyphon again attempted to gain control during the Winter War but was thwarted by Tuckerby Underbank. Also known as the Great Deceiver, the Great Enemy, the Great Evil, The Greatest Evil, the High Vûlk, the Master.

Haddor: a Man of Valon. One of the riders in Brytta's force. Slain in the Battle of Stormhelm Defile. One of the Five Riders (q.v.).

Hai: a Free Folk exclamation of delight, surprise, or fierce exultation.

Hai roi: an enthusiastic call of greeting, probably Valur in origin but common to all tongues of the Free Folk.

Hál: a Free Folk greeting: hail.

(the) Hall: a term applicable to many of the chambers in Kraggen-cor: e.g., the Great Hall, the Hall of the Gravenarch, the War Hall. Also, a term by which Woody Hollow Hall (q.v.) is known.

(the) Hall of the Gravenarch: a long, low, narrow chamber in Kraggen-cor with a rune-engraved arch supporting the roof. Site of Braggi's demise and Braggi's Rune. The Deevewalkers strode through the Hall of the Gravenarch. Brega broke the

Gravenarch to thwart the Gargon by blocking the way. Thus, this part of the Brega Path could not be traversed, but a way around the blockage (the two-mile detour) was found by the Squad of Kraggen-cor.

(the) halls of the dead: the underworld (Hèl) of Valonian myth.

(the) Hammer: the Common-Tongue name given to Rávenor by the Dwarves because of the sudden storms that whelm its slopes. (See Stormhclm.)

Hammerer: a Dwarf whose craft is hammering, one of the skills of stone delving.

hammer-signalling: a Dwarven method of signalling one another by tapping out coded messages—hammer striking stone.

(the) Happy Otter Inn: a Boskydell inn in Greenfields. Also known as the 'Otter.

Harl. See Strong Harl.

Harlingar (Valur: Harl's line of blood): the lineal descendants of Strong Harl. Also the name given to horse-borne warriors of Valon.

Harl the Strong. See Strong Harl.

Harth: a Realm in Mithgar, south of the Wilderland, west of Rell, east of the Boskydells, north of Trellinath.

Hâth Ford: the ford across the Hâth River north of Gûnar Slot.

(the) Hâth River: a river flowing west from the Grimwall Mountains to the Rivermix north of Luren.

hauk (Châkur: advance): a Dwarven term meaning advance.

healer: a physician. A term also used to mean a battlefield helper who binds wounds and dispenses medicines and unguents.

hearthtale: a fairy story or adventure tale told for amusement or for illustrative purposes. So named because these tales were usually told in the evening around campfires, or around the fireplaces of dwellings.

hearthtale hero: a hero of a hearthtale. A term sometimes used to ascribe atypical powers, characteristics, or fortunes to a person. A person whose abilities or fate does not conform to reality.

Hèl: Hell. Also known to the Vanadurin as the halls of the dead, the Realm of the Underworld, and the Underworld.

Hèlarms (Sylva: Hell-arms): Elven name for a Kraken (q.v.).

Hèl's spawn. See (the) undead.

Hèlsteeds (singular: Hèlsteed): horse-like creatures with cloven hooves, long scaled tails, yellow eyes with slitted pupils, and a foetid stench. Slower than horses but with greater endurance. Ridden by Ghûls. Also known as 'Steeds.

(the) hemidome: a great cavernous arch of mountain within which the Dusken Door is situated. Also known as the Great Arch of the Loom and the great hemidome.

(a) Hero of the Realm: an honor bestowed by the High King upon extraordinary heroes.

(the) hidden language. See Châkur.

(the) hidden linchpins: linchpins set in strategic passages in Dwarven caverns which, when pulled, cause the collapse of the passage. A Dwarven defence.

(the) Hidden Refuge. See Arden Valley.

(the) Hidden Stand. See Arden Valley.

(the) hidden tongue. See Châkur.

(the) Hidden Vale. See Arden Valley.

High Adon. See Adon.

High Adon's Ban. See (the) Ban.

High Adon's Covenant. See (the) Ban.

(the) High Gate: a secret door from Kraggen-cor into Quadran Pass. Situated on the western side of the col. Also known as the Gate.

(the) High King: the Liege Lord of all of Northern Mithgar, to whom all other Kings swear fealty. He holds Court at Caer Pendwyr in Pellar, and in Challerain Keep in Rian. Also known as the High Ruler.

(a) High King's Ceremony: a Ceremony ordained by the High King.

(the) High Leader. See Durek.

(the) High One. See Adon.

High Plane: one of the three Planes of creation, holding the High Worlds.

hight: command; order; call; called; name; named.

(the) High Vûlk. See Gyphon.

his Nibs. See Gnar.

(the) History: generally taken to mean the written body of work of the Ravenbook Scholars.

Hlōks (singular: Hlōk): evil, Man-sized, Rūck-like beings. Though fewer in number, Hlōks were masters of the Rūcks.

Also known as Drōkha (Valur), Hlōks (Châkur), Loka (Sylva), Lōkha (OP).

Hlōken: a term meaning "of the Hlōks."

(the) hoard of Sleeth: the treasure trove of Sleeth the Orm. Originally stolen by the Dragon from the Dwarves of Blackstone, centuries later the trove was won from Sleeth by Elgo. This treasure became a bone of contention between the Dwarves and the Men of the Steppes of Jord, leading to War and to the Quest of the Black Mountain.

Hogon: a Man of Valon. One of the riders in Brytta's force. A lead scout.

Hola: an untranslated exclamation, common to all tongues of the Free Folk, used to express surprise or to call attention.

(the) Hollow. See Woody Hollow.

(the) Hollow Commons: an open wooded parkland in Woody Hollow where the citizens gather for special events or to have picnics and games. Also known as the Commons.

Hollow End: the northwest end of Woody Hollow. Also named Hollow End because of the many burrow dwellings there.

Hollow Hall. See Woody Hollow Hall.

Holly Northcolt: a damman Warrow of the Boskydells. Wife of Peregrin Fairhill. Dam of Dando, Pippen, Silver, and Petal.

(a) Horde: usually taken to mean ten thousand or more maggot-folk ravaging across the land. In the time of the Fairhill Chronicle, however, Gnar's Horde was one that had been trapped in Drimmen-deeve at the end of the Winter War and remained there until destroyed in the War of Kraggen-cor.

(the) Horn of Narok: a Dwarven horn carfted by an unknown hand. A great token of fear to the Dwarves. Lost to Sleeth the Orm when he took Blackstone as his lair. Won by Elgo. Given to Patrel, as a token of his office, by Vidron. Used to rally Warrow forces in the Struggles during the Winter War. Kept on display at The Root until the Quest of Kraggen-cor. Returned to Kraggen-cor, by Cotton Buckleburr, where it called forth the Doom of Narok. Also called the Horn of the Reach and the Horn of Valon.

(the) Horn of the Reach. See (the) Horn of Valon.

(the) Horn of Valon: a Dwarven horn found in the hoard of Sleeth the Orm by Elgo, Sleeth's Doom. The horn was passed down through the generations until it became Vidron's property. For reasons unexplained—perhaps in a sweeping gesture of generosity but more likely because the horn sought to fulfill its destiny—Vidron gave the horn to Patrel as a token of the Warrow Captain's office. It was used by Patrel to rally forces during the Winter War, although a greater destiny for the horn lay in future events. Also called the horn of Narok, the Horn of the Reach, and the silver horn of Valon.

(the) Horror. See (the) Gargon.

(the) horsefolk: a term used by Cotton to mean the Vanadurin.

(the) Host: an army (or armies) of a leader of the Free Folk. Also known as a Legion.

(the) House of Aurinor: a branch of weapons-making Lian Elves in Duellin, a lost city of Atala.

(the) House of Valon: the ruling House of the Kingdom of Valon.

Hoxley Housman: a Man of New Luren. Owner of the Red Boar Inn during the time of the Quest of Kraggen-cor.

Hoy: an untranslated exclamation, common to all tongues of the Free Folk, used to express surprise or to call attention.

Hrōks (singular: Hrōk) (Châkur: vile-vermin). See Hlōks.

Hrōken: a term meaning "of the Hrōks."

Hunter's Moon: the first full Moon after the Harvest Moon.

Hurn: a realm of Mithgar situated at the eastern reach of the Avagon Sea.

Hyree: a southern Realm in Mithgar allied with Gron during the Winter War. Bounded on the north by the Avagon Sea, on the east by Karoo, on the south by wasteland, and on the west by the Weston Ocean.

Igon: a Man of Pellar. Youngest son of Aurion. A Lord and Prince of the Realm, Brother of Galen. Hero of the Winter War. A member of Brega's squad.

Inarion: an Elf. Lian warrior. Elf Lord of Arden Vale. Leader of the Elves in Weiunwood during the Winter War. Fought in the Battle of Kregyn.

(the) Inner Sea: a brackish-water inland sea joined to the ocean through an extraordinarily long, narrow strait. Bounded on the east by Garia and on the west by Riamon.

(the) Iron Tower: Modru's fortress in the Wastes of Gron. Also known as the Cold Iron Tower, the dark citadel, the Kinstealer's holt.

(the) Ironwater River: a river originating in the Rimmen Mountains and flowing southeasterly to the Inner Sea.

(the) Isleborne River: a river running south and west from Luren to the Weston Ocean. So named because of the many islands in the river. Also known as the Fainen (Sylva) River.

(a) jam: a mountain-climbing/stone-climbing device that is lodged in crevices and used with a snap-ring and a rope or climbing harness, giving purchase to climbers. Shaped like irregular cubes, jams are known as "nuts" by modern-day climbers. Used in Mithgar primarily by Dwarves.

Jayar Northcolt: a buccan Warrow of the Boskydells. Husband of Dot. Sire of Holly. Ex-postmaster. Squire. Owner of Buttermilk Springs, near Thimble. Also known as Squire Northcolt.

Jeering Elgo: a name given Elgo by the Dwarves after their dispute over Sleeth's hoard.

Jugo: a Realm of Mithgar bounded on the north by Gûnar; on the east by Valon, the Red Hills, and Pellar; on the south by the Avagon Sea; and on the west by Hoven and the Brin Downs.

Kachar: a Dwarvenholt in the Grimwall Mountains above Aven. Here it was that Elgo came to face Brak in the dispute over Sleeth's hoard.

Kala (Châkur: good): a Dwarven exclamation meaning good.

(the) Kammerling: a silveron hammer said to have been forged by Adon Himself. Used to smite Black Kalgalath, a Fire-drake.

Khana (Châkur: breakdeath): a Dwarven term meaning breakdeath; refers to the Dwarven belief in reincarnation, that the bonds of Death are broken as each spirit is reborn to walk the earth once again.

Khana Durek (Châkur: Breakdeath Durek): a Dwarven title for Durek; i.e., Khana Durek = Breakdeath Durek. (See Breakdeath Durek.)

Khōls (singular: Khōl) (Châkur: reaving-foe): Dwarven term for Ghûls (q.v.).

Kian: a Man of Riamon. Prince of Riamon during the Quest of Kraggen-cor. Realmsman. Guide to Anval and Borin, and to the

Squad of Kraggen-cor. The Leader of the Squad of Kraggen-cor. Hero. King of Riamon after the War of Kraggen-cor. Also known as Lord Kian and later as King Kian.

(the) Kindred: generally taken to mean Châkka Kindred (q.v.).

King Kian. See Kian.

King's business: the specific purpose with which a King charges his emissaries.

(a) King's Ceremony: a Ceremony ordained by a King.

Kingsguards: the personal guards of a King.

Kingsmen: agents and soldiers of a King.

King's Messengers: couriers or heralds of a King.

King's-soldiers: warriors of the army of a King.

Kinstealer: a name given to Modru when his forces took Laurelin captive.

Kistan: an island Realm in the Avagon Sea north of Karoo and south of Vancha. Ancient enemy of Pellar. Home of sea rovers (pirates). Allied with Gron during the Winter War.

Kop'yo (Valur: now): a Valonian term meaning "now" or "go now."

Kraggen-cor (Châkur: Mountain-strength, Mountain-might): the Dwarven Realm mined under the Quadran. Mightiest of all Dwarvenholts. Lost to the Dwarves for more than a thousand years while ruled by the Ghath. One of the rare places in Mithgar where silveron is found. Also known as the Black Deeves, Black Drimmen-deeve, the Black Hole, the Black Maze, the Black Puzzle, the Deeves, Drimmen-deeve, the Mines.

Kraken (plural: Krakens): an evil creature of the sea. Huge. Tentacled. Some Krakens are said to live in the Great Maelstrom. Krakens are perhaps the female mates of Dragons. Also known as Hèlarms.

(the) Krakenward: a Kraken, living in the Dark Mere, guarding the Dusk-Door. Controlled by Modru and borne to the lakelet by Skail the Cold-drake in preparation for the coming of the Dragon Star. Slain by the Dwarves during the Quest of Kraggen-cor. Also known as the Hèlarms (Sylva), the lurker, the Madûk (Châkur), the Monster, the Monster of the Dark Mere, the Monster of the Mere, the Warder, the Warder from the deep black slime.

Kruk (Châkur: untranslated interjection): Dwarf oathword of rage.

* * *

(the) Lady of the Root: title given to Holly by Perry.

(the) Lair. See (the) Lost Prison.

Land of Galion: Holly's name for Darda Galion.

(the) Land of the Waldana. See (the) Boskydells.

(the) Land of the Wee Folk. See (the) Boskydells.

(the) Land of the West: taken to mean the island of Atala.

Landover Road: a great east-west road of Mithgar, running eastward from the Crestan Pass in the Grimwall.

Landover Road Ford: the ford across the Argon River along the Landover Road.

Larkenwald. See Darda Galion.

(the) Last River Camp: the place where the Squad of Kraggen-cor last camped along the Argon River. It was there, on the west bank, that they fought with Spawn in the Battle of the Last River Camp.

Laurelin: a Woman of Riamon. Princess. Betrothed to Galen in the time of the Winter War. Modru's captive during the Winter War. Wife of Galen after the Winter War. Mother of Gareth.

Lawks: a Free Folk interjection of surprise or awe meaning "Lord," "Mercy," "Lord of mercy," or "Lord have mercy."

leaf: apparently tobacco. Smoked in pipes usually made of clay.

(a) Legion. See (the) Host.

Levels: taken to mean the tiers or floors within Dwarvenholts.

Lian (Sylva: first): one of the two strains of Elves, the other being the Dylvana. Also known as Eld Ones, the First Elves.

(the) Lian Guardian(s): Elf warder(s) of Mithgar, guarding against evil. Also known as Guardian(s).

Lianion (Sylva: first land): Elven name given to Rell, where the Lian once dwelled.

Lianion-Elves: the name given to the Lian when they dwelled in Lianion.

(the) Line of Durek: the lineage of Durek and of Durek's Folk.

Line of the Châkka Kindred: any one of the five strains of Dwarves.

little uns. See Warrows.

Littor: a Dwarf of Durek's Folk. One of Bomar's cooking crew. Slain in the Battle of Kraggen-cor.

Loftcrag: the northeasternmost of the four mountains of the

Quadran, beneath which Kraggen-cor is delved. A mountain whose stone is tinged blue. Also known as Chagor (Sylva) and Ghatan (Châkur).

Loka (singular: Lok) (Sylva: vile-ones). See Hlōks.

Loken: a term meaning "of the Loka."

Lōkha (singular: Lōkh) (OP: ones-of-filth). See Hlōks.

Lōkken: a term meaning "of the Lōkha."

(the) Lone Eld Tree: a single Eld Tree growing among the pines in Arden Valley near Arden Falls. This tree was the only known one of its kind in Mithgar other than those in Darda Galion.

(the) Long Hall: one of the chambers in Kraggen-cor along the Brega Path.

(the) Loom: a massif; the western sheer stone flank of Grimspire Mountain, containing the cavernous hemidome at Dusk-Door. Also known as the great flank, the Great Loom, the Great Loomwall, the Loom of Grimspire, the Loomwall.

(the) Loom of Grimspire. See (the) Loom.

(the) Loomwall. See (the) Loom.

(the) Looser of the Red Quarrel. See Tuckerby Underbank.

Lord Kian. See Kian.

Lost Duellin. See Duellin.

(the) Lost Land. See Atala.

(the) Lost Prison: the place in Kraggen-cor where the Gargon was trapped for three thousand years. Also known as the *Draedan's* (Sylva) Lair, the Gargon's Lair, the Lair.

(the) Lower Plane: one of the three Planes of creation, holding the Low Worlds.

Lumme: a Free Folk interjection of surprise meaning "Love me."

Luren: a great city of trade situated on the west bank of the Isleborne River in the Riverwood Forest. Suffered through the Dark Plague; destroyed by fire and abandoned. Centuries later, the hamlet of New Luren was founded among the ruins of Old Luren, for at that place is the only river ford in the region.

Luren Ford: the ford across the Isleborne River at Luren.

Lurenites: citizens of Old Luren and of New Luren.

(the) lurker (in the Dark Mere). See the Krakenward.

Luthen: a Man of Valon. One of the riders in Brytta's force.

Slain in the Battle of Stormhelm Defile. One of the Five Riders (q.v.).

Madûk (Châkur: evil monster): the Dwarven name for the Krakenward.

(the) Maelstrom. See (the) Great Maelstrom.

maggot-folk: a Warrow name for Spawn.

maiden (plural: maidens): the age-name given to a damman Warrow between ten and twenty years old.

Market Square: a town square in Woody Hollow with stores and an open market.

Marshal of the North Reach: the rank of the Valonian governor of the North Reach of Valon. Brytta was the Marshal of the North Reach in the time of the Quest of Kraggen-cor.

Marshal (of the Valanreach): any of the Reachmarshals (q.v.).

Mastercrafter: a Dwarven master of a craft.

Masterdelver: a Dwarf who has mastered the skill of delving the stone of a Dwarvenholt.

Master of the Ravenbook Scholars: a scholar-moderator elected by the Ravenbook Scholars (q.v.) to chair meetings, direct studies, and in general to guide the activities of that historical society. In the time of the Quest of Kraggen-cor, Gerontius Fairhill was the Master.

Master of The Root: the Ravenbook Scholar chosen to be the curator of The Root.

Master Perry. See Peregrin Fairhill.

(the) Memorial. See (the) Monument at Budgens.

Men: Mankind as we know it. One of the Free Folk of Mithgar. Allied to but separate from Dwarves, Elves, Warrows.

mian: a tasty Elven waybread.

(the) Middle Plane: one of the three Planes of creation, holding the Middle Worlds.

(the) mill: taken to mean the mill on the banks of the Dinglerill in Woody Hollow.

Mineholt: a term meaning a Dwarvenholt.

Mineholt North: a principal Dwarvenholt in the Rimmen Mountains in Riamon. Also called the Undermountain Realm of Mineholt North.

Minemaster: a Dwarf who has mastered the skill of mining.

(the) Mines. See Kraggen-cor.

Mister Borin: an appellation given to Borin by Fennerly Cotter.

Mister Cotton: an appellation given to Cotton by Fennerly Cotter.

Mister Perry: an appellation given to Perry by a number of Warrows of the Boskydells.

Mitheor (Châkur: mid-earth): the Dwarven name for Mithgar.

Mithgar: a term generally meaning the world. Also can refer to the Realms under the rule of the High King. Also known as the midworld, and as Mitheor (Châkur).

Modru: an evil Wizard. Servant of Gyphon. Master of the Myrkenstone. Slain by Tuck in the Winter War. Also known as the Enemy, the Enemy in Gron, the Evil in Gron, the Evil One, the Evil up North, the Foe, the Kinstealer, the Master of the Cold, Modru Kinstealer.

Modru Kinstealer. See Modru.

Modru's Dread. See (the) Gargon.

Modru's Horde: all of the forces of maggot-folk commanded by Modru.

Modru's Mines: Spawn caverns thought to be in the Grimwall Mountains in the vicinity of Crestan Pass.

Modru's minions: all of the forces commanded by Modru.

Modru's Reavers. See Ghûls.

Mog: a Cave Ogru of Kraggen-cor. A Troll in Gnar's Horde.

Molly Brewster: a Woman of Stonehill. Wife of Aylesworth.

Monarch: generally taken to mean the High King, but also can mean any King.

(the) Monster. See (the) Krakenward.

(the) Monster of the Dark Mere. See (the) Krakenward.

(the) Monster of the Mere. See (the) Krakenward.

Mont Coron. See Stormhelm.

(the) Monument. See (the) Monument at Budgens.

(the) Monument at Budgens: a Boskydell monument in the hamlet of Budgens commemorating the first battle of the Struggles. Also known as the Memorial and as the Monument.

Monument Knoll: the hill in Budgens on which is situated the Monument.

Mountain (Châkur: MOꟼA = living stone): a Dwarven word represented in the translation of *The Raven Book* and of *The Fairhill Journal* by the word Mountain. The symbol M indicates a special word for "mountain" signifying Châkka reverence for the living stone of Mitheor (Mithgar).

(the) Mountain Throne: a natural quartzen outcrop shaped like the bench of a great throne high upon the side of Stormhelm. From it can be seen the Châkkacyth Ryng.

Mount Redguard. See Redguard (Mount/Mountain).

(the) Mustering Chamber (of the First Neath). See (the) War Hall.

(the) Mustering Hall. See (the) War Hall.

myrk (Sylva, OHR: myrk = murk): murk.

(the) Myrkenstone: the piece of the Dragon Star that fell to Mithgar; used by Modru to create the Dimmendark. Destroyed by Tuck. Also known as the 'Stone.

(the) Myrkenstone Slayer. See Tuckerby Underbank.

Naral: a Dwarf of Durek's Folk. One of Bomar's cooking crew. Slain in the Battle of Kraggen-cor.

Nare: a Dwarf of Durek's Folk. One of Bomar's cooking crew. Slain in the Battle of Kraggen-cor.

Narok (Châkur: Death-War): a Dwarven term meaning Death-War. The Staves of Narok (q.v.) foretold of a Death-War (an apocalyptic struggle) in which the Dwarves would reap great sorrow.

Neaths: the name given to the levels in Kraggen-cor deeper than the entrance at Dawn-Gate. (See Gate Level.)

Neddra: the name of one of the Untargarda, whence came the Spawn.

Ned Proudhand: a buccan Warrow of the Boskydells. The wheelwright that was paid a gold coin for repairing the waggon used by Anval, Borin, and Lord Kian on their trip to the Boskydells.

New Luren: the settlement built upon the site of Old Luren. (See Luren.)

Nightwind: a horse of Valon. Brytta's great black stallion, trained for War.

ninnyhammer: dolt.

(the) Nith River (Sylva: nith = rising): a river in Darda Galion flowing east to plunge down the Great Escarpment at Vanil Falls into the Cauldron to join the Argon River.

(the) Northern Wastes. See Gron.

(the) North Reach (of Valon): the northern quadrant of Valon.
North Riamon. See Riamon.
(the) North Route. See (the) Post Road.

Ogrus (singular: Ogru) (Twyll, Valur: Trolls): evil creatures. Giant Rūcks. Twelve to fourteen feet tall. Dull-witted. Stonelike hides. Enormous strength. Also known as Cave Trolls, Cave Ogrus, Ogru-Trolls, Trolls.
Ogruthi (Sylva: Trollfolk): Elven name for the Ogru Folk.
Ogru-Trolls. See Ogrus.
Old Luren: a city of old, destroyed by fire. (See Luren.)
Old Man Tumble: Cotton's name for the Tumble River.
(the) Old Rell Spur: the ancient road joining the Old Rell Way to the Dusk-Door. Also known as the Old Way Spur and as the Spur.
(the) Old Rell Way: an abandoned trade road running south from the Crestan Pass down the west side of the Grimwall Mountains to Luren. Also known as the Old Way and as the Way.
(the) Old Way. See (the) Old Rell Way.
(the) Old Way Spur. See (the) Old Rell Spur.
O Mighty One. See Gnar.
(the) One-Eyed Crow: a Boskydell inn in Woody Hollow. Also known as the 'Crow.
Oris: a Dwarf of Durek's Folk. One of Bomar's cooking crew. Slain in the Battle of Kraggen-cor.
Orm. See Dragon.
Orn: a Dwarf of Durek's Folk. Glain's son. Slain by the Gargon shortly after it burst free of the Lost Prison.
Othen Warrows: one of the four northern strains of Warrows. Othen Warrows traditionally live in fen stilt-houses in marshlands.
Othran the Seer: a Man from Atala, the Lost Land.
Othran's Tomb: a rune-marked stone tomb at the foot of Mont Challerain. Here lie the remains of Othran the Seer. Tuck found the Red Quarrel and the Atalar Blade in Othran's Tomb. Also known as the barrow of Othran the Seer.
(the) 'Otter. See (the) Happy Otter Inn.
Outside: a Boskydell Warrow term meaning the Lands beyond the borders of the Boskydells.

Outsiders: a Boskydell Warrow term meaning people living beyond the borders of the Boskydells.

(the) Oval Chamber: one of the chambers in Kraggen-cor along the Brega Path.

(the) Over Stair: the portage-way up the Great Escarpment at Bellon Falls.

Paren Warrows: one of the four northern strains of Warrows. Paren Warrows traditionally are field dwellers living in stone field-houses (stone dwellings and stone farmhouses situated in open fields).

(the) Path. See (the) Brega path.

Pathfinder: a name given to Cotton by Bomar.

pathfinder: a guide.

Patrel Rushlock: a buccan Warrow of the Boskydells. Hero of the Winter War. Captain of the Company of the King. A leader of the Struggles. One of Tuck's companions. Wearer of the golden armor. Bearer of the Horn of Valon. A member of Brega's squad. Also known as the Captain of the Infant Brigade, Captain Patrel, and Paddy.

Pellar: a Realm of Mithgar where dwells the High King in Caer Pendwyr. Bounded on the north by Riamon and also by Valon across the River Argon, and on the east and south by the Avagon Sea, and on the west by Jugo.

Pellarion: the common language of Mithgar. So named because it originated in Pellar. Also known as the Common Tongue. (For various words and phrases in Old Pellarion, see Appendix: Translations of Words and Phrases.)

Pendwyrian: a term meaning "of Caer Pendwyr."

Peregrin Fairhill: a buccan Warrow of the Boskydells. Raven-book Scholar. Curator of Sir Tuckerby's Warren. Member of the Quest of Kraggen-cor. Member of the Squad of Kraggen-cor. Brega-Path guide. Wielder of Bane. Drimmen-deeve Rück-fighter. Scriber of *The Fairhill Journal*. Hero of the Realm. Also known as Friend Perry, Master Perry, Mister Perry, Perry, Wee Perry, and Wee One.

Perry. See Peregrin Fairhill.

Perry's map: Perry's drawing of the Brega Path.

(the) Pitch: a great slope of land falling away to the east of the

Quadran. Also known as Baralan (Châkur) and Falanith (Sylva).

Plooshgnak: a Hlōk of Gnar's Horde.

(the) Plow. See Rhone.

(the) Pony Field: a large field in Woody Hollow where ponies are kept.

(the) Pony Field stable: a common stable of Woody Hollow, situated on the southern edge of the Pony Field.

(the) Post Road: the road between Luren and Challerain Keep. Also known as the North Road, and as the South Road.

(the) Purging: the successful efforts of the Lian Guardians and the Men of the Wilderland to drive dire creatures from Drearwood. Also known as the Great Purging.

(the) Quadmere: a pure lakelet on the Pitch one mile from Dawn-Gate. Also known as Châk-alon (Châkur) and as the 'Mere.

(the) Quadran: the name collectively given to four of the mountains of the Grimwall: Greytower, Loftcrag, Grimspire, Stormhelm. Herein Kraggen-cor is delved.

Quadran Col. See Quadran Pass.

Quadran Gap. See Quadran Pass.

Quadran Pass: the pass across the Grimwall through the Quadran. Also known as the Col, the Gap, the Gap of Stormhelm, the Pass, Quadran Col, and Quadran Gap.

Quadran Road: the road from Quadran Pass down the west side of Stormhelm.

Quadran Run: the road, and the stream, from Quadran Pass down the east side of Stormhelm.

(the) Quadrill: a river flowing southeasterly from the Quadran through Darda Galion and into the Argon River.

(the) Quartzen Caves: a Dwarven mineholt of Durek's Folk, east of the Rimmen Mountains, delved in the Quartzen Hills.

(the) Quartzen Hills: a range of hills east of the Rimmen Mountains. Here are delved the Quartzen Caves.

(the) Quest of Black Mountain: the quest of Elyn and Thork to find the Kammerling.

(the) Quest of Kraggen-cor: the quest of the Dwarves and their allies to regain Kraggen-cor from Gnar's Horde.

(the) Quest of the Green Stone: the quest of Arin and of Egil One Eye to find the Green Stone of Xian.

(a) quilted down-suit: special quilted, down-filled clothing worn to withstand the bitter winter cold of the mountains.

Quiren Warrows: one of the four strains of northern Warrows. Quiren Warrows traditionally are tree dwellers living in wooden flet houses.

(a) Race. See Folk.

(the) Race: a narrow, high-walled river canyon through which the Argon River thunders at a great speed. Situated south of the Dalgor Marches.

Rach (Valur: untranslated interjection): oathword of Valon, used to express frustration.

Raech: a Man of Valon. One of the riders in Brytta's force. Slain in the Battle of Stormhelm Defile. One of the Five Riders (q.v.).

Rael: Lian Elfess. Consort of Talarin. Mother of Gildor and Vanidor. Seeress and soothsayer.

Raffin: a Boskydell village along the Crossland Road in East-dell.

Ragad Vale: a western Grimwall valley leading to Dusk-Door, at the base of Grimspire Mountain. Also known as Ragad Valley and as the Valley of the Door.

Ragad Valley. See Ragad Vale.

Ralo Road: the road between Luren and Gûnarring Gap.

Rand: a Man of Riamon. Prince of Riamon. Kian's younger brother. Guide to Durek's Host. Realmsman. Troll-slain in the Battle of Kraggen-cor.

Raven (Underbank-Greylock): a damman Warrow. Wife of Willen Greylock. Dam of Robin. Dammsel of Tuck and Merrilee. Raven was instrumental in the recording of *Sir Tuckerby Underbank's Unfinished Diary and His Accounting of the Winter War*. Also known as Raven the Scholar.

(The) Raven Book. See *Sir Tuckerby Underbank's Unfinished Diary and His Accounting of the Winter War*. Tuck named the journal after his dammsel, Raven; hence, it acquired the name *The Raven Book*. Also known as the *'Book*.

(the) Ravenbook Scholars: a continuing group of Warrow historians originally organized by Willen Greylock to carry on the recording of the history of Mithgar. This group continued the work started by Tuck, who had been commissioned by King Galen to record the events of the Winter War, and other history as well. Also known as the Scholars.

Rávenor (Châkur: storm hammer). See Stormhelm.

Raven the Scholar. See Raven (Underbank-Greylock).

ravers: ravagers.

(a) Reach (of Valon): one of the four quadrants into which Valon is divided (North Reach, East Reach, South Reach, West Reach). The term "Reach" translates into "Reich" in Valur.

Reachmarshal (from Reich-marshal): the Vanadrin rank below Hrosmarshal (Valur: hros = horse). Also known as Marshal and as Valanreach Marshal.

(the) Realm: generally taken to mean that part of Mithgar ruled by the High King.

(the) Realm of Death: the dwelling place of spirits in the time between death and rebirth—a Dwarven belief.

(the) Realm of the Underworld. See Hèl.

Realmsmen: agents of the High King. Defenders of the Land. Champions of Just Causes.

Realmstone: any one of the obelisks marking the boundaries of Kingdoms; e.g., there is a Realmstone on the west bank of the Quadmere marking the Realm of Kraggen-cor.

reavers. See Ghûls.

reaving-foe. See Ghûls.

(the) Red Arrow. See (the) Red Quarrel.

(the) Red Boar: an inn in New Luren.

(the) Red Caverns. See (the) Red Caves.

(the) Red Caves: the Dwarven mineholt in the Red Hills. A famous Dwarven armory. Also known as the Red Caverns.

Redguard (Mount/Mountain): a small mountain just to the west of the Quadran. Also known as Mount Redguard.

(the) Red Hills: a north-south range of mountains between Jugo and Valon.

(the) Red Quarrel: a red arrow, made of a strange, light metal (perhaps coated lithium or magnesium), found by Tuck in the tomb of Othran the Seer. A token of power loosed by Tuck in the Winter War, the Red Quarrel destroyed the Myrkenstone. Also known as the Red Arrow.

(the) Refuge. See Arden Valley.

Rell: an abandoned Land of Mithgar. Bounded on the north by Arden, on the east and south by the Grimwall, and on the west by the River Tumble along Rhone.

(the) Rest Chamber: one of the chambers in Kraggen-cor along the Brega Path.

Rhondor: a city of commerce on the shores of the Inner Sea at the outlet of the Ironwater River. Because of the scarcity of nearby forests, the city was made of tile, brick, and fireclay.

Rhone: an abandoned Land of Mithgar. Bounded on the north by the Rigga Mountains, on the east and south by Arden and the River Tumble along Rell, and on the west by the River Carie along Harth and Rian. Also known as the Plow because of its shape.

Riamon: a Realm of Mithgar, divided into two sparsely settled Kingdoms: North Riamon and its Trust, South Riamon. Bounded on the north by Aven, on the east by Garia, on the south by Pellar and Valon, and on the west by the Grimwall.

(the) riddle of Narok. See (the) Staves of Narok

(the) Riders of Valon: Men of Valon. So named because Valon is a nation of horsemen.

(the) Rigga Mountains: a north-south chain of mountains between Rian to the west and Gron to the east, running from the Boreal Sea in the north to Grūwen Pass in the south.

(the) Rillmere: a lakelet along the southwestern side of Budgens.

(the) Rime of Narok. See (the) Staves of Narok.

(the) Rimmen Mountains: a great ring of mountains in Riamon.

(the) Ring. See (the) Châkkacyth Ryng.

Rises: the name given to the levels in Kraggen-cor higher than the entrance at Dawn-Gate. (See Gate Level.)

(the) Rissanin River: a river running southwesterly from the Rimmen Mountains to the River Argon.

Rith: the trothmate of Seventh Durek. The only female Dwarf named in either *The Raven Book* or *The Fairhill Journal*.

River Drummers: merchants who ply their trade on the rivers of Mithgar.

(the) Rivermix: a great swirl of water where the Hâth River meets the Caire River to become the Isleborne River, just north of Luren.

Riverwood (Forest): a great forest, along the Rivers Caire and Isleborne, extending into the Lands of Trellinath, Harth, and Rell.

rock-nails: pitons.

Rolf: a Baeran Man. Middle son of Baru, the Passwarden of the Crestan Pass in 5E231.

(the) Room: a term applicable to many chambers in Kraggen-cor; e.g., the Grate Room.

(The) Root: the name of Tuck's burrow in Woody Hollow. So named because it lies at the root of the coomb in which Woody Hollow is situated. After the Winter War, The Root came to be known as Sir Tuckerby's Warren and as Tuckerby's Warren.

(the) Rothro River: a river originating on the wold east of Dawn-Gate and flowing south into the Quadrill.

(the) Round Chamber: one of the chambers in Kraggen-cor along the Brega Path.

(the) Rovers of Kistan: reavers of the sea whose pirate holts are in the wild southern coastal lands of Kistan. Ancient enemies of Pellar.

Rucha (singular: Ruch) (Sylva: foul-ones): Elven name for Rūcks (q.v.).

Rūcken: a term meaning "of the Rucha."

Rūck-doors: hidden doors, Rūck-made, along the mountain slopes, opening into the caverns of the maggot-folk. Also known as Rūck-gates, Rutch-doors, Spawn-doors, and Wrg-doors.

Rūcken: a term meaning "of the Rūcks."

Rūck-fighter: a term generally taken to mean any person of the Free Folk who has fought the maggot-folk.

Rūck-gates. See Rūck-doors.

Rūckish: a term meaning Rūck-like.

Rūcks (singular: Rūck): evil, goblin-like creatures from Neddra, four to five feet tall. Dark. Pointed teeth. Bat-wing ears. Skinny-armed, bandylegged. Unskilled. Also known as Rucha (Sylva), Rukha (OP), Rutcha (Valur), Ūkhs (Chākur).

Rūckslayer: a term used to describe any warrior who has slain several Rūcks.

Rukha (singular: Rukh) (OP: filthy-ones): Pellarion name for Rūcks (q.v.).

rune-jewel: a jewel inscribed with runes of power. Such a jewel was embedded in the blade of the Elven long-knife Bane.

Rûpt (Sylva: corpse-worms): the Elven name for the maggot-folk.

Rutcha (singular: Rutch) (Valur: goblins): a term used by the Men of Valon meaning Rūcks (q.v.).

Rutch-doors (Valur: goblin-doors). See Rūck-doors.

Rutchen: a term meaning "of the Rutcha."

Rutch-pace (Valur: goblin-pace): the running lope of the maggot-folk.

(the) Ryng. See (the) Châkkacyth Ryng.

(the) Scholars. See (the) Ravenbook Scholars.

(the) Scroll. See (the) Brega Scroll.

(the) Secret Seven: Cotton's name for the Squad of Kraggen-cor (q.v.).

Sentinel Falls: a waterfall of the Duskrill near the Dusk-Door. So named because of the sentinel post above the falls.

(the) Sentinel Stair: the carven stair up the bluff of Sentinel Falls and to the top of the Sentinel Stand.

(the) Sentinel Stand: a guard post atop a tall spire near the Dusk-Door where Dwarf sentries kept watch over Ragad Vale.

(the) Seven. See (the) Squad of Kraggen-cor.

(the) Seven Dells: the Boskydells (q.v.). Called the Seven Dells because the Realm is divided into seven major districts, each called a Dell: Northdell, Eastdell, Southdell, Westdell, Centerdell, Updell, Downdell.

(the) Seven Penetrators. See (the) Squad of Kraggen-cor.

Seventh Durek: the Dwarf King of Durek's Folk during the Quest of Kraggen-cor. Renowned for wrestling Kraggen-cor from the maggot-folk and forging it into a mighty Realm as of old. The seventh to be named Durek (q.v.).

Shadowlight: the spectral light of the Dimmendark (q.v.).

(a) shadow-mission: a false mission or a mission of little or no hope.

Shannon. See Vanidar.

Shannon Silverleaf. See Vanidar.

(the) Shelf. See (the) Broad Shelf.

shok (Châkur: axes): a Dwarven term meaning axes.

(the) Side Hall: one of the chambers in Kraggen-cor along the Brega Path.

(the) Signal Mountains: a north-to-east-to-south arc of weatherworn, sparse, widespread mountains. Mont Challerain is the northernmost mountain, Beacontor the southernmost. So named because signal fires upon their crests were used to pass along news of import.

(the) silver armor. See silveron armor.

(The) Silver Call. See *(The) Fairhill Journal*.

(the) Silver Call: the sound of the Horn of Narok—mentioned in the Staves of Narok—which caused the fulfillment of the ancient prophecy.

(the) silver call: generally taken to mean the lure of a quest or a venture, said to fetch with a silver call. Also can mean the sound of the Horn of Valon.

silver coin. See silver penny.

(the) silver horn (of Valon). See (the) Horn of Valon.

Silverlarks. See Vani-lērihha.

Silverleaf. See Vanidar.

silveron: a rare and precious metal of Mithgar. Probably an alloy. Also known as starsilver.

(the) silveron armor: the armor worn by Tuck during the Winter War and by Perry during the Quest of Kraggen-cor. Originally made by the Dwarves of Drimmen-deeve for Princelings of the Royal House of the High King, the armor was given to Tuck by Laurelin to wear at her birthday feast. The armor was ultimately placed on display at Tuckerby's Warren, where it was to remain in possession of the Warrows until recalled by the shade of Aurion. Also known as the silver armor, the silveron mail, the starsilver armor.

(the) silveron mail. See (the) silveron armor.

silver penny: one of three types of coins used for commerce in Mithgar (gold and copper being the other two types). Also known as a silver, a silver coin, and as a silver piece.

sipar: a Rūcken shield with three strap-handles positioned such that it can be used either as a target shield or as a buckler.

Sir Tuckerby's Diary: the original diary kept by Tuckerby Underbank during the Winter War. (See *Sir Tuckerby Underbank's Unfinished Diary and His Accounting of the Winter War*.)

Sir Tuckerby's Warren. See (The) Root.

Sir Tuckerby Underbank: a title given to Tuck by Laurelin and by other members of Royalty.

Sir Tuckerby Underbank's Unfinished Diary and His Accounting of the Winter War: the chronicle compiled by Tuck and various scribes to describe the Winter War. Tuck's diary was unfinished, for he was blinded by the Myrkenstone and wrote in it no more. Yet it, plus Tuck's accounting of his memories, and the accounts of others, made up the history of the Winter War. The chronicle was commissioned by High King Galen, and funds were set aside to hire scribes to assist Tuck in this work. Raven aided immeasurably; hence, the history is also called *The Raven Book*. Also known as Tuck's chronicle.

Siven Warrows: one of the four strains of northern Warrows. Siven Warrows traditionally live in burrows dug into hillsides.

Skail: the Dragon that bore the Hèlarms to the Dark Mere at Dusk-Door.

skut (Twyll, Valur: untranslated interjection): oathword used by Warrows perhaps to mean filth. Also an oathword of Valon used to express anger.

(the) Sky Mountains: a southwesterly-northeasterly chain of mountains between Gothon to the west and Basq to the east.

(the) sleep of Elves: the manner in which Elves slumber, which is different from that of other Folk: Elves can rest their minds in gentle memories; however, after a prolonged time, even Elves must truly sleep.

Sleeth's Doom. See Elgo.

Sleeth the Orm: the Cold-drake that captured Blackstone, the Dwarvenholt in the Rigga Mountains, and took the Dwarven treasure as its hoard. Slain centuries later by Elgo.

slowcoach: sluggard.

slugabed: layabout; one who lolls in bed.

Slûk: a foul-sounding common tongue of the Spawn. First spoken by the Hlōks. Even with Slûk, however, Hlōks, Rūcks, and perhaps Ghûls and Ogrus, at times also used a debased form of Pellarion. (For various Slûk words and phrases, see Appendix: Translations of Words and Phrases.)

snap-ring: a mountain-climbing/stone-climbing device that clips onto pitons and "nuts" to fasten ropes and straps to in order to support climbers. Primarily used in Mithgar by Dwarves.

Sons of Harl: the lineal descendants of Strong Harl. Also the name given to all Men of Valon and Jord.

Southdell: one of the Seven Dells of the Boskydells.

South Riamon. See Riamon.

(the) South Route. See (the) Post Road.

Sovereign: generally taken to mean the High King, but also can mean any Lord or King.

Spaunen (Sylva: filth of the Untargarda): Elven term for Spawn (q.v.).

Spawn: the collective name given to all the Folk and other creatures of Neddra who came to live in Mithgar; e.g., Rūcks, Hlōks, Ghûls, Gargons, Ogrus, Vulgs, Hèlsteeds. Also known as maggot-folk, Wrg (Valur), Yrm (OP), *Rûpt* (Sylva), *Spaunen* (Sylva), Grg (Châkur), and Squam (Châkur). Also known as Winternight Spawn during the Winter War.

Spawn-doors. See Rūck-doors.

(a) spelldown: a spelling bee.

(the) Spindle Ford: a Boskydell ford along the Upland Way across the Spindle River.

(the) Spindle River: a river forming the northern and eastern border of the Boskydells. In the valley of the river grows much of the Spindlethorn Barrier.

Spindlethorn: an iron-hard thorn growth of great density reaching to heights of fifty feet or more. Found in nature only in the river valleys around the Boskydells. Also known as 'Thorn.

(the) Spindlethorn Barrier: a barrier of thorns shielding the Boskydells. The thorns, called Spindlethorn, grow in the river valleys surrounding the Bosky. The thorns have been cultivated to grow along the boundary in those places where formerly there were gaps in the barrier. Forty to fifty feet high, the barrier width varies from one mile at its narrowest to ten or so miles at its widest. Also known as the Barrier, the Great Barrier, the Great Thornwall, the 'Thorn, the Thornring, the Thornwall, the 'Wall.

(the) Spiral Down: one of the legendary features of Kraggen-cor.

(the) Spur. See (the) Old Rell Spur.

(the) Squad. See (the) Squad of Kraggen-cor.

(the) Squad of Kraggen-cor: those persons whose mission it was to enter the Dawn-Gate, pass secretly through Gnar's forces, and make their way undetected through the length of Kraggen-cor to the inside of Dusk-Door to repair it (if broken) and let in Durek's Army. The Squad originally consisted of Anval, Barak, Borin, Delk, Kian, Perry, and Tobin. But Barak was slain and Tobin disabled before reaching Kraggen-cor. Shannon Silverleaf and Ursor joined the Squad to bring it up to seven strong again. Also known as the Secret Seven, the Seven Penetrators, the Seven, the Squad of Seven, the Squad.

(the) Squad of Seven. See (the) Squad of Kraggen-cor.

Squam (Châkur: Underworld foul ones): Dwarven name for Spawn (q.v.).

Squam-War (Châkur: Underworld-foul-ones War): War with the Spawn.

Squire Northcolt. See Jayar Northcolt.

starsilver. See silveron.

(the) starsilver armor. See (the) silveron armor.

(the) Staves. See (the) Staves of Narok.

(the) Staves of Narok: an ancient legend, set to verse, foretelling of great sorrow to befall the Dwarven Folk during the Death-War. The Horn of Narok was intimately entwined with the fulfillment of the Doom spoken of in the Staves. Also known as the Doom of Narok, the riddle of Narok, the Rime of Narok, and the Staves.

Stel (Valur: steel): a Valonian term meaning steel, weapons.

(the) Steppes of Jord: a northern Realm of bleak, high plains in Mithgar. Bounded on the north by the Barrens, on the east and the south by the Grimwall, and on the west by the Gronfangs and the Boreal Sea.

(the) 'Stone. See (the) Myrkenstone.

(the) Stone-arches Bridge: the bridge over the River Caire along the Crossland Road.

Stone Giants: a Dwarven name for the Utruni (q.v.)

Stonehill: a village on the southern margins of the Battle Downs in the western fringes of the Wilderland between Rian and Harth. Situated at the junction of the Post Road and the Crossland Road. Also known as the 'Hill.

Stonehiller: a resident of Stonehill; the argot of Stonehill.

stone or fire: the way of a Dwarven funeral, in which the dead are placed on a fitting pyre or are buried in stone.

(the) 'Stone Slayer. See Tuckerby Underbank.

Stoog: a Hlōk of Gnar's Horde.

Stormhelm: the northwesternmost of the four mountains of the Quadran beneath which Kraggen-cor is delved. A mountain whose stone is tinged red. Said by Dwarves to be the mightiest mountain of the known ranges in Mithgar. So named because of the many storms that rage at its peak. Also known as Coron (Sylva), the Hammer, Mont Coron, and Râvenor (Châkur).

Stormhelm Defile: a steep-walled canyon on the road up the western flank of Stormhelm to Quadran Pass.

stripling (plural: striplings): the age-name given to a buccan Warrow between ten and twenty years old.

Strong Harl: The great leader of the Vanadurin in ancient times when they rode the Steppes of Jord. Also known as Harl and as Harl the Strong.

(the) Struggles: the general name given by the Warrows to the struggles to overcome Modru's forces in the Boskydells in the Winter War. Also known as the War of the Boskydells.

(the) study at The Root: one of the rooms in The Root. The study is considered a curiosity among Warrows since few, if any, other Warrow dwellings have studies.

(the) sundered causeway: the shattered causeway along the Loomwall near the Dusk-Door.

Swarm: a thousand or more maggot-folk.

swordthane (OHR: sword warrior): warrior of the sword.

Sylva (Sylva: our tongue): the language of the Elves. (For various Sylva words and phrases, see Appendix: Translations of Words and Phrases.)

tag-along: one who follows closely. In *The Fairhill Journal*, two younglings (q.v.) were called tag-alongs.

Talarin (Sylva: steel-ring): an Elf. Lian Warrior. Elf Lord. Consort of Rael. Sire of Gildor, Vanidor, and Faeon. Leader of the forces in Arden Vale during the Winter War. Fought in the Battle of Kregyn. Also known as Alor Talarin, Lord Talarin, the Warder of the Northern Reaches of Rell.

Teddy: a buccan Warrow of Budgens in the Boskydells at the time of the Quest of Kraggen-cor.

theen. See Wizard-metal.

Thief Elgo: a name given Elgo by the Dwarves after their dispute over the hoard of Sleeth. (See Elgo.)

Thimble: a Boskydell village south of the Tineway in Southdell.

Third Glain: a Dwarf King of Durek's Folk. Father of Orn, and slain with him by the Gargon shortly after it burst free of the Lost Prison.

(the) Thirsty Horse: a Boskydell inn.

Thork: a Dwarf. Companion of Elyn in the Quest of Black Mountain.

'Thorn. See Spindlethorn.

(the) Thornring. See (the) Spindlethorn Barrier.

thorn tunnel: a passage through the Spindlethorn Barrier.

(the) Thornwalkers (of the Boskydells): bands of Warrow archers set along the entry ways into the Boskydells in times of trouble to keep out all but those on legitimate business. These archers also patrol the borders of the Boskydells (i.e., the Spindlethorn Barrier), thus are said to "walk the Thorns."

(the) Thornwall. See (the) Spindlethorn Barrior.

Thuuth Uthor (Slûk: dread striker; fear lash): Gargoni words meaning dread striker or fear lash. Scrawled by the Gargon on a large stone block in the Lost Prison.

Tillok: a Boskydell village along the Crossland Road in Eastdell.

Tine Ford: the ford along the Tineway across the Spindle River.

Tineway: the northwesterly-southeasterly road between Rood in the Boskydells and the Post Road in Harth.

Tobin Forgefire: a Dwarf of Durek's Folk. Gatemaster. One of the Squad of Kraggen-cor. Tobin's leg was shattered during the Battle of the Last River Camp. Cared for by the Elves, Tobin recovered, though afterward he always limped.

Tovit (Valur: ready): a Valonian term meaning "ready" or "stand ready."

Trell: a Man of Valon. One of the riders in Brytta's force.

Trellinath: an abandoned Realm of Mithgar. Bounded on the north by Wellen and the Boskydells, on the east by Rell, on the south by the Grimwall, and on the west by Gothon.

Troll-dam of the Black Mere: a Troll-made dam blocking the Duskrill and creating the Black Mere at Dusk-Door.

Trolls. See Ogrus.

Troll's Bane: taken to mean Bane (q.v.), the Elven long-knife.

Troll War-bar: a massive iron bar borne as a weapon by an Ogru.

Tror: a Dwarf of Durek's Folk. Masterhammerer. Warrior in the Battle of Kraggen-cor. Tror and his Hammerers helped break the Troll-made dam to empty the Dark Mere during the battle with the Madûk.

trothmate (Châkur: true-pledged mate): a Dwarven term meaning "husband" or "wife."

Tuck. See Tuckerby Underbank.

Tuckerby's scribes: the scribes hired by Tuckerby Underbank to work on the History. Also known as Tuckerby's scriveners.

Tuckerby's scriveners. See Tuckerby's scribes.

Tuckerby's Warren. See (The) Root.

Tuckerby Underbank: a buccan Warrow of the Boskydells. Husband of Merrilee. Raven's sire. Hero of the Winter War. Thornwalker. Deevewalker. Bane Wielder. Wearer of the silveron armor. Arrow Bearer. Bearer of the Red Quarrel. A member of Brega's squad. Looser of the Red Quarrel. Myrkenstone Slayer. Slayer of the Myrkenstone. 'Stone Slayer. Modru's Doom. Modru's Slayer. Died of an illness at age 97. Also known as Friend Tuck, Master Tuck, Master Waerling, Sir Tuck, Tuck.

Tuck's chronicle. See *Sir Tuckerby Underbank's Unfinished Diary and His Accounting of the Winter War.*

Tuck's diary: Tuck's journal. The blank diary was given to Tuck by his cousin Willy upon Tuck's departure from Woody Hollow to join the Eastdell Fourth; the diary formed the basis for *The Raven Book.*

tulwar: a curved Rūcken sword (sabre).

(the) Tumble River: a north-south river of many rapids and falls, originating in the Grimwall Mountains and flowing through Arden Gorge and south to join the River Caire above Luren.

Tunnelmaster: one who has mastered the Dwarven craft of tunnel making.

Turin Stonesplitter: a Dwarf of Durek's Folk. Minemaster and Delfshaper. Slain by the Krakenward.

turves: squares of sod cut from turf.

(the) Twilight Path: the way of the Twilight Ride (q.v.).

(the) Twilight Ride: a way of passing from Mithgar, on the Middle Plane, to Adonar, upon the High Plane. Elves riding on horses can somehow pass between the Planes. Brega observed that a ritualistic chanting and a pacing in an arcane pattern were used to achieve passage. Other Folk know not how or perhaps are incapable of passing between the Planes, since only Elves and their horses, and perhaps the Vanilērihha, seem to make this journey. There is, however, evidence that Adon and Gyphon can open the way for others.

(the) two-mile detour: the detour taken by the Squad of Kraggen-cor to get around the wreckage of the Hall of the Gravenarch and back upon the Brega Path.

Twyll (Twyll: our tongue): the ancient Warrow tongue. (For various Twyll words and phrases, see Appendix: Translations of Words and Phrases.)

Uchan (Châkur: anvil). See Greytower.

Ûkhs: (singular: Ûkh) (Châkur: stench-ones): Dwarven name for Rûcks (q.v.).

Ûkkish: a term meaning "of the Ûkhs."

Uncle Bill: the name of a Man in the song "The Battle of Weiunwood." Uncle Bill in fact may have been an actual participant in the battle.

(the) undead: those of Valonian legend who dwell in Hèl. Also known as Hèl's spawn.

(the) Underbanks: the Underbank lineage.

(the) Undermountain Realm of Mineholt North. See Mineholt North.

(the) Underworld. See Hèl.

(the) 'Unicorn. See (the) White Unicorn Inn (of Stonehill).

(the) Unknown Cavern: a Dwarven term meaning a place of uncertainty.

(the) Untargarda (OP: Under Worlds): all the worlds upon the Lower Plane.

(the) Upland Way: a northeasterly-southwesterly road running between the Cliffs in the Boskydells and the Post Road near the Battle Downs.

(the) Upward Way: a long, upward slope in Kraggen-cor between the Broad Hall and the Great Chamber of the Sixth Rise. A part of the Brega Path.

Ursor: a Baeran Man of enormous size and strength. Ursor's wife, Grael, and child were slain by maggot-folk. Seeking revenge, Ursor used a great black mace to slay many of the Foul Folk. Ursor became a member of Shannon Silverleaf's Elven Company and then a member of the Squad of Kraggen-cor. After the Quest of Kraggen-cor, Ursor was made Captain of Kian's Kingsguards.

Utruni (singular: Utrun) (Sylva: stone-giants): one of the Folk of Mithgar. The Utruni comprise three strains. The adults range from twelve to seventeen feet tall. Gentle. Shy. Dwellers within the stone of Mithgar (the continental bedrock itself). Keepers of the 'Stone. Jewel-like eyes. Shapers of the land. Able to move through solid stone. Also known as Giants and as Stone Giants.

Utruni eyes: jewel-like eyes. It seems that the Utruni can see through solid stone. Their eyes resemble actual jewels, and they see by a "light" different from that seen by other Folk. (Modern-day physicists have speculated that perhaps the Giants see by neutrino-like particles.)

Valanreach (from Valon-reich): the name generally given to the grassy plains of Valon.

Valanreach long-ride: a method of varying the gait of a horse such that a pace of forty or even fifty miles per day can be sustained over a considerable number of days.

Valanreach Marshal. See Reachmarshal.

Valki: a Dwarf of Durek's Folk. The greatest Gatemaster of the Dwarves, who in the First Era, with the Wizard Grevan, constructed the Dusk-Door.

(the) Valley of the Door. See Ragad Vale.

(the) Valley of the Five Riders: a valley of lush grass and clear water named for the five Riders of Valon slain in the Battle of Stormhelm Defile. This vale is situated on the western side of the Grimwall Mountains and is the first valley south of Ragad Vale. Here were buried the Five Riders.

Valon: a Realm of Mithgar noted for its lush, green prairies and for its fiery horses. Roughly circular and divided into four Reaches (quadrants), the Land is bounded on the north-to-east-to-south margin by the River Argon, beyond which lie Riamon and Pellar; on the south-to-west margin by the Red Hills, beyond which lies Jugo; and on the west-to-north margin by the Gûnarring and by the Great Escarpment, beyond which, respectively, lie Gûnar and Darda Galion.

Valonian: a native of Valon. Also a term meaning "of Valon."

Valonian Battle-tongue. See Valur.

Valonners: Cotton's name for the Riders of Valon in Brytta's force.

Valur (Valur: our tongue): the ancient War-tongue of Valon. Also known as the Battle-tongue of the Valanreach, the Valonian Battle-tongue, and the War-tongue of Valon. (For various Valur words and phrases, see Appendix: Translations of Words and Phrases.)

Vanadurin (Valur: bond-lasting = our lasting bond): Battleword of Valon meaning Warriors of the Pledge.

Vanar: the capital city of Valon, central to the Realm.

Vanareich (Valur: our nation): a battleword of the Valonian War-tongue meaning Men of the Land of Valon.

Vanidar (Sylva: vani = silver, dar = leaf): an Elf. Lian warrior. One of the Squad of Kraggen-cor. Also known as Alor Vanidar, Shannon, Shannon Silverleaf, Silverleaf, Vanidar Shannon Silverleaf, and Vanidar Silverleaf.

Vanidar Shannon Silverleaf. See Vanidar.

Vanidar Silverleaf. See Vanidar.

Vanidor (Sylva: vani = silver, dor = branch): an Elf. Lian warrior. Elf Lord. Son of Talarin and Rael. Twin brother of Gildor, brother of Faeon. Hero. One of four Elves sent on a mission into Gron to spy out Modru's strength at the Iron Tower and to rescue Laurelin, if possible; Vanidor was torture-slain by Modru at the Kinstealer's holt while on this mission. Also known as Alor Vanidor, Lord Vanidor, Silverbranch, and Vanidor Silverbranch.

Vani-lērihha (Sylva: silver-larks): silvery songbirds that disappeared from Darda Galion ages agone. It is told among the Elves that when the Vani-lērihha return, dire times will be upon Mithgar. Also known as Silverlarks.

Vail Falls (Sylva: vanil = silvery): a cataract where the Nith River plunges over the Great Escarpment to fall into the Cauldron. Also known as the Falls of Vanil.

Vidron: a Man of Valon. The commander of the army of

Challerain Keep, and of the Alliance of Wellen and Arden during the Winter War. Hrosmarshal. Reachmarshal. Fieldmarshal. Kingsgeneral. General. A member of Aurion's and then Galen's War-councils. Hero. Also known as the Whelmer of Modru's Horde.

Vidron's Legion: the Alliance of Wellen and Arden. Also the name given to the Wellenen who rode with Vidron to the Boskydells, to Gûnarring Gap, and to Grûwen Pass.

(the) Vorvor (Châkur: wheel): a whirlpool on the edge of the Pitch into which First Durek was cast by Squam. Durek was drawn under the surface and into the caverns of Kraggen-cor. Also known as Durek's Wheel.

V'ttacku (Valur: strike, attack): a battleword in the Valonian War-tongue meaning attack.

Vulgs: large, black, Wolf-like creatures. Virulent bite. Suffer the Ban. Vulgs act as scouts and trackers as well as ravers. Also known as Modru's curs, and as Vulpen (Slûk).

Vûlks (Sylva: Vûlk = dread power): a class of evil creatures having special powers; these powers range from those of Gyphon (nearly equal to Adon's) to the minor effects of the Ghûls. Another creature, the Gargon, was a major Vûlk with power equal to that of a Wizard.

Waerans (singular: Waeran) (Châkur: wary-ones): Dwarven name for Warrows (q.v.).

Waerlinga (singular: Waerling) (OP; Sylva: caution-small-ones = cautious-wee-folk): Elven and Pellarion name for Warrows (q.v.).

Waldana (singular: Waldan) (Valur: wood-ones): the name used by the Men of Valon to mean Warrows (q.v.).

Waldfolc (Valur: wood-folk = folk of the woods): the name used by the Men of Valon to mean Warrow Folk.

(the) Wanderjahren (Twyll: wandering-days): the time in Warrow history when they wandered restlessly over the face of Mithgar seeking a homeland.

(the) War-banner of the House of Valon. See (the) War-banner of Valon.

(the) War-banner of Valon: the battle flag of Valon: a white horse rampant on a field of green. Also known as the green-

and-white of Valon, and as the War-banner of the House of Valon.

(the) Warder (of the Dark Mere). See (the) Krakenward.

Warder of the Northern Regions of Rell. See Talarin.

(the) War Hall: one of the chambers of Kraggen-cor on the Brega Path. A vast hall, it was used to muster the Dwarven nation under Kraggen-cor when war threatened. Also known as the Mustering Chamber (of the First Neath), the Mustering Hall, the War Hall of Kraggen-cor, and the War Hall of the First Neath.

(the) War Hall of Kraggen-cor. See (the) War Hall.

(the) War Hall of the First Neath. See (the) War Hall.

(the) War Horn. See (the) golden War Horn.

(the) War of Kraggen-cor: taken to mean collectively all the skirmishes and battles fought in the Quest of Kraggen-cor.

Waroo: the Baeron name given to a mythical white Bear, bringer of winter storms. Also known as Waroo the Blizzard. Akin to the White Bear (q.v.).

Waroo the Blizzard. See Waroo.

warren: a large burrow (q.v.).

Warrows (singular: Warrow): one of the Folk of Mithgar. For a description of Warrows, see Appendix: A Word About Warrows. Also known as little uns, Waerans (Châkur), Waerlinga (OP, Sylva), Waerlings (Warrow corruption of Waerlinga), Waldana (Valur), *Waldfolc* (Valur), Wee Folk, Wee Ones.

(the) Wars of Vengeance: the battles fought in the millennia-long conflict between the Dwarves and the Squam, beginning when the Foul Folk hurled First Durek into the Vorvor, and ending at the conclusion of the Great War.

(the) War-tongue (of Valon). See Valur.

(the) Wastes of Gron. See Gron.

(the) Watchtower: taken to mean the watchtower (now ruins) upon the crest of Beacontor.

waugh (Slûk: untranslated cry of startlement): a maggot-folk squall of startlement and fear.

(the) Way. See (the) Old Rell Way.

waybread: a nutritious, dense, biscuit-like bread carried by wayfarers.

wayleader: a guide.

(the) Wee Folk. See Warrows.

Wee One: a name often given to one of the Wee Folk by other Folk of Mithgar.

Wee Ones. See Warrows.

Wee Perry: Ursor's name for Perry.

Weiunwood (Stonehiller: Wei = wee, un = one, wood = forest; Weiunwood = wee-one-forest): a large, shaggy forest, in the Wilderland north of Harth and south of Rian, where Warrows live. Also known as the 'Wood.

Weiunwood Alliance: the alliance of Men (of Stonehill and the Wilderland), Elves (of Arden), and Warrows (of Weiunwood). In the Winter War, this alliance successfully fought one of Modru's Hordes in the Battle of Weiunwood. Also at times known as the Alliance.

Wellen: a Realm of Mithgar bordering on the Boskydells to the east, Dalara to the north, Trellinath to the south, and the Ryngar Arm of the Weston Ocean to the west.

werelight: a spectral light.

(the) West Hall: one of the chambers in Kraggen-cor, just inside the Dusk-Door, in which the Deevewalkers sought refuge from the Krakenward. The first chamber on the Brega Path.

(the) Wheel of Fate: usually taken to mean the inexorable turnings of Fortune that lead toward some great, foreordained event.

(the) Whelmer of Modru's Horde: the name given to Vidron by Talarin after the valiant stand in the Battle of Grűwen Pass.

(the) White Bear: a mythical Bear of Riamonian legend, bringer of winter storms. Akin to Waroo (q.v.).

(the) White Unicorn Inn (of Stonehill): an inn in Stonehill. Also known as the 'Unicorn.

(the) White Wolf: a mythical Wolf of Warrow legend, bringer of winter storms.

(the) Wilderland: the wilderness between Harth to the south and Rian to the north, Rhone to the east, and the western edge of the Battle Downs to the west.

(the) Wilderness Hills: a low range of inhospitable hills in the Wilderland bordering on the River Caire.

(the) Wilder River: a river between the Dellin Downs and the Wilderness Hills. Running southeasterly from the Crossland Road, the river eventually flows into the River Caire.

(the) wild kine of the south. See black oxen.

Willen Greylock: a buccan Warrow of the Boskydells. Husband of Raven (Underbank) Greylock. Sire of Robin. A scholar, historian; founder of the Ravenbook Scholars.

Willowdell: a Boskydell village along the Crossland Road in Eastdell.

Will Whitlatch, the Third: a buccan Warrow of the Boskydells. Mayor of Woody Hollow in the time of the Quest of Kraggen-cor.

Winternight: the cold darkness that grasped the land within the bounds of the Dimmendark in the time of the Winter War. Also known as 'Night.

(the) Winter War: the War between Modru and the Alliance. Fought in the Fourth Era. Called the Winter War because of the bitter coldness that gripped the land within the Dimmendark.

(the) Winter War Quest: generally taken to mean the events involving Sir Tuckerby Underbank and his friends during the Winter War.

(the) Wizard Grevan. See Grevan.

(the) Wizard Grevan's rune: a rune *G* inscribed in theen upon the Dusk-Door.

Wizard-metal: a special metal used by Wizards to form runes, sigils, glyphs, and lines that glow when evoked by words of power. Wizardmetal, like silveron, is probably an alloy, rather than an element. Also known as theen.

Wizards: persons of arcane lore and power. Said to live in, on, or near the Black Mountain of Xian.

Wizard-word: a word of power; e.g., Gaard is a Wizard-word.

Wolf Patrol: one or more patrols of Thornwalker archers guarding flocks against Wolves during times of winter famine.

woodsmen of the Argon vales. See Baeron.

Woody Hollow: a Boskydell town north of the Crossland Road and inside the western edge of Eastdell. Also known as the Hollow.

Woody Hollow Hall: the town hall of Woody Hollow. Also known as the Hall and as Hollow Hall.

Woody Hollow Road: the road between Woody Hollow and Budgens.

Word from the Beyond: a Boskydell phrase meaning news not to be trusted until confirmed.

Wrall: a Baeran Man. Youngest son of Baru, the Passwarden of the Crestan Pass in 5E231.

Wrg (Valur: foul-worms): the term used by the Men of Valon to mean maggot-folk.

Wrg-doors. See Rück-doors.

Wrg-lope: the loping run of the maggot-folk.

Wylf: a Man of Valon. One of the riders in Brytta's force. Noted for his ability to find comfort.

Xian: a Land far to the east in Mithgar where Wizards are said to dwell.

Year's End Eve: the evening before Year's End Day; December 30.

Year's Long Day: the longest day of the year; June 21. Also known as Mid-Year's Day.

young buccan (plural: young buccen): the age-name of a buccan between twenty and thirty years old.

young damman (plural: young dammen): the age-name of a damman between twenty and thirty years old.

youngling: the age-name of a buccan or damman between birth and ten years old.

Yrm (OP: worms of corruption): the term used by Men of Pellar to mean maggot-folk.

ziggurt (Châkur: shatter-rock): a Dwarven term meaning stone that is cracked and crazed.

AFTERWORD

I hope you enjoyed reading The Silver Call as much as I enjoyed writing it. For those of you who may be wondering, I have in rough outline another Mithgarian tale. I don't know how long it may take me to see if it's any good. But I'll tell you this: if I become as enraptured with this new saga as I was with The Iron Tower and The Silver Call, then it might take quite a while; for it will be a soft-blooming love, requiring much nurturing, and its many manifestations will be revealed to me only in their own true time.

D. L. McKiernan
Westerville, Ohio—1984

When I wrote the above, little did I know that the Mithgarian Saga would cover the span that it does (see the list at the front of the book). It certainly has been fun.

D. L. McKiernan
Tucson, Arizona—2001

About the Author

Born April 4, 1932, I have spent a great deal of my life looking through twilights and dawns seeking—what? ah yes, I remember—seeking signs of wonder, searching for pixies and fairies and other such, looking in tree hollows and under snow-laden bushes and behind waterfalls and across wooded, moonlit dells. I did not outgrow that curiosity, that search for the edge of Faery when I outgrew childhood—not when I was in the U.S. Air Force during the Korean War, nor in college, nor in graduate school, nor in the thirty-one years I spent in Research and Development at Bell Telephone Laboratories as an engineer and manager on ballistic missile defense systems and then telephone systems and in think-tank activities. In fact I am still at it, still searching for glimmers and glimpses of wonder in the twilights and the dawns. I am abetted in this curious behavior by Martha Lee, my helpmate, lover, and, as of this writing, my wife of forty-four years.